#Fic 5-19-10

Sha

Shaw, Patricia
Valley of Lagoons

S0-BXV-433

# VALLEY OF LAGOONS

# VALLEY OF LAGOONS

## Patricia Shaw

HEADLINE

Copyright © 1989 Patricia Shaw

First published in Great Britain in 1990
by HEADLINE BOOK PUBLISHING PLC

All rights reserved. No part of this publication may be
reproduced, stored in a retrieval system, or transmitted,
in any form or by any means without the prior written
permission of the publisher, nor be otherwise circulated
in any form of binding or cover other than that in which
it is published and without a similar condition being
imposed on the subsequent purchaser.

All characters in this publication are fictitious
and any resemblance to real persons, living or dead,
is purely coincidental.

British Library Cataloguing in Publication Data

Shaw, Patricia
Valley of Lagoons
I. Title
823'. 914 [F]   # Fic 5-19-10

ISBN 0 7472 0200 1

Typeset in 11/12 pt Plantin
by Colset Private Limited, Singapore

Printed and bound in Great Britain by
Richard Clay Ltd, Bungay, Suffolk

HEADLINE BOOK PUBLISHING PLC
Headline House,
79 Great Titchfield Street
London W1P 7FN

3 6000 00109 8308

'Australian history does not read like history, but like the most beautiful lies . . . It is full of surprises and adventures, and incongruities and incredibilities, but they are all true, they all happened.'

Mark Twain, *More Tramps Abroad*, 1897

# CONTENTS

# PART ONE
## UNITED STATES, 1957

# CHAPTER ONE

A black limousine glided through the VIP entrance to La Guardia airport and was waved on by the guards at the second checkpoint. Eduardo Rivadavia leaned forward and tapped the driver on the shoulder.

'Do you know where to go?'

'Yes sir,' the chauffeur assured him. 'We're right on time.'

Eduardo shook his head and settled back. Airports this size were still a maze to him, and now, driving between rows of private planes, their noses stuck in the air, he wondered how the owners ever located their crafts.

He lit a cigar and leant further back, out of sight of the passers-by. He hated this car; it made him feel like a gangster, and he supposed his fat cigar wasn't helping. But, as Argentinian Ambassador to the United Nations, he had to submit to being chauffeured around New York in this long ugly ominous-looking limousine.

Had it not been for the misty rain he might have taken the opportunity to examine some of these small planes. His sister, Maria, was at him all the time to buy one. She had married a Texan and lived in Dallas. With the rest of the family remaining firmly in Argentina, Maria fretted that Eduardo in New York might be lonely.

He sighed. Now that his only child was to be married he expected Maria would become even more insistent on the need for that plane. He could not convince her that such extravagance would create problems. With the depression in Argentina, news of one of their diplomats swanning around in a private plane would only invite scrutiny and inevitable criticism. She could not understand that an ambassador is not Caesar's wife. The Rivadavia companies would purchase this plane, she argued, it would not cost the government a cent. He could not make her see that the public would not want to know the truth. The Opposition would see to it that rumours of corruption reached out to him; it was hard enough to keep clear of their smear tactics without handing them the ammunition. Anyway, he rather liked the big commercial aircraft and the busy efficiency of airports.

Maria had always been the same, whatever she had, she wanted the others to have too; her surges of enthusiasm for new toys, as Eduardo called them, had become a family joke. And since her husband, Hank Wedderburn, had a private plane, then the Rivadavia family would be nagged until something else took her fancy.

It was still raining, that flat grey subdued rain which seemed almost

2

apologetic, as if hoping that the bombastic New Yorkers would not notice. He put out his cigar and closed the window, feeling isolated and depressed.

I should be happy, he told himself, my daughter's wedding day. I hope the rain stops in time. They say it will. She's marrying a fine young man who cares for her; a sensible sort of fellow, with a background not unlike our own, but from so far away! Who would have dreamed she would marry an Australian?

Elena had laughed at him. 'Daddy! Why do you keep saying "so far away". Argentina is a long way from everything too, so what's the difference? And we're going to live on a ranch. I'm the one in the odd spot. I leave the ranch to come to New York, and end up living on another ranch.'

Another ranch, she had said, as if it were just down the highway. Young people! They have no idea what they are getting into half the time. What sort of a ranch he had not yet discovered, except that they ran cattle too. He hadn't liked to quiz her fiancé too much, and so far had only worked out that it was unmarked on any map and far from a township.

Luke MacNamara had told him the house was very comfortable, that Elena would live well, but standards differ. What did he mean by well? His daughter Elena Maria Rivadavia de Figueroa was accustomed to a high standard of living, as the Rivadavias had been for generations; but this pair, so excited with their marriage plans, would not take his questions seriously. He wished his wife were still alive, he needed her now; she would have been more forceful, more forthright.

Normally he would have spoken to the young man's parents before giving his permission, but Luke's father was dead and his mother was due in from Australia this morning, so there had been no opportunity to enquire further, apart from his own embassy's discreet check.

Ah well. Let them be happy. Let them all be happy today! Eduardo preferred to feel depressed. Hank and Maria were as excited about the wedding as if she were their own daughter. He estimated that he had only a few minutes of peace left in his day.

Last Easter they had taken Luke home to meet the family and Luis, Eduardo's brother, had been impressed with his knowledge of cattle. This had given Eduardo heart. 'Offer him a job!'

'I did,' Luis had told him, 'but he wants to go home.'

'What in damnation is he doing in North America then?'

'Things are not so different in his family,' Luis said gently. 'Like you, he wanted to go out into the world, but now he realises that his heart is in the land. We don't all have the talent that you have, to take so easily to the world of commerce. He is more like me, more suited to country life. We are all so very proud of you, Eduardo; you are a man of great distinction and that young man respects you, but let him go home. Let them go. I don't think you need worry about Elena. If he has to stay on working in New York to marry Elena, he'll be miserable. Could you imagine me working in New York?'

'Why not? You could handle the sort of job he has in the Trade Commission, dealing with primary producers and outlets.'

Luis laughed. 'But I'd have to live there – that's the problem. They want to live on a ranch. I don't blame them. You can keep New York.'

The chauffeur brought him back to the present. 'There's the plane, sir. They're coming in now.'

Eduardo watched as the small plane swept neatly down to the runway and rolled to a stop. Hank and Maria came down the steps and dashed across to the car in a flurry of umbrellas.

Maria threw her arms around him. 'Eduardo! It is so good of you to come to meet us. You shouldn't have! You must have so much to do today.'

'Not me, I was in the way. It was my escape to take a drive.'

Hank leaned over to pump his hand. 'We still appreciate it Eduardo. And what about little Elena getting married? We haven't bought her a present yet. We thought we'd wait and see what they wanted. Maria thinks a cheque might be bad manners. Different people, different customs. And she's marrying an Aussie? How about that?'

Eduardo produced a thin smile. He was fond of Hank but the Texan's exuberance always left him at a loss for words.

'Hank's got a soft spot for Australians,' Maria said.

'Oh yes,' Eduardo replied. 'Why?'

Maria blinked in surprise. 'Why? I don't know. Why Hank?'

Hank shrugged and his wife, taking that to mean it was of no consequence, hurried on, 'Aunt Cecilia tells me she is sure that there was a branch of the Rivadavia family in Australia a long time ago. Last century, she thinks.'

Her brother smiled at her, patronising. 'I never heard that one before. Aunt Cecilia finds branches of the family everywhere, when it is convenient.'

'She could be right. You never know. But tell me, what's happening with the wedding? Is everything organised? I wish I could have been here to help Elena. Now who is coming?'

'The usual people. Family. Friends. His and hers. Luis and Isobel and their children are staying at the Waldorf, making a holiday of it. The aunts are with friends in Connecticut. The Garcias and others from Buenos Aires have taken apartments somewhere and Grandpapa Batiste is staying with Uncle Julio on Long Island . . .'

'But,' Maria interrupted, 'not *our* family Eduardo, the other side! I heard there's a Lord and Lady coming!'

'Yes, Lord and Lady Heselwood.'

'I didn't know Australians went in for lords,' Hank said.

'They're not Australian, they're English. Friends of the MacNamara's. Luke's family.' Eduardo spoke as if he had already gone through this explanation too many times.

'Luke must be well connected, to have friends in the peerage,' Maria said, sensing that Eduardo wasn't overjoyed at the prospect of this marriage. She looked out of the window. 'I love New York, it's such a stolid

4

place isn't it? Everyone putting one foot after the other with such intensity.'

Hank laughed. 'Eduardo, this sister of yours has the strangest reactions. Most people say New York is exciting.'

'Oh bosh,' she cried. 'It is too predictable to be exciting. Everyone who comes here knows exactly what to expect. Australia is exciting. I'd love to go to Australia. Pioneer country . . . it must be like North America was in the movies of the Wild West; all that space.'

'And no water,' Hank said. 'That's the difference. Our pioneers were fortunate they found well-irrigated country. The further west you go in Australia the drier it gets; a lot of their rivers flow inland and just run into the sand.'

'Rivers can't flow inland Hank,' his wife said.

'They can, can't they Eduardo?'

Rivadavia was curious. 'Have you been to Australia, Hank?'

'Yes, during the war.

'Have you ever been to this country, this part that Luke comes from, Queensland? I've never heard of it before.'

'Eduardo, for once I'm way in front of you,' Hank said. 'Sure I've been there, but it's no big deal. I reckon more than two hundred thousand GI's and fly-boys know that part of the world. There were enormous US bases in Australia, but the biggest concentration of fighting men was based in Townsville, on the coast, a jumping-off spot for the Pacific war. I often wonder if any of them went back; there were big opportunities in that country in those days, still are for that matter.'

Eduardo was at last finding the conversation more interesting. 'What sort of prospects?'

'Plenty of them, in all directions. Fantastic, endless grazing country – they've got cattle stations there, ranches, as big as Texas.'

His brother-in-law was stunned. He had been taught to believe that everything in Texas was the biggest. 'You are joking with me?'

'No I'm not. What size is this station, the ranch your future son-in-law has?'

'I didn't like to ask.'

'You should have. Aussies don't mind. They'd tell you if their grand-pappy was Jesse James. Half of them are descended from convicts – they don't care. In fact, they're proud of it.'

'Oh, my God!'

Even Maria was aghast. 'I'm sure Luke MacNamara isn't descended from a convict.'

'How do you know?' Hank was enjoying himself, teasing them. He loved them all dearly; they had taken him to their hearts and given him a sense of belonging, something he had not experienced before, but the Rivadavias took their family line so seriously they were vulnerable to a little gentle needling.

5

Hank still recalled with rage his homecoming from the war after months of hospitalisation. He had called his parents from San Francisco to tell them what bus he would be on; he had travelled across country for two days, too excited to read the magazines he had bought to fill in the time, and had stepped out at the old bus station, home at last after two years. There was no one to meet him so he had walked right across the town, experiencing a sense of surprise that it seemed so much smaller than he remembered. The front door was locked but the key was in the same place so he let himself in the back door and found a note on the kitchen table, anchored by the sugar pot, where his mother always left her notes. It said his parents had gone to the movies.

He had wanted to leave right then, but his need to be home, among family, was too great. He desperately needed to tell them what had happened to him, to be rid of it. But when he spoke of the war and they saw him begin to shake, his father told him, 'The war's over boy. Put it behind you.'

Eduardo cut into his painful memories. 'If you have been to Townsville, have you been to Luke's home town, this Valley of Lagoons?'

'Valley of Lagoons,' Maria repeated, 'it's such a romantic name. I adore it.'

Hank shook his head. 'No. I don't think it's a town. I looked it up on a map but I couldn't find it.'

'Neither could I,' Eduardo groaned. 'Luke circled it with a finger for me, but one can only guess. It looks to be hundreds of miles inland from Townsville, which is on the coast.'

'Not so different then from Argentina or Texas is it?' Hank laughed.

Eduardo scowled and changed the topic. 'Here we are. Look at all the cars in the street. The residence is a madhouse today, photographers, dressers, hairdressers, squealing women. Why don't we keep going and lunch somewhere quiet?'

'No,' Maria cried, almost leaping from her seat. 'I must go and help Elena. There must be a million things I can do.' She was climbing out even as the limousine glided to a stop at the front portico.

Maria and Hank took the same car to the church just minutes ahead of the bridal party. Hank was irritated; he hated to be late at any time.

'There's no hurry,' Maria said; 'they can't start without the bride.'

'That's not the point,' he complained. 'I like to get places early so I can see who's who. Now look, they've all gone inside. We'll only see backs on the way in.'

The usher took them down the long aisle while Maria admired the flowers and Hank looked around for familiar faces.

'There's the groom's mother,' Maria said as they sat down, and Hank glanced over at an attractive woman with a slightly suntanned face and blonde hair rolled gently under a pillbox hat. He noticed her strong

6

competent hands as she placed her gloves and prayerbook on the narrow ledge in front of her and saw the contrast in his wife's olive-skinned elegantly manicured hands. 'Where's her husband?' he whispered to Maria.

'Sssh. He's dead! Killed in the war. Luke is such a nice young man isn't he?' She was looking towards the bridegroom and, even though they could only see his back, Hank nodded approval. In the way of all tall men, he appreciated that this lad was a good six foot, wide shouldered, but still lean and lanky, needing more years to fill out. He smiled. The groom was obviously uncomfortable in his formal clothing, jerking at his coat and straightening the tie. He looked again at young MacNamara, trying to see his face; there was something familiar about him, about his stance. What was it? Hank searched his brain. The way the shoulders moved? The slight lean, a cowboy lean. Maybe it reminded him of some of the boys back home. He felt a strange nervous roll in his stomach and perspiration stood out on his florid face. Looking down he saw that his hands were shaking.

Maria, who missed nothing (he always said), took his arm. 'What's the matter Hank? Are you all right?'

'Yeah, I'm okay. It's just a bit hot in here.'

She looked at him sharply as he took out a handkerchief and dabbed at his face and neck.

Getting old, that's my trouble, he told himself. He stood as the first chords of the wedding march peeled triumphantly through the church. There was Elena standing with her father at the top of the aisle, framed in light.

Hank's troubling thoughts were forgotten as he turned and was briefly lost in the beauty of this woman he had watched grow from a child. Her lovely face was misty under the veil that fell in a cloud of tulle from the same mantilla Maria had worn on their wedding day.

'Isn't she beautiful?' Maria was ecstatic, clutching at Hank.

'She sure is,' he said, turning to catch the bridegroom's reaction.

Luke MacNamara had turned, as all bridegrooms do, to steal that first glimpse of his bride. His nervousness left him and his face broke into a wide grin, then he remembered to turn back to the altar.

He saw the tall man standing in the front row and guessed it must be Hank Wedderburn, Elena's favourite uncle, so he acknowledged Hank with a conspiratorial wink before resuming his correct stance with the groomsmen, facing the priest.

Hank staggered as if struck. His knees buckled and he clutched at the pew for support. His eyes clouded. The bride went past with Eduardo and the organ music seemed to rise to a roar.

'What is it?' Maria's voice was fearful. 'Are you all right?'

'I'm not too well. I think I'll just get outside for a minute.'

'I'll come with you.'

'No, you stay here.' He stepped from the pew into the side aisle, trying to look as if there were some rational purpose to his exit. Heads turned, curious, as he disappeared through a side door.

Outside he braced himself and walked away to stand under a tree, fumbling for a cigarette. Instead, the pack fell to the grass from his trembling hands. In the privacy of the deserted courtyard, Hank Wedderburn gave way to tears.

By the time the others emerged from the church he had washed his face at the drinking fountain and forced his cheerful self to return, but Maria noticed the redness of his eyes. His sudden 'turn' had given her a fright. He had to promise to see a doctor as soon as possible because he could give no explanation for the lapse.

# CHAPTER TWO

During the reception Hank made up his mind to act on something he had let lie dormant for fourteen years.

But it wasn't until he was back in the privacy of his Dallas office some weeks later that he picked up the phone and called a firm of private investigators.

That afternoon, Thomas J. Clelland travelled up in the lift of the prestigious Wedderburn Building to see Hank Wedderburn himself, wondering what this assignment might be. Checking up on a business associate? Hardly. Wedderburn could do that better through his own contacts. Wife trouble? Unlikely. Those sort of arrangements were made well away from the office. Smart wives were friendly with secretaries.

Wedderburn was polite. He wanted quiet enquiries made on a matter of minor interest. Curiosity. He had heard that Clelland had been with Army Intelligence during the war.

'I wouldn't make much of that, Mr Wedderburn. It sounds impressive, but I was based in New Zealand. Didn't have much to do except move files around and enjoy the lifestyle. At the time I resented being stuck there, but now that I look back I was lucky.'

'Did you get to Australia?'

'No. Missed out on that too.'

'My enquiries would take you to Australia. Would you be free to go? All expenses paid.'

Clelland kept the excitement out of his voice. 'Yes sir. If I can be of assistance to you there.'

'You can. I want information on an Australian soldier.'

Clelland knew it had been too good to be true. He couldn't jeopardise the firm's first contact with Wedderburn by wasting his time and money. 'I hate to knock back a trip to Australia Mr Wedderburn, but if that's all you need we could get that information from here.'

'That's just what I don't want. It's a personal matter. I don't want to offend anyone. I can't have someone lead-footing it around the Army records. This family has got its own contacts in the Australian Embassy here. I don't want anyone to pick up that there's a "need to know" going through on one of their people. The man is dead and he was not a criminal, it's nothing like that. I just want you to trot quietly along and bring me back his case history. Nice and neat. I don't want the family to hear of it.'

'Army files are a bit hard to get into without family approval.'

'You'll find a way. Bribe somebody if you have to. You needn't scrimp. But I do want discretion.'

He handed Clelland one sheet of paper on which was printed . . . JOHN PACE MACNAMARA. VALLEY OF LAGOONS. QUEENSLAND. AUSTRALIA . . . and he apologised, 'It's not much to go on. He was "killed in the war" as people say. He could have been run over by a jeep in Perth for all I know.'

'Sure. I know one guy who came home with a Purple Heart. He was gored by a bull taking a short cut through a farm outside Auckland.' He looked at the page. 'Where is this Valley of Lagoons?'

'That's a good question in itself. I'm not exactly sure, but it's inland from Townsville, which is a town on the north coast of the eastern state of Queensland.'

'Oh yeah. I know where Townsville is. Big US wartime base wasn't it?'

'That's it. I don't really think you're going to have much trouble finding out about this guy. If you subtracted all those troops from that little town, I think it would have just gone quietly back to sleep.'

He escorted Clelland to the door and then, suddenly, he felt the need to say more. 'Listen, I don't want you to be flying blind on this. I stumbled on this guy's name recently. Out of the blue. I think he was a guy I met during the war. That guy, that Aussie . . .'

Clelland stared, embarrassed.

Wedderburn had tears in his eyes. 'I'm sorry. I've never been able to talk about it.' He took a deep breath. 'I think he saved my life.'

That damn war, Clelland thought. So many men came home with terrible memories buried deep inside them. He checked his impulse to say, 'That's okay pal. I know how it is.' He did not know. It was an easy thing to say, a cliché. He waited for Wedderburn to speak.

Hank appreciated his silence. 'Thanks. You see, now this has confronted me I have to know. I don't want to discuss it with his family. If I'm wrong, I'd make a goddam fool of myself. If I'm right, it could be worse. Why resurrect all the pain again? Put his wife through it a second time. This is a private matter, between me and a guy who has been dead for fourteen years. It's not just that I owe him – and I like to pay my debts – it's not knowing who that digger was that has been bugging me all these years.'

'I hope I can help Mr Wedderburn. Do I need your service record to tie up this enquiry?'

'No. You bring me home all you can on the late John Pace MacNamara and I'll know.'

Clelland retraced his steps through the Wedderburn offices with a heavy heart. The trip to Australia was a bonus, but he felt sorry for Wedderburn. Guys like that carried guilt around with them like lead weights. The real guilt was that their buddies had died and they had lived.

10

He was surprised that a positive guy like Wedderburn couldn't see that these things happened all the time in battle. It was the name of the game. He walked across the foyer, glancing at the list of Wedderburn companies displayed on the wall, and pushed out into the heat of the day.

When he returned from Australia, Clelland delivered his report to Wedderburn's office. Weeks passed, and though the account was paid in full without a query, he heard nothing. Then Wedderburn called, 'Can you meet me for a drink?'

'On one condition,' Clelland said. 'You tell me whether we hit the right button or not.'

'I'll tell you. I feel like some of God's fresh air. What about Lindy's there, by the park? We can sit outside.'

Hank was seated at a table under the trees when Clelland arrived. Hank already had a drink so Clelland bought himself a bourbon and carried it down with him. 'I've come armed,' he said, waving his drink. 'I'm sorry that report only had one blurred photo, lifted from a battalion magazine. All the guys in that photo look alike to me and I didn't want to go to the family.'

'That's okay Tom. I didn't need a photo. It was the timing that was important. You ever heard of the Kokoda Trail before this?'

'Oh Jesus, yes – the arse end of the war.'

'Sure was. It was a hot steaming hell on those New Guinea mountain trails, nothing but jungle, and Japs behind every bush.'

'Yeah, I remember. They were always screaming for supplies from up there but it was hard to get to them. A drop would end up down some ravine or in a Jap camp. But I thought it was only Aussies in that fight.'

'There weren't too many Yanks around; it was just our bad luck to draw the short straw. God knows how we got into it, we were raw GI's straight from the good old USA into Port Moresby and on to Kokoda. I can still see those big tough-looking Aussies tramping past us. They looked older than us, or something; I couldn't figure it out at the time. They had those sweaty slouch hats pulled down over their faces, granite faces, and their sleeves rolled up, looking like battalions of lumberjacks. It threw us. They looked so bloody sure of themselves. The jungle was alive with Japs and there were no real battle lines; you fought where you stumbled into them, with bayonets, and, oh Jesus, it was a bloody business.'

'Now I've learned something. I had no idea any of our guys were on the Kokoda Trail,' Clelland commented.

'By Christ they were, and died there too. But your report taught me something about that campaign I never knew before. Now I realise why I felt so inadequate beside those Aussies; a lot of them had been fighting for years. They just brought them back from Tobruk and pointed them at the Japs. They were the famous Rats of Tobruk, and I never knew. They were battle-hardened men, no wonder they looked older. Anyway, our officers were raw too; they'd had no combat experience and we got into a hell of a mess, lost too many guys, so we were pulled out and sent around to a place on the coast not far from Buna, and went inland from there.'

'That wouldn't have been much better would it?'

'We still had the stinking jungle and plenty of Japs, but more chance to get our act together. We could use the rivers, move faster, and see what we were about. Kokoda was no place for raw recruits. Anyway, we seemed to be going well after that, until one day I was with a patrol near the Adai River and the Japs jumped us. Two of my buddies bought it right then and they caught another of our guys. I could hear him screaming all night. I took off into the undergrowth; I didn't care where I was going. In the morning I could hear the Japs beating the jungle looking for me.' He finished his drink and signalled the waiter. 'Same again. To cut a long story short they caught me, stuffed a pack of leaves in my mouth, trussed me up and marched me into a clearing where they had three Aussies tied up. They were gagged too so we couldn't communicate, but I felt better for their company. I didn't want to die alone. They left us there all day, no food, no water, and that night the Japs got stuck into the booze and the prisoner nearest them got roughed up a bit. And then two Jap officers started leaping around, showing off with the swords. It looked like some sort of play acting.

'The next thing they came sauntering over, crocked to the eyeballs, rocking on their heels and lurching all over the place. They stood us up, pulled out the gags, but left our hands tied behind us, and started to walk us along a trail from the clearing. One of the Aussies must have known what they were talking about. All of a sudden he lashed out with his boot at the nearest Jap, screaming at us to run. I can still hear him. "Get the hell out of here. We're for the chop, the fuckin' bastards." '

'We didn't need any more telling. We split! I went head first back into that undergrowth crawling for my life and I could hear them all shouting and yelling behind me. The Japs were so drunk it took them by surprise.

'So there I was back in the jungle again, handicapped. My hands were still tied behind me, but I was luckier this time. I fell down a hollow. It was full of ferns so I moved along an inch at a time, keeping my head down. I thought I was going great, getting further away from them, but I must have gone around in an arc. They had caught the Aussies again. I didn't have to look up to see that; I could hear them swearing, abusing the shit out of the Japs, and it frightened me. I was so close to them, but I was too scared to move. I could hear the Japs beating them to get them to shut up. Finally there was quiet, and I couldn't stand it, so I lifted up my head just enough to see what was going on.

'The Aussies were lined up again, ankles hobbled and their wrists tied together in front of them, and one of the Aussies started this crazy row. "Give us back our hats you bastards. We have to die in uniform." It was all crazy, but one of the Japs must have understood and, this sounds insane,

12

but they were big on protocol or whatever they call it, and he sent his men scurrying around for the hats – they found those goddam slouch hats.'

He stopped and drank his whisky in a gulp. 'I've never told anyone this before.'

'You'll get through,' Clelland said, 'even if I have to buy you another ten drinks. You're not leaving me halfway through *this* story.'

'Yeah . . . well they gave them their hats and the diggers were laughing and exchanging hats, and the most insulting remarks they could think of about the Japs, who were standing right in front of them, rifles and bayonets to all sides. And I'm staring and thinking they were all mad when one of these Aussies turned, pretending to be straightening his hat. And for a second he looked right at me. He winked and said "Lower mate" and went right on with a string of cuss words that would make your hair curl, and his mates joined in and the Japs started belting them again while I took off again, going backwards, getting further away into the jungle.

'Do you think that hat business was just a decoy?'

'I'm sure of it. I didn't think anyone could see me, but they could.'

'Did they get away in the end?'

Hank rested his chin on his clasped hands and stared over the neat green lawns and carefully trimmed hedges for a moment before answering. Then he cleared his throat, and, straining his voice to reply, said, 'They were beheaded. All three.'

'Jesus!'

For a long time the two men sat watching the sun go down.

Hank was the first to speak. 'The file you brought me back says that Sergeant John Pace MacNamara was executed by the Japanese in the Adai River area, New Guinea, 22nd December 1943.'

'And he was one of those three men?'

'Yes.'

'Do you know which one?'

Hank paused and smiled sadly. 'It was MacNamara who winked at me. MacNamara who said . . . "Lower mate".'

'How do you know it was MacNamara?'

'Because as long as I live I'll never forget that face. And only a few months ago it walked back into my life and winked at me again.'

Clelland stared.

'No. I'm not seeing ghosts. I met his son, the spitting image of him.'

'God Almighty! Did you mention this to him?'

'No. That's where you came in.'

'Back there in New Guinea. How did you get away?'

'Natives found me. I'd been crawling around that jungle for nine days, covered in leeches, bitten by everything that creeps and crawls and burning up with malaria. I was a mess. I must have come to enough to tell someone in the field hospital about the Aussies, because later on an officer came in to see me. He told me they had located the bodies and asked me if I

13

wanted to know their names. He started pulling out this notebook. That cracked me wide open. They tell me I screamed the place down. They put me on a ship and I ended up in hospital in Townsville. I hung around there for months and then went on to the Philippines. So that's the end of the story.'

Clelland leaned back in his seat and tapped the table. 'No it's not. If I were de-briefing you I would say that is a half-assed report soldier, try again. You left something out.'

'No I didn't. I don't remember much about crawling around in the jungle . . .'

'You said they were beheaded. Don't look away. If you left the scene, how did you know? That's the part you've got buried. You might as well get it out now and be done with it, you've come this far. Did you see it happen?'

Hank's face had turned a sickly grey. 'I heard it. I heard the Japs jabbering and then I heard the Aussies shouting again and then, whatever was decided, there was this dead silence again. I lay in the swamp and I prayed to God to take me away from there and I cried and cried, I was only twenty-three, and then I heard the Aussies starting to scream. And I heard the chop and this terrifying silence. Then I heard one of the Aussies shouting at them to leave his mate alone . . . not to do it, but they did . . . that chop again. And the last one never said another word. I heard them chop him too. I think I'm going to be sick.'

When Hank came back the colour had returned to his face. 'That load must have been sitting on my stomach for years. I'm sorry I put you through all that.'

Clelland smiled. 'I asked for it. I'm pleased my report answered your question.'

'It helps to know who he was.' Wedderburn looked up and smiled, 'There was also a good side to my story of Down Under. While on leave in Townsville I went wandering around the countryside with three other guys, and we all came home rich men.'

'I often wondered how millionaires got started.'

Hank laughed. 'You need that stroke of luck, it's rarely done with bare hands.'

'So I've noticed,' Clelland said ruefully.

'Now to go back to where you came in. Sometimes I think happenings have a purpose. Or even another dimension, I don't know. But John Pace MacNamara had a son. I didn't. And his son turned up in New York and married my niece.'

Clelland gulped his drink. 'You're kidding?'

'I'm not. I think I'll take a trip to Australia and have a look around MacNamara's territory, this Valley of Lagoons. I have the feeling he's sent me an invitation.'

14

# PART TWO

## ARGENTINA, 1825

# CHAPTER ONE

In the year of 1825 Viscount Forster accompanied the British trade delegation to Buenos Aires to meet with members of the Assembly of the United Provinces of La Plata. Although he held no official accreditation and was listed at the embassy only as an observer, Forster's height of six foot three and his bearing made many mistake him for the leader of the delegation.

Over the centuries the Forsters had managed to remain both staunch Catholics and staunchly loyal to their country. As a Catholic, Forster could hold no public office, but the British government had found his services useful. He had served his country well in a less formal, even shadowy, capacity. As a private citizen he could often travel more freely and gather more information than those appointed by the government, and his religion gave him common ground with many who would look with suspicion on a Protestant. His role suited Forster. He enjoyed being involved in diplomatic affairs free from the leaden hands of bureaucrats, and as an intrepid traveller he endeared himself to everyone he met with his enthusiasm and charm.

On this expedition, once again, he needed all those attributes to deal with the proud and prickly South Americans. His religion, he knew, had already assisted him in establishing a basis of trust. Now it would be up to him to discreetly sound out the feelings on the subject of the Islas Malvinas. The British government was intent on annexing these islands with a minimum of fuss and there was reason to believe that the La Plata Assembly would acquiesce.

It was not enough that in the eyes of those who counted in Buenos Aires the British were supporting them in their struggle against the Spanish. There were past conflicts which had not been forgotten. In 1806 the British had invaded this very territory, the Spanish viceroyalty of La Plata.

The Spanish viceroy had packed his bags and fled, and so the people themselves had sprung into the breach and fought off the British. From that day on, encouraged by their success, the descendents of the Spaniards saw themselves as patriotic Argentinians. It was this that gave them the incentive to turn on the Spanish and embrace the revolutionary spirit aflame in this region. They determined to rid themselves of the Spanish yoke.

Forster had been enjoying the social life of Buenos Aires. As an aristocrat he had been welcomed into the homes of the rich and powerful. His socialising like most things in Forster's life was not without a purpose. He was on the lookout for a high-ranking Argentinian who might support the annexation by Britain and encourage others to as well. His choice had fallen upon Jorge Luis Rivadavia.

The Rivadavias, he had learned, were wealthy landowners of Spanish descent. The main hacienda was up-river at Rosario. There they lived like the Russian aristocracy with serfs, not slaves, but were far more industrious than the Russians. The main source of wealth was silver mines in the North, but they also had huge estates where they maintained herds of fine pure-bred cattle. Their farm hands, or cowboys, of mixed origin, Spanish and Indian, were known as gauchos.

Jorge Luis, now in his early fifties, though not a member of the Assembly, exerted power commensurate with his position in society. He was also regarded as something of a hero, having left his estates and gone to the wars. He had fought in the north against the Spanish and had marched in San Martin's army from Mendoza across the Andes to Chile to strike at Spanish bases.

The wars had secured independence from the Spanish but violence and chaos now reigned as provincial leaders fought for supremacy and disagreed on the form of government. The caudillo (military) element began to take control. This added urgency to the British plans for the Malvinas. Juntas were notoriously difficult to deal with.

In his unobtrusive way Forster had encouraged the company of Jorge Luis during his stay in Buenos Aires and was delighted to find him an interesting and intelligent companion. They dined together on several occasions. The Argentinian, although well educated having attended the University of Cordoba, was anxious to learn more about England and its constitution, and wanted to understand more of the complexities of European trade. Forster was happy to oblige, subtly and indirectly building a case for the British annexation of the islands.

When he was invited to spend a few days at Jorge's hacienda the roles were reversed and it was Forster doing the learning. He found Argentinian lifestyle fascinating. Leisurely meals were enjoyed in the cool white courtyard which was shaded by a pergola massed with red roses. At these gatherings Jorge introduced him to members of his family and Forster was surprised that most of the men spoke English. Jorge's beautiful wife though, spoke only Spanish, but their eldest son Juan, was always there ready to translate for her. They were a handsome family, Forster noted. Jorge with his black hair greying at the temples, slim dark moustache and white even teeth was very much the suave Latin but Forster also noted that with his stocky build he looked as strong as a bull. His son Juan was very like him, but his dark eyes, like his mother's, were wider, brushed by incredibly long eyelashes.

At the first opportunity, when his mother was absent from the table, Juan questioned Lord Forster about his opinion of the government, but

17

his father intervened. 'Lord Forster is a diplomat. He would not wish to comment on our internal politics.'

'One is still interested,' Forster said, in deference to both of them. 'I believe you are related to the Minister, Senor Rivadavia? He seems to me to have sensible, farsighted policies.'

'He will be President soon,' Juan said quickly, and Jorge shook his head.

'You don't think so Father?' Juan challenged.

'I didn't say that. It is possible, but I fear for him; he is an excellent minister with a sure grasp of commerce and a true vision for our country, but that will not make him the leader. I think he will be overrun by Colonel Rosas.'

Juan protested. 'Impossible! Rosas is not fit to lead. He turns gauchos into brigands.'

'No matter what we think of him, the man has an immense fortune and vast estates where he can recruit and train men.'

'Only fools would follow him,' Juan cried.

'You call them fools; they think they are patriots. We all have our dreams.' Jorge turned to his guest with a note of sadness in his voice. 'We had ours. There was dancing in the streets when our dream came true, our independence. We saw a glorious future, and what have we got? Anarchy. There is conflict between the central government and the provinces, between city and country. Caudillos like Lopez in Santa Fé set themselves up as dictators of provinces in order to attack the government. It is very difficult for estancieros like ourselves. We have had to organise to protect our families and our lands against Indians and hordes of militant gauchos, and, as well as that, to maintain order, we must send money and men to Buenos Aires to fight off the caudillos and their troops.'

'Could Rosas be classed as a caudillo?' Forster asked.

'Yes,' Juan said.

'No,' his father disagreed. 'He is more powerful and more dangerous than that. Also his mother is of the family Anchorena, the richest in the whole of the Rio de la Plata. As you would know Lord Forster, the next step for ambitious men after money is power. He will not be content with one province.'

'But I understand he fought with the central government against these provincials?'

'That is true,' Jorge said. 'You do not strike with a hammer a work of art that will be yours in time. He fought on the side of unity; he defeated Lopez and for that he became a hero, and was presented with even more land by the grateful government.'

Forster heard a mutter of irritation from Juan. 'I fought against Quemalcoy, sir, and I saw what Rosas's men were, murderers and plunderers, not soldiers.'

Jorge smiled proudly. 'Yes. My son fought in the Indian wars when he was seventeen and acquitted himself well, but the men from our contingents fell foul of Rosas. When they came back, hotheads like this son of mine began to speak out in the capital against Rosas. They say he stands over the estancieros with his gauchos and lets the gauchos loose in the city like barbarians, and that he should be stripped of his wealth and power.'

'And we will go on shouting it from the rooftops,' Juan said.

'And when Rosas comes to power you will be in certain danger,' his father replied.

'What would you have us do Father? Turn a blind eye? The people must be told about him. Anyway, we have won. He has retired to his haciendas. Bernadino Rivadavia will never allow him a position of power again.'

'Bernadino will have no say in it,' his father said quietly. 'Rosas is not sitting quietly on the pampas, he is gathering strength, becoming the popular hero. He is becoming everyman's dream.'

The musicians came out to play for them and a violinist strolled by.

Forster was disappointed at the interruption; he would have liked to have heard more about this man Rosas, obviously a man to watch.

The next day Jorge invited him to ride out with them to inspect the estate. He noticed that Jorge and his two sons were armed, even the younger lad who was only about thirteen. And they travelled with a bodyguard of gauchos.

'I am worried about Juan,' Jorge said, riding alongside Forster. 'We will have enough trouble on our hands without provoking Rosas.'

'Perhaps he might like to come back with me to visit England and Europe?'

'That is kind of you, but he will know I'm sending him away. Wars are unsettling; a soldier comes home and life is not the same again. He needs a challenge. My father had died just before I returned, so I had big responsibilities. If Rosas comes to power I will have to get Juan out of the country quickly, but it would be easier if I had something in mind for him.'

A great herd of cattle was being mustered into a forest of high-fenced stockyards ahead of them and ranch hands were waving to them, acknowledging Jorge with proud grins. Forster admired their colourful ponchos and wide hats and the brilliantly striped horse-blankets.

The stockyards covered a large area and the cowboys skilfully manoeuvred the cattle into the various sections with a great deal of shouting and cracking of whips. 'Very impressive Jorge,' Forster said but he found the choking dust and the noise of hundreds of beasts trying. He longed to return to the calm of the hacienda. As if he had read his visitor's thoughts, Jorge suggested they might visit a pulperia for lunch.

Forster agreed, silently hoping the place was clean, these shanty inns were not noted for their cleanliness.

When Rivadavia's party rode up there was cheering from villagers. A long table was set out under a spreading tree with exquisite lace-bordered tablecloths and gleaming crystal glasses. Forster noticed familiar faces among the serving people. He realised that Jorge had had his servants bring across all the necessities for a classic luncheon on the chance that it would please the visitor to attend. As the party dismounted and were seated, guitars began their romantic music then violinists played strident tunes while gorgeous women came out to dance, their skirts a mass of swirling red petticoats and heels tapping staccato on the worn hard ground.

Jorge joined in, matching the lead dancer, his precision and control bringing shouts of delight from his people.

Forster applauded, relaxed now and enjoying the scene, hungrily sniffing the aroma of beef on the open grill. He began to eat the stiff breads and the spicy creams and cheeses that were handed to him by attentive servants, washing them down with red wine from a glass that was refilled every time he drank.

Juan was dancing too. He was the image of his father, strong, medium height, good carriage, heavily-muscled shoulders taut under the well-cut richly embroidered jacket. His black eyes, concentrating on the dance, gave him an air of great seriousness until the dazzling white teeth lit up his swarthy face in a smile. Handsome indeed, like his father, Forster thought, and the mother of course.

Jorge came back to the table, his arms around two women, whom he dismissed to rejoin his guest. 'Ha!' he cried to Juan who was nearby. 'Pour me some wine. I am over-excelled.'

'Exerted,' Juan said and his father grinned.

'See how good is his English, and he loves to correct his father.'

He sat down beside Forster. 'Are you getting enough to eat?'

'Indeed I am. And the wine is superb.'

'Good. It is our own wine.' He watched Juan moodily for some minutes and then turned to Lord Forster. 'Have you ever been to New South Wales?'

'No I have not. I had hoped to go there from here and return home via the Cape of Good Hope, but it is not to be this journey. I must return to England.'

'I have been studying the map. It seems that they have grazing lands there on the same scale as we have here, lands that can be bought for a pittance by the first man who claims them.'

'Yes, I believe so. But why would you be interested in New South Wales when you have the same opportunities here?'

Jorge tapped a finger on the table. 'I might be just a man of the country, but for our family to survive over the generations, and to achieve our present situation, we have had to be political, to watch and to know what is coming. For instance, I know that you British have your eyes on the Islas Malvinas and that there are men in our government who will say: "Let them have those islands, what are they? Just rocks in a great ocean." But I say they are land and land is a birthright. Every inch of land should be defended. Good friend that you are, I will oppose you on that.'

Forster adopted an appearance of studied interest while he worried about getting back to Buenos Aires and finding another champion for his cause. The British would have those islands, they would not allow Spain to take them and neither of the great nations was interested in the Argentinian point of view.

Jorge was still talking . . . 'We have problems at the highest political level and at the other end of the scale the people are beginning to ask why they too do not have land. If I were a peon, I might be asking the same questions, but I am not. I am of the great families which built this country and we say the land is ours while we hear the sounds of revolution.'

'Your people here seem very content Jorge.'

'So they do, but will their children be or their children's children? I doubt it. And tell me this? Why are you British so confident you will be able to retain New South Wales when you have failed in North America?'

'Aha!' Forster smiled. 'We shall not make the same mistake this time. We intend to keep a firm hand on this colony. It *will* remain British.'

'I am pleased to hear that. If it does, it will have a stabilising influence. That colony will prosper.'

'You intend sending Juan there?'

'Yes, if necessary for his safety. Also to invest in land there. If the Rivadavias owned cattle ranches in New South Wales as well as in Argentina we would be more secure. If we were forced to leave Argentina . . .' Jorge shrugged.

'I am sure the Governor of New South Wales would welcome investment from our friends in Argentina,' Forster said. 'And if there is anything I can do to assist, do let me know.'

'I shall. It is a challenge that will intrigue my son. I know it will. He can go out into the world a conquistador, instead of being the small voice here trying to stop the thunder.'

# PART THREE

## IRELAND, 1825

# CHAPTER ONE

The streets of Dublin were furled in dank grey fog, making it hard for Pace MacNamara to keep his guide in sight, the shambling figure looking no different from the rest with his coat collar turned up and cap pulled down. Pace had not been told where the meeting place would be, only to follow this fellow. 'But the way he is going,' Pace muttered to himself, 'skulking down alleyways like the devil is following him rather than a friend, it'll be my luck to end up following the wrong man.'

The guide turned yet another corner and Pace hurried after him, dodging oncoming pedestrians, losing him for a minute in the fog and then spotting him again in the dim yellow light of a tavern doorway as he disappeared inside. What does he think I am? A bloodhound? Am I supposed to sniff his trail?

He hunched his shoulders and walked steadily down the narrow lane as if he intended to pass the tavern and then turned abruptly and went inside to a gloom of low flickering lamps and the smoke of peat, as misty as the streets outside. Moving quietly through the crowd, but not searching, he was waiting for a familiar face or voice. When he reached the bar, he ordered a porter. The barman nodded, poured the drink, and without a backward glance took it to a booth at the far end of the room. Pace followed.

Behind him, some lads celebrating spread across the aisle cutting off access to that part of the bar. Casual it seemed, but it was not missed by MacNamara as he slipped into the booth, facing them, his eyes wary, skimming the company, you cannot tell friend from foe in this town. He took care to note it was only a few yards to the unbolted side door. Not reassured, he wondered if he had walked into a trap.

An older man came wearily through the side door, taking his time. Pace, pretending to stare at some brass plates on a far mantelpiece, saw the floor bolt drop into place as the man closed the door. He flexed his muscles, ready to catapult himself out of the seat if need be, but the newcomer shuffled over, rubbing his black-mittened hands, and slid into the seat beside him.

The barman found a path through the noisy revellers and delivered another glass of porter to the booth. Not lifting his head, the older man watched the white apron disappear before he spoke. 'Do you know me?' His voice was harsh.

'Yes,' Pace nodded, although he had given no sign of recognition until now. Dan Ryan was one of the organisers of the opposition to the British. No-one seemed to know exactly where Ryan stood in the scheme of things and few had ever clapped eyes on the man. Pace had seen him twice at clandestine meetings.

'They're onto you boyo,' Ryan said.

'They've been saying that for a long time now.'

'But they know who they're looking for this time. You're a marked man.'

There was no change of expression on MacNamara's face. 'Is that so?'

'It is so. You've been warned and you won't listen to sense. That's why I had to come myself.'

'You shouldn't have gone to the trouble.'

By the saints, Dan thought, studying him. You never can tell. This one's looking at the last of his twenties, a professional killer, and still has the face of an altar boy, black curls and all. 'I'm carrying your orders,' Ryan said. 'You are to leave Ireland.'

MacNamara showed no reaction but Ryan could almost feel the heels digging in. 'I'm taking a risk coming here to save your skin. You must go. You're no use to us dead and they won't let you be a martyr if that's what you're thinking. You'll just disappear. Dumped out to sea with a bullet in your back.'

He waited for an answer. It'll be a crying shame to lose a marksman like MacNamara, never mucked up a job yet, but if we can get him out we've still beaten them. A morale booster for the boys; a victory however small can raise cheers. Even the mother's darling of a MacNamara isn't safe from informers when the screws are put on; if they get him it will make a lot of others twitch and think about going back to the farm.

'I'll not go,' MacNamara said. 'They won't be forcing me out. Let the English get out. I'll just lie low for a time.'

'Too late. The hue and cry is on to ferret you out. There's no place for you now. We can't stop them and we can't put our safe houses in jeopardy. You're going and that's flat.' He put up his hand to stifle any further argument and pushed a slip of paper across the table. 'The boys are waiting for you outside. Two of the lads will take you to a ship to see you get there safe and sound.'

'To see I get there don't you mean?'

'The ship sails tonight. Its name and the name of the captain are on the paper. If anything goes wrong and you get separated from the boys, keep on going.'

'Tonight? I'll not go tonight. The parents . . . I would have to see them . . .'

'We'll let them know. They'll be glad of the news that you got away safe. Would you rather they hear you were dead?'

'Where is this ship going?'

25

'This one will take you out of Dublin to Bristol, and then the captain will take you to London and put you on another ship for New South Wales. The captain's a good man; he'll set it all up. Your passage will be paid and he'll see you have some spending money.'

'New South Wales! That's the end of God's earth. And it's ruled by the English anyway. You're putting me out of the fat into the fire, man.'

'We're not! You'll be free there. You'll be able to live your life in peace. Listen boy, we're not forgetting what you've done for us here. For once we can pay back. Most of our boys don't live long enough for that. If you stay here, you throw your life away. Do you want me to send a message to anyone else after you've sailed?'

'I do not.' MacNamara's voice was resigned and wistful and Ryan remembered the raid that had led Pace to join them. British soldiers had stormed the bottom end of Mary Street in Kildare, routing families out of their homes and shooting up the place. Two women were killed by stray bullets, one of them the young wife of Pace MacNamara. Though the British never knew it, they had done themselves a bad turn that day, Dan thought. It was a pity they would never know what that raid had cost them in British lives at the hands of the grieving husband. Revenge was never sweet to the likes of MacNamara, only never ending.

# PART FOUR

## ENGLAND 1825

# CHAPTER ONE

Huddled in the ankle-deep filth of a dark corner, Jack could not decide which was worse, the foul stink of the overcrowded cell or the biting, sleet-laden wind sweeping in from the open barred window above him where a hag was wheedling the prisoners to buy her beggar scraps. He kept his head down, afraid someone might recognise him as Jack Wodrow, highwayman. So far he had been able to pass himself off as Jack Drew, charged with a lesser offence. He studied the men who were to be his fellow travellers – trans-portees to New South Wales – and wondered why the government would be bothered shipping out such a miserable, useless lot, a good few of them half dead already.

Felons, the judge had called them and that tickled Jack. Most of the scavenging scum would give a true felon a bad name. The poor sods were being banished for stealing barely enough to survive one day. The bloody hulks and prisons were full to overflowing with the sweepings of the slums and poorhouses and now the government was spending a fortune shipping them to faraway lands instead of using the money to feed them, which was the root of the trouble in the first place.

It was rumoured around the prison that they would be tossed overboard out at sea, and the more gullible were crazy with fear already. Jack dismissed that story. The landowners, the gentry, and their hangers-on in the courts were too stupid to think of that solution. Had it been up to Jack he might have considered disposing of the dregs that way, nice and easy. Keep the healthy ones and sling the rest into the briny and good riddance. A prisoner stumbled past him in the darkness and Jack lashed at him with his boot. 'Get your plague-ridden bloody sores away from me,' he snarled.

He amused himself choosing the men he would keep and the men he would consign to the deep. If there were a few hearty ones around, might not there be a chance to take over the ship? He had never been to sea before but the idea struck him as a possibility. He would have to give it more thought.

For the present there were other problems. Jack believed he had no place among these wretches. He had seen his career as a highwayman as strictly business, a stepping stone to a better life. He had not been greedy; the wealthy merchants and travellers he robbed could well spare the contents of their purses. For years he had been cautious, trusting no-one and then mis-fortune had come upon him, tumbled on him like rocks from a cliff.

He had built a sizeable fortune in coin, almost enough to buy a tavern and live grand but while he was out one day, for less than an hour, a thief had broken into his lodgings and stolen his savings. His savings! Jack Wodrow, Black Jack, had been robbed! If he ever found the bastard, but there was little hope of that.

As a result of that loss, he had redoubled his activities, and one night on the Birmingham Road a merchant had lunged at him. Jack had only intended to shove him aside but his musket had fired and he could still see the fellow sinking to the ground, astonished. After that he had gone hotfoot to London, lying low in the rockeries around St Giles. Then the next bit of bad luck had descended.

He was walking home through the mists of a dark alleyway when he saw a dandy come stumbling, drunk, out of Minella's house. Easy pickings. In a flash Jack was upon him and was rifling his pockets when the dandy's friends rushed out of the bordello and fell upon Jack. They delivered him to the parish watchman under the name he had given them, Jack Drew, and the high mincing voices, so self-assured, had saved his life. A parish watchman was unlikely to question information given to him by gentry, and Jack entered the criminal lists as a thief, not as a highwayman wanted for murder.

He pulled his coat around him. The judge had sentenced him to be transported to New South Wales, better than a hanging.

The next morning they were taken to the blacksmith's shop for their chains. There were complaints among the prisoners at the use of bolt locks on their ankles but Jack adjusted to the stiff shuffle, forcing himself to submit without protest. Do what they tell you, he told himself, they'll not hear a word from Jack Drew until he is well clear of these shores. With the chains on their wrists linking them fore and aft the prisoners were marched down the street to the river and onto the barges.

Jack listened to the talk around him while the same questions were asked over and over. 'What ship is it to be?' 'How long will it take to get to New South Wales?'

A prisoner chained two-down answered. 'About four months,' and Jack was shocked. 'How do you know?' he growled.

'Because I been halfway there already,' the man replied. 'I sailed in the Royal Navy.'

'What's halfway?'

'The Cape of Good Hope, down at the bottom of Africa.'

Africa? He'd heard of Africa with lions and tigers. He wondered if New South Wales had lions and tigers. He could read, and write a little too, but this information was beyond him. He had a thousand questions to ask but concealed his ignorance. He decided to stick by this sailor. He could be useful.

The barge took them down the Thames to a landing where they were pushed ashore to be joined by another twenty heavily chained prisoners, some of them weedy little lads hardly more than a couple of years into their second decade on this earth.

'What'd you do?' Jack asked one of them. 'Rob the Bank of England?' And the prisoners laughed but a truncheon laid across Jack's neck from the back sent him flying. He hit the rough boards of the landing and blood ran down his face. 'No talking!' the guard shouted.

The sailor helped Jack to his feet and held him upright while the chains were removed so that they could climb into the long-boat which was to deliver them to their transport ship now at anchor in the wider reach of the river. 'You all right mate?'

Jack scowled. 'I think so. For a minute there I thought he'd knocked my head off, the bastard. It's a bloody fitting farewell to the filthy shores of England. The next place can't be any worse.'

All faces now turned into the biting wind to crane and peer at their ship, its masts tall and stark against ominous grey skies. As they bumped across the choppy waves, spray blew over the bow and the sailor rubbed salt water into his face. Jack copied him, washing the blood from his cheeks, enjoying the fresh feeling of the salt water. The sailor grinned at him. 'That's it mate. Never fight the sea, make the most of it.' He nudged and Jack looked back at some prisoners who were already turning green.

They scrambled up the rope ladders to the deck but before they had a chance to look back they were forced down through a hatch into the bowels of the ship. When the ninety-strong contingent of prisoners was below in their quarters a heavy wooden gate was bolted behind them. Jack stayed by the gate. He heard orders being shouted, the answering cries from the crew and the slap of the great sails as they unfurled into the wind. He heard the smooth slip of the winches and the grinding of the anchor as it lifted from the depths, setting the ship loose into the outgoing tide.

He turned to find the sailor standing next to him. 'My name's Jack Drew. What's yours?'

'Scarpy. Just call me Scarpy. I can't make out what they're doing here. There aren't half enough bunks. In the Navy some got hammocks and you shared, two up and one down, some sleeping while his mates were up working, but here, we won't be doing any work. I can't figure it out at all. And look . . .' he showed Jack iron rings set at intervals along the bunks. 'Look at this. The only place I ever seen these before was on a slaver.'

Jack eyed the rings. 'Are they going to chains us down here, the bastards?'

'Looks like it.'

'We're not bloody slaves. We won't bloody let them.'

'Not much we can do about it.' Scarpy fished in his pocket and brought out a small parcel of cheese. 'Here, have some,' he said.

Jack took a piece and ate hungrily, surprised that this fellow would share when he had so little for himself. 'What did you get?' he asked.

'Fourteen years. Striking an officer. The navy flogged the arse off me and threw me out. I should have made a better job of it. What did you get?'

'Me? I got life,' Jack replied, feeling superior.

30

'Four months in this hole with this filthy mob will be as bad as life,' Scarpy warned. 'And I reckon we've got a few butchers down here with us too.'

Jack nodded moodily. He was not concerned about the threat of violence, he could take care of himself, but those iron rings worried him. What if the ship sank? A shudder of fear ran through him. Who would spare the time in a shipwreck to release prisoners? A flush of sweat ran from his pores. Four prisoners were sitting in sullen silence on an end bunk. 'Who are they?'

'Irish. Politicals,' Scarpy told him.

Jack sneaked another glance at them trying to work out what sort of crimes they would have committed to become politicals. They were all clear eyed and healthy looking. He put them on his list of possible allies, wondering if they had noticed the rings.

'Where'll we kip?' he asked Scarpy.

'The best spot's there by the scuttle. Get some fresh wind we would and a look at the sea.'

'Water might get in there.'

Scarpy laughed. 'You'll be glad of it in time.'

'Good then, we'll clear them sparrows off that perch.' Jack walked over to the bunks and pulled three youths and an old man out of their places.

'Ay!' a small man with a squint yelled at him. 'They was there first!'

'Shut your gob, ferret face,' Jack told him.

Scarpy prowled between the benches. 'By Jesus we could suffocate in here. I seen horses travel better than this.'

31

# PART FIVE

## THE VOYAGE OF THE
### *EMMA JANE*

# CHAPTER ONE

The *Emma Jane* was a sturdy eight hundred ton square-rigger that had sailed for many years under the banner of the East India Company, but the new owners, W & A Stuart and Company of London, preferred their independence. This firm was a branch of the prestigious Stuart Shipping Line of Aberdeen.

In purchasing the *Emma Jane* they had retained the services of the Captain, Hector Millbank, but only after some persuasion, because of a change in policy. Millbank, a fine navigator, had spent a lifetime at sea, beginning before the mast in His Majesty's ships. He had sailed the China Seas and rounded the Horn many times, but more importantly from the Stuarts' point of view, he had twice completed voyages to Sydney Town around the hazardous seas off Van Diemen's Land where many a good ship had been wrecked.

When they informed Millbank that his first voyage under their flag would not be to carry cargo outward bound but to transport convicts to the penal colony of New South Wales, he was outraged. A heavy set man, with black stubbled hair going steel grey at the temples, and a trim beard, Millbank looked the part of the old sea dog, bristling with authority. His keen eyes snapped at the Stuart brothers as if they were his junior officers, not his employers, and his roar could be heard all over the building.

But Walter Stuart had anticipated this reaction. The meeting was deliberately informal, around a bottle of their finest Scotch whisky. He waited while his brother Angus soothed the captain, admitting this was a great deal to ask of him, a radical change from a merchant ship to a transport ship, but reminding Millbank that even though he was transporting prisoners, he was taking these men to a place where, once they had served their time, they could go on to lead full and productive lives in the colony. Many of them were already doing so.

'It is the *Emma Jane* we are talking about here,' Millbank had countered. 'I'll not see her turned into a prison ship!'

Because the brothers needed this man, they avoided the obvious reply that such matters were for the owners of the ship to decide. Walter knew Millbank's reputation as a responsible captain who treated his crew with consideration. He was a far cry from some of the tyrants who sailed the southern seas, and it was this compassionate streak in the *Emma Jane*'s master that he hoped would win the day.

'It is not the thought of a prison ship that worries me,' he said. 'These people are being transported against their will so it is up to us to see that the ships are seaworthy and in the hands of experienced masters. I don't need to tell you, Captain, that many of these voyages have proved disastrous. Incompetent command has resulted in a high death rate among the prisoners.' He had Millbank's attention now. 'Don't you see, sir,' he continued, 'the *Emma Jane* must have an efficient master and one who possesses sure knowledge of those seas.'

Later he explained that there would also be paying passengers on the *Emma Jane*, only a half dozen or so, and it finally seemed, as they reached agreement, that Millbank's main concern was to make certain he had adequate supplies. Walter assured him that they would spare no expense to meet his requirements.

Some measure of satisfaction came the Captain's way. Under the new owners, the *Emma Jane* would now have the full refit he had been requesting for years. The British Government, in the terms of the contract with Stuart, had agreed to underwrite the necessary renovations.

A few days before sailing date Millbank stepped aboard the *Emma Jane*, still harbouring misgivings about this voyage, but he had given his word. The prison quarters shocked him. Carpenters had turned the hold into a maze of timber ledges.

'What are you doing?' he shouted at the foreman. 'This won't take ninety men!'

Each bunk was divided from its neighbours by criss-crossed slats, giving the appearance of pigeon holes.

'Aye Captain, it will,' the tradesman replied. 'We're working to specifications. Four men to each bunk, head to toe. It will work out fine.'

The first mate Palmerston, who had sailed with Millbank for many years, was just as gloomy. 'It'll be a cess pit within a day,' he said, 'but there's nothing we can do about it.'

'Yes, we can,' Millbank told him. 'Once we get under way we'll have them up top to take the air, in shifts maybe, and we'll put some of them to work.'

But as he watched the prisoners come aboard he was not so sure. They were a wretched lot, some of them had a wild-eyed look, half crazed. He began to have second thoughts about letting them loose on his ship. He went down to his cabin already planning to take on extra supplies at the Canary Islands so that they could bypass the Cape of Good Hope and make a run across the southern ocean with the winds. Every day saved was one less day of certain misery for the men chained down below so there was no time to waste in Capetown. It would cause complaints among the passengers and crew but *all* souls on board were his responsibility.

And the passengers . . . thank God there were only five of them, not counting the doctor and his wife. One double cabin was empty. The booking had been cancelled when the prospective travellers had discovered the

*Emma Jane* was a transport ship. As far as Millbank was concerned, that was a blessing. He would use that cabin as an infirmary.

He wrote his first entry in the ship's log before giving the order to sail. 'Ship in fine shape. Officers and crew accounted for. Dr Brooks and his wife aboard. Five passengers: The Honourable Jasin Heselwood and wife, Mr Pace MacNamara, and Mr Dermott Forrest and wife. Ninety prisoners quartered in inadequate space. It will be a sore trial of a voyage, this one. Pray for good winds.'

As the ship heaved forward into the Channel, prisoners began to scream and weep, throwing themselves against the gate, but the two guards outside ignored them. They were more interested in the commencement of a journey that would take them to join their regiment in the far-flung colony where they would find adventure and, they hoped, promotion.

They nursed their pistols and listened to the swish and surge of the sea. Their temporary appointments on this voyage, as jailers, seemed to them a soft job to fill in time until they stepped ashore to military duties in Sydney Town.

Most of these soldiers had been trained by officers who had served in the European wars or the more exotic east and they looked forward to romantic lifestyles and deeds of heroism for the glory of the British Empire. They had no conception of the reality of New South Wales, that they were to become nothing more than uniformed warders, impressed to continue guarding prisoners, hunt absconders and patrol boundaries; they had no idea that it was more than likely convicts would become the front line troops fighting beside their masters on the New South Wales frontiers, receiving only bed and board for their labours and nothing for their fighting abilities.

The further north the pastoralists pushed in this new colony, the more dangerous became their expeditions, but all they saw was a vast empty land ahead of them. They failed to understand that it was part of the Aboriginal culture not to disturb the land they had inhabited for thousands of years and the general opinion was that this country was inhabited by nomads who had no territorial claims.

At the time the *Emma Jane* was sailing south from the English Channel, the Aboriginal tribes of the north lands, which stretched more than a thousand miles from the furthest boundaries of New South Wales, had never seen white men. They were fierce strong people, content to live their lives as their laws decreed, but tribal travellers on the great trade routes around the Continent brought news of white invaders who had no respect for boundaries, the worst of crimes. They listened in great sadness to the stories of death in the south lands and wailed at the fate of those tribes whose people had become displaced, and when big corroborees were held to discuss this tragedy, the men of the north came to listen; the men of the Tiwi tribe and the Tingum and Kabis and the Mandanggia and the

Kungai; and the Banjin men came from their island and the six-foot men of the Keramai with red and yellow painted shells around their necks and immense spears and woomeras. Newegi tribesmen came with their dangerous hardwood weapons, and the Kalkadoon and the Mijamba and Wannamara and even the bloodthirsty Kebishus sent envoys from their islands far to the north, to trade pearls for stone tomahawks. And many more came, from the mountain country and the channel lands and the gibber deserts, and then they returned home and they waited. They would not be taken by surprise like the gentle tribes in the south.

Meanwhile the white men spread out across the land, confident, ignorant, bringing their women and children and their herds. They worried about astonishing droughts, and dingoes that killed their sheep, and floods and fire, and they dreamed of gold and they dismissed the owners of the land. And here on the *Emma Jane* were passengers, in chains or in the sedate saloon, who were going to war. They were destined for roles in a war that is rarely mentioned in the history books, and the battles have a name. The Black Wars.

# CHAPTER TWO

Late in the afternoon of that first day at sea, the gate to the hold was thrown open and all prisoners were taken up on deck. From their vantage points around the decks, armed crew members watched the first mate Palmerston introducing the jailbirds to shipboard life.

Roley Palmerston, known to the crew as 'Roley-poley' because of his rotund figure, was a florid-faced man with a wide smile and a jovial air which gave the lie to his true character. Son of a Welsh coal miner he was a hard, tough man, feared by the crew, many of whom had been preparing to sign off if Millbank left the ship.

One by one the prisoners were stripped to the skin and a seahose was turned on them, sending them slipping to the decks in a scramble of white arms and legs and behinds while the crew roared with bawdy laughter at this unexpected entertainment.

Jack Drew was in the first contingent and after the water assault he ran back to retrieve his clothes.

A sailor barred his way. 'Leave the filthy rags. We don't want those fleabags on our ship.' And the lot went overboard.

He was handed a rough towel, a bar of soap, a shirt and trousers plus a pair of canvas shoes. 'These won't take us far,' he grumbled, examining the thin soles.

The sailor grinned. 'You're ridin' not walkin' mister. Get yourself dressed.'

Down below he found that long chains had been threaded through the iron rings and from them, single chains hung ominously.

'Line up here,' a guard ordered and once in place, each man was chained near his bunk.

'What if the ship sinks and us chained up like this?' a prisoner whined, but the guard laughed. 'What difference would that make to you? You can't swim anyway!'

Jack stood in a fury as a chain was locked to his ankle, accepting it helplessly but with murder in his heart.

All night long he lay in the blackness listening to the swish of the sea and the moans and sighs and vomits of the wretches incarcerated with him, feeling the cold steel on his ankle, and his rage was so great he felt he would have a seizure. There was a price on his head for shooting that fat merchant but now he wished he had shot every last one of his victims to make this sentence worthwhile.

His head ached even more and the farm boy next to him was snoring. 'Wake up,' he said, thumping the body, 'the inn's on fire!'

The lad sat up with a jerk. 'What? What's going on?'

'You,' Jack growled. 'Stop your bloody snoring!'

'I might be snoring mister, when I get some sleep, but you've been tossing around all night there like a woman in her throes.'

Before first light, prisoners were clanking about trying to ease the stiffness from the discomforts of the night, queueing for privy buckets.

Jack sat up and threw his blanket aside. His mouth was dry and his first breath filled him with the stench of human excrement. 'Jesus wept!' he cried and spat on the deck as if trying to rid himself of the taste. He rolled his blanket to keep it clear of the deck which was running with urine. During the night men had urinated on the floor from laziness or from fear of disturbing the others in the search for buckets and others had added vomit to the slime.

The gate opened and the Captain entered the prison unable to hid a grimace of revulsion at the suffocating stench.

'Lovely, isn't it?' Drew shouted and the others took up the call shouting abuse, while the guards cocked the pistols, ready to fire.

'I am Captain Millbank,' he announced, waiting while a mutter of anger rolled around the tiers of human beings crammed into their timber catacombs. 'This is the first time the *Emma Jane* has carried transportees . . .' he began.

'First time for us too, mate,' a voice shouted followed by a wave of raucous laughter.

'I will do all I can to help you,' Millbank continued, surprised that the smell of these wretches overshadowed his pity for them. He was already in a hurry to get away from them. 'I propose to remove all chains now we are on our way . . .' The prisoners rattled the irons in response, pleased at this concession, but Jack was not impressed. 'Why wouldn't you?' he roared. 'We're not bloody slaves!' And immediately the mood of the prisoners swung back to rumbling resentment, but Millbank stood his ground, shouting above the din until curiosity forced them to listen.

'Any breach of the rules by any prisoner and all chains will be replaced for forty-eight hours. When the weather permits, you will be taken on deck while these quarters are cleaned. You will be able to get some exercise up there. You will be fed the same meals as my crew and fresh lime juice will be distributed every day. You must drink this juice to avoid a serious sickness called scurvy.'

'We got sick men already Captain,' Scarpy called. 'What about them?' He was feeling chirpy. It was the first time he had ever dared shout back at a ship's captain but he now figured he had nothing to lose.

Millbank had intended to say more but the stench was too much for him. The question had given him an excuse to leave.

Up top in the clean air he caught hold of William, the cabin boy. 'Tell Dr Brooks I want to see him in my cabin.'

'I don't think he has risen yet sir,' William said.

'Then shake him up. It's all hands on deck today.'

'And that's no understatement,' he muttered as he made for his cabin. It was only just beginning to dawn on him how much extra work these convicts would cause.

The wind was brisk and a running swell had them scudding along in fine style. A good start, but the presence of the convicts nagged. He would have to keep a tight rein on them, they were a dangerous presence and by the looks of them there were quite a few cutthroats in the ranks. He sighed. He had not even had time to think about the passengers yet.

Doctor Brooks tapped on his open door.

There was a dignity about this grey-haired little man, despite a slight stoop, that gave Millbank promise of good company on the voyage.

'You wished to see me, Captain?' Brooks asked, clutching his plaid cloak with one hand and reaching unsteadily for a chair with the other.

'Yes Doctor, sit yourself down. You're still not feeling too bright eh?'

'Better today than yesterday,' the Doctor gave a wan smile, 'and then perhaps, better again tomorrow than today.'

'That's the spirit, then you will enjoy the voyage. Have you sailed these seas before?'

'I fear I have not sailed any seas before, sir. My legs seem to be made of rubber.'

The Captain laughed. 'Ah well, I hope we will not have to keep you too busy.' He noticed an inexplicable blink behind the horn-rimmed glasses, but continued, 'We already have some patients for you. Among the convicts I am sorry to say.'

Since the Doctor appeared surprised, Millbank presumed an explanation was in order. 'They were not in the best of condition when they were brought aboard and some of them were overtaken with seasickness, even at the docks . . .'

Brooks was clearly agitated. 'I think there is a misunderstanding. I am not a doctor of medicine!'

Millbank gaped. He shuffled papers on his desk until he found what he was looking for. 'It says here, "Dr Brooks". The owners of this ship, the Stuart Brothers, assured me you were a doctor. You sir, and your wife, are travelling on a grace and favour passage. Who else but a doctor could expect not to pay the fare? I ask you!'

Brooks's face reddened while the Captain waited for his reply. 'I am sorry Captain,' Brooks managed to say at last. 'There has been a mistake. I am a Doctor of Astronomy. Read at the Edinburgh University.'

'Good God!' the Captain exploded, 'And the Stuarts gave you a passage believing you were a doctor of medicine! How did you manage that? Did you not have to show them verification? Do you realise you have endangered the lives of all souls on this ship?'

'Captain,' Brooks said quietly, 'I should appreciate it if you could give me a hearing.' He took his time before proceeding, waiting for Millbank's anger to subside.

Millbank coughed. 'Go on then.'

'I must tell you that at no time was it mentioned to me, when our passages were arranged, that I should take up the role of the ship's doctor. I assure you Captain, I should have protested most vigorously. It is ludicrous. You must believe me. I would not have you think that I have taken up this voyage under false pretences. The fact of the matter is that Governor Brisbane of New South Wales invited me to join him. He is most interested in astronomy and the skies of the southern hemisphere intrigue me, so I was delighted to accept. And, very kindly, the Governor extended the invitation to include my wife. We will be staying at Government House until suitable accommodation can be found for us. If you wish I shall go to my cabin this instant and bring you my correspondence with Governor Brisbane.'

He searched Millbank's face for some reaction but met only a cold stare. 'And besides, Captain, grace and favour though it might sound to you, your ship owners do not count to lose by this arrangement I am sure. I do not imagine the Stuarts give away passage with no return, especially passages at the request of His Excellency, the Governor.'

'No, not them,' Millbank said bleakly.

Having made his explanations, Brooks took out a large white handkerchief and dabbed at his face. He was a gentle person and had managed to go through life avoiding confrontations. He shifted uneasily in his seat, wanting to leave, but lacking the courage to get up and go.

'The bloody misers,' Millbank muttered. 'Do you know what has happened? Those Scot bastards thought they were getting two for the price of one. They spotted "Doctor" on the manifest and thought, with one doctor on board why send another?

'Perhaps so,' Brooks whispered.

'So what's to be done?' Millbank barked, and his passenger, having no idea, stared back at him. 'We must not let this out,' Millbank continued. 'Dr Brooks, until we reach Port Jackson, for all intents and purposes you *are* a doctor of medicine, astronomy is only an interest. Is that understood?'

'Yes Captain, the intent makes sense, the actual purpose may not. What if I am called upon to practise?'

'You will be called on. But you're an intelligent man, between us we should find some answers.'

'I shall be pleased to help where I can, but what if an operation is required?'

'We pray,' Millbank said.

'I shall have to tell my wife about this new status,' Brooks still looked bewildered.

'Of course,' Millbank agreed. 'She'll have to know. We'll muddle along somehow. I've had doctors on board who wouldn't know a neck from a knee bone and others who saw nothing but the bottom of a rum bottle. I'm grateful to you sir and I apologise for jumping to conclusions.'

That evening the Captain dressed with care. There was a long and difficult voyage ahead and he wanted to keep the passengers content. Some of them, he hoped, might even enjoy the experience. He trimmed his beard and moustache and the bushy hairs in his nostrils and stood back to examine the result, but found himself thinking of the passengers again.

The Honourable Jasin Heselwood could be a difficult one. Standing staring into the mirror he pictured Heselwood again. A fine-looking gentleman, tall and slim with longish fair hair. From one side of the parting a swatch of blond hair hung half across Heselwood's left eye, giving him a rakish air, which Millbank thought might not be undeserved.

He always made a point of meeting his passengers as they boarded and Heselwood had seemed genial enough then, attentive to his wife, a good-looking woman, expensively dressed, who, at the time, was more concerned with their belongings. This couple had brought enough trunks and pieces of furniture aboard, including a piano, to fit out a village. The bosun had decided that the best place for the piano was in the saloon and carpenters had to be called in to make a way for it.

There were only three women on board and he hoped they would get along well. Mrs Heselwood and Mrs Brooks should hit it off, he believed, and they would probably make allowances for Mrs Forrest.

Dermott Forrest was a bootmaker from Norwich, off to make his fortune in Sydney Town. His wife, a plump little woman, with pretty brown curls bouncing out from her large blue bonnet, had already told him their plans in her enthusiasm for this great venture. He admitted to himself that she talked a lot but what was that but cheerfulness, which would be needed in the months ahead.

William brought in his blue jacket, well pressed now, gold buttons gleaming.

'Are the passengers assembled?' he asked the lad.

'Yes sir, as many as will be up. Only four of them. Mrs Heselwood and Dr Brooks and Mr Forrest are all feeling too sick.'

'Damn!'

To start on the right foot he had instructed the cook to prepare a special four-course meal. 'Oh well. It can't be helped. Tell them in the galley I want the food served hot and no grease. Now get along with you.'

When he entered the dining saloon Jasin Heselwood was explaining his wife's absence to the group. 'Mal de mer! My poor dear wife is suffering greatly. And our cabin is stifling. One wonders how one will survive the tropics. Ah Captain! How are we progressing? Will the seas become calmer?'

'They're fair enough now Mr Heselwood. Too much calmer and we'd be in the doldrums.' He turned to Mrs Brooks. 'I'm disappointed. I was hoping Dr Brooks could join us this evening.'

She picked up his emphasis on the word 'doctor' with a small smile. 'Yes it's a pity but he is only taking tea and biscuits this evening to be on the safe side.'

He placed her and Mrs Forrest at the top of the table, either side of him, and Heselwood took the chair beside Mrs Forrest. 'No point in leaving spaces,' the gentleman commented. 'Makes a table look like a wake for the dear departed.'

MacNamara, the fourth passenger to brave the first dinner at sea, moved into the seat beside Mrs Brooks.

Millbank smiled at his little party. 'I hope the others find their sea legs soon, it is always very enjoyable to have the full complement to dinner.'

Heselwood leaned forward. 'Tell me Captain. What if the other passengers do not find these sea legs? What if the mal de mer persists?'

'That rarely happens but if it does then the patient has to give consideration to discontinuing the journey. Ship sickness can be debilitating and for some, the only cure is dry land.'

Mrs Forrest gulped, and did not look at all well but Millbank decided not to draw attention to her.

'You seem to be faring well, Mrs Brooks?'

'Yes,' she replied. 'I've never felt better. I think sea life might agree with me.'

Mrs Forrest looked up.' My husband is mortified to miss our first dinner party. He did not count on suffering mal de mer. But he sends his greetings to all.'

'Thank Mr Forrest for his kindness,' the Captain said, nodding to William to begin serving. Mrs Forrest had said they were joining Dermott's brother in Sydney Town and it was Millbank's guess that the brother was a former convict, since both had glossed over how the brother had happened along to the colony in the first place. But good luck to them, tradesmen were needed in New South Wales, they should prosper.

Mrs Forrest began dropping lumps of bread into her soup so he addressed the Irishman. 'You're not bothered by the swell of the sea? You've sailed before perhaps?'

'I have not,' MacNamara muttered.

Millbank was curious about MacNamara, as handsome as they come, with smooth skin and soft brown eyes, but rather gaunt, half starved in fact. In which case, how could he afford to be travelling cabin class? There were other ships that carried Irish emigrants below decks for a much cheaper fare. This fellow had arrived at the gangplank of the *Emma Jane* with only a few belongings wrapped in a bundle, as if he intended to be away overnight rather than years.

'And where are you from, Mr MacNamara?' he asked.

43

'Ah – the Curragh sir,' the Irishman replied, caught off guard, his concentration engaged in the enjoyment of the meal. Millbank heard the hesitation, a note of suspicion in the voice, that it might not be safe to speak of background, and guessed the reason.

Mrs Forrest paused in her open-mouth chewing. 'Captain, I have not been introduced to this gentleman.'

'I beg your pardon madam. Might I introduce Mr Pace MacNamara. And this young lady is Mrs Dermott Forrest.'

The Irishman bobbed his head at her without getting up and Millbank saw the scorn on Heselwood's face. He hurried on. 'Have you met the other passengers yet Mrs Forrest? Our absent friends?'

'Not yet and I confess to curiosity since we shall be travelling companions for many months.'

'Ah then, Dr Brooks will be joining us and then there is Mr Heselwood's good lady. You are all free to use the saloon at any time. It is a change from the cabins.' He went on to explain procedures on the ship, the duties of the steward, William, and other matters.

Jasin Heselwood listened in silence, appalled that he should be travelling on a prison ship. He, the Honourable Jasin Heselwood, gentleman, was offended by the ship, the hoary old captain, this disgusting dining room with its warped floor, musty rags of draperies and blood-curdling food. The smell from the convicts' quarters was already overpowering but it was not a subject one could discuss at dinner, let alone in front of ladies, such as they were, but he vowed to speak to the Captain at the earliest opportunity. And the company! The Forrests were common tradespeople and that bog-Irish fellow! Georgina would not take kindly to these acquaintances. The next few months would be a nightmare, no a rolling, pitching hell! He now regretted his hasty decision to run for New South Wales to be out of reach of his creditors. He should have given the matter more thought.

However, the damage was done, and he supposed he could at least look forward to staying with his friend John Horton, who, by all accounts, was doing well for himself in Sydney Town.

By the time they had finished the dessert of heavy pudding marooned in a moat of custard, the face of the woman beside him had turned pea soup green.

When Milly Forrest staggered from her chair, Jasin was on his feet and the Captain leapt up, calling on William to assist the lady outside, but Jasin's gallantry had almost cured her. She leaned heavily on his arm, her eyes downcast, until he handed her over to the steward. 'Thank you kindly, dear Mr Heselwood,' she managed to gasp before the bile began rising in her throat, forcing her to clamp her jaws shut and allow herself to be wheeled away by the steward.

As soon as the door closed behind them, Jasin leant against it, laughing. 'My God! I didn't think she'd make it out of here. Every mouthful she swallowed sent her greener.'

'Poor Mrs Forrest,' Mrs Brooks said.

'Poor nothing! The woman ate like a pig. It's a wonder she lasted as long as she did. Still what can one expect, having to dine with tradespeople? They tell me New South Wales is awash with them, aping their betters.'

Adelaide was disappointed. Mr Heselwood had been so charming all evening and now he was spoiling it with these cutting remarks. She felt he needed correcting. 'My husband says the tradespeople are the mainstay of the colony.'

'Is that so? God forbid! But what would a doctor know about the business of maintaining a colony? Of controlling a population of convicts and their camp followers?'

She blushed and clutched her napkin. She had not realised he would react so badly to her small rebuke.

'There's not a lot to know,' MacNamara said in his quiet voice. "It's just who controls the firearms.'

Heselwood scowled. 'I think sir, your remarks are uncalled for.'

'As were yours,' MacNamara replied. 'Maybe you should listen to Mrs Brooks. You British have a lot to learn.'

'We are all British subjects Mr MacNamara. Even you.'

'I am not a British subject by choice. Might be one day this colony will see sense and banish the British.'

Heselwood laughed, aware the Captain was not appreciating this turn of events. 'Like the Irish have?'

'Like we will!' Pace corrected.

'If you gentlemen are interested,' Millbank intervened, 'I should like to show you my charts of the route we shall be taking.'

When Heselwood left, Millbank was relieved. Having this pair either side of his table did not augur well for the coming months but he decided, for the time being, to ignore them.

'Did you enjoy your meal Mr MacNamara?'

'It was the best meal I've had in a month of Sundays, thank you Captain. And call me Pace.'

'Pace? That's an unusual name. Where did it come from?'

'My mother found it. A bit of a mix-up of the Latin I think, but it means peace.' He looked at the Captain with a wry smile. 'We are at heart a peaceful race you know.'

Millbank laughed and rose from the table.

'I've enjoyed your company,' he said, 'but now I must be off. Mrs Brooks, may I escort you to your cabin?'

As he left with Adelaide he turned back to the Irishman. 'It's fine up top Pace, if you want to get some air.'

Pace got to his feet to bid them both goodnight and then wandered around the saloon examining the carved furnishings and the pictures of ships on the walls. It was a grand ship, indeed, but no place for him, his place was back in Ireland, and every press and dip of the ship was taking him further and further away.

'Ah dear God,' he said. 'They've turned me into a man without a country.'

# CHAPTER THREE

By the time the *Emma Jane* reached the Canary Islands, Millbank realised
that the voyage would be even more difficult than he had first thought.
The crew complained at the extra work caused by the prisoners, not the
least their constant spitting on the scrubbed decks and companionways,
the passengers were miserable and the prisoners a constant worry.

At first there had been some scuffles with the guards and crew when
they were allowed up top and then more marked aggression had followed.
But no matter what the Captain tried to do for the welfare of the prisoners
they did not stop blaming him for their miserable state and took delight in
shouting obscenities at every turn, especially when they sighted the cabin
passengers. Millbank had been forced to order the passengers to stay out of
sight until the prisoners were returned to their quarters which brought
more complaints from Jasin Heselwood.

Dr Brooks was managing well in his sick bay, assisted by his wife
Adelaide, who was an obliging woman, but did not seem to be able to get
along with Heselwood's wife.

Millbank was certain that Adelaide Brooks's impish nettling of
Georgina Heselwood was deliberately designed to offset the simperings of
Milly Forrest who had appointed herself handmaiden to Mrs Heselwood,
dressing her hair and sewing for her. The imperious tones Georgina used
to address Milly often made Millbank wince.

But these were only minor matters. With the ship at anchor, he made for
his cabin having decided not to go ashore on this occasion, admitting to
himself that he dare not turn his back on the ship even for a few hours.

Palmerston put his head in the door. 'We've been taking stock Captain and
the quarter-master says if we keep using supplies at this rate we'll be
outspending our allowance. We'll have to cut back on rations to the
prisoners.'

'We will not. They promised me adequate supplies. The Stuarts will
learn not to play tricks on me. They want these prisoners to make a good
showing when we get to Sydney, so be it. The only way I can do that is to
put some condition on them or they won't last the distance. Tell him to
order as much as we can carry.'

Palmerston shook his head. 'Very well but you won't get any thanks
from that scum down there.'

'You let me worry about that. Get extra rum for the crew, that might compensate them for our difficult cargo.'

The ship's bell tolled. 'There's the pilot. Send the passengers ashore in his boat. I don't want to linger here any longer than necessary in case some of our below decks passengers get the idea they might swim for it.'

When Palmerston departed, Millbank called in McLure, the bosun. 'I was thinking I might have a talk to some of the prisoners, just one or two of them. It is important they understand what we are trying to do for them.'

'I don't know about that,' McLure said. 'They'd never recognise sweet reason if it was fed them on a plate.'

'It's worth a try. If I can get them to co-operate it would make their lives easier. Who could I talk to? Ringleaders I'm looking for, so the sheep will follow.'

McLure lit his pipe. 'Let's see. There's one fellow they're all scared of, Big Karlie, they call him, but he rules with the fist, no brains. And an Irishman with a following, he's gathered a few into his clan. O'Meara. He never gives any trouble, just watches.'

'Get him up here then. Who else?'

'There's another one, Jack Drew, a lifer. A bit too street-sharp for my likings, but he comes up a boss among them.'

'An Englishman?'

'Yes.'

'Good. I'll start with him.'

As he waited he was certain he could get better organisation for the rest of the voyage with some co-operation. The odd job details had been a disaster; the prisoners had been worse than useless and the daily excursions on deck were trying the patience of everyone on board. If they could behave when they were allowed out he might be prepared to bring them up of an evening. On the lovely tropic nights the crew often had concerts with a few songsters and the scrape of a fiddle and some to dance a jig. The last thing he wanted to do was to keep the prisoners down there like animals, but they were becoming increasingly troublesome and punishments were well overdue. So far he had refused to order any floggings but his alternatives were running out. His passengers were now on their way into Tenerife and Millbank wished he could sail away without them to give him a chance to bear down on these prisoners without an audience.

The guards, looking more sullen than their captives, brought in Jack Drew, a tall lantern-jawed fellow with lank brown hair tied at the nape of his neck, his pockmarked skin stretched over high cheek-bones. He held his head high and stared boldly at the captain. 'What do you want me for?'

'You will speak when you are spoken to, not before,' Millbank growled, and motioned the guards to leave his cabin. 'Your name is Drew?'

'Yes.'

Millbank refrained from ordering the guttersnipe to address him as 'Sir', there were more important battles to be fought. 'I want to see what I

47

can do to make this journey easier for the prisoners.'

'What has this got to do with me?'

'Mr Drew. I hear you are well thought of among the prisoners. If I can explain to you what I have in mind, you could put it to them. I want them to understand that I am trying to help.'

Drew laughed, a hard sneering laugh. 'Even by bringing me up here you'll have them thinking I'm a snitch. You're soft in the head.'

Millbank was patient. 'Mr Drew. We have a long way to go, about four months of sailing ahead of us . . .'

'Four months?' Jack interrupted. 'I heard that before but I didn't believe it. Is that the royal truth then?'

'Yes it is.'

Jack whistled and Millbank saw a chance of breaking through the hard shell that encased the prisoner. 'Would you like to see our route on a map of the world?'

'I wouldn't mind,' Drew said, 'and I wouldn't mind a tot of rum either.'

Millbank grinned. 'Why not?' He liked to see a man with a bit of ginger in him.

He poured the rum and handed it to the prisoner who drank it in a gulp, wiped his mouth and clucked with pleasure. 'That was all right.' Then he turned his attention to the map, and watched carefully as the captain pointed to the Cape of Good Hope and then to the long run across the southern seas. 'There are winds racing across that ocean called the roaring forties,' Millbank explained, 'they come right from the Horn at the southern tip of South America here, on past Africa across the Indian Ocean – see there, and they'll take us right past Van Diemen's land and from there we run up north to Port Jackson, Sydney Town.'

He watched as Jack scrutinised the map, his nose almost upon it. 'It's about as far as we can get from England, I'd say,' the prisoner commented and Millbank nodded.

Jack was still staring at the wall map. 'Where's India?'

'Here,' Millbank pointed. 'But we don't go anywhere near India.'

'What about the Far East?'

'Here. A long way north of Port Jackson.'

Drew walked back to his chair, he seemed to have found out all he needed to know, so Millbank turned the conversation to the matter in hand. 'Now what about the prisoners down below?'

'What about them?'

'Mr Drew. Don't you care what happens down there?'

'All I care about that lot is to get as far away from them as possible. Most of them don't know no better. No matter what sort of a nest you give them they'll poop in it, so what's the difference? You shift me up here away from that filth and I might be able to think up some advice for you.'

Millbank was stunned at the audacity of the man. 'I couldn't do that, I couldn't make any exceptions. No.'

48

'Well ain't that your bad luck! It was English law put us on your ship so don't go belly-achin' to me about how to run it. You're getting paid. You're just as bad as all the rest so no milk-sop talk will get you off the hook. Find yourself another pimp.'

Millbank banged on the timbers summoning the guards who came rushing in. 'Take him away,' the Captain said, but Drew was in full force now, shouting. 'You can shove me out to New South Wales, I don't care, but a prison without walls won't hold me! And there'll be some bloody reckoning one day too. You English!' he spat. 'Don't call me English anymore! You'll find out we're not slaves!'

As the guards dragged Drew away, the bosun came into the cabin, grinning. 'Tough nut that one!'

'Yes,' Millbank said. He wasn't concerned at the outburst, he'd met harder men than Drew in his day. A crew member would have earned the lash for that behaviour but the Captain didn't want the first flogging entry in the log to be listed merely for insubordination. The legal position of these prisoners was ticklish.

'I sent him to solitary for a few days,' McLure said. 'That'll rest his tongue for a while. I told you you won't get any sense out of the bastards.'

Millbank sighed. 'I don't know. Perhaps you're right. If you are, then we'll have to lower the boom on them from now on. But I'll have a talk to that other one, O'Meara. I might as well see what he has to say.'

When the bosun returned he was red-faced and angry. 'I've got O'Meara outside but he wouldn't come on his own. Insisted on bringing a witness. I don't know what the world's coming to.'

'Let's have them both then,' Millbank said, determined to keep his patience with them.

'Aye aye, sir.' McLure pushed the two prisoners in the door. 'This one's O'Meara and this one's Brosnan. Stand up straight for the Captain.'

The two men touched their foreheads in a mark of respect but there was hostility in their eyes. They stood in silence while Millbank outlined his plans for rosters and better conditions for the prisoners. At first they listened in amazement and then, glancing at one another, began to laugh.

'You want us to jolly up the lads, is that it, Captain?' O'Meara broke in, his voice silky. 'Sure then, I tell you what to do. You put us ashore and let us find out own way to the colony. We don't wish to be a trouble to you now. Do we Pat?'

'Not at all,' Brosnan said. 'This looks a nice place out here.' He wandered over to the open porthole and peered out. O'Meara followed him, looking over his shoulder, their backs to the Captain.

'Stand to attention!' Millbank roared, but the two men ignored him.

'They say it's the Canary Islands,' Brosnan continued in a conversational tone. 'It looks a darlin' place.'

'I'll have the both of you flogged,' Millbank warned and suddenly O'Meara turned on him. 'You try that with us mister! You lay a hand on us

49

and we'll teach your villains down there tricks they never heard of.'

Brosnan turned back to them. 'Ah now Dinny,' he chided, 'don't be getting upset. The Captain's doing his best. You see sir, what Dinny is saying is this . . . you've got four Irishmen in your prison, and the rest are your own, you understand? What you do with your own countrymen is not our business. As for us, you don't bother us and we won't bother you. We'll weather it down there without your help.'

Millbank gave up and sent them back below but not before the cheeky Brosnan had the last word. 'You've got some real bad lads down there, Captain. But what would you expect? This is a transport ship not an honest merchantman.'

The studied insult hit home and the contempt he saw in their eyes hurt him far more than Jack Drew's ravings. Brosnan was right. To be the master of a ship with men crushed down below in quarters worse than for livestock, dishonoured all Millbank's proud years at sea.

That night he stayed in his cabin alone and took out a bottle of Jamaican white rum. He made up his mind that if the *Emma Jane* remained a transport ship he would retire.

As the voyage progressed each week became worse than the last. The crew were resentful and the prisoners became more and more belligerent. At one stage they smashed their bunks and the Captain finally had to agree to Palmerston's urging. Ten prisoners were pulled out at random and flogged since none would give the names of the ringleaders.

Heselwood complained incessantly and threatened to demand an inspection of the ship by the British authorities when they reached Capetown. Millbank had made no comment. He understood Heselwood's anger but he could allow no interference. He saw to it that they swept past the Cape of Good Hope during the night.

Looking back on it now, he smiled grimly. The good Lord had stepped in just as the hostility of the prisoners had reached a stage short of mutiny. Hurricane winds had come howling from the dark reaches of the Antarctic and battered the ship for days. It had been a frightening experience for all the passengers but the force of the storm, felt from the bowels of the ship, had sickened and terrified the convicts. Fear had quelled the fires of revolt and their only interest, after that, had been in reaching port safely. They began to treat the crew with more respect and at last the ship's company settled down, but it had taken half the journey to achieve this sullen truce.

Supplies were dangerously low by the time they sighted the wild west coast of Van Diemen's Land and Millbank had been forced to cut the water ration again but the sight of land softened the blow.

As the *Emma Jane* plied up the east coast of the great southern land the weary little group of passengers stared in awe at the rolling green hills and the misty blue of mountains beyond.

'Why! It's quite beautiful,' Adelaide said. 'I half expected to see deserts like the Sahara.'

'Doesn't anyone live here?' Milly cried. 'We have been following this coast for days, and not a single cow or a horse have I seen, let alone a settler.'

'Perhaps they're late risers, my dear,' Heselwood said, and Milly burst into peals of laughter.

'He's calling her "my dear" now,' Adelaide Brooks whispered to her husband. 'There's a turnabout. Of course Milly keeps on about all the money she and Dermott are bringing with them, that would keep Heselwood friendly.'

'You're not being very kind,' Brooks murmured.

'Kind or not, it's the truth. Heselwood is a gambler. The only thing he cared about the whole trip was his card games and his wagers with Palmerston and McLure. Let's hope they get paid.'

'I'm sure that's the least of Mr Heselwood's worries,' Brooks told her primly.

'Well I'm not. If the Heselwoods are as important as they would have us think, why are they travelling on a ship like this . . . unless they are short of money?'

'I really don't know,' Brooks replied.

Adelaide was looking forward to farewelling Georgina and Milly, both of whom had tried her patience to the limit. She had been forced to sit with them day after endless day, sewing or reading, or playing cards, which often ended in an argument since Milly hated to lose. She had found Georgina a stiff person, difficult to get to know, and Milly just the opposite, rarely quiet.

The evenings hadn't been much better. They dined with the gentlemen every night trying to find some suitable conversation beyond that of the food which had really become appalling. They had all lost weight. Heselwood held the floor most of the time, self-opinionated and tiresome, while Dermott Forrest sat like a dummy letting his wife speak for him. Pace MacNamara could be entertaining when it suited him. He had a repertoire of intriguing Irish tales, and sometimes he sang for them. Adelaide smiled. She had often played the piano, accompanying Pace, which annoyed Georgina since it was her piano. Even Brooks admitted that she was a better pianist than Mrs Heselwood.

There had been other nights though, when Heselwood would so annoy MacNamara that the Irishman would disappear for days, taking his meals with the crew.

The only really enjoyable times were when the Captain dined with them, and he and Brooks were able to bring some sense into the table talk.

Millbank came out to join them on deck. 'We made very good time,' he said, looking pleased with himself.

'At our expense Captain,' Heselwood reminded him.

51

'Oh Jasin, look on the bright side,' Adelaide chided him. 'Had we called in at the Cape we should still be out on the high seas, not drawing close to Port Jackson. When are we due for land Captain?'

'In the morning. I shall not enter Port Jackson until sunup so that you can all have a good view of one of the most splendid harbours in the world. It is a great experience to sail down Sydney Harbour and you will be able to see some of the fine mansions lining the shores.'

Pace MacNamara was surprised. 'It has fine houses you say? The colony?'

'By Jove yes. And the colonists will be watching us sail in too because we are carrying mail for them. The arrival of mail is always a great event in Sydney Town.'

'I can understand that,' Georgina said. 'One feels if we went one more mile we should fall off the end of the world. I cannot understand how people could want to live so far from civilisation. I had no idea we should have to travel so far. One absolutely dreads the return journey.'

They were all quiet at lunch, relieved to be in sight of their destination and perhaps nervous of what lay ahead in this strange country. Adelaide could feel the presence of the great landmass, as the ship forged northwards hugging the coastline. 'I had no idea this continent was so immense Captain. Ever since we left the southern Indian Ocean it has been looming somewhere there beside us. It has an air of mystery, of foreboding . . .' She shuddered. 'I find it rather frightening.'

If Adelaide had some forewarning of tragedy, her husband did not. 'Surely not frightening my dear. Interesting. Mysteries are the spice of life and should be embraced. Most of this continent has not yet been explored. We could be witness to some wonderful discoveries.'

Even Jasin was in high spirits. 'Who knows? We might outdo the Spaniards and find cities of gold and all go home as rich as Croesus.'

'It's not beyond the bounds of possibility,' Brooks said. 'An ancient continent like this . . . it would be most unlikely if it did not contain gold. What do you think Captain?'

'I would agree. But where to look? That's the spinner.'

Jasin was surprised they had taken his joke seriously. 'I say. This is a turnup for the books. Why haven't I heard of this before? I shall immediately start searching for my very own goldmine.'

'We will too,' Milly giggled. 'Won't we Dermott?'

Dermott agreed.

Adelaide noticed that Georgina's smile was thin and guessed that she had had enough of the Forrests. During the voyage Milly, an excellent dressmaker, had made Georgina some dresses from bolts of cloth Georgina had with her, and had also made herself useful in smaller ways, insisting on running and fetching for Georgina, but it appeared now that Georgina was preparing to drop Milly. Not surprising of course, she mused, they had nothing in common.

Before she went to bed Adelaide brushed her hair out, letting it fall into shoulder-length golden ringlets. She did have pretty hair but she envied Georgina her smooth blonde hair that was always so neat.

'You are looking very lovely tonight,' Brooks interrupted her thoughts.

'Thank you,' she said. 'But I shall have to do something about my skin, it has become quite weather-bronzed. Heaven knows what the Governor will think. I feel more like a farm girl than the wife of the distinguished astronomer.'

'You look well. No-one could complain of that. We have all been fortunate to arrive in good health. So dear, let us retire. Tomorrow will be an exciting day for us. I am looking forward to meeting Governor Brisbane. What luxury to have his own observatory in the grounds of Government House.'

Out on deck after dinner, Pace MacNamara looked at the dark shadow of this mysterious land. For himself, the voyage had been time spent in limbo, neither here nor there. He had sought out the Irish political prisoners, not surprised to find that one of them, Caimen Court, was an acquaintance, and had tried to help them, but their leader, Dinny O'Meara, had rejected his offer. 'I thought I knew the face of you! What are you doing travelling in style? Are you an informer or just a deserter? We don't want your help. We don't want nothing of you!'

'You mind your mouth O'Meara,' Pace had shouted at him.

Court, the peacemaker, had intervened. 'Leave us be, Pace. O'Meara won't see reason.'

'He'd be the sniper would he not?' Their other friend Brosnan asked Court in a whisper that would wake the dead and that had angered O'Meara even more.

'Then why is he on this ship behaving like an earl? We give him our backs, do you hear me?'

Annoyed, Pace left them to it, but it still hurt him that brave men who had fought for Ireland should be forced to live in such squalor among felons. Especially Court. He had been at Maynooth, studying for the priesthood, but after a year or so he was forced to choose between his country and his church. In the end, he chose Ireland. It was Court who wrote the pamphlets, operated printing presses and kept an eye out for recruits until he was caught red-handed with his offsider, Jim Connelly, who was also on board. They had both been charged with treason and remembering the furore over it, Pace grinned. The magistrate, casting a fatherly eye on the two fine young men, who, their solicitor claimed, were simply 'misled' by their elders, could not bring himself to condemn them to death in the flower of their youth. Instead he sentenced them to life imprisonment in New South Wales.

What might have coloured the magistrate's decision was an 'anonymous' letter informing him that if Court and Connelly were hanged, his own son, also in the flower of his youth, would die the same day. Pace knew all about it, only too well. There was no doubt the threat would have been carried out, they had shown him his target.

And so here they were, he mused, all in together, bound for Botany Bay, He began to hum the song sailors had taught him on the journey and then it did not seem to make sense. He called to a sailor on watch.

'Aren't we going to Port Jackson?'

'Yes sir.'

'Tell me then, why do we sing the song "Bound for Botany Bay"?'

'Botany Bay was the first port sir, but there was no water, so they moved north to the next harbour called Port Jackson There's still plenty of them as come out on these ships thinking they're off to Botany Bay though.'

There was not a cloud in the bluest of skies as the *Emma Jane* neared the jutting sandstone headlands at the entrance to Port Jackson. Sails were slackened and small coloured flags signalled to land and then a cannon fired a welcoming shot, booming out across the ocean and down the harbour to alert the residents. A cutter came out and a boat was lowered to take the pilot on board; the sails were set again and the *Emma Jane* rode past the white tower of Macquarie's lighthouse ready for the six-mile run westwards down the great harbour to Sydney Cove. The sailors sang as they worked as if they were returning home triumphant from a great victory and the passengers lined the rails as excited as the crew.

Captain Piper, the Customs Controller, was an old friend. As the Customs rig approached, Millbank was pleased to see that Piper himself was on board.

'Welcome back,' he called to Millbank as the sailors hoisted him up to the deck.

'I'm pleased to be back,' Millbank said, shaking his hand, 'Sydney Town seems to have doubled in size since we were here last.'

'Aye, that it has,' Piper said. 'She'll be a fine city one day. But I hear you're carrying convicts now?'

Millbank's face darkened. 'First and last time,' he said, 'we've got new owners. I'm thinking of retiring if this is to be the way of it.'

'Sorry to hear that,' Piper said. 'What would you do? Take a little cottage in the country?'

'Not me,' Millbank smiled. 'I was thinking more of Buenos Aires. I've always had a soft spot for South America.'

'By heavens, I wouldn't mind joining you,' Piper said following him down to the cabin. 'I'm retiring too.'

The Captain had the ship's manifests ready for Piper's inspection but his visitor didn't seem to be in any hurry.

'Is there anything wrong?' Millbank asked.

'Oh no,' Piper said. 'I'm just a bit tired. Had a few financial worries that's all. Had to let my harbourside house go. Wentworth's purchasing it from me, and I'll be taking the family and moving out to Bathurst.'

'That's a shame,' Millbank said, feeling depressed.

'It's not so bad,' Piper said. 'Sydney has become a dreary place since Darling took over. Dour little bureaucrat, I'll be pleased to be out of his clutches.'

'Darling?' Millbank said. 'Who's he?'

'Why sir, our new Governor. Lieutenant-General Ralph Darling. The squatters got the better of Brisbane and had him recalled.'

When Piper departed and his ship was under way again preparing to dock in Sydney Cove, Millbank went in search of Dr Brooks and his wife. They were packed and ready to leave the ship, the Doctor in his tweeds and soft cap and Adelaide looking her best in a neat brown bonnet and billowing cape. Standing there by the rails anticipating exciting days ahead, they took on the aspect of a tableau. He walked towards them, the bearer of bad news.

'Would you take one last turn around the ship with me Doctor?' he asked, and Brooks, obliging as always, agreed. When they reached the stern he stopped and took Brooks by the arm. 'I have some news for you and I'm afraid it will be rather a jolt.'

'What could it be on such a beautiful day Captain?' Brooks said, as lighthearted as Millbank had seen him all these months. The Captain, never noted for his diplomacy, tried to think of some words that might soften the blow but gave up. 'Governor Brisbane has left the colony.'

Brooks was still smiling as if his face were suddenly frozen and in a vague movement he turned to look towards the shore.

'Did you hear me?'

'Yes.'

They stood in silence and a light squall blew across the water on its way out to sea. Brooks clutched his cap and then gave a nervous laugh. 'That can't be right Captain. Governor Brisbane has years of his term yet.'

'It is right. He has been recalled. Piper told me. It was rather sudden he says.'

Seagulls wheeled overhead and Brooks seemed to be following their flight. 'Do you know anyone else in the colony?' Millbank asked.

'No,' Brooks said. 'We're not adventurous people, we lived very quiet lives at home. I don't even know anyone who has visited the colony. Not a soul. What shall we do?'

Millbank, always practical, had to be abrupt; he had a great deal to do. 'Well, you can't turn up at the Governor's mansion unless you're sure this one's expecting you. I'll make some enquiries for you. I think you should let the others go ashore, and wait until I can find out what's happening.'

They looked back at Adelaide who was still watching the activity in the harbour.

'What am I going to tell her?' Brooks asked. 'She'll be devastated.'

'The truth, man. What else?' Millbank said. 'Now don't worry. We'll work something out.'

He hurried away, skirting activity on the decks as the crew lowered the sails, anxious to tread dry land again.

The Heselwoods and the Forrests were waiting, portmanteaux and cabin boxes arranged around them, and he wondered what lay in store for them in this outpost. To avoid these passengers he doubled around the starboard side of the ship and came across Pace MacNamara who looked a different person from the morose suspicious fellow who had come aboard in the dark of the night.

'Ha, MacNamara! How have you enjoyed the life of a seaman?'

''Twas an eye opener, sir,' Pace said, 'good enough but I'll be glad to be off.'

'You'll not consider signing on? We had hoped you might want to become a sailor. You were a good hand for a passenger.'

'I would not, thank you all the same. You've been very kind sir. I only did a bit here and there to fill in time.'

'Right you say. See Palmerston before you leave and he'll refund your passage money in return for your labours.'

He brushed off MacNamara's thanks, put aside the problems of Piper and Dr Brooks and went down to speak to the guards in charge of the prisoners. As soon as the passengers were out of the way he wanted the prisoners cleaned up before being issued with prison garb. No matter how long it took, they would walk off the *Emma Jane* looking as respectable as he could make them and that'd be the end of it. He hoped Brooks would have the good sense to keep his wife out of the way during that process because port or not, he had no control over the vicious tongues of some of the wretches.

# PART SIX

## SYDNEY TOWN

# CHAPTER ONE

It had not been the Governor's intention to be part of the welcoming committee for such an assorted collection of arrivals. He had just happened on the scene on his way home to Government House with his Secretary, Macleay, after a meeting of the Australian Agricultural Company. The Macarthur cousins and a brother-in-law, Bowman, had formed the company with formidable old John Macarthur and others of importance such as Forbes, Oxley and the cantankerous Reverend Marsden. They had asked for grants of land outside the proposed boundaries of location, and as they could call on considerable funds and influence from their backers in London and Scotland, Governor Darling doubted that he could resist them. The colony desperately needed more investment, but he did not intend to be instructed by them.

What he would demand in return was more discipline and an understanding that these colonists, no matter who they were, gave more regard to the dignity of his office. And, by God, he would see that they did!

As he took his leave of them he told Macleay to instruct the driver of his carriage to take him home via the waterfront. Though not much of a sailor, Darling was fascinated by ships.

The well-sprung coach and its escort of cavalry from the 40th Regiment clattered down George Street and Darling sat well back to avoid the stares of the rabble.

It was tricky trying to do business with these native-born squatters who had no sense of propriety where his high office was concerned. They believed themselves to be high society, quite preposterous in a colony, and worse, had the temerity to squawk that they were building a nation. He wished there was not such a need to rely on them for finance. Whaling fleets provided exports too, but they slipped away from Sydney to keep the profits to themselves. No. Wool was the answer.

'Very well,' he said to Macleay abruptly, 'if they want grants of thousands of acres beyond the settled areas I'll give them to them.'

'Yes sir,' Macleay said.

'If they're foolish enough to want to go there, what with blacks and bushrangers and God knows what, let them go. I sometimes wonder if it would be possible to force the emancipists and ticket-of-leave men to go out too. After all, they were transported as criminals.'

Macleay hoped the Governor would not attempt such a radical plan, it would cause riots, but he had discovered that this Governor was never interested in the opinion of his Colonial Secretary.

'Tell them to stop here,' Darling instructed, and Macleay knocked on the window.

The carriage and entourage came to a halt, the horses stamping impatiently. Darling stared out to sea. It was one thing to consort with these squatters as if they were gentlemen from his own club but quite another to allow them to believe they had any real power.

'What ship is that?' he asked, looking at the newcomer in the harbour. 'I haven't seen that one before.'

'The *Emma Jane*, sir, from London. Came in just this morning.'

'Is she carrying mail?'

'Yes sir. I believe so.'

'Ah. My wife will be pleased. I think I'll stretch my legs. Get the official mail. We shall take it with us.'

'I believe it would have gone off by this time, sir.'

Darling stepped out of the carriage. 'I said to go and get it!' He strode away enjoying the fresh breeze which cleared his head of the cigar smoke, and stepped out firmly, his back straight, aware that inquisitive eyes were upon him. He passed some wharf-workers and one tipped his hat, 'Gooday Guv.'

The Governor lowered his eyelashes just enough, perhaps, to acknowledge, having discovered that in this country it was not uncommon for the lower orders to address their betters, but he would bend no further to their customs. Hotheads were beginning to emerge, even among the moneyed class, requiring democracy, whatever that might mean. But he, Darling, would not encourage them. He turned to look back at the township. 'You can demand all you like,' he said. 'While I'm here we'll go by the book. All I need to do is to hold the status quo for six years and then take myself back to London for a knighthood. The next Governor can deal with democracy.'

Macleay, returning, pretended not to hear. The Governor often talked to himself, which was unnerving for a secretary who had to guess when he was being addressed and when he was expected not to be listening. But it was all of one to Alexander Macleay, he had his own plans. Macleay had leapt in station from secretary to the London Transport Board to the lucrative office of Colonial Secretary and knew better than to endanger his career by a wrong word to his superior. He was fifty-nine years old with no time to waste and a large brood of children to support. He had already taken up his grant of twenty hectares of land in Onslow Avenue, Elizabeth Bay, and planned to build a Regency mansion equal to any of those occupied by the gentry.

Sightseers were straggling from the wharf, fish and fruit vendors trundled past and the Governor, standing erect, was taking his breathing exercises when Macleay saw a customs officer pointing him out to a

59

bearded sea captain. He too struck a pose suitable to his high office.

'Excuse me, sir,' Captain Millbank said, 'but I am told I am addressing the Colonial Secretary?'

'You are, sir. Alexander Macleay, at your service.'

Millbank eyed his fellow Scot, hearing the words but understanding that this one was by no means at his service. 'Now here's a stroke of great good fortune. You are the very man I needed to see. I have a rather delicate matter on my plate . . .'

'My office is the place for business,' Macleay interrupted.

'But this is a matter of urgency.' Millbank proceeded to explain to Macleay about Dr Brooks, still waiting on board the *Emma Jane*.

Macleay looked nervously over at his Governor who had gone pacing off in the other direction. 'The Governor and his lady do not put up strangers.'

'No, I suppose not,' Millbank said. 'I shall find accommodation for them, but what about this position at the Observatory? Perhaps you could advise where Dr Brooks should present himself to continue with his work.'

'Captain, the Observatory is closed. It is in the grounds of Government House and the Governor will not have strangers wandering about. Another one is being built in a more suitable location but we have all the astronomers we need. There will be no vacancy I assure you.'

'But we can't leave them stranded, Mr Macleay, after all Dr Brooks did come to Sydney on a viceregal invitation.'

Macleay was pleased to see the Governor returning. 'I have no idea what they can do, sir, and I really don't see that this concerns the present administration.' Just when he had almost broken away from this persistent fellow a couple came towards them and Macleay noted that this pair were gentry and, judging by the cut of their clothes, fresh from London. The young man was tall and fair in a fine cloth coat and grey waistcoat with pearl buttons; his trousers looked to be cashmere, the most expensive available, and his lady, almost as tall as he, was very elegant in a dark blue travelling suit with a pert hat placed atop her thick rolls of hair, a new fashion perhaps for the Sydney ladies who still clung to their blinkered bonnets.

Governor Darling, also impressed, signalled to Macleay, who hurried over to him. 'Who are they?'

'I don't know, sir.'

'Then find out. Use your discretion, I may care to be introduced.'

Within minutes Macleay was back with the new arrivals. 'Your Excellency might I introduce the Honourable Jasin Heselwood and his lady Mrs Heselwood. Mr Heselwood is the third son of Sir Edward Heselwood, Earl of Montone.'

'Of course,' Darling said, dismissing Macleay. 'Know your father, sir, know him well. Colonel in the 27th?'

'Yes, Your Excellency. How kind of you to remember,' Jasin replied.

The Governor addressed Georgina. 'The latest fashion from London, I suspect, Madam. You must come to Government House and tell Mrs Darling all the fashion news. She likes to be the first to hear. I am afraid we are quite behind the times, so far away from the hub.'

'We should be delighted, Your Excellency,' Jasin said, placing Darling as rather an upstart. He could not recall him ever having been received at Moor House, but an invitation to Government House before taking the first step in Sydney Town was a lucky start.

Just then Milly Forrest came rushing over, dragging her husband, to prevail on Jasin to introduce them to the Governor, which he did as stiffly as he dared, irritated by interruption.

Darling nodded bleakly to the Forrests and left.

They watched as the carriage drew away and the brilliant horse guard in gold and scarlet fell in behind.

'How absolutely thrilling to meet royalty as soon as we arrive,' Milly cried. 'What a letter I shall write home.'

'He is not royalty,' Jasin said, 'and now we must go . . .'

'Oh no, you can't go yet. Dermott's brother and his wife are back there collecting our baggages. Come and I will introduce you.' Milly was so excited she took hold of Georgina's arm but Georgina eased away. 'Not just now thank you. We really must leave.'

'Where are your friends?' Milly wanted to know. 'Didn't they turn up?'

Jasin lied. 'We had a message to say they are detained but they are waiting for us.' He snapped his fingers at the baggage carriers to follow them.

'The news is not good,' Millbank reported to Adelaide and Dr Brooks in the privacy of their cabin. 'I met the Colonial Secretary on the wharf. He didn't offer much hope for an appointment for you, Dr Brooks, under this administration. Perhaps it might be better for you to call on the Governor yourself when you are settled.'

Adelaide was tense but the full implications of this setback had not yet dawned on her. 'Aren't we going to Government House? We were invited! We are expected, Captain.'

'It doesn't seem so,' Millbank said. 'It's a new crew so to speak.'

Dr Brooks sank onto his bunk, his face ashen.

'What shall we do then?' Adelaide cried. 'Where can we go?'

'I know a place where you can stay,' Millbank offered. 'The proprietors are friends of mine, the Misses Higgins. They have a respectable boarding house. I am sure you will find it pleasant.'

Brooks stood up. 'Very well. We shall go to the boarding house and stay there until the *Emma Jane* sails. Captain Millbank, you have been very kind. Could you give us a cabin for the return voyage?'

'We will not!' Adelaide cried. 'How can you say such a thing Brooks? I will not let you humiliate us like that. We sold up everything before we

61

left, our house, our furniture, have you forgotten? If we went back now, we'd be a laughing stock.'

'What else can we do?'

Millbank interrupted them. 'It's too early to say. If you wait for me I'll take you to Macquarie Street and introduce you to the Misses Higgins. You've come so far, you should give the colony a chance.'

'I suppose we should,' Brooks said. 'Some say Sydney Town is quite exotic.'

Adelaide sniffed. 'I should hardly call it exotic. It looks rather plain if you ask me.'

# CHAPTER TWO

For a change the convicts were assembling in an orderly manner, like waifs who might be denied an outing. The short-term men were feeling light-hearted, boasting that they would only have to stick it out in this sunny town for a few years and then they could take off, back to the old country.

Jack Drew, the lifer, had no such expectations. He had heard the rumour that a man could get over the hills and away to China, and he was anxious for the slow-moving line to take him up onto the deck so that he could see these hills for himself.

Chains clanking, he climbed in his turn to the deck, and there under the impossibly blue skies of New South Wales, Jack had his first glimpse of this new prison. He looked around him in amazement.

There were people on the dock, waving and cheering, to them, prisoners! Shouting encouragement to them, laughing, while bored troopers, their shore escort, stood in an untidy line awaiting instructions. On from them an array of tall masts lined the wharf like an avenue of willows in winter.

And then a strange thing happened. Jack found himself smiling. There hadn't been much to smile about for a long long time. He looked out over a stretch of the great blue harbour, and back to the white buildings of Sydney Town and off to the distant ring of hills and he experienced a sense of space, of being able to reach out endlessly in an uncluttered world.

Overhead, gaudy birds wheeled lazily and then swept away towards the hills, disappearing into a haze of blue. All around him now the *Emma Jane* was bustling with activity and he stumbled ashore among the ranks of prisoners but he was no longer part of them; to him all of these people were intruders on this grand landscape.

Men in cotton smocks ran forward to fix linking chains to their wrists while the troopers stood guard, and an officer in a drab black uniform stepped forward to peer at the prisoners.

'Who's he?' Jack asked one of the workers.

'Captain Noble. Superintendent of the convict barracks, and noble he ain't,' the man whispered and scurried on.

Big Karlie was in the row ahead of Jack. He cleared his throat and spat, from habit, but Noble saw him.

'Get that man's name,' he shouted to the guards. 'I won't stand for insolence. Forty lashes.'

63

'Are you a magistrate?' one of the Irishmen, Connelly, yelled. 'Does a man get flogged for clearing his throat of the stink of that ship?'

'Forty lashes for him too,' Noble called, and Jack looked at O'Meara, who seemed ready to spring, but the troopers were now alert, surrounding the band of chained men, their muskets ready to fire. The men who were employed to fix the chains crouched low to keep out of the line of fire.

Noble was given the two names. He called to a young officer standing nearby. 'Send this pair to Moreton Bay, and . . .' he looked at the prisoners now sullen and quiet. 'The ten men in the front row. Send them there too. Logan's doing a fine job in Moreton Bay. He can do with a few more.'

'Where's Moreton Bay?' Jack asked one of the workers as he lugged the heavy chains forward.

'Somewhere in the north,' he replied. 'Keep your head down mate, Moreton Bay's a hell on earth. You don't want to even know about it.'

# CHAPTER THREE

Pace MacNamara was in no hurry to disembark. When Roley Palmerston finished his duties he would go ashore with him. Pace had watched the Heselwoods leave the ship, their high-pitched voices giving orders to the cargo master about the unloading of their piano, and listened to the remarks of the men working the docks; much more of Georgina's nagging and the instrument would have landed in New South Wales with a bump.

Then the poor prisoners came creeping up like old hermits from their caves and were whisked ashore by the same uniforms that had invaded Ireland. Pace had no idea how a penal colony operated and those uniforms made him uneasy. He was glad to wait for Palmerston in case he put a foot wrong on his first day. He now had two ambitions. To learn as much as he could about this place and find out where they had taken Caimen Court and the other three Irishmen.

It was late afternoon before Palmerston was ready and the docks were crowded with strollers. At the end of Campbell's Wharf, Pace hesitated. 'I'm still not too sure,' he said. 'It's like plunging into the O'Connell Street Barracks. I never saw so many soldiers in my life.'

'You can still sign on with us.'

'No. I'm on the run, Roley. I can't be making any return journeys.'

'Then don't worry about Sydney. Put all that behind you. You're an immigrant here, no-one will bother you. Half the nobs here are on the run themselves, cashiered out of the army or fleeing creditors.'

They crossed the road and headed up George Street. As they walked further into the town the streets became more crowded: ladies walked with their gentlemen, business men in silk hats and frock coats discussed matters of importance on the sidewalks, men in moleskins and high-heeled boots strode by and vendors' carts barred their way, their owners calling out the prices of their vegetables, fish and oysters; Pace felt as if he were attending a village fair where people from all walks of life mingled on the one day of the year.

Phaetons rushed along the sandy road dodging lumbering carts, and horsemen trotted past while Pace turned about to marvel.

'I never thought to see such fine horses here,' he said, walking towards a grey stallion tethered at a hitching rail. 'But now here's a strange one.'

Palmerston was impatient. 'Come on MacNamara. You're holding up my drinking time.'

65

Reluctantly, Pace turned, and bumped into a fellow who looked for all the world like an English squire. 'I'm sorry, sir,' he said, backing away.

The gentleman grinned. 'You like the horse?'

'Indeed I do,' Pace said.

'Do you know about horses?' he asked.

'A fair bit, but this one's got me tossed.'

'That's understandable,' the stranger said. 'He's our own breed. He won't win any bloodstock prizes but he's what we need in this country, strong animals for the distances we have to cover. You must be new here?'

Pace nodded, still interested in the horse.

'Well then, do you want a job?' the gentleman asked. 'We're always looking for good stablehands.'

Pace looked up, surprised. 'I suppose I do.'

'Good, what's your name?'

'MacNamara sir.'

'Right, MacNamara. I'll meet you here in four days' time. At noon. My name's William Macarthur. We've got a station at Parramatta and a good horse stud. You won't find a better job.' He swung onto his horse and with a casual wave to the pair of them, trotted away.

'Talk about the luck of the Irish,' Roley said. 'You're not here ten minutes and you've got a job and a roof over your head. Now it's Jack Boundy's hotel we're making for if you've finished all your business arrangements.'

The foyer of the little two-storeyed corner hotel was deserted when the two men stepped inside so Roley peered into the bar, looking for his friend Jack Boundy.

'Not there,' he said. 'He might be in the office.' He went down a passageway and knocked on a door.

A woman came out, stared at him, and then threw her arms around him. 'Roley! You're back! Well for God's sake, you're a sight for sore eyes.'

'It's great to be back. Now here, Katrin, this is Pace MacNamara, new to Sydney Town.'

'How do you do?' Pace said. She was a fine-looking woman, only about thirty, with jet black hair piled high on her head. From the way Roley had spoken of her husband, Pace had expected an older woman.

'Now where's Jack?' Palmerston was saying. 'He owes me a tankard or two from last time.'

'Jack?' she queried. 'Jack's dead.'

'Oh no!' Palmerston was stunned. 'What happened to him? When did this happen? Katrin, I'm sorry, barging in like this.'

She sighed. 'You weren't to know. He died about four months ago. Drowned. Remember he bought a run out past Parramatta, for sheep. He liked to go out there and look it over, every so often. But there were floods. Jack drowned trying to get back across the river.'

'Well if that doesn't beat all!' Palmerston said. 'Poor Jack! But what about you now?'

'I run the pub, that's all,' she said. 'It's no use moping. Come now and I'll buy you a drink.'

Their first night in Sydney Town was a riotous occasion, with Mrs Boundy turning on the generosity of the house to welcome Roley back. Never had Pace seen widow's weeds look better than on this stately lady in a black silk dress with just a pearl brooch at the high collar. She had an infectious laugh too, a surprising laugh for a woman, a rumble that burst forth into a throaty sound; but he heard her voice change into a rasp when one of the maids spilled a tray of drinks.

He gave no hint of his reaction to the harsh instructions issuing from this sweet-faced lady but her sudden change in tone startled him, disappointed him. Ah well, he told himself, you're either the boss or you're not. She's just playing her part.

In the morning he awoke with a raging headache from too much grog, and found he was not in the hotel bedroom Katrin had allotted him. He shook his head, trying to recall the night, and then lay back on the hard little cot he now occupied, and laughed. Of course! Sometime during the night he had found his way out here with Gwynneth, a Welsh woman, one of the maids, who had let him know that for a price he could share her bed. He'd forgotten to enquire the exact figure but since Gwynneth had gone about her duties he left ten shillings under the thin scrape of pillow. Well worth it. He'd spent nought else last night and had a grand time.

He washed and went back to his own room to find a clean shirt and then wandered down to the kitchen since no-one else in the hotel was stirring.

Gwynneth was already at work peeling vegetables and he noticed now, in the light, she had a wide scar across her face, but he made no comment. Poor woman, he remembered now that she had said all the staff in the hotel were convicts transported from their homelands. The cook came bustling in and insisted on serving him a huge breakfast of porridge and eggs and a large slice of beef, which was too much for him after months of lean meals on the *Emma Jane* but he did his best. The two women seemed to know everything about Sydney Town and were eager to answer his questions.

By the time he walked out the back door of Boundy's Hotel he knew exactly where he was going: to the convict barracks near the park; it was from there that the convicts were sent out to their assigned jobs. He would take up a vigil outside the gates for days, if necessary, to see what he could discover about the movements of the inmates.

He walked up a long street, with the sun on his back, past rows of shops that would do Dublin proud, and then on, peering in at markets and pawnshops and pubs. He cut across a vacant block where fat cows and goats grazed and nodded to washerwomen hauling out their baskets, and kept walking, getting the feel of the town. And he grinned to himself. 'This place is no penance.' But as he rounded the corner he came to the prison and its gallows, with a body still hanging black against the innocent blue sky.

67

'Oh Jesus Christ!' he said. He had been deluding himself. Drunk with the good food and wine and romping with the girls, besotted with the beauty of Port Jackson, and now look at this! They were here too, contaminating this fair land as they did Ireland, with gallows at crossroads to warn of their savagery. He could see the high walls of the barracks and the guards at the heavy iron-grilled gates, and he could hear the voice of Dan Ryan urging him to turn away, but the sight of the gallows had rekindled the anger and he was now determined to find his countrymen.

All morning he sat on a bench across the road from the barracks, watching chain gangs shuffle past, scrutinising every face. The women had told him that only local work gangs lived at the barracks, most convicts were sent away to live at their assigned places of work.

The sight of men struggling down the road in heavy chains infuriated him but he kept his mind on the matter at hand. He could not afford to miss a face.

Around noon two civilians rode into the barracks and not long after that a heavily laden dray stopped outside the gates. The horses stood patiently, flicking at flies while the driver fussed, securing the ropes and checking the canvas cover.

An hour or so later the two civilians rode out again, followed by two mounted troopers. Pace watched them swing out onto the road and halt by the dray.

Two men sauntering along the street stopped to watch the proceedings.

'Who's that feller?' Pace asked them, pointing to the older civilian who was dressed in fine clothes and had a riding crop tucked under his arm. 'He looks like a military man.'

'That's Major Mudie,' one of the strangers replied. 'A squatter and rich as the king, but a fair devil. A cruel bastard.'

'And a magistrate too,' the other man said. 'So there's no arguing with him.' He spat on the ground to emphasise his disgust. 'He owns a big station he calls Castle Forbes. The one with him is Larnach, Mudie's son-in-law and foreman. And he's no better.'

Soon the gates swung open again and four prisoners, their heads shaved to a stubbled baldness, were led out.

'Ha!' one of the strangers pointed to them. 'See! Mudie picks the eye teeth out of them. He always gets first choice. A new lot came in yesterday.'

Pace was confused. 'How is that?'

'Mudie pays the superintendent, Noble, and gets first choice of workers for his farm. He picks brawn. He works them like horses so he needs them big and strong.'

They watched as the prisoners were shoved towards the dray and their chains latched onto the back board. The driver jumped up into his seat and flicked his whip. 'Giddy-up there!'

Mudie rode forward leading the little cavalcade and the dray jerked into action, heavy metal-bound wheels creaking, and at the back, the convicts lurched forward. The troopers did not seem to be in any hurry; their horses reined, they were still talking to the guards while Larnach, his hat set square on his face, trotted out to catch up with Mudie.

Pace was staring at the prisoners and as they came closer he recognised the hawk-face of Jack Drew, the one who had given the Captain a piece of his mind. The next man he was unable to make out but on the other side there was a prisoner who looked like O'Meara. He stepped onto the road to get a better view and saw Brosnan. He ran forward. 'Hey Brosnan! Where are they taking you?'

Brosnan stared at him in astonishment and stepping sideways nudged O'Meara, pointing to Pace.

O'Meara's bull head came up, his face full of anger. 'Erin go Breagh!' he shouted in defiance.

Larnach heard the shout, wheeled his horse and cantered back pulling a stockwhip from his saddle. With a crack like a pistol the stockwhip flew through the air and ripped across O'Meara's back, slicing a bloody red line on the coarse shirt.

'You bastard!' Pace shouted, his reactions as quick as they had ever been, too fast for Larnach. He grabbed the stockwhip. 'You bloody little pig,' he yelled, pulling the whip down and the man with it. He smashed his fist into the rider's face. 'You keep your bloody whip to yourself.'

By then they were all upon him, the troopers and guards, while Larnach screamed abuse. Heavy boots kicked and pummelled him and as they dragged him away O'Meara yelled at him: 'You're a bloody fool, MacNamara!'

He was in a cell, bruised, battered, one eye closed and with excruciating pain in his groin. It was dark, windowless, but the stone floor was dry. He felt around the walls, finding only new pains in his body, and wondered hazily why he bothered and put his head on the cold floor again. To move was to invite more pain. It'll pass, he told himself, just stay still awhile. A door opened near his face and a pitcher of water and a chunk of bread were placed on the floor. He sipped a little of the water but ignored the food, the thought of any food sent waves of nausea through his system. There was no sound at all, and no light and he was grateful, nothing to set his head aching again. A blessing.

He climbed to his feet. His bones creaked and his muscles had no give, like dried-out ropes. He had no remorse for striking Larnach and grinned remembering that crazy O'Meara calling him a bloody fool. Typical of those one-eyed buggers; they liked to run their own wars those fellows, they were never much use in the fight, no discipline, but they had plenty of spirit and their hearts were for Ireland.

At least now he knew where two of them were going though, if he was not too sure what was to become of Pace MacNamara. Even in the colony, he figured, the grand old British justice must have some sway. They had no right to imprison him without trial and this was not a proper prison anyway, it was a barracks. They were up to the same tricks here as at home; take prisoners to military barracks where they were out of the main-stream of the legal system. The only difference now was the convict barracks. Sooner or later he would have to surface, he reasoned. They would have to release him or take him before a court and he'd have plenty to say then.

Upstairs in his office Captain Noble chewed his knuckles. He did not know who the prisoner was and to bring him up for questioning would be dangerous, there were too many eyes around the barracks and the convicts had pipelines to friends in the outside world. The sooner Mudie got the fellow out of the barracks the better, someone would surely be looking for him.

They were. Palmerston and Katrin Boundy were searching everywhere for him. It came out that he'd been drinking late, out in the servants' quarters with Ruby and Gwynneth, and ended up with Gwynneth, and that Mrs Boundy was furious, but so far had not meted out any punishment. Between them the girls gossiped that Mrs Boundy had an eye for the Irishman herself, while it was plain to see that Roley Palmerston would like to court her.

Some of the staff thought MacNamara might have wandered down to the Rocks district and been murdered but Ruby said he was too smart for that. Katrin was on good terms with the local constabulary so they made a search of the area but not a trace of him could be found.

Days later Palmerston remembered William Macarthur, and stationed himself outside the offices of the Australian Agricultural Company until the squatter arrived.

'Could I have a word with you, sir?'

'Do I know you?'

'I'm the first mate from the *Emma Jane*, sir. You hired my friend MacNamara to work at your place, with the horses.'

William nodded. 'That's right. And I'm as good as my word. Where is he?'

'He's missing, sir. We can't find him.'

William shrugged. 'That's the end of it then,' he said and pushed open a door to a drab staircase which led up to the boardroom.

'No it's not,' Palmerston insisted. 'MacNamara's a good man. Something's happened to him, I'm sure.'

William continued up the stairs and Palmerston, frustrated, shouted after him, 'It's your loss, mister.'

'You can't lose what you never had,' William chided but Palmerston knew the bait had been taken, curiosity stirred. 'Pace MacNamara is missing, sir! He wanted that job with you.'

'But what can I do?'

'You know his name and what he looks like. You could claim him as one of your employees. You could make enquiries where I can't.'

'Very well, I'll ask around. Where can I find you if I hear anything?

'At the Nelson Hotel in King Street.'

'Ah yes. Poor old Boundy's place. Now I really must go.'

Two weeks later the *Emma Jane* sailed out of Port Jackson with a welcome cargo of grain and wool. All on board from the Captain down were sorry to have to sail without news of MacNamara but Katrin Boundy had promised to keep up the search. The bosun seemed to think that Pace must have met attackers and that his body had been dropped into the deep of the harbour and, regretfully, Palmerston was inclined to agree.

But Pace MacNamara was taken before a magistrate friendly to Mudie late one night and for six fat lambs from the Mudie station he was found guilty of assault and battery and sentenced to fourteen years with hard labour, to be served in the Bathurst jail.

# CHAPTER FOUR

Having escaped from the Forrests and made certain their belongings were stored securely Jasin managed to find a carriage to take them out to Wilkin House, which, he explained to the driver, was on South Head Road.

'I know it,' the driver said. 'Jimmy Wilkin's place.'

Jasin was startled. 'I was under the impression it was owned by Mr John Horton.'

'It does now. He married the daughter when the old man croaked.'

Jasin ignored him and handed Georgina into the carriage. 'It is a poor show that Horton isn't here to meet us but there must be a good reason.'

'There would need to be. It is very disconcerting. He could at least have sent a carriage for us. I'm inclined to think we should go to an hotel.'

'It would be a waste of money. After all Horton has invited us. We might as well go on out. A drive is what we need after that foul ship.'

Once through the town the road became little more than a track and strange slim trees with high dappled foliage took command of the country-side. Beyond them small farms and cottages looked idle and deserted in the noon-day heat. Save for the rhythmic clop of the horses' hooves and the spinning crunch of the wheels, the air was still, with hardly a breath of a breeze.

Jasin had a lot on his mind; he was now forced to address the problem of how they might live in the colony for the next few years, before returning to London. Georgina's inheritance had dwindled to an alarming state and he knew he could expect no further assistance from his father.

Apart from trusting his luck at the gaming clubs or a few flutters on the horses, Jasin had no idea what he might do to raise money but he was optimistic. At least his London debts were far behind. He was reminded of Horton's letters which had informed him that many people had made great fortunes in New South Wales. He now supposed it was just a matter of finding out how they did it.

They passed some rather presentable houses set well back from the road and as they turned a corner they saw a large house in a very attractive garden setting.

'Is that it?' he called to the driver, who shook his head. 'No, about another mile further on.'

Jasin took Georgina's hand. He never minded her complaints; he agreed with her. He believed she was entitled to better than he had been able to

72

provide so far, and it was right that she should demand to maintain her standards. In fact it was decent of her to agree to come out to the colony at all, although she had been honest enough to admit that her only other choice would have been to return to her mother in Sussex. Their home was a dreary cold place where Georgina's mother was constantly in mourning for some distant relative. Sometimes he wondered if she ever removed the black drapes in that house.

'Here we are,' the driver called and jumped down to open gates.

Georgina took out a tiny bottle of perfume and touched at her face with a delicate lace handkerchief. 'I must look a sight,' she worried, but Jasin disagreed. 'My dear, you look positively splendid.'

The carriage followed a winding drive among straggling trees to the house. It was as strange a house as Jasin had ever seen, built of stone, like a large workman's cottage, but rather attractive sand-coloured stone, and sheltered on all sides by a wide verandah.

A woman came dashing out of the open front door and down the steps. 'The Heselwoods! My goodness, you must be the Heselwoods!'

Jasin bowed and gave her his most charming smile and the woman giggled, her curls bobbing. 'Oh how awful! I mean . . . John is away!'

Jasin turned to assist Georgina down. He was staggered to find that Horton was not in residence but he could not afford to revise his plans at this point. 'I take it we are meeting the lady of the house, Mrs John Horton?'

'Oh yes, I'm Vicky. Do come in. I am so sorry. I wasn't expecting you so soon.'

Georgina gathered her skirts and followed her up the steps. 'I hope we are not inconveniencing you, Mrs Horton. It is true, our ship did arrive ahead of the scheduled time . . .'

'And there was no-one to meet you!' Vicky interrupted. 'That is terrible. John will be so upset.'

'No harm done,' Jasin said, relieved to find that the inside of the house was rather pleasant.

Vicky guided them around wide cool hallways to their room, talking all the time, and Jasin stole a glance at Georgina. It was the first time for either of them, that a hostess, herself, had shown them to their room and they were embarrassed.

'I've heard so much about you,' Vicky said, 'I've been dying to meet you, Jasin. You don't mind if I call you Jasin?'

'Not at all,' he murmured.

'John has told me so much about your schooldays together and what fun you had. One day he is going to take me to London. And Georgina, he said you were the toast of London society. Oh I am excited! He said you were the handsomest pair in town, and so you are, I am sure.' She burst open the door and ran inside to draw back the curtains.

A mahogany four-poster bed dominated the long room, and french windows opened out onto the verandah. A thick moss-green carpet square covered most of the floor and soft lounging chairs were placed at the far end of the room.

'I hope this is suitable,' Vicky cried. 'If you need anything at all, just ask. Oh I do feel a fool not being ready for you.'

'I feel like a show pony,' Jasin whispered to Georgina but she refused to acknowledge his remark, standing stiffly, waiting for Vicky to withdraw. Jasin could almost hear her foot tapping.

But finally Vicky was on her way. 'I'll send around your luggage. And you must be dying for a cup of tea. Just come to the parlour when you're ready.' She closed the door carefully behind her.

Georgina flung her hat on the bed. 'Really! What a person! I thought she was the housekeeper at first. But she is Horton's wife. His mother will have a perfect fit.'

'Well they don't seem to be short of money, judging by these furnishings,' Jasin said.

'No,' Georgina replied. 'As a matter of fact this bed looks so inviting I'd prefer to take tea in here, but our hostess might join us.' She sat on the bed admiring the plump eiderdown and pillows in their white covers which were edged in fine lace. 'I must say her linen is quite exquisite. And the room is so clean, not a speck of dust anywhere.'

'Yes, it's such a relief after that awful ship I can almost forgive Horton for not meeting us. I wonder where he is.'

'John is out at our property in the Hunter Valley,' Vicky explained over tea, pushing a platter of sandwiches towards them. 'You must be starving.'

Hot scones with jam and thick cream were followed by dishes of jelly and an array of mouth-watering cakes.

Jasin ate well, delighting his hostess, explaining that it was such a change to have decent food after the vile stuff they had been forced to endure on the ship.

Two maids hovered around them, pouring more tea and whisking plates away, and it was an effort for Georgina to keep a straight face when Vicky introduced them. 'This is Lettie and this is Bridie. They'll look after you if there's anything you want.'

The girls bobbed and smiled and Georgina, watching Jasin's surprised blink, was highly amused. She realised that this was the first time she had felt even remotely cheerful since they left London, perhaps this colonial visit would not be so bad after all.

'When do you think he'll be home?' Jasin asked.

'In a day or so I expect,' Vicky said. 'Otherwise I shall have to send a messenger to him to let him know you are here. But you will wait, won't you?'

'If it is convenient,' Georgina answered.

'How far away is this property?' Jasin was still confused. 'Do you have a farm there?'

'No, a station, Chelmsford. A sheep run. My father bought it in the first place but he didn't like the bush much. He missed his pub and all his friends.'

Jasin coughed. 'Your father owned an hotel?'

'Yes, that's where he met John. He was looking for someone to manage Chelmsford for him and John took it on.'

'Horton's running a sheep farm?' Jasin was amazed.

'Oh yes, my word. It's much bigger now, carries a few thousand sheep. It's doing extremely well. John and I lived there when we were first married but when my father died we moved in here. It was sad really. Daddy always wanted a house like this but he died before it was finished. We sold the hotel and put a manager on the station. Lately, though, we've had a few problems with the managers, that's why John is out there now.'

'And where is the property?' Jasin asked.

'The Hunter Valley, a hundred miles or so north of here,' Vicky said. 'Now I wonder if you would excuse me for a while. I have a few things to do. You just make yourselves at home. Is dinner at eight convenient for you?'

'Yes, of course,' Georgina said, thinking of that soft inviting bed. She would rest in comfort for the whole afternoon.

Jasin walked out onto the verandah and Georgina followed him. 'Now what do you make of all that?' he said, but Georgina put her fingers to her lips, french windows were open all along the verandah and they could be overheard.

They strolled down to the steps at the far end. 'I shall take a walk down to the gate,' Jasin said. 'Stretch my legs. Do you want to come along?'

'No, thank you, I'm going to rest.' She watched him set off and, turning about, peered into a comfortable little sitting room, surprised to see Vicky working at a desk just inside the door. Vicky looked up and smiled. 'I like to work here because I can see the gate from here and watch for John to come home.'

At breakfast the next morning Jasin was bored and restless. Georgina had remained in bed, claiming to be exhausted, and he faced Vicky across the table alone. He was tired of her chatter, and irritated by the impossible meal of beefsteak and eggs that now confronted him.

He could not imagine what Horton must have been thinking of to marry such a common person, except, of course, for the money. Even so, it seemed a desperate measure. Georgina had told him that it seemed the Hortons were happily married, according to the wife, but why wouldn't she be happy? Horton was a gentleman, and a fine stamp of a fellow at that. A good catch for her.

'Do you ride, Jasin?' she asked interrupting his thoughts again.

'Indeed I do.'

'Well, unless you have other business, why don't you take one of the horses out? It will make you feel much better.'

He glared at her. How dare she patronise him like that! But the chance to get away for a while overcame his irritation. 'That's an excellent idea. I shall go and change.'

Vicky headed for the kitchen. 'I'll tell Fred to saddle up Dossie. She knows her way around.'

Jasin gritted his teeth. Even when Horton came back he couldn't see them staying on here, but where to go next was the problem. He decided not to mention his worries to Georgina but she had her own revelations. 'Jasin, I've had the most frightful morning. Those two maids brought in my breakfast, they seem to have the run of the place. And listen,' she lowered her voice to a whisper. 'They are convict women, they told me so themselves. They were transported here from God knows where and as bold as you like about it too. And if that's not enough, all the servants here are convicts!'

He changed his clothes as quickly as possible. He could give no explanation for the strange employees, except to say that they looked harmless. 'How is this?' he asked, straightening his jacket and setting his cap firmly in place.

'Very correct,' she told him. 'But I nearly forgot . . . there's more. Poor Horton is out in the wilderness where there are wild natives, those maids said, and hundreds of highwaymen, all escapees from the prisons. They say Mrs Horton worries the whole time he is away that he might be killed.'

'My dear Georgina,' he drawled, 'since when do you listen to the idle chatterings of servants?' He picked up his riding crop and left, but as he closed the door it was as if he were shutting off insurmountable problems. He was now fully aware of the foolhardiness of this sudden decision to make for New South Wales, and he was angry with Horton for suggesting it in the first place. He was angry with his father too, blaming him for this predicament.

It was his father who had insisted that he join Harrald's regiment, but unlike his brother, Jasin hated military life; he could not stand being ordered about all the time, so he quit. That had sent his father into a rage followed by accusations that Jasin was living a useless life in London, spending too much at his club. But what else was there? No Heselwood could contemplate trade. And if there were not enough funds in the family coffers to support the three sons then it was not his fault. He couldn't see any point in hanging about at Moor House, since the eldest son, Edward, already had the title, and the estate, well within his grasp.

All very well, Jasin thought, to expect one to keep up the manners befitting one's station in life but no-one had ever explained to him how this might be done without money, except by marrying a fortune. He had rebelled again by marrying Georgina, who had little to offer in the form of a dowry, except a great name, and he had no regrets on that score but it had further alienated his father.

Now, worrying that Horton might be in danger, he blamed all this on

76

his family. It was their fault he was in such a vulnerable situation.

He skirted the courtyard and made for the stables. His brother Edward was a good type, rather spoiled because he had always been sickly. His father had insisted on the first son's favoured position as inheritor and this had driven a wedge between them. Edward was content to interest himself in rural matters but why should he, Jasin, bother? When his father died Edward would get the lot, he could not even lay claim to his own bedroom.

'Oh God,' he groaned, praying for the safety of John Horton, who could be relied on for a loan when the situation deteriorated, as it surely would. It was only ten o'clock but he would have given anything for a stiff bracing whisky. His nerves were shot. Months at sea, preoccupied with the rights and wrongs of this mad venture, had been a strain. He was feeling desperate and edgy.

When he saw the horse, saddled and ready for him, he was furious. It was a nondescript mount, thick around the girth and dull as a potato, a horse for matrons to ride. If this were Mrs Horton's assessment of his experience with horses, she had better think again. He strode past the stablehand, stopping at each stall, examining all of the horses.

'Who is this?' he asked pointing his crop at a frisky black Arab with a white flash on his head.

'That's Prince Blue, sir,' the stablehand said.

'Saddle him up.'

The stablehand cringed. 'That's the missus's horse, sir.'

'Really? I'm sure he could do with some exercise.'

'Mrs Horton don't like no-one else to ride her horse,' the man argued, while the horse stamped and snuffed noisily, smelling an opportunity.

'Nonsense,' Jasin walked away. 'Saddle him up and bring him out here.'

Out on the road he felt free at last. A cool breeze sprang up, bringing with it the pungent aroma of eucalypts, which he found strange but not unpleasant. Rather a cleansing scent. He let the horse out into a steady canter, delighted with its easy gait, and patted it in appreciation. At a crossroads he turned inland and gave the horse his head. Prince Blue galloped eagerly, surging forward to release some of the energy stored in his powerful muscles, and Jasin laughed, urging him on. 'You're too good for a woman,' he cried. This was a mount he would dearly love to own. He reined the horse to a slow trot and followed the sandy roads, getting to know the countryside.

At luncheon he could see Vicky was not pleased that he had ridden Prince Blue, but she made no comment, obviously not wishing to upset Horton's friends, so Jasin pretended to take it for granted that Prince Blue was his to ride each morning.

Georgina rode with him the next few days, accepting Dossie with good grace, although she was, herself, a fine horsewoman and used to better mounts. At one stage she did ask Jasin to let her ride Prince Blue for a while, but he would not hear of it.

'My dear,' he laughed. 'I saw him first. You'll have to learn to get up earlier.'

On the Saturday, Jasin went riding alone because it looked like rain. It was his only excuse to get away from the boring household. Since Horton was expected each day, they had postponed any plans to explore the town.

At an imposing gateway further down the road he was hailed by Horton's neighbour, Lachlan Cormack. 'You must be Mr Heselwood, Horton's friend. Do come in and meet my wife.'

Jasin found this lack of formality odd but with little better to do, he dismounted and walked up the drive to the Cormack House, a two-storeyed mansion which, he discovered when they walked out to the rear of the house, had a grand sea view.

Mrs Cormack was a quiet, reserved person but she charmed him by bringing out some chilled white wine, even at that hour, to celebrate their meeting. They were Scots, both of them, he heard, having come to New South Wales some ten years earlier to invest in sheep. Jasin guessed they would now be in their forties and was intrigued that this sheep business seemed so rewarding but he could hardly question them about it. Besides they were more interested in news of the Old Country.

'Would you care to lunch with us?' Mary Cormack asked but Jasin declined.

'Some other time then,' Cormack suggested. 'You must bring your wife and dine with us when Horton returns.'

Jasin agreed to that, thinking that everything lately seemed to revolve around Horton.

He continued his ride after leaving the Cormacks' house, but on the return journey a sudden sweep of rain sent the dust dancing and a bolt of lightning rent the darkening sky, followed by the loudest clap of thunder he had ever heard in his life. At the ear-splitting noise Jasin jumped in fright but, except for an angry toss of his head, the horse did not falter. Within minutes the sky was black and a wall of rain surrounded them but the sure-footed horse cantered steadily on. Jasin was so impressed with this sturdy horse he was determined to own him. In his praise of Prince Blue, he had already mentioned he would like to purchase him but Vicky had not taken him seriously.

Through the torrential rain Jasin saw that two workmen had opened the gate so he cantered past them pleased to be spared that chore in the wet. They were a rough-looking pair, heavily bearded, protected from the rain by lopsided blankets and dripping leather hats. As he passed he noticed that their saddles had packs strapped to them and rifles were slung in heavy holsters by the necks of their horses and he wondered if these fellows might be bandits. He thought he heard one of them call to him but preferred not to turn back in case they were dangerous. It would be better to raise the alarm at the house. But then Vicky came running down without cloak or brolly, like a mad woman, her curls plastered wet to her head and her face running water. He reined in his horse, but she ran on past him.

The leading horseman spurred his mount up the drive and bent down to sweep up the drenched woman, placing her side-saddle in front of him.

'Great heavens!' Jasin cried at this spectacle.

A voice yelled to him: 'Heselwood, you villain!'

Staring, Jasin saw it was Horton behind the preposterous beard, unmistakably the merry eyes of the dandy he had once known.

'Upon my life,' he cried. 'Is it you?'

Horton reached out and took his hand in a strong clasp, while Vicky, ecstatic, clung to her husband.

'Dear friend,' Horton called through the rain. 'What a happy home-coming.'

The Horton household sprang into life. The new John Horton, whiskers trimmed, rough clothes discarded for fashionable attire, reigned over dinner parties, luncheons, gay picnics and late night card games with his cronies. Friends and neighbours came from all over the district to join in the celebrations and meet the English visitors.

Each morning Horton retired to his office to work on his books and to receive a procession of visitors, business bent. Jasin watched as riders, messengers, agents and squatters tramped confidently past the main house around to Horton's door. He felt left out.

Georgina was enjoying the envy of the colonial women, who admired her stunning clothes, and found herself the centre of attraction, even trading conversations with the men, some of whom were only rough farmers as far as Jasin could make out. To his astonishment, Vicky and Georgina, who prior to Horton's return had been set on a collision course, were inseparable. In a cranky moment he mentioned this to his wife, who calmly explained, 'My dear. Do you realise that for the first time in our married life we don't have a care in the world? No creditors, no cold rooms to suffer. Do enjoy it my darling. The day of reckoning must come.'

'I don't know what to say to that.'

'Then come to bed,' she giggled, 'and you won't have to say anything.'

'Georgina! I do believe you're tipsy.'

'Probably.' Her voice came from deep in the warm white bed.

'Horton's changed,' he growled, pacing the room. 'He's not the same any more. Housebound, that's the trouble. Do you know he belongs to a gentlemen's club in Sydney and hasn't set foot in it since he came in from the country?' He stared out at the dark blue starry skies. 'I mean to say, he could at least have introduced one. I've got things to do.'

'Like what dear?'

'Well you know I play a good hand at cards.'

'Not from what I hear now. They fleeced you the other night I'm told.'

'What do you mean fleeced? Where are you picking up these dreadful expressions?'

'I gather it has something to do with sheep. But you know what I mean Jasin. You lost, dear. They're too good for you here. Not the easy mark you thought you'd find.'

'And you choose to believe that?'

Georgina chose not to reply. When Jasin and his friends had gambled at the Devonshire Club in London, no word of the results ever leaked out. No gentleman bothered the ladies with sordid details. But the games they played in Horton's house were talked about openly. Everyone was interested, even the servants. And Jasin had consistently been losing to Horton and his friends. She wished she had not mentioned it now, too much wine had loosened her tongue and nettled him.

'It's steamy weather,' he said. 'I'll take a turn outside before retiring.'

He breathed in the fragrant night air with a snort of disgust and watched a squeaking bat flap across the dark sky to a huge fig tree. They had explained to him that these things were flying foxes, not the goat suckers found in Europe, but he still ducked his head when one winged over the house. It was only eleven o'clock now, when the gaming houses would be in full swing, and here he was sitting watching bats!

'Ha Jasin! I thought you had gone to bed!' Horton came tramping out and flung himself into a nearby chair. 'Great night!'

'It's a superb night,' Jasin said. 'Why don't we ride into the township for a flutter at the tables?'

Horton was quiet and Jasin waited, feeling as if his life depended on the answer, until he could stand it no longer. 'Be like old times,' he prompted. 'Kick up the heels again.'

'Jasin, I feel I've let you down. It must be damned dull for you out here, but I don't gamble much any more.'

'Aha! I thought I spied a reformed character.'

'Not quite. But let me explain. Gambling in the clubs here is very different from home. Entrée to the clubs depends on two factors, good name or money. I mean there really are not enough gentlemen around Sydney to support the clubs so they have widened the membership to some appalling types.'

'As long as they don't cheat . . .' Jasin began.

John interrupted him. 'No. Wait. What happens is this, the nouveau riche try to outdo the gentlemen and they play for big stakes. High stakes, out of my league you see. Quite mad. And they play for cash. There are no gentlemen's games, it's cash up. Why, they wouldn't even take my note when I first arrived.'

'Deuced bad form,' Jasin said. 'I say, that presents rather a problem, I had hoped to augment the coffers at the tables.'

'Let me warn you, with your background you'd be a prime target for some of these upstarts. They have money to burn. They'd challenge you off the tables. It's damned annoying and not a thing the club can do about it. And anyway, if I might make so bold as to ask, old chum, how are you placed?'

'In practical terms, one could say one is hardly placed at all,' Jasin said with a grin. 'One really must get cracking at something.'

'You could always invest in land. You can take up thousands of acres here beyond the boundaries of location for next to nothing.'

'If beyond the boundaries of location means what I think it does Horton, you must have lost your wits.'

Horton laughed. 'Forget the land then. You know the Governor, you should talk to him about finding a place on his staff.'

Jasin stared at him. 'Now I think you have truly mislaid your senses. First you want to push me off into the jungle and then you suggest I sit in a dingy office kowtowing to that upstart.'

Horton strode down the verandah. 'Now listen, Jasin, it's time we talked straight. Come and we'll find a brandy.'

His guest followed him inside, sulking. Horton had become quite bourgeois, but a brandy would be appreciated. 'What about a game of cribbage?' he asked.

'Very well, but first things first. I wanted to tell you,' Horton began, as he poured the drinks, 'that, like it or not, I've had to change my ways here. Now I'm glad of it.'

'Spare me the tale of the honest toiler, old boy, you'll have me weeping for you. Mrs Horton's dowry must have come in handy.'

'It did, I'll make no bones about that, but I have worked hard and I know what I'm doing. So now I have a proposition for you.'

'I'm sure you have, what is it this time?'

'I need a manager for Chelmsford Station.'

'Are you seriously suggesting that I should go off into that wilderness and run your farm?'

'Yes. I am offering you, as my friend . . .' Jasin was counting cards. 'In the name of God, Heselwood, stand still and listen to me! My late father-in-law couldn't run Chelmsford because he couldn't read and write. Educated men are needed to run the big concerns here. There's a lot of bookwork. Many a squatter has lost his land because he didn't understand all the regulations. You can't run these stations in an ad hoc way. You have to keep a tally on the stores and the stock and pay the wages and keep a daily journal, all sorts of things. Why do you think I wrote to you to come out? I want you to manage Chelmsford, I need you, someone I can trust.'

Jasin shook his head. 'It's all too absurd. I appreciate the honour but do give over. No hard feelings, but it's not for me. I say, I'm parched. That's a damn good brandy.'

'Won't you even consider it?'

'Not in a thousand years. I'd rather go back to London.'

'With your tail between your legs and the bailiffs waiting?'

'Steady on!' Jasin cried. 'That's a bit below the belt.'

'You're right. Forgive me. I went too far in my enthusiasm, but do think about it. The offer will stay open until I do find a manager.'

'What happened to the last one?'

'He died.'

'What of? A spear?'

Horton burst out laughing. 'You are the end, Heselwood! No, he died of sickness. His wife is staying on for a while to look after the homestead.'

'His wife? I forgot about that side of it. Horton, could you see Georgina as a farmer's wife?'

'Don't be ridiculous. It's not farming. And you'd have an overseer. Just forget it now and we'll play cribbage.'

'Good idea. I'm still wide awake.'

When the sun gave notice of the day, streaking the pale grey skies with rays of pink, magpies warbled their tone-perfect notes from the high trees; Vicky woke, surprised to find her husband had still not come to bed. She put on her dressing gown and padded out to the kitchen, where the servants were already at work, and then walked along the verandah, taking pleasure in the fresh dewy air. Cows were trundling up from the back paddock for milking and a flock of white cockatoos sped overhead on the way to rob the cornfields.

As she approached the open doors she heard the shouts and laughter of the two revellers and, peering in, was amused to see the usually stiff-shirt Heselwood, now unshaven, his fair hair hanging over his face, letting his guard down for a change, and her husband as he climbed unsteadily to his feet to proclaim, 'One more game and we'll call it a night.'

'One more game,' Jasin agreed, and Vicky tiptoed away.

Horton cleared the the cribbage board. 'Why don't we make this one a good wager?'

'Surely,' Jasin said. 'But what shall we wager?'

'A good wager must have an element of risk,' John said.

'But if we raise the bets and I lose I shall have to borrow from you to pay you,' Jasin said 'Because you won't accept my note,' he added, and they both hooted with laughter at this witticism.

Horton banged on the table as if calling the room to order, and Jasin sat up. 'Yes,' he said, 'so to the business at hand. Now we really must think of a fine wager here.' His eyes roved around the room.

'The barometer,' John said. 'I'll put up my barometer against . . . what have you got?'

'I don't want the damn barometer. We have to make the game worthwhile.'

'I know,' John cried and bent over to whisper to Jasin. 'It's Vicky's birthday next week. She has always wanted a piano. You've got a piano in storage. We'll play for your piano.'

'Oho! Just a minute, that's Georgina's piano. She'd flay me alive.'

82

'You agreed high risk,' John challenged. 'What more risk than being flayed alive?'

'Well you needn't think I'll settle for your damn old barometer,' Jasin said.

'What then? Against the piano?'

'Is the bet on?' Jasin asked, an idea forming in his mind.

'Of course it is.'

'Very well,' Jasin said. 'The piano for the horse.'

'What horse?'

'Prince Blue.'

'Oh, Christ, no. That's Vicky's horse.'

'It's Georgina's piano,' Jasin reminded him.

'But Vicky can shoot. She'd come after me with a shotgun.'

Jasin laughed. 'Then we have our high risk. Being flayed alive or shot down on the run.' He tapped his fingers on the table, staring at Horton through the haze of blue smoke. 'If you aren't game, we might as well turn in now.'

'Cut for deal,' Horton said, slapping the cards on the table.

When she heard the two men lurching around the passageway singing a bawdy version of 'Cockles and Mussels', Georgina slipped out of bed and sped into the bathroom. With a large towel around her shoulders and her face dripping, she called to Jasin, who waved happily, and still mumbling his song, fell across the bed. She pulled off his shoes, pushed him further onto the bed and threw a cover over him, leaving him to snore away the morning.

She dressed quietly and wandered outside, marvelling that here was she, who rarely rose before ten or eleven, actually up and about at seven in the morning, and finding new pleasure in early morning rising. She had even begun to look forward to eating her first meal of the day in the breakfast room, a pleasant corner of the house.

Vicky was laughing at the state of their husbands when Georgina arrived, but with the servants in the room Georgina could not bring herself to unbend to that degree. She was shocked that Vicky should allow them to be giggling too.

'It must have gone off well,' Vicky said when the maids left. 'It will be simply ideal for you two to be managing Chelmsford.'

'I don't know. It still concerns me. We know so little about such an endeavour. Nothing really.'

'Don't worry, Georgina. There's an excellent foreman in the station. He knows what to do and his wife does the cooking. We just need a manager to live in the homestead and run the whole show, keep an eye on the lot of them.'

Earlier Vicky had explained the offer to Georgina but the two women had decided to keep their knowledge of the proposal to themselves until the men had discussed the matter.

'The homestead is comfortable,' Vicky said, 'but you can furnish it as you wish and there are carpenters on the station. You can write to me for anything you need and I'll be happy to help. Horton will pay for anything you require to get the house into good shape, it all adds to the value of the property.'

Although nervous of such a radical plan, Georgina saw it as their salvation. A roof of their own for a start. And Vicky had told her, without any embarrassment, that they would make enough money to purchase their own property in time. It sounded to Georgina quite an outrageous thing to do, but after all, she recalled, her Great-aunt Cecilia had run off to the deserts of the Levant to live with a sheik, a story that was never discussed with outsiders but made lively gossip within her family circle. And sheep farming seemed to be the only occupation for a gentleman in these parts.

'I can't say what my husband will decide,' she said, 'but if he believes this arrangement to be an amiable one then I suppose we can only try.'

Georgina was envisaging an English country estate with green fields, neat hedges and a gentle stream with, as she understood it, a great many more sheep than were usual at home.

'Don't forget we have that garden party at Government House tomorrow,' Vicky said. 'It will be a bit chaotic but the Governor particularly wants you along.'

'It should be quite pleasant,' Georgina replied. She was looking forward to the party and had already decided she would wear her apricot crepe de chine with its rich Brussels lace trim and matching bonnet.

The following morning she was early to breakfast again, leaving Jasin to another sleep-in. As she had hoped, Horton had already breakfasted and gone off to his office at the back of the house, which gave her a chance to question her hostess. 'Vicky, did John mention the Chelmsford proposal to Jasin? He hasn't said a word.'

'He turned it down,' Vicky said, her voice tight with anger.

'Oh.' Georgina took some bacon from the sideboard and sat down to an unusually silent room. She was a little relieved and at the same time disappointed. No doubt Jasin had considered the idea impossible and he was probably right, in which case there had been no point in discussing it with his wife. Jasin could be silly at times, she admitted to herself, but he was not a stupid man. It had been foolish of her to get carried away with the proposal like a romantic schoolgirl. Nevertheless, she could see no reason for Vicky to be sulking about it, nor would she make any apologies for her husband's decision. She ate her breakfast in dignified silence. It was up to her hostess to speak if she wished. If not, then so be it.

Vicky did not have her second cup of tea and she did not offer one to Georgina. Instead she rose and replaced her chair with a noisy scrape of the floorboards, banging it into place. 'We have to be ready to leave for Government House at two o'clock!'

'Thank you,' Georgina replied calmly, wishing her cranky hostess would leave the room so that she could take some more tea for herself, since even the brash maids had disappeared this morning, like birds when there is a hawk around, she thought, keeping out of danger. But Vicky still stood in front of her, fuming, while Georgina took a tiny piece of toast and spread a skerrick of jam on it.

Unable to cope with the strain as easily as her guest, Vicky finally broke. 'If your husband did not tell you about Chelmsford, then I presume he did not tell you about their wager?'

Georgina put down the empty tea cup with care. 'No, he did not,' she said quietly. 'Should he have?'

'Oh!' Vicky cried in frustration and ran out of the room and Georgina was able to get that second cup of tea. She found Vicky's tantrum tiresome. Whatever the wager, it was none of their business. Horton and Jasin had been making silly wagers all their lives, no-one took any notice of them. It was extremely ill-bred of Vicky to be inflicting her bad temper on a guest. Still what could one expect?

When Jasin came in, Lettie appeared with fresh servings of bacon and eggs and bolted from the room again but Jasin was in great good humour.

'Vicky seems a little upset,' Georgina commented.

'She'll get over it.'

'And what is it she is expected to get over, might I ask?'

Jasin wrestled with tough bacon rind, which gave him an excuse not to look up. 'Horton and I played a game of cribbage the other night, for a prize, and I won. It was a good game. He nearly beat me.'

'What was the prize?'

'The horse. Prince Blue.'

Lacking experience in gambling Georgina failed to enquire about the rest of the wager. 'But wasn't it Vicky's horse?'

'The horse belonged to them. She hardly rode the thing. He's too good an animal to be treated like a toy. Horton will get her another one.'

Georgina shrugged. She was still cross with Vicky for her rudeness. Besides she was pleased that Jasin had acquired a good horse, a saving indeed.

In the carriage on the way to Government House, Georgina began to have misgivings about the wager. Vicky was taking it very badly, and cold-shouldered all of them, refusing to be cheered by the too-obvious solicitude of her husband.

As the carriage turned into the driveway of Government House, pedestrians peered in the windows, trying to identify the passengers, and Georgina was relieved when they parted ways, the pedestrians directed by the sentries to walk down the side of the house, while the important guests drove to the main entrance.

Liveried footmen stepped forward to open the carriage doors and they made their way up the steps to be greeted enthusiastically by His Excellency and Mrs Darling. After a quick chat they moved forward through the house to the garden and grounds beyond, where the festivities were in progress.

There was a magnificent view out over the glittering harbour, and the band of the 40th Regiment was playing a martial welcome, dress uniforms resplendent in the sun. Chairs ringing the bandstand were occupied by guests content to enjoy the concert but others of the common throng were already crowding damask-covered tables to take their share of the afternoon tea while it lasted.

A footman handed Horton four gilt-edged tickets which would allow them entry to the inner sanctum, a large colourful marquee where tea would be served formally.

John and Jasin led the ladies across the lawns, greeting friends and acquaintances, and Georgina was enjoying the occasion until the heart-stopping moment when Milly Forrest, her husband trailing, came bustling across the grass, delighted to see them again.

When Georgina made no attempt to introduce them, the Hortons moved on and Jasin, nodding curtly at Dermott, stood by while Milly talked shrilly of her pleasure at receiving an invitation to Government House and of the wonderful time they were having in Sydney Town, hardly drawing breath.

Feeling something was required of him, Dermott addressed Jasin. 'And how are things with you, Mr Heselwood?'

'Quite well thank you.'

'That's good. It's a fine place the colony, isn't it?'

'Yes.'

Since Jasin was not contributing to the conversation Dermott rambled on. 'It's a funny thing. Milly and me, we worked hard and saved to get out here. We wanted to have plenty of coin in our pockets, see, before we got here, just in case. But we should have come out years ago. The cash is pouring in. The bootmakers' shop is going so well we had to employ a couple of tradesmen and we've opened up a saddlers too. There's a crying need for good saddlers in our district. And what are you doing Mr Heselwood?'

Jasin raised his eyebrows. It didn't take these people long to pick up colonial manners. Back home this fellow would never have dreamed of asking such a question. He gave a bored sigh. 'I'm thinking of taking on a rather large sheep station, property you know.'

'Oh! You're going to be a squatter eh? Well of course that's only fitting for a man in your position,' Forrest said heavily. 'And excuse me Mr Heselwood, now that we've come across you again sir, I wonder could I ask your advice?'

'What about?' Jasin asked, noticing the Governor had entered the grounds.

'Well you see sir, I've got quite a bit of money lying idle and I should invest it but it's hard to know who would set one right. One day when you are not busy you might be able to give me some direction.'

Jasin was suddenly listening carefully but he smiled and spoke to a passing acquaintance before he replied in a bland and patronising voice. 'If you think I could help.'

'I'd be very grateful. We're in Quay Street. You'll see the shop any time you chance to call.'

Jasin frowned. 'We'll see what we can do. But now I really must take my wife away, there are people waiting for us.'

'Yes, of course.' Dermott stepped back a few paces. 'Come on Milly. Mrs Heselwood has to go.'

Jasin grinned as they walked away. He would certainly call on Mr Forrest, he had some thoughts on how Dermott could invest his money.

Just then Secretary Macleay approached Jasin with a request for the Heselwoods to join the Governor at the official table, and Jasin replied with exquisite regard for protocol. 'Would you be good enough, sir, to thank His Excellency for his courtesy. We are pleased to accept but are unable to do so because we have attended today with our hosts Mr and Mrs John Horton. We can hardly forsake them.'

Macleay retired with the message and a loud imperious voice sounded nearby. 'Well said, sir. Loyalty is a rare commodity these days!'

An elderly white-haired man marched over, his hand outstretched. 'Macarthur, sir, John Macarthur. You must be young Heselwood and this lovely lady must be Mrs Heselwood.'

'You're too kind, sir,' Georgina said and Jasin looked on with interest. The Macarthurs were talked about in the colony as if they were royalty.

'Not at all,' Macarthur beamed. 'I'm enchanted. Your wife, Heselwood, is even better-looking than I had heard. I shall have to chastise my informants. Are you coming in to tea?'

They both nodded. 'Well, come on then. We must go with the throng. They eat like grasshoppers at these events you know. I hear you are interested in running Chelmsford Station, Heselwood?'

With an effort Jasin refrained from showing irritation. He had never known such a place for everyone knowing everyone else's business. 'Horton did mention it,' he said.

'Big job you know,' Macarthur told him. 'You should come to Camden and see how things are done. Too many new chums come out here thinking they know everything and end up making a mess of things.'

Jasin wondered if this old boy were trying to provoke him, one never knew with these native folks. But Macarthur was continuing with his advice, still talking as they entered the marquee. 'As I said, too many Englishmen turn up here thinking they know everything and they know nothing. And that goes for viceregals too,' he added loudly, watching the Governor and his wife moving by the tables.

Jasin smirked. He found that remark quite hilarious in this company, and, noticing his amusement, Macarthur raised his voice. 'One day,' he said for all to hear, 'we shall have Australian governors. Native-born people who know what they are doing.'

His pronouncement had the desired effect upon nearby guests who nudged and fidgeted in embarrassment.

Jasin nearly laughed outright. He did not care who they had as Governor, he realised Macarthur's remarks were designed to shock and he liked him for it.

'When are you coming to Camden then?' Macarthur asked.

'One of these days, sir.'

Macarthur glared. 'Don't give me that talk! You can come out next week. I am sure your lady can spare you. The wool clip is important to this country, we can't have waste. We all suffer. Ah, there's Mrs Macarthur, I must heed the call.'

The Hortons were waiting too. 'I say,' John said, 'we're all to sit at the Governor's table.'

Jasin smiled. 'Good. And by the way, Horton, does that offer to manage Chelmsford still stand?'

'Yes. Changed your mind?'

'I believe I have,' Jasin replied, and John clapped him on the back, pleased that his plan was working. Jasin, however, was thinking only as far as Camden, the Macarthur stronghold. It would be interesting to mix with the so-called elite of the colony, one never knew where that would lead. And it would be a change from the confinement of Horton's household. But this still did not mean that he would be burying himself out on Horton's farm.

Pressing on through the crowd towards the official table, he missed the sharp exchange between Horton and his wife.

'Good news Vicky!'

'What good news?'

'Heselwood has agreed to take on Chelmsford after all.'

'Has he? Well, he can go there on one condition. That he gives Prince Blue back to me. Otherwise I won't have it. Do you hear me, John? I won't have it!'

'You *will* have it madam. I need them out there. It was I who made the offer and I will not go back on it. You will kindly leave the management of the properties to me. Now, if you please, we are keeping the Governor waiting.'

# CHAPTER FIVE

Outside on the lawns two other people had arrived much earlier and seated themselves in front of the bandstand.

Dr Brooks insisted that Adelaide remain seated while he fetched tea and cakes. She knew she should be more appreciative but it was hard to rid herself of this depression. Brooks was trying to please, wanting her to enjoy the outing, but Adelaide had found nothing to enjoy since they came to Sydney.

They had both been under a strain since they discovered that Governor Brisbane had departed, and neither of them could cope with the difficulties that now beset them. The room at Bligh House was clean, the meals frugal but adequate, and the Misses Higgins were kind, but it was peculiar to be living in a room with nothing to do all day. No work for Brooks and no household for Adelaide to manage.

They had explored the town from end to end, walking to save expense, but could not find cheaper, clean lodgings, and as the weeks passed, were eating into their meagre capital.

Brooks had finally obtained an audience with Governor Darling and had achieved nothing but the invitation to this garden party.

As the band struck up, he touched her arm. 'They are really quite splendid aren't they?'

Adelaide nodded. She knew Brooks was doing all he could to cheer her up but the band held no interest for her. Not a whit. He was talking again and she wished he would stop, just be quiet for a while, and then she realised what he had said. 'Who?' she exclaimed.

'Milly Forrest. Look over there!'

And it was. Milly Forrest in full sail in a cluttered pink crinoline.

Adelaide stopped Brooks just in time. 'Where are you going?'

'I thought I'd bring her over. It is nice to see someone we know.'

'Don't you dare bring that woman here to be crowing over us. Pretend you don't see her.'

'But why, my dear? We have nothing to be ashamed of.'

'Really? Well if you recall we should have been staying at Government House, not sitting here in the grounds. I do not wish to see her.'

Brooks settled back in his seat and began to nibble at a cake while Adelaide feigned interest in the music.

They stayed until the band packed up, and walked home in silence.

After that Brooks redoubled his efforts to find work. A skilled

89

mathematician, he had applied to every school within range for a teaching appointment but, being a truthful man, he had refused to jettison his beliefs, and doors were slammed in his face. When the question of religion came up, Brooks had answered simply: 'None'. No school boards would contemplate hiring an atheist.

He answered advertisements, tried the banks, tried everywhere but could not find employment of any sort, and Adelaide was becoming angry with him.

'It is your own fault,' she cried. 'Why can't you just say you are Church of England or some religion, what does it matter?'

'It matters to me,' he said apologetically. 'My dear, I think we should return to England while we can.'

'No! We can't. We had the send-offs and all that fuss leaving home, we can't go back yet.'

She recalled too that she had insisted on buying fashionable clothes and luggage before they left London so that they could look the part mixing in Sydney society, and had spent more than she had intended. And now all those fine clothes were crammed into the small boarding-house wardrobe.

Weeks passed and each time he went down to pay their rent Adelaide saw the anxiety on his face and she despaired.

Then one afternoon he came home with a grim smile on his face. 'Well, I've found a job.'

She was so relieved. 'Oh Brooks, I knew you would. Where?'

'I am now the clerk at St James's Church, hired by Deacon Tomlinson,' he said. 'I gather I am to take care of the bookwork and transcribe the gentleman's sermons into a volume for posterity and other such odds and ends.'

'But how? I mean, what about the religion? What did he say about that?'

'He didn't ask,' Brooks said, dropping his cape wearily on the bed. 'He's an impossible creature, so pompous, it didn't occur to him to ask, so I didn't volunteer.'

The idea of Brooks working at a church made her nervous but she dismissed her worries. 'How much is he paying you?'

'The princely sum of thirty shillings a week,' Brooks said bitterly. 'And I hope you're satisfied, it's the best I can do. I pawned my watch this morning, that was quite an experience, I can tell you.'

Adelaide put her arms around him. 'Don't be angry with me. Everything will be all right now. We just needed that start, something better will turn up in time.'

Brooks liked to think he was a humble man and, as he set off for the church on his first morning, he tried to condition himself for this very real test of humility. To be a clerk, planted in the steamy church annex among all the religious paraphernalia, he told himself, was not only a comedown, it was some form of retribution. No, he smiled, it was just a marvellous irony and he should recognise the situation as simply that. He was desperate for employment of some sort and this job he could handle easily. At least he had a place to go each day now and that was important.

His new job lasted but a few hours.

On examining the ledgers he found himself staring at years of clumsy larceny perpetrated by the Deacon. Altered receipts, totals of donations that did not match bank pay-slips, forged pay-slips, everything was wrong. He was shocked.

Tomlinson had boasted that he owned a sheep-run out at Bathurst, explaining that the Archbishop, Dr Scott, who now resided at Parramatta, also invested in rural affairs for the good of the colony, and, although Brooks had thought it all rather strange from his own special view as a non-religious man, it did not concern him. But now he saw that Tomlinson, instead of putting his trust in God, was siphoning off God's funds to underwrite his business activities. That situation was ludicrous, and his own situation was hopeless. There was no point in confronting Tomlinson, it was too sordid and he would have to leave anyway.

He collected his hat from the peg behind the door. His own life had become sordid, living in that sad little room, debarred from the continuation of his studies, existing in a most pointless manner. He walked out of the annex leaving Tomlinson's ledgers spreadeagled on the desk and headed down for the quiet solace of the sea at Darling Point, to wait for nightfall and his last look at the wonders of the universe.

Adelaide screamed and screamed until the Misses Higgins quietened her with doses of medicinal brandy. She would not have it that her husband had suicided, had thrown himself in the sea.

Olive Higgins agreed with her. Dr Brooks would hardly have taken his own life on the very day of commencing work at the church. The women insisted that he must have suffered a heart attack and fallen into the harbour, but the coroner returned a verdict of suicide. There were witnesses, he said.

Adelaide burned the death certificate.

The funeral was a miserable affair held out on the windswept sand flats in the no-man's land of the cemetery. Because no clergyman would officiate at the funeral of a suicide, Olive Higgins read the service and her sister gave the responses, and they took Adelaide back home to Bligh House where she sat down and wrote to family and friends in England that dear Brooks had died of a heart seizure.

That evening, bringing tea up to Adelaide, Olive Higgins vowed she would have something to say to the Archbishop about Deacon Tomlinson refusing to officiate at the funeral of such a good and gentle man, and Adelaide began to laugh hysterically. She had been so shocked she had hardly known what was going on around her but now her mind was clearing. Brooks had been an atheist, he would have deplored a religious service, he would have hated it. But he got one anyhow, such as it was.

After the mourning came the reckoning. When the baker began to whistle his way to the kitchen again and the maids stopped tip-toeing past her door, Adelaide forced herself to face the world. Her first call was to the bank where

91

she discovered the true state of their finances and fled back to her room in a panic.

Encouraged by the Misses Higgins, she decided to take up dress-making since that had been her occupation before she married Brooks. She made dresses for them and for Mrs Kelso, who occupied a room on the first floor with her husband, a retired Army major. Mrs Kelso only gave Adelaide the work under pressure from the landladies but was so pleased with the result she then introduced several of her friends.

Months later with her little business progressing, Adelaide had adjusted to her new life and was beginning to be pleased that she had chosen to stay on in Sydney. She felt free, almost anonymous, able to come and go as she wished, and her health improved. The colour came back into her cheeks as her nerves settled down and her fair hair lost its lack-lustre appearance.

And one day a new customer turned up on her doorstep. Milly Forrest.

Adelaide was surprised. 'But Milly, I saw the dresses you made on the ship. You are a far better dressmaker than I am.'

'I don't make my own clothes any more,' Milly told her, picking up Adelaide's sketches. 'I don't have to. Dermott and Fred have two saddleries as well as the shop. Isn't it strange how things work out? On the ship we were just a bootmaker and his wife coming out in the hopes of doing well and you were practically gentry, going to stay with the Governor.'

Adelaide looked at her, wondering if there were malice in the silly woman's talk but either way it was of no consequence to her. She would simply make Milly pay more in retaliation.

Milly chatted on. 'We just love Sydney town. And, oh! Adelaide. I am so sorry to hear the Doctor died, he was such a nice man. Is it true he took his own life? I can hardly believe it.'

Adelaide snatched the sketches from her. 'I would appreciate it if you didn't mention that again for his sake. I told people he died of a bad heart.'

'That's a good idea. You can count on me. I liked your husband. How he died doesn't matter, he's dead, that's the sad part. But you seem to be getting along all right.'

'Oh yes,' she said wearily. 'It was a shock for a start but one has to persevere.'

Before they began their discussions on the style of Milly's dresses, she had one more item of interest to impart.

'Remember our friends, the Heselwoods?'

Adelaide nodded.

'Well, we are going into business with the Heselwoods, partners you know. Jasin is looking into it right now. We are thinking of buying a sheep station.'

'That's wonderful,' Adelaide said, and she meant it. Milly could turn into a good customer. As for the Heselwoods, Adelaide wished dear Brooks were alive so that she could say, 'I told you so.'

# CHAPTER SIX

Sometimes Jasin felt that nothing ever went right for him. Nothing that he organised ever turned out exactly as he had planned and he was constantly forced into spur-of-the-minute alternatives. He had left Horton's place and ridden off on Prince Blue feeling pleased with himself. Georgina was comfortably placed for the time being and this was his first lone endeavour in the colony. He was looking forward to visiting Camden and would make the most of his time to secure connections with the right people.

The journey to Parramatta, following the river, had been most pleasant and he had broken the trip with an overnight stay at an inn where he had enjoyed a good supper and convivial company. The Macarthur property was well-known and directions freely given so he rode up to the house with confidence.

A manservant opened the door.

'Mr Macarthur,' Jasin requested.

'Which Mr Macarthur, sir?'

'Mr John Macarthur.'

'I'm sorry, sir. Mr Macarthur is not at home.'

'When will he be at home?'

'I do not know, sir. Mr Macarthur has been taken ill. He is in Sydney and will not be returning for a while.'

Jasin stood dumbfounded. What a bloody nuisance.

The servant was ready to close the door on him. 'Will that be all sir?'

'I should like to speak with the other Mr Macarthur.'

'Which other Mr Macarthur sir?'

By God this man was insolent. How many Macarthurs populated this place? 'I suggest you fetch me the nearest one,' he drawled.

The servant took himself off and Jasin turned to look at Prince Blue who was standing quietly at the hitching rail, and over at the greenery of a large orchard. This seemed to be a very big establishment but the house was a disappointment. Jasin had expected a mansion, he had noticed that the wealthy colonists went in for rather spectacular houses, and now he wondered if these people were as well-off as the gossips made out. He hoped he had left the world of the impoverished gentry far behind him.

A man not much older than himself came dashing out of the door in his shirtsleeves. 'I'm sorry to keep you waiting sir. I'm William Macarthur. You wished to see my father?'

Jasin was surprised. Except for the telltale flatness of some of the vowels he could have been addressing an English gentleman. 'I'm afraid I have come here at an inconvenient time,' he apologised. 'The name's Heselwood. Mr Macarthur invited me here this week to learn about agriculture so that I don't go off causing a nuisance of myself.'

William grinned. 'Yes. That sounds like my father. He should have been a teacher. He has no intention of taking his knowledge to the grave. I'm very pleased to meet you, Mr Heselwood.'

Jasin nodded and looked back down the driveway with calculated vagueness. 'Oh well. I'd better push off back to Sydney.'

'No. You can't do that. You've come all this way. You must stay. Although my father isn't convinced, my brother James and I are quite capable and we'd be happy to tell you all we can.'

'If you're sure I wouldn't be in the way?'

'Not at all. We often have people like yourself staying here to learn the ropes. Do you know Percy Dalgleish? He only left last week.'

'Can't say I do,' Jasin said and then tried a new tack. 'But I have the impression we have met somewhere before.'

'Maybe we have. My father took me to England when I was nine and I lived there for some time.'

'The Devonshire Club perhaps?'

Jasin's question was studied but William for all his English education had the disarming candour of the native born, the currency lads, a term Jasin had already learned.

'Never been there,' William said, cutting short that avenue of finding mutual acquaintances. 'Come on, we'll get your horse and I'll take you around to the bachelor quarters. Now are you serious about wanting to learn?'

Jasin, taken aback, assured him that he was.

'Good. You must dine with us this evening and tomorrow you can begin in earnest. We rise at five in the morning I have to warn you. There's a lot to do. We are just about at the end of the mustering so you are in good time. I hope you will find Camden interesting. There's nothing remotely resembling our sheep stations in England so it will be strange for you at first.' The brothers were very kind to their guest but they were not gentlemen farmers as Jasin had expected. The first morning the foreman woke him at dawn and dumped some moleskins and a check shirt on his bunk. 'The boss says you'll need these, Mr Heselwood. You can't be spoiling your good city clothes out here. Stick them on and I'll wait for you.'

Jasin clambered up wondering if he had stumbled into a prison instead of a gentleman's country estate, but he dragged on the working clothes, relieved that they smelled new, and reached for his riding boots.

'Hey whoa!' the foreman cried. 'We'll have to get you another pair of boots.'

'These will do perfectly, thank you,' Jasin said firmly but the foreman explained. 'It'd be a crying shame to wear them out there in the mud, sir. I never seen a finer pair of boots. You'll ruin them and you won't be able to replace them.'

He spoke to Jasin more like an uncle than one of Macarthur's employees. 'We'll get you another pair from the storeroom.,' he said. 'They call me Slim by the way.'

Jasin looked at the man in his fifties with dusty grey hair and at the long frame with narrow hips that almost seemed disinclined to hold up his trousers, but the foreman had no time to waste. 'Come on, son. Say farewell to your bunk. You'll be huggin' it tonight like it was your best girl.'

The guest was appalled at the cheek of the man but plodded along behind him in his socks, to be shod.

For the rest of the week he had good cause to remember Slim's warning. Each night he fell into his bunk exhausted and aching in every limb. He had hardly been out of the saddle in all that time, travelling for miles across this great property, trailing behind the foreman and his men who dashed into gullies and into the bush gathering stray sheep. Then they were down at the river bank running thousands of sheep into the pens and out again in a confusion of shouts and smells, with the dogs whipping around and other men standing waist deep in the water washing the sheep.

They invited Jasin to try his hand, daring him, so he waded in, took the soap they handed him and lathered the sheep's wool, not believing that anyone in his right mind could contemplate such a ridiculous operation. One had seen plenty of sheep at home but to wash them like fat babies was unheard of. When a stockman pushed another sheep towards him he pretended not to see it and staggered up the river bank hardly able to straighten his back and wondering if he would be able to mount his horse.

He felt his life was running out of control and and could not believe how he had come to walk into this school for farmhands. He rarely saw James Macarthur who was the estate manager but William Macarthur was everywhere. More of a bushman, he preferred to ride with his men.

Jasin was flattered that the two brothers expected him to fit in so easily. It was the only thing that kept him from fleeing the place. But they both had great humour. They laughed with him when he made mistakes, never at him, and they were proud to show their stockmen that an English gentleman could ride as hard as them, even if the gentleman's inner thighs were red raw. Jasin's painful secret.

They set great store by their horses, which Jasin could understand, but they loved their sheep dogs just as much. Strange animals bred from the wild dingoes, Jasin found the dogs vicious and ugly, which he would never dare to say, but agreed that they were clever; like earnest little pupils they loved to learn new tricks and were cocky in their mastery of the sheep. He learned to treat them politely for fear of incurring their masters' wrath but he would as soon have owned a wolf.

At sundown he was released from the clutches of the workers to bathe and rest before stepping up to the house to dine with William and James, the civilised part of the day. As he dressed he was surprised that his aches and pains had left him at last, but was still determined to quit Camden. A week was enough.

This very night he would give notice that he was returning to Sydney on the morrow, but as usual his announcement was pre-empted.

'And how is Jasin doing?' James asked William.

'Not too badly at all,' William said, to Jasin's amazement. 'I must apologise Jasin that I haven't had much time to spend with you but I'll rectify that in a few days. He's had to fend for himself,' he told James, 'and he's hanging on quite well. I have to admit Jasin, I thought a couple of days would see you running back to Sydney. Remember Wylie Mills, James?'

Both men laughed and William explained. 'He came here straight from a ship, deciding he would be a squatter. He didn't last a week. He was quite certain every bone in his body was broken. And he never even learned to saddle his own horse.'

'Poor Wylie,' James said gently. 'I felt sorry for him. He did have a few nasty falls. And he did try. This wasn't the life for him that's all. And the boys can be merciless when they spot a victim.'

'Oh yes. They had a few go's at Jasin but gave up when they saw they weren't rattling him.'

This was news to Jasin. He hadn't noticed the stockmen had stopped annoying him. But here were James and William laughing about a fellow who had chucked it in and he was about to do the same. He munched on his lamb chop and reconsidered his announcement.

'One does not wish to impose on you for too long . . .' he began, trying to find a way out.

But William insisted he was welcome. 'We start shearing next week, you have to stay for that. I'll have more time for you and then James will take you over to explain the bookwork, without which all of my endeavours would end up a tangle.'

Jasin was too tired to argue with them. 'I shall have to advise my wife. How long do you think one should stay to get some understanding of the procedure? I fear it is all odds and ends to me.'

'Make it a month at least,' William told him 'I assure you, you won't regret it.'

Jasin took a deep drink of their excellent claret to cover a groan at the thought of a month's sentence.

'Besides,' William continued, 'we are glad of your company. And you must meet our friends. We have promised them we shall not let you go until you have done the rounds of Parramatta society. As soon as we get the shearers on the job we shall begin with a dinner party. What about that James?'

'Capital,' James said. 'And next time you come Jasin, you must bring your wife. Make it a social visit.'

Jasin sighed. A social visit. Would he survive for it?

That night he wrote to Georgina that he must stay on at Camden for a few more weeks, and for her to tell Horton that he was being put through his paces like a draught horse and that he feared he would return bandy of leg. That would amuse Horton. Since there was no way to beat a dignified retreat Jasin resigned himself to suffering it a bit longer but his plans were beginning to take shape. By the second week at Camden he realised that he was finding the farm a damn sight more interesting than moping around Horton's household all day.

The countryside was ugly and dull, scarred by ragged creeks littered with untidy tree trunks. It was infuriating to have to associate with the patronising stockmen and listen to their rude humour and rough talk but James and William were excellent fellows. It was just that they strode a world that he was unable to appreciate. Jasin had already decided that on his return to Sydney he would sell their furnishings and sail for London in a decent ship, shaking the dust of this land from their boots forever. Horton could keep his sheep station, and all the work it entailed running about after stupid sheep.

The schooling went on relentlessly and the genial William took Jasin further afield. Jasin was astounded to discover that this man was widely travelled, spoke fluent French, and was an accomplished botanist. Under William's tuition he came to grasp the size of this enterprise, more than thirty thousand acres. The station had a dairy herd, some beef cattle, orchards and vineyards and about seven thousand sheep. There were three hundred acres under produce and they employed an average of one hundred and twenty workers, most of them convicts.

The Macarthurs clothed their staff in dull white 'Parramatta' cotton shirts and shifts, supplied their rations and gave each man an occasional dram of spirits or common wine and some tobacco. A warehouse carried every possible farm implement and the storehouse contained supplies of clothing and food, including dried meats, herb-flavoured sausages, cheeses, jams and preserves.

William showed Jasin how to follow the process from lambing to shearing and the washing was explained. 'Our brother John releases the wool in London for us and there's hell to pay if we send dirty fleece. The sheep get filthy in the dust and dirt in this country, and they pick up burrs and twigs and everything else in their wool to make our lives miserable so we have to wash them several times to clean them to make them ready for the shearers.'

To William, the production of fine wool was an art; to him the countryside was not stark, but rich and generous. He took Jasin to the vineyards and the wine cellars and out to the mustering yards to examine a herd of horses brought in by a horse dealer. And they watched the shearers, joining in the excitement each evening as the men took bets on the tally and speed of individual shearers.

Gradually Jasin came to meet local people who visited Camden and they

97

accepted invitations to Parramatta homes where he listened to the squatters, taking careful note of their casual wealth and the size of their estates. James introduced him to the stud books, and to the neat efficient journals which recorded the size of their wool clip and the returns they achieved. And he began to understand that they were simply following in the footsteps of their formidable parents.

'Australia sent one million pounds of fleece abroad last year,' James told him proudly. 'That made them sit up and take notice, coming from their convict colony.'

Jasin was sitting up and taking notice too. He had found the source of money in the colony and would not easily be turned away from it.

The brothers did not forget their promise. They arranged a splendid dinner party in Jasin's honour, inviting people from all over the district. The food was excellent as was the wine, and after dinner William took their guests down to the woolshed where the annual dance was being held for their employees. Some of the male guests, including Jasin, were a little drunk. The plunged into the crowd, grabbing at girls to swing onto the oily dance floor, prancing madly to the footstamping rhythm of the fiddles and accordions while the workers clapped them on.

Jasin had found himself a pretty girl with a mass of tawny-orange hair and gold-flecked green eyes and at the end of that dance, he refused to let her go. 'No. I've found the belle of the ball. You're mine.'

The girl laughed, impressed that the gentleman should make such a fuss of her and willingly stayed with him to dance a polka and a reel.

Sobering in the alcohol-free environment, Jasin began to take more notice of her, the supple back, the small waist, the full taut breasts, and he kept glancing at her face, the skin like rose petals.

'A face to launch a thousand ships,' he told her and she giggled.

'What's your name?' he called and spun her around.

'Dolour Callinan,' she said.

He pulled her closer to him, dancing nearer the door and out into the night. They were both laughing and puffing and he drew her over to a heavy dray that was propped against the wall, edging around the big wheels, under the shafts into a small private space, and afraid she might run away, Jasin gave her no time. He kissed her, holding her tight, drinking in the softness of her lips. His hands covered her breasts cupping them and caressing them but she made no move to pull away, so braver now, he slid a hand under her skirt feeling the bare thigh. Her tongue tantalised him and her arms were around him pressing his body to her in an urgent rhythm and he felt strong and sure of her. 'Come with me Dolour,' he whispered.

'No. I can't. Not now.'

Jasin groaned, both arms holding her into him, the light perfume of her hair brushing his face. 'You have to,' he insisted.

'No. They'll catch me. I'll come later.'

'Where will you come?' he murmured, unwilling to give up this warmth even for a moment.

'To your room Mr Heselwood. I'll come there tonight.'

Jasin was surprised that she knew his name and she took that for hesitation. 'Don't you want me to come to you?' she asked.

'Yes, and don't you forget or I'll come looking for you.'

In a second she was gone and he stood leaning against the wall, taking out a slim cigar to settle himself. A little Irish miss, he mused, but born for the cot.

The rest of the night dulled. He jogged around the hall with another lass and then accompanied the ladies back to the homestead while William and his friends followed discussing their favourite subject, sheep. For supper a delectable combination of peeled fruits and cheeses was served with more wine and Jasin nibbled and drank to pass the interminable hours before the carriages finally came to the door to carry away the visitors and he was able to escape to his room, worried that she might have come and gone, and worried that she might not appear at all.

Dolour Callinan had known who he was. Everyone on the station knew about him, especially the women. The handsome English gentleman was the talk of the place and all of the younger girls and a few of the older ones too, went out of their way to have a look at him. Dolour worked in the laundry and she had seen his fine silk shirts before she managed a glimpse of the owner. She had always dreamed of marrying a gentleman like him and living in a fine house. To date there hadn't been any opportunities for an Irish maid to find her fortune in the colony, but she lived in hopes.

Mrs Macarthur had rescued her from the Female Factory where all convict women were sent until they could be placed and the superintendent, in Dolour's hearing, had warned that this girl was fiery tempered and brazen, she had been transported for striking her mistress.

Dolour smiled at that. She had been caught canoodling with the son and heir, nothing but a few kisses, and the mistress had beaten her with a heavy stick until Dolour had grabbed the stick and fought back. The first part of the story was never told and Dolour at nineteen had been banished.

When Mrs Macarthur had taken a chance on her, Dolour, from contrariness, decided to prove the superintendent wrong, a meddling old woman with never a good word for any of the convicts, and now for eighteen months she had worked at Camden quiet as you like and the housekeeper gave good reports of her. But Dolour was biding her time; she thrust away the advances of the workmen, who were no better off than she was, and kept her eye out hoping to meet one of the single currency lads who often came to Camden from the township but luck had not been with her. She had years to go of her sentence and yearned to be free of this bondage. Many a time she had thought of running away but she knew she would be found and it would be back to the Factory, so she had hung on, hoping and dreaming.

And this night, when she wasn't expecting any such thing, who should rush in and grab her, just as she was walking over to get some of Mrs Henry's strawberry punch, but the English gentleman himself, more beautiful, close up, than ever; and he had slipped her outside to be kissing her, falling for her. Of that she would not tell a soul. Someone would pimp and they would have her out of the place in no time.

He was still up at the house when she slipped into his bed without a stitch. He wanted her and this might be her only chance. No-one knew how long he was staying. She lay in his bed, smelling his presence, thinking of him and the loving she would give him, to make him love her, unafraid of the possibility even of a pregnancy. It didn't matter. Nothing mattered except that she had chosen her lover.

And when he did come in and find her warm body ready for him he was overjoyed; he took her in his arms with such passion that she became alive and hot and gave him so much that he begged her not to leave him before the dawn.

'I have to go,' she said to him again. 'Do you want me to come back tomorrow night?'

When she left him the room was empty and desolate. He lay on the bed reliving every detail of the night. Never had he taken a woman like that, with so much skill and abandon, and he would teach her more. He wondered if he had reached his sexual peak and how he could maintain this new surge of passion. Georgina would not approve of that sort of love-making, she would not tolerate it; besides, she was not stupid, she might question him. That day he rode out to the horse paddocks where he could appear interested but he could think of nothing but Dolour, of the hours he had to wait to see and touch her again.

He had a letter from Georgina to tell him that there was much excitement in the Horton household. Vicky had announced she was with child. Horton was pleased that Jasin was taking his visit to Camden seriously. Jasin rushed off a note congratulating the Hortons on the forthcoming event and saying that he was looking forward to taking on the management of Chelmsford. This time he meant it. The Macarthur brothers had convinced him that it was a great advantage to be able to take over a going concern, and Jasin was determined to have his own station one day. At Chelmsford he would be the boss, with an experienced foreman, a wonderful opportunity, he now realised. It made him nervous to think he had almost passed it up. But he blamed Horton for not explaining in better detail.

William urged him to purchase his own land as soon as possible. 'Not far north of the Hunter Valley, where you will be situated, there are millions of acres that are going for next to nothing.'

Jasin shook his head. 'I've been studying your maps. That land is outside the boundaries, not even civilised country.'

'Exactly. It is there for the taking. It will be like picking up gold. I wish I could go north but we have too much to do here. A friend of mine, a fellow botanist, has explored that country and he says it is magnificent grazing country. Great rivers and wonderful pastures.'

'How does one go about it?'

'Take guides. Go north of that Valley and mark out your run. Keep some men there to hold it for you. When it is surveyed you can register it in your name and lease until you are able to purchase it.'

'If I did that, how much land should I claim?'

'We'll talk to James about it. At least several thousand acres.'

Jasin's head was swimming. 'Is that how your father got started?'

'Yes, and there's still half a continent north of the Hunter Valley, land ready and waiting for the men bold enough to grasp it.'

His guest laughed. 'I hardly see myself in that role. I really don't think I'm the pioneering type.'

William looked at him seriously. 'Maybe not. But you don't have to swing the axe. Labour's cheap. All you have to do is find the land and claim it. The rest, with good management, will look after itself.'

Had Jasin been able to think of an excuse to stay on he would have, but his time was almost up. For a week now Dolour had been coming to his bed and their love-making had become more intense. He was frantic at the thought of leaving her. Even thinking of her during the day made him want her so much he wished he could go to her but he had to continue to walk around Camden as if she didn't exist.

'I love you,' he told her that night, 'and I shall never let you go.'

But Dolour was quiet. 'You're married. They told me you are married.'

'And is that my fault? How was I to know I would meet you and love you? My marriage is just a marriage of convenience.'

She was pulling away from him, shocked to find it was true but he refused to let her go, and Dolour knew it was too late. She loved him too much to waste this precious time with him.

It was James who sought him out after his discussion with William about acquiring land. 'If I were you Jasin I would go into cattle. I think you find all this fiddling around with the sheep and the wool rather boring.'

'Chelmsford carries sheep. I have to know about it.'

'Yes, but when you go north, stock your runs with cattle. The population is increasing. They'll have to be fed. We need the sheep for their wool.'

Now Jasin was thoroughly confused. 'I'll have to think about it.' The whole idea of chasing north after land was receding.

'Yes, give it some thought,' James said. 'But sheep take a lot of handling. You need shepherds and stockmen, and the further out you go the harder it is to find workers. Cattle are easier. You just have to fatten them up and sell them.'

They rode into Parramatta the next day and while the brothers attended to business Jasin wandered into a tavern where he struck up a conversation with another Englishman.

'Where are you from?' the Englishman asked him.

101

'Camden,' Jasin said, deliberately misunderstanding the question and his reply impressed the stranger.

'My name's Pelham,' he said. 'Captain Pelham. I've quit my regiment, taking a look around. There are pickings here we'd never find at home.'

'What sort of pickings?'

'Quick turnover. Buy and sell.'

'Buy and sell what?'

'Cattle. Horses. And I'll tell you something else. I am absolutely convinced there is gold out there somewhere.'

'Gold. Well I hope you find it old chap. Where are you going from here?'

'Back to Sydney, I have to find a backer. Are you interested?'

'I might be. Where can I find you in Sydney?'

'Here's my card. The York Hotel, Phillip Street. Look me up.'

Jasin could see the Macarthurs across the road. 'Yes, I will. I'm interested in cattle. Thinking of going north, you know.'

'That's the shot. You're looking in the right direction,' Pelham said.

At lunch with William and James, Jasin didn't mention his encounter with Pelham. Besides it was all too far into the future. He would simply go to Chelmsford and think about his next move from there. One thing at a time.

'Jasin, you came into Sydney in the *Emma Jane* didn't you?' William asked.

'Yes.' It was no use denying it.

'I thought so, I've a strange story for you.'

'Everything about the *Emma Jane* was strange. It was a positively foul voyage. My wife is still recovering.'

'Did you know a fellow called MacNamara?'

'Vaguely.'

'Oh good,' William said. 'It appears that Mr MacNamara has got into some bother, and his friend, the first mate Palmerston, was looking for him.'

'Ah yes, I remember Palmerston. What has this got to do with me?'

'Well you see Jasin, at Palmerston's request I've been trying to locate MacNamara and I've found him but the news isn't too good. Apparently he fell foul of Mudie, a squatter from the Hunter Valley. A poor type I'm afraid even if he is a magistrate. Mudie is full of his own importance, but he does have friends in high places. They've got MacNamara in Bathurst jail, but my sources tell me the case wasn't handled legally.'

Jasin laughed. 'What did MacNamara do?'

'I believe he punched Mudie or his son-in-law quite heartily, for which a lot of colonists would give him a medal, but Mudie's a vindictive piece of work, a very unwise thing to do.'

'That's typical of the Irishman.'

'I was thinking,' William said, 'since you know him . . . when you get back to Sydney would you call at the Nelson Hotel in King Street and let his friends know where he is? They're very concerned for him.'

'Of course,' Jasin said. What else could he say to his hosts? He'd try to remember but there would be so much to do when he returned to Sydney, and much to think about. He turned to James. 'You were talking about my taking up new land. Where would I find trustworthy guides?'

'That's always a problem,' William said.

'Not this time,' his brother put in. 'What about Clarrie Shipman and his mate Snow?'

'Ha, yes! They'd jump at the chance,' William laughed. 'Give them something to do. They're a couple of old bushmen, Jasin, and they live at Camden now, when they're not off on their walkabouts. They're just the pair you want. All they'd need is their keep and a bottle of rum for highdays and holidays. Just let us know when you need them.'

They celebrated Jasin's last night at Camden with a quiet dinner and the Macarthurs presented him with a fine pistol and a set of maps of the explored areas of New South Wales in a leather cylinder, and gave a toast to his success at Chelmsford and to his future, eventually, as a cattleman.

As he walked back to the bachelor quarters he was feeling on top of the world. The family unity and determination of the Macarthurs fascinated him, they made it all sound so easy, which he was sure it was not, but he had cemented a good relationship here and before he made any new move he would seek out their advice. If old John Macarthur could reach such heights then a Heselwood could too. He was so carried away with his ambitions, he forgot, until he opened the door, that Dolour would be waiting for him.

This was their last night together and caught up in his passion for her he begged her to leave, to come with him.

'I can't,' she said, 'it would look bad for you. But in a few weeks I'll run away.'

'Yes you must. And you must let me know where you are.'

'You won't have any trouble finding me,' she said, with a trace of fear in her voice. 'They'll put me in the Female Factory.'

'No. You must hide from them. I'll help you.'

'It's not as simple as that. They'll find me sooner or later, so I'll give myself up.'

He sat up in the bed. 'Why would you do that?'

Dolour smiled. 'Because they won't have me back here. And you can come and claim me as your assigned servant. Then I can go wherever you say.'

'But what if someone else claims you?'

'Ah there's the beauty of it. I don't have to go. They can't make me. I'll just wait for you. But it's an awful place darling. You wouldn't leave me there too long? I'll be dreaming of you every night.'

Her fingers dug into him, reminding him, and he went back to loving her, at peace with the world. And all the time he talked to her of what they would do when they were together, free of this secret little room, of the nights and the days they would have together and he found yet another plane of love-making, one that he could never have imagined, one that left him bereft from the minute she slipped away from him into the night.

In a dream the next day he took his leave of William and James, thanking them for their great kindness to him. It was a different Jasin Heselwood who swung into the saddle, and rode down the slope across the creek to the gates of Camden. He was confident now, and ambitious, no longer the nervy gentleman waiting to be introduced to the colonists, sure of nothing except his social standing. That, he now knew for certain, would stand him in good stead in New South Wales and the rest he could achieve on his own.

He stayed overnight at the same inn and left the next morning with his plans clear in his mind. It was essential that he take on Chelmsford as soon as possible, that would move him north with no expense and give him a base from where he could lead an expedition to find his own land. He cantered towards Sydney with Prince Blue in fine form after all his exercise in the country. The colony had become an interesting place.

The road to Sydney was busy with loaded drays heading for the markets but Jasin rode past them engrossed in his own thoughts. He did not see Lachlan Cormack coming towards him until he reined in and called his name. 'Mr Heselwood! Jasin!'

'Why Cormack! It's you! One hardly expects to see a familiar face along these highroads. Is anything the matter? You look quite agitated.'

'I've come to fetch you Jasin. I'm afraid I have sad news for you. I'm sorry to be the bearer of bad tidings, but – John Horton is dead. God rest his soul.'

Jasin was stunned. 'Horton? No! Are you sure? Did he have an accident? A fall from his horse?'

'It wasn't an accident. He came down with influenza and he seemed to be getting better and then he took a turn for the worse. The doctor said it was double pneumonia. He did all he could. Vicky and your good wife, Georgina, nursed him day and night but he died suddenly in the early hours of yesterday morning. It is a terrible thing. Vicky is taking it very hard.'

Jasin, still not able to accept that Horton had gone from his life, was more amazed than grief stricken. Horton had seemed indestructible; a man who had taken hold of a new way of life and gathered great strength from it. How could he have succumbed to such a stupid and untimely death? He had noticed the way the colonists had looked up to Horton, people like Cormack, for instance. Strangely he had been thinking about Cormack this morning, realising that Horton's friends belonged to the same wealthy group of squatters to whom he had been introduced at Camden.

Cormack had fallen back but Jasin kept going, Prince Blue galloping as if he knew there was an urgency about this ride now. As the hours passed, Jasin became genuinely upset at Horton's death but when the finality of it began to reach him, he thought of Chelmsford and Horton's other holdings and saw that Vicky would need him more than ever now. A woman could not run the stations.

The funeral was well attended but the widow had refused to allow any of the mourners to return to the house afterwards.

'I can understand her,' Georgina said. 'I could not bear to have people drinking and chewing and haw-hawing in my home after a death in the family. Quite insensitive.'

'It's their custom,' Jasin murmured, disappointed to have missed the opportunity to better acquaint himself with Horton's friends.

'It's an Irish custom, not ours,' Georgina said.

They sat alone in the parlour while the red-eyed maids served tea. 'Did you take tea to Mrs Horton?' Georgina asked them.

'She doesn't want any ma'am. She's just sitting in her room staring. Won't say nothing.'

'Knock on the door gently. Take the tea in and leave it there. And don't be bothering her.'

'Yes ma'am.'

When they left Georgina looked at Jasin. 'I must say Heselwood, you look well. You are even sunburned.'

'It's a wonder I'm not burned to a crisp. But the activity did my constitution good I suppose after all those months cooped up on the ship.'

'You know that Vicky is expecting?' she asked.

'Yes you told me that in one of your letters.'

'There was so much excitement. Poor Horton was ecstatic and now he'll never see his child. It is sad. And they were all so up in the air, I felt it would be untimely, even a little embarrassing to mention my news.'

'What news?'

'I too am expecting.'

'You are?' Jasin nearly spilled his tea. Suddenly she looked vulnerable, searching his face for his reaction, and his old fondness for her returned. 'That is good news. I shall have to make even greater efforts now, with a son and heir of my own. I think we shall do very well here after all.'

'But I don't feel like staying on at this house much longer. Even before poor John died I felt we were outstaying our welcome.'

'My dear Georgina. We might be accused of many things, but never bad manners. We would never outstay our welcome. Everything is under control. As soon as Vicky is up to it, I shall have a talk with her. There is nothing to stop us leaving for Chelmsford right away. It will be one less worry for her to know that she can rely on us. It is what Horton wanted. In the meantime I have quite a bit of business to attend in the township, commencing with the Governor. I must establish my right to take up land, and be a little kinder to the poor fellow.'

'Jasin. You can't see him now. Haven't you heard? His little son died of the influenza too. They're in mourning.'

'Good Lord! Has there been an epidemic? Well I simply have to see him before we leave.'

105

'You could see Macleay. He seems to do most of the work.'

'I will not see that bumptious fool. I don't talk to underlings.' He lit his pipe and thought about the problem for a while. 'Tell you what! I shall pay a call on His Excellency to deliver my sympathies in person. Offer him my solicitude and company. And when I have wrung out my hankie I can turn to him for advice on the matter of the land. Quite opportune really.'

'Jasin! That's very harsh!'

'My dear. Life must go on. Like here. I shall be glad to get away. Horton has taken the life of this household with him. I hope she doesn't keep herself locked up too long.'

Governor Darling did make an exception to see the Honourable Jasin Heselwood and was grateful that this young man, the son of an earl, should make such a thoughtful gesture. 'Young people these days,' he told Jasin, 'do not seem to have any respect for the proprieties. And out here there are few who even understand what is expected of them.' It was the Governor who brought up the subject of land. 'Have you given this matter consideration, Mr Heselwood? Your father would never forgive me if I were not to offer you some guidance.'

'Not as yet. One does wonder what to do for the best. But I would not wish to detain you with mundane affairs at this time.'

Jasin rose to leave but the Governor stopped him. 'Come with me. We shall look at the charts. It will take my mind off my sorrow for a little while.'

They studied the maps and Darling pointed out the areas that could be bought cheaply because the owners had relinquished or been forced to withdraw for non-payment of lease charges, or failure to fulfil leasehold obligations.

'What about up here?' Jasin pointed vaguely at the northern areas outside the boundaries.

Darling was startled. 'Those areas have not been surveyed. I am trying to keep the squatters out of there.'

'Nevertheless they are going. And I am told that every Tom, Dick and Harry who blazes his mark on that outlying country ends up keeping it. That is rather unfair on people like myself who prefer to keep within the law.'

'It is a very difficult situation. I wouldn't want to hold you back Mr Heselwood but I can hardly approve of any expansion until I have proper control. You are still entitled to a land grant within the boundaries. Why don't you take up a property at Bathurst or Goulburn?'

Jasin looked disappointed. He would not allow this fool to encourage him to waste his time on the leftovers, now that he was fully aware of what was really offering. 'Your Excellency. Let us not be bothered for the moment. Unless I could compete with the rest I should be hobbled. It is a pity. I was thinking of asking the Earl to form a syndicate, a family syndicate, to invest here.'

The Governor racked his brains searching for an answer. He did not wish to offend the Heselwoods. A word at Court from that quarter could guarantee his knighthood.

Jasin had a suggestion. 'What if I have a look around up there later on, and send you back my findings? All I ask is a little advance notice of when the land will be thrown open. I think I could be entitled to that courtesy, since one is quite determined to do the right thing.'

Darling knew it was more than a courtesy but he would prefer the Heselwoods in his domain to the unruly colonists who were already stampeding past his boundaries. Far better English gentry out there than emancipists. 'I suppose we could do that without upsetting the apple-cart,' he reflected.

'It being only hypothetical at this stage anyway.' Jasin finished the sentence for him and then switched the conversation away from possible misgivings on Darling's part. 'The tragedy of Horton's death – I'm sorry Your Excellency, I keep coming back to it – is that his family won't hear about it for months. Even now they will be still thinking he is alive.'

The Governor's eyes clouded with tears. 'You are right. It is quite horrible to think that everyone at home will be writing and sending greetings to my little son for months yet. And my poor wife and I shall have to go through this again when letters of condolence start coming from home.'

'Ah yes. One feels marooned at a time like this. They do not understand what sacrifices we have to make to stay out here in the colony.'

The Governor, now thoroughly upset, took his arm. 'My dear fellow, you must excuse me. I do thank you for coming and for your understanding. Pray do keep in touch with me. One can take so few people into one's confidence.'

Before he left the township, Jasin called in at the York Hotel on the off-chance of sighting Captain Pelham as a relief from Darling's maudlin company. He was feeling pleased with himself at having established a head start in the land race, with the Governor leaning over backwards to please.

'Syndicate, my backside!' he snorted. 'My father offered me nothing, he'll get nothing from me. Except his first grandson.' He wondered what he would name his son. It would be a son, he was sure of it. Why not Edward? The first sons in the Heselwood family were always called Edward. His brother Edward had so far only produced a daughter.

Pelham was not at home and Jasin didn't bother leaving his name. The wall-eyed hotelier would no doubt describe him and Pelham would work it out. Make him curious. Keep him interested. If he were to strike north, Pelham could be a useful companion.

It was days before Vicky emerged from her solitary vigil, and Jasin found her in the parlour, with all the shades drawn, looking white-faced and bleak. 'Are you feeling better my dear?'

'Yes.' Her voice was hard.

107

'We are immensely grateful for your hospitality and feel now, that if you wish we should be on our way.'

'Very well.'

'We shall make straight for Chelmsford and I can assure you that we will do our best to look after your interests as Horton would have wished.'

'You never look after anyone's interests but your own Jasin Heselwood. Don't try to fog me. And you've still got my horse.'

'My dear! Surely . . .'

But Vicky cut him short. 'Oh it's all right. You can keep the horse since he means so much to you. But you caused the only disagreement John and I had in our married life. I won't forgive you for that.'

'Perhaps it is just as well then that we are leaving.' Jasin spoke soothingly since she was still distraught. 'This is a very difficult time for you. But you are young. You will get over it in time. When we are settled at Chelmsford I shall write to you straight away.'

'Yes. Chelmsford. I shall not be needing your services there.'

Jasin was stunned. She was addressing him as if he were a servant. Dismissing him! 'Madam. It was Horton's express wish that I should take on Chelmsford. Surely you will accept his choice of manager.'

'You have missed the point. I won't need anyone for Chelmsford. I intend to sell that station and the other runs too. The sales will leave me comfortably off and I shall be able to stay on here without worrying about what is happening out there.'

'It would be very foolish of you to act so quickly. You should seek advice on this.'

'I don't need advice thank you. If you're so interested in Chelmsford, Heselwood, then you buy it.'

She picked up a prayerbook and deliberately began to read while Jasin, furious, stood stock still, wishing he could strike her. 'In that case, you will excuse me. We will leave as soon as possible.'

Vicky inclined her head in agreement, refusing to look up.

Outside, one of the maids scuttled away and he felt sure she had been listening at the door.

Georgina didn't seem too surprised. 'I knew there was trouble between them over the horse. I couldn't very well mention it in a letter but Vicky was rather terse while you were away, making it very uncomfortable for me. I'm glad we're leaving, I shall try to talk to her. It would be a pity to leave on a sour note.'

'Do you think you could persuade her to change her mind about Chelmsford?'

'I doubt it. It really seems the most sensible thing for her to do in the long run, even though she thinks she is using it as a stick to beat us with.'

'Thinks! She has done an excellent job of lashing at me as if it were my fault her husband died. And she knows we don't have anywhere to go. The little bitch is mad with power now. Ah well. I shall have to look around and find us lodgings. Do you think we could put up at an hotel for a while?'

'No. It would look too much of a retreat. Our plans have changed. Vicky is selling Chelmsford and our attitude should be complete agreement with the good sense of that. And allow her no room to whisper that she has dispensed with our services as she insinuated.'

'Try spat! The little brat positively spat at me.'

'It doesn't matter now. Chelmsford is out and our first requirement is a roof. I think I already have a solution. As I told you, her sulks included me while you were away. Unless Horton were around, she hardly spoke to me.'

'I am sorry about that, Georgina. Had I known the upstart would dare to treat you in that manner I should have come right back.' Suddenly Dolour's face came to his mind and he flushed. He felt his cheeks and made a quick excuse. 'I feel quite hot and embarrassed to think of you being in such a spot.'

'We won't worry about it. I wasn't prepared to sit back and be snubbed. I have become quite friendly with the neighbours. Mary Cormack is a charming woman. It was she who sent Lachie off to fetch you.'

'Aha! Lachie is it?'

'Jasin. Please don't trivialise the conversation. Let me finish. Now you've been to the Cormack house. It is quite large with a view over the bay. But at present that house is the worry of their lives. They intend to go to England for a year or so and it is a long time to leave a house unattended.'

'Are they looking for tenants?'

'My dear no. They are extremely wealthy people. They just need someone to live in the house and mind it while they are away. Mary said she would keep on three of the staff, a cook, a maid and a gardener, all assigned servants, but she couldn't leave them on their own. She has already mentioned to me what a pity we are going out to Chelmsford, we should be ideal to look after the place.' Georgina sat back in the chair and smiled. 'I should rather enjoy living there. What about you?'

'What a laugh! We should become neighbours of Mrs Horton! My dear, it is the answer. You are a clever girl.'

'I am feeling quite stuffy in here today Jasin. Why don't we take a walk across the fields and call on the Cormacks?'

'Excellent. And tomorrow I shall go back into Sydney and have that talk with Dermott Forrest. He doesn't know it yet, but he is going to invest in cattle. A lot of cattle.'

Georgina gathered up her shawl. 'Really Jasin, it is hard to keep up with you. I thought it was sheep.'

'No. We are going to buy cattle with every penny we can find.' He was already thinking Georgina would not need all their furnishings, which were still in storage, at the Cormack house. And he would have to arrange a loan. Mrs Horton would discover that the Heselwoods could do quite well without her.

109

# CHAPTER SEVEN

Jack Drew watched Pace MacNamara's attack on one of the bosses outside the barracks and agreed with O'Meara. The man was a fool to stick his nose into someone else's fight. But for now, he was more concerned with the chains that held them to the dray, and his own fate.

Brosnan was standing impatiently between O'Meara and Scarpy. 'Will you look at us lads? Hanging off the bloody back of the wagon like tails on a kite, the bastards they are.'

'Shut your gob, Brosnan,' Jack snapped. 'We're getting out of the prison. If you don't shut up, you bloody Irish, we'll end up back in there. What'd you expect? They'd put us in a carriage?'

While they waited, the dray driver climbed down again and came back to the prisoners. 'Who was the bloke that punched Larnach?'

No-one answered and he shrugged. 'Well he'll be in a decent spot of trouble now.'

Jack looked at O'Meara and decided if the Irish were not talking it was no business of his. 'Where are we going?' he asked the driver.

'Castle Forbes,' the old man said. 'In the Hunter Valley.'

'How far's that?'

The old man chewed on his pipe. 'About a hundred miles with the arounds and uphills and down dales.'

'God save us!' Scarpy exclaimed. 'And we're walking? It'll kill us!'

The driver laughed. 'Do you the world of good son. Get some fresh air in your lungs. The march is the best part. Once Major Mudie gets you there he'll work your backsides off.'

Jack studied the old fellow with his thinning hair and tobacco-stained beard, a possible ally. 'Do you work there?'

'No fear. I just do haulage with my wagon. I don't hang about Mudie's place. He's as mean as a drover's dog. And he's got a terrible scourger out there, a big black nigger called Jeremiah. They say he hails from Jamaica. He's the blacksmith on Mudie's station when he's not swinging the cat. Rip the skin off your back.'

'He's trying to cheer us up lads,' Brosnan said and then he turned back to the gate. 'Ah now, here comes the boss himself.'

Major Mudie rode out of the gates with Larnach who was now featuring a dark bruise down one side of his face, and Brosnan laughed.

'You'd have to say, Dinny, that MacNamara did a fine job there.'

The troopers swung onto their horses and the cavalcade set off with the four prisoners trudging behind.

As the days went by, their muscles became tuned to the new rigours and the prisoners became adept at handling the dray and keeping away from the heavy wheels. Striding along, Jack watched the countryside and took notice of everything they passed. It was strange country, dead trees standing mulishly as if they had as much right to be there as the live ones, their white trunks jagged and menacing. Nothing soft about this land, Jack thought, and he didn't mind that; it gave him a comforting sense of pay-back that the jailers had to live here too.

The strange group trailed north, living like gypsies, sighting Mudie and Larnach only on rare occasions. Jack found that the troopers and old Tom the driver were easy-going. Tom cooked for them when they made camp, and good grub too. O'Meara was quiet, brooding; Scarpy still complained at everything and Brosnan, in between asking questions of old Tom and teasing the life out of Scarpy, who was terrified of snakes, joked all the way. Jack could not remember when he had ever met such a merry customer as this, and despite his avowed intention to eventually keep well clear of the Irishmen, he liked Brosnan.

It was a week before they saw any of the wild blacks Tom had been telling them about. His stories around the campfires had given Scarpy the horrors. Brosnan said he did not believe a word of it but Jack was not so sure. When they finally came across an Aboriginal camp in a pleasant copse of trees by a river, he laughed in relief. There were women and children cooking nothing more than sweet-smelling fish on the coals of their fire, and they sat nervously waiting for the white men to go away. Only the old men came up to talk to them.

Scarpy couldn't take his eyes off the women. 'Will you get onto them? Stark naked. And look at the bubbers on them, knock your bloody eyes out.'

The troopers, indifferent, rode on down the track but the sight of this paradise was an agonising frustration for the prisoners.

'It's a hard life we lead,' Brosnan said wistfully and they all watched intently as a girl, her dark body sleek and shining, walked over to the sandy bank and began digging with a small wooden scoop.

One of the old men, his leathery skin as dusty as his hair, examined their chains with sadness in his eyes. 'Chains no good. You poor fella white man,' he said and grabbed Tom by the arm, accusing him. 'Chains no good,' he cried, but Tom shrugged. 'Nothing I can do about it.'

Sometimes the track broke out into open roads and passing horsemen paused to talk to the troopers. Long bullock wagons pulled aside to let them pass and the bullockies shook their heads in sympathy for the convicts, but the troopers were alert and would not permit any interference.

They were ferried across wide rivers on barges and at Singleton they waited for the ferry to take them across the Hunter River.

'This is as far as we go,' Corporal Mitchell, the senior of the troopers, told

111

them. 'Mudie's men are waiting for you on the other side.'

The ferry was met by Mudie's overseer, Jock McAdam, a dour thin-faced Scot with muscles like ropes under his leathery flesh, and a rough-looking bully-boy called Lester. Their new guards rode behind the dray with guns resting on their saddles.

Tom opened and closed the gate with no help from the riders and followed a track skirting the main homestead which Jack was surprised to see was not a castle at all but just a large house set in a grove of trees. At the back of the house was a collection of buildings which looked more like a village than a farm but as they padded up the worn dry hill a tall iron triangle stood sentinel and beside it Larnach sat on his horse, waiting for them.

'You know what this is?' he yelled, pointing at the triangle with his whip, and the prisoners nodded.

'Yes sir,' Larnach yelled. 'Do you hear me? Say, yes sir.'

'Yes sir,' they all said through their teeth.

'Right. The four of you now listen to me. You're nothing but dirt. Felons work here for one reason. To be punished for their crimes. You are still in jail. Keep that in mind. We haven't got any boundary fences but we've got a lot better than that. No-one has ever escaped from here.'

The prisoners stood listening while the station manager ranted like a hellfire preacher. 'God has delivered you here to atone. On Sundays you attend Church services which will be held by Major Mudie himself and that goes for any Popish dissenters too. We've had them before, and sooner or later they all go to church. You will work hard, and you will give thanks to the Lord for bringing you to Castle Forbes.'

He turned to McAdam. 'Tomorrow put them on the clearing work in the west paddock and get them straight to me if they buck. Lester, you put them away now.'

Jack could feel the anger emanating from O'Meara and Brosnan as they were led away but for a change they said nothing.

Their first stop was at the blacksmith's to release the chains from their calloused wrists and they studied Jeremiah while he worked, measuring the strength of his brawny shoulders and his great arms.

'We heard of you,' O'Meara said. 'You're the flogger. You must be proud to have such a fine job.'

Jeremiah didn't bother to lift his eyes from his work. 'I'm better off than you are,' he said.

Lester threw some shirts on the floor. 'Put these on.' They were the same rough cotton but each one carried a number on the back. 'From now on you don't have names, just numbers. Like the boss said. You're still in prison, now get going.'

He took them out past the dairy and the milking bails and across a paddock to the convict quarters, a long hut with a shingle roof.

'We got four more,' he shouted in the door and the Chinese cook came screaming out, his pigtail flying, waving a meat cleaver. 'Wong no magician! No can feed four more. Too many jumpee up,' he shrilled.

Lester leapt out of the way. 'You'll cook what you're friggin' told, you yeller monkey!' He flipped his rifle and fired at the Chinaman's feet which sent him flying back inside, still shrieking.

Lester leaned against a woodheap facing his prisoners. 'You blokes set down there. We have to wait for the rest of them to come up.'

The newcomers dropped their seabags and slid to the ground by the cookhouse wall. They could see men working in the sheds and others helping Tom unload the dray but the gunshot hadn't caused a ripple. Three milkmaids emerged from a lane between the stone sheds with their buckets, and Scarpy nudged Jack but Lester was watching. 'Take your eyes off them. They're not for you. And something else. Up there's the main house. See that white fence. Everything past there is out of bounds, so you keep away. If any of you go past that fence we don't ask questions, we just shoot. The Major and his family live up there. They don't want none of you lags anywhere near them.'

His listeners were indifferent to Lester's lectures. All of their lives had been concerned with boundaries of some sort and each one had crossed them regardless of the danger. The neat white fence held no attraction for them, the wide stretch of country bordered by forest, and the dark hills in the distance were far more interesting.

Brosnan stretched his legs in front of him. 'It looks a fine farm boys. I wouldn't mind owning a place like this.'

Lester glowered at him, gritting his teeth and fingering his gun and Jack groaned. They were supposed to be in hell not heaven, the trick was to look like a sufferer, it kept the guards happy. Brosnan was going the right way to invite trouble. And he did.

When the other convicts, about forty of them, came in from the fields the new numbers joined them to be fed watery mutton stew and muddy tea and then marched off to the bunkhouse for the night. Jack heard the heavy wooden bolts drop and looked along the long dormitory to see that the windows were barred. The thin and weary workers crowded around them hoping for news but there was not much the newcomers could tell them so they crept away to their bunks.

Jack managed to strike up a conversation with Polly Phipps, another Londoner who occupied the next bunk. 'What's it like here?'

'About as bad as it can get. Not enough to eat, they work you until you drop and flog you up again. Mudie's a magistrate but he is not supposed to order floggings for his own convicts. He should send us to another magistrate for trial and sentencing. But he ignores all that. Does what he wants and straightens the books later.'

'Why don't you mutiny?'

'Most of us are too sick. He keeps us weak, we wouldn't get far. Down the bottom of the hut there's four of our blokes with their backs just about ripped off for trying to escape.'

113

It was an odd work party that went out the next morning to clear the virgin bush about a mile from the main house.

'All the new chums get this job,' Polly Phipps told Jack, 'while they're still fit enough for the hardest work. I've only been here a month and it's wearing me down I tell you.'

The prisoners were roped together like a mountain-climbing party, and their picks and axes were brought along in a cart, under guard. Lester and two other guards rode beside them hurrying them along and shouting at them to take a good look at the bush. 'If you've got any ideas about running off into the scrub you new blokes, just try it.' Lester laughed.

Jack was given a crowbar to grub out stubborn roots behind the axe-men who were forging ahead through the scrub, felling trees. At the edge of the cleared tract, men were burning off, while birds wheeled and squealed in protest and small furry animals rolled and ran in panic. A kangaroo dashed out to stare at them and bounded away as Lester, not the best shot in the world, Jack noted for future reference, tried to shoot it.

Keeping to his plan to be seen to be suffering, Jack worked with the pick and crowbar, struggling with the gnarled roots that clung tenaciously to the hard earth, groaning that his back was aching, his hands blistered and that smoke was burning his eyes and all the time he was studying his guards, his surroundings and that mysterious bush. Country bred, O'Meara and Brosnan put their backs into the work from habit and were soon promoted to axemen, while Scarpy stumbled and complained and Lester's stockwhip cracked dangerously close to his back to keep him working.

It was no more than Jack had expected. Dry bread and tea at dawn, dry bread and cheese with water at midday and the same mutton stew every night. Then they were locked in for the night. Farm work was hard, there was no doubt about that. He had always contended there were better ways of making a living; he couldn't imagine how anyone could volunteer for this sort of work. Besides, he thought, this is still better than England, while he dug the pick into the crumbling soil. This is going to be my country when I get away and, forgetting his place, he stared out across the fields until a stockwhip lashed across his shoulder, the fine hide leaving a weal that stung for days.

After weeks of monotonous work, all four of the newcomers were feeling the strain of the hard work without enough nourishment to sustain them. They were thinner and complained of headaches which Lester told them was just sunstroke, and the Irishmen were getting desperate enough to make a run for it when bad luck struck Brosnan.

Jack was working at his usual job when there was a shout from the bush and O'Meara came stumbling into the clearing dragging Brosnan.

'Oh Christ,' Brosnan cried, 'the bloody axe slipped. I'm out of practice boys.'

Blood was streaming from his foot and O'Meara pulled off his shirt to wrap around it but Lester snatched it away. 'You don't go using good shirts for bandages,' he shouted.

'Well give us something to stop the bleeding,' O'Meara shouted. 'He's cut his bloody foot open.'

Lester ordered them back to work but O'Meara refused to budge. 'That cut will need stitching. He can't sit there holding it together with his bare hands. Do something!'

'Take him up to Laidley in the storehouse,' Lester yelled.

A guard swung onto his horse and Lester pulled Brosnan to his feet. 'Get going!'

'He can't walk with his foot like that,' O'Meara protested and Lester levelled his gun at him. 'You get back to work or I'll put a hole in you.'

The others watched while O'Meara, his face blazing with rage, stood towering over Lester, but Brosnan called back to him. 'There's no time for martyrs Dinny. I'll make it on me own.'

Whenever there were floggings, which was every second or third day, all the convicts were required to watch before they left for work. The victim, after being doused, screaming, in a salt bath, was permitted the day off to recover and contemplate crime and punishment. The next morning the prisoners were marched up to the triangle where Mudie was waiting with Jeremiah. Mudie, being a magistrate, always liked to be present at the floggings.

Brosnan, his foot stitched and bandaged and wedged into his boot, was limping along with them.

'You should have told them you can't work today,' O'Meara said. 'You've got to give it a chance to heal.'

'Don't you think I did? They told me to get on the line. They'd make you work here if your head was cut off.'

'Then we'll speak to Larnach after this affair. What poor lad is getting it today?'

'Halt!' Mudie cried as if they were a military unit. 'All atten-shun!'

The convicts shuffled to a stop and Mudie rode over to the triangle where Jeremiah waited. He called to his son-in-law, Larnach. 'What are the charges?'

'Prisoner twenty-eight step forward,' Larnach yelled and a small ferret of a man cringed out a few steps. 'Ah no, sir, not me. I didn't mean nothing.'

'Broke a settling dish in the dairy sir,' Larnach reported.

All faces turned to Mudie who deliberated on this. 'Ten!' he called suddenly and Jeremiah acknowledged, inclining his head while two men added scoops of salt to a wooden vat of water to make it ready for the victim.

'Next,' Mudie shouted.

'Prisoner number twelve, step forward,' Larnach called and the guards pushed out a barefoot young man, his arms bound behind him.

'Attempting to escape,' Larnach intoned.

115

Mudie straightened his hat, his fingers curling the wide brim. 'Ah! The bolter! This is his second go isn't it?'

'Yes sir,' his son-in law grinned.

'Very well. He learned nothing from forty, make it fifty lashes.'

'Prisoner number thirty-four step forward,' Larnach shouted but this time no-one moved. Some hands behind him started pushing at Brosnan, who looked around, bewildered, and Jack leaned over to peer at his back. 'They're calling your number Brosnan,' he whispered.

'What for?' Brosnan asked.

'Buggered if I know,' Jack said but Larnach was already calling the guards. 'Put him out.'

As they dragged him from the ranks Brosnan shouted at Mudie. 'What's the bloody charge?'

Mudie pointed his whip to Larnach to proceed.

'Self-inflicted wounds,' Larnach yelled.

'Don't be bloody stupid man!' Brosnan shouted at him. 'I wouldn't cut my own bloody foot!'

Jack could have told them what would happen next, and it was almost as if he were counting: five, four, three, two, one – and sure enough there was O'Meara out front roaring at them to get their hands off Brosnan, and Larnach blew a whistle which made Mudie's horse rear.

The bolter was off again across the paddock in a crazy wobbly run, his hands still tied behind his back, and guards, taken by surprise, went after him on foot, but Jeremiah, not to be done out of a customer, had the little dishbreaker clasped, kicking and scratching, in his brawny arms.

O'Meara had moved so swiftly past Brosnan that Larnach missed the chance to grab for the pistol hanging low on his hip, before his attacker, not forgetting the stockwhip incident in Sydney, punched him in the face and again in the stomach sending him toppling back into the salt water vat, then O'Meara turned back to assist Brosnan who was wrestling with two guards.

It seemed that the attempt by the Irishman to prevent the flogging would only delay proceedings but out of the corner of his eye Jack saw Polly Phipps and some of his mates backing away, and at the same time, the excitement was too much for the prisoners near Brosnan. They jumped into the fight with whoops of joy.

Jack decided to follow Polly's example while he could and he raced towards the nearest building and around a corner, across a yard and over a fence, dashing for a haystack. He could hear shots and shouts and saw one convict escaping bareback on a horse and he could have kicked himself for not making for the stables. He tried to burrow into the haystack but it was too tightly packed, so he shinned up the ladder and pushed it crashing to the ground, settling himself on the top. From there he could see two guards riding fast after the barefoot bolter with dogs racing along behind them. The flogging area was hidden from him by the storehouse so he edged over to the other side to see what was happening.

116

Convicts were dodging quietly now, between the buildings, making for the outskirts of the station and Jack watched them with interest. There was a lot of open country to cover before they reached the shelter of the bush. Horsemen could easily run them down. Their only chance would be to get hold of some guns. It was a pity he thought, that O'Meara had triggered this confused breakout. In time, he, Jack Drew, could have worked out a plan to take over the whole place. That house, out of bounds! He laughed. There'd be some good pickings in that place judging from the cut of Mudie and his gold watch.

He heard some shots in the distance and below him three stockmen strolled calmly towards the stables; their spurs jingling, as if this rumpus had nothing to do with them. Polly had told him there were about ten stockmen out and around the station, men who had done their time and who preferred to stay and work in the bush. Jack could understand that, with a good horse you could go where you liked in this country. Mudie and Larnach were mean with the stockmen too he had heard, but the free men knew what they were doing. They either walked off the job or delivered a pay-back by cutting out some of Mudie's sheep.

Larnach himself came galloping after the stockmen. He had lost his hat and his stockwhip but he was waving his pistol about, shouting at them. 'Get mounted and get after the bastards!'

Jack expected them to break into a run, but instead they stood insolently in their tracks, looking up and down to see no-one was watching, and then, suddenly, they leapt at Larnach and pulled him from his horse. They punched and kicked him mercilessly while he rolled on the ground trying to protect himself and when he tried to lift himself up, one of the men, a lean ginger-headed fellow, motioned to the others to stand back. He picked up a long-handled spade and swung it around with both hands batting Larnach to the ground.

Interested, Jack wondered if they had killed him.

He watched them amble on their way in their high-heeled boots and a few minutes later come riding out of the stables, with their tools of trade, the guns and ropes, in place, without a glance at the unconscious Larnach. They stopped to discuss his horse standing waiting for its master, the bridle dangling to the ground. Then the ginger-haired stockman laughed and whistled to the horse which dutifully trotted up to him. He grabbed the bridle, dug in his spurs and all three horsemen plunged forward with the spare horse, galloping towards the last of the buildings and racing around the corner heading for the road.

It was only a matter of time before someone found Larnach and it had to be the Chinese cook who screamed and shrieked and ran around in circles calling for help, making it hard for the convicts who were still lurking in the sharp shadows of the whitewashed buildings. One man, whom Jack could see at a distance, was making a good job of it, dodging for the stables. Jack

117

decided that if he could last up here until nightfall he would grab a horse too. If they caught him in the meantime, nothing was lost. He would say he climbed the haystack for safety.

Guards had come for Larnach and were picking him up while further down the convict made his run for the stables. One of the guards, seeing the yellow garb running from the scene of the crime, lifted his rifle and fired. The convict threw up his arms, spun around and fell on his face in the grey dust.

'Ah struth!' Jack said, disappointed.

They carried Larnach into a shed and Lester arrived, shouting instructions. Across in the paddocks, at least a dozen convicts were making for the bush. Jesus, Jack thought, they look like getting away, annoyed now that he had not made the effort, but Lester was talking to two black trackers while a group of horsemen lined up behind them. Convicts were loading a wagon with chains and Jack nodded, understanding what the procedure would be. The black men would find the absconders and the white men would bring them home.

The rifleman had gone down to inspect his prey. Guards pulled a slab of bark from the stable wall making a stretcher, and dumped the body onto it and two more convicts were impressed to carry it away. As they trudged past his haystack Jack saw the number clearly. Thirty-four. Wasn't that Brosnan's number? He craned out again and there right under his eyes was Brosnan, brown hair falling over his face, his mouth open as if he were just about to say something. Tears of rage smarted his eyes and he choked back a shout of pain. Brosnan, of all the rummy lot, it had to be him! Never before had death hurt Jack so much, though he had walked beside it in the dark violence of the London wharves. He had seen murders and he had heard rattling death but this time, he felt pain and it scorched. He told himself that Brosnan had won a clean swift death, hardly a mark on him, he had heard that said often enough, but it did not help. He tried to recall the face of the shooter, the one who had killed Brosnan but he could not see it, only the gun.

Curled up in the warmth of the haystack he began to wonder what was happening to him. Getting soft? He made up his mind to wait until all the bolting and shooting had stopped and he would go down and give himself up. There was always another day. Jack Drew was too smart to go racing off into the countryside like a headless chook. When he went he would know where he was going.

Major Mudie took his time. Each one of those felons would rue the day they crossed their employer, making him the laughing stock of the district. 'They will pay,' he told his wife. 'Oh how they will pay!' And as she had always done, she crept away to warn their daughters not to upset the Major.

In his study, Mudie checked the list of convicts and Evan Laidley his storekeeper, bookkeeper and part-time physician, stood awkwardly behind him, picking at his nails. The Major in his kindness had brought him out from

England to make his fortune and so far he had not progressed but he did earn twenty pounds a year and his keep and he lived in the big house away from the workmen and the felons. Every single one of those men frightened the life out of him, from the convicts to the swaggering stockmen.

The Major rarely came down to the workplace, except to pass sentence on the convicts but Mr Larnach had always been there, and Laidley had felt safe with him around, but now Larnach was laid up, attacked by the same monsters they expected the storekeeper to associate with every day of his life. And every one of those days Laidley expected to get an axe in his back, the mood of the convicts was so vicious.

It had been four weeks since the riot and they still hadn't settled down. A procession of prisoners had been led into the Major's court and he, Laidley, had been seconded to assist the clerk of the court, as if he didn't have enough to do. Had it not been for that youngish daughter of the squatter at the adjoining station, Miss Jemima Cooper, he would have taken leave of Castle Forbes long before this.

Two of the convicts had been hanged and were still swinging from a tree near the slaughteryards, the storekeeper had been told, but he never went up that way. Mr Larnach had been lucky, there was no doubt the felons had tried to kill him even though they had cried out in court that they had not put a hand near him. Three stockmen had stolen Larnach's horse and the troopers were after them. Stealing a horse in this country rated as high as murder so their days were numbered too.

'Your report sir?' the Major snapped without turning from his desk.

'Yes sir. All convicts accounted for except three. They are still missing.'

'Then they are not all accounted for. Who is missing? Names?'

Laidley struggled with his book, passing his finger from the numbers across to the names. 'Smith. O'Meara. Johnson.'

'Have you notified the authorities that they are still at large?'

'Yes sir.'

'What about the rest?'

'Punishments are in order for nineteen more sir. The ones who ran off but were caught.'

Mudie stared out of the window at his second daughter who was rocking gently on the swing in the garden. 'We can't have them all out of the work-force at the same time. We shall have to stagger the floggings. Have they nearly finished the new courtyard?'

'Yes sir. I believe so.'

'What do you mean you believe so? As soon as you leave here go and see for yourself and report back to me.'

Mudie went back to his writing, dipping his pen into the ivory inkwell and adding flourishes to his letters, and Laidley waited. He knew better than to leave without being dismissed. The courtyard Mudie was referring to was nothing more than a flogging yard. Since the riot, floggings had been postponed because the Major wanted them carried out in future in a secure

119

enclosure. Laidley had asked the workmen, convicts of course, when it would be completed, having seen the triangle set-up in the centre, but his question had brought a string of vile oaths down on his head.

'You may go,' Mudie said. 'And tell Mrs Mudie I will take tea now.'

The convicts knew the floggings would be resumed as soon as the courtyard was finished so the stone masons were taking as long as possible about it. There was still no sign of O'Meara and two others but the rest of the absconders had been rounded up from the bush, Scarpy being the first, after only two days.

'To tell you the honest truth,' he told Jack, 'I'm bloody glad to get back. They're right. There's nothing out there but trees and at night it was so blooming dark I sat on a log too shit-scared to move, listening to wolves howling and seeing their red eyes looking at me.'

'They're not wolves,' Jack said. 'They're wild dogs.'

'What's the bloody difference?'

Polly Phipps lasted two weeks before they dragged him back half-mad with thirst. Jack listened to all their stories of the bush and it seemed to him that the only way to escape and not starve was to go back to Sydney Town and hide out there. He was still working on the clearing job with Polly and Scarpy but the men were nervous and jumpy. The hangings had frightened them and the floggings were still to come. Each day there were accidents and incidents, and at night, with everyone on edge, there were fights in the bunkhouse.

Strangely, when the floggings did begin again, they seemed to relieve the tension, but the workmen were then sent to build another familiar apparatus. Stocks! Jack watched in amazement as they erected solid pillories in the middle of a paddock and wondered why Mudie would bother when there were no passers-by to taunt the wrong-doer.

Each night he lay on his bunk listening to the moans of Jeremiah's victims, waiting his turn, and wishing that Scarpy with his whines and miseries had been left in the bush. He missed O'Meara's unrelenting anger, and Brosnan's goodwill that had made life bearable. A shepherd was brought in for a flogging, having lost some sheep, and Jack went down to talk to him but after a few minutes he realised he was wasting his time. The man was demented.

Polly Phipps laughed. 'You'll get nothing out of him. All them shepherds have to be mad to take it on.'

'But they're free out there. Why don't they bolt?'

'Ah give over Jack! If a shepherd bolts there's trouble. The squatter goes raving mad if any of his woollies get lost. They hunt the shepherd down like a plague carrier. But you'd have to be soft in the head to take the job, sitting out there on your own talking to sheep. They stay out there in the wild you know, no horse, no gun, no nothing and every few weeks a stockman comes by to take the count and throw them some beef and some plugs of tobacco. It the blacks don't get them the loneliness does.'

Jack shook his head. There had to be an answer. 'It looks as if O'Meara got away.'

'Go on, he's probably dead out there in the scrub.'

Then the floggings began again and every few days punishments were meted out to the failed escapees. Jack had insisted that he had only been keeping out of the way of trouble when he had given himself up, and now it seemed that his excuse had been accepted, but one morning he was dragged up to Larnach who had his arm in a sling and was still limping.

'I didn't bolt,' Jack was quick to tell him. 'I stayed right here.'

'You would have,' Larnach shouted. 'I know your type! But you're not going to be flogged. The Major's making an example of you. A lesson for anyone who even thinks about bolting. Bring him down here,' he said to the guards. 'I never seen one of these things working but the Major knows all about them. He said to put this man in the stocks for two days.'

They marched Jack across the paddock and fastened him into the stocks. Larnach walked around examining the wooden structure, intrigued. 'You're sure he can't get away?'

'No sir,' the guards said, throwing the bolts.

Larnach peered into Jack's face. 'There you are. You can watch the ants, and the crows can watch you. Keep your eyes closed or they'll pick them out.'

When they left Jack swore and swore, licking the spittle from his lips. Two days! Mudie was mad. The flogging would have been better. Maybe. He did not know. Crows cawed above him and he shut his eyes tight in panic. Do they pick out eyes or was that a joke? The sun was hot on his back and he eased his legs, stretching them one at a time, then tried to rest his arms, looking for some small degree of comfort. He tried to doze to pass the time but the wood cut into his throat.

The afternoon sun came over the sky to beat down on his head and hands and his eyes burned, and then his eyelids, and his lips cracked. By the end of the day, when the guards came to inspect him, his face was beetroot red.

'Water,' he croaked and a guard poured his waterbag over Jack's head, laughing as the victim stuck out his tongue to catch the drops and then the dinner gong was heard and the visitors left.

No-one came with food for the prisoner and as darkness closed in, he heard squeaks and flurries from the bush and saw night birds flapping high over the trees. It began to rain, cooling his face and freezing his body, and he hung limply, in agony, through the cold wet night. He opened and closed his hands to keep the circulation going and then he stopped. He thought he could feel movement around him, a difference in the wind, and he turned his head in the blackness but he could see nothing. Fear struck at him like a cramp and he hardly dared breathe, afraid that the stories of the blacks were true, that a spear would be plunged into his helpless body, or that wild dogs were prowling, ready to lunge at him. He forced himself to stay alert until the first pale rays of the sun came to rescue him.

121

A large black and white bird flew down and ambled nearby, picking at grass seeds but every so often it cocked a black, glinting eye at him and came a little closer. He hoped it was not an eye-picker too. He shook his head and waggled his fingers to keep it away but the bird was patient. It waited until his antics had died down and swooped in to pick up some shavings from the woodwork and flew away with its treasure. Several times that morning the bird came back and the prisoner began to look forward to its visits.

Another guard came up at sunset with some bread and water and he was released for fifteen minutes with his ankles hobbled but when it came time to put him back in the stocks the guard felt sorry for him. He placed a tin of water on the ground under Jack's face, and dousing a strip of canvas left one end in the tin and stuffed the other end in Jack's mouth. 'Keep that in your mouth, mate. It'll keep the moisture up to you.'

Darkness came again but the clouds had gone and the moon rose across the sky like a giant orange penny and the eerie howl of dingoes lifted into the quiet air. Jack's head dropped and he dreamed muddled dreams of strange places and deep forests and he awoke to find he had dropped the piece of canvas. All he could do was eye the cloth as the bird had eyed him. There was no retrieving it. Salty tears scalded his eyes and then he was aware of movement near him again, a new warmth in the air and he groaned, helpless against the monsters of the night.

Turning his head he realised he was looking at feet, black feet and two strong black legs, right in front of his face. The shock caused him to recoil and bang his head against the timbers, and forcing himself to get a better view, he saw a long spear and a fierce-looking blackfellow standing above him. This was one of the wild blacks he had heard about, stark naked and streaked with white paint. It was too much of an effort to hold his head at that angle any longer. He let it drop again waiting for the inevitable spear.

And then the blackfellow spoke. 'Plurry funny lockemup this!'

The convict roused himself at this unexpected tone of curiosity and realised what had been said to him. Confused, but recognising that the voice was not hostile, so far, he made himself speak even though his tongue felt too big for his mouth.

'It's killing me,' he said.

'Him Major killem you?'

'Yes.'

'Him Major bad man.'

Jack's eyes closed. He was too tired to carry on a conversation. He heard the bolts jerk loose and the top board lift off, the voice commenting, 'Plurry funny trap'. Jack lifted his head and rolled free.

The black man took his arm and pulled him up. The last thing Jack remembered was leaving the stocks like a deer on a poacher's shoulders, except that these shoulders were bare and smooth and smelled of fat. Was he now in the hands of cannibals? He was past caring.

# CHAPTER EIGHT

The whole of Sydney Town it seemed, had turned out to watch the majestic Argentinian brigantine sail down the harbour, a splendid sight on a gusty day, the square sails taut and the rare flag matching the brilliant colour of the sky. Georgina, awaiting the birth of her first child, saw it from the bay windows of the Cormack house and Milly Forrest, out walking with her sister-in-law, waved madly from their vantage point on Kings Wharf.

They watched some passengers disembarking but none of the officers came ashore so they lost interest and left. Had they waited they would have seen an elegant young man leave the ship dressed in black trousers, black shirt and a black jacket with a high embroidered collar and a cascade of white lace at his throat. Other ladies noticed his swarthy complexion, the dark eyes and his flashing smile as he took his leave of the companions of the voyage and set off for Sydney Town.

He walked a long way on this his first morning in New South Wales before deciding to take a cab. 'I wish to go to . . .' he examined his notebook. 'Bligh House in Macquarie Street.'

'Certainly sir, hop in,' the cabbie said.

The elder Miss Higgins opened the door to the stranger, a Mediterranean type she assumed and her face showed she was unimpressed.

'Might I speak to Miss Higgins?' he asked.

'I am Miss Higgins.' She did not ask what she could do for him and she held her hands tightly in front of her as if to bar his way.

'I have a letter of introduction from Captain Millbank.'

Miss Higgins took the letter and withdrew into the lobby to examine it, leaving him standing at the front door.

Millbank spoke highly of this young man. He said he came from one of Argentina's most respected families, and was a rich man in his own right. Miss Higgins frowned. She hardly thought it was necessary for Millbank to have added that, very poor taste. The young man's affairs were his own. But she supposed the Captain had meant well. He also sent his regards to Dr and Mrs Brooks if they were still in Sydney. She sighed. Poor Brooks, dead and gone.

She returned to the door. 'Will you be wanting a room?'

'Yes madam.'

'All right. Come along in. Where is your luggage?'

'Still on the ship. I thought it would be best to discover if you could take me

123

before arriving with my possessions.'

She smiled, pleased with his good manners. 'Come along Mr Rivadavia, lunch is ready. Then I shall show you to your room.'

By six o'clock he had settled in and when a bell rang he enquired of a maid what that might be.

'That's the dinner bell sir. Dinner is served every night at six o'clock except Sundays when it is high tea and served at half-past five.'

He thought it was early to dine, but he went in to dinner to answer questions in his very correct English. 'Yes, Captain Millbank is well. He is a friend of my father's. Captain Millbank intends to retire to Argentina I believe.'

'Peculiar thing for a chap to do,' the Major said. 'And what brings you here, young fellow?'

Juan would not discuss his family business with strangers but his reply was polite. 'Curiosity sir. To see a new land. To meet new people.'

'Humph! Not the sort of place I would choose for a holiday! You should have gone to England. Closer than here. Have you ever been to England?'

'No, sir.'

'What a shame. It is much more interesting than Sydney,' the Major's wife told him.

'Then why do you stay here?' Adelaide asked her.

'The climate my dear. It is so much better for the Major's chest.'

Each morning the maids brought tea and biscuits to the guests at seven o'clock, the wake-up tea they called it, but, weather permitting, Adelaide preferred to take hers in the courtyard. And the new boarder, Rivadavia, did the same, strolling down in an open-necked, gleaming white shirt and black trousers. He wanted to know all about Sydney, and Adelaide, who now considered herself practically a colonial, was able to enlighten him. He was a good listener and she went on to tell him her own impressions of Sydney and how different it was with the seasons reversed. She saw him smiling and then laughed at herself. 'I completely forgot that Argentina is in this hemisphere also. My late husband, who was a Doctor of Astronomy, would have been surprised at me.'

She explained to the Major's wife. 'He is most interested in everything, a well-educated young person as far as I can make out. He is fascinated with England too, with all our kings and queens, so it is fortunate I do know some history.'

With a sly smile the Major's wife looked over at Adelaide, her eyes narrowing the way they always did when she was ready to deliver a catty remark, arching her little pointed chin. 'We were wondering what you two whisper about downstairs in the mornings.'

Adelaide reacted angrily. 'Mrs Kelso, we do not whisper! Since the courtyard is directly under your window you'd be the first to complain if we talked at the top of our voices!' But she was embarrassed and she felt herself blushing, seeing his soft white shirt again, always open almost to the waist in the mornings, showing his smooth brown chest. Flustered, she said, 'Juan is a gentleman I'll have you know and I think that remark was uncalled for.'

'Oh? Juan is it?' Mrs Kelso asked.

'Why not?' Adelaide retorted. 'If you'd take the time to talk to a lonely young man on his own in a strange country he might pay you the same compliment.'

'I only asked,' the Major's wife replied and whisked away in a huff.

There were times when Adelaide hated living in the boarding house with everyone prying. Why shouldn't Juan talk to her? At least she wasn't an old frump like Mrs Kelso. She brushed her hair back with the palm of her hand tucking in loose stands, and stroked her neck. They were just jealous. It was a pity Juan was so young, he really was a very attractive man. Young man.

She shivered and wondered if she should take her morning tea in her room in future, but then she decided she would not allow Mrs Kelso to tell her what to do. To retreat now would give entirely the wrong impression.

'Oh blow!' she said to the cat that was rubbing itself luxuriously against her leg through the silky folds of her skirt.

Adelaide's life had settled into a routine. Every day after breakfast she went to her room, leaving the door open so that she would not be cut off from the world, and concentrated on her dressmaking. Every day except Sunday, of course. She wondered where Juan went during the day. Business, he said, but what kind of business she did not know, nor would she dream of asking.

He returned late in the afternoons by which time Adelaide had changed for dinner and was sitting in her favourite chair on the porch, taking the air.

She began to look forward to seeing him come in the gate because more often than not he would pull up a chair and join her. The more she looked at him, the more she felt mesmerised by him, his physique, his charming smile, his sultry accented voice, and of course, the flattery of his attention. Sometimes in the deep of the night she thought of him and realised she had a silly fancy for him, so foolish, but a harmless daydream, and she yearned to touch him, just to take his hand, an elegant hand, but full of strength. The thought of him warmed her, but other times it caused her to despair, wondering if she would end up a cold old woman, relegated to a back room somewhere. And pitying herself, she wept for Brooks, poor dear gentle Brooks. They had had such high hopes.

The Major gave her the newspapers when he finished with them and she read of Georgina and Jasin, 'the darlings of the Darling set', but she never mentioned that she knew them. Seeing how successful they were in society and what a happy life they were living, depressed her. Life could be so unfair.

After dinner Juan always went out alone. 'Taking his constitutional', the young Miss Higgins explained. Adelaide found his comings and goings mysterious but dared not ask for fear that she too was becoming as inquisitive as the other boarders.

She began to take more care of her appearance and in between orders ran herself up some light dresses of Swiss voile that were more in keeping with the climate of Sydney town, cool dainty dresses with velvet bows and flounced hemlines, ideal for warm evenings on the porch.

# CHAPTER NINE

When the Heselwoods left, Vicky Horton felt that a burden had been lifted from her shoulders, their presence had caused her to be more morbid and irritable than was good for her. She could now take control of her household again.

There was a great deal to do before the birth of the baby and while John's death still caused spasms of tears, she determined to overcome the depression. She decided that if she had a son he would be called John, but a daughter would be Marietta after a song Horton used to sing.

The sheep runs at Bathurst sold quickly but it was taking time to dispose of Chelmsford Station. At times she thought the station agents had forgotten her, but they assured her they were looking for the best possible price, and in the meantime, the station foreman Andy, and his wife, were keeping the place in good order. She was grateful to Andy and Dora, a good reliable couple, and hoped the new owners would keep them on.

Through the servants' grapevine, Lettie kept her informed of the goings-on next door since Mary and Lachie Cormack had left for London. The Heselwoods were now installed there, which Vicky found annoying, and Georgina too was having a baby. Not that Vicky cared. They were out of her life forever. She knew John would not want her to mope about so she was already planning the christening to celebrate the birth of his child.

A letter came from her agents stating that they had a possible buyer but he wished to meet the present owner. Due to her condition they had refused to meet this request but they assured her that negotiations were in progress. Vicky replied that she would see this person. She found his request quite sensible.

The appointment was made and she dressed in her best black dress of watered silk, and she sat at the table in her sitting-room to receive him.

Her first impression of Juan Rivadavia was disturbing. She had been expecting a much older man and here was a gentleman nearer her own age and so handsome as to cause a blush to tingle on her cheeks. She frowned at Lettie who was casting admiring glances at him. 'That will be all Lettie, thank you,' she said and stayed in her chair rather than allow him to see her ungainly figure.

He took the chair at the end of the table. 'Mrs Horton, I hope you will forgive this intrusion when you are in mourning but I am a stranger to

126

your country and I believe you could tell me more about your ranch than any of the agents.'

'Oh yes,' she replied and heard herself explaining and then babbling on about the station, the staff, the stock, the lovely Hunter Valley and trivial things she had not meant to say and all the time he sat quietly, listening, not interrupting. As she spoke she studied the careful folds of his high collar and the lace-edged cravat that was held in place with a ruby pin so that she wouldn't have to look into his dark eyes, and when she finally came to a halt, he was smiling. 'I had no idea that Mrs Horton would be so young. They should have warned me.'

'I am not so young,' she replied, 'that I cannot discuss a business arrangement.'

'Of course not,' he said. 'I didn't mean to offend you. I just meant that it makes it much easier for me to talk to you. We can look at this from our point of view and you can tell me if you think I will make a success of it.'

'I see, I suppose so. Would you like coffee?'

'Yes. Thank you.'

They talked more like conspirators than business associates, and Vicky, forgetting her figure, jumped up and led him out to John's office where she showed him the stock tallies and projections and not once did he apologise for intruding on her because of 'her condition' as everyone else did. She was disappointed when he left, she felt as if she could have talked to him forever.

'Do you think you'll buy the station?' she had asked.

'I think so. But you understand Mrs Horton, I have to see it first, that will take a little time. But once I have seen it I will let you have my answer right away.'

She shut herself away from Lettie's grins and sat brushing her hair in her bedroom, confused. She had not thought she would ever look at another man after John Horton but here she was already half-smitten with this man from Argentina. 'You must be going mad,' she told her reflection. 'Who would be interested in you in your state?' She was sorry now that she had allowed him to come to the house. It would have been much better to meet a man like that after the child was born. Now it was too late. Then again, he could be married. He had told her little about himself, she realised, and he had heard her life story.

She had already forgotten about the sale of Chelmsford. It did not seem to matter any more.

# CHAPTER TEN

'I've bought a horse,' Juan told Adelaide one evening. 'Would you like to see it? The stables are only around the corner.'

'I'd love to. But they don't like us to be late for dinner.'

He looked at his watch. 'We've got time.' He offered her his hand and she stood up to go with him, feeling very daring.

The stablehands welcomed Mr Rivadavia and they all went down to admire his horse.

'He looks very strong,' she said. 'What's his name?'

'They call him Rex, so I leave it at that, but it seems a very plain name for such a handsome fellow.'

'Oh no, it suits him,' Adelaide cried. 'He's beautiful. And that saddle in the stall. Is that yours?'

'Yes.'

Adelaide examined the big black embossed leather saddle with its intricate silver trim. 'It's magnificent. Where did you buy it?'

'I brought it with me.'

The stablehands, too, were impressed with the saddle and they showed her the silver-trimmed bridle and colourful blanket that went with it. 'Rex'll be the best dressed horse in town,' the men laughed. 'We'll take good care of him Mr Rivadavia.'

Juan nodded. 'Do you like to ride, Mrs Brooks?'

'Yes. But I haven't sat a horse since I got here.'

'That is a shame,' he said.

As they hurried back, Adelaide thought what a strange young man he was sometimes.

One night he came back later than usual when all the boarders had retired and knocked softly on Adelaide's door.

She opened it anxiously and peered out. 'Oh, it's you Juan. Is something wrong?'

'May I come in?'

'Well, Juan, I was in bed . . .'

She pulled her dressing gown around her not sure what to do with a young man who perhaps did not know that it was not proper to knock on a lady's door at this hour, even if the lady were several years his senior. But she invited him in and closed the door quickly.

'What is it Juan? Wait until I light the lamp.' She felt her hands shaking

128

as she fished around on the table but he stopped her. 'No. Leave it.'

He put his arms around her and stroked her hair. 'It is beautiful, your hair.'

'Juan. What are you thinking of? You mustn't!' Adelaide could not believe this was happening and she was afraid someone would hear them. Even her whispers sounded deafening in the slumbering household. She tried to push him away.

'You don't like me?' he asked.

'Of course I like you, but not this way.'

'Just let me kiss your hair and your soft neck,' he murmured, his strong arms holding her lightly, not forcing her and she attempted a light laugh while still trying to extricate herself. 'You must understand, Juan. I like you. But not this way. Why, I am so much older than you.'

'Just kiss me once,' he said, 'and we'll see.' His mouth moved across her cheek to hers and he was so warm and loving she responded for just that minute, one kiss could not matter.

'Are you sure you don't like me this way?' he asked, kissing her again and pressing her towards the bed, and then he drew back to undo her dressing gown, take it from her and place it carefully on a china knob at the end of her brass bed.

Adelaide waited. She felt guilty, like a silly young girl, unable to take control of the situation. She wanted him to go, she was sure he was only teasing her and perversely she also wanted him to kiss her again but when he did, he held her so close to him that she could feel the hardness of him and it shocked her. But he was so warm, so lovable, she pretended not to notice.

When he let her go she straightened her night gown, trying to think of something appropriate to say, since she thought he was now leaving but he was removing his clothes and she panicked, shifting away from the bed. 'Please Juan. You mustn't.' But he kissed her again and stroked her face and her hair and gently pressured her to her knees and Adelaide wondered what he wanted of her, this strange beautiful young man, and he drew her face into his belly and she could smell the faint perfume she was sure he used and she was amazed at her own wanton behavior.

He slipped with her into the bed and Adelaide was impatient for him now and breathless at being naked next to a man, skin to skin, something she had never contemplated before, not even with Brooks.

'Do you want me now?' he asked and she slid closer to him, her whole body wanting him.

'No,' he said. 'You have to tell me.'

She dropped her head back to the pillow. 'What do you mean?'

'Unless you ask. Unless you say to me you want me to make love to you then you will convince yourself that I forced this on you, and your Anglo-Saxon morality will be appeased. You do not really approve that I am in your bed. I have shown you that you are a desirable woman and I want you. You will pay me the same compliment.'

129

'Don't be silly Juan.' Her hands caressed his back. Surely he could not expect her to beg him to stay. After all it was his idea. He had come to her room. They both lay very still.

'Very well,' Juan said. 'I shall go.'

He threw back the covers and stood up, his body silhouetted against the light filtering through the lace curtains.

'No Juan. Don't go. Please. I want you to stay.'

Juan leaned over to smile at her. 'That wasn't so hard was it. Now I will make love to you.' He began stroking her body slowly and gently, kneeling on the bed beside her and the pleasure was so new to her, so exquisite she came up to him wrapping her arms around him.

'You are beautiful,' he murmured.

Despite his lessons in honesty Adelaide was petrified when he left the soft feather bed, that someone in the house might see him leave, and she waited, expecting to hear voices but all was quiet and as she settled down into the bed she hugged a pillow. He really was adorable, she felt like a young girl again.

In the cold light of day, remembering her total abandon of the night, Adelaide was too embarrassed to face him, and that afternoon she found she was far too busy to waste time sitting on the verandah. At dinner she was quiet, and careful not to catch his eye until he addressed her directly. 'You look enchanting this evening Mrs Brooks,' and ignoring her consternation turned to the younger of his landladies. 'Does she not Miss Higgins?'

'Yes, you do, Adelaide. You are looking so much better these days.'

'It's the wind,' the Major announced. 'I always say that people are much healthier in windy weather. Blows away the germs, smartens up the blood. You should take more walks Mrs Brooks. Why, back in the old country I used to walk ten miles a day and the colder the better. It's only this gammy leg stops me walking these days.'

For once Adelaide was glad to have the garrulous Major at the table. Once he started it was an end to conversation. She finished her meal and took her tea upstairs claiming she had work to finish by morning, and spent a long humiliating night waiting for Juan to come back to her door.

Three more nights passed, an eternity, until she was driven to resuming her place on the verandah before dinner, waiting for him to come home.

When he did push through the gate, he waved to her and strolled down the tiled verandah to take his usual place in the cane chair next to her as if nothing had happened. 'The garden is looking splendid isn't it? What is it you say? The ladies have green hands?'

'Green thumbs,' she corrected.

'Ah yes. Green thumbs. A strange expression. Have you had a busy day with your sewing?'

'Yes.' She thought she would go mad. She wished she had the courage to reach out and touch him but she did not dare. Someone might see her, or worse, he might repulse her.

'Aren't you feeling well?'

'I am quite well, thank you, Juan.'

'What is the matter then?'

It took some time for her to ask the question, but she had to ask it, driven to it she felt by a sudden madness. 'Was I a disappointment to you?' and when she whispered it she could have bitten her tongue.

He laughed. 'No.'

'You haven't come near me since.' She heard herself hissing at him like a fishwife but his reply was casual. 'I have not seen you for days. Do you want me to?'

Adelaide looked furtively around her. 'Yes.'

'Then why didn't you say so?'

They watched a colourful gypsy wagon trundle past.

'Adelaide is a very stiff and serious name,' Juan remarked. 'It doesn't suit you at all. I shall call you Dell.'

Nothing escapes the eagle eyes of housemaids or the wagging tongues of boarders and before long they were all about with the scandal. Mrs Brooks was having improper relations with that young man. The Misses Higgins were greatly concerned since the young man had been placed in their care by Captain Millbank, and they were very disappointed in Adelaide who had no idea that everyone in the house knew. They discussed confronting her with the matter and then shrank from that. What if she denied it? They were certain she had seduced the young man and they prayed for him.

In the kitchen the maids kept the cook informed. 'Half her luck,' old Maisie said. 'They say them Italians are a fiery lot. Warm-blooded you see. And that Mister Rivadavia is a bit of all right, no getting away from that. He could put his boots under my bed any time,' she laughed and waved her big hips. 'But fancy Mrs Brooks getting on to him. You'd think butter wouldn't melt in her mouth. See. You never know with them quiet ones.'

While the Misses Higgins worried and the boarders talked in whispers, Adelaide went on with her sewing, dreaming of the nights in his arms, unaware that she had become a scarlet woman in danger of eviction.

Her best customer, Milly Forrest, came by. 'Did you know Georgina Heselwood had a son? She called him Edward. He's a dear little baby, very pretty. I've been over to visit her, she lives in a mansion but she's very lonely. She misses Jasin.'

'Did he come back for the birth?'

'No, he couldn't, he's too far away, out in the country.'

'What a pity, poor Georgina.'

'Why do you say that Adelaide? You never liked her.'

'I didn't mind her, I don't like to see anyone lonely.'

Milly looked at her. She had heard a few tales lately about Adelaide and some young buck but she doubted it could be true. 'I suppose you get a bit lonely yourself, being a widow?' she tried, but Adelaide doubled back.

'What is Jasin doing in the country this time?'

'He and a friend of his, Captain Pelham, are buying cattle in Bathurst and they are taking them north to start a cattle station.'

'Jasin Heselwood! I don't believe it! I didn't think he'd move out of a drawing room.'

'Jasin has changed, he has been out in the bush. He knows what he is doing. Not that he still hasn't got his lovely manners when he is back here. he's our partner you know.'

'Yes. You told me. What about your house? Have you bought the new house yet?'

'No. Dermott says that would be dead money for the time being. We will make a lot more in the cattle business.'

'Is Dermott going with Jasin?'

'No, he's making too much money at the saddlery just now. You keep promising to come to see it but you never do.'

'Yes. I must one day, but I seem to be kept too busy here. Your blue dress is finished, you can take it with you today.'

Milly, who hated to miss anything, missed Juan Rivadavia for the second time, by only a few minutes. He came up from the stables just as her carriage spun away, for which Adelaide was thankful.

'You're looking very pleased with yourself Juan,' she smiled.

'With good reason. I have finished my business in Sydney. I will be leaving tomorrow.'

Adelaide's face turned brick red at his casual news. 'You're leaving? You can't! Where are you going?'

'First to Newcastle by ship and then on into the Hunter Valley.'

'How long will you be away?'

He looked surprised. 'How long? I am going for good. I think I will buy a ranch up there but first I have to look at it. I have examined details of a lot of ranches but this one seems the best.'

The dinner bell rang. Adelaide jumped up and ran past the dining room and up the stairs to shut herself in her room. How dare he say he was leaving her? Just like that! It was plain to see he did not care about her. And the way he had told her, not even bothering to break it gently. Well she would show him. She would lock her door tonight and he could stay out. She paced the room for hours trying to maintain her anger but as the night dragged on she began listening for him again and when he came to her door it was open.

Adelaide clung to him, their last night together, and kept him with her as long as she could but the dawn was coming and he had to go back to his room before the others began stirring. At the door, shivering and wrapped only in a sheet, she still would not let him go. 'Juan. I can't bear to be without you. Please don't go, don't leave me.'

132

'Come with me then.'

'What did you say?'

'I said come with me. Why not? Unless you want to stay in this ugly little room for the rest of your life.'

She hadn't realised he thought her room ugly. It confused her. 'Juan. Are you asking me to marry you?'

'No Dell, I'm not. But we are good together. I will look after you. You deserve better than this. If you want to come with me, start packing.'

She looked wildly around the room. Was it any more precarious to rely on her few dressmaking customers than to take her chances and go with him? God knows, it would be unbearable here without him. She would miss him so much. But he was so young, would he keep his word? And even if he did how would she look in public with such a young man? What would people say? Oh my God!

She ran to her wardrobe and began pushing things aside as if she were looking for something, searching frantically for her answer. What would become of her if she stayed on here? She'd not looked that far ahead before. She was alone in the world, quite alone, just managing to keep ahead of the rent – her room now seemed a prison, a place of confinement. Would she one day reach such a point of desperation as had Brooks? Oh God no! But Juan was probably right, they did not really know one another well enough yet to discuss marriage; she turned to look at him, waiting by the door somewhat ungenerously she felt. 'Don't stare at me like that!'

He grinned and spread his hands, palms out. 'You can't want to stay here!'

'I don't know what I want,' she cried. 'You tell me I can come with you in such an offhand manner, as if you're taking pity on me. It is not good enough. Do you really want me to come with you?'

He came back into the room and put his arms around her. 'Of course I do. I want you,' he added with a laugh and his hands slipped through the sheet.

Adelaide pulled away and slumped into a chair. 'Now you're teasing me. I'll think about it and perhaps I'll join you later.'

'No. You walk out the door with me or you do not come at all. You are ashamed of us. You worry about them, all of them here, that they should find out about us. They all know, Dell. They have known all the time. I don't care. Why should you?'

Adelaide felt her face freeze. 'They don't know! They couldn't know!'

He shrugged.

She looked around her room. 'What about the work I am doing here? The dresses. They're only half finished.'

'Leave them. It's work for peasants anyway.'

'But what will I say to Miss Higgins? What on earth can I tell them? And I have to pay my rent.'

'But, but but! That's all you can say. I will tell Miss Higgins we are leaving and settle your account. Does that make you feel better?'

'Yes,' she whispered but she didn't appear for breakfast.

Juan took her luggage down to the vestibule and came back for her. 'Are you ready to leave?'

'Yes.' She still hadn't dared to step out the door that morning and now the time had come. She followed Juan down the stairs relieved that there was no-one in sight.

'Wait here Dell,' he told her. 'I will call you a carriage. You can take the luggage to the ship. I will ride my horse down.'

The elder Miss Higgins appeared. 'Surely you would not leave without saying goodbye Mrs Brooks?'

'No. Of course not. I was just coming to look for you.'

'Well, here we are,' the other Miss Higgins came down the passage looking very prim and the maids ducked past behind her.

'Thank you very much for all you have done for us, I mean my husband, Dr Brooks and myself . . .' Adelaide's voice was trailing.

The two women who had been her friends now seemed turned to stone. 'There are some dresses left in your room. Did you forget them?'

'No, they belong to customers. I have pinned names to them. Would you tell them I am sorry I couldn't finish them?'

There was no sign of the carriage but Adelaide could not endure this any longer. She decided to wait in the street. 'Well, goodbye.' She turned to escape from them but the elder Miss Higgins spoke, her voice stern. 'Just a minute.'

Adelaide's heart pounded. Didn't he pay the bill? He had said he would.

'You haven't left a forwarding address Mrs Brooks. Where shall we send your mail?'

'What? Oh yes. I shall write to you from Newcastle.'

'Is that where you will be getting married?' Miss Higgins the younger asked and the question was loaded with disapproval.

'Yes,' Adelaide lied but she was in a state of panic. What on earth was she doing? The Misses Higgins were standing, waiting to be rid of her, severe censure plain on their faces, but there was the carriage at last, and riding behind it, Rivadavia on the bay horse, in his flamboyant riding clothes and a black, silver-edged sombrero, the focus of all eyes. She hadn't realised before how different he looked. The Major and his wife were on the verandah but as soon as they saw Adelaide, they turned their backs. Her humiliation was complete.

On the ship, at Juan's insistence, they shared a cabin and the short voyage was pleasant. He put her on the packet boat to travel up-river to Singleton while he rode the rest of the way. At the Singleton Inn they shared a room and Adelaide wondered if he had signed them in as a married couple until the publican stumbled and stuttered trying to think what to call her, and she knew he had not.

The next day he took leave of her. 'I have to go now and view this

134

property. It will take about a week but I'll be back. They will look after you here.'

Adelaide was terrified. 'I don't want to be left here on my own.'

'Dear Dell. They tell me there are no inns from here on. I want you to be comfortable.'

She saw him off, believing that would be the last she would see of him and when she returned to the bedroom she found fifty pounds in a drawer, and burst into tears. It was so much money she was convinced he had abandoned her.

The money was still there when he returned. She had waited and worried each day for the innkeeper to present the bill and ask her to leave but nothing had happened. He and his wife were as kind as they could be, since their guest avoided any attempt at conversation.

'I have bought the ranch,' Juan said when he returned. 'Now I begin. I hope you have had a good rest because we must be going. I must find you a suitable horse, we will ride the rest of the way. A cartage contractor can deliver our belongings.'

She handed him back his money but he laughed and rolled her on the bed. 'It's yours Dell. Now take off that dress, I have been away too long. Did you miss me?'

For Adelaide it was a relief to be riding away from Singleton but once out on the road, secure in Juan's company, she was happy. The country-side seemed to crackle with energy and she noticed for the first time that the leaves of the native gums were tinged with red, she had always thought them to be flat green, and the huge wattle trees were in bloom lighting up the bush with their glorious yellow fluff.

They stopped for refreshments at a rough shanty inn where the inn-keeper's wife produced a china cup and saucer for Adelaide's tea. 'I keep them for best,' she said. 'Tin mugs does most of our customers.'

'You're very kind,' Adelaide replied.

The woman was watching Juan who was outside talking to some men. 'That's a flash-looking gent of yours,' she said and Adelaide was thankful for the dimness of the room to hide her embarrassment. She had become accustomed to Juan's eccentric clothes, she had even begun to appreciate them as being quite attractive and superbly tailored but now she realised that talking to the dusty bushmen he stood out like a peacock among the hens.

'He's from South America,' she said, her tone an apology.

'Ah yes,' the woman said, obviously none the wiser.

Juan had warned it would be a long and tiring ride for her and by late afternoon when they were travelling across open pastures, seeming to be alone on the planet, Adelaide found herself bumping along, every so often losing the rhythm of the horse. Her knees were stiff in the side-saddle and she longed to be able to stretch and stand in the stirrups as a man could, or better still get down and walk awhile.

Noticing her distress, Juan took them into the shade of a clump of trees and helped her down. 'How do you like it?' he asked.

'Like what?'

'The ranch. We have been travelling over it for six miles or so now. It goes right back there into the hills and it has plenty of water from the river. And there is the house.'

She saw a large movement of sheep on a shadowed hill and in the distance a long windbreak of tall willows leading to the house, only the red roof visible reflecting the setting sun.' 'Juan! All this land! Is it all yours? And that's our house! I can't wait to get there.'

'My house,' he said quietly and Adelaide flushed at the rebuke. She felt a rush of tears and searched in her sleeve for a handkerchief.

Some riders were coming out to meet them.

'The station has an English name,' Juan said, seeming not to realise that his correction had been hurtful. 'It is called Chelmsford. What does that mean?'

'I don't know,' she whispered. She pulled her hat further down over her eyes and tightened the muslin scarf around it, to hide her confusion and waited dully while he went forward to speak with the horsemen.

# CHAPTER ELEVEN

Bathurst was hot and dusty and the locals were already beginning to worry that another drought might afflict them this year. Clarrie and Snow, the two old stockmen from Camden, waited for Jasin outside the inn.

'If I were you I'd get the herd going while you can,' Clarrie said.

'I'm trying to,' Jasin replied. 'But every day something seems to go wrong.'

'Something always goes wrong Mr Heselwood. You just git and go. If you'd gone last week we wouldn't be looking for a new lot of drovers. Those blokes don't hang about.'

Jasin hurried down the main street looking for Pelham and spotted his horse outside the blacksmith's. 'Anyone here seen Captain Pelham?' he shouted over the noise.

'Around the back,' a voice called.

He found Pelham squatting over a mudmap drawn in the dust, with four stockmen. 'Here's the boss now,' he said. 'These boys are willing to go, Heselwood.' He introduced them: 'This is Nick, and Bobbo and Tommy and Lance – Mr Heselwood.'

'Good day boss,' they all replied but their spokesman was Bobbo who looked to have Aboriginal blood. 'It's gonna be a long drive eh boss?' Jasin nodded. 'Yes. But you do your work well and you'll be well paid. Where's the cook?'

'We haven't got one yet,' Pelham said.

Bobbo looked up in surprise, 'What happened to the Chinee?'

'He's run off on us.' Pelham didn't seem concerned.

'Oh God!' Jasin was furious. He had a herd of six hundred cattle waiting in the stockyards with the manager charging him for every extra day, and the horses were all in a paddock with broken-down fences and he was forced to pay a lad to watch them.

'I've got a German mate,' Lance said. 'He says he's a good cook. Do you want me to round him up?'

'Yes, get him,' Jasin said. 'Tell him we leave first thing in the morning.' Jasin was annoyed that he had to do everything himself. He was beginning to wonder if taking Pelham were such a good idea after all. The man was unable to make any decisions, even to buying the cattle. In the end Jasin had to do that himself too, with the help of Clarrie and Snow.

William Macarthur had kept his word. He had sent the two old bushmen to report to Jasin at the Queens Hotel in Bathurst and they had come riding in eager to get on the road again.

'I'll show you on the map where we intend to go,' Jasin had said but Clarrie had grinned. 'Mr Macarthur told us where you want to go boss. We'll get you around the ranges and then we'll see what we've got after that. Anything you want us to do while we're waiting?'

'Would you check the supplies and see if we have all we need?'

The supplies and equipment ordered by Pelham had turned out to be inadequate and Jasin was forced to spend a day at the store while Clarrie and Snow unloaded the wagon and reordered. Pelham, who was to be the boss drover, waited in the bar next door.

'One thing he has got, plenty of guns and ammo,' Snow commented. 'Enough to start a war, but he's light on flour, tea and sugar.'

'I suppose it is difficult to know what we'll need,' Jasin said.

'No it's not,' Clarrie said. 'The old six, four, two pound for each man still works, and he's got tools and horseshoes all right but he's forgot the horseshoe nails. And we need axes. Don't worry boss, we'll get it right. Might cost you a bit more.'

Snow disagreed for which Jasin was thankful. 'You don't have to pay any more. We'll swap some of the guns for what we need.'

Jasin felt comfortable with the two old men. Loyal to Macarthur, they would be loyal to him. The stockmen were an unknown quantity. He had seen Pelham buying them drinks and making a good fellow of himself, but that did not worry him, he needed them as workmen not bosom friends. Pelham talked big. They had envisaged taking a thousand head of cattle north, to put out to pasture, and then with natural increase they would have plenty to stock a sizeable run and begin marketing next year. Jasin had bought five hundred at an average of one pound per head but Pelham could only afford one hundred.

'There are wild cattle on the route, I'll pick up strays on the way,' Pelham had argued and later Clarrie nudged Jasin. 'He might if he's a good enough horseman to ride them out of the brush, but he won't get none of us to go chasing wild steers for him.'

And that, thought Jasin, will be Pelham's problem. For the time being he needed him as a right-hand man, a go-between. Pelham could communicate with these people better than he could. But all night he tossed and turned in his bed while Pelham snored on his side of the room. The imbalance was worrying. He had invested a lot of money, all of it borrowed, in the herd and the spare stock horses, wagon and provisions, not to mention the wages that would have to be paid, and after that he would need funds for a house and improvements; too much money to let a sharp-Jack like Pelham get the edge on him. He argued with himself that he was probably worrying for nothing, but Pelham's investment was now minor instead of being fifty-fifty as they had first discussed. Pelham had admitted in the end that he had no interest in taking up land, only in the turnover of

138

cattle and out there in the wilds what would stop him from taking the whole herd if he could get the others on his side, leaving only the two old men to back up the owner? Jasin now had the impression that Pelham thought he was a chump and as he waited for morning, an idea that had been at the back of his mind became more and more attractive. He would do it.

At first light he watched the herd leave with everyone in good spirits and the German cook, Otto, riding the wagon. Clarrie and Snow had taken out the remount horses and Pelham was in high good humour in the lead.

'I'll catch up with you later,' Jasin called and rode back into the town. There was plenty of time, the herd could only travel about ten miles a day. He was pleased about that. Every day they would have new pasture and if they took it quietly the cattle could fatten up along the route.

The owner of the Queens Hotel, Jim Moran, came running out into the road to stop him. 'Hey, Mr Heselwood. Just as well you came back. We were going to send one of the lads after you. You got a telegraph. You've got a son called Edward.'

Jasin smiled, surprised. 'I have? Well now I shall have to write to my wife before I go.'

'You'll have to have a drink on the house more like it. Not every day a man becomes a father for the first time.'

Jasin sighed. They knew everything. But then that could be handy now.

'Jim,' he called to his host. 'Do you know the superintendent of the jail here?'

'Old Rufus Donoghue. Know him well. He likes a spot. Comes in here every Saturday.'

Jasin dismounted and went into the hotel, suffering the enthusiasm of locals who bobbed up from nowhere to toast his newborn son and get in on the free drinks, their bushy faces clamouring at Jasin to shout another round, but he took the publican aside, ignoring them. 'You might be able to help me. There's something I nearly forgot to do while I was here, I've had so much to think about . . .'

'And with a kid on the way too, eh?' the publican reminded him.

Jasin frowned at the interruption and at the noise the louts in the bar were making, and continued. 'While I was staying with the Macarthurs at Camden, William asked me to locate a prisoner by the name of Pace MacNamara who, he believes, is in the Bathurst jail. Apparently he is a great friend of theirs, very highly thought of, and was jailed because of a fight, I'm told, with a fellow called Mudie.'

The publican laughed. 'That one! Yeah I've heard of him. They should of given him a medal instead of putting him in jail.'

'I promised William Macarthur that I would get MacNamara assigned to me if I could. I already have two others of Macarthur's men.'

'Yeah, Clarrie and Snow. Smart old bushies those two, you won't get better guides than them. You go on up to the jail and make yourself known

139

to Rufus. He'll sort it out for you.' The publican winked. 'He's partial to whisky.'

Jasin took the hint. 'Then you had better sell me a bottle of your best. Why don't you come with me? Mr Donoghue might not believe me, coming out of the blue as it were.'

They went through the side gate of Bathurst jail and found the superintendent at breakfast but not against a few shots of whisky to start the day. In explaining about MacNamara, the publican laid it on even thicker than Jasin would have dared but he need not have bothered. Donoghue had his own opinion of the prisoner. 'Lovely feller, MacNamara. Comes from the Curragh, same as my dear old Dad.'

Jasin picked up on that point. 'That's why I need him, I'll be buying horses along the route. I can't claim to know as much about horses as the Irishman.'

'That'd be right,' Donoghue said, reaching for the bottle. 'And you want him assigned to you?'

'He'll take him off your hands Rufus,' Moran said. 'Mr Heselwood's cattle have gone on, he nearly forgot this poor feller.'

The bottle went around again and Rufus said to Jasin, 'I'll send someone to bring him up. Convicts can't be made to go past the boundaries. You're headed right out west aren't you?'

'North-west,' Jasin said.

'Well it's all the same. You can't work them outside the limits unless they're willing to go. You can ask him yourself.'

Jasin was escorted into a small courtyard with high walls and one stone bench and a warder unlocked a heavy door and disappeared into the prison.

When MacNamara arrived he was hardly recognisable behind a thick black beard, and looked thin in the shapeless faded convict garb.

'Well MacNamara! We meet again,' Jasin said.

'So we do. They said you've got a job for me. What sort of a job?'

'I need a stockman. We're taking cattle up north.'

'*You* are?' the brown eyes glistened with mirth.

'Yes.'

'And you want me to work for you?'

'Yes.'

'You can go to hell. I'll not work for any bloody Englishman. It was another one of you bastards put me in here on a play-act of a trial.'

'Don't be such a fool MacNamara. I'm offering you a way out.'

'I know. Assigned to you like your servant.'

Jasin was beginning to think this was a mistake. 'Take it or leave it!'

'And what's in it for you Mr Heselwood? It's not the kindness of your heart would have you venturing into a prison.'

'I have to buy horses on the way. You know about horses.'

'Try again. There'd be fifty men in this jail and plenty more outside that would know more about their bush horses than I do,' MacNamara said. He sat down on the bench in a small patch of sunlight, appreciating the warmth.

Jasin searched around in his head for another story. He couldn't tell MacNamara that he was uneasy about Pelham. Attack, he remembered, was the best line of defence. 'Stay here then you fool. You can rot for all I care.'

Pace grinned. 'That's more like it. Now if you can get me out I should be grateful but I can't help thinking there's a catch to it. A stockman you say?'

'Yes. But don't get any ideas about taking off on your own, or I'll notify the authorities and you'll be back here post-haste.'

'I'm sure you will Mr Heselwood. And where might we be going?'

'To the north beyond the range. Out on the Liverpool Plains I would think.'

'You're going to claim land?'

'That's what I said.'

'Not quite, but we won't worry about that now. You're an unlikely explorer Heselwood. Are you sure you know where you're going?'

'Of course I do. I have reliable guides. Are you coming or not?'

'I don't have much choice, sure I'll come along. I have to see what it really is you want of me.'

Donoghue had found another bottle of whisky so Jim Moran was in no hurry to return to his pub which suited Jasin. He signed the necessary papers and went around to the front gate to wait for his assigned servant.

MacNamara emerged dressed in a rough shirt, moleskin pants, home-made riding boots and a battered wide-brimmed hat. 'They dressed me for the job you see. They were very kind.' He grinned at Jasin. 'Now do you want to put a rope around my neck and tie me to your stirrups?'

'You won't bait me MacNamara so don't waste your breath. You go out to the pound and get yourself a horse. I'll bring you down a saddle and bridle.'

'The pound eh? That's fitting I suppose. But that's a fine horse you got there,' he said, admiring Prince Blue. 'An Arab no less. Where did you get him? Win him at the tables?'

Jasin was startled. That was only a wild jab at him but close to home. He wheeled the horse and looked down at MacNamara. 'I've got a lot to do. I'll meet you back at the pound.'

'And where would the pound be?'

'Ask someone!'

He rode off leaving MacNamara to walk down the wide dusty road into the town. The man was infuriating but the law would keep him in place and his hatred of the English was exactly what was needed now. Jasin laughed. Wait until he finds out his other boss, the second-in-command, is English too, and worse, red rag to a bull, a military man, one who had

141

served in Ireland for years. Oh no, MacNamara would never throw in his lot with Pelham.

He had the drive planned. He would ride on ahead with Clarrie and Snow to work out the route for the herd. He would stay at stations along the way, having been advised that visitors were welcome, and at each stop would be able to learn more of what lay ahead. Otto would follow with the wagon to make camp and have the meals ready for the men and Pelham with the stockmen would bring up the herd. It would be up to him to keep the stockmen on the job and he was welcome to MacNamara. Jasin worried that he should have gone back to Sydney once more to see Georgina but there hadn't been time. She would understand. He would like to see his son but a man can't be everywhere.

And then there was Dolour. He wondered if she had really run off from Camden. Probably. She was a strong-willed little miss but he had not had a chance to check at the Female Factory. It all seemed so long ago now, what with Horton's death and their sudden change of plans. The months had passed too quickly. When he came back to Sydney he would find her. He would be in a better position then to make some arrangements. But for the present, the drive: the most important thing was to get his own run and to establish himself, nothing would be allowed to interfere with his plans.

'Who's he?' Pelham asked when Jasin rode up with a new stockman.

'MacNamara,' Jasin said, straightfaced, 'this is the boss drover Captain Pelham.'

Unimpressed, Pelham looked MacNamara over and then ordered him to take up the rear. As MacNamara rode away he turned to Jasin. 'Where'd you get him?'

'Bathurst jail. Cheap labour. If I'd thought of it before we should have had a few more assigned to us.'

'I thought of that,' Pelham growled. 'But they're no use. They'll bolt. You have to have experienced men.'

'It was worth a try. Another hand. I thought you'd be pleased Pelham.'

'I suppose so.' Pelham looked back at the clouds of dust as the big herd swayed steadily on. Tommy and Lance were riding quietly on the flanks with their ever watchful dogs loping along beside them. 'Pray they stay as quiet as this and we'll do jolly well.'

Free of the confusion of the mustering yards the cattle sniffed the breezes from the open plains and trotted resolutely after their leaders. Tailing them with Bobbo, breathing the choking dust, Pace smiled. So that's your game is it Mr Heselwood? He whistled at the gall of the Englishman to have walked into Bathurst jail and plucked him out just as illegally as he went in with some cock-and-bull story about the prisoner having friends in high places. And for what? To bring forth an antagonist, turn him into a protagonist and set him against his black knight.

'Oh well played sir,' he said aloud, mimicking the British voice. 'I wouldn't trust the bastard either. But then can you trust me?'

142

# PART SEVEN

## THE WOMEN

# CHAPTER ONE

Georgina Heselwood rang for the maid to show Milly Forrest out.

'I'll come again as soon as I can,' Milly said making for the door at last. 'But wait a minute Georgina. I have been so busy admiring the baby and this lovely house I forgot to tell you the gossip. Adelaide Brooks ran off with a foreigner.'

'What do you mean, ran off? The woman is a widow. She is entitled to marry anyone she likes.'

'But she didn't marry him. She just up and went. She left my dresses half-finished. Some people!'

Georgina accompanied her to the front door to keep her moving and went back to the sitting room. The baby was asleep in his pram and she rocked it more to comfort herself than her son. She had never dreamed it would be possible to be so lonely. She had even dismissed the nurse so that she could look after Edward herself, for company. It was humiliating that Milly Forrest could call on her whenever she pleased and always find her alone, without an excuse not to receive her, and more annoying that at times Milly's company was better than none.

Heselwood had written when he could but the letters were taking longer and longer to reach her and the only address she had now was care of the store at a place called Singleton, on the Hunter River. Letters would be forwarded from there.

Since the Cormacks left, few visitors had called, and Vicky Horton, living just a half-mile down the road, was silent. When Vicky's daughter Marietta was born, Georgina sent their congratulations and a set of silver tea spoons but the gift was neither acknowledged nor rejected, and there was not a word from her when Edward was born.

Georgina felt disloyal to Jasin for being so miserable in these comfortable surroundings while he was putting up with all sorts of privations, doing his best for them. She wandered into the formal dining room, toying with the idea of having a dinner party, for the umpteenth time. She had heard about the magnificent christening party that Vicky had given for Marietta, the servants said half Sydney was there which made her feeling of isolation even more acute. But among strangers, it was hardly the right thing to do, to be entertaining in her husband's absence.

At least Jasin was trying to do something constructive. His father, old Lord Teddy, had never done anything in his life but inherit and then spend, leaving little for his sons. If Jasin succeeded in this plan Teddy was in for a shock, he had no confidence in his third son. Georgina had written to him to tell him of the birth of his first grandson, and had informed him that they were living in a gracious mansion with magnificent views of the harbour, but nothing more. She had not mentioned a word about Jasin's expedition.

Her letters to Jasin were different, she tried to keep the loneliness out of them but it was a depressing task. Sometimes she thought she might just pick up Edward and return to London but she could not let the side down. He would be away for months, there was nothing she could do but sit and wait.

His wife might have been vexed with Jasin for leaving her to her own devices in Sydney but Dolour Callinan had worked herself into a rage. She had carried out her side of the bargain and as a result, was now working in the steamy laundries of the Female Factory in Parramatta in the company of the worst women in the colony. They began work in the bleak dawn at scrub boards with hard caustic soap and as each load went out more came in. They ate their meals in the laundry and at night they climbed the rickety stairs to the dormitory to sleep on mattresses of straw.

There were no friends in the factory. Every woman had to look after herself, and the women in charge, convicts themselves, pushed the extra work on to newcomers, but that ploy failed with Dolour. She challenged Flora, one of the supervisors, who gave her two hard slaps across the face and sent her back to work while the other women laughed.

Dolour walked to the end of the stone laundry, picked up a broom and came back. She swung the handle of the broom across Flora's back and the older woman went down with a crash. Dolour stood over her. 'You put me in you old bitch and you'll be getting the same over your skull one night.'

After that they left her alone. She did her own work but no more. Dolour had things to think about. Jasin had not come for her as he had promised and there were times now when she planned to kill him and other times when she made excuses for him and daydreamed about seeing him again. But then as the days grew colder and the misery of the factory pressed in on her, she became thinner and her hands were red raw. She went to the foreman and put her name down for assignment.

'Fat chance you'll have,' he said. 'They don't like bolters.'

'Write it down,' she instructed and stood watching to see that he did. There was no-one to be trusted in this world.

Katrin Boundy was surprised to receive a letter out of the blue from Pace MacNamara, when they had given up on him. He had been in jail he told her, over an altercation with the wrong man. He was out now and working as a stockman. He sent his greetings and hoped she was well and the hotel was prospering. The best address he could offer, if she cared to reply, was care of the store at Singleton. As for the clothes he had left at the hotel, they could be given away. She was relieved to hear that, she had already done so.

MacNamara also asked if she would keep a kindly eye out to see what might have happened to some fellows who had come in as prisoners on the *Emma Jane*; two Irishmen, Caimen Court and Jim Connelly.

Katrin replied immediately, relieved to hear from him, promising to make enquiries about the people he mentioned and reminding him to call next time he was in Sydney.

Anxious to please she began to search for his friends. Connelly, she found, had been sent to Moreton Bay but Court was working as a clerk in the offices of the Female Factory at Parramatta, so she went to find him. She had a good excuse, since she was always on the lookout for good staff for the hotel, but she admitted to herself there was more to it. MacNamara was a handsome man, and single. Having his friend working at the hotel would draw him back to her at the earliest opportunity. The more she thought about him the more determined she was to marry MacNamara. She had been taken with him the first night, even allowing for his fall from grace playing around with the servants, both of whom she had replaced as soon as Palmerston left.

Caimen Court was cautious. 'MacNamara sent you, you say?'

'Yes, he was worried about you.'

'And you're offering me a job on his say-so?'

'On my own say-so. I need a barman.'

'And where's MacNamara now?'

'Up north somewhere. He has a job as a stockman.'

Court laughed. 'You don't say? Well it's no sillier than me working here counting lengths of cloth, who could never measure a thing in me life. But it's kind of you Mrs Boundy. If you can swing it I'd be pleased to work in your bar.'

'That's settled then,' she said. 'And you knew Pace back home did you? What did he do back there?'

Caimen's blue eyes opened wide and he smiled at her like a cherub. He had no idea what MacNamara did beyond pull the trigger of a gun. 'He was a farmer,' he said and the lady seemed satisfied with that.

Katrin applied to have Caimen Court assigned to her employ as a ticket-of-leave convict. Eventually her request was refused so she went to see Macleay but he informed her that His Excellency did not have to give reasons, and rejected a second application.

Then she discovered that political prisoners had less chance of getting out than murderers, so she boarded the packet for Parramatta to tell Caimen Court herself, and to have a day out away from the hotel.

He took the disappointing news philosophically. 'I thought it was too good to be true and I'm thankful to you for trying. But while you're here Mrs Boundy, if you want to do a good turn, there's a young Irish girl in the

146

laundries who shouldn't be here. It they leave her with those women she'll end up as bad as them. Could I bring her to meet you?'

'If you like.'

Caimen hurried away and Katrin groaned. She felt cornered. She didn't want the girl but Caimen had the persuasiveness of a parish priest, and when he returned with a doll-faced redhead, she knew this one would be trouble, even though the girl stood with downcast eyes.

A female superintendent came in. 'You taking her?' she asked Katrin.

'I might.'

'She's a bolter,' the woman laughed and Katrin saw a defiant toss of curls as the Irish girl was led away.

But Caimen pleaded. 'Think on this Mrs Boundy. If she runs away again it won't be the Factory, it'll be jail. None of them want to go to jail, she won't run off again. And it's a beautiful girl to be thrown in among women almost beyond redemption.'

'That's just it. She is good looking. Would she be better off in my hotel with all the men around?'

'Sure she will. You can find her a husband. There'll be plenty offering for her hand I'd say, and then she'd be free and have a place of her own and children to keep her occupied.'

Katrin laughed outright. 'So now I'm a matchmaker?'

'You won't be sorry, you'll see. A good turn never goes astray.'

Dolour Callinan settled in well and Katrin was surprised to see that she gave the men short shrift, not like the procession of hussies who came through the Nelson. She went about her work methodically and except for being a bit on the moody side, was no bother to anyone. The hotel was running smoothly and she soon forgot about Dolour. There were other people to think about, like Pace MacNamara. Katrin looked forward to his homecoming, because that was what it would be. A homecoming. Katrin Boundy had a lot to offer a man.

# CHAPTER TWO

Jasin Heselwood took a detour from the stock route to investigate Chelmsford Station. Even though Vicky had sold it, he was curious to see the place since he was in the vicinity. Clarrie had described the route and he cantered on with one last creek to cross and a storm rumbling and echoing in from the hills.

Just as Clarrie had said there were two tall wattle trees ahead marking the turnoff to Chelmsford and Jasin breathed a sigh, relaxing in the saddle. This was the first time he had ventured into the countryside without his guides, and even though the journey was only thirty miles, Clarrie's instructions had been littered with forked trees, jutting rocks, three point hills and waterholes which Jasin had been sure he would never identify. He didn't really believe that one could find one's way around this land by means of old trees and bogs and he considered his success in finding the track more good luck than good management.

So far he had found the cattle drive quite easy, not as hazardous as he had expected. The station owners along the route had been helpful and on a number of occasions he had been able to stay over with them for two or three days waiting for the herd to catch up. Then after conferring with Pelham he had journeyed on again as the advance guard with either Clarrie or Snow to show him the way. The squatters and their families had been most agreeable and all was going well except that Pelham was becoming terse that he was roughing it while Jasin slept between sheets, but Jasin would make no change in his plans. 'You said you would take charge of the cattle. I never claimed to be a stockman. Besides, when we get beyond the boundaries I shall have to camp out too. You must admit the station people have been extremely accommodating. They've steered us away from bogs and quicksands, and sent men to help us through that scrub country. They saved us a day there, and gave us extra supplies at each point. I don't think you can complain about that.'

He noticed Pace MacNamara was quiet and the other stockmen were working well although full of complaints about Otto's cooking. Two Aborigines had joined the trek, relations of Bobbo's they said, and they loped alongside the herd laughing excitedly as if they were all on some great noisy parade. Jasin had come across a lot of blacks now, camped on the stations or working around the homesteads, and their presence was of no interest to him except to reinforce his opinion that stories of their ferocity were all fabrication. More amusing to him were some of the families he had encountered in the outback. At one station, an English family, living in a large ugly house with a thatched roof, dressed for dinner every night and sat sternly and interminably at their long dining table being waited on by excruciatingly slow black girls. He wondered what sort of a family he would find at Chelmsford.

The rain began to fall, great splotches that gave notice of a downpour and Jasin patted Prince Blue, to reassure himself as the landscape darkened and the bush shook with thunder. In the teeming rain he took a wrong turning and had to double back again so by the time he found the creek it was late afternoon.

Merri Creek they had said was shallow and easy to ford, but this was a raging torrent rushing through a deep-sided gully. He rode along the bank in the gloom turning away time and again to avoid the twisted tea-trees that hung wantonly across his path.

The rain was pelting down and Jasin searched for a sandy bank, worrying that within the hour it would be pitch dark. He would have to find a safe place to cross or stay out here all the damn night. Around another bend in the creek's endless twists and turns he saw a large tree hanging out over the water and thought this might be the answer. Dismounting he led Prince Blue to the edge of the bank but the horse was nervous, jerking away, refusing to be dragged to the creek.

'Come on!' he told it. 'We've got this tree for a life-line, it's holding back the current. Now come on!' The horse tossed its head and snorted so Jasin swung into the saddle and snapped at it with his whip. Prince Blue reared angrily and dropped forward down the bank attempting to dislodge the rider but Jasin hung on and dug in his spurs forcing him into the creek. Prince Blue pranced into the water but it was deeper than Jasin expected and the horse began to swim strongly for the other shore.

'Good boy,' Jasin said, and heard himself using the stockmen's words, 'You beauty! Keep going.' They were halfway across the stream when he heard a wrench and a rushing sound. The tree had snapped away from the banks and was thrown into the stream releasing a torrent of water. Jasin was dragged from the saddle and branches swept against them, tangling man and horse in a newly created underwater snag.

Suddenly Prince Blue's head jerked up and he began to surge strongly towards the bank and Jasin grabbed the saddle, feeling the horse pulling him free. He could hear men shouting and saw other horsemen in the creek pulling and heaving on ropes.

Jasin lay on the bank, coughing creek water from his lungs, exhausted.

'You all right mate?' a voice asked and he managed to nod.

Three men were staring down at him, and he heard them talking. 'Just as well for him Mr Rivadavia came along and roped the horse. Bloody stupid place to try to cross.'

'Yeah. Pity about the poor horse though. A bloody shame.'

149

Jasin lifted his head to look at them. 'What about the horse?'

Then a foreign voice spoke. 'I'm sorry sir, but your horse has broken a leg. He will have to be shot. Do you want me to do it?'

Jasin was glad of his soggy appearance, that they could not see his sudden tears. He could only nod and bury his face in the wet earth waiting for the fearsome sound, and when the shot rang out he jumped as if it had entered his back.

Shattered, Jasin allowed them to help him onto a strange horse, and he hung on, being led by these misty figures as they rode in silence towards the distant lights of the homestead.

And at Chelmsford, Adelaide was waiting for Juan to come in. It was a dark wet night and she worried about him, although she knew she should not. She recalled her needless embarrassment on their first days at the station when she had seen the men nudge and grin at the new boss's fancy clothes and what they called his 'circus' saddle. She had watched the station hands, even Andy the foreman, with their battered hats pulled down, studying Juan's working clothes, from the wide black hat with a trailing chin cord to his highly polished boots. He wore a soft, hide waistcoat over a black shirt and over his riding trousers, a strange pair of cow-hide pants, cut away to fit a saddle. When he walked the odd overalls flared so that he seemed to sway along, bandy-legged.

In those early days he had been the joke of the station and Adelaide had stayed in the homestead with her own problems, wondering what they thought of her, being with a man ten years her junior. She had her own room, but Juan treated it more like her sitting room. She slept in his bed and he did not care who knew it.

But their first impression of him was way off the mark as Dora, the cook, was quick to report. The laughing stopped and the jaws dropped when they saw him handle the horses in the mustering yard. He'd take on any buckjumpers with the rough riders and he could crack a whip with the best of them, but it was his roping prowess that won him a place in their hearts. They had never seen anyone as accurate with a lasso, and one day he had shown them a string of tricks with the rope. They said he could just about make a rope sing and it became all the rage at Chelmsford for the stockmen and farm hands to practise the tricks too.

Dora's admiration for the boss now knew no bounds and Adelaide found her tactless talk unnerving. 'We thought he was a real mother's boy when he first turned up Mrs Brooks, no offence you know, but didn't he put all the men back in their box? My Andy's taken a great shine to him. I reckon we'll all get along well here now. It's great relief to us to know we can stay on and a good boss makes all the difference.'

Thunder rolled across the hills and the black girls, Mary and Libbie, came running around the passage. 'Boss comin missus.'

'Him just in time. Big tree crackem on head spose he don' come in.'

'Boss comen alonga nother boss.'

150

'New boss got plenty cattle, seven miles past creek.'

It was always a competition between them to get to Adelaide first with the news and it was becoming easier for her sort out their chatter. She knew they had no conception of distance, any of them. Seven was Mary's favourite number and Libbie liked eleven. As far as she could make out the language needed a vowel between each consonant so seven and eleven were melodic words that rolled easily off the tongue.

She wondered who the visitor was and how the house-girls knew he had a herd out there somewhere. They seemed to know everything that was going on in the district.

Juan tramped down the hall and sat on the high rosewood chair while Adelaide dropped to the footstool to help him off with his boots. 'Juan, you're soaked to the skin. You must hurry out of those wet clothes.'

'We had to pull a man out of the creek. And I had to shoot his horse. I hate having to do that.'

'Oh no. How awful for you.'

'Andy's taken him out to the bath house, will you send him out some dry clothes? And tell the cook one more for dinner.' He handed her his boots and went down to his bedroom.

Adelaide took the boots to the kitchen and gave them to Billabill, the black house 'boy'. Dora already knew there would be a third for dinner and Andy had found dry clothes for the gentleman.

'Who is he?' Adelaide asked.

'I don't know. Andy says he's real posh gent. Talks posh.'

Glad that she had lit the fire in Juan's room and set out a change of clothes for him, Adelaide hurried back to have her talk with him.

He had stripped to the waist and washed at the basin.

'Do you want some more hot water?' she asked.

'No thank you Dell.' He unbuttoned his pants and took them off towelling himself dry and she marvelled again at his lack of inhibition, and her new-found ability to enjoy watching his naked body. She tried to keep her mind on the news she had to tell him.

The rain pounded down and he called her to the window. 'Look at the hailstones, they are covering the ground like snow.'

She peered at the glittering hail on the dark ground and he pulled her to him nestling her head into his neck, whispering to her. 'It isn't fair for you to have so many clothes on. Why don't you take them off and warm me up? I've had a cold cold day.'

As they lay curled together in the bed Adelaide worried. 'I love you Juan. Every time you touch me it is like making love to you for the first time again and I never want it to stop.'

'But we must. We have a guest for dinner. But we won't stay up late.' He began caressing her again, 'I will put out some good wines, they always make my lady more exciting.'

She took a deep breath. 'Juan. I have something to tell you.'

151

'Yes?' he mumbled and she could feel him arousing her again. 'Stop a minute.' But he ignored her.

'I'm going to have a baby.'

He kissed her. 'I know.'

'You do?'

'My Dell, you are blooming. There are roses in your cheeks and a softness in your loving. Of course I know. Everyone knows.'

'What do you mean, everyone knows?'

'Everyone, even the black girls, the natives. They live close to the earth, birth, death, they feel it. But they don't feel what I feel do they?' He was laughing, the last reaction she had expected. 'Are you happy about it?'

'Of course I am. It is my child. I am very proud. Let me feel where my child is.'

'Juan. We are not married. We can't have a child.'

'But we are, see. We are very clever.'

'You're making fun of me.'

'No I am not. What do you want me to do, be unhappy?'

'The child will be a . . . it won't have a name. Don't you understand Juan? For the child's sake we will have to get married.'

'No.'

Adelaide lay very still, her mind in a panic. 'If we don't get married people will say the child never had a father.'

'People will say! There you go again. And it is stupid to say no father. The child will be Rivadavia and that is that. What are you making such a fuss about? If you are unhappy here you can leave, I will provide for you. I will always look after you.'

Adelaide knew she would never leave him voluntarily but she had always believed that he would marry her sooner or later even though it would cause talk, the age difference being what it was. She had hoped they could marry in a quiet ceremony here at Chelmsford. A dullness entered her spirit. She now had to face the fact that she was his mistress, nothing more, take it or leave it.

She inspected the dining table. Juan insisted that it be set formally each night and the girls were learning to get it right. She put some more wood on the fire and lit the candles, turning as the men came into the room to find herself facing Jasin Heselwood.

'Why Mrs Brooks! I do declare!'

Adelaide was so surprised she felt a flush of crimson on her face and Juan, who had brought up two bottles of wine from the cellar and was dusting them, looked up sharply.

Jasin retreated, making things worse. 'I'm sorry. Is it no longer Mrs Brooks? Is it . . .'

'You know Mrs Brooks?' Juan interrupted, supplying the answer.

'Yes, we came out on the same ship.'

Juan jerked the cork from a bottle and Adelaide was nervous. The way Jasin had put that, gave the impression that they had almost been travelling companions. She hurried to correct it. 'Jasin and his wife had the cabin next to ours. How is Georgina? I would like to see her again.'

'I am sure you would,' Jasin said with that on-and-off smile of his, that had always irritated her. 'Next time you are in Sydney you must call. We have a son now. Edward is his name. I haven't even seen him yet.'

'Your first son and you haven't seen him?' Juan said. 'I would ride day and night to see my first son.'

'Unfortunately I am riding in the wrong direction,' Jasin said and Juan shrugged, a gesture that expressed disapproval and was not lost on his guest, who turned to Adelaide. 'And how is Dr Brooks?'

She was sure, by the sudden flutter of his fair eyelashes, by his feigned solicitousness that he already knew what had happened to Brooks. 'My husband passed away,' she said.

'Oh. I am very sorry to hear that. But then one supposes that all doctors run a certain risk from their own patients. I should think it must be rather horrifying being a doctor. What they must see! My God!'

'Brooks was not a doctor of medicine,' she said. 'He was a doctor of astronomy.'

Jasin peered at her, this time genuinely astonished.

'Dell,' Juan's voice was low and controlled, a danger sign. 'If you are ready would you tell them to serve? Mr Heselwood has had enough today. He doesn't need to be kept standing in a doorway with his dinner cooling.'

During the meal Adelaide was quiet, aware that Juan was upset. He is jealous, she thought, and of all people, Jasin Heselwood. To make matters worse Heselwood had sized up the situation and was enjoying it. He kept trying to draw her into the conversation, talking about the ship, knowing it was making her uncomfortable and annoying Juan. She wondered what he would tell Georgina when he got back to Sydney. At least he did not know she was pregnant, that was one small mercy, she doubted if she would have been able to face him. And she drank more red wine than usual to settle her nerves.

Looking at Jasin now, dressed in borrowed duds, he seemed more like a country man, his face and hands bronzed by the sun, so different from the perfumed dandy she had known on the ship but for all the apparent metamorphosis the real Jasin Heselwood had not changed a scrap. He still considered himself a prince among lesser mortals and he still had that adolescent streak of meanness. The strain and the wine were making her tipsy. 'Jasin. I am not sure that I am hearing correctly. Don't tell me *you* are travelling north with a herd of cattle? You?'

'Wonders will never cease Adelaide,' he returned with a smile. And she felt the thrust of his words turn on her and her own situation. And at the same time she saw Juan's eyes flash knowing that he had misinterpreted Jasin's mischievous glance.

'What would you know about cattle Jasin?' Her voice sounded spiteful and she did not care. She wanted Juan to know she disliked this man and his suspicions were groundless.

'I don't claim to know a great deal, Adelaide, but I have good workmen. One of my stockmen is in fact a friend of yours, Pace MacNamara. You remember him from the ship?' He turned to Juan. 'Adelaide used to play the piano for him when he sang for us. They were very good together.'

The last line was added with an ingenuous smile and Adelaide sucked in her breath. She watched him talking to Juan, listening to the drawl of his voice and the insufferably superior tone and then she realised that he was not provoking her he was provoking Juan through her. She wanted to warn Juan, to tell him he should have left the dog to drown. To this aristocrat, Juan was a foreigner, lower in his eyes than any English peasant. There would be no gratitude for saving his life, no gratitude for shelter in Juan's house. Adelaide thought it might be a good idea to appeal to Jasin's better nature if he had one. 'You intend to go into unknown country Jasin. Aren't you worried about wild blacks?'

'We are looking for pasture land. We won't bother them, they have no interest in pastures.'

'You surely don't believe that,' Juan said.

'Believe what?'

'That you simply need their land for pasture.'

'What else should we need it for?'

'To conquer. To conquer their civilisation.'

'My dear Juan. I have absolutely no ambition to conquer as you say. They can share the land, that won't hurt them.'

'Share means equal return. What return shall they receive? It is their land.'

'It is not their land. They have no towns and villages. No land under crop. It is empty.'

'It is far from empty. I have been making enquiries. They have defined tribal territories.

'Tribal indeed! Your wine is excellent Juan but your understanding of this land is lacking,. The relics of a race that never achieved so much as a village cannot be called tribal. We British understand them. The Spanish by-passed this land.'

Juan thumped his fist on the table. 'You keep referring to me as a Spaniard. I am not. I am Argentinian. We regard Europeans as decadent.'

'So you might. I could even agree with you. We British do not regard ourselves as Europeans either. God forbid!'

Juan began to lecture him. 'If you will take the time to remember that I am Argentinian and my family before me for generations, you will understand that we have had experience with Indians, like these blacks, who had no apparent civilisation of their own except a distant connection with the Incas. Now, you are not going into this land for pasture alone, you will build your houses and villages, you are invaders.'

'Come now. That is a hard word. We have already colonised a large part of New South Wales and except for a few minor incidents the blacks don't care.'

'That's where you are wrong. They did not understand what was happening, but I believe they are now very much aware. And colonising is the wrong word too.'

'What else would you call it?'

'The truth. I have already told you. Conquering. You are here for the same reason as I am, to conquer and these unfortunate people must succumb to our superior weapons because we want their land.'

'You are dramatising.'

'I am not. I don't like pretence. I am trying to point out that if you want to conquer these northern lands you shall have to fight for them.'

'Dear me. You are getting morbid. I am a peaceful man.'

Juan laughed. 'Are you? When I have completed all I have to do here I will strike north too, but I recognise the danger.'

'You jest?'

'No. I am honest. You might go on calling it colonisation but you will fight the war.'

Adelaide was frightened. 'I don't understand. Why go at all Juan? You have this big station, what more do you want?'

'Ask Mr Heselwood. He knows. He understands what it is, this desire for land, a desire that can push a man forward into mortal danger.'

'It's hard to explain,' Jasin said, not so sure of himself now and Adelaide was pleased. Juan had him rattled.

Later that night Juan exploded. He accused her of having had Heselwood as her lover and he wanted to know who this other man was, this MacNamara. Adelaide noticed he even remembered the name and she argued with him without success.

'I don't like Heselwood. How could you think I would have anything to do with him?'

'Why don't you like him? He is very handsome in a wishy-washy sort of way.'

'Because he is so superior. He thinks he is better than everyone else.'

'He has a right to do that,' Juan said 'He *is* better. Breeding is important. He is bred to the upper classes, you can't take that away from him.'

'Oh, I see,' she said. 'And is this why you won't marry me? Because I'm only a middle-class person, not highborn enough for you?'

Juan placed the pearl studs from his dress shirt in a polished silver box, closing the lid firmly. 'And yourself Dell? Are you proud to be my lady? Did you stand with me tonight before your friend Mr Heselwood? Or did you avert your eyes from me? I cannot make an honest woman of you Dell, you have to do that for yourself.'

He put on his dressing gown. 'Go to sleep Dell. I have some work to do in my office.'

# CHAPTER THREE

Mrs Horton had launched herself back into society and her friends had rallied around. They took her to balls and parties and for gay weekends at the country homes out at Emu Plains, and all the time she thought of Rivadavia. She wrote him a long letter explaining various things about Chelmsford that she hoped he would like to know, and he wrote back thanking her and congratulating her on the fine station which was all he had expected. He was putting in vineyards and would personally deliver to her his first wines.

Vicky wrote again telling him he must not wait until the wines were ready but he must call personally, next time he was in Sydney, and tell her all the news of the station. It had been part of her life for so long, she was finding Sydney rather dull, she said.

That was not quite true. Sir Percy Rowan-Smith had fallen madly in love with her and was on her doorstep from dawn to dark. He was much older than her and sweet, in a bumbling sort of way, and very rich, but Vicky kept thinking of Rivadavia, the Argentinian. Until the day Dora came to visit.

It was the first time Dora had been to Sydney for years and she had only come now for her brother's funeral but she felt she could not leave without calling on her former mistress to see the baby and say how sorry she was about Mr Horton's death, though it did seem a long time ago. Mrs Horton was pleased to see her, taking her into her little sitting room and insisting she stay for lunch.

'And how's your new boss Dora? Does Andy like him?'

'Oh Mrs Horton, he's very nice and Andy thinks the world of him. And he's good with the men too. He can out-ride the lot of them, and that's saying something up there isn't it? And he's rebuilding the house, It'll be a show place when it's finished, I'm sure. Andy thinks in time he'll let us manage Chelmsford, he's more interested in cattle. He's bought a couple of runs out on the plains and he is stocking them with breeders.'

Vicky was delighted to hear all this information about Rivadavia first hand.

'You know he's Argentinian don't you?' Dora asked.

'Yes, I met him, to discuss the sale. Of course it was just a business meeting, before Marietta was born.'

'You've seen him then?' Dora's eyes twinkled. 'He's a handsome man isn't he? And I'll tell you something else, he likes everything the best and blow the cost. He's very fussy about his meals, likes big steaks and sees they are hung first. For that matter he's fussy about his clothes and the house, even the sheets, they have to be the best.'

'Is he married?'

'No.'

'It's a wonder one of the squatters' daughters from up that way hasn't been on his track. He sounds like a good catch for them.'

Dora looked away. 'I don't think so Mrs Horton.'

'Why ever not?'

Dora fidgeted. 'I don't know as if I should say; he's a very good man, good to us you understand. Andy mightn't be too pleased at me for mentioning this so you never heard it from me.'

'Heard what?'

'You see there's Mrs Brooks. She lives there too.'

'Who's she? His housekeeper?'

'She's more than that. I'm not one to criticise, none of my business, but you know what I mean.'

'How interesting!' Vicky did find it interesting but also irritating. 'How long has she been there?'

'He brought her with him. She's his lady so to speak. A lot older than him mind you, and she's having his child so there's not much point in the local girls coming around.'

Dora's visit seemed to last for hours while Vicky controlled her anger. She was angry with herself for imagining that a man like that would not have a woman around somewhere, and disappointed. Very disappointed.

But Dora had more news. 'You know that Mr Heselwood? Andy said it was the same one as was staying here with you when Mr Horton died. He saw him here one time.'

'Yes, what about him?'

'Well he came by Chelmsford. Stayed the night. He was riding Prince Blue – your horse, Andy recognised him right off, no mistaking Prince Blue.'

Vicky sighed. She still missed Prince Blue.

Dora was quiet for a minute. 'I've got some bad news for you now. Prince Blue's dead. Mr Rivadavia had to shoot him. He had a broken leg.'

'What?' Vicky jumped up? 'What happened to him?'

'I'm sorry Mrs Horton. The gentleman got into trouble in the creek. It was a bad night, they had to pull him out. Andy said it was a stupid place to cross with the current running and the creek full of snags . . .' She stopped, worrying that she had said too much now by the look of Mrs Horton.

'He killed my horse!' Vicky was livid.

'Not Mr Rivadavia. He had no choice.'

'I know that,' Vicky shouted. 'That imbecile Heselwood! I will never forgive him. Prince Blue! My beautiful horse!' She burst into tears and Dora tried to console her. 'I'm sorry, I shouldn't have told you. Don't cry Mrs Horton, these things happen.'

For Vicky, the rest of the day was grey and depressing. The house seemed empty, echoing, and she felt nothing would ever cheer her up again. All her grief at Horton's death came flooding back again and she walked out onto the deserted verandah. She wished she could get away from them all, somewhere different.

When Sir Percy Rowan-Smith arrived that evening she accepted his hand in marriage and agreed to go with him to England. Marietta's grandparents, the Hortons, would be pleased to see them.

Months later, Juan Rivadavia came to Sydney to purchase some thorough-bred horses for his stud, and with time to spare he decided to ride out to visit Mrs Horton, who had told him to call at any time. She was a very attractive woman, he mused, so young to be a widow.

On his arrival at Wilkin House he was met by a caretaker who informed him the house was locked up.

'Is Mrs Horton away?'

'She's not Mrs Horton anymore, she's Lady Rowan-Smith. Got herself married and went to England.'

Juan smiled. 'Good for her.' The ride had not been wasted, it was better than sitting in a hotel room and he had enjoyed looking at all the fine houses again after the empty roads of the valley.

'Can't tell you any more,' the caretaker said. 'Mrs Heselwood at the next house over there might know her address.

'Who?'

'Mrs Heselwood. The English lady. Lives over there in the house on the cliff.'

'Thank you,' Juan said, and kept going down the road. This must be Heselwood's wife. Since he was out that way, it could be acceptable to call. He had gathered from Jasin that she was also from an aristocratic family. The English aristocracy intrigued him.

Georgina was surprised but made him welcome since he had news of her husband. She was pleased to hear that Jasin had been looking well, last seen, and that this young man had every confidence that he would succeed in his venture. He cheered her immensely explaining Jasin's plans even better than her husband had, in his formal way, and Georgina invited him to stay to lunch.

Juan enjoyed her company and found they had a mutual friend in Lord Forster who had first encouraged him to come to New South Wales.

Aware of the proprieties he did not stay long after the meal. Observing her address the servants, he appreciated what Dell would call her haughty ways. He never mixed socially with his staff and they worked well for him, he was unable to understand why Dell should be forever standing around the kitchen talking to the cook. He could not imagine Mrs Heselwood making friends with the servants. He made up his mind that the Honourable Jasin Heselwood, and his charming wife, would always be welcome at his home whether Dell liked it or not.

158

# PART EIGHT

## THE LAND

# CHAPTER ONE

Jack Drew waited, squatting on a low tree stump. He had been travelling through the bush with the blackfellow for three days now and the troopers were still on their trail, so they struck higher into the mountains and it was hard going for Jack. He understood now that the black man was trying to save him and he co-operated by eating anything that was handed him and following instructions without question.

The Aborigine seemed to regard the chase as a personal contest, covering their tracks with care and easing through the brush, but Jack was a handicap, stumbling, breaking twigs and once, when he had held onto a branch to lever himself up and the branch had snapped, his escort had hissed his irritation through clenched teeth. When Jack's feet bled, leaving telltale bloodstains, the black man had shaken his head. 'No good boss. Troopers catchem up your tracks easy.'

'You're not going to leave me?' Jack whispered but the Aborigine shook his head, grinning.

Jack watched him now, standing motionless, almost invisible near a tall gum, the white markings on his face and body melting into the silver of the tree trunk. He had been standing in that position for a long time. Jack was anxious to get on but he did not speak, everything was so deathly quiet. And then he thought he could make out three more blacks, they were hard to distinguish against the background. They came out cautiously, each one as tall as his friend and all armed with spears. Their hair was twisted into topknots and their wiry beards made them look so ferocious he shuddered.

His own black man called out to them but the newcomers stood their ground, spears raised, pointing at Jack, who was ready to run, back to the troopers if necessary.

The four men talked in low guttural tones, the strangers were still suspicious of the white man but Jack's escort was laughing and Jack could see he was describing the stocks to them, copying the position of a prisoner in the stocks. As if to prove it, he brought them down to examine Jack's neck and wrists. They stared at the raw skin and began to laugh. Jack grinned too but did not move. Then they became serious again, pointing back down the mountain, and they sat down to confer on the problems of the chasers and the chased.

One of the men fished a dead possum from his dilly bag and threw it onto their small fire while they talked. Jack was not invited to join them

160

but the delay was causing him to worry. Shouldn't we be getting on? Would they hand him over after all and claim payment from the white men in reward? Why should they care about him?

A wind blew up and the high gums swished overhead making an eerie sound in the half-light of the forest. Jack examined his feet, wiped his nose on his sleeve and sniffed the air. Whatever they were cooking smelled good but surely the smoke and smell would carry. They gave him a piece of meat and he ate it hungrily nodding his appreciation, expecting the troopers to come charging into the quiet glade any minute.

At last they picked up their spears and walked over to him. 'We go now,' his escort said. Jack jumped up, pleased to have a bodyguard of four, but the other three blacks smiled and patted him, each one in turn, and went back down the trail.

'Where are they going?' he asked, thinking they might tip off the troopers.

'They killem those blackfella trackers. Plurry nuisance them. Killem troopers too if they don't git going quick smart.'

Jack was full of admiration for them and the simplicity of the solution to his problem. He would have liked to have gone back to watch.

'Good on you,' he said, clapping his friend on the back. 'You're a man after me own heart.'

He loped along after his guide, feeling stronger now with the fear removed. They began to climb higher into the rocky slopes where it became harder for him to keep up. He envied the blackfellow's agility and strength but struggled on cursing his own weakness.

That night they sheltered in a cave and the black man lit a fire and brought in strips of bark for them to lie on, as protection against the damp.

'What's your name?' Jack asked.

'Dimining. Who's your name?'

'Jack Drew.'

The black man copied the sound and it came out Jackadoo and that became his name. Jackadoo.

'Where did you learn to speak English?'

'On the stations. Our mob camp on stations. Some white man not mind. Come on down to our camp sometimes and say, "You boys want work one day get tucker?" and we givem hands chasem sheep and things. But Major Mudie he chasem us all off his station. Bang, bang, killem fambly people.'

'He killed some of your family?'

Dimining nodded sadly.

'Why don't you kill him then?'

'Too many guns. We killem his sheep. Payback allatime.'

'Where do you live?'

Dimining waved his hands around and Jack wasn't too sure he understood that but he resumed his questions.

'What's the other side of these hills?'

161

'Plenty big country.'

'White men out there too?'

'Some.'

Jack sighed. That was disappointing. 'Where are we going?'

'We wait for them other blackfellas then we go far away. Them Kamilaroi too.'

'What's that?'

'Mob. Us Kamilaroi mob. You want comen with us?'

'Yes. I'll be Kamilaroi too.'

Dimining rolled on his side laughing and slapped his thighs. 'You good fella,' he said, still chuckling.

Jack stayed in the cave the next day while Dimining hunted and the other three natives arrived in his absence, pleased with their exploits. They spoke no English but from their excitement and their actions Jack learned that they had speared the trackers, one in the head and one in the back, and the troopers had fired on them but they had disappeared into the bush. It seemed then that the troopers had run for their lives, not knowing how many blacks had attacked them.

When Dimining returned with a catch of wallabies he too was pleased at their success. 'Us warriors. Kamilaroi warriors. White men say he give Dimining job watching sheep.' He turned to the others to translate and they laughed. 'Killem sheep more like it.'

One of the warriors reached down into his dilly bag and threw four oddly shaped objects on the ground and Jack leaned over to have a look and then pulled back in shock. They were ears. The blacktrackers' ears, proof of the kill.

They left the cave the following morning and they reached the crest of the range and were now looking out over a vast plain with more hills in the far distance. Jack was disappointed. There didn't seem to be an escape from the country that way. He pointed to the north. 'What's up there? Why don't we go up there?'

Dimining gaped. 'You don't go too many far up there. That Tingum country. Better you go back along Major Mudie. Tingum choppem off head.'

Jack felt like a scrubby old man beside these tall strong blacks and he realised why it was always said that convicts would die out here. 'You teach me to hunt, Dimining?'

The black drew lines in the dust with his big toe. 'Dunno. We take you to the camp. Better you stay alonga women.'

It was six days before they came to the camp on the banks of the Namoi River. They had been travelling fast and Jack was ready to drop. There seemed to be about sixty blacks living in the camp of bark humpies. Skinny dogs came out to snap at him followed by a group of women who screamed and ran away when they saw him and one even ran up a tree. The children huddled together and gave him shy little smiles. Dimining spoke to a group of old men who sat by a fire and explained who the stranger was. They all turned around to study Jack and then went back to their discussions.

The white man moved down to the water's edge to soak his burning feet. They've walked my legs off to get to their home, he grumbled to himself, and it's no different from being out in the bush. He had imagined a village with large huts for shelter and a market place, not this rough camp. The water was cool and fish jumped and birds dived under the surface on fishing forays emerging well away from their original point of entry. Black swans sailed majestically past. A young woman ran towards him, dropped a wooden bowl near him and then ran away again. Jack studied the bowl which was full of nuts and berries and then began eating them while he tried to work out what his next move would be. The blacks looked the same as the group they had encountered on the way to Castle Forbes, the women sitting in languid circles pounding powder in wooden gourds with the children climbing and clambering over them, and the old men were at the camp fire, but this time their young men were with them, their warriors, and there was an entirely different air about this camp. Jack knew he had better watch his step.

# CHAPTER TWO

The big herd stumbled and shouldered and pushed a track through Dart's Pass, crushing bushes and small trees, breaking lowhanging branches and treading them into the dust. Fresh from the night's rest, they trotted after the horsemen, hurrying, smelling the chill mountain breezes, the leaders snorting their superiority over the mob, nudging and butting the would-be leaders back into place and lashing out with both heels at the more persistent. Stockmen rode quietly with them, watching over the bobbing heads, whistling, chucking and coaxing, to keep them steady, afraid of a stampede in this confined area, and the dogs, sensing the need for restraint, padded stiffly over the rocky ground, leaping across boulders and onto ledges to look over the sea of movement.

Once through the pass and onto the plains, the mob surged out, running free, until the leaders decided they had been travelling long enough and slowed to graze. Most of the mob followed suit, spreading out to choose their own pasture and resisting combatants who butted in on their territory.

The stockmen took no notice of minor altercations, their keen eyes watching for the inevitable next move and sure enough a rogue steer took this opportunity to dash away. Nick was after him at the same instant, his horse galloping across the plain at breakneck pace, then wheeling expertly as the steer changed course, and wheeling again to catch the runaway before he could crash through a clump of trees; he headed him off, matching the steer's zigzag course until suddenly the steer stopped in his tracks to stare at the horse and rider. The crack of the stockwhip turned him back to the mob. Curious cattle wandered to the edge of the herd to watch, and far to the back, the slow and the shy, the tail-enders, finally caught up with the rest.

Pace MacNamara and Bobbo brought the spare horses through the pass and moved out, skirting the noisy, slow-moving cattle. The lead horse, a big chestnut Waler, was well in command of his small herd.

Snow caught up with Pace. 'We're outside the boundaries now, son. This is where it gets interesting.'

'What happened to the two black boys, Bobbo's mates?'

'They chucked it in. They won't come into this territory. Wrong totem. Bad medicine. They've all got their own districts and God help them if they set foot in another without permission.'

164

'Is that right? It looks fine country doesn't it? I've a mind to take up some myself when the Englishmen look the other way.'

'What do you know about Pelham?' Snow asked.

'Nothing much. I heard him talking the other night, his regiment was in Ireland, so I'd just as soon keep me distance.'

Snow lit his pipe and rode beside Pace. 'I reckon Mister Heselwood has been sold a ball of string there. As a boss drover he'd make a good trapeze artist. It's my opinion he's a man of considerable stupidity. It's just as well Lance and the boys know what they're doing.' He squinted at Pace from under his dusty hat. 'Why did Heselwood spring you? You a mate of his?'

'Far from it. The opposite you could say. He's a contrary feller, I don't think he trusts his mate Pelham and he probably thinks the devil he knows is better than the devil he doesn't. But this beats Bathurst jail so I'm not arguing.'

Snow left it at that. 'Clarrie and me haven't been on a drive for years. You miss the good life hanging about a station growing old. When this is finished, if you want to get a run of your own say the word, we'll give you a hand.'

'It's a good idea but how do you do it without money?'

'There are ways and means. Wait and see how you take to the bush. If it doesn't suit you then you're better off making for Sydney. I can't see Captain bloody Pelham lasting out here too long.'

'What about Heselwood?'

'He's a different story. He's like a dog with a bone, he won't let go of his, but he wants the other dog's bone too. There's bosses and workers. Me, I've always been a worker. Heselwood will always be a boss, but that Pelham he's only a worker and he doesn't know it.'

He whistled to Bobbo who seemed to be dozing in the saddle and waved to him to keep the horses on course. Bobbo cantered away.

'The thing is,' Snow continued, 'what are you? A boss or a worker?'

'I can't say I've worked that out myself yet,' Pace said.

'Time you made up your mind. You're getting on. And I'll tell you something else. This is dangerous country, you need a gun.'

'They won't give a convict a gun,' Pace said bitterly.

'Yes they will or me and Clarrie might go bush and bugger the lot of them.'

The issue of the gun for MacNamara caused a row in the camp that night. 'I'll not let him have a gun to put a bullet in my back,' Jasin said and the bushmen exchanged glances at this strange retort.

Clarrie stood up. 'Mister Heselwood, do you want your herd looked after or not? There are so many dingoes out there they hunt in packs. What's he supposed to do if they attack? Spit on them? And if he doesn't have a gun you've got one less guard for night work and the boys are not going to like that.'

165

They finally convinced Jasin but Pelham resisted and they left the two of them to argue it out.

Three days later they were still travelling across land that had been taken up by illegal squatters and discovered that runs were already operating sixty miles beyond the boundaries and there were probably more further out that no-one knew about.

'We'll just keep pushing out until we come to the end of it,' Clarrie told Jasin. 'There's no end to the land so it doesn't matter and the cattle are getting plenty of good food on the trail. And by the way, MacNamara still hasn't got a gun.'

Jasin shook his head. 'I can't undermine Pelham's authority. He knows what he's doing.'

'That's your opinion,' Clarrie said sourly. 'But a man's entitled to defend himself. If we run into trouble with wild blacks and he hasn't got a gun he's in danger.'

'I thought you said if we treat the blacks well they'll leave us alone.'

'So I did. No-one's looking for trouble but if trouble comes looking for us, we might need him. Try it this way Mr Heselwood. I'm not one for arguing. You arm the man or we quit.'

Jasin stared at him. 'Are you giving me orders?'

'No. Just telling you the way it is.'

Pace was given a gun and Pelham became suspicious of him, wondering about the connection between Heselwood and the Irishman.

A few days later Clarrie rode into the camp to find the fire lit, the supply wagon unhitched, and the horses hobbled and grazing nearby, but no sign of Otto, the cook. In his quiet, matter-of-fact way Clarrie put the billies on to boil and began to unpack supplies for the evening meal. Snow and MacNamara were at the waterhole with the horses and the herd would be along in another hour or so. To have hungry men come into camp and find no tucker cooked was a good way, he knew, to stir up tempers. They were travelling north through rough, patchy country with scattered eucalypts, acacias, and tussocks of grass. They had been keeping within range of a river to the east in case the waterholes ran out, but were preparing to strike west again. The eastwards detour had annoyed Pelham but Clarrie had insisted the country was too dry to risk the herd yet.

There had been no need to ask permission to cross these runs because the claimants were illegal but Heselwood had still made a point of searching out the men holding the land and asking for permission to cross, to promote goodwill and to pick up information about the 'further out'.

The land they were presently crossing belonged to a brawny Scot, Hughie McPhie, who had marked off two thousand acres for himself and his sons. Hughie had built a long slab hut with a timber roof lashed on with rawhide, to house his family.

Clarrie grinned as he soaked the salt meat. Heselwood had turned his nose up at the rude shelter with a hard floor made from anthill mud and the Scot had caught him.

'It's no palace Mr Heselwood,' he had said, 'but it's a start. Like you, we're taking the first step. And it is still a better life than we had back home. My sons will go back to Scotland wealthy men.'

The bush was dense towards the river even though it was a mile or so away, indicating a flood plain, and it fanned out inland making a fine breakwind and border for McPhie's land.

Pelham and Heselwood rode in. 'Where's Otto?' Pelham asked.

'He's probably gone looking for wild honey,' Clarrie said. 'But I'd call him if I was you or the silly bugger'll get lost.'

When the other men came into the camp, hearing Pelham shouting in the bush, they laughed.

'Otto's gone walkabout,' Lance said to Bobbo. 'We might get some decent tucker tonight with Clarrie on the job. I never seen a man who could make such a bloody mess of a meal as Otto. He was your idea Bobbo.'

'He told me he could cook. How was I to know he can't even boil water?'

Pelham returned leading his horse. 'I can't find him. You go after him Bobbo and bring him back here at the double.'

They could hear Bobbo calling and cooeeing in the bush until the sounds became fainter, and they had finished their supper by the time Bobbo rode in. 'Otto will have to stay out there tonight unless he finds his own way back. We'll get him out in the morning. You buggers left any tucker for me?'

'Did you see any sign of blacks?' Pelham asked him.

'What signs would that be boss? If there are any friendly blackfellers around they'd have paid us a visit to get some of Clarrie's tucker. If there are any bad blokes around there won't be no tracks.'

There was trouble the next morning when Otto still had not returned. Both shifts of stockmen had finished their breakfasts and Pelham was issuing his instructions.

Lance interrupted him. 'We only need a couple of blokes to watch the herd. The rest of us can spread out and find Otto.'

Pelham rounded angrily on him. 'You'll do nothing of the sort. We're moving out. Bobbo can stay behind with a spare horse until he finds the bloody fool.'

'It'll take more than one man to search him out in that bush,' Lance persisted but Pelham ignored him. Jasin was aware a confrontation was looming and, anxious though he was to get the herd on its way, he judged it a good time not to interfere.

Pelham mounted his horse and looked down on his men. 'Get going you fellows. Clarrie can drive the wagon, he doesn't need you.'

Lance stood squarely in his path. 'We aint going no place until we find Otto mate, so you better get that through your head right now.'

'When I give an order I expect it to be obeyed,' Pelham shouted. 'I'm not leaving Otto, Bobbo will find him.'

'Bobbo could take a bloody week to find him on his own,' Lance said stubbornly.

'That's my affair, not yours,' Pelham snarled. 'Now get out of my way.' He swished his riding crop at Lance who moved back a few steps away from the horse, his eyes on the whip. 'You touch me with that bloody woman's whip you got there mate and you'll get the belting of your bloody life.'

Pelham turned to shout at Jasin. 'This is your drive Heselwood. Do you intend to let them pull up every time they feel like it?'

Jasin watched all the men mount up including Clarrie, which meant the wagon wasn't going anywhere either. 'It's a damn nuisance but perhaps Lance is right. If we all go in and find the fellow we can put him back on his wagon and get going.'

Pelham fumed. He was inclined to tell Heselwood to run the whole bloody show himself but if he did that, he'd be relegated to the status of a stockman. And he couldn't leave. Not with a hundred cattle of his own on the drive. 'One day!' he told Lance. 'You've got one day to find him and no longer.'

Jasin tried to be optimistic. 'We should find him this morning, wouldn't you say?'

'Who bloody knows?' Lance replied. 'If he's travelling in the wrong direction he could be ten miles from here by now and that's thick scrub in there.'

Clarrie was tired of the delay. 'Let's go then.' He turned his horse into the long grass and scrub trees making for the tall timbers beyond.

They searched all day, keeping in contact with shouts and whistles, widening the arc for the return journey in the afternoon, scouring every gully and dried-out creekbed but there was still no sign of Otto.

Snow met up with Jasin. 'Looks as if we'll have to follow the river downstream tomorrow, he could be walking in circles.'

'What a bloody nuisance. The drive has been going so well.'

Snow shrugged and rode on ahead. Jasin was furious with the stupid German for getting himself lost. By this time they should have been a day out across the plains heading for the Namoi. That was the river McPhie had told him was the next one ahead, and he had said it watered good land.

Jasin's horse picked its way through the untidy bush, skirting straggling logs and avoiding broken ground. He peered ahead of him through the drab trees, there seemed to be no sounds at all except for the crunch of horses' hooves on dry foliage until suddenly he heard a gunshot. He wheeled his horse back towards the sound and met up with Lance and Snow.

'Over that way,' Lance said and led them through the bush. They found Pelham, white-faced and shaking, pointing into a small clearing.

'Did you find the German?' Jasin asked and Pelham nodded.

Otto was sitting propped against a tree, his body covered in a mass of buzzing black flies. A spear had entered his chest and he was pinned to the tree.

'Ah Jesus, the poor bugger,' Snow said, and Jasin stared, shocked.

Snow broke the spear and removed it from Otto's body. 'Give me a hand, we'll take him back to the camp.'

Jasin heard himself whispering. 'What for?'

'To bury him of course.'

'Why can't we bury him here?'

'Because we haven't got a bloody shovel!'

They buried him on the outskirts of the scrub and the stockmen piled timber on his grave to protect it from dingoes. Clarrie carved Otto's name and the date of his death into a nearby tree, since that was all they knew about him.

'Should we shift camp now?' Jasin asked.

'Not much point,' Bobbo said, 'they wouldn't have any trouble finding us, but we'll have to post guards.'

'I doubt anyone could sleep tonight,' Jasin said. 'I say Pelham. We should bring our tent closer in to the wagon. Make a tighter camp.'

'Good idea.' Pelham said. 'I'll take Snow and we'll go back and report this to Hughie McPhie so he can warn the other squatters.'

Pace grinned. Pelham had just outmanoeuvred Heselwood. The captain was not the type of man to be concerned about the other pastoralists or their families. He was off to spend the night in the safety of a homestead.

Early the next morning, after an uneasy night, they packed up the wagon and Clarrie went on his way, now the cook for the outfit. As the stockmen moved the herd out, a wind blew up and the cattle reacted to it, trotting briskly as if it were whipping them along. In the afternoon the sky on the uneven horizon took on a dull-red colour and as the wind increased it changed to a bright orange, the sun hidden in the haze.

Jasin watched his men tying handkerchiefs around their faces and rolling down their sleeves. 'It's a peculiar light,' he said to Lance.

'It'll be more peculiar soon boss, there's a dust storm coming.'

'Should we make camp?'

'No, we'll push on. That last waterhole was dry, there's no point in stopping until we have to. The cattle will play up all night.'

'Should I ride on and see what's ahead?'

'No fear, you stay put, when that storm gets here you won't be able to see a thing. You could get lost.'

Jasin was worried. The wind was building up and already dust was whipping around his face, thick, choking dust, and it was a strange colour.

'Where is all this red dust coming from?'

'Far inland I'd say,' Lance said. 'I never believed the stories about an

169

inland sea, I think it's one big dust bowl, and every so often a million tons of it gets dropped on us.'

'Don't tell me we're headed towards a dust bowl?'

'No. If Hughie says there's a big river ahead of us, it's there. You can tell by the horizon, and how long it takes to hit us, that dust storm built up hundreds of miles further out.'

Further out. Jasin rode on into the stinging wind thinking about that. Lance was right. Dust like that would have to come from deserts – once he claimed his land on the Namoi he would start looking to the north. The others could have the west . . .

Then the full force of the dust storm descended on them, the wind howling and the dust so thick it blotted out the light. The herd came to a standstill turning in to one another for shelter, their hides matted in red dust. The stockmen covered their horses' heads with hessian bags, drew blankets around themselves and stayed at their posts.

Jasin clambered under the wagon with Clarrie who had dropped canvas around them for shelter, but the dust was still thick, stinging their eyes, and making them cough with every breath. Huddled against the wagon wheels they could only sit and wait until the storm abated.

By nightfall it was over.

The cattle were restless during the night, having missed their watering, and Nick rode slowly around the herd playing softly on a tin whistle and the other stockmen could be heard humming as they patrolled in an effort to keep the thirsty cattle calm. There was no sign of Pelham and Snow, and Jasin cursed, spitting dust.

Since they were shorthanded he had had to take a shift with the stockman and was now struggling to stay awake in the saddle. The perseverance of the stockmen in pacifying the herd impressed him, but the cattle were still on their feet, a danger sign, Lance had warned, anything could stampede them at this stage.

He could see MacNamara keeping a solitary vigil on a rise, silhouetted on his horse against the night sky, and he hoped the Irishman was finding it as arduous as his employer was. For the last few days Jasin had been feeling the strain and had been tempted to ride in the wagon but he knew he would lose face with the men. Each day now seemed harder than the last, but he kept his spirits up with the thought that he was almost at his goal.

In the morning the cattle did not need any urging, they surged forward and the tired men rode with them. Jasin and Bobbo took fresh horses and raced ahead searching for waterholes and at last they came to a pool of slimy green water in an old creek bed. Jasin rode down towards it eagerly but Bobbo cautioned him. 'Steady on boss. That green groundcover there could have water under it. This creek has stopped flowing, it's dry further up so the pool would have to be deep to hold out.'

Bobbo dismounted and walked towards the weeds, feeling the depth of the water ahead of him with a sapling and Jasin was shocked to see the improvised measuring stick sink into the depths.

'How do we water the animals?' Jasin asked.

'We'll water our horses from the other side and we'll have to dig this out,' Bobbo said. 'But she's a sweet little billabong; she's all we need for today. We just have to hold the herd back and let a few of them go at it, at a time, otherwise they'll get themselves into a horrible mess.'

By the time the main herd was allowed closer to the creek the stockmen were working hard, their whips cracking and their horses wheeling to keep the cattle disciplined. It was a long slow process releasing cattle to make their eager lumbering dash to the water and then forcing them out again to make way for the next batch. Nick and Tommo kept watch at the water's edge, wading in to rescue the calves which became separated from their mothers, while the dogs patrolled the other side of the creek to keep the satisfied animals from wandering away.

Jasin was exhausted. He went back to the camp, found a blanket and lay down to rest, his head on his saddle. There would be no meal until the herd was settled for the night.

When Pelham rode in, having followed the wagon tracks across country, he had to shake Jasin to wake him. Bleary-eyed and with a few days' growth of beard, Jasin sat up and stared at him taking a few minutes to get his bearings. He washed his face in water Clarrie had drawn from the creek before the animals waded in, spluttering at the taste of it.

'About time you got back,' he snapped.

'We couldn't get back any sooner. That dust storm was frightful. Had us all confined to the homestead back there.'

Jasin nodded. He did not care now that they were over the worst. It was a relief to have Pelham back, he felt more confident with him around; someone to talk to on common ground. The two men shared a tent which was always pitched a little way from the main camp to give them some privacy. The stockmen travelled with swags which were tossed on the wagon during the day and slept in the open or under a tarpaulin lean-to in wet weather. He stretched and pounded the dust from his breeches. 'You were lucky. It was absolutely bloody. I believe I have a stomach full of dust. We had to stay out all last night to keep the cattle from bolting. I almost felt like chucking it in.'

Pelham agreed. 'I can understand that. This is no place for a gentleman. As a matter of fact I have news for you. I have chucked it in.'

'There's no point in giving up now. We're almost there.'

'*You're* almost there. You're the one who wants to take up land. I'm only dealing in cattle and I've sold mine to McPhie. He paid five pounds a head for them so that's a grand profit.'

Jasin felt a roaring in his head and fought to control his rage. 'You have no right to sell those cattle!'

'They're mine, I can do what I like with them,' Pelham laughed.

171

'You bloody well may not! They are to be the nucleus of a herd up here. If you sell you destroy the purpose of the drive.'

'Don't be greedy Heselwood! You've got plenty left.'

'That's not the point. I put up the money for the drive. I should have first claim on them.'

'Will you pay me five pounds a head?'

'Why should I? I could have bought them in Bathurst for under a pound.'

'There, you see. You are annoyed that I've made a good business deal. And I'll accept one hundred pounds from you for bringing you this far. Wages.'

Jasin heard himself shouting. Never in his life had he imagined he could get into such a rage. 'You brought me this far Pelham? Who paid for the supplies and the drovers? You couldn't have brought your cattle this far without help. You've been fed, you've had a change of mounts. I refuse to allow you to sell any of those cattle. The purpose of this drive is to stock the run. You'll get a better return in natural increase later on and you'll still own your original herd. You can tell McPhie there is no sale.'

'I'll tell him no such thing! I've sold my cattle. We'll build some mustering yards in the morning and run the herd through, cut mine out, the brand is clear, and that's the end of it. McPhie's boys will be here tomorrow to help me bring back his cattle.'

To Jasin, that was the last straw. That operation would cost him another day. And for that matter, his drovers were out there working their behinds off watering Pelham's cattle.

Pelham reached into his saddle pack. 'Here, I've brought you a bottle of McPhie's wine, it's powerful stuff. We'll drink on it.'

Jasin shoved the wine away angrily and brought his whip across Pelham's face. 'You've just used me!'

Pelham reacted swiftly. A punch sent Jasin sprawling and when he jumped to his feet Pelham was facing him with his pistol. 'How dare you strike me? Arm yourself Heselwood. I won't shoot an unarmed man, but you apologise or you are dead.'

Jasin dived for the tent, grabbing his pistol and loading it, his hands shaking. Neither man intended to wait for the sobering decorum of a duel and in his fury Jasin gave no thought to the fact that Pelham was a crack shot and he was not.

Pelham waited outside, standing feet apart and steady, his pistol aimed at the tent knowing that Heselwood would come out firing. A rifle shot cracked and Pelham's pistol flew from his hand. He screamed in pain, the top of a finger shot away, as Pace MacNamara walked down into the camp.

'Shoot him!' Jasin shouted. 'He tried to kill me.'

'Shoot him yourself,' Pace said, picking up Pelham's pistol. Jasin raised his gun, wavered, and put it down again.

Pace leaned against a tree, his rifle still ready to settle any further argument and Lance came galloping in. 'What happened?'

'The gentlemen here had a disagreement.' Pace grinned and left Heselwood and Pelham to do their own explaining to Clarrie and Snow who had also arrived on the scene.

When McPhie's sons rode up the next day the drovers had no choice but to wait while Pelham's cattle were separated from the lazy H of Heselwood's brand. Rather than watch, Jasin rode ahead with Clarrie, leaving Lance in charge of the sorting. His own men were annoyed at the delay and he knew they would see to it that Pelham got not one steer or heifer that was not his. He did not bother to thank MacNamara for intervening, believing that, had he been given the chance, he could have disposed of Pelham himself and kept the cattle.

They went westwards through dry country for long empty days until Jasin began to worry that they were off course but at last they topped a rise and the Namoi River could be seen in the distance, a shining ribbon threading through long belts of trees.

'There it is,' Clarrie said and Jasin gulped. He was looking on past the river to endless miles of tree-studded plains. 'Where does this country end?'

Snow laughed. 'God knows! And He ain't telling.'

Jasin felt weak. For the last few days it had only been his pride that had kept him on his horse; he was sure now that he looked as old and weather-beaten as Clarrie. His fair beard was caked with mud that no river water seemed to be able to remove, and his hair, bleached white by the sun, was greasy and hung in thick matted strands. His skin felt like sandpaper.

Clarrie shaded his eyes and squinted around him. 'Any amount of game here, we'll be eating wild duck for dinner.'

But Jasin was still in a daze. All this land was his. His father's estate would look puny compared to these holdings. He looked down at the herd spreading out in the man-high grass. 'One thing worries me Clarrie. If the drovers come back with me, how will three men watch all these cattle? Wouldn't they stray without fences? I mean to say, look out there, God knows where they'd get to.'

'They'll be all right. You've got to train them, like horses. The boys can knock up a fence down by the river. It won't keep them in, but it just lets them know where home base is. Then while you're marking out your territory they'll train the cattle – take them out every day and bring them back every night to the same place until they get to know their own run. Animals understand territory.'

'Even cattle?'

'Sure they do. Some of the bolder ones might roam but you'll flush them out of the bush come mustering time. It takes some fancy riding but if you get good stockmen they can handle it.'

Jasin supposed they could. 'I was hoping Lance and the boys would stay on and work for me but they don't seem to be interested.'

'No. They're drovers. But any time you're moving cattle you know who to ask. Lance and his mates are good value. Get them to round you up some stockmen when they get back to Bathurst.'

The men seemed to be very defensive about convicts but Jasin asked Clarrie anyway. 'Most of the squatters seem to employ convicts?'

And Clarrie surprised him. 'Nothing wrong with that. Gives those lads a chance at the good life, but you better feed them well and treat them right or they'll burn your house down.'

The surveying took weeks. Jasin worked with Clarrie and Snow hammering saplings into the long grass and blazing trees with an 'H' and numbered arrows to mark out the boundaries. They climbed into overgrown gullies and to the tops of hills, and at night they shone lanterns from one point to another to get a straight line, and they cleared scrub for access to waterholes, until Clarrie eventually convinced Jasin that enough was enough. 'Twenty square miles is a good run to start with in anyone's language. To get a proper go on here you'll need at least a dozen men to build your yards and your sheds and to get the plant operating before mustering time next year.'

While the surveying proceeded, the stockmen built a timber cabin, taking care to leave slots for firearms in case of a native attack, and they fenced a home paddock for the horses with split logs. The cattle Jasin had acquired along the route were branded and the herd settled down in its new home.

Pace MacNamara agreed to stay on with Clarrie and Snow until Jasin returned with his workforce. On condition . . .

'On what condition?' Jasin growled. 'I got you out of jail.'

'Not good enough. When you go back to Sydney Town, I want a remission of sentence, not a ticket-of-leave but cleared off the books.'

'Don't give me orders MacNamara. As soon as I turn my back you'll be marking out a run of your own.'

'That thought had crossed my mind, but if I don't get your word on it I might go about my business right now.'

Lance promised to take back and mail two letters for Pace. On Clarrie's advice he had written a letter to Katrin Boundy.

'Don't you know anyone who has a few bob to put up cash for a hank of land? A couple of thousand acres,' Clarrie had asked him.

'A partner are you saying?'

'No bloody way! You mark off your own land and mark off another run as well. That's where you'll get the dough to stock your own. Sell the spare.'

'I know a lady who might be interested.'

'Write and ask her then. No harm in asking.'

The second letter was to his parents in Ireland to advise them he would be taking up land in New South Wales and to send his sister Mary and his brother Brenden out as soon as possible for he would be needing their assistance in this land of plenty.

174

Heselwood had taken up a big run and had his herd in place. Now that he had seen how it was done Pace was anxious to claim his land too, he would not let this opportunity slip away. If Mrs Boundy declined then he would have to find another investor or take a job until he could raise the money to purchase cattle. In the meantime he would keep his side of the bargain and remain here until Heselwood returned; he owed him that much. And he would learn as much as he could from Clarrie and Snow.

He watched Heselwood and the four drovers saddle up and gallop away to the east, the drovers ready for the hard ride back to where they could spend their pay. Pace was relieved to be rid of the Englishman. The man irritated him and, for a reason he was unable to fathom, depressed him too. He had the knack of making Pace feel that he was worthless and would never amount to much. That in itself was a challenge Pace was willing to take up. 'We'll see,' he said to himself. 'I'll find the money somewhere. If you can be a cattle king, so can I.'

A few days later Clarrie suggested Pace should start surveying land for himself, but Pace was apprehensive, 'I wouldn't like to leave yet, there's a lot to do here.'

Clarrie grinned at him. 'The work won't go away MacNamara. We're not the only ones on the trail. No use sitting around here thinking about it. I'll come with you.'

'But what about Snow here on his own?' Pace worried.

'I don't need no nursemaid in the bush,' Snow said. 'The black boys from the camp over the rise will give me a hand until they get sick of it. And you'll be back in every night. Where do you reckon he should set down Clarrie?'

Clarrie drew a map of the river as they knew it. 'The boss put his markers here, so you've got one boundary marked out already. We take up from there. And the first block is the one you sell, so you two won't be neighbours. You don't seem to be the best of mates. Then we'll go a few miles further on and look at the country and if it's any good we'll blaze out a run for you.'

Pace looked down at the river where the tea-trees were flowering in their strange way, like everything in nature here, white blossoms crowning the foliage like snow. He was grateful to the two old bushmen; without them he would never have had the confidence to try such a move.

'What about the other side of this river? It looks to be good pasture over there too.'

Snow shook his head. 'Don't push your luck mate. There's a lot of blacks out there. I've seen their fires in those hills at night. The mob we've got on this side are quiet enough if we let them have a bullock or two, but I've always had the feeling there's a lot more where they come from. Leave 'em in peace while we can, I say. Anyway, you've got a good trail back through to the Hunter from here.'

Pace smiled, feeling a little foolish. 'My own land! It's hard to believe I'll have a property as big as Dublin itself.'

'You won't get it if you stand around talking about it,' Snow commented.

175

# CHAPTER THREE

Edward Heselwood had colic and a running red nose. It was a cold day with blustering winds sweeping up the harbour and small sharp gales slamming into the bays. Georgina was finding that this house had been built for summer, not winter, with its marble floors and few fireplaces. The Cormacks withdrew to their country house at Parramatta over the winter months.

Windows rattled and shutters banged at night, keeping her awake and nervous; the floorboards creaked, doors would not close properly and the passages were draughty. She had taken to wandering the house in her dressing gown, rising late and retiring early. Every day she wrote letters, but letters that were rarely posted because they were so full of gloom.

On two occasions she had taken a carriage into Sydney Town to look at the shops but was repelled by vulgar people in the streets.

Milly Forrest, who still claimed Georgina as her friend and called too often, was equally indignant. 'The convicts hate immigrants,' she had explained. 'They call us legitimates.'

Georgina winced, remembering. She had never regarded herself as an immigrant, it had never entered her head. But Milly had kept on: 'They say they built all the roads and public works for no pay, and they say we've got no right to just walk off the ships and get everything for nothing.'

Every time Georgina thought about that it made her angry. It was perfect nonsense, utter rubbish. She wondered how Jasin would react to being called an immigrant. But when all was said and done if they stayed in the colony as it seemed Jasin might yet do, then they were immigrants.

She had written to Jasin, wherever he was, to insist that her financial situation was desperate. On the Cormack name, in their absence, Georgina had obtained credit at the stores and had made some payments but since she was occupying the house she was expected to feed the staff too. This was not a small expense. The dairyman and the butcher and the storekeeper terrified her. Were it not for the Cormacks' wily maid, Tess, they would surely have confronted her in person.

She was appalled at the cheek of them to be demanding money from her. She had turned to Tess: 'Don't they know who I am?'

The housemaid had looked at her sorrowfully. 'Madam, if you don't mind me telling you, they don't care.'

For all of her days Georgina would remember the shock of that reply.

176

Not just the jolt that it gave her but the sudden awareness of her vulnerability in this country, no longer protected by title and family ties. She
realised that if she were to stay she would have to adjust to an entirely
different situation. If she stayed, that is, and as the days passed she was
tempted more and more to return to England.

That night, sitting alone at dinner, she had drunk a full bottle of claret.
It had taken her a long time to choose the very best she could find from the
Cormack cellars and it was a fine French wine.

Heselwood had been gone five months now. She rose to pour herself
another glass of wine, astonished to find the silver-encased carafe was
empty. She could hardly go down to the cellars herself at this hour, past
the servants in the kitchen and yet if she wanted more wine there was no
reason not to have it.

She rang the bell and Tess came in. 'Refill the carafe with the same
wine, please.'

'Yes madam.'

When Tess delivered the wine to the dining room, the baby began to
cry.

'You finish your dinner madam, I'll see to Edward,' she said and
Georgina was grateful. The child had been perfectly wretched for days.

She looked down the table and addressed the empty chair facing her at
the far end. 'I will not put up with this isolation any longer Heselwood.
Either I join you in the country or I take the child and return to London. I
cannot even write to my parents of your whereabouts. It is a state of affairs
that cannot be tolerated . . .'

There was a loud banging on the front door and Georgina's monologue
ended abruptly. It was a strange hour for anybody to be calling. She stared
out into the gloomy passageway as the knocker banged again, waiting for
one of the servants to see who it might be. She heard the door being opened
and firm footfalls cross the marble-floored entrance hall. A bearded man in
a dusty cape loomed up in the doorway without waiting to be announced.

Georgina stood. 'Sir!'

And then she stared at him. 'God in heaven. It's you! Heselwood!'

The argument began at breakfast the next morning. All the time he had
been in the bush Jasin had thought, ruefully, of the comforts of this house,
and of how fortunate Georgina was to be so well placed. It irritated him to
come home to her complaints.

'I am not unmindful of what you have achieved Jasin,' she said, 'but
now that we have land I want to live there and be beholden to no-one.'

'Do try to imagine how primitive it is, Georgina. It is no place for a
woman.'

'It will be Jasin. There will be other settlers. And it is our house you will
be building there. I want it to be built to my specifications. I shall not leave
it to some convict carpenter.'

'And where will you sleep in the meantime? Under a tree like Eve? It is no garden of Eden and no place for a lady. You are staying in Sydney.'

'Then I shall return to London with Edward on the first ship.'

'You shall not. My son stays here with me.'

'Your son will not be with you. You said yourself your next visit to this station of ours could take six months.'

He sighed. 'It will take six months because I have to build the house and get the station under way. I will have a great deal to do.'

'Of course you will. And I shall be there to assist you. It will save you a great deal of journeying back and forth. I wish you would stop worrying about me Heselwood. I am your wife, I am here to help you. I don't wish to be left here like some hothouse flower.'

Georgina knew she would persuade him in the end and changed the subject. 'Now that you are back we must do some entertaining while we can. We must not lose what place we have in society here.'

The next few months were exciting for the Heselwoods. Jasin renewed his friendship with Governor Darling and the vice-regal personages were the first to accept Georgina's invitations to dine. After that, many callers left their cards, and invitations to one of Georgina's soirees became greatly sought after. Their names were mentioned in the newspapers as the 'darlings of Darling's set' and reports from unnamed sources told of their parties. In the meantime Jasin discussed his claim for land with the Governor who instructed Macleay to attend to it. He also obtained substantial credit from a bank manager pleased to be included on their guest list.

Once he had accepted that Georgina and the child would be accompanying him, Jasin began to appreciate his wife's assistance. They would need to assemble equipment and household goods which would be forwarded by bullock train. Jasin had arranged to meet up with Lance and his drovers in Bathurst and send them ahead with another herd. And at Bathurst he would sign on the workmen he needed for the station. He tried to persuade Georgina that she should go as far as Newcastle by ship and then go inland. At first she would not hear of it. She had read about the sinking of the *Mandalay* and, after their voyage on the *Emma Jane*, that was the last straw.

'Madam. You may not accompany me on a cattle drive, it is out of the question, and since you refuse to go by ship to Newcastle and you have no wings to fly then you stay in Sydney Town . . .'

'Then ship it will be. I will brave the elements.' Georgina smiled. She thought he looked rather dashing these days with longer hair and his face bronzed rather like that of a buccaneer, one imagined. And he was stronger now, more aggressive. She would see that his favourite dishes were served this evening, that no-one would be allowed to disturb them, and that their bed was turned down early. She had discovered over the long months of deprivation a yearning for him to come back to her bed. Before, she had taken him for granted, rarely encouraging his attentions. Today, Georgina decided, I will spend preparing myself. I shall bathe and wash my hair and wear the soft blue décolleté dress.

She remembered that when he came home from Camden he had murmured in his sleep, with his arms around her, the name of another woman. She would not allow him to disappear again for six months or more. Next time he might forget to come home.

Their arrangements were moving steadily along until the morning when Milly and Dermott Forrest presented themselves at their door. Exasperated with them for calling without notice Georgina told Jasin to hurry them off, she was busy organising a luncheon for that very day, but when she dashed in to have a few polite words with them she found the Forrests firmly planted in their seats.

'I see you have been having a very social time,' Milly pouted.

Georgina feigned boredom. 'Yes. Since Heselwood returned all the world and his wife seem to call. It is very tiring.'

'I notice that we were not invited to any of your parties,' Milly said and Dermott flushed.

Jasin stepped forward and took Milly's gloved hand. 'My dear Milly. I was just saying to Georgina last night, "we really must have the Forrests to dinner one evening. Just the four of us." This place,' he shrugged, 'is hardly adequate for the sort of entertaining we are used to, so one has to keep restricting numbers.'

'We were friends before you met any of them,' Milly said. 'I don't see why we shouldn't have been the first on the lists.'

Georgina, appalled at Milly's crassness, kept a light smile on her face but refused to answer. She noticed that Jasin's mouth had popped open like a fish.

There was a nervous cough and some throat-clearing from Dermott as he prepared to contribute to the conversation. 'Ah now Milly, Mr Heselwood just said they'd be inviting us to tea one night on our own. That'll be much better than sitting down with a band of strangers. Won't it lass?'

Milly sniffed and wriggled. She tapped her foot. 'I suppose so. Now Dermott, you tell Jasin what you came about.'

Jasin sprang into the breach. 'Yes Dermott. What can I do for you? I was looking forward to seeing you as soon as I could to find a minute to tell you about the awful time I had getting the cattle up to that place. Our cook was speared to death by blacks. Another feller, you met him, that blackguard Pelham, tried to shoot me, and ran off with a hundred of the best cattle. I was nearly drowned in a river, I rode for days on end through dust storms, without water. It was absolutely harrowing. I tell you I was lucky to have survived.' He continued with a highly coloured description of his experiences, which emphasised the risks and expense he had undergone and Dermott listened open-mouthed while Milly sneaked a better look around

179

the drawing room. On their other visits she had been put in the little sitting room over at the side, Georgina not being one to show a person around. She thought it was a fine room, despite Jasin's criticism of the house, but she supposed coming from castles, they would find this a bit of a comedown. The drawing room, she would not forget to mention to Bess, was as big as their entire house. It had cold floors with big rugs and stiff uncomfortable furniture. The chairs were highly polished with green silk upholstery but everything was separated by great distances. She was still balancing her cup and saucer on her knee but Dermott had put his on the floor. It seemed a useless sort of a room but it was accepted practice in society to have a drawing room, so, when they built their house Milly was determined that they would have a drawing room too. These grand thoughts brought her abruptly back to her present situation.

They were still sharing the house with Bess and Fred. The brothers worked well together, but the dispositions of the wives were beginning to sour. Milly found Bess dull, and Bess complained that Milly put on airs.

'Two mistresses in the one house is bound to cause a little friction,' Fred had said.

But Bess corrected him. 'I am the mistress of this house. She is a visitor.'

Milly's one ambition was to have a fine house and Dermott had promised her that, but all of his spare cash had gone into the partnership with Jasin. The house had to be postponed. Milly still had no regrets about that transaction, it placed her on a social level far above their other friends.

At Dermott's urging Jasin was recounting how he lost his magnificent horse Prince Blue and Milly became impatient. Her husband was sitting there looking as sorrowful as a cow that had missed her milking. He was supposed to be talking business so she interrupted them, and by doing so missed the juiciest gossip of the day – the whereabouts of Adelaide Brooks.

'Excuse me Jasin. You did say you were having visitors shortly. You can tell us all about the rest when we come to dinner. Right now Dermott wants to talk business.'

'Of course he does. But Dermott if you are worried about the cattle through all my adventures, do not. I got them there safe and sound. Out onto the wilds of the Liverpool Plains.'

Dermott twisted the brown gloves Milly had insisted he wear. 'I know you did Mr Heselwood. It's a bold thing you did, but – about our investment . . .'

'The investment is safe. You can't expect a return on your money for a year. I told you that. The herd now has to stay up there and multiply and then I shall take some to the markets and sell them. Immediately I do I shall see that you are paid with interest on your money. I am the one risking life and limb.'

Jasin thought he had put that rather well. Forrest would get a modest return on his money. No need to mention top price for beef cattle to a

180

bootmaker. A modest return for a modest man would suffice.

'I know that Mr Heselwood, but there was the other part,' Dermott continued.

'What other part?'

'When we first made the deal you said we would be squatters too, that we would share the land.'

Jasin threw up his arms. 'Oh God! Think of that! It seems years since I first rode into the wilderness. We all get a bit carried away thinking a grubby piece of land out there would make a Camden. One hardly knew what one was talking about.'

'I did,' Dermott said.

Milly's little black eyes spun from one to the other and Georgina rang for Tess to collect the tea trays.

Dermott continued. 'When I put up the money I wasn't just looking for a return. I could have got that here, lending out through any lawyer, but you said we'd have a partnership. We'd share the land. The land is what I want to know about.' He dragged a crumpled map from his vest pocket and walked over to one of the small round tables. 'Now Mr Heselwood I'd like you to show me on here. Where is our land?'

'My dear fellow. You are as naive as I was about this land. Now see here, here are the boundaries of location. I see they are marked on this map. Good. Now our cattle are out here on the plains, about here I'd say, just running wild. Not a fence in sight. I've left two old bushmen to keep an eye on them.' He was careful not to mention Pace MacNamara who could tell them exactly where, and would too, given half the chance. 'Now you have to understand . . .' He straightened up to address the room. 'It is illegal to be out there in the first place. The Governor will not recognise any claims to that land until it has been surveyed by his own men. All we have is free grazing land for our cattle.'

'Why spend all that money and nearly kill yourself taking the cattle up there then?' Milly asked sharply, not letting the point slip.

'Where else would we put them my dear?' Jasin laughed. 'But we do have to wait the Governor's pleasure to claim land.'

Dermott was trying to work this out. 'Other people have done it. That's why they call them squatters. Why can't we?'

'Because we don't want to do anything illegal and find we've got a bag of nothing when the land is opened up. If I were you I would forget about land and concentrate on your shops. Georgina tells me you are doing very well indeed.'

'That's so. But I can't forget about the land, Mr Heselwood, and neither can you. That's our agreement. I think you've been taken for a ride, listening to this talk about illegals. There's land out there. When you go back, claim it anyway. We'll worry about the legal situation later. It says in our agreement that we are partners and any land you lay claim to is half mine. I'm disappointed.' He stuffed his map back in his pocket. 'I was

181

looking forward to showing Milly where our land is.'

He took his wife's hand. 'Never mind love, Mr Heselwood will do it next time. The trouble with you, Mr Heselwood,' he said, 'you've been brought up to do the right thing and it doesn't work out. Here it's first up best dressed.'

After that long speech, Dermott shook his partner's hand warmly. 'Don't let it worry you. I say you've done a sterling job so far and it's not too late to stake a claim. Mrs Heselwood it has been nice to see you and my congratulations on your little son. One day I'll make him his first little saddle with my own hands.'

Georgina stood as they left, a regal figure in a grey serge skirt and white satin blouse, her only jewellery a rope of amber beads. Milly noticed how plain her clothes were and yet they looked so expensive and wondered how this was achieved. Jasin was in a good mood. He escorted them right down to the front gate past rows of snapdragons and poppies that bordered a thick green hedge.

'Do they really think they own half of our land?' Georgina asked Jasin when he returned.

'It seems so. I must get the loan papers. I don't remember the wording.'

Georgina handed the papers to him. 'I thought you would want to study them again.'

'No, not at the moment. Take them away, they're such a bore.'

His wife began reading a single-page document. 'Here it is. Clause five. And you've signed it.'

'I didn't sign it, I signed at the bottom of the page.'

'Well it is one of the conditions but surely they won't hold you to it after all you have been through. No-one could have foreseen the difficulties you had to overcome to find and survey that property. And we can't have them to dinner, we're far too busy. I can't believe you invited them Jasin.'

'What choice did I have? That woman forced herself on us!'

'She thinks she has forced herself on us. There will be no invitation.'

'Good God! They'll be monstrously offended.'

Georgina put the loan papers back into his desk. 'What if they are? I see that as a blessing, we will be rid of them once and for all as soon as you can pay back their loan. Why not pay them now?'

'No. I need the money I raised from the bank for expenses and to buy cattle and equipment. There will be wages to pay, and the house to build. We will not run ourselves short on their account. By the way I heard a rumour that our friend Governor Darling is in danger of being recalled.'

'Why? What has he done?'

'He has upset practically everyone. He's offended Macarthur and the "exclusives", and also angered Wentworth and the "radicals". He tried to muzzle Wentworth's newspaper, the *Australian*, among many other things. But I'm not fussed as our application is with Macleay, so it will go through whether Darling stays or leaves. It is just a formality. The minute

182

the boundaries are extended the land is officially ours.'

'How wonderful. We must give the property a name. Have you thought of one yet?'

'I've thought of hundreds. It occupied my time riding back to Sydney but I can't make a decision.'

'What about calling it Carlton Park? That will please the King. When we christen it we should tell your father to let His Majesty know.'

'An excellent idea. Carlton Park it is.'

# CHAPTER FOUR

In the daily routine of the Nelson Hotel, Dolour Callinan found the tranquillity she needed to summon her strength again. She was by nature a solitary person and the last few years had been agony for her, from the crowded jail in Dublin to the horrors of the ship and on to the Female Factory in Parramatta. At Camden it had been peaceful enough but Jasin had disrupted that life for her. She still blamed herself for being so stupid as to end up back in the Factory, where that old hag, Meg, had made matters worse.

After her attack on Flora, Meg had warned the women. 'She's Tuatha's brat. Stay clear.'

'I am not,' Dolour had said. 'She was my grandmother.' And Meg had screeched like a night-owl and fled to her own end of the dormitory. Dolour heard them whispering but her mind was searching for the solace of her grandmother's words, recalling the nights she had sat by the hearth listening to the mystic tales, trying now to conjure up the face of the old woman who had been her only friend.

In the village they had said that Tuatha was a witch but none would dare test her powers. Not even the priest. Dolour remembered the day he had come stooping into the cottage. 'Give us the girl,' he had said, but Tuatha had refused. 'She is not ready.'

Tuatha had told her the stories of the magic people, for was she not herself a direct descendant of Dana, of the Druids, the people who know, the privileged ones? And Dolour had listened, curled up with the gentle goats that slept with her for warmth.

This day at the Nelson Hotel there was no-one around. The bars were closed, they had all gone to the Show Society carnival. It was a great day in the colony, the King's birthday. Dolour had pleaded a sore throat and a headache and Katrin Boundy had allowed her to stay home, relieved that someone would be about the hotel as it could be a good time for robbers.

'Very well, you can stay home. But give those rooms upstairs a good going over. And my room could do with a sweep and a dust . . .'

Sometimes Katrin wondered about the competence of the people in charge of the Female Factory. Some of the girls who had come from there highly recommended had been slovenly wretches, and yet Dolour, with her bad reputation, had proved to be a good worker. Well trained too. She also wondered why this girl had run off from the Macarthurs, everyone said they treated their convicts fairly. Dolour would not talk about Camden.

She gave the keys to Dolour. 'Don't serve anyone or I'll lose my licence. Everything's closed for the holiday,' and went out to the horse-drawn bus with her staff and boarders and a few customers.

Dolour watched them pull away, the bus decorated with red, white and blue banners, and the horses trotting proudly in front, their manes plaited and garlands of patriotic rosettes draped around their necks. She waved to the excited passengers with no regrets. A whole day to herself!

The throat was cured instantly and the headache gave way to joy. She decided to hurry through the work and then make herself a cup of tea and a lunch of cold meat from the safe. The boarders' rooms were small and easy to do but Mrs Boundy's large bedroom took longer. Meticulously Dolour moved the furniture and swept the room and began to dust with an oiled cloth irritated at all the knick-knacks that cluttered the room. She walked to the window, pulling aside the drapes and stared down at the deserted street. If Jasin went to the Factory looking for her now he would not be able to find her.

She picked up Mrs Boundy's silver-backed brush and swept her hair from her face. 'Don't be such a lump Dolour Callinan. He won't come looking for you. Not now. You're only teasing yourself hoping he might. He's ditched you good and proper. You were a fool to believe him.'

Her anger returned and she stormed around the room cleaning with a vengeance. Mrs Boundy was an untidy woman. Clothes were dumped on chairs and thrown into the bottom of the wardrobe; shawls hung over the mirrors and the drawers Dolour closed were stuffed to overflowing. Ready to leave, she stood at the door contemplating the superficial tidiness of the room, feeling that something was holding her there, telling her not to leave. Weren't you trained as a lady's maid? Wouldn't it be a grand idea if Mrs Boundy had a lady's maid? She'd never think of it herself, not born to it.

Dolour plunged back into the room and set to work.

When Katrin Boundy came back from the races she was astonished. The furniture in her room had been re-arranged making it look more spacious. The clothes in her wardrobe now hung in neat rows with the shoes in tidy rows beneath. All of her drawers had been emptied and cleaned, the clothes sorted, folded and replaced. The room gleamed and a bowl of pink roses with feathery ferns reflected in the dressing table mirror.

She called out over the bannisters. 'Mickey! Send Dolour up here.'

When Dolour came running, her mass of red hair tied back with a patriotic ribbon, Katrin threw open the door. 'Who did this?'

'I did madam. I hope you don't mind. I had nothing to do.'

Katrin walked around the room opening and closing doors and drawers, the perfume of the roses adding to the freshness of the room. 'Thank you

Dolour. It's nice to see someone do something, for a change, without having to be asked.'

'I like to do it madam. I was a lady's maid in Dublin. And she was never as busy as you are, with no time to look after yourself at all.'

'Yes,' Katrin murmured. 'It's a pleasant surprise.'

Dolour retreated. For the time being that would do.

Katrin poured herself a glass of wine from the cut-glass decanter, now free of dust. Dolour was right. Since Boundy's death she hardly had time to think about herself, having to run the hotel on her own. It might be a good idea to bring Dolour upstairs to look after her clothes and keep the place tidy. It would save a lot of time. Dressing, these days, meant rifling through drawers trying to find things that matched and had already been ironed, a flurry of clothes pulled from a heap and discarded again.

But there were other things to think about. Pace MacNamara's suggestion that she purchase the land next to his was interesting. Surely it was not just a business proposition? It was nice to know that she was one of his few friends in the colony. Reassuring. Tomorrow she would get a map and see how far out this land was.

Downstairs her friends were calling for her. She had invited them back for champagne and supper and by the sounds of things there would be more drinking than eating. They were good cheerful friends but there was no-one among them to fill a need. She didn't want to be a publican all her life. She wanted her own home and a husband. And she wondered what it would be like to live out west on a station.

# PART NINE

## THE SETTLERS

# CHAPTER ONE

Pace MacNamara stood in the sluggish creek sluicing himself down with the cool water, it had been a long hot day. Above him crows cawed, posing on dead white trees, three to a branch in mournful trinities, their glossy feathers like black reeds, and their black eyes as patient as Job without his guilt. Pace hated them. They picked the eyes out of bogged, helpless animals and they spooked the horses.

A sharp whistle from the hut told him that Snow had their meal ready. He walked out of the creek and pulled on his dungarees, not caring that he was still wet, he'd stay cooler that way, picked up his gun and pushed through the scrub to their base.

For weeks they had been splitting iron bark and building solid two-rail fences for home paddocks and Pace would be glad to see the end of that job. Digging postholes and grubbing the bush was the hardest work he had ever done. He stared out over the dry scrappy landscape. 'This country looks as tired as I feel. Those gum trees, you'd think a good wind would blow them down.'

'They're hardier than that,' Snow said, handing him a plate of beef stew.

'Where's Clarrie?'

'He's out tracking the brumbies. He reckons they hole up in the little valley to the east, he likes to keep an eye on them. You want to take a look at them tomorrow?'

'I'd love to catch a few of them.'

'We can do that if you feel like building a good strong yard.'

Pace groaned. 'When I get that run of mine going I'm giving the fence building to the first one who wants it. Can't you rope those horses?'

'No, you've got to trap them, they're too smart. And they're suspicious. Your fences have got to be stronger than a prison wall or the stallion will throw his mares at it. He doesn't care if they get hurt just so long as they smash a way out. And the buggers will get right down on their knees and smash a fence up and out of the way.'

'You're joking?'

'No fear I'm not. Getting them into your trap is a dance all of its own. Fencing off their waterhole is a bit of a mean trick but it's one way of grabbing them if you're patient. They'll hang out for days, knowing it's a trap, until the thirst beats them.'

Snow sucked on his pipe and Pace settled down to listen. He liked to

188

hear these old men tell their bush stories. They had a timelessness about them, as if, like this land, they had not gone forward to old age but back to meet it. The old men Pace recalled from his village back home were men who expected to be defeated by the years but these two were tough, light on their feet and quick into the saddle. They had an eagerness about them that contradicted their age and their eyes were bright, constantly alert.

'I caught one of those big stallions one day,' Snow was saying. 'Thought I did a great job of roping him and tied him to a tree to let him settle down but he bucked and screamed and no-one could get near him, and he ended up choking himself. Crashed down and just lay there with foam still dribbling out of his mouth. We finally went over to him, felt his flanks even and we were sure he was dead. But he was pulling the lizard trick. The rope had torn into his neck so I cut it and then he was up again and lashing out in all directions. We scattered I can tell you, he'd have killed us if he'd got a chance and then he was off. I saw him around plenty of times after that, but I left him alone. Too bloody good for me.'

'It's hard to believe that there are horses out here for the taking. That'd be a good business to have for a sideline,' Pace said.

'I'll tell you what's a better business boy. I took myself a ride into that territory you've marked off and you've got some beautiful red cedar stands in there. Worth a fortune. Always keep your eyes peeled for good timber, learn about it. Trouble is these rivers don't flow to the sea so you'd have to overland the timber but it'd be worth it. Hire yourself a bullocky and a couple of timber-getters and you're in business.'

Pace laughed. 'And here I've been worrying about the forest on my land and how the hell I'm going to clear it all and looking at Heselwood's run which is more open country, and envying him.'

'Yeah, things even out,' Snow grinned. 'Anyway what about the boss? Do you think he'll let you off the hook?'

'He's a foxy feller. Not if he can help it. And we won't mention to him about my runs for a while. He'll throw convulsions if he finds out his assigned servant has taken up more land than he has.'

Snow stood up and poked at the fire. 'Here comes Clarrie. And there's someone with him.'

'Who would that be now?' Pace asked but Snow shook his head. 'I can't make it out just yet. Ah, wait on, it's one of McPhie's lads. He makes them wear those red shirts all the time in case they get lost in the bush. And he's got a packhorse with him. About bloody time. We'll get some supplies at last.'

Young Jock McPhie was a welcome sight. He also carried some rum, a few old newspapers and some precious green vegetables grown by his mother. And two letters for Pace. The first one, from Heselwood, Pace read to them. Heselwood was sending on a bullock train with equipment and supplies and on his return journey he would be bringing another herd. It was all interesting enough but it made no impact on their immediate situation.

The second letter was from Katrin Boundy who was enthusiastic about the land claim and who would, if invited, come to Newcastle to discuss the matter.

Pace grinned and stuffed the letter in his pocket. Everything was turning out well. He would sell Mrs Boundy that land, she'd make a good profit on it in a few years, and the money for it would start the MacNamara cattle station.

'I'll reply to this letter tonight,' he said to Jock, 'and will you take it back with you in the morning?'

'Sure will Mr MacNamara. And my Pa sends his greetings. You had any trouble with the blacks out here?'

'No.'

'There's been some real trouble down our way. Blacks killing off cattle and sheep. Two of our stockmen got speared. The troopers came in to find out about that cook of yours that got speared and they started shooting up the place. They knocked off a couple of blacks marching through Stanton's place, that's the run south-west of us, and old Stanton skinned one of the blacks, stuffed him, and hung him on a tree to frighten off the rest of the mob.'

Clarrie spun on his heel. 'He did what?'

'I told you. Hung him up like a scarecrow.'

'The bloody bastard. I hope the blacks get him.'

'Fair go Clarrie. The blacks are no good. You should hear what they do to white women.'

'Listen you bloody . . .' Clarrie's face was purple with anger. 'How old are you?'

'I'm eighteen I think.'

'Well you better wake up to yourself.'

'Give over Clarrie,' Snow turned to Pace and talked to him as if Jock were not there. 'You waste your time talking to these blokes. They breed them to hate the blacks and they go on hating them because they've not been bred to think. I never heard of any of the blacks bothering to molest a white woman. If they're in a killing mood they'll kill all right, women too because we kill their women. But this little whippersnapper, when he learns how to do it he'll be down by the creeks of a night looking for the gins . . .'

Jock opened his mouth to speak but Clarrie stopped him. 'You've said enough tonight, now just shut your trap.'

'I was just gonna say,' Jock whined, 'I remember I've got a message for Mr MacNamara. It's in the saddlebag. One of the boundary riders brought it in only the other night.' He dragged a crumpled letter out and handed it to Pace. 'It's from a lady at Chelmsford station.'

The envelope was greasy from being handed on by men who understood the importance of any message in the outback.

Pace was surprised. It was a note from Adelaide Brooks.

*Dear Mr MacNamara.*

*I hope you remember me from the* Emma Jane, *Jasin Heselwood told us you were working for him. I am living at Chelmsford station in the Hunter Valley and I desperately need to talk to you. Can you come?'*

Adelaide had written the note on impulse. Now she was embarrassed. Diagnosing her own actions, she thought it was probably because she longed for a familiar face.

She had been feeling so well during the first months of her pregnancy that she had almost overcome the worry of having a child at her age and out of wedlock but now her worries had returned.

Juan had been very kind and had ordered anything she needed to be sent out to the station. From a catalogue he had selected a cot and he had made a grand occasion of its arrival on the bullock wagon. His enthusiasm had generated great excitement on the station. This was to be a special baby, the boss's child and they all seemed to forget, or not to care, that he was not married to the mother. All except Adelaide.

Dora was a midwife and that had made Adelaide feel more confident but the last few months had been difficult, she had felt heavy and listless and suffered pains in her back and severe headaches which brought on a depression she was unable to control. She forced herself to take walks around the station, down to the empty shearing sheds or to the vineyards where she sat pretending to read. She thought of friends back in England, of Brooks, even of the Misses Higgins. It was then she thought of Pace MacNamara.

Dora had begun to worry about her. 'You should see a doctor, Mrs Brooks. Do you want me to get him out here?'

To have to face a stranger and explain the situation would be unbearable. 'Of course not. What could a doctor do?'

'I don't know, but he could make it easier for you. I reckon you should go into the hospital in Newcastle while you've still got time.'

Adelaide was nauseous with fright. A hospital would be even worse with everyone knowing about her. She shook her head in a definite 'no', unable to stop the tears.

Dora guided her to a kitchen chair. 'Sit down and I'll make you a nice drink. Don't be worrying, you're getting yourself into a real state.'

Suddenly Adelaide ran outside behind a shed, dry-retching, her body convulsed and shaking, her eyes and nose streaming as heavy sobs replaced the paroxysms. Dora, who had followed her out, held onto her while a sorrowing Billabill stood by, his dusty face creased with worry.

The black girls came running up. 'What's up missus? Him birrahlee in there playem up?'

'Go away,' Dora shouted at them. 'Come on Mrs Brooks, we'll get you to bed.'

She sponged her and puffed up the pillows to make her as comfortable

191

as possible and tucked the net around the bed. 'Now you get some sleep Mrs Brooks, you're just tired out.'

Outside she took hold of Billabill. 'You get a horse and ride to Mr Anderson on Big Sal station. Tell him to send for the doctor, quick.'

The old man cringed. 'Not me. Boss say I stay with the Missus. Him say Billabill stay here and mind the missus.'

Dora ran outside but there was no sign of any of the men. The homestead was quiet, even the blacksmith's shed. All hands were needed for the mustering. Two horses, both shod and ready for emergencies, grazed in the home paddock. She raced out, grabbed a bridle and saddle, and whistled to the nearest horse. Then she called Billabill. 'Come here. I can't leave the missus. You get on this horse and bloody go or I'll get the gun out.'

Billabill was on the horse in seconds.

'Now get going,' Dora cried and slapped the horse on the rump.

Pace MacNamara was riding back across the plains with Jock McPhie.

'You're a ticket-of-leave bloke aren't you?' Jock asked.

'That I am,' Pace said, it was easier than an explanation.

'What about Mr Heselwood? If he comes back and finds you gone he could have you run in.'

'I wouldn't be worrying about it. Clarrie'll tell him where I am. And I'll be back as soon as I can.'

'You're still breaking the law. They got a constable's station at Jerry's Plains. If you haven't got a pass they'll nab you. And if I was you, seeing any troopers around, I'd dodge off!'

A pass. Pace hadn't given any thought to that. 'Have you got pen and ink at your place Jock?' he asked.

'My word we have. My Pa writes real good.'

'Then the problem is solved. I'll write myself a pass and get your Pa to witness it.'

'You can't write one for yourself.'

'I can if I sign it Heselwood,' Pace grinned.

All around them the ranges in the distance looked the same, no matter how far he travelled in this country there were always more hills on the horizon. They were taking a cross-country route now, climbing through dense scrub in rocky hills. Pace marvelled at the way Jock pushed his horse through miles of bush. He might be a bit thick in the head, he thought, but sure as God there's room in there for a compass.

The McPhie homestead seemed deserted when Jock and Pace rode in but they found Mrs McPhie digging in a vegetable patch at the back.

'Where the bloody hell is everyone?' Jock called and his mother, a weatherbeaten woman with fierce eyes, glared at him. 'I told you before. You stop that swearing!' She pushed wisps of hair from her face and dropped the front of her black skirt that had been hooked up to give her kneeling room. 'Who's this?'

'That's Mr MacNamara. Going through to Chelmsford station. He works for Mr Heselwood.'

She acknowledged Pace with a jerk of her chin. 'You can stay over in the bunkhouse. And if you've got sticky fingers keep them in your pocket if you know what's good for you.'

The yard was a scrapheap of odd pieces of rusting farm implements, and rubbish lay scattered about. Chooks and goats picked their way through the tufted grass that met the back door of the main house. He peered inside as he passed. The dirt floor was carpeted with hessian and it looked as gloomy as the woman herself. Heselwood had stayed here, he recalled. He must have enjoyed that. Get him used to the fleas. This was the land of fleas he had discovered, and great biting ants, and spiders and snakes. He was glad he had not mentioned them in his letter home or none of the family would venture out.

'Those devils of bushrangers duffed your father's cattle,' Mrs McPhie decided to tell Jock.

'How many'd they get?'

'A good twenty he says. Picked the best of them too. He's taken the boys and gone after them.'

Jock was clearly disappointed to miss the fun of chase. 'Oh Jeez!' He glared at Pace as if it were his fault. 'Where'd they go? I'll catch up with them.'

A flock of pink galahs wheeled overhead creating glorious colour against the blue, in contrast to the drab creations of man below them. Mrs McPhie leapt for her gun and fired at them. Pace was amazed that anyone could fire into a flock of hundreds of birds and not hit one but was careful not to smile.

Chelmsford Station, established for many years, was the opposite of McPhie's rough beginnings. There were plenty of fat sheep on the slopes and the homestead charmed Pace. Two stockmen rode out to check on the stranger. 'The name is Pace MacNamara. I've come to visit Mrs Brooks. Is she still here?'

The men glanced at one another, their faces serious. 'Yes. She's up at the house but she's bad, poor lady, real bad. You might be able to see her though.'

Whispering, the foreman's wife took him into the parlour. 'The doctor and Mr Rivadavia are with her now.' She shook her head.

'What's the matter with her? What happened?'

'The baby. She had a fine girl but a lot of trouble. It went on too long. She's very weak.'

'Where's Dr Brooks?'

Dora stared. 'Dr Brooks? I don't reckon you've seen Mrs Brooks for a good while. He died. Heart, she said. Long before she came here.'

Pace was confused. This talk of a baby and Brooks dead? She must have married again. But why was she still called Mrs Brooks?

'It's Mr Rivadavia's child,' Dora whispered.

'Ah dear God.'

'It distressed her an awful lot to be giving birth without a wedding ring. I told her not to worry about it but I know she did.'

Pace thought of Adelaide as he had known her on the *Emma Jane*, bright, confident. What misfortunes had come upon her? He was angry with the squatter, the fellow who owned this station, who had obviously taken advantage of the woman. He looked around the parlour. The fine furnishings could not have been cheap. He wondered how long it would take him to build and furnish his house . . .

The parlour door opened and a well-dressed young man walked in. He looked worried but even allowing for that, this meeting was more of a confrontation. 'I am Rivadavia.'

'MacNamara. Is this your station or your father's?'

'I own the station.'

'I see. I believe Mrs Brooks has had a child?'

'Yes. A daughter.'

'And it is your daughter?'

'Yes. But I cannot see that it is any business of yours.'

'That's true enough, but I would like to see Mrs Brooks.'

'How did you know she was here?'

'I received a note,' Pace said.

Rivadavia shrugged, satisfied with that explanation. He opened the door and called to Dora. 'Show this gentleman in to Mrs Brooks.'

The doctor was just coming out of her room. 'How is she?' Pace asked.

'She's very low. Are you a friend?'

'Yes. We came out on the same ship.'

'Ah, that's good. You might cheer her up, Mr Rivadavia has done all he can.'

Pace stepped quietly into the room and was shocked at the wasted appearance of the woman in the bed, her face drawn and grey against the whiteness of the linen.

'Mrs Brooks,' he whispered. 'It's me, Pace MacNamara.'

Adelaide opened her eyes slowly and Pace took her hand. Tears slid from her eyes and she sobbed, but the effort was too great; she lay quiet again, her eyes on him.

'There now,' he said awkwardly. 'Everything's all right and you have a lovely daughter. You've got to get yourself strong again. It's a good world out there.'

'Not for me,' she whispered.

'Ah now, you're just feeling low and that's natural. The hard part is over and you should be proud.'

But she pressed his hand. 'I'm not married, Pace. The child has no name.'

'It'll have a name. Here in the land of convicts you're a saint so don't be worrying about a piece of paper no-one is ever going to read.'

But she would not be consoled, she closed her eyes as if to ward off his comforting words.

Pace smoothed her hair and whispered to her and held her hand again.

Later he sat in the kitchen while Dora set out a meal for him, and he was grateful. 'Thank you Dora. I hope that boss of yours doesn't mind. I think he didn't take too kindly to me visiting. Not fancy enough for him.'

'Mr Rivadavia's different, Argentinian he is. Once you get to know him he's a fair boss. Bit standoffish but he's gentry you see.'

'He wasn't too standoffish with his housekeeper.'

'Who? Mrs Brooks? She wasn't his housekeeper, she came with him when he bought the place.'

'Is that so? Where'd she meet up with him?'

'In Sydney. He was always very good to her. Bought her everything she wanted and she never had to lift a finger unless it suited her.' She hurried out and came back with the baby. 'This is Rosa. Look at this little mite. Isn't she beautiful?'

'That she is,' Pace said. 'A sweetheart. Surely a little one like this can make her mother happy?'

'She's too weak and when you get down like that all your worries seem fifty times bigger. We've got a black girl wet-nursing this little one.' She hugged the child. 'One good thing, Mr Rivadavia's made no bones about claiming her and he's a very rich man. She'll want for nothing.'

'As long as it suits him,' Pace said.

Dora looked at him wearily. 'You could say that about any kid, Mr MacNamara. At least Rosa will have a good start here which is more than a lot of poor beggars in the colony get. And if you don't mind me saying, Mrs Brooks should have gone to hospital but she wouldn't go. Mr Rivadavia tried to take her in himself but she wouldn't have a bar of it. You can't help people who won't help themselves. And now she just wants to roll over and die. More worried about what people will think than about the baby.'

'That's a harsh way of looking at it.'

'It's a harsh country this. If she only knew she was living well thanks to Mr Rivadavia. And he treated her like a lady.'

'She is a lady.'

'I didn't say she wasn't. I'm just saying Mr Rivadavia was good to her, seeing as how he's only a young man and a handsome one at that. He never looks at other women.'

'A paragon,' Pace murmured.

That night Rivadavia ate alone and Pace had supper with the stockmen. Andy offered him a bed in the bunkhouse but he preferred to doze in a chair on the verandah outside the kitchen. Inside, lights were still burning while Dora hovered around and Rivadavia kept vigil beside the bed.

195

'Mr MacNamara!' Dora, in her nightdress and shawl, shook him awake. 'She's gone. Mr Rivadavia said to come in.'

He stumbled inside. By the lamplight Adelaide looked peaceful and Rivadavia, beside her, his face suffused with tears, seemed now to be very young, no longer the confident head of the household.

Pace knelt down and began to pray aloud and was surprised to see Rivadavia threading silver rosary beads through his clasped hands.

At sunset the next evening all hands on the station including the Aborigines attended the burial of Adelaide Brooks. Rivadavia led the mourners but it was Pace who read the service. Dora wept quietly while the black girls cried out their grief and Billabill spilled large tears down his polished face.

The next morning Pace went to find Rivadavia to take his leave. 'I'll be going now,' he said, and Rivadavia made an effort to be civil. 'Thank you for coming to see Dell. She should not have died. I blame myself for not making her go to hospital.'

'I blame you too but I don't know if the hospital would have made any difference. She died of a broken heart.'

'Mrs Brooks came here by choice and she stayed here by choice. People do not die of a broken heart.'

'What about the child?'

'The child is mine. I will care for her.'

'And her name?'

'Her name is Rosa Rivadavia.'

'Not by law. Not unless you draw up legal papers.'

'I will do that.'

'Then why couldn't you have done that for her mother?'

'This is none of your business. You were her friend, you can see she was held in high esteem here.'

'And is that why she died weeping. She was so happy?'

Rivadavia turned and walked back into the house and Pace went around to the stables where he found the foreman. 'I've come this far,' he said. 'I might as well go on to Newcastle, I've land out west and I need to find out about claiming it, but I'm strapped until I get paid. Could you lend me a pound or so?'

'Sure I can,' Andy said. 'We're glad you came to see Mrs Brooks. Would four pounds do?'

With the four pounds in his pocket and food for the journey in his saddle-bag Pace rode up for a last prayer at Adelaide's grave and then turned his horse towards the Hunter River and followed it south. At Singleton there was a letter from Katrin Boundy. She was in Newcastle, staying at the Globe Hotel. He stabled his horse and hurried down to the dock. He was just in time to board the crowded river boat for Newcastle.

That night he slept on the deck huddled under a canvas, with the other travellers who could not afford cabins. Cold winds blew in gusts, as if from bellows, across the wide reaches of the river. The next day was sunny and as the deck passengers warmed, their dispositions improved. Men and boys trailed lines from the stern of the boat, ladies came up from their cabins to stroll on deck and enjoy the scenery; a barber sat his customers on a pile of ropes allowing the breeze to act as his broom.

'What about you mister?' he called to Pace. 'You grow any more hair, you'll need shears to find your face.'

Pace laughed. 'I'll have a haircut, then, and you can trim my beard.'

'For another threepence I'll shave you clean.'

'No thanks. I've got used to the beard.'

Hawkers spread their wares on blankets – cloth, beads, combs, false teeth, needles and cotton and boxes of clothing. Pace bought a shirt and a pair of dungarees and bargained with a fat lady who sat cross-legged on the deck, for a sheepskin jacket.

'Made it meself love,' she roared in a voice that would have done an auctioneer proud. 'Learned me trade in London Town. Ten bob for this beautiful garment.'

Pace examined it. 'I'll give you five.'

'Five bob? Did you hear that? After me making it from the squatter's pet merino.'

Her audience erupted with shouts of laughter. There was nothing they liked better than to 'see off' the squatter.

'Try it on love. Put it on. Warm as your mother's heart.'

He put on the jacket. It was the strangest coat he had ever seen but it fitted well and was warm and snug and the collar turned up high, the very thing against the cold of the plains.

'Just the right length for sitting a horse,' the woman cried. 'Now look at him, fits him like a glove! Come on angel-face, ten bob. Look at the stitching, you'll never get better!'

The audience joined in. 'Pay her,' they shouted. 'It's a bargain.'

Pace agreed but spending another ten shillings worried him.

The fat lady grinned and winked at the audience. 'Look at the eyes of him. The big brown eyes! Break your bleedin' heart wouldn't they? You can have it for nine bob!'

Pace leaned over and kissed her sweaty cheek. 'You're a fine lady. I'll take it,' and the watchers clapped their approval.

Katrin Boundy saw him walk into the hotel lobby, looking huge in a sheepskin jacket and she thought it was Pace but it was hard to tell with that black beard. Then he spoke to the publican and she recognised his voice, the soft Irish brogue.

'Mr MacNamara?' she called, and he turned, so obviously pleased to see her she was thrilled. 'I got your letter Mrs Boundy,' he said, 'but what are you doing up here so soon?'

'Oh, I needed a holiday and I thought I'd take a look at this land.'

He laughed. 'It's not just down the road, there aren't any coaches running past. But now that you're here that's good. I'l be able to explain it all to you properly.'

She took him into the ladies' lounge, a small windowless room designed for privacy, with a few hardbacked chairs and a central table. Brass jardinières over-flowed with lilies and gum-tips, and a barman ducked his head through a hatch to take their orders.

With so much to discuss, they talked like old friends. He explained his disappearance and how he came to be out in the bush now and stumbled across this new land. Eventually their conversation came to their mutual interest.

'I have been to see a lawyer here while I was waiting to hear from you,' Katrin said. 'And he thinks our arrangement is fair. I purchase two thousand acres which you hold for me until we can register the run. He is working out the details. So if it suits you, it is fine with me.'

Pace beamed. 'That calls for another drink Mrs Boundy. Pastoralists we shall be and please call me Pace.'

Katrin smiled joyously. 'Of course and I'm Katrin.'

The morning passed quickly. 'Pace, do you intend to live out there or will you just use it as grazing land like my husband did? I sold his runs by the way and made a good profit, so that shows what can be done.'

'I'll be living out there, building my house, and never looking back.'

'It's a hard life, starting cold.'

'So it is I've already seen but it's a good start.'

'I suppose you're right. Why don't you stay and have lunch with me?'

'That would be very nice, but I must be off. I've little time to spare here and a lot to do.'

She took his arm. 'If you're worrying about money Pace, don't. I'll pay.'

'Now Katrin, that wouldn't be right.'

'Ah goodness me Pace. I can afford it. I'm doing so well I even travel with a maid these days.' It was important for her to impress him with her wealth. She wanted him to know he would be marrying money and life would be a lot easier for him. 'It wouldn't be right for a lady to be travelling on her own in these frontier towns, now would it?' she asked.

'Maybe not,' he replied.

'And you can't leave me here to eat alone.' She smiled archly at him.

He laughed and pinched her on the cheek. 'You won't be alone Katrin. You can eat with your maid. I'll be back later.'

He examined Newcastle from the wharves to the outlying farms. It was a busy place with an earnestness about it, as if everyone had a job to do and no time to waste and that pleased him. This would be his market place. Wool bales lined the wharves, and coal dust blew from open wagons. Squatters mingled with miners in the streets and few convicts were seen.

He asked about this and was told that their services were too much in demand in the mines and on the stations.

There were two banks in the town already, a good sign, a small hospital and three churches and plenty of pubs. The saleyards bustled and bulged with fat woolly sheep and there were some cattle around but not too many. He passed a butcher shop with a slaughter yard at the back and went in to find the butcher was an Irishman from Tipperary and they had a long and interesting talk, after which they adjourned to a pub to eat hot pork pies and discuss future co-operation.

When he trudged back up the main street light rain sprinkled the air, the shops were closing and taverns lighting up. At the entrance to a dance hall a spruiker was calling one and all to roll up, and an organ grinder's monkey put out his tiny hand to Pace and lifted his bellboy's cap with the other. Pace found a penny for him. He was enjoying the sights of town life again, enjoying the smiles of anticipation of the passers-by as they threw off the work day. Newcastle seemed a husky town to him, vibrant, a place for the young and the strong, and it gave him confidence. He strode into a small hotel and took a room for the night and then he went back and stood across the corner from the Globe Hotel. 'It surely is a grand place,' he said to pedestrians who were waiting to cross the road, 'lit up like a church at benediction.'

'If you go over now,' he told himself, 'they'll be sitting down to dinner and you'll be back where you started, with Katrin wanting to pay for your meal like you're the poor relation. You'd better wait awhile.'

He retired to a bar and talked to a group of timber men, burly fellows, just passing through the town on their way to set up their own logging operations and sawmills up river. There seemed to be no end to the opportunities in this country. Dan Ryan had done him a good turn after all.

It was after eight, well after eight, later than he had intended, when he returned to the Globe Hotel, pushing aside the glass doors with their etchings of white swans. The dining room, he was relieved to see, was closed and the ground floor of the residential section was deserted. A piano thumped a catchy tune from the bar as a woman came out of the office behind the small front desk. 'I'd like to see Mrs Boundy,' he said.

The woman took her time to answer, carefully locking the office door. 'I haven't seen her around. Wait on and I'll find out.' She walked around the corner and down a corridor to the kitchen and Pace heard her calling to someone. 'Ay, there, you! There's a bloke here to see your mistress.'

'She's gone to bed,' a voice called back.

'You better come out and talk to him then, I'm busy.'

He could see Katrin's maid walking towards him. He paid little attention to her until her voice jerked him out of his reverie.

'Well! As I live and die! Pace MacNamara. I thought they'd hung you by this!'

Pace stared at this girl who was standing, laughing at him. 'God Almighty! Dolour Callinan!' He stood back and looked at her again. There she was. Dolour in a black dress with a white collar looking as prim and proper as a novice, when at home she had been a holy terror. 'Don't be telling me you're the maid?'

'Lady's maid I'll have you know, MacNamara. And what can I do for you?'

'I came looking for Katrin Boundy. I have business with her.'

'You won't see her tonight. She's gone off to bed. Took her supper in her room and in a right royal rage she was too. Hurling all my good ironing into heaps. Now would you be the cause of the tantrums? What did you do to her?'

'Nothing. It doesn't matter, I'll see her in the morning. Now Dolour we can't stand here. Come in and I'll buy you a drink.'

'Not me. They've got their rules here. But I'll get my cloak and meet you at the back gate.' She tapped him on the arm like a grandmother sending a child on its way and as she walked away he remembered the skinny girl he had known at home. New South Wales had not done her any harm by the look of it, put meat on the bones and rounded her off nice and neat. Dolour Callinan, all the way from the Curragh! Last he'd heard of her she'd gone to Dublin to find work like so many others from the poor families.

They walked down one block and around another and then along the docks past the noisy waterfront taverns, treading the rough boards with the water glinting below them. Ships' bells rang the watch and men rowed ashore in dinghies, swinging lanterns, their voices echoing in the wind with the rustle and surge of the tide.

'Are you going back to Ireland when you're free?' he asked her.

'I might. I don't know.'

'Don't you miss your family?'

'Is it possible to miss people who don't miss you? To care about people who don't care about you? I don't think so.' And she found herself thinking about Jasin again. It was a pleasure to hate him now for making such a fool of her but at times he was there in her dreams, his arms around her, and she awoke confused. The hurt was deeper than she wanted to admit. Pace was talking about this farm of his and his grand plans. When he first said the name it seemed a natural part of their conversation. 'Who was that you said?'

'Heselwood. This English fellow. Cunning as a bag of monkeys he is, and I'm assigned to him but not for long. It's all a game to Heselwood but two can play so I'm not worrying about him. He's the sort of fellow who'll pull a fast one if your back is turned but you're safe enough facing him.'

'Where is he now?'

'He'd be in Sydney still I'd say. Getting ready for another drive.'

'Where's his wife?' She corrected herself. 'Has he got a wife?'

'Ah yes, she's in Sydney. Very much gentry that fine lady.'

'Will he be taking her out to the station?'

'Who, Georgina? I don't know. He doesn't confide in me. When he builds his house I suppose he'll bring her out. Her and the boy.'

The road took them back into the town and Pace stopped at his hotel. 'This is where I'm staying. Do you want to come in and have a drink?'

'I'll come in and have a glass of wine to warm me up but don't go getting any notions Pace MacNamara.'

'God forbid that I should try to take advantage of a lady's maid,' he said. 'But I've been thinking. The notion I did have was we ought to get married.'

Dolour was dumbfounded and then she pushed past him in the door. 'And don't be pulling my leg either. I'm tired. You've just about walked me down to my knees as it is.'

'I'm not pulling your leg. I'm going back to build my house. You'll have your own home. If you marry me you'll be free, emancipated. Now isn't that a nice word? It sounds more like a dance. The emancipation reel.'

They sat in a corner of the tavern and talked some more. 'It's a strange sort of courting,' Dolour observed.

'I'm sorry about that but I'm only here a few days.'

'And where does the love come in? You've said nought about that. Is it a housekeeper you're looking for?'

'Come now, you're just being stubborn. You know yourself we're half-way there already.'

At the back door of the Globe Hotel, he kissed her. 'You've kept me waiting hours Dolour, what's your answer?'

'I'll have to think about it.'

She climbed into the small bed allotted her in the maid's quarters and worried. Pace MacNamara was a good man and handsome, and he would be loving too but now she was afraid. Wasn't it always the way for her? Something always went wrong. Marriage to Pace would be perfect. She would make him a good wife but with Jasin on the doorstep it would be impossible. She was unsure of her own feelings towards Jasin and uncertain of how he would react to having her turn up as Mrs MacNamara. By the sound of things, those two men disliked one another already, not that it made any difference. If they had been best friends it would have been worse. Of course she could tell Pace about Jasin. And then she shuddered. No, never. All night long she dozed and worried and dozed again.

When Pace MacNamara arrived precisely at the business hour of nine o'clock the next morning Katrin was in a bad mood. 'Oh, you do deign to come and see me.'

'I'm sorry Katrin, I did come to see you last night but you had gone to bed. I didn't want to disturb you.'

Katrin gritted her teeth, this time angry with herself. She should have had supper downstairs and then she could have spent the evening with him. 'Well if you're ready now can we get on with our business affairs? Shall we go over to the lawyer and draw up the papers?'

'You're sure now that this investment suits you?'

'Of course I am,' she said.

'Good. I'll lodge all the details with him so that he can register the land in our names as soon as the boundaries are extended. And from what I've seen of the settlers moving west that's not too distant. They'll have to open up the Liverpool Plains and the adjacent areas soon, but we've already got our land, we've beaten the rush.'

Mr James Batterson of Batterson and Fleury agreed, and considered that five shillings an acre was a fair price for her land at this stage. He took details, as precise as Pace could supply, of both properties, so that he could register them. 'I should not make any improvements on the properties until your leases are approved,' he said. 'Sometimes, quite often in fact, settlers claim the same territory, either from ignorance or larceny. You would not want to waste your energies on land that could end up belonging to someone else. I doubt this will happen in your case Mr MacNamara since you are in a position to defend your own land against intruders. But it does happen to speculators. And I take it you will also keep a weather eye out to see that no-one tries to usurp Mrs Boundy's claim.'

'Of course. I would like to put two provisos on this contract if Mrs Boundy agrees. First, that if Mrs Boundy decides to sell her land then I should have first option to buy.'

'That's reasonable. Does it meet with your approval Mrs Boundy?'

'Yes.'

'And secondly,' Pace said, 'that I be allowed the timber-getting rights on your land Mrs Boundy.'

Katrin was uncertain. 'What would I get in return?'

'You would have your land cleared of heavy timber, I'm not sure what yet, cedar and pine I think, I haven't taken a good look at it. We wouldn't be turning it bald by any means but there's a lot of land there that has to be cleaned up for pastures anyway so it's a saving for you.'

Batterson was interested. 'Where would you market this timber? It would take a lot of hard work.'

'I'd have to hire timber-getters and bullockys but in time when more settlers come out that way they'll need timber so I was thinking I'd build a sawmill myself, and sell it locally.'

'Yes. I'll agree to that,' Katrin said. She was becoming bored with this meeting.

'Very good. Now I have to impress on both of you that when the lease is finalised you must pay the yearly rent to the Lands Office and make improvements as well as stock the runs. At the end of five years your land will be inspected and if your management of the runs is approved you will receive clear title. Is that understood?'

They both nodded.

'And also for the sake of identification in the district it is as well to name these runs which will become stations. Do you have a name in mind Mrs Boundy?'

'I hadn't thought of it. Just call mine Boundy.'

Batterson wrote the name. 'What about yours Mr MacNamara?'

Pace smiled. 'MacNamara doesn't roll off the tongue as easy as Boundy. I was thinking of calling my run Kooramin station. There are a lot of kangaroos out that way and the blacks tell me that Kooramin is their word for kangaroo.'

'We'll spell it as it sounds then,' Batterson said and spelled the word out to Pace. 'Does that sound right, with a "k" and the double "o"?'

'I think so. That's how I'd spell it too.'

The lawyer promised to have the contracts ready for them the next day, and Katrin took Pace's arm as they left the office. 'I thought we'd never get out of there. Old Batterson with his wherewiths and wherewithalls and fixing every dot and blotting every word.'

'He's careful. Better than slapdash. I think I'll go out to the saleyards now. I want to look at the cattle and get the hang of it. And I have to ask around for some good lads. By the sound of things I'll need them sooner than I thought.'

'Oh no you don't. You can do all that this afternoon. Right now I insist we celebrate. I have ordered a special meal for us with champagne and everything at the Globe. I'll bet it's a long time since you tasted champagne Pace.'

'To tell you the truth Katrin, I've never tasted champagne. But time's getting away on me. There's so much to do.'

'Don't be so difficult. We're partners now Pace. The least you can do is make a happy occasion of it.'

He thought it would be unkind to remind her that the contract was for the sale of land, not a partnership. She could sell her share the next day if she wanted to. He begrudged the time but since they would be neighbours he felt it would be churlish to refuse. Besides it would give him a chance to tell her about Dolour.

But choosing the right time was difficult. Katrin was excited, and bolstered by the champagne, began complicating the agreement. 'I think I'll come with you as far as Singleton.'

'Why would you want to do that? Pace said, surprised. 'It's only a raw village. And travel on those boats is no pleasure for a lady. They're rough and overcrowded.'

'I won't mind. I'm thinking of selling the hotel. It would be nice to live out in that country if you say it is so peaceful.'

'Katrin. In time there's nothing to stop you doing that but not now. It's too soon. What I'm doing is a gamble, any number of things can go wrong. But you've got your hotel, don't let that go. I don't want you doing anything you might regret.'

'And what about you?'

'I don't have any choice. I have to keep going in that direction.'

'But you do have a choice Pace. Why don't we join forces properly?'

For a minute he sat there stunned, hoping she wouldn't take this idea any further. But she did.

'I'll take your advice. I won't sell the hotel. I'm a wealthy woman Pace. We could be married and there would be no need for you to break your back out there in the bush. We could pay men to open up that grazing land like Boundy did, and build a house out there in our own sweet time. Come back to Sydney with me Pace. We'll buy off that Englishman.'

Pace shook his head. 'Katrin, I am sorry. You're a fine woman and any man would be proud to take you as his wife, but you belong in Sydney and in grand places like this. I belong in the country.' He tried to make light of it. 'I'm just a farm boy at heart. You wouldn't want someone like me.'

'But I do,' she whispered.

He sighed. Ah well, here it comes. 'Katrin, I have something to tell you. Something that has just happened, a strange thing. I didn't even know Dolour was here. I just met up with her last night when I came looking for you . . .'

'Who?'

'Dolour. Dolour Callinan.'

Katrin was staring at him.

'Your maid.'

Her eyes blazed. 'Are you trying to tell me you've taken up with my maid? A servant girl? Oh yes, I remember. The first night you were in Sydney you bedded with my maids. Is that all you're good for? Servants?'

Her voice grew louder. 'You tell your slut she's fired. You want her? You keep her!'

She was standing now and shouting at him and the other diners turned to watch.

'I don't think I'm worth all this fuss,' he said quietly but she snatched at her handbag, knocking over her wine glass. Pace picked it up and stood it in place again, so she took his glass and threw the champagne in his face and stormed from the room. At the door a nervous waitress took the empty glass from her as she swept past.

Pace wiped his face with a napkin and grinned. 'Dolour Callinan,' he said to the empty chair. 'You always were trouble. I should have known.'

The branches of a tree brushed against the coloured glass of the dining room windows decorating it with moving forms and figures, and old Tuatha, Dolour's grandmother, long dead, came into his mind. 'I wouldn't mind betting your gypsy hand's somewhere in all this,' he murmured.

'You did what?' Dolour cried. 'You told her? Oh you fool of a man MacNamara! You should have waited until you got her signed up. Now what'll we do?'

She slammed the kitchen door behind her and came out onto the back verandah where bushmen sat yarning in the afternoon sun and a boot-maker, nails in his mouth, tapped at a lady's shoe on a rickety bench. Washerwomen trudged past on their way to the flapping line and children dashed madly about, dipping their fingers in the drip from a wine cask and reeling around in a merry game pretending to be drunk. A barman pulled a hand-lorry past the steps. 'Ay, Miss Callinan. Your mistress is looking for you!' He grinned at her and winked at Pace. Everyone in the hotel had heard about the row in the dining room.

Pace took Dolour's arm and marched her across the yard to stand under the eaves of the stables in relative privacy. 'Now let us get a few things straight here. I don't take kindly to being called a fool. Just remember that. And if she does give you the sack I'll find another job for you and somewhere for you to live until I come back for you.'

'And when will that be?'

'I'd say about six months.'

Dolour could see the Heselwood experience happening to her all over again. Jasin had promised to come back for her. Was Pace any different? Would he too go off into the wilds and forget her?

'No,' she said. 'If you want to marry me Pace MacNamara, you take me with you or I won't be sitting waiting. You'll marry me right here in Newcastle.'

'We'll get married right enough and we'll go up river and that's where you stay, probably Singleton. But no further, it's too rough on past the Hunter. There's nothing out there.'

She knew she had allowed herself to be provoked into demanding he marry her when she had not made up her mind what to do about Jasin Heselwood. It made her anxious. It's done now, she thought. God help me.

The scullery maid put her head out of the window. 'Dolour! Your mistress is yelling for you.'

The turbulence of the day drew them closer together. Pace recalled the happiness of his first engagement and marriage, and felt sorry for Dolour, and angry that she should be deprived of those good times and the good will a young woman might expect at this time. They called on the priest, an irritable old Irishman, who insisted on the banns being posted for three weeks until Pace roared at him and had the marriage date set for the following Saturday.

Katrin had sent Dolour packing which necessitated a visit to the Police Magistrate who kept them waiting for an hour until he had time to talk to them. He was suspicious of the convict Callinan. 'I'm inclined to send you back to Sydney. You come back tomorrow and bring with you permission to marry, from Mrs Boundy. You're still assigned to her.'

Dolour's instinct was to run but Pace refused. 'We can't do that, we'd not get far. It's bad enough me travelling on a forged pass.'

'I'm not going back to her for permission. She'd never give it to me.'

'Then I'll have to see her myself,' Pace said.

'Go and beg for me?'

He smiled. 'It's little enough wouldn't you say for a man to do for his bride?'

In deference to a fellow hotelier, the owner of the Globe Hotel had instructed Dolour to vacate the staff quarters and now Pace carried her cardboard case to his hotel. 'You can have my room. I'll let Katrin cool off for today and talk to her tomorrow.'

'What about your business deal with her?' Dolour said. 'That will be off now and we're both out on our ears. What will become of us?'

'Let me do the worrying. We might go out somewhere. Would you like that?'

'Go out? Where?'

'There's a concert on down the street, we could go to that.'

Dolour was startled. She looked at him, unsure of herself. 'We could too, I suppose, but it's a strange feeling. I haven't been free to go where I please for years, me being a convict woman. It has been so hard trying to keep going. I never really understood what they've done to folk like me. Isn't that stupid?' She was crying. 'I'll get my own back one day.'

Pace put an arm around her. 'Ah now, you can forget all about that, it's over now Dolour. I won't let them take you back even if I have to hide you out in the bush under a coolabah tree.'

The appointment with Mr Batterson was for eleven in the morning and Pace was punctual. He brought Dolour's papers with him for Katrin's signature, having decided that if she failed to appear he would take them over to her at the hotel. He would not allow her to punish Dolour even if she reneged on the purchase of the land.

Mr Batterson welcomed him with small talk about the weather while he placed the contracts on the desk. 'As you see Mr MacNamara, Mrs Boundy has signed everything and the cheque is here.'

'When was this?'

'Why, she came in early this morning. Said she had to board ship for Sydney and no time to waste. But everything is in order.'

'What ship?'

'The *Rose*. Mrs Boundy sailed in the *Rose* at 10 am.'

Pace stood staring at the contracts. 'And she signed them? She still wants to go ahead with buying the land?'

'Of course, Mrs Boundy said to apologise to you for rushing off. Business, she said.'

'Did she now?' And what was to happen with Dolour? He could feel the vindictiveness of Katrin's presence in the room. She knew that Dolour was dependent on properly certified papers, without them she could be arrested.

The lawyer hovered over his desk like a pelican coming in to land, his white sideburns fluffing down to a bushy white moustache. He waited for Pace to be seated and then dropped the rest of the way into his chair. 'Is there anything wrong Mr MacNamara?'

'Mr Batterson, everywhere I turn I seem to be going wrong, so I might as well go the whole hog, I won't be signing those papers. Thank you for all your trouble. Would you send that cheque back to Mrs Boundy?'

'If that is what you wish, but it seems an extraordinary thing to do. Perhaps we should discuss it further?'

'I don't know. If you've a little time I could explain my situation from landing in Sydney. I certainly could do with some advice on the strange meanderings of the law in New South Wales.'

Three days later Mr and Mrs MacNamara boarded the schooner *Dove* for Singleton, Dolour as an emancipated convict and Pace as a parolee, no longer assigned to Jasin Heselwood but required to report his movements to a Newcastle magistrate, Mr Batterson's partner. The lawyers agreed with Pace that his conviction was illegal and promised to take steps to right the wrong. He also learned that as a convicted first offender, not a transportee, his assignment to Heselwood was also illegal. He decided it would be a fine joke not to mention this to Heselwood for the time being.

After they had sorted out his domestic problems there was the matter of his land claims. Batterson himself decided to invest in the land on the Namoi and took up the buffer zone between the Heselwood and MacNamara properties which Pace found a comforting thought.

With money in the bank and more to come when Heselwood paid him off, Pace booked a private cabin for their honeymoon voyage.

'I never knew marriage would be so easy,' Dolour said candidly. 'I thought it would be an awkward business of running about trying to please everyone.'

'It is. God forbid that I should start you off on the wrong foot.'

'Be serious. I feel as if I have been married to you for years already.'

'And has the bloom left us yet?'

Dolour shook her head. 'You're a warm lovely man, and I feel so much at home with you.'

He opened the door of the cabin. 'As me old mother used to say . . . marry the girl next door. Even when you're not speaking there's always something to talk about.'

# CHAPTER TWO

Jasin Heselwood was ready to leave Sydney at last. Georgina had refused to allow him to sell any of their furniture, including the piano, when he'd first begun his search for cash, and her foresight now gave them the basis of household effects needed for their future home on the Namoi.

When he had discovered that there was talk of Governor Darling being recalled to London, Jasin had quietly shifted his allegiance to the Colonial Secretary, feigning interest in the house Macleay was building at Elizabeth Bay. He took Georgina to visit the site, where they could examine the plans in perspective and they were astonished. Macleay had taken up fifty-four acres on the harbourside and the proposed two storied 'Grecian villa' promised to be the finest mansion in the colony.

Georgina found the design of the house, to be called Elizabeth Bay House, and the scope of the landscaping, quite breathtaking, and she lingered on chatting to Macleay while Jasin wondered how a civil servant could afford all this. He decided the Scot must be a wise investor since he was not the type to stoop to bribes, so he redoubled his efforts to make a friend of Macleay.

'When do you think the boundaries will be extended?' he asked the Secretary.

'They should have been extended by this but Governor Darling procrastinated. He has a lot of problems and his health is not good. Your run is out on the Namoi isn't it?'

'Yes, and I'm anxious to get back there.'

'I quite understand. You're very wise to keep an eye on it, settlers are moving out there all the time, jumping claims. And there's a move by the Australian Agricultural Company to claim land up towards the Gwydir River, something like 300 000 acres.'

'What? That's impossible!'

'Not at all. Henry Dangar is after several runs of that size.'

Jasin was dumbfounded, and angry with himself. He should have taken up more land. What a fool he was! 'That makes my claim look positively puny.'

'I don't think so. It is realistic. Only a syndicate could afford the legal costs and lease fees, not to mention the workforce they would need to staff such an enterprise. They usually cut up those runs into several stations operated from the head station. Keep in mind, they're a powerful company, they get what they want. And their demands will be in the best interests of other squatters in the area. For instance the Governor wanted to raise the Crown lease fees so you can be sure they'll oppose that. But there is plenty of land to the north, it is endless. When you are settled at Carlton Park you should look north again but take my advice, form a syndicate.'

'Thank you. I'll have to look into it.'

Jasin had no intentions of forming a syndicate. Why should I? he thought. I do all the work and the other investors sit pretty in Sydney. No, when Carlton Park is established I'll raise a mortgage on it and proceed north. And this time it won't be the ridiculously small run I've got now.

'I am in a quandary,' he said to Macleay, 'I have to leave Sydney and the boundaries are likely to be extended any day. I'll be the last to know.'

'Don't worry about that Jasin. When the Governor puts his signature on the proclamation, I'll register it for you. Just leave me the details before you go.'

'That's extremely kind of you, it takes a weight off my mind.' He was delighted. Who better than Macleay to handle the paperwork for him? And Macleay had solved another problem. His friend John Burnett was Commissioner of Lands in Newcastle and he assured Jasin that the Burnetts lived very comfortably in the northern village. He had elicited an invitation from Burnett to put up Georgina and Edward until the Heselwood residence at Carlton Park was built. 'I am sure all Newcastle will be delighted to have you visit their little community,' he had told Georgina.

When Georgina boarded the coastal ship with their son, Jasin teased her. 'You're becoming quite adventurous, old girl.'

'I believe we both are,' she replied. 'How long will we have to stay in Newcastle?'

'One can't say as yet but I shall take carpenters out to Carlton Park and will make the house first priority.'

To keep Milly and Dermott Forrest in good temper, he invited them to his club for dinner, knowing that would impress them.

'Georgina didn't even say goodbye,' Milly accused.

'There was no time, my dear. You know Georgina, she travels with so much luggage, and more now with the child. She had to take the first cabin available or wait for months.'

'What about our land?'

'Yes?' Jasin raised an eyebrow and Dermott coughed.

'You're building a house out there aren't you? Since Georgina is going north, you must be,' Milly said.

'Of course we are. I shouldn't expect my wife to live in a tent.'

'Is it on your land or our land? We are half shares don't forget.'

'How can I forget?' He ordered more wine. Dermott had his head down, eating as if it were his last supper but Milly chewed defiantly, poking at the

209

air with her fork. 'What if we want to build a house there?'

Dermott explained. 'She's got the idea in her head that we can afford to be station people too.'

Milly flushed, gulping down some wine. 'And why not? They say they live like kings on those stations, plenty of servants to do all the work in their big houses. I don't like Sydney anyhow, riffraff on the streets worse than London. If your brother wants to stay here, he can Dermott, Bess likes being a bootmaker's wife. I want better than that.'

'I'm sure you do,' Jasin murmured. 'But Dermott's saddlery business is doing well isn't it?'

Dermott nodded enthusiastically and Jasin distracted them from the other subject by engaging in a discussion of the various saddles used in the colony. 'I notice the stockmen use a different type of saddle from mine. They're lighter but they seem to be packed higher in the rear.'

'Yes, you come by the shop Mr Heselwood and I'll show you. We're making them now. You should have one, they're more restful for long journeys, support the back.'

Jasin kept him talking about saddles and riding boots while Milly sulked and drank more wine.

An attendant came to the table to tell Jasin a gentleman wished to see him in the small parlour and Jasin excused himself, glad to get away from them for a while.

Macleay was waiting for him with news. 'The Governor has signed the proclamation Jasin, I have registered your claim and it has been approved.'

'Jolly good, it's damn'd decent of you to let me know. A great relief, and thank you for your assistance. When we are settled you must be our first visitor, and bring your wife of course.' While he talked Jasin worried. This news was more of a shock, with his so-called partners sitting in the next room. He knew he should invite Macleay to join them but it was out of the question, so he broached the subject himself. 'I do wish you could join me for dinner but I am caught with the most tiresome people, my wife's dressmaker and her husband. You know how kindhearted Georgina is, she insisted I take them to dinner, a night out for them don't you know. But it is a fearsome experience and I'm afraid the wife is getting tipsy.'

When he returned he saw Milly was still drinking wine but was remarkably sober. 'I thought you must have left,' she snapped.

'My dear lady, I would not dream of doing such a thing but I have a lot of business interests that have to be attended to at the last minute.'

Dermott was apologetic. 'Milly, Mr Heselwood was kind enough to invite us here. Don't spoil it.'

'I'm sorry Jasin,' she said. 'I'm having a lovely time, but the thing is we would like to build a house on our land and we want to do it right away.'

Jasin lit a cigar and sat back in his chair. Did she think this was checkmate? Not by a long shot. An idea was forming that would allow him the freedom to find more land, this time of a decent size. 'I don't see why not,'

210

he said. 'As a matter of fact, Georgina would much prefer to live in Newcastle.' He would worry about Georgina's reaction later. 'But do you think you could run the station Dermott?'

Dermott gave him a small smile. 'I think we're all new at the game but as long as we get good workers I don't see why not.'

Jasin could almost hear Milly crowing and he had not missed the inference that if he could run a station so could they. He hoped they could, he was now banking on them. Milly was too clever, bullying her way into the show, now they would have to build the house, not him; and later, well, it was Heselwood land, house or no house. 'If you manage Carlton Park then, it will give me a chance to attend to my other business affairs.'

'Carlton Park? Is that what it's called?' Milly said. 'Oh I like that! What a good choice of name.' She was excited now.

'At the end of the year we share profits of course,' Jasin told them, 'fifty-fifty, which is more in your favour since you will be able to live off the property. You'll only need to buy a few basics.'

'That's very generous of you Mister Heselwood,' Dermott said, astonished at their sudden good fortune.

'It's what we always wanted,' Milly said, breathless.

'Well Dermott, I am leaving on the morrow. If I were you I should make your way out west as soon as possible. You had better see if you can find some workmen to take with you, preferably convicts, but investigate them carefully. We don't want any thieves or murderers.'

'I'll attend to that,' Dermott said.

'Good. Bring them on to Bathurst and I'll meet you there, but you'll have to get moving. We'll be taking another herd north so I don't want to delay.'

'I'm coming too,' Milly said and Jasin laughed. 'I hardly think so. It is hard riding and we have to camp out. It is very rough out there.'

'I'm coming,' she said.

Jasin had planted Georgina in Newcastle but Dermott was no match for Milly.

'Other women have gone out to the west. If they can do it so can I,' she insisted.

'By all means,' Jasin said. He was tired of arguing with this woman. What did it matter? If she found the journey arduous, it was by her own choice. He rather hoped she would; serve her right.

As he waved their carriage off Jasin considered going to the gaming room but lately he had found little spice in cards. The stakes were bigger and the game more exciting on the frontiers of the colony. He would push on to that country they called the Darling Downs. He had heard it was magnificent pasture land with plenty of water.

And then there was the other interesting piece of information. Left to himself he had taken the Rose Hill packet up river to Parramatta and called at the Female Factory to enquire after Dolour Callinan. He had intended giving a false name but no-one enquired as to his identity. He discovered she had been assigned to a Mrs Boundy, the licensee of the Nelson Hotel in Sydney.

Now, with Georgina out of the way he could go to see Dolour, and at a loose end, with only one night left to spend in Sydney, why not? He could easily explain why he had not been able to come for her. She would understand. If not, it did not really matter. It was just a whim, he had a bit of the devil in him tonight, she would never turn him away. And at the thought of her his whole body tingled, she was surely the most passionate woman he had ever bedded. He was sorry now that he had not called on her sooner; perhaps he could stay on in Sydney for a few days to spend more time with her.

The hotel was still open but there was a sombre note in the bar, replacing the usual raucous tone of these places. Men muttered and gossiped in tight groups. He ordered a brandy and walked down to a quiet corner where he felt less conspicuous among the workmen.

A scrawny old man served him, spilling the drink and mopping at it with a grubby cloth. 'Sorry sir. I'm not too good at this. Not my job, you understand. I'm only helping out here tonight. We're all at sixes and sevens, it's the murder you see.'

Jasin jerked to attention. 'A murder you say? Who?'

'Why Mrs Boundy. On her way to the bank with the takings she was. I always said she shouldn't go the short cut, down those back alleys, but you couldn't tell her. And her just back from her nice holiday. Bashed and robbed she was and left to die in the street like a dog. That's her brother over there talking to the police.'

Jasin realised the police were interrogating the customers and had no wish to become involved. As soon as the garrulous barman moved on he swallowed his drink and slipped out the side door. Some other time he would call on Dolour Callinan.

# CHAPTER THREE

Dolour had persuaded Pace to let her travel with him as far as Singleton but he refused to allow her to go any further. 'This is a poor enough place for a woman to be living.'

'Ah but you're seeing it in the wrong light altogether MacNamara. If you look about you it's a pretty place with the woods and the stream and there are plenty of other women around.' She watched a convoy of wagons leaving the town laden with household goods, the women striding along beside them and children sitting atop, and her face darkened. 'If they can go, why can't I?'

'Because they've got nowhere else to go.'

'Is there nothing at all past here?'

'I've told you a dozen times woman, there are no towns, only a few store-houses and inns. We would pass through stations but they don't take in boarders.'

'Then I'll get a job on one of them and I'll be close to you.'

'My wife will not work for any of them. You have to let me go and sort things out with Heselwood.'

At the mention of Jasin's name, Dolour shuddered and she realised she was now mortally afraid of him, afraid he would spoil everything with Pace. As Pace had predicted, the love had come easily and she adored him, but it was hard to tell him so, besides his head was filled up with all this complicated talk of land and cattle. He was a great one for ferreting around the place talking to people and finding out what was going on and he met a fellow who had been prospecting for gold.

'A fool's game if ever there was one,' she said.

'He doesn't think so but since he hasn't dug up his fortune here he's off to America to start digging again.'

'The silly man!'

'I'll thank you not to be telling him that because I've just bought his house and I don't want him asking for it back.'

'You bought a house? Our own house? What did you pay for it?'

'Fifteen pounds, a bargain! I wrote him a please-pay letter to give to the bank in Newcastle. He wasn't too keen on that, he examined the paper like it was gold and I thought he was studying the writing but it seems some of the swindlers have learned a new trick. They cook the paper so that by the time the owner presents his IOU to the bank it has crumbled into nothingness; but mine passed inspection.'

They ran like urchins through the street that ended abruptly in bush and followed a track a hundred yards further on to the prospector's house. Dolour walked around the house with a keen eye. 'What about water?'

'I suppose he brought his water up from the creek.'

'The lazy old villain, he should have sunk a well and put in a tank for rainwater.' Inside she scratched her legs. 'He had plenty of company here with the fleas.'

'If you don't like it I can easily sell it again and make a profit.'

Dolour was shocked. 'You'll do no such thing.'

'If there's so much to complain about . . .'

'I'm not complaining. I said he was lazy. Look, not a sod turned around the house!'

They walked into the bush searching for the surveyor's pegs and Dolour hugged him. 'Is this all ours? A half an acre did you say?'

'All yours Mrs MacNamara but it's nothing. I keep telling you we've got thousands of acres out west.'

'I don't care about that. You couldn't see all that land, I can see this, it's real.' They stayed until dusk and went back to their shanty room at the back of the tavern.

'It's the best surprise of my life,' she said, 'and I'll clean it up and make it a home.'

'I had to do something,' Pace explained. 'I couldn't leave you here at the tavern, my darling and the only other course seemed to be a back room in someone else's house . . .'

'Or take me with you?'

'That was beginning to be a possibility,' he said, 'but now I'll leave you money and here's your chance to show off. I haven't time to dig a well. I'll send someone to put a water tank in for you and when I come back there will be my wife under an arbour of roses.'

Pace was determined to keep the mood light because he planned to leave in a few days. It was his misfortune to be parted from his wife so soon, but it had to be. He had bought her a gun for protection against snakes and taught her to shoot.

On the morning he rode out, leading a packhorse, he felt guilty at leaving her but when he crossed the river, heading north, there was that surge of excitement at being on his way. As the horse cantered down the road, he realised he was looking forward to the wide open country again.

With well-worn tracks to follow he made good time and detoured to Chelmsford station to repay Andy his four pounds. A station hand directed him to the stables where he found not Andy, but Rivadavia himself in one of the stalls administering to a sick horse.

'What's the matter with him?' Pace asked.

Rivadavia, surprised to see the visitor, answered civilly. 'Swamp fever.'

The horse lay sweating in the straw and Rivadavia worked gently sponging him and wiping the mucus from the dull eyes.

'Ah the poor feller,' Pace said and went back to his saddlebag where he kept sugar lumps for his own horse. He took some sugar into the stall and knelt beside the sick horse, stroking its head. 'Here's a little bit of sugar for you now and more when you get better.'

The horse sighed and took the sugar in his lips.

'They get depressed when they're sick,' Pace said.

'He was bad last night but I think he's a bit better today.' Rivadavia prepared to leave the stall.

'Get someone to stay with him. When they're sick they get frightened and lonely,' Pace said.

Rivadavia stared at him. 'Have you come here to tell me my business again?'

'I have not. I was thinking I was a bit hard on you and maybe we should start again on the right foot.'

Rivadavia seemed uninterested, rolling down his sleeves and buttoning them at the wrists.

Pace persisted. 'I'm not too good at apologising and by the sound of things neither are you. But I'd come a long way to see Mrs Brooks and a tiger snake would have got a better welcome.'

They watched some black children playing with two puppies at the door of a shed.

'Would you like coffee?' Rivadavia asked, and Pace nodded.

Rivadavia called to the tallest of the back boys who came running, pleased to be chosen. 'You go in and sit with the sick horse. He's lonely.' As the boy went to dash away, Juan grabbed him. 'Don't run, go quietly, you'll frighten him.'

'You have a sheepwalk?' he asked Pace.

'A run so far, but I'm for cattle.'

'Ah! That's what I intend to do. I'll keep this place as my home and I can use it for a depot for cattle passing through. Where is your run?'

'On the Namoi.'

'And I have taken up some land on the Peel River.'

Pace stayed overnight enjoying the company of the young Argentinian and appreciating that he had at last found someone with an expert knowledge of cattle.

He arrived back at Heselwood's station long before his employer, and Clarrie and Snow were pleased to see him and hear all the news. They sat over the campfire late into the night yarning with him.

'If you're legally free, why did you come back?' Clarrie asked.

'I promised I would, and to be fair, he did get me out of jail. And then I'm doing an apprenticeship here with you lads, getting the hang of it. You've been busy yourselves by the look of things.'

'Just filling in time,' Snow said. 'The blacks brought us all the bark we needed and gave us a hand to build the bunkhouse. We made it longer than

215

usual so we could partition off one end for the boss. And I'll tell you what we did find, limestone in the low hills down there so we'll be able to make a proper chimney for the cookhouse.'

The resourcefulness of these two men impressed Pace once again, and the next morning they were up at dawn splitting logs for the never-ending fences before they rode out to check on the calves, keeping the count of the cattle in their heads.

Leaving Snow at the camp Clarrie took him bull-herding, warning him to stay out of the way and watch until he got the hang of it. The old bushman rode after a stray bull at a frightening rate dodging through the rough scrub, twisting and turning with the bull until he turned it around and drove it out into the open to rejoin the herd.

'Stubborn old bugger that one,' Snow grinned when Pace caught up with him.

'So are you,' Pace said. 'I thought you'd break your neck! That was fancy riding!'

'No. All I've got to do is stay on. The horse knows what he's doing. Get to know your own bush so you don't run into any thick stuff or knock your head off on an overhanging tree. The old bulls'll run you right at them if they can, but you've got four eyes watching and he's only got two.'

Two months later Jasin Heselwood rode in with his men and two wagons and far in the distance a high cloud of dust signalled the arrival of another herd of cattle.

Pace stared as the wagons rolled up to the gate. There was a woman on board! He walked down to greet them and saw the woman was Milly Forrest being assisted from the wagon by her husband Dermott. Milly looked tired and dusty and her long skirt was bordered with dried mud.

'Am I seeing things?' he cried, 'It's you Dermott, and Milly! What are you doing out here in the back of beyond?'

'We've come here to live,' Dermott said in his shy voice but Milly bounced past him to embrace Pace. 'How pleased we are to see you Pace!' And then she whispered. 'He didn't tell us you were here until we were half-way out.'

'That'd be right,' Pace grinned. 'But for you to make such a journey Milly, you must be worn out, girl.'

'I could drop right here on the spot,' she whispered again, 'but he didn't want me to come, so don't let on.' She nodded at Heselwood who had ridden on to talk to Snow and Clarrie.

'Well come now and sit down, and we'll find you some tea.'

Still mystified he escorted them up to the bunkhouse and Clarrie called him aside. 'What's a woman doing out here?'

'Don't ask me,' Pace said. 'But they're people I know from the ship.'

'Then there goes the boss's room,' Clarrie grinned. 'We'll have to give it to the marrieds. He'll have to bunk in with us or stay in his own tent.'

216

The bunkhouse the men had built had no furniture but even then Milly didn't complain. 'We've brought some furniture with us,' she said, 'not much, a bed and a table, that will do for a start. Dermott is a very good carpenter.'

Pace shook his head and waited for a chance to talk to Dermott who explained that they were Heselwood's partners.

'You could have knocked me down with a feather,' he told Clarrie afterwards. 'And if my wife finds out there's a woman here and she got left behind there'll be hell to pay.'

Heselwood's drovers were staying on as stockmen and the other men accompanying the wagons had been employed by Dermott to build the house so there was a surge of activity as they all began the real work of establishing the station. Snow took over the cooking and Milly attached herself to him and since she did as she was told he approved.

'She's a bold little thing,' he told Pace. 'I reckon she's got more gumption than her old man.'

Both Milly and Dermott were shocked to hear of Adelaide's death. Pace told them it was from heart trouble.

He saw Heselwood watching and waited for him to ask, 'How do you know all this Pace?'

'She sent for me and I went down there.'

'Who gave you permission to leave here might I ask?'

'I did. And what did you find out about clearing me?'

'It's not possible at this stage.'

'You're a bloody liar. I found out for myself that you haven't got anything to hold me with.'

'So you've been minding everyone else's business but mine?'

'You'll find no complaints about this place.'

'I suppose you'll be leaving now?'

'No point in leaving empty-handed,' Pace said. 'You've got some cattle ready for market. For two pounds each Clarrie and Snow and me will drive them down for you.'

'Two pound each? Not a chance!'

'Then drive them back yourself. These other fellers are needed here.'

'I'll think about it,' Jasin said.

'While you're thinking about it think of twenty pounds each for our pay as well.'

'Clarrie and Snow didn't want any pay. They agreed to come for their keep.'

'Look around you, you mean bugger, they've done the work of ten men.'

'You were engaged as a convict, you can't expect pay.'

'It's all or nothing. You pay us or we leave and you get your own cattle in.'

The next day Jasin agreed to the arrangements as Pace knew he would. 'Twenty-two pounds each and no more.'

217

Dermott was sorry to see Pace go. 'I had hoped you would stay. It is nice to have a friend to rely on. Stay with us, you'd be one of the family.'

'Keep it to yourself Dermott,' Pace said, 'but I've got a place of my own north of here so I'll be back.' He still wondered why Heselwood was allowing the Forrests to take over the run. He could remember Jasin's excitement when he had first marked out his boundaries, and his talk about building his house here. It was a lovely station. Why would he leave it to them? There must be something better on the horizon.

'Where are the roses?' Pace called as he tramped across the small verandah. At the sound of his voice his wife came flying out to greet him.

'Ah you silly man I have to grow them not create them,' she said, reaching up to kiss him. 'Look at that beard! You look like a wild man.'

'I feel like it too. It was a hard drive back, the rivers were up and the trails bogged and it never stopped raining.' He put an arm around her and took her inside. 'I'm looking forward to a dry bed and some company.'

Dolour ran inside, ahead of him. 'What do you think of the house? Does it look better? Are you staying now? Oh Pace, it's so wonderful to see you and look at me all of a mess. Are you hungry?'

'Whoa now.' He kissed her again. 'You'll always look beautiful to me. And the house looks very grand, with curtains and all.' He walked through to the back step and pulled off his boots, laughing. 'One of our neighbours out there, old McPhie, has got a troop of sons, and the eldest fellow brings home a wife. And she makes some curtains and puts them up in the homestead and her mother-in-law, Mrs McPhie, who scares off the crows by just standing there, pulled them all down and ripped them up. She said they keep out the light.' He looked up at her with a twinkle in his eyes. 'But yours can stay up.'

'Oh you're a tease MacNamara. Are you staying now?'

'For a while. We had some luck. We were supposed to take the cattle right on to Bathurst but Heselwood got his price and sold them here.'

Her heart skipped a beat at the mention of that name and she hurried to change the subject. 'I got some work cooking at the inn. They couldn't pay me but they gave me things for the house, some chairs and some bed linen that I patched up, and I collected all the feathers from their chooks and made us a feather-down mattress and all sorts of things. Come and see, Pace.'

He walked through the little house with her, pleased at the transformation. 'It's as clean as new,' she said proudly, 'and I've dug a vegetable garden out the back and flower garden in front.'

She so desperately wanted to please him he was touched. 'I wouldn't have known it was the same place. You've done a grand job of it, I'm proud of you. We'll get a good price for it now.'

'What do you mean? This is our house! We're not going to sell it?'

'Dolour, the boundaries have been extended. By this Mr Batterson

218

would have registered Kooramin Station in my name. It's time to claim our land. I thought you'd be wanting to come with me?'

'Of course I want to come with you, but it seems such a shame to sell this, I've grown fond of it.'

'We need the money,' he said simply, 'but we won't be leaving for a while yet. I'll have to go back to Bathurst again and buy cattle.'

'Why can't you buy them here?'

'Because the only cattle they sell here are those ready for slaughter. You can enjoy your house for a little while longer, then when I come back we'll be on our way. And before you say anything, I have to tell you there's a woman out at Heselwood's station.'

'Who? His wife?'

'No. Milly Forrest, with her husband.'

'Who are they?'

'Heselwood's partners, but I knew them on the ship. It's a long story, I'll tell you later. Right now I need a good wash and that meal you promised me and time with my wife.'

# CHAPTER FOUR

Georgina felt stifled in Newcastle. She had come from the loneliness of the Cormack mansion to the madhouse that was the Burnett household, with dogs and cats and screaming children running everywhere, and an endless stream of visitors who wanted to meet her, forcing her to sit for hours at tea, day after day. It left her exhausted, and the dinner parties were not much better.

Her son, Edward, kept her occupied, she took him for long walks to get away from them all, wondering about mothers who claimed it was essential to have a nursemaid. She was sure she would have gone mad without Edward for company, and wondered if she were becoming too colonial, finding it was not necessary to keep to the conventions. In England she would never have dared to try to bring up a child without a nurse, but from her own experiences she now believed the nurse got the better part of the deal. She adored her son and hated to have him out of her sight, she had never dreamed a child could be so absorbing.

When at last Heselwood came to Newcastle from Carlton Park she was shattered at the news that he had allowed the Forrests to take over their station. 'I have been sitting in this lunatic establishment for months, waiting to get away and you tell me that upstart woman is living on our property! This is too much Heselwood! I shall book passage and return to my mother's house until such time as you make up your mind where we shall live.'

'You talk as if it were my fault,' he said angrily. 'I had no idea that pair would fasten themselves onto us like leeches. But madam, if you insist, I shall build you a house at Carlton Park forthwith. There is plenty of room. And you will have them right smack on your doorstep for eternity.'

'Or I can return to London,' she reminded him.

'Listen Georgina. I shall leave them to run Carlton Park and take on more land up north. Right away. I have heard talk of magnificent country only a few hundred miles further on, even better than our own land, and once again, there for the taking, and this time I won't be so delicate about it. We'll have a really big station.'

'We already have Jasin. You seem absolutely determined to build our house as far away as possible from civilisation. I do not intend to be a recluse.'

'And you will not be. There are rumours that the convict settlement in

220

Moreton Bay will be opened up as a port in few years. That will cause a stampede for the good grazing land which is at a place called the Darling Downs, named after the departed Governor. We shall have stolen a march on them.'

'But what about Carlton Park?'

'Carlton Park belongs to us, but if the Forrests want to work there and share the profits with us then why should we complain? That Milly person is quite determined to be a squatter's wife, thinking it will push her up the social ladder. She is living out there in squalor waiting for her husband to build a house around her.'

'She must be mad!'

'Well, of course she is. I tried to explain to her that a lady would not expect to go near the place until her house was ready but not her, you can't tell her a thing. Georgina, just give me a year. That's all I ask. By that time I will have the new station and will have built a decent house, and have a good income. We will then own two properties and be set for life.'

Georgina was still dubious. She walked over and looked down at Edward who was sleeping soundly in his cot.

'Think of the boy,' Jasin said. 'Think of all the land he will inherit. By the time he grows up these two cattle stations will be worth a fortune.'

'That doesn't alter the fact that Edward and I do not have anywhere to live at present. I told you we will not remain here.'

'You don't have to. I shall find a house for rental. You can get your own furniture and take up residence here in Newcastle where you know people, until our house it built. That is all I can offer. Will you give me just that one year?'

'It depends on what house you find to rent I would suppose,' she said, but her answer was not promising.

Neither was the choice of accommodation in Newcastle; the few houses Jasin could find were hovels. He gave up and went out to the saleyards, which were always busy, to look over the stock and talk to other cattlemen who were few and far between in the district since most of the stations ran sheep. It was essential to keep in touch with them, not the least to keep informed on the available bloodlines. He needed to buy bulls for his next herd and the cattlemen would give him an indication of what he should expect to pay for the best stud animals. He was finding a camaraderie with these men that he had never experienced before, and he knew that he had earned their respect by his own physical efforts, which would have surprised his father. He shared the old man's grief for his brother Edward who had died at Christmas in the bitter English winter, but with Harrald coursing around Europe looking for a war Jasin felt it was high time the Earl was shown what his third son could do. He had intended inviting his parents to visit Carlton Park when they settled there but that plan would have to be postponed. How much better to show them two estates as big as English counties.

221

He was enjoying conversations with John Appleby and his sons, cattlemen with a big spread on the Goulburn River, sipping brandy from silver flasks which seemed to be standard equipment for these occasions, when he saw Rivadavia. He could not help seeing Rivadavia, who, he thought, looked as if he were going to a fancy dress party in his black riding habit and that impossible mile-wide hat decked in silver. He turned slowly away to avoid the necessity of speaking to him but Appleby was already claiming the fellow. 'I say, Rivadavia! Juan! Over here!' and his sons were all smiles as he approached, as if he were some potentate.

'Juan, what good fortune meeting you here! Might I introduce the Honourable Jasin Heselwood?'

'We've met sir.' Juan seemed pleased to see him and Jasin was placated. If Appleby accepted the Argentinian then he supposed he could; come to think of it Horton's station was rather impressive. He had not mentioned to Rivadavia that his original plan had been to manage Chelmsford and the thought of that plan annoyed him now. He realised that the Macarthurs had been right. How much easier his life would have been if he had been able to take over that station – a home for Georgina and the boy, with time to search out his own runs and a steady income. He envied Rivadavia and was reminded of Vicky Horton who had married old Sir Percy and gone to England. Well, good luck to her; she would hate England and be quite out of place in that family.

'And how is Mrs Heselwood?' Juan asked.

'Extremely well thank you. I had quite forgotten you had met,' Jasin said, deciding not to remark on his extraordinary visit to the Cormack house, since Georgina liked him. 'She is in Newcastle at present.'

'Your wife is here?' Appleby was surprised. 'Well you must bring her out to the station, my wife would be delighted to receive you.'

'I shall,' Jasin said, 'but I am preparing to go north just now.'

'Where are you going?' Juan was interested, and Jasin considered whether or not he should tell them, but there seemed little choice. 'The Darling Downs I believe they call it.'

'Oh well done,' Appleby said. 'I've never met anyone who has been there but its reputation is preceding it. Good country I'm told.'

'It's very high country,' Juan said. 'I hear it is rather difficult to approach.'

'How could a Downs be high?' Jasin laughed.

But Juan was serious. 'I have met bushmen who have seen that high plateau in the distance, but have never approached it. Though the explorers' maps show that it is good land with fine rivers. If you can get to it, you should find excellent cattle country.'

'I'm pleased to hear that,' Jasin said, reminding himself to have a talk with Burnett about the approach. He would need good maps.

'I wouldn't mind coming with you,' young Arthur Appleby said shyly. 'Do you reckon I could come along?'

Jasin was taken aback but he looked at Arthur who was about twenty, and strong.

'I'd work my way Mr Heselwood. I wouldn't be a burden,' the young man said.

'Well if your father agrees?'

Appleby beamed. 'My word! There's an opportunity for you boy. Get to see what's up north. If you're sure you want him, by all means Jasin.'

Arthur was thrilled. 'When do we leave?'

Jasin laughed. 'Not for a while yet. I didn't feel up to another trek down to Bathurst so I put a cattle buyer on the job. He's bringing a herd up as far as Singleton. I'll pick them up there. But I'll let you know well in advance Arthur, and you might keep your eye out for some stockmen to come with us. I can't see much point in making two trips.'

The group moved across the yards to watch the auctions and Jasin remembered he still had to face Georgina with his failure to find a house. She would be very put out and start that nonsense about going back to England again. He saw Rivadavia deep in conversation with Appleby about the merits of the few cattle that were for sale and smiled. Of course! Georgina liked the fellow. Perhaps he could head her off for today. He tapped Rivadavia on the shoulder. 'Juan. If you have no other plans would you care to come back with me? I'm sure Georgina would be pleased to see you again.'

As they rode back into town Jasin complained that he was having trouble finding decent accommodation in Newcastle. 'Georgina finds it tiresome living under someone else's roof no matter how kind they are. I begged her to stay on in Sydney where she was perfectly comfortable but she insisted on coming up here and I think she is regretting it now.'

'I have bought a house here,' Juan said. 'It was the homestead of the big sheep station that belonged to the Matsons. The station was broken up into smaller sections but the house is very solid with a view to the ocean. I always wanted a summer house by the sea and it was too good to miss.'

Jasin was sorry that he had mentioned the matter now. Juan's answer annoyed him, the fellow seemed to have more money than he knew what to do with. 'How nice for you,' he commented.

'You would be welcome to it.'

'I beg your pardon?' Jasin said.

Juan was quick to explain. 'I will not be occupying it for some time. But you may inspect it and if you find it suitable then I would be pleased to have someone living there. There would, of course, be no rent or anything of the sort.'

Jasin was astonished. He could hardly believe the offer. 'My dear fellow, that's generous of you. I shall be in your debt again, but of course it would be up to Georgina.'

He prayed that this house was suitable. Georgina was in no mood to be put to more discomfort. He felt better now that he had something to offer

223

her and rode cheerfully in the gate with his Argentinian guest.

The grooms in the stables were subdued and Georgina herself came out the back of the house to meet them, kissing Jasin gently, which he thought was rather odd of her, and greeting Rivadavia with the barest enthusiasm. She deposited their guest in the parlour, since the Burnett family seemed to have disappeared altogether.

'Would you excuse us a minute?' she asked Juan, and led Jasin outside to the garden.

'What is going on Georgina?' he cried. 'It's hardly the way to greet him and I have some good news for you.'

'I will apologise to him Jasin but I have bad news. A letter from your mother. It is very distressing so brace yourself. My dear, your brother Harrald was killed in battle fighting the Turks.'

Jasin staggered. 'Oh my God! Harrald! Poor Harrald. Are all the Heselwood sons doomed? What was he doing there anyway?'

'Your mother said he was fighting on the side of the Greeks. She sounds very bitter about it, "a fashionable war",' she said.'

'Ah my poor mother, first Edward and now Harrald. How is my father taking it? The bloody fool encouraged Harrald in that madness, the glory of war! I blame him for Harrald's death. Well now he's stuck with me! And he'd never even give me a kind smile!'

There were tears in his eyes. Georgina knew Jasin had been fond of Harrald, who had always been so full of fun. Edward had been different, pleasant but aloof and always rather sickly; that he had succumbed to consumption had not surprised her.

'Do you think you should rest Jasin?'

He heaved a sigh. 'I don't know what to do. But I don't want to see anyone at the moment. I might go to the room and write to my parents. So now I am the heir. I'm the one to inherit the title, but by the look of things he'll outlive all his sons.' His voice held a strong note of bitterness.

'I don't think so,' Georgina whispered, 'when the Earl heard the news he had a stroke, he's recovering but he's frail.'

'Oh Jesus!' He turned away from her and walked down a path, seeming to be trying to get his breath.

Georgina followed him. 'Jasin, do you think we should return to England?'

'We should,' he said, looking distraught, 'but if we go we are ruined. I won't be able to pay the banks and all my work will have been for nought. No, old dear, we're just going to have to stick it out here. I have the opportunity within my grasp to establish great estates in New South Wales and I cannot stop now. The old boy will pull around! I'll write to Mother. Oh my God, I forgot about the Spaniard. Would you go and talk to him? He's got a house for us.'

'A house, where?'

'If you don't mind, I'm not up to discussing it right now.'

224

When Georgina returned to the parlour she saw that Mr Rivadavia was still standing. They had not invited him to sit. She smiled, he did have impeccable manners, a change in this rough community.

Georgina had never seen Jasin so depressed.

Some days later she asked Juan Rivadavia to take her out to see the house. Jasin was immobilised by shock and possessed by a fear that his own death was imminent. Juan was as usual very polite. He seemed to have a natural tact for which she was grateful.

When the carriage took them up a weed-covered drive her heart sank, the old house looked windswept and decrepit.

'Don't judge it yet,' Juan said. 'Come and see the view.' And from the wide verandah they stood looking out to sea. 'You can see ships passing by and whales. It is never dull looking at the sea.'

'Yes I know. But I don't think the house would be suitable, really Juan.'

His face lit up in a wide smile. 'But that is why I am so pleased you came to see it. Tell me, what would you do to restore it?'

She looked around her wondering where to start. 'Well, I don't know. I've never done this sort of thing.'

'Try.' His eyes were on a level with hers and as he looked at her she felt encouraged. It was not a challenge, it was as if he were offering her support, and friendship.

'I wouldn't presume.' Then she smiled. 'I have a feeling Juan that you could do a far better job of it than me.'

'But it would lack the woman's touch. I am making my house at Chelmsford to my tastes and there I see myself copying my mother's ideas. This is very different from a hacienda, this is a summer place, not a country house.' He waited. 'Come now, you have been to English summer houses, I have not. What would you do?'

She tried. 'Well they don't have these wide verandahs but I rather like them for shade.'

'Good, the verandahs stay.' He opened the creaking front door.

They spent the afternoon walking through the musty house, discussing its good points and its bad points. The timber floors were of excellent quality and the high ceilings gave it an air of spaciousness. 'I don't like those dark panelled walls in a seaside house,' she ventured.

'We'll throw out the panelled walls,' he said, and they went down to the kitchen, an ugly stone room under the house.

'It must be freezing down here in winter,' he said.

Georgina added, 'And look, they have to go outside to bring up the food. It would be cold before it got to the table.'

'Or rained on,' Juan laughed, wandering further into the maze of rooms. 'The furnishings are hideous. I think we should throw it all out and start again. I'm fortunate you are here to assist me.'

Georgina coloured. His use of 'we' embarrassed her a little.

They walked outside again.

225

'Gardeners will clean up out here,' he said. 'So don't worry about the grounds. There's even a bush walk down to the seashore but you can see that another time Mrs Heselwood. I should be very grateful if you could supervise the renovations for me.'

He had asked her to address him by his Christian name, which in view of his age seemed appropriate but Georgina was relieved that he had the grace to stick to her married title. He was extraordinarily attractive and everything about him gleamed, even to his buffed fingernails, a fastidious person. She appreciated that but she still felt nervous with him. It was difficult to put aside thoughts of Adelaide, of them together, as lovers; the thoughts lingered like the perfume of an exotic flower almost revealing the shape of the bloom which she did not want to see.

'I should be delighted,' she said. 'It will give me something to do while Jasin is away.' Georgina noted another change in herself. Before she came to this country she had never thought of having or wanting something to do. Something constructive that is. And she was even looking forward to it.

'Would you still wish to live here when it is convenient?'

'We should be most grateful. Thank you.'

He whistled to the carriage driver which she found amusing, and as he helped her inside she felt a warmth at his touch and she understood what had attracted poor Adelaide.

'Tell the tradesmen to send their accounts to my bank,' Juan was saying. 'I am very excited about this house now, I think it will be the best house in Newcastle.'

Georgina agreed, thinking ruefully that money could work wonders. She hoped that by the time they came to building their own house in the north, they would have the cash to build something half as good. She already knew that tradesmen in this country would not work on account, and worried that her husband had not really grasped some of the facts of life in the colony as she had.

Juan seemed to be absorbed in his own thoughts again and she was thinking of Edward. She remembered Juan's child and decided to comment. The subject could hardly be kept under the mat forever.

'Edward will be wondering where his mother has got to,' she said. 'I believe you have a daughter Juan?'

'Yes. Dell's daughter,' he said candidly. 'You knew Dell?'

'Yes we did. She was a very sweet lady. But by the time I heard of her passing, well, you know, I was the last to hear,' she said lamely.

'That's all right,' he said. 'You know I loved Dell, but she didn't love me enough to marry me.'

Georgina didn't want to delve into his relationships but she felt it would be discourteous not to appear interested.

'I'm so sorry to hear that.'

Juan continued, sadness in his black eyes. 'Her friend Pace MacNamara accused me of making her unhappy by not marrying her, especially as she was carrying my child, but he didn't understand.' He looked at Georgina, choosing his words. 'You see Adelaide was ashamed of us. She wanted to be married for the piece of paper. She loved me, but she didn't want to be seen with me. I was too young and I am not English. She would never come into town with me or visit other stations, she was only happy on our station among the people who she thought didn't count. And it is true, all the time she talked of marriage, but she didn't love me enough. I knew the marriage paper wouldn't make any difference. She would always have compared me in company to her professor husband who was not different like me. There was love, beautiful love, but in her heart Dell never really accepted me and I could not permit that.'

'I am so sorry,' Georgina said again, careful not to utter a word that might sound patronising, or critical of either of them.

Then he cheered up. 'But my daughter, Rosa, is beautiful. I will bring her in to meet you one day and we will buy her some fine clothes. She is well cared for on the station, everyone loves her.'

With Georgina busy restoring the Argentinian's house, Jasin found himself at a loose end. Burnett was away at his office all day which left him, as he told Georgina, 'like a piece of furniture to be shifted every time they clean or sweep.' He urged her to get on with it so they could move in and have some privacy. On the one occasion he had visited the place walls had been torn down and clouds of dust misted the rooms and outside the men clearing the grounds and had been burning off. The smell of the burning leaves had reminded him of the back country where there was always smoke drifting in the air towards the end of summer, sweet-smelling fumes from burning eucalypt trees that lingered for weeks after the fires and travelled on the wind.

One of the first things Macarthur's two old fellows, Clarrie and Snow, had done out at Carlton Park was to set fire to a large stretch of pasture land. The stockmen had seemed unconcerned but both he and MacNamara had been surprised and nervous.

Clarrie had laughed. 'We're just burning off this old sour grass so good sweet pastures will have a chance to grow. The blacks do it all the time, they taught us. Fire cleans out the rubbish, this country thrives on it. But you have to be careful when Nature takes a hand. You mind out you haven't got a house in her road, or crops, or they'll all go up. Clear a firebreak well away from the homestead when you build her.'

Jasin remembered that advice and wondered if someone had told Dermott Forrest. He would go out and inspect the place as soon as possible, but then that was a good way off, there were other things to do first.

There were no clubs in Newcastle and only one hotel that aspired to a fairly decent standard but it was the haunt of sheepmen who regarded cattle men as intruders. He found their attitude incredibly stupid since they were growing wool not meat, and both were needed. But he realised he stood to benefit from their hostility towards cattle. It would keep cattle numbers down and keep prices up.

The days dragged and he was tense and nervous. He brooded on his brother's death and the bad luck that seemed to be dogging his family. But he couldn't make any arrangements for his expedition to the north until his cattle arrived. He wanted to see for himself what the cattle buyer, Slater, had bought for him before any payment was made. Then he would take them north in more or less the same manner that he had done before, except this time he would start them on the road and go ahead non-stop with Arthur Appleby and a few other fellows until they reached the Darling Downs.

When the cattle were due at Singleton he was relieved to have an excuse to leave Newcastle. 'I won't be away long this time,' he told Georgina. 'I have to check the cattle and see that they pass the inspection point and find somewhere to park them and then I'll be back to gather up men and equipment for the trek.' He was looking forward to the journey north. Arthur had enlisted some friends of his to come with them for the adventure into unknown country and they could assist him in the surveying. This time there would not be the tensions of the first trip. He knew the stockmen could be relied upon to do their jobs quite well without him.

It was a cold and miserable ride out through Maitland and he stayed overnight in the town hoping the rain would ease but a new storm blustered in and he passed wagons floundering in the mud as his horse plodded on.

His heavy cloak was soaked as he dismounted at the trooper station, the fount of all information in the Singleton district.

The sergeant was pleased to see him. 'Ah Mr Heselwood! A rider brought a message in for you. Now where did I put it?' He pulled papers out of pigeon holes. 'Good bit of rain eh? Ah! Here it is. A stockman left it here a few days ago. I wrote it out myself. He couldn't write you understand. Here it is. It's from Harry Slater, the cattle buyer. Harry says the Macquarie River's in flood and your herd's stuck there. That's a bit of bad luck.'

Jasin was furious. 'It's not bad luck! He should have been well on by this. What's the bastard doing? How long do you think it will take them to get here now?'

'Christ knows. The country's one big bog. Best rains we've had in years. I'd give them another few weeks.'

'Damn!' Jasin had no wish to hang around this shanty town for weeks. 'I'll have to come back. Where'll we put the cattle when they turn up? I wanted to arrange that while I'm here.'

'Slater's got a small run a couple of miles out on the trail. It'll hold them for a while. You taking them out to the Namoi?'

'No. Further north, a lot further north.'

'They'll be here for a while then eh?'

Jasin glanced blankly at him, not understanding that remark, but there were other things to think about. 'Here's my address in Newcastle. Tell

Slater to let me know when he does get here. And do you know a fellow called Pace MacNamara? Where I could find him?'

'Sure do. He lives at a place down the end of North Road.'

'Thank you.'

It didn't take long to locate the house, shack rather, he mentally corrected himself. MacNamara wasn't coining money, probably renting this hovel and working at odd jobs if he were working at all. He wondered if the Irishman really had taken up land out west. Nothing had been said about it and he would not stoop to enquire. He'd probably spent his pay at the tavern by now and could be amenable to a droving job. He tapped on the door with his whip and a woman opened it, a woman with a mass of tawny red hair, and Jasin stepped back in astonishment. 'Dolour! Is it you?'

She was as surprised as her visitor. She blushed and her soft pink lips formed a round 'oh' but no sound came out.

'My dear Dolour!' he cried. 'What good fortune! I've been searching for you everywhere. I went out to Parramatta and to the Nelson Hotel . . .'

'In your own good time,' she snapped. 'What can I do for you Mr Heselwood?' He pretended not to hear the angry tone and moved quickly to slip an arm around her waist, his desire for her rekindled. 'Oh my dear, you're more beautiful than ever.' But she pushed him away.

'Don't Dolour,' he murmured, his face in her hair and his arms now pressing her body into his. 'Feel how much I want you now. Remember how we were together? I've missed you so much.' His strong hands were moving over the familiar body through the thin dress and the urgency he had always felt with her was on him again and he wanted to make love to her there and then. They had been too long parted.

She was fighting him, her mouth firmly shutting out his kisses, her body twisting away from him. He felt blurred and confused as she shoved him away and stood back straightening her dress. 'Go away Jasin. That's finished!'

He reached for her again, smiling, loving her. 'No it's not Dolour. It'll never be over.' He was gentler now, coaxing her, after all it had been a surprise for her too. 'Come and make love with me and you'll see nothing has changed. I want you more than ever now. We're free of them all. I'm on my own here and we've got all the time in the world.'

'No!'

She pushed her hair back from her face and he saw the thin silver band, grabbing her hand angrily. 'Is that a wedding ring? Why did you do that? I'd have come for you! I did!' It was beginning to dawn on him now whose house this was and even before she said it he knew.

'I am married to Pace MacNamara and you'd better get used to it.'

He stared at her speechless and walked away from her feeling his insides shaking from frustration. 'When did this happen?'

'None of your business. Now did you come here to see my husband?'

'I came to offer the stockman a job,' he said icily.

'You'll find him at the saleyards, there's a horse sale on.'

Jasin recovered quickly. He wasn't about to give up that easily. He forced a laugh. 'Thank you Mrs MacNamara. But now that we are formally introduced and you have done what is expected of the little wife, come here to me.' He opened his arms to her, palms out. 'I'm married too, you know that. It didn't make any difference to you, why should it matter to me? You're still my beautiful Dolour, we are lovers still.'

In a defensive movement Dolour pulled the door towards her. 'Please don't say those things Jasin. You must go away and leave me alone.'

He could hear fear in her voice and he thought he understood it. 'Don't worry about MacNamara. I'll send him away with my cattle. I intended to do that anyway. Then I'll come back to you.'

Instead of closing the door she threw it open and stormed at him. 'Can't you get it through your head? Whatever feelings I had for you are gone. Six months in that Factory beat them out of me.'

'That wasn't my fault.'

'It doesn't matter whose fault it was. It was stupid of me too. Now I want you to leave.'

'I could do that,' he said, grinning at her. 'And I could tell MacNamara about us. I'll wager you didn't. And if I tell him, your precious marriage won't be worth a pinch of salt.'

Dolour reacted angrily. 'This is the day I knew would come and I've been preparing for it.' She reached inside and confronted him with a rifle. 'I always warned you, you were not dealing with a milkmaid. If you ever tell MacNamara about us I'll put a bullet through your head.'

'Don't be so melodramatic woman. Put the gun away.'

'I will not! I mean it! Now get off my property. If you want to talk to my husband go and find him.'

Jasin made a point of strolling casually away and turned to wave back at her, admiring the curve of her figure and the sensual defiance in her stance. 'You little minx,' he muttered to himself. 'There's fire in that body. It's a trial having to walk away from you but there'll be other times. I'll come back.' There was a new lift in his life now that Dolour was back in the scene, more colour in the landscape.

In this frame of mind he felt he would do anything to get Dolour back. His wife seemed to pale against the bursting vigour of the Irish girl. He planned to re-employ MacNamara, double his pay if he had to, but send him away. And time was with him.

But the meeting with MacNamara achieved nothing. The Irishman did not want his job, and was himself bidding for stock.

'What are you intending to do with these cattle?' he asked.

'Put them on a little farm.'

'So you did take up land on the Namoi. How much land?'

'Enough.'

'Next to mine?' Jasin asked, seeing some humour in that.

'No. The land neighbouring your Carlton Park has been taken up by a Newcastle lawyer. But why are you buying again? I'd have thought that station of yours was well stocked, until they can clear more land.'

'We can always do with more.'

Pace didn't believe him and made some enquiries of the friendly sergeant who advised that Heselwood had a pass to take stock far north to the Darling Downs.

'I heard of this place. Could you show me where it is?'

The trooper station also served as a branch of the Lands Office. He showed Pace the newest maps. 'It's a hard climb to get up to the plateau but once there they say it's as green as the meadows of England.'

'You don't say?'

So that was it. Pace mooned about the house for days trying to work out how he could be in two places at once. He had to stock his property and build his house as well as make the required improvements or he would lose it.

'Be satisfied with what you've got MacNamara. If you keep up with this sort of thinking you'll fall off the end of the earth before you settle,' his wife told him.

They sold their house, packed up their few belongings and travelled north-west to their Kooramin property on the Namoi in the company of six stockmen and a great swaying herd of cattle. Ahead of him her husband could see years of hard work but Dolour was triumphant. She had beaten Heselwood. He had not dared mention their relationship to her husband and she thanked the Lord they were free of him forever. And she praised Mary in her innermost thoughts that she had been speaking the truth, that she no longer cared for Heselwood, no longer found him appealing. He was not a patch on her own man, for which she would be eternally grateful. That had been her greatest worry.

But for Jasin that was by no means the end of it. He had found Dolour now and he would see her again. At first he had planned to report the Irishman as a ticket-of-leave who had broken his agreement but he decided against that, it would draw attention to himself, besides the Irishman would talk his way out of it.

He would have to come out this way again in a few weeks thanks to Slater's tardiness and he guessed MacNamara wouldn't be idling around the town. It was after all only a staging point. MacNamara had no money, that he knew, it would be years before a fellow like that could raise enough money to equip a station for habitation. Next time he came to Singleton he would call on Dolour again and talk some sense into her. One day they would be neighbours so to speak, they should be friends. After all, wasn't he the one who retrieved her husband from Bathurst jail? He might even apologise, explain that his reaction on seeing her again was understandable;

a gentler approach was needed now to ease her into the same clandestine relationship they'd had before, because in effect nothing had changed. And their mutual attraction could never change, of that he was sure. His mind seemed to roll back to Dolour as if he were once again rolling over in that bed with her and the memory of her and thoughts of her sustained him, helped him to overcome his disappointment at the wasted journey, which now he realised was far from wasted.

Rivadavia's summer house was habitable and Georgina had moved in with Edward, a maid, a cook and a gardener, and Jasin shuddered, extra wages when he needed every penny he could muster, but she was in her element and that was a blessing. He decided to call on Burnett in the peace of his office to get specific information now on the northern route which would assist him to estimate the supplies he would require.

Burnett was surprised. 'I thought you were going out to the Namoi, Jasin.'

'No. Plans have changed. I put people out there. I'm after land on that Darling Downs place.'

'My dear fellow, it's a bit early to go that far.'

The comment the sergeant had made about his trip north being 'a while yet' flashed into Jasin's mind. 'I don't see why not. I've a herd of cattle arriving from Bathurst shortly. I'll collect them and we'll be on our way with the winter over.'

'Jasin, I have been studying Cunningham's notes as well as his maps. It seems the best time to go up there is in the winter, further north they have summer rainfalls, more than we'd get in years down here.'

'Why is that?'

'Because you are going towards tropical country.'

'Nonsense. The equator is a thousand miles or so to the north.'

'Well, sub-tropical. But besides that, the route is as yet undefined. In this game it is not always the wisest course to be first.'

'I was first out at the Namoi.'

'You crossed a plain with stations in relative proximity. This is different, there are mountains to overcome, there's land closer in the New England area, look at that first.'

'It has been picked over already. I would end up with the worst of it. No, I am set on winning my share of the Darling Downs.'

'So you can, but not just yet Jasin. It is one thing to be a pioneer, quite another to be a frontiersman. It is far too dangerous to venture that far yet. The blacks there are still in a wild state and belligerent. They murdered the Commandant of Moreton Bay Captain Logan, while he was out on survey. Decapitated the poor fellow, an appalling thing to happen.'

'You're saying I should just sit back and let someone else have it.'

'My dear fellow, you said yourself there are thousands of miles of unclaimed land up there. It's safer to wait.'

'What if I go anyway?' Jasin asked, still stubbornly refusing to give up.

232

'I could forbid you. You are planning to go far beyond the boundaries. I won't do that, being a friend, but what I can say to you is, that no-one will come to your aid if you strike trouble, not one trooper.'

'But it is so close to that port on the Brisbane River.'

'Which is not yet a port, Moreton Bay is a penal settlement. Do give over Jasin, I do admire your spirit but it is out of the question. You won't lose by waiting.'

Jasin was thunderstruck. Everything depended on finding new runs as soon as possible, before his credit ran out. He had mortgaged Carlton Park to equip this expedition, banking on his return as an even bigger land-holder, with more collateral. This plan had seemed as simple as his first expedition. How could it be going so wrong? He thought of the Forrests sitting smugly on his land. He should not have made such a hasty decision. Nothing ever seemed to go the way he planned. His head ached and the room seemed to spin.

'You have to expect setbacks,' Burnett was saying. 'I'm sorry if this is a disappointment but if you wait a year or even more we'll have some idea of the country leading to the big plateau of the Downs when we get time to survey the new claims along the route. I do know there are big rivers to cross, we'll be able to tell you more about them . . .'

'What about my herd? I've got a big herd of cattle on its way.'

'You won't lose there. Send them out to your own station on the Namoi. I don't know why you are worrying about them.'

'No!' Jasin would not permit the Forrests to get them as easily as that, after his own efforts. They could claim half of the profits.

'Then sell the cattle as soon as they arrive, Appleby for one would be pleased to get his hands on them. Here, join me in a drink old chap. How is that seaside house going? We miss you and Georgina at home now.'

Jasin rose shaking. 'If you will excuse me, I must be getting along. Actually I am rather tired.' All he wanted to do now was to get home. And home, he thought bitterly, belongs to Rivadavia.

It was raining as he rode home and again he was soaked to the skin. He shivered convulsively as he rode. He could not clear his mind of doom-laden thoughts.

For weeks he was very ill and Georgina herself nursed him. The doctor diagnosed his fever as influenza but his wife was not so sure. Except for the fever he had none of the symptoms of influenza, and as she listened to him muttering and worrying and calling out she realised he was suffering a nervous collapse. When the fever left him he was morose and withdrawn one day, and cranky and demanding the next, not knowing what he wanted to do. Georgina was patient with him. She understood. No-one could know how hard it had been for Jasin in this country, what physical hard-ships he had endured as well as the ever-present worry of finances. His upbringing had not prepared him for this strain. She told their friends that he was still weak from the severe attack of influenza and would not allow any visitors to see him. She could not permit anyone to see Heselwood in that state.

A message came from Harry Slater. The cattle were at his run and he was waiting on instructions. Carefully Georgina raised the subject with Jasin, but he didn't want to talk about it. His expedition to the north was off so nothing else seemed to matter. He had lost interest in everything, sitting quietly with a rug over his knees wherever she chose to place him. She appealed to Burnett for advice and he arranged the sale of the cattle, assuring her that it had been Jasin's intention to do so.

Rivadavia's house was finished and she thought it looked beautiful, and she persuaded Jasin to take walks with her to the beach as the weather improved and he seemed to be more cheerful but he would not discuss business, leaving his letters lying around unopened.

Their bank accounts had been transferred to Newcastle and in desperation she went to see the bank manager herself. He was a thin little man with a bald head and large moustache and protruding eyes. Pop-eyes, she told herself, that gave the lie to his smarmy talk, cold eyes.

'My dear lady, what an honour to meet you. I am sorry to hear Mr Heselwood is ailing. Do give him my best regards. Now I see here that payments are overdue but don't worry about them, I'm sure Mr Heselwood will settle up when he is feeling better. And of course there is the extra loan Mr Heselwood arranged for his expedition. I am sure he is making good use of that, and when he has title to his new land then Mr Heselwood's assets will be excellent collateral. We are very progressive in our attitudes as you can see. We are prepared to stand behind our pastoralists, give them some leeway, so to speak, so don't let it worry you dear lady. Just tell Mr Heselwood to call on me when he is feeling better.'

He escorted her to the front door snapping his fingers to a teller who rushed forward and handed her an envelope which she guessed would be a statement of their indebtedness to the bank, not for her eyes obviously. Then he took her to her carriage and stood in the street to wave farewell. She ripped it open and felt sick. She could expect little from Carlton Park and that was their only income. Their living expenses were rapidly whittling away the loan raised for the northern expedition. And then of course there was the original loan and the money borrowed from the Forrests. That had to be repaid somehow to get them off the place. It was all a dreadful mess. She wondered if they should sell to the Forrests, let them have Carlton Park. That would solve it all.

But when she mentioned the idea to Jasin he got himself into such a rage it took the rest of the afternoon to calm him down, and she realised he was not ready for such discussions. She thought of returning to England but if they simply disappeared the bank would foreclose and they'd lose Carlton Park, probably to the Forrests anyway.

Nevertheless, she kept the household cheerful around her husband and

234

encouraged him to walk Edward about on his little pony and read him stories finding that the only one to profit from Jasin's enforced idleness was their son. He adored his father and trotted behind him everywhere.

When Juan Rivadavia came back into Newcastle, he called at the house. Georgina was nervous that Jasin might resent him, but he was affable enough. Then uninterested, he went off to have a nap while Georgina and Juan toured the house, both of them pleased with the results.

They took tea in the front parlour and Juan's bland expression gave no hint that he had noticed a change in Jasin. Having exhausted the subject of the house, Georgina was finding their conversation a strain. 'Do you ever think of going back to Argentina, Juan?'

'No. Argentina is now run by the dictator Rosas. It is very difficult for my family at present so it is much better to remain here.' He smiled. 'But you have left your country behind too. Don't you wish to go back sometimes?'

She looked at him, needing someone to talk to, and decided this was no time to be squeamish. 'I would like to take Jasin back to England for a holiday. He is not himself after the influenza.'

Juan nodded and she had the feeling he understood that there was more to it.

'His sickness has caused him to have to postpone all his plans which have in their turn placed us in a rather precarious situation.'

'Yes. Arthur Appleby said the plans to go north had been postponed, but that's not a bad thing. I thought at the time it was a bit soon to be going out too far. There is still land in Argentina beyond the limits but if you go too far away from markets and into Indian country you can't grow, you understand? It's the same in this country.'

'I realise that and it would be a good time to go to England. His father is not well after Harrald's death and the other son some months prior. I would love them to see Edward, he is their only grandson.'

'Then go, don't worry about this house. I hope you are not staying here just to mind a house.'

'No, it's not that. Jasin has to be patient and that is irritating him, he is sitting around feeling useless. But to be quite truthful the banks are not so patient. Impatient is a better word. They are hanging over our heads like hawks. I want Jasin to sell Carlton Park but he won't hear of it.'

'Good God! You must not sell! That land will grow in value and to sell it now would be to throw away all he has worked for. Never!'

Georgina blinked. She reached for a small cake and put it down again. She had hoped he would be an ally to persuade Jasin to sell.

'Since Jasin is not well, why don't you let me talk to your bank? I think I could persuade them to be patient.'

'How? We can't make the payments they demand. You can't alter that.'

'I could guarantee you. Make them extend your loan. And then when you return from England, Jasin will be ready to claim land on the Darling Downs. I intend to do the same in the future, it will be well worth the effort, I can assure you.'

She studied her hands, worried. 'I don't know. Jasin might not approve.'

'Then don't tell him until he is feeling better. On your voyage to England would be a good time,' he grinned.

'Would the bank accept your guarantee?' she asked curiously. 'I didn't mean that to be as uncivil as it sounded. I mean can you afford to do this for us?'

'It will not cause me any concern. You see my family, and their friends now, are investing in this country, through me. Their money is safer here where there is no interference from the Government. In Argentina the dictator is bleeding pastoralists like my father of all the money he can get out of them. Over here the Spanish dollar is most welcome, so I am in great favour with the banks.'

'Oh I see. Excellent! What do you invest in?'

'For them? Coal, wool, shipping – for myself land, cattle, because I intend to stay. I like this country, it is not as complicated as Argentina, not so many levels to deal with.'

'That must be very interesting for you.'

'Yes I find it so. Now getting back to your holiday, there is nothing to stop you. Don't let the banks dictate your life. You do have the collateral, every year land within the boundaries becomes more valuable.'

Long after he had gone she sat on the verandah, thinking. He had the ease and grace of good breeding but he was different from the young men she had grown up with. Vastly different. There was a seductiveness about him, a maturity that made him seem so much older, mysterious even, but he was too flashy for English men. She wished Jasin would stop referring to him as The Spaniard, it was so unnecessary.

The following afternoon she took a drive in her carriage and when she came home she carried a tray with a bottle of champagne and two glasses out to Jasin who was dozing in the little summer house. 'My dear, I have decided we are going home for a holiday with Edward, so we must celebrate.'

'What a good idea,' he said, accepting the champagne. 'Jolly good.'

It was not until she poured the third glass that he came back to reality. 'It is an excellent idea, but quite impossible under the circumstances, you forget we are near paupers living on the Spaniard's charity.'

This was no time to argue with him, to remind him he had had no objections to living in other people's houses in the past.

'I called on the bank manager to ask him and he said we should go, the sea air would be the very thing with the hot summer coming on here, and we would then be in London for the spring.' She lied airily about the bank manager and his splendid advice. 'He said it is quite the thing to do since

236

you have had to postpone your expedition and not to worry about finance, your assets are . . .' Georgina was faltering, she couldn't remember Juan's words. 'Oh, I don't know Jasin, I can't recall, but everything is in order. There is nothing to worry about.'

'Humph! Changed his tune hasn't he? Probably just woken up to who one is. Very well, we shall go. But for God's sake Georgina, do see that he books us passage on a decent ship, first class. I think we ought to have another bottle to celebrate.'

Now that he had accepted the idea Georgina was looking forward to their holiday. It would be a proud day to step ashore in England again with her little son and her husband who was more handsome then ever, and not to be forgotten, the owner of an estate called Carlton Park which eclipsed his parents' holdings. The Earl should be proud of his son. She knew how important this was to Jasin.

With the financial strain removed and the prospect of a voyage, Jasin's recovery was swift. He was soon up and about again giving orders, and organising his affairs. He said he had some business to settle up-river in Singleton, some odds and ends to do with the cattle or Carlton Park, Georgina wasn't sure. Since it would remove him from the household and allow her to get on with the packing and the arranging of her wardrobe with the dressmaker she had installed for the remaining weeks, then it was a blessing.

There were no odds and ends for Jasin to settle up-river, he wanted to see Dolour again.

He rode boldly up to her house, not caring whether MacNamara was home or not. He had a number of reasons he could advance for wanting to see him, if he were there; and if he were away, which was more than likely, he would have that talk with Dolour. With his gentlest persuasions he would have her in bed. He wanted to let her know he was going to England but would come back to her. He would never risk leaving her in the dark about his whereabouts again.

The yard was empty of horses. That was a good sign. He tapped on the door with a smile on his face. A man appeared, unshaven, in a flannel shirt and battered trousers. 'What do you want?'

'I was looking for Pace MacNamara,' Jasin said carefully.

'You a friend of his?'

'Yes.'

The man hitched up his pants and walked outside. 'Sorry mate, they're not here. The missus and I bought this house. They went off a few days ago, out to their station. You going out that way?'

'Yes. I must have missed them. Good day to you.'

As he climbed on his horse the fellow shouted after him. 'If you ride hard you'll catch up with them, they're driving cattle!'

'Thank you,' he said and turned back down the road, anger churning his

237

stomach. She'd gone. This trip had been wasted. MacNamara was heading for the Namoi, to his own station, taking Dolour with him. As he rode away his rage grew, he was so jealous of the Irishman he felt he could kill him. If he had known this was going to happen he would have let him rot in Bathurst jail. That Irish bastard was too smart for his own good.

He stayed in Singleton for days, drinking in the taverns, drowning his miseries in their bad whisky. When he came out of his alcoholic daze with a ferocious headache and two days' stubble of beard, he was among the deadbeats and riff-raff who camped at the edge of the town within walking distance of the last tavern which was nothing more than a stone shed. They shared their fiery liquor with him and persuaded him to pay for more and in a confused state he sat with them listening to their yarns and whines.

A few days later he awoke again to find the camp fire ashes scattered and his companions gone, not a sign of any of them. Gone also was his purse and saddlebag.

Cursing himself for his stupidity, he washed up in the creek and rode into Singleton where he sold his horse and boarded the river boat for Newcastle.

With time on the boat to recover he arrived back at the household in a fair humour and was pleased to see that Georgina had everything under control.

They had a few days in Sydney to shop for more fashionable clothes and then the Heselwoods stepped on board to their comfortable cabin in the East India Company ship *Spennymoor* bound for London. The afternoon sun had more colour than warmth as it hung, ready to drop behind the Blue Mountains, glistening gold on departing clouds but the passengers looked to the east as the *Spennymoor* ran before the wind down the Harbour towards Sydney Heads, the gateway to the Pacific Ocean. They were sailing east this time, with the winds, down and around the Horn and north into the Atlantic and for England.

# CHAPTER FIVE

Dinny O'Meara, as he put it himself, 'got clean away from the Mudie bastard' but in doing so branded himself as an escaped convict, a man who could be shot on sight. He made for the hills where he was held up by three wild-looking fellows with beards like birds' nests. Starving and barefoot, O'Meara collapsed on the ground laughing. 'You'll never make your fortunes robbing those with nothing!'

He had already decided his only chance of survival was to become a bush-ranger, until he could find himself enough money to bribe his way out of the colony and make for America. If he were caught as an escaped convict, he had a good chance of swinging anyhow, and he felt he may as well be 'hung for a sheep as a lamb'.

The three would-be robbers, also escaped convicts, were the first members of his gang. Not only were they failures as bushrangers but they knew nothing about the bush and were hard pressed trying to find enough food to barely survive. They were willing to follow O'Meara because he seemed to know what he was doing. And as lean as he was from convict rations O'Meara gave orders in his bull voice that made them jump and run. 'We'll need arms first,' he said, 'I'm never holding anyone up with a shillelagh like you fellers. I have more respect for my skin. And we need horses. Then we'll go north and find ourselves a safe camp way out of reach of the troopers.'

'I ain't going that way, there's cannibals up there,' said Jimmy Sims, the oldest member of his little troupe.

'You'll go where we go or you're out right now,' O'Meara told him. 'We'll deal with the blacks when we come to them. Our first move is to get the troopers off our tails.'

Jimmy acquiesced. 'All right then, but what's your name?'

'John Minogue, from Dublin,' O'Meara lied, thinking how the Minogue family would be interested to know they now had a bushranger in their clan. He grinned to himself, he had always had it in mind to marry one of those Minogue girls, give her his name, now the reverse had happened. But if he were to be on the run again, not even his own men would know his real identity.

His plans worked well. He staked out trails for lone riders and ambushed them one by one until the gang was equipped to hunt and travel. Then he returned to the Hunter Valley.

On a hill overlooking the valley his men watched astonished, while he sat down with a stolen razor and shaved off his beard and cut his shaggy hair, collecting all the hair on a piece of bark. He fashioned the hair into a false beard with the aid of sticky sap and fine strips of hide. They clapped their hands when, with a whistle and a flick, he suddenly became a different person. 'You boys stay up here in the hills until I get back,' he said, 'and don't show your noses. I have to go back for a mate of mine and then we'll be off at the gallop.'

Posing as a clergyman, clean-shaven and Protestant to boot, he rode down into the Hunter Valley to find Brosnan. At the inns they were still talking about the riot at Castle Forbes and Mudie's revenge. Three of the convicts had been hanged and one sent to the dreaded Norfolk Island, and word had it that convicts were still being flogged for the rioting. But no-one remembered any names.

He decided then that there was nothing for it but to bless Mudie with his presence. Not knowing any Protestant prayers O'Meara amused himself on the trail by inventing exhortations of hell and brimstone that would have done a mission priest proud.

Major Mudie and Mr Larnach were away in Sydney looking for workers, Mrs Mudie told him as she welcomed him into her home. It was getting more and more difficult to obtain labour, she explained. By which you mean free labour, O'Meara thought meanly, but he flattered the woman outrageously and prayed with her.

While she and her servants were preparing his dinner, he sailed outside, ostensibly to bless the tobacco and corn crops, studying the workers as they filed back from the fields, all of them gaunt and starved, dragging up the hill to their barracks.

He had acquired a black hat from a traveller and pushed the crease out of it, sitting it straight on his brows, 'for all the world,' he laughed, 'like the village idiot,' but it gave him just the sombre touch he needed. And now he pulled the hat further down over his eyes more to hide his anger than his identity, and he had almost given up hope of finding a familiar face when he saw Scarpy.

A week later, just as the convicts had been locked in for the night a bearded stockman came galloping down the hill past the stables. 'Fire! Fire! In the tobacco fields!'

Clouds of smoke were already billowing over the paddocks as pandemonium broke loose. To the east the cane fields were smouldering ready to explode. Men tore from the kitchens and bunkrooms, and bells clanged.

Dinny watched as the convicts tumbled out, caught up in the rush, and someone shoved heavy bags at him so he began issuing them to the convicts shouting at them to hurry, to add to the confusion, until he saw Scarpy. 'Grab these bags,' he said, 'and keep running behind me.'

'Who the hell . . .' Scarpy cried, but O'Meara grabbed his shirt. 'Shut up and run you fool or I'll leave you here.'

'Jesus, it's you O'Meara!' Scarpy puffed, but he kept moving.

They raced behind the stables, and O'Meara turned urgently to Scarpy. 'Where's Brosnan? I haven't sighted him.'

'Brosnan's dead!' Scarpy said. 'Didn't you know?'

O'Meara was shocked but there was no time for discussion. He leapt onto his horse and reached down for Scarpy. 'Quick, get on behind me.' He wheeled the horse and rode fast in the direction of the fire, galloping past the men running in the same direction, seeming to go after the horsemen who were racing ahead but once through the second gate he turned towards the open road under cover of the smoke.

'So Brosnan's dead,' he said heavily when they were safe in the bush on the way into the hills.

'Yeah, bad luck that was, poor Brosnan. Jack Drew got away too but they say he is dead. 'Course, they say you're dead too.'

'What happened to Brosnan?'

'One of Larnach's men shot him, trying to escape that day.'

'Jesus, Brosnan! He was the best friend I ever had. If I'd known that I'd have burnt the whole bloody place down.'

Scarpy was the only one of the bushrangers who knew O'Meara's real identity and he would never tell. He was grateful to the bold Irishman for rescuing him and indebted to him more than he could ever repay for bringing him to a new life. O'Meara taught him how to ride. 'There's nothing to it,' O'Meara said when he discovered that Scarpy had never ridden a horse. 'Come on now, I'll leg you up.' But Scarpy shied away from the great beast. It had been bad enough bumping around on the rear in the escape from Castle Forbes when he could at least hold on to O'Meara, but to sit up there alone, at the end where the teeth were – Scarpy was not too sure.

'You'll ride or you'll starve,' O'Meara shouted at him, and then he was up and being led around by Dinny, quietly at the beginning, and then slipping and bumping at the trot. Days later he learnt to lift and sink with the horse as it cantered and all of a sudden Scarpy got it and he was sure O'Meara had been right all the time, he truly was a horse rider. To be up there gave him a marvellous feeling of confidence, he was a man among men, a swashbuckler with his gun and rope, and galloping cross-country he could go like the wind.

As O'Meara and his bushrangers moved north they ambushed riders and coaches for money, supplies and ammunition. With money they could buy food from poor settlers. O'Meara appeared occasionally as the clergyman to keep an eye out for the law and pick up information on what lay ahead of them. One time while posing as a clergymen he met a genuine one.

The day Deacon Tomlinson joined him on the road O'Meara's first reaction was to bolt in case he was found out as an imposter but his

241

instincts told him there was something odd about this one too. There was no doubt Tomlinson was an ordained minister but he seemed to O'Meara to have a shady side to him and before long he discovered that the Deacon had grazing properties and was on the lookout for cheap cattle.

'Not that I know much about it,' he told Tomlinson. 'I'm from Van Diemen's Land myself, new here you understand, just visiting. But I heard some lads on the trail talking about having a herd of cattle and nowhere to place them. They may be able to help you. I'll put them in touch with you.'

He rode back to the camp with a new career in mind. 'Time we were done with this bushranging, boys. There's too much competition and they're all getting too rough. We'll end up getting blamed for something we didn't do. We're going into the cattle business.' He sent Scarpy back to meet up with Tomlinson and make certain that their buyer would take unbranded cattle off their hands and Scarpy reported that the Deacon was 'awake-up' that the cattle would be stolen since he asked no questions.

'And I've gone one better,' Scarpy cried. 'He's given me a branding iron, his own. It's registered and all. So any cattle we find without brands on or off somebody's land will be ours. We could pass anywhere with his brand.' He demonstrated the inverted double 'T' by scorching it onto a tree. 'See T T, Tom Tomlinson.'

O'Meara gathered more men as they rode north and they rustled young steers, bulls and breeders until they had their own herds well out of range of the settlers and could keep the Deacon supplied with cattle at half the going rate. With permits supplied by the man of the cloth they brought the cattle down to the extended boundaries of settlement and handed them on to Tomlinson's drovers, and when the squatters began moving onto the Darling Downs thinking themselves to be the first cattlemen in the district, they were surprised to see cattle trails.

'We're practically legal now boys,' O'Meara said. 'It's time we marked out our own land and keep other buggers off.' They moved down to the west of the Brisbane River and built their own settlement. 'Mark every tree that pleases you lads,' he told his men. 'Put a double "X" on them and hang a few "keep out" signs. We don't want any visitors. But give the blacks anything they want.'

The Aborigines in the district were hostile at first, shaking their spears at the outlaws to leave but under O'Meara's orders no-one was permitted to fire on them. Instead O'Meara's men left gifts of meat and tea and sugar and tobacco for the tribespeople, who noticed that these strange white men made no attempt to chop down the trees or dig up great tracts of their land. The locals became more curious and they ventured closer but no-one bothered them so they went about their own affairs and moved away again when the time came.

Scarpy and the other men were satisfied with the life. They were free to come and go as they pleased, and, on average, O'Meara had about twenty men at his settlement. They traded with the Aborigines, meat for fish, and in a spirit of goodwill the blacks loaned them their women. O'Meara had been long enough in the bush to know the rules and he impressed on his men that the Aborigine women were on loan, they could not stay in the white men's camp nor could they be taken away or the blacks would turn nasty.

O'Meara was amassing money. He paid his men for any cattle they brought in and paid the drovers for the long trek south to meet up with Tomlinson's drovers but he made no attempt to politicise the settlement. He expected the outlaws to hunt and forage for themselves, and share if they wished, and they could buy supplies from the timber-getters on the Brisbane River. When they decided to build a stockade around the camp as a protection against a future raid by troopers, he had no objections and lent a hand building the high log fence. By the time it was finished half of the original workers had left, bored with the little outpost. He did not blame them; he was becoming restless himself. He knew it wouldn't be long before the squatters reached them, and after them would come smaller settlers and troopers and then a local constable would be appointed and it would be time to move on again. He was getting tired of keeping a jump ahead of civilisation, he wanted to be part of it, not locked out forever.

He often rode down to the timber-getters' camp and became friendly with one of the camp bosses, Jock McArdle, who knew he was the leader of the bushrangers but it didn't worry him.

'We don't meddle with that hornet's nest any more than we do with the blacks,' McArdle told his men.

'So what's a man of your intelligence doing wasting his life up here?' he asked O'Meara.

'I'm saving my life, that's what I'm doing. If they catch me they'll string me up.'

'What for?'

'For escaping. I ran off at the first chance.'

'But what did they transport you for in the first place?'

'Something called treason,' O'Meara laughed.

The Scot nodded. 'I thought so.' He fossicked in the bark lean-to that was his home and his office. 'Would you join me in a whisky?'

'Nothing I'd like better. But why do you do this? It's a terrible place here on the river and dangerous work. And I'll tell you something else, I'd rather try to keep my mob of fellers in order than the lot you've got here. Meaning no offence but you've got your share of cutthroats I'd say.'

'Ah some of them can work, some of the others aren't worth the skin they live in but I keep them at it or shove them on a raft out of the place. I don't care if they fight among themselves, but not on my time, and they won't buck me. Some of them think they're smart, turning up here with knives in their boots, thinking they'll be the boss but I've got their measure. See that silver gum back there?'

Before O'Meara could answer he heard the swish as McArdle's arm swept the air beside him, and an axe flew past him embedding itself in the tree trunk.

The timber man retrieved the axe and walked back smiling. 'It puts the fear of God into them laddie. And it keeps my quotas up. I've got contracts to fill, and we're always working against time. We go off in the wet season, we can't work in that weather, the river floods.'

'Where do you go then?'

McArdle looked surprised. 'Home. I've my family in Sydney. I'm doing well in this business. Another couple of seasons and I'll be out of it, then I'll be the middleman. I'll sell timber not cut it.'

'Good for you,' O'Meara said but it depressed him. He had almost forgotten normal life and families and homes. He studied the quietly flowing river. 'That goes down to Brisbane, a port. Could you smuggle me onto a boat leaving the country?'

'Not from the prison, Moreton Bay's as tight as a drum. It's been tried a dozen times. There are always troopers on board and the captains have got to keep sweet with the authorities. They'd throw you overboard rather than lose their tickets. You'd be better to try to get out of Sydney.'

'I can't go down south, I've no papers.'

'If you've got some money, I could buy you some papers.'

O'Meara was drinking from a tin mug. He choked. 'What?'

'Papers,' McArdle said. 'They're turning them out for a price in Sydney. The powers-that-be were very smart. They deported scores of forgers and diddlers with the pen, and when they got here, they were the very ones that were needed. They got good soft jobs for their penmanship and in no time at all they got off for good behaviour, all ready to go back into the forging business. The trade's flourishing. There's free men and women too wanting forged papers, to show they were never convicts, never a blemish on their names.'

'Could you buy me some papers, and some for my mate Scarpy? You met him.'

'Consider it done. I'll buy them when I go down at Christmas. I'll give them your descriptions and they'll write you out a nice new name and pedigree.'

'Well I'll be damned!'

'I could find you work in Sydney if you want it.'

'No way. I'm still an escaped convict, there's no forgiveness for me. I want to go to America where I won't have to be looking over my shoulder. But I've been thinking about that Moreton Bay place. When we first landed in Sydney one of our lads was sent off to another prison. The names were all Dutch to us then, we didn't know where we were, but the name Moreton Bay rang a bell. Lately I've been thinking he might be there.'

'God help him if he is. It's a shocking place.'

'So I hear. Do you think you could find out if they've got a fellow called Jim Connelly there?'

'No harm in asking.'

McArdle had the answer for him a month later. 'Your mate Jim Connelly was there but he scored a ticket of leave. He's been sent to the Newcastle District. He can't leave that district without permission, so you could probably track him down.'

'Bloody Connelly free and me still sweating it out! He always was a lucky bugger!'

Jock shook his head. 'He'd have earned it.'

When the rains came O'Meara moved the cattle to higher country and returned to the stockade to wait. With the cedar cutters out of the area and a visit to the penal settlement out of the question, they lived in total isolation until most of his men, unable to stand it any longer, decided to take their chances in the little frontier town of Limestone to the south-west, promising to return in the dry season.

'Why don't we go too?' Scarpy asked. 'There's nothing to do here.'

'Because we don't want to get caught now. When Jock comes back we'll have papers and we can ride free. I just have a couple of things to do and then we'll make for America. We're safe here and we're making money. When the squatters come, we'll have to go anyway, so we might as well earn as much as we can, while we can.'

It was the blacks who brought them the news that the timber men had returned. McArdle had brought the new identification papers with him. Now O'Meara and Scarpy could 'prove' that they were free immigrants. O'Meara began the long ride to the south leaving Scarpy in charge of the settlement.

As he travelled south he noticed the heat didn't ease but the country grew drier and he couldn't decide which was worse, the mouldy humid heat of the Brisbane Valley or the searing white heat of the southern plains that would have a long wait for their winter rains. He followed the rivers and their tributaries and was surprised to find that little townships were springing up. He was headed for Newcastle to search for Connelly but talking to the men in a shanty pub he was told that the Newcastle district had been divided up and he would be better advised to start his enquiries at Quirindi since most of the ticket-of-leave men were working on the stations. It would save him, perhaps, the ride over the hills to the Hunter and on to Newcastle, and he decided it was worth a try.

Three days and a great thirst later he rode into the parched little town and made for the pub. 'Connelly can wait,' he said to himself. 'A man could die of thirst in this country.' He was still uneasy about walking in cold to a police station to ask about a convict even with his precious papers, so he asked around the bar if anyone knew Connelly.

A young stockman turned away from his contemplation of a fly drowning

245

in beer. 'The Irishman? The one that was in Moreton Bay?'

'Yes,' O'Meara said eagerly. 'Where would I find him?'

'Out on Kooramin Station.'

'Where's that?'

'You've come a bit far mate,' the publican said. 'It's north-west of here, out on the Namoi.'

'Well I'll be damned!' O'Meara said. 'And I'll have another. Pour yourself one sir and the lad there too.'

It was an easy road to follow, well-worn with wagon tracks and he camped on high ground beside the road that night.

In the morning he was intrigued to see a lone bushranger preparing an ambush. Two riders came by, squatters for sure, O'Meara told himself, good pickings, only trotting slowly along, but the bushranger allowed them to pass, perhaps not confident enough to take on two men. He looks a bit old for the job anyway, O'Meara thought and picked up his rifle to move down very quietly so that he could watch the fun.

He could see a lone rider coming down the trail and the bushranger was preparing to make his move. Suddenly O'Meara jerked back to take another look at the horseman coming towards them, and he stared amazed. It was that bloody fool MacNamara!

Then a shot rang out and MacNamara spun out of the saddle and crashed to the ground. 'Hey! That's not the way it's done!' O'Meara shouted. He aimed carefully and shot the bushranger in the leg. Then he pushed his way down through the scrub, took the assailant's gun and walked back to MacNamara, who recognised him immediately. 'You murdering bastard O'Meara! I might have known.'

'Sit yourself down and shut up and I'll have your gun for safe-keeping,' O'Meara said. He hitched Pace's horse to a tree and dropped the weapons beside it. 'Let's have a look at that shoulder of yours.'

'You won't get away with this,' Pace fumed as the other Irishman wadded his shirt to staunch the blood. 'Give it to me. I'll do it myself.'

O'Meara ignored Pace's angry rejection. 'I'll get a strap and make a sling for you. Have you got any bones broken?'

'I have not, no thanks to you. It's gone in through the muscle and out under my armpit. Now get away from me!'

'Get away from you? You're lucky I happened along. There's a gent in the bushes over there with a hole in his leg. He shot you, not me.'

He tramped over to the bushwhacker who was lying groaning in the thick grass and Pace dragged himself to his feet to follow him. 'So who is this?' he asked angrily.

'You tell me. It's a funny business. Why did he want to shoot you?'

'Easier to rob a dead man.'

'That doesn't make sense. You don't get a murder charge for a few pickings on the road. He was trying to kill you MacNamara!' he laughed. 'Just as well he's no marksman.'

Pace leant against a tree to steady himself. 'Who is he?'

O'Meara kicked the old man in his bony buttocks ignoring his screams. 'Who are you, you old goat? Tell us what you're up to or we'll take your horse and leave you out here for the crows.' He peered down at the old man cringing at his feet. 'Hey, look at him MacNamara! He's just an old tosspot! Friend of yours?'

Pace stared at the rheumy frightened face. 'I've never seen him before.'

O'Meara kicked him again. 'Speak up before I put another bullet in you.'

'I was paid to shoot him,' the old man cried. 'Him!' He pointed at Pace.

'You were what?' Pace shouted. 'Who paid you?'

'The Englishman. He gave me five pounds and said I'd get five more when the job was done. I've been watching you for a good while. He said there was no need to rush it.'

O'Meara roared laughing. 'You're not worth much are you MacNamara?'

'What Englishman?' Pace snarled.

'I told you, the Englishman. Captain Pelham.'

'God Almighty!' Pace said, stunned.

'Do you know him?' O'Meara was fascinated.

'Yes I know him. I shot the top off his finger the last time I saw him but that was years ago.'

'Well he hasn't forgotten has he? You can't go around shooting off fingers MacNamara and expecting to get away with it. I'll tie up this old bugger's leg and put him on his horse and send him on his way unless you want to take him back to the local constable, in which case I'll not be joining you.'

'No he can go. But just a minute you bloody old mongrel. What's your name?'

'Walter Smith sir, they call me Wally.'

'Where do you come from?'

'Singleton sir, but what'll I tell the Englishman now?'

'I don't bloody care what you tell the Englishman,' Pace yelled. 'For Christ's sake, O'Meara, get him out of here!'

O'Meara sat the attacker on his horse and Pace warned him. 'If you ever come out this way again you'll be shot on sight.' He slapped the horse on the rump and it galloped away down the road. 'I suppose I have to thank you then,' he said to O'Meara. 'We'll go back to my place. You can meet my wife and sons. I've got twin sons. And by the way Connelly's there too.'

'Kooramin Station is it?' O'Meara asked.

'How did you know?'

'It so happens I was on my way there. But I can't figure how Connelly got out of Moreton Bay. I heard convicts only leave there with their toes turned up.'

'Caimen Court fixed it. He's a great one for writing letters. He claimed Connelly and his mates should never have been sent there, that it was illegal. It's only a place for those convicts who commit another crime in the colony. Caimen plagued the Governor and got nowhere so he went to the newspapers and that worked.'

'He's healthy then?'

'Sure. He took a bit of feeding up but he's all right now. He says that big feller from the ship, Big Karlie, was in Moreton Bay too and they gave him hell until he turned on a guard. Killed him with a mattock. They hung him.'

'Ah Holy Mary, the English have got a lot to answer for. But what's Court doing handing out all this cheek when he's a convict himself?'

Pace laughed. 'Now there's the silver lining to the story. Court got the powerful arm of our Holy Mother the Church on his side. The Church soon had him freed when they found out he'd done two years at Maynooth. He's studying for the priesthood again. Staying put in New South Wales now to save all our souls.'

O'Meara frowned and went off to get the horses, and Pace called after him. 'You know I'm still confused about why that old man tried to shoot me. Pelham must be mad. I thought I did him a favour.'

'If you shot my finger off I wouldn't consider it a favour.' O'Meara laughed.

'It wasn't my fight. He got into this barney with the boss on a cattle drive. They were partners, sort of, I never did get the full gist of it, both English. The boss went diving for his gun but Pelham had the drop on him. Now if he'd shot the boss the boys would have strung him up, that's a certainty. But if the boss had shot him, and mind you I think that would have been unlikely, they were ill-matched, but if he had, it would never have been in the finger. The way I saw it bloody stupid Pelham would have been dead either way. I thought I did him a favour. They're a peculiar race the English.'

'They haven't got the logic we've got,' O'Meara said wisely.

'That's right,' Pace agreed. 'Give us a hand to get up here.' He climbed onto his horse, grimacing with the pain. 'As a matter of fact,' he said wearily, 'I didn't mean to take his finger, I was just trying to knock the gun out of his hands.'

'Losing your touch are you MacNamara?'

'Not at all,' Pace said. 'Strange weapons. Hard to gauge.'

O'Meara urged his horse on, thinking grimly how easy it was for men to speak of things never discussed when they were off guard and how that sort of interrogation, so simple, had led to his own arrest, and to Brosnan's. 'You know Brosnan's dead?'

Pace groaned. 'No. I didn't know. What happened to him?'

'He was shot trying to escape.'

'God help us – and what about you? Did you get a ticket of leave?'

'You might say that, I wrote my own.'

'Well, that'd please Brosnan. You're on the run then?'

248

'As long as I stay in this country. But yourself MacNamara? How come you were on that ship with the nobs?'

'Oh Christ. Do you ever let up? They sent me away. Dan Ryan and his lads got me out of Ireland with nothing but my coat in my hand. I thought it was the worst day of my life. But listen here now, I'll thank you not to be mentioning Pelham to my wife or any of them at home. We'll say it was just an altercation with some bushwhackers and they got away. But, by Christ, when I catch up with Pelham, he's a dead man.'

'You'd better think on that. They'll hang you for murder.'

'I can't go around waiting for a stranger to put a bullet in my back . . .'

'I suppose not, but it might be easier to knock a bit of sense into the bastard, instead.' Ahead he saw a collection of cottages shimmering in a mirage across the open plains with a blurred backdrop of faded green bush. 'Is this your place now?'

'It is,' Pace said. 'But we're going to build the homestead up on that rise where we can get a bit of a breeze. I'll be bloody glad to get home. It feels as if he hit me with a cannon ball.'

As O'Meara told Scarpy later, their arrival at Kooramin Station was '. . . something like a cross between Good Friday and Saint Patrick's Day, with Dolour wailing her husband had been shot and Connelly cheering and declaring a party because I'd returned to the land of the living! And it was a grand party with everyone joining in and singing the songs and drinking the whisky I'd bought for Connelly. But MacNamara didn't enjoy it much. After we'd operated on him, and his wife bandaged him up, he lost interest in the day and passed out.'

In the morning Dolour fussed over O'Meara cutting thick slices of bread to go with a hearty serve of eggs and bacon. 'Eat up Dinny. We don't often have visitors. That's our own sugar-cured bacon.'

'And delicious it is too,' he said. 'It's a long time since I had bacon. We eat strange fare where I'm living.'

Pace loomed up in the doorway with bandages covering his shoulder and swathed across his bare torso.

'I was bringing breakfast over to you,' Dolour said.

'Well I'm here now girl, to save you the trouble. Have you had a look around O'Meara?'

'I have indeed. It's a good spread you've got here but the country's not a patch on my place.'

'Your what? I thought you said you were on the run.'

'So I did but I haven't been doing too badly just the same. I've got my own cattle run in the north.'

'Where in the north?'

'In the Brisbane River Valley, on past the Darling Downs.' He laughed. 'If you could see your face MacNamara. You look like a trout out of water.'

'How the hell did you get up there?'

'Easy. There wasn't anywhere else to go.'

'And have you got stock there?'

'I've got fat cattle, they make your herd look a skinny lot.'

'How many cattle have you got?'

'Two or three hundred, not many by your standards but I don't keep them around long.' He walked over to the bench. 'Could I have a drink of this milk, Dolour.

'Sure you can.' She handed him a cup.

Pace stared at him. 'You're duffing cattle!'

O'Meara grinned. 'A man has to make a living somehow.'

'Madness,' Pace muttered. 'Jesus, O'Meara, it's hard enough to start herds here what with the blacks using them for target practice and no water in summer, without you blokes cutting out prime beef.'

'You're breaking my heart squire,' O'Meara laughed. 'Now give over lad. We're not bothering you.'

Pace shook his head. He had no answer for O'Meara who seemed doomed to stay on the wrong side of the law forever. But he was curious about this northern land. 'There's a lot of talk about that country you're living in. I've been wanting to get up there for a long time. I'd love to establish a run in that country.'

'Haven't you got enough here?'

'Not nearly enough. They're always talking drought down this way. They say the rains are better to the north. Is that true?'

'I never seen rain like it in me life. When it rains, it pours, for days, even weeks at a time. In the summer too, not the winter. Warm rain though, so everything grows like fury.'

'So there's my point. If I had more runs to the north I could move my cattle into the rain belts in the dry seasons.'

'There are good lakes up there too,' O'Meara said. 'It's better country than this all round.'

'Many squatters moved there yet?' Pace asked, almost afraid to hear the answer.

'No, not up my way. But they are starting to come through. I saw a lot of sheep headed for the Darling Downs just lately. I daresay another twelve months and we'll have neighbours.'

'Would you consider selling me some of your land?'

'It's not mine to sell, I was only needling you.'

'Who owns it then?'

'No-one. I've just got it marked off to keep strangers out. None of my boys want anyone nosing around asking questions.'

Pace shook his head. 'In that case it's yours Dinny.'

'And how would I go about registering my ownership? I've got forged papers to get about with but I wouldn't like to put them to the test. If I try to register I could end up in jail again.'

'Perhaps I could do it for you?'

'It wouldn't work. There are men up there who know it's outlaw territory. If I hang around too long someone will talk and they'll catch me in time. Anyway I don't want to be a farmer. I've got my heart set on going to America. I just came down here looking for the lads.' He walked to the door and stared out. 'And now I find you've all given up on Ireland.'

Behind him Dolour was nonplussed. 'Oh Dinny, that's a cruel thing to say.'

'Well Connelly tells me you'll be making him foreman here so this is where he's staying. Brosnan's dead and Court's gone back to the Church, and you MacNamara, you never mention Ireland.'

Pace pushed his plate away, his meal unfinished. 'We can't go back.'

'But you can fight them from here and I can fight them from America. We can raise money and arms for the lads. Have you forgotten so soon?'

'I haven't forgotten,' Pace said gloomily, 'and there's no use making excuses. We've got a new life here and a new country to deal with. Maybe we'll do better this time. We didn't come here by choice but it's our destiny.'

'I didn't come here by choice either,' O'Meara cried. 'This is just another English county, it's not my destiny.'

'Then I wish you well,' Pace said, 'but I won't let you make us feel guilty.' He changed the subject. 'How many acres have you got up there in the north?'

O'Meara had to force himself to reply, knowing his cause was lost in this company. 'How would I know? We're itinerants you see. We never intended to stay too long. We've got about ten miles marked off along the west bank of the Brisbane River.'

'That's a good start,' Pace said. 'Now I've got a proposition for you. You hold onto that land up there a while longer and I'll buy it from you. Then you'll have your money for America.'

O'Meara's broad shoulders shook with a rumble of a laugh. 'If that doesn't beat all! I make money selling cattle I don't own and now I'm selling land I don't own.'

'I keep telling you, you do own it,' Pace cried. 'Possession's not nine points of the law here, it's the full ten. You found it, you claimed it, and you are entitled to be paid for it.'

'How much?'

'I'm not sure. How far are you from Moreton Bay?'

'About fifty miles.'

'By God I'll take it. How far inland does your claim go?'

'We never measured it. You'd have to do that yourself.'

'So then what about five hundred pounds?'

'Five hundred pounds you say? For that sort of money I'd wait till hell freezes.'

Pace looked at Dolour. 'I can see this lady scowling at me. I promised I'd build her a proper homestead this year in return for getting two sons in one go, so I have to do that first, but I'll write you an IOU for the sale.'

'Where will you get five hundred pounds?' Dolour was worried.

'I'll find it. I've got some maps Dinny, come over to the house and you can show me where you are.'

Dolour sighed. 'Will you look at him! The eyes as bright as pennies and the shoulder forgotten. He'd rather read a map than a prayer book.'

# CHAPTER SIX

Milly Forrest walked out of her house into the silent hot night, singing little snatches of tunes when she could remember the words. She stood under the big wattle tree and looked back at the house, her house. It was finished at last and just in time. She had lit the oil lamps in the parlour and the entrance hall and the two bedrooms along the front of the house to get the effect and it was beautiful. There had been arguments with Dermott at first but they had compromised and now she was happy. The wide veran-dahs which made the house look more flat than stately did give it a cool air but she would have preferred a single portico. Dermott had insisted that everyone built their houses in the country with verandahs, for the climate, but she had had her way refusing to allow him to put the ugly auger holes in the walls and insisting that they have a drawing room.

She gathered her skirts and walked sedately to the front door pretending she was a guest, stepping inside to admire the glow of the polished yellow-wood floors, and the new furniture, some of which she had ordered by catalogue and some Dermott had made himself. The walls were papered but they still looked bare, they needed family portraits but the Forrests had none as yet and she couldn't think what else to put on them. It didn't matter, the walls were so clean and smelled new. Milly did not regret the months she had spent living in the rough hut the men had built. It had been worth it to keep an eye on every piece of wood and brick that went into the house.

Dermott was at his desk in the sitting room. 'Are you still going over to MacNamara's tomorrow?' she asked.

'Yes. I told him I'd go over every Sunday until their house is finished.'

'Well you can't go next week.'

'I know that.'

'I suppose they have copied our house?'

'Most houses out here look the same from the outside, you know that Milly. But it will be much smaller.'

'What are they doing about furnishings? Dolour says she hasn't ordered any yet.'

'They're going to make do with what they've got for the time being. Pace hasn't got money to spare. And he said they'll be pleased to come next Saturday night.'

'I sent them a written invitation. It's manners to write back.'

'Oh well, you know Pace doesn't worry about things like that.'

Milly curled up in the big chair facing him. 'I can't get over Jasin Heselwood being a Lord now. Do you think we should still call him Jasin?'

Dermott frowned. 'I never called him Jasin. They are more friends of yours than mine, and he never invited me to. But I don't think you should now, love, you could offend him. And Mrs Heselwood too, she's a Lady now, I wouldn't go calling her Georgina again if I was you.'

'If we ever see her again. I'm still cross with her, they just went off to England without a word.'

'His father was sick. They seem to do everything in a hurry those two.'

'But we had to read in month-old newspapers that they are back on our "sublime shores".'

Dermott shook his head and went back to his journal. He worked hard and he loved the station life. He got along well with his men, taking advice from the experienced hands and keeping a meticulous record of the stock and daily activities of the station.

Milly interrupted him again. 'Show me that letter from Jasin saying he is coming out. What did he sign himself?'

He took the letter from a drawer and handed it to her.

'Oh! He just signed it J. H. I thought Lords might put something better than that. It's a pity the Pagets from Blair Station can't come on Saturday night, they seem to be the king pins around here, but did you read her letter Dermott, she was practically weeping that they couldn't come since we are entertaining a Lord.' Milly giggled. 'And don't forget, she sent us an invitation to Blair. We'll take them up on that.'

'Yes dear.'

She went out to the kitchen to see what her staff were doing. She had been assigned two convict women and had recruited two girls from the blacks' camp to assist them. Efficient herself, Milly followed them around to see that everything was done properly and she complained to Dermott that they were all so slow, but it was delicious to be a squatter's wife and have a household to run. Milly too loved Carlton Park and the life they led. Bess had said that with all those servants she would have nothing to do but it was quite the opposite, they had to be watched all the time and the providing for the household and for the men had to be done. The garden had to be watered, she couldn't trust anyone to remember to do that, and there was the linen and laundry.

Now that the house was finally complete their entertaining would begin. She had given up riding since she found she was with child, a condition that neither excited nor depressed her but Dermott was pleased enough for both of them.

And now the most important event of her life was imminent. Not only her first dinner party, with a Lord no less as guest of honour, but also the first proper dinner party in the lower Namoi district. She spread a cloth on the gleaming dining room table and sat down to study her list again, getting up to wipe a smudge from the far end of the table first.

Lord Heselwood, the Earl of Montone! She could have cried with the joy of it. Who would have thought that she, Milly Jukes, would be one day entertaining a Lord? She had written to her parents telling them of the great good fortune that had blessed them in New South Wales, but the few replies from them and from her sisters had been terse, even rude. They had said, 'out plain' as her mother had put it, that she sounded as if she was getting too big for her boots and had inferred that she was lying. Dermott had suggested that they bring them out here to a better life, but then Dermott and Fred were orphans. To them family life was a kingdom of the happily-ever-after, like fairy stories. Milly knew better. Pace MacNamara had the opposite trouble. He had written for his brother and sister to come out and God knew he needed the extra hands but they had declined.

The MacNamaras . . . Pace had told Dermott they would be coming. It was a pity that Pace had once worked for Jasin but Dermott had insisted and Milly supposed it didn't really matter since Pace was a neighbour. And Dolour was a very beautiful woman. Milly had noticed that all the men gaped at her, even Dermott, but fortunately Dolour saw no-one else but Pace.

She had not invited the McPhies . . . the woman was a hag and the whole family were too rough. Dermott was certain the McPhie sons were stealing his cattle, he had had several rows with them and it was getting to the stage he might have to fence the south-east boundary. He would discuss it with Jasin.

The Pagets were away and couldn't come, but the invitation had made its mark, as it had on the people from the big station on the Peel, run by Henry Dangar. He had sent a formal regret and his best wishes to Lord Heselwood whom Milly knew for a fact he had never even met.

Then there were the Craddocks, the little couple who were managing the lawyer's property between Carlton Park and MacNamara's Kooramin. They had accepted, of course.

And Bess and Fred Forrest were already on their way. Fred liked to come out and help Dermott whenever he could. The two men had put their heads together and decided that Bess and Fred should come to stay. They would open up a saddlery and bootmaker's business out here. 'There's plenty of call for it,' Dermott had told Milly, 'and the business will grow as more people come this way.'

'Where will they live?' Milly had asked.

'Here. The house is big enough surely.'

'Let me remind you Dermott Forrest, that it was Bess herself who said there should only be one mistress in a house. Let them build their own house.'

'But they can't build here. Jasin might object.'

'They should have bought their own land when we did.'

And at the bottom of the list was Milly's surprise guest. The man who was becoming quite famous in the district. As well as his sheep station, vineyards and horse stud at Chelmsford, he had cattle runs on the Peel River not far from its junction with the Namoi, and although there were a lot of rumours, no-one knew for sure what else. On a visit to the Hunter Valley, Milly had insisted that Dermott take her to Chelmsford so that she could pay her respects at Adelaide's grave. Mr Rivadavia, whom she discovered was not a Spaniard but an Argentinian, had been charming. He even invited them to stay overnight and introduced them to his little daughter.

'The homestead,' she told Bess later, 'is absolutely gorgeous. Completely rebuilt, they say, in sandstone, and inside there is a courtyard with colonnades like a nunnery. The walls are all white with flagstone floors and huge pieces of furniture and glorious rugs on the floors and hanging on the walls. Our bedroom was the same, with a big bed and black furniture, Dermott knew what the wood was. And there was a cross on the wall over the bed. I think he's a papist but you should see him! He is utterly divine! How someone like Adelaide Brooks could have nabbed him I'll never know. She was years older than him.'

Only Dermott knew that she had invited Mr Rivadavia and only Dermott knew that he had accepted.

It didn't matter that the three couples who had accepted were people who would be just as happy eating in the kitchen, what mattered, Milly knew, was that news travelled fast in the bush. Carlton Park would become the social centre of the district when everyone found out that Lord Heselwood and Mr Rivadavia had both attended. In her way Milly understood people: sometimes being there was not as important as having missed out.

# PART TEN

## THE BLACK WARS I

# CHAPTER ONE

Upon their return to the colony of New South Wales, a carriage was waiting to escort Lord Heselwood, Earl of Montone, Lady Heselwood and their entourage to Government House, where they were welcomed by Governor Bourke and his daughter. Jasin had decided it would be appropriate to cut short their time of mourning as irrelevant in the colony where few had even heard of his late father and when they stepped ashore the elegance of their fashionable London dress turned heads. Jasin in his grey cutaway with a top hat and Georgina in a ruby silk morning dress and a feathered, velour chapeau.

Governor Bourke, an Irish Protestant, was a far cry from the stiff pomposity of Darling. A man of intelligence and good taste, he charmed them both on the first sunny days, while they regained their 'land legs'. He was not a man to encourage social activities which interfered with his workload, but also, as he explained to Jasin, 'there are so many factions here one is better to keep clear of them, it is so easy to stand on toes.' His daughter, a quiet girl, was too shy to invite ladies to her home, so the first few weeks gave Jasin time to observe the colony after more than a year's absence, and proceed with his preparations.

His late father had always cried poor-mouth, and indeed, he had discovered that the family estate was in poor shape, but Jasin had been surprised at the doors that opened to him once the title had been conferred, important doors to important financial institutions.

After examining various propositions in London, which would have gained him little more than seats on boards, acting as a rubber stamp and pursuing a long slow road to prosperity, he declined them all. Offers were also made to him by syndicates willing to invest in his New South Wales enterprises. These too he steadfastly resisted. He would share with no-one. But in their wake, credit was established, invaluable credit, backed by the benign directors of the Bank of England. He realised that the courtesy he was shown would turn sour if he were not able to meet his commitments, but at least it would enable him to move faster in his search for a northern station. It was unfortunate that his father's death had occured just before they were due to return, causing a considerable delay in his plans, and he worried that the prime land would have already been taken up, but he also remembered Burnett's advice, that the scope was endless and neighbours were needed. He was glad now that Burnett had turned him aside from that foolish idea of going too far beyond the boundaries, and his first thought had been to look up Macleay and find out how far they had run in his absence, but Georgina cautioned him.

'I should be careful. I have heard that a new Colonial Secretary has been appointed and is coming out from England. There is also talk that the Governor himself will be replaced.'

'Bourke hasn't said anything.'

'If you notice, the Governor does not weary us with his problems, I believe he would consider that in poor taste, but if you were to raise a question or two I'm sure he would oblige.'

Jasin did not have to bother, the Governor had invited a visitor to lunch. 'A good friend,' he had told them and Lord Heselwood was shocked to find it was the bombastic noisy Wentworth. He and John Macarthur were the wealthiest landowners in the country but their politics were poles apart.

Wentworth flattered Georgina outrageously, at the same time launching into one of the political diatribes for which he was famous.

'I don't know if Lady Heselwood is ready for this, William,' Bourke said gently, but the rebuke was tempered by a smile.

'Nonsense! The woman's got a brain. I can see that from here.' He tossed back his mane of white hair. 'Why does everyone assume that women are born sans intelligence? Now, do you think we should have a House of Assembly madam?'

'I don't see why not,' Georgina replied. 'It will have to come sooner or later as long as the colony follows the Westminster system.'

'Ha! See, I told you so,' he cried, pleased at her reply and then he focused on Jasin, his eyes challenging. 'But I see Milord disagrees.'

Jasin leaned back easily in his chair waiting for a lead from the Governor but Bourke gave no hint of his opinion. 'I should have to study the ramifications first,' he stalled.

But Wentworth attacked. 'What's to study? Are not the people of this colony as free as the people of England?'

'A good percentage of them are not, one would have to say. Do you intend to have convicts represented?'

'That is exactly the sleight of hand reply one would expect from you,' Wentworth said rudely, 'pretending the middle class does not exist.'

'Ah now steady on William, everyone is entitled to an opinion.' Bourke said.

Wentworth barked his reply: 'That is Macleay's view too, word for word! Governor, that man has to be put out of action, he's nothing but a jumped-up clerk, telling us we should not have a House of Assembly and daring to defy your endeavours for trial by jury.'

Jasin was astounded at Bourke's good humour. The man should have been put in his place but Bourke's reply stunned him. 'Patience William, we shall have trial by jury and we shall have a House of Assembly, it all takes time.'

259

Mollified, Wentworth turned to his meal and Bourke changed the subject. 'Lord Heselwood has a station out at the Namoi, William.'

'Yes I know. Is it going well? It can get dry out that way.'

'I believe so, I shall be visiting there shortly,' Jasin said, 'but I am looking to the north.' He forced a smile to keep the fellow in good temper and noticed that Georgina seemed to be quite enjoying the conversation.

'Where in the north?' Wentworth asked.

'The Darling Downs I believe it is called.'

'Humph! That country. It's got a bad name. That Moreton Bay is a disgrace, Governor.'

'But the prisoners in that penal settlement are incorrigibles,' Bourke protested. 'What are we to do with them?'

'You've got more than a thousand men up there doing nothing but growing enough corn to keep themselves half-fed. They should be put to work, why should the colony support them and the English army loafers put there to mind them? They can't all be incorrigibles.'

'It's difficult to say who is and who isn't these days,' Bourke commented.

'Anyway, Governor, what's this I hear, that you are talking about stopping land grants?' Wentworth asked.

Jasin place his knife and fork carefully on his plate and took a sip of wine, listening intently. He had obtained Carlton Park on a grant and he intended to claim another grant in Edward's name, since he was born in the colony.

'We need money for public works,' Bourke said, 'it makes more sense to charge an upset price of a few shillings an acre. It's not much to ask.'

Wentworth exploded. 'Not much to ask for a pipsqueak little farm but a murderous imposition on men of foresight who need, require, large runs to make their investments economical! This isn't England, this country will only take a few sheep to the acre and less cattle. I'm warning you Governor, I'll oppose you on this.'

Bourke smiled. 'We'll see.'

Jasin hoped he would. He could not fathom Wentworth at all, the man seemed to be packed with inconsistencies, making it difficult for listeners to know which way to step.

They waited while the dessert was being served, and Jasin frowned at Georgina as she re-opened the conversation. 'Is there much information to be had on the Darling Downs, Governor?'

'Not a lot I'm afraid,' Bourke replied.

Wentworth turned an approving smile on her. 'Then we should give the lady what little information we do have. Dangers aside, there is no doubt it is excellent country, and even though it is years since the unlamented Captain Logan received his just fate at the hands of the Aborigines on the Brisbane River, there aren't too many willing to take up land in that direction, but a syndicate of Scots is planning to establish a large sheep station up there. They are the ones we know of, so there are bound to be other men staking their claims, waiting once again for our trembling government to extend the boundaries.'

Jasin was appalled. Wentworth seemed unable to make a statement of any sort without taking a jab at someone, it was quite extraordinary. No wonder the Macarthurs had no time for him.

'Why don't you just throw the whole country open and be done with it Governor?' Wentworth asked.

'We've been through all that before. It would be an administrative nightmare and I don't have the staff.'

Wentworth turned to Jasin. 'Don't tell me *you* are seriously considering venturing into the northern wilderness? I should have thought a soft seat to sleep in at the House of Lords would be more to your taste.'

'Do you indeed?' Jasin drawled, refusing to allow his anger to show. 'There are some of us who find it more entertaining to take up the challenge of unknown country rather than sit still and inherit the spoils of our father's endeavours.'

The statement was not true, Jasin would have preferred to inherit, but it hit home. Even Governor Bourke was taken aback at the insult thrown at the formidable Wentworth, whom they all knew had inherited a vast fortune in New South Wales from his father. Only Georgina seemed to be enjoying the sparring match. She looked to Wentworth as if to say 'your move sir?' and Wentworth rallied. He twirled his empty glass and the Governor indicated to the footman to replenish the glasses.

'Bravo!' Wentworth shouted suddenly and the Governor blinked as though a strong light had suddenly struck his handsome face.

Jasin grinned. I'm a match for this bastard, he thought, hating the strong jutting face that was only softened by that thick womanish hair.

But his victory was short-lived.

'Then prove it sir!' Wentworth said, leaning across the table.

Bourke intervened. 'Lord Heselwood has already proved it. His own station at Carlton Park is proof of that. He was the first to open up that country.'

'A hop step and a jump!' Wentworth cried. 'I know that country. Move from one station on to the next until you stumble on free ground. I'll wager you lived well most of the way?'

'Is that a crime?' Jasin asked still smiling.

'It's not a challenge.'

'What is challenge then?' Jasin affected a bored look, tiring of this conversation and making it plain that, to him, Wentworth was simply punching air.

'Going north,' Wentworth was smiling.

'But sir, you seem to forget I have already said I am going north.'

'By what route?' Wentworth's voice was silky as if he were in a courtroom.

261

'By the same route I presume those Scots you referred to, will take. North through New England and up the range, and from what I hear it is hardly a main highway,' Jasin replied.

'Then take the other route.'

'There is no other route,' Bourke said, 'so don't confuse the issue William. You lawyers are good at that.'

'But there is.' He was excited now. He moved silver condiment pots on the table to demonstrate. 'Here is Sydney. Down here with the mustard. Now up here under the pepper is the Moreton Bay penal settlement with the Brisbane River spilling into the sea.' A crested fork marked the Brisbane River. 'Now, do you realise that it is about eight hundred miles, less maybe, I'm not sure, from Sydney to Moreton Bay?'

They all nodded and the lesson continued. 'Now a little way southwest of the penal settlement is Limestone.' He plucked a tiny flower from the centrepiece. 'That's Limestone. Not important in this discussion except to demonstrate distance. Now up here, and lady and gentlemen I have studied these maps cautiously, is that place we all refer to as the Darling Downs.' For a bulky man he was light on his feet. He jumped up and took a small figurine of priceless china and dumped it on his starched white map. 'There it is, the Darling Downs! Now take note. It is a vast distance from Sydney, from where flows all our benefits, perhaps seven hundred miles. You agree?'

His audience nodded again.

'But,' he continued. 'Look at it in relation to the Moreton Bay Settlement. And Limestone. Do observe Limestone. You will notice the Darling Downs is only about ninety miles from Moreton Bay.'

He sat back satisfied that his point had been made, but Jasin, glad the geography lesson was over, raised his eyebrows and said simply: 'So?'

'So there's your route!' Wentworth cried, stabbing at the table.

'You forget sir,' Jasin reminded him, 'that Moreton Bay is a closed settlement. Civilians cannot use that route.'

'And you forget Lord Heselwood that you are sitting at the Governor's table. With the sweep of a pen he could give you permission to take that route. Isn't that right Governor? If Lord Heselwood wishes to travel via Moreton Bay you surely would not deny him that simple request.'

'I don't suppose so,' Bourke said, walking into the trap.

Jasin, seeing an easier way to get to the north by ship, to save those months on horseback, looked to the Governor. 'Would you give me that permission?'

Bourke was troubled. Wentworth was not usually so helpful to people he obviously disliked. There was a catch to this, but he could not place it. 'If you wish,' he said.

'Then that's settled,' Jasin said, pleased at the way things had turned out after all. He would go by ship and have his cattle brought overland. It was too simple. He wondered why other men had not thought of it before and he had to admit that Wentworth for all his reputation, well deserved, of being an obnoxious person, was a clever fellow.

'Good!' William Charles Wentworth beamed. 'Take the Moreton Bay route and follow Logan!' He waited with the practised skill of a debater for the impact of his words to sink in. 'Follow Logan!'

In the privacy of their room at Government House, Georgina rounded on him. 'You can't Jasin! You must not!'

'Oh yes I will, he won't get the better of me.'

'Don't you understand he was baiting you? Governor Bourke has apologised. He said not to take any notice of him.'

'Then why is he such a good friend of the Governor's?'

'I don't know. I'm sure I don't know. He is a most volatile person. It defeats me that Bourke puts up with him.'

'Well there's one thing we have discovered. We have to get out of here as soon as possible,' Jasin said. 'This Governor may be a very likeable fellow but he's completely at odds with our own friends. No wonder we haven't seen anyone. It is quite obvious that the Macarthurs don't call.'

'I don't know about you,' Georgina said, 'but I had enormous trouble following what Wentworth said and he seems to hate the Macarthurs and yet he is one of them.'

'Don't try,' her husband said. 'Wentworth is quite mad.'

'But Miss Bourke told me in great confidence that John Macarthur senior is certifiably mad.'

Jasin paced the room, 'They're all mad out here, but Wentworth has thrown down the glove and I have to pick it up.'

'You don't! He tricked you into it.'

'Yes I do. He owns newspapers. He could make a laughing stock of me.'

'What do you care?'

'One has to care. But smart as he is Wentworth has not got the better of me. I said I would go, but I didn't say when. We have a lot to do. First we shall rent a house and enjoy life in Sydney and while keeping on good terms with the Governor, distance ourselves. He might be popular with some in the colony but I doubt he will be appreciated at home by the gentlemen who hold the purse strings. And then of course at some stage I must go out and inspect Carlton Park. Do you want to come with me?'

'No I do not.'

Jasin laughed. Georgina had not forgiven the Forrests. To him they were simply a convenience; to her, an irritation.

# CHAPTER TWO

Mr and Mrs Fred Forrest were the first visitors to arrive at Carlton Park, rumbling over the track in their buggy because Bess did not like to ride long distances.

The drive from the gate to the house had not yet been laid down but the area had been flattened by the passing of horses. It didn't matter much in summer but in winter it would be a bog. Milly planned in time to have a sandy drive, encircling an ornamental garden. Now she waited at her front door in a brown linen dress with a cream lace collar and cuffs, smoothing the front of the dress that she had cleverly lifted a few inches at the waist to allow more fullness and disguise the thickening of her figure.

Rehearsing her role as hostess, she waved and smiled as Fred helped Bess down, but they hurried up the steps, their faces grey and worried.

'Where's Dermott?' Fred cried, rushing past her.

'He's putting on a shirt. What's the matter?'

'Oh Milly,' Bess said, embracing her tearfully. 'We've got some bad news.'

'What's wrong?' Milly demanded, forced to follow them into the house. 'Were you attacked on the road? The constable was only here yesterday and he said things were quiet out this way.' Her voice trailed off as she watched Fred grasp hold of Dermott and steer him towards the parlour. 'I'll just have a few words with Dermott,' Fred said over his shoulder, but Milly strode after them. 'Whatever you've got to say, you can tell me too Fred Forrest.'

'Yes, come on in and sit down Fred,' Dermott said. 'Poor Bess must be worn out. Do you want a drink before you tell me all this startling news? It can't be all that bad.'

'I'm afraid it is,' Fred said. 'I think this will be a shock for you, brother, but you have to know. Remember you asked me to go to the Lands Office and get a copy of the title deed to Carlton Park so that you'd have one here on the station, now that you've got a child, an heir, on the way?'

'Oh yes,' Bess said. 'How are you feeling, Milly?'

But Milly ignored her. 'What about it, Fred?'

He shook his head and put his hand out to Bess who withdrew some papers from her large brocade handbag. Solemnly he took the papers and handed them to Dermott as if observing a form of protocol. 'That's a copy of the deed and the government surveyor's report and it cost me a few quid to get my hands on it too.'

'Do they charge for such things?' Milly asked.

264

'Not if it's yours but if you're snooping into someone else's business they're not obliging.'

Milly sighed. Fred could never get anything right. 'I think they put one over on you Fred,' she laughed. 'Let me see the deed Dermott.'

But Dermott kept staring at it. 'You've got the wrong place Fred, our names are not on it.' He looked up and smiled. 'Easy enough to do.'

'It's not the wrong place,' Bess said. 'You can see it is called Carlton Park and the description is this property.'

'Let me see.' Milly snatched the papers and sitting down spread them flat on her lap to study them while the others waited. 'It's our place all right,' she said at length. 'It's Carlton Park, you can see by the shape of the drawing, but they've just made a mistake. They've put Jasin's name on it and forgotten to put Dermott's on. Might be they only put one name on.'

'Read the wording of the title deed, the ownership papers, that's what counts. It says this place is owned by the Honourable J. Heselwood. Your name's not there Dermott! Believe me I had them go back and look and look again. This land was given to him as a free grant, most of it anyway, he hardly paid a ha'penny for it. And look at the signature of his witness, it frightened the clerk. When he saw it he just wanted to get rid of me after that. Heselwood's grant of land was arranged by Macleay, the Colonial Secretary himself.'

'What does it mean?' Milly demanded, bewildered.

'It means you've been tricked.' Fred said flatly.

Dermott took the papers back, his hands trembling. 'I wouldn't go as far as to say that. Mr Heselwood will be able to explain it. He'll be here on Friday. He'll sort it out.'

'Are you saying, Fred, that we don't own any of this land?' Milly whispered.

'Yes.'

'But our house is on it! We own this house!' She was shouting. 'Tell me we don't own this house!' She jumped up and stood glaring at the men who were too upset to reply and burst into tears of rage. 'Dermott, what have you done? You've let him rob us. And we've built our house, our beautiful house on his land. I'll kill him!' She was hysterical and they found her some brandy.

'He won't get away with it,' Milly yelled, storming around the room. 'He still owes us money. We'll demand our money!'

'Then he could demand you leave,' Fred said. 'You're on thin ice, Dermott.'

'How could he do this to us?' Milly cried. 'Why would he do this? And what about my dinner party? How can I have a dinner party for a Lord when he's nothing more than a thief!'

At the same time another argument was in progress, at Kooramin Station: Dolour was refusing to attend Milly's dinner party.

265

'But I said we'd go,' Pace told her. 'And Milly will be hurt if we don't turn up. Dermott says she's been planning this for weeks.'

'There's too much to do here,' Dolour cried. 'We'd have to stay over the night and there's the milking.'

'Connelly said he'd do the milking.'

'I can't add on to his work, he's got enough to do. And what about the work on the house? It's a day wasted there.'

'The house will keep. Dolour, you work too hard as it is. I'm always telling you to rest. You're going from dawn to dark. It'll be a little holiday for you and a chance to dress up. You're not shy of them are you?'

'Of course I'm not,' she said miserably. 'But we don't need to go Pace. Milly won't miss us, she probably only invited us to be polite.'

'That's as good a reason as any to go wouldn't you say? We'll turn up and give them a little bit of support. If she wants to put on a good show for Heselwood, why not? God knows he won't appreciate it, but if she's got her friends around we'll make a good night of it. And anyway,' he laughed, 'what's the use of having a beautiful wife if I can't show her off?' He put his arms around her and kissed her.

On the Friday night when Dolour was still refusing to go, he said to her, 'Dolour. I'm not asking any more, I'm telling. We need neighbours out here, we have to help each other. We must not let Milly down, if she's good enough to ask us then we're good enough to go. You have to put yourself out for other people sometimes.'

Dolour squirmed in her chair, white-faced and anxious. From the minute the dinner party had been mentioned along with Jasin's name she had worried herself into a state of panic. Now Pace was angry with her, and she had run out of excuses but she would not go, not with Jasin there. It was too dangerous, you never knew what he'd say. Pace was waiting for an answer and with all her heart she regretted her affair with Jasin but it was no use fretting over that. She had prayed that she had seen the last of him but every time his name was mentioned she felt sick. It was terrible to live with this cloud hovering over her all the time, and it made her angry now. Why should I have to live like this? she asked herself, worried at each turn that the tale might come out, squalling inside like a weak little goat. I won't have it any longer.

'I'll not have it any longer!' she said and Pace looked at her, surprised. 'Have what?'

'I've got something to tell you Pace and it might as well be now and get it over and done with, I love you and it's killing me the worry of it. It's about Jasin Heselwood . . .'

He sat in the big old canvas chair on the verandah all night. He had not said one word to her. He did not trust himself to say anything in case it released the rage in him. Every word that she had said seared into his heart and it was no use thinking he might have reacted differently had it been someone else but Heselwood. It was Heselwood! And another mystery was solved now.

As soon as his shoulder had healed he had ridden down to the Hunter Valley searching for Pelham and he had found him. In a cemetery at Maitland.

'Died in a fight some time back,' the constable told him. 'Got into an argument in a bush pub and challenged a man to a duel. But the bloke he picked on didn't know what he was talking about; he'd never heard of a duel. Pistols at forty paces or whatever they do! He just turned around and belted Pelham and the next minute the Captain's outside waving his pistol around and threatening to shoot Silver, that was the stockman's name. Well! Silver went for him with his stirrup iron. Killed him stone dead. We had an inquest but as Silver said, "If someone's half-charged and pointing a loaded pistol at you, you don't waste time asking questions!" Plenty of witnesses, Silver got off.'

Then Pace went to Singleton and found the old fellow who had been hired to kill him and dumped him head first into a horsetrough until he sobered up enough to talk to him.

'I never seen him again,' he whined. 'He didn't come back to give me the other five pounds he said he was gonna give me when I pulled it off.'

'You didn't earn it, you old bastard.'

'I wasn't gonna tell him that.'

'Then let me tell you something. His name wasn't Pelham. Captain Pelham was already dead. Now who the bloody hell was he?'

'I don't know. How should I know? That's the name he gave me. He was an Englishman I swear. A real toff, he was drinking with us boys one night.'

Pace had decided that it was a case of mistaken identity. The old drunk had gone after the wrong man, which wasn't surprising. Whoever chose him for the job must have been tarred with the same brush, a fellow winebag. Since there were no other attempts on his life, he had forgotten the incident.

He had other things on his mind. His herds were improving and the station taking shape but he still hadn't been able to fulfil his promise to O'Meara. He knew he couldn't ask O'Meara and his mate to wait much longer, but he had as yet been unable to raise the cash to buy the northern land. That thought had depressed him. If he could not buy it, the least he could do for O'Meara would be to arrange for him to sell it to someone else. But he had not managed to bring himself to do anything about it.

But coming back to that fellow who tried to shoot him, and the mysterious Englishman, in the light of Dolour's confession it was becoming clearer. In her anxiety to show him that it was all over with Heselwood, (he winced at the thought of them together) she had told him of the encounter at their house in Singleton and how she had sent Heselwood packing.

It had not helped. He had sat there, stony-faced, letting her talk. There was no doubt in his mind now that Heselwood was the instigator of that shooting. His fingerprints were all over it, in the stupid amateurish way he went about it. Typical of him! Pace laughed but it came out a growl. Heselwood was not the heart of the matter. Dolour had been living a lie. She'd made a fool of the husband she said she loved. She had bedded with a man known to him and said not a word about it. All those times he had talked about Heselwood, she had let him go on, never once saying she already knew the man. And better than her husband did! What a fool he must have sounded!

And the Forrests! She had listened to them talking about their partner The Honourable Mister Heselwood, with the secret up her sleeve. Or did they know that Heselwood and MacNamara's wife had been lovers? She'd make him a laughing stock yet.

The grief and anger he felt was a torture to him and he hated them both. Dolour for deceiving him, for making him their dupe, and Heselwood for getting his hands on Dolour, and thinking he had a royal right to her still. Calling on her when her husband's back was turned. And what about that story? That Heselwood had called on her and talked to her and she had sent him packing. What else had happened? How much of that was true? The fury was in him again and he slammed a fist into the palm of his hand.

Dolour was at the door in her nightgown. 'It's very late Pace, aren't you coming to bed? I'm sorry, I wouldn't have put you through this for the world but I didn't know what else to do.'

He felt a huge sigh or even a sob building up in him and stifled it, causing his chest to ache, but the bitterness was so overwhelming he could not even turn his head to look at her. After a while she went away and he stayed out in the night.'

In the end he decided he would go to Carlton Park without her. He would attend Milly's party. He had accepted the invitation. There would be time afterwards for him to settle the score.

There was pandemonium at the Carlton Park homestead when Pace arrived. They didn't even notice that Dolour was not with him. Dermott had suffered a heart seizure! Heselwood had departed after some great upset with his partners, and Pace couldn't get any sense out of Milly who seemed to have gone to pieces altogether. The doctor emerged from the sick room to speak to the family and since he was still standing in the passageway Pace was included.

'He's in a bad way,' the doctor said, and Milly's' weeping increased. 'I think you'd better lie down, Mrs Forrest. I'll give you some laudanum to put you to sleep.'

'I don't want to go to sleep!' she shrieked. 'What's wrong with Dermott?'

'Hush now, you must be quiet. I'm afraid he is paralysed down his right side. He's had a stroke.'

'Will he get over the paralysis?' Fred asked and the doctor shook his head. 'I can't promise that. It'll be a long time before he can walk again, if he does at all.'

'Oh that Jasin Heselwood! He's the cause of this! He's done this to my Dermott!' Milly was shouting again. 'I must go in to him.' She made for the door but the doctor held her back. 'No. He's sleeping now. Let him rest.' With Bess helping him he led Milly off to another room.

'What's happened here?' Pace asked Fred.

'Everything!' Fred said. 'I could do with a drink, what about you?' Without waiting for a reply he headed for the dining room and Pace followed. As he passed the parlour door he saw the Craddocks from Batterson's station sitting nervously on the edge of their chairs in the parlour. He nodded to them and hurried after Fred.

Over Dermott's best rum Fred told Pace the cause of the upset in the first place. Heselwood! Pace wondered if he should be surprised. To find you had no equity in your own land and worse, that you'd built a house on someone else's land was enough to give anyone a heart attack.

'It's a bad business,' Pace said to Fred. 'But Heselwood was here yesterday I gather. Did Dermott quiz him on it?'

'Oh he did all right. But, do you know that Lord Heselwood just looked at Dermott as if he had no right to be questioning him. He ignored him. Then, of course, Milly had her say. He told her it was all a misunderstanding, that there was nothing to worry about. Well you know Milly, she's got a temper that girl. She hurled pages of the title at him as well as a few nasty words; she said she didn't care if he was a lord or what he bloody was, she wanted that title fixed, and the money he owes them paid.'

Despite his own misery Pace couldn't help smiling. He was sorry he had missed that.

'But do you know what Heselwood did? He got up cool as a cucumber and looked down that skinny nose of his. "I did not come here to be insulted," he says, "I have seen over the station Dermott, you seem to be keeping it in splendid order." And he stalked out. The next thing we see him riding off with a pair of stockmen who looked more like bodyguards. Then Dermott suddenly collapsed – and you know the rest.'

The doctor was leaving so Fred went to see him off and Pace wandered into the parlour.

'Do you think we should leave?' Bill Craddock asked him.

'I'm sure I don't know,' Pace said. 'But if you want a drink, you'd better get yourself one. No-one will notice. The drinks are out ready in the dining room.'

'Get me a sherry while you're about it,' Mrs Craddock whispered to her husband.

'All right,' Craddock said. 'What about you Pace?'

'A rum thanks. I haven't been drunk for a long time and I'm fast beginning to think today's the day.'

269

Fred and Bess Forrest came in to join them and it was an awkward, subdued group until Milly loomed up in the doorway, her face washed and her hair combed.

'You were supposed to be sleeping,' Bess cried.

'I won't take that laudanum stuff, it tastes foul. I threw it out.' She looked at Pace as if he had just arrived and went over to take his hand. 'Oh Pace. I'm so glad you're here. Did you hear what that Heselwood has done to us?'

'I heard. But you mustn't let him get away with it. You need a good lawyer and who better than Batterson?'

'Yes. He'd be the one,' Bill Craddock echoed. Batterson was his uncle.

'But what about Dermott? He can't run the station any more and I wouldn't know what to do. Pace you've got to help me.'

Pace looked at Fred. 'I've been thinking about that. Milly's got to hold on here. Could you and Bess stay with her? If she vacates, there's no case at all for the courts.'

'We'll stay Milly,' Bess said stoutly. 'Won't we Fred?'

'My oath we will. As long as Dermott's not well enough to work we'll look after things.'

Pace turned back to Milly. 'I don't know what a lawyer's advice would be but I think you'll have to take him to court to prove your half share in the station, but in the meantime I wouldn't pay him a penny for any stock you market. Don't give him a penny. Since he owes you money I think you'd be within your rights.'

Bess found this a drastic step. 'But Pace. What if he is right and it is just a mistake after all? What if some clerk just forgot to put Dermott's name on the title?'

Pace looked at her, his face grim and his eyes hard. 'Never give a Heselwood the benefit of the doubt.'

There was a cough at the back of them and a voice said. 'Good evening. I was knocking but nobody seemed to hear.'

The special guest, Juan Rivadavia, had arrived, looking splendid in a short cut black-embroidered jacket, a white shirt with a lace jabot and wide cummerbund over immaculately fitting trousers.

Milly stared at him and burst into tears. She had forgotten the dinner party.

They did not dine. They ate. Bess had the the courses sent in to them in swift succession, while Milly presided, stiff and silent as if this were a dream sequence in which she had no speaking part. Within the hour, the Craddocks had fled. Milly walked out of the dining room and did not return, Bess disappeared into the depths of the kitchen and Fred went to sit with Dermott.

'It is very sad for Dermott,' Rivadavia said to the last remaining guest, Pace MacNamara.

'You don't know the half of it.'

'Oh? What else is wrong?'

Pace shook his head. 'Let's not spoil a grand evening,' he said with a grin, and Juan, who was still immersed in the cataclysmic atmosphere, glanced at him, not too sure of what he had heard, and then he too began to laugh.

He walked down to the sideboard and picked up a bottle of wine as the clock chimed eight. 'It's going to be a long night.'

Left to their own devices they talked of the weather and stock improvements and their stations.

'I've got a run far to the north,' Pace said, 'but I'm going to lose it because I can't raise enough cash. You wouldn't be interested in going halves?'

'Where is it?'

'On past the Darling Downs, in the Brisbane Valley.'

Juan was immediately interested. 'That far? I'd like to get hold of land up there.'

'I'll be going up there when I can,' Pace said. He didn't know whether it was the liquor talking or his bitterness towards Dolour.

'I'd like to come with you. But I've bought the property next to mine for a horse stud. There's too much to do. It's a pity, I've always wanted to explore that country. But I promise you, as long as it's good land, I'll invest in it.'

'As far as I can make out it is valuable land, and there's at least twenty square miles staked out and waiting.'

'That's a good start,' Juan said, echoing Pace's own thoughts. 'We might even get more.'

Pace remembered the homestead he was building. He felt bound by his earlier promise. 'Right then, we'll go fifty-fifty. I have to finish my house and then I'll get myself up there.'

Back at his own station he commandeered more hands to work on the house and he kept at it himself from dawn until late at night, working with lanterns when necessary. He still refused to speak to Dolour and although she tried to talk to him he ignored her. He knew it was hurting her, and saw that her eyes were constantly red from crying, but he could not look at her. As the days wore on, his attitude towards her hardened. He was still angry that he had missed the chance to give Heselwood his just desserts and vowed to catch up with him again and his fury remained. Since his return from Carlton Park, he had been sleeping on the verandah and he knew there had been talk around the station, but no-one dared mention it to him; they were all becoming very quiet in his presence, wary of his sudden bursts of anger, and he looked forward to getting away. It'll be a more cheerful place without me around, he thought bitterly, and the night before he left, he called Connelly in.

'I'm going north to claim that land O'Meara's holding for me,' he said, and thought he spied a look of relief on his foreman's face. 'You'll be able to run things while I'm away?'

271

'Yes, it'll be fine. I hope to God O'Meara's still there.'

'So do I. I wouldn't blame him if he's given up on me. Now you and the boys fix up the inside of the homestead and move Dolour and the kids in, and if you want, you can move in here.'

'I don't mind being in the bunkhouse. We could turn this cottage into a creamery, they need more space.'

'No. If you don't want it, keep it as an office and turn the bedroom into a storeroom.'

'All right. How long will you be away?'

'It's hard to say,' Pace said thinking perhaps he might never come back. 'A couple of months at least. It'll be good practice for you, to keep the books in order.'

'We still need more hands. Why don't we get some convicts out here?'

'I don't know how you can say that Connelly when you were one yourself.'

'But they'd have a better life here than in prison. And we'd pay them the same as free men. They use them at Carlton Park.'

'There'll be no serfs on my land. We'd have Government officials around the place checking on them and if anyone ran off we'd have to report him or be charged ourselves with aiding an escapee. I'll keep a lookout on the trail and if I meet any likely fellows I'll send them down. In the meantime you'll just have to do the best you can.'

He packed a swag and put supplies aside to be loaded on the pack-horse and went to bed very late and tried to sleep.

'You're going away tomorrow?' Dolour was standing beside his bunk, a blanket wrapped around her.

'I am.'

'Without saying goodbye?'

'Go back to bed.'

'What do I have to do? I have said I am sorry. Do you want me to go down on my knees? I will Pace, but I beg you, don't go off like this. I have a terrible feeling you're not coming back. Are you coming back?'

'I don't know.'

He heard her catch her breath. 'Thank you for building the house, it's a beautiful house. But without you it's worth nothing.'

She sat down on the steps near the foot of his camp bed and looked into the night and he could feel her desolation, huddled there like a deep shadow, but he would not speak. The things that came into his head to say were far worse than his silence.

In the morning she was still there her face white and pinched but he dressed, pulled on his boots, went into the bedroom for spare clothes and his sheepskin jacket, stood and looked at his sons for a few minutes and then left by the back door.

# CHAPTER THREE

Dimining's tribe were Kamilaroi but his mob, he said, were Warrigal people and Jack soon learned that the warrigal was the dingo which, being their totem was never to be harmed. They allowed Jack to stay with them, sharing with him, and he tried to teach them English but they made a joke of it, another game, they liked games, so he was forced to learn their words and suffer their laughter when he made mistakes. They even shared their women. Ngalla and Kana were permitted to come to him but Dimining explained that he would have to wait his turn for a wife.

Jack had not thought that far ahead. He intended to leave one day, but for the present, the easy-going life pleased him. They seemed to have more rules than the army but he listened politely while Dimining outlined this important matter regarding wives. He could not take a wife, even when one was available, until he had been initiated into the clan and when Jack saw evidence of the necessary ceremonies he decided he would be better off remaining an outsider. The young men showed him their scars with pride and pointed to the gap where a front tooth had been knocked out by their betters and Jack retired to his humpy, happy to have the women on loan. The elders had first choice of wives, some had two or three, and there were no unmarried women so the young men had to wait for the girls to reach marriageable age or be widowed. Jack thought the old men were randy to have so many wives but he soon began to see the wisdom of their ways. The women searched for roots and honey and berries keeping the old men fed once their hunting skills failed.

Gradually Jack learned to fend for himself, foraging a little and fishing which gave him a better standing in the community and every time he thought about leaving he wondered why and the weeks turned into months. He learned to smear himself with emu fat to keep out the cold and to pat dust on his skin to deter mosquitoes and as his body browned in the sun and his hair grew into a thick mat, the women painted him with red ochre and trimmed his beard with sharp shells into a jutting extension of his jaw.

He loved the lazy life. Each day began with a search for food and when enough was found the remainder of the day was given over to rest and enjoyment.

One morning he awoke to shouts of 'Bullara! Bullara!' and rushing out he saw them all excitedly pointing to a rainbow. It didn't seem to Jack to

273

warrant such attention but then he realised they were packing up the camp.

'Where are we going?' he asked Dimining.

'We go walkabout now,' Dimining said, and Jack was none the wiser.

'What's the name of this river?' he asked, so that he'd know where he was when he got back.

'Namoi River. This man run on fast now. You stay with Moorego and Kamarra. They mind you,' he laughed, 'like a birrahlee.'

Jack knew a birrahlee was a baby and he grinned and shoved at Dimining, amazed at his ability to mix in with this tribe of people who were as fierce as they looked, high spirited in good times but with nasty ways of settling arguments. He was always careful not to offend. A spear in the thigh was the usual punishment for men and the wrong-doer was expected to stand there and take it. Even the women could be savage. He had seen them fly into rages and fight, taking turns to crack each other's heads with waddies until one dropped, half-dead. Then the victor would nurse the loser back to health. It was all too complicated for Jack who stayed well clear.

The women packed up their dilly bags and digging sticks, carrying their babies in slings around their necks and Moorego whistled to Jack to hurry along. He was about forty years old with a gammy leg and Kamarra was his son. The hunters had gone on ahead and now the women and children and slower men gathered around expectantly as Jack approached. Moorego stepped forward and with extravagant formality presented him with a new spear.

Jack thanked him with a courtly bow which raised gales of laughter and held it aloft understanding that this was not only a gift but acceptance. Somehow he knew this was to be a long walk.

'Plurryell!' Moorego said with a grin and Jack nodded, pleased. Moorego had picked up a few of Jack's words but his favourite was 'plurryell', learned when Jack had walked barefoot into a thornbush shouting 'bloody hell!' Moorego had split his sides laughing and pounced on the words to be used on special occasions. They didn't seem to have any 'swear' words in their language or if they did Jack had not been able to discover them.

He ascertained from Moorego that they would be following the river south and then heading east towards the morning sun and it made him nervous, they were taking him back towards white man's country. Across the plains and on the other side of the ranges was the Hunter Valley. He'd have to drop out before then.

Moorego drew mud maps for him so he was beginning to learn a little about the country and the names of the places they came to. Baddawaral was a place to keep away from, a plain with no water, so they skirted it for miles. And at the entrance to a small valley was Girrawheen, place of flowers. Every landmark had a name and they delighted in pointing them out to him. As they trekked on he said the names over and over, trying to keep them in mind. Each night the hunters returned with kangaroo or possum meat and the women threw roots onto the fire with the meat and they sat around their camp fires singing or listening to stories and then they rested preparing for the next long day of travelling.

One afternoon as they filed through heavy scrub everyone stopped, waiting, and Jack sat down thankful for the delay. The waiting went on for more than an hour until they heard a 'cooee', a strange carrying call from the distance. Moorego replied and answering calls came back and then strangers suddenly appeared, their faces and bodies decorated with feathers.

'Bralga men,' Moorego said and Jack watched while the leaders talked and then there were smiles all around. The trek continued through the bush until it thinned out and they came upon a large camp scattered among the sparse trees. The Warrigal people ran forward and there was much laughter and excited talk. The women plodded through with their children to squat by the fires. Jack hung back, unsure of this new mob but Moorego came to collect him, showing him off like a trophy and the Bralga people were fascinated. They examined every inch of him, even the embarrassing parts and laughed at the diminutive size of his big toe. Their big toes were huge, from a lifetime of climbing trees.

He complained as they left the shelter of the bush and headed out across the plains even though they were travelling in high grass, and he lagged behind wondering if he should try to get back to the Bralga people, but in the end he had to keep up because he had no water. For a reason he could not as yet fathom they considered it bad form to carry water so he plunged after them wishing he had a hat. Nobody ever seemed to be leading and the lines straggled but the course was always dead straight as if they knew exactly where they were going and by the end of the day, sure enough, they came to a waterhole. Closer now were those hated mountains that he had struggled through with Dimining, whom, Jack suddenly realised, he had not seen for days. He tried to tell Moorego that he should not go any further but the Aborigine could not understand. He wished Dimining would come back; he knew the danger.

There didn't seem to be any hurry to leave this waterhole, for which Jack was grateful. There was plenty of game including flocks of wild birds and bats that could be knocked out of the trees with sticks. Everything else they ate he had learned to appreciate but Jack drew the line at bats. It was superstitious of him, he knew. The blacks themselves had plenty of superstitions but he was unable to explain about the bats because he had yet to learn the Kamilaroi words to describe superstition.

One morning Kamarra woke him, indicating that they should leave quietly, and took him to a place well away from the camp where Moorego and some strangers were waiting. He wondered what they wanted of him, but with Moorego leading they set off running across open country and

Jack went after them until at last they stopped, pointing down at some strange tracks.

Proudly Moorego pushed Jack forward to see if he could identify them and the others stood back respectfully, but Jack didn't need a second look. 'Oh Jesus,' he said. 'Wagon tracks!'

It was a shock to him that white men had already come out this far but it was difficult to explain the tracks. 'Wagons,' he said to blank stares, and then scratched his head for the word for horse, he must find out from Dimining. 'White man,' he said, holding up his spear like a rifle. 'Bang. Bang!'

Moorego's face was creased with worry and they all sat on the ground in a small circle to discuss this problem. Jack felt important. The sight of the wagon tracks had given him no pleasure. He lived among friends and he did not want anyone to intrude and spoil things. He was becoming adept with the billah, spear, and could hunt when he needed to. His muscles were hardier and he felt stronger than he had ever been in his life.

For the first time since he had been with the blacks he made a decision for them. 'We will follow these tracks and see where they go,' and they nodded in agreement.

The trail led them across the plains for two days and they stood in the bush, out of sight of the white men who were building stockyards near the river.

Jack pointed. 'Wagon. Over there. Wagon.' And the black men gaped.

Kamarra pointed at the horses. 'Yarraman,' and Jack snapped his fingers. 'That's it, Yarraman. Yes, horses.'

When they returned to the place where the people were sitting down Jack was relieved to see that Dimining and his friends were back. They already knew about the wagons. 'The white men have found the getting-through-place in the mountains. There is nothing to stop them now. They'll be bringing their sheep and cattle as well as horses and they will sit down and live here on our land.' He turned and called to Jack who always sat at the back. 'Am I right?'

'Yes,' Jack called, feeling a nervous tightening of his stomach muscles as he always did when they got onto the subject of white men.

A speaker stood by his fire and made a long speech. It was listened to in silence and then another man stood and spoke and afterwards voices began to shout angrily. Even the women joined in. They were all talking too quickly for Jack to understand.

'What's happening?' he asked Ngalla.

'One man said we must go back, get out of here quickly. That other man says no. This is our country we stay, kill the white men.'

Another man stood, an old man called Jung Jung. There was no chief among this mob but Jung Jung was highly respected and he had three wives. He spoke quietly and slowly and Jack understood him. 'We don't take any notice of the white men. They don't matter. Why are you all getting so angry?'

Jack Drew had no qualms about the killing of the white men. He saw them as a procession of landowners like Mudie who ruthlessly used the convicts.

Dimining came back and squatted beside him. 'What do you think?'

'I don't know. You can't fight the troopers and their guns if they come out here.'

The debate raged and Dimining waited until the people were quieter. He stood by his fire and told them about the guns, explained to the people exactly what a gun could do. They slept that night, frightened and confused, but the next morning they continued their trek along the ancient trails, which Jack was relieved to see did not go through the Hunter Valley this time.

They passed by the wagons and everyone took turns to creep up and take a good look. They forded the river and turned away from the plains, and went on inland to the cool mountains to escape the heat and mosquitoes. As they entered small valleys they lit fires and walked through the smoke to rid their bodies of the mosquito pests and keep the valleys free of them. They swam and fished in mountain streams and in the pools at the base of waterfalls. They roamed the forests, held meetings and visited other mobs. They showed Jack the taboo areas where all life was safe, no animals were killed, no birds hunted, no honey could be touched nor any roots of the earth disturbed because this land was set aside to regenerate life. When winter came they turned north into the sun.

When Ngalla's husband died she begged to be permitted to marry Jackadoo and it was allowed because Jackadoo had become a great hunter as well as an object of great interest among the tribes. Several lighter-skinned babies were born over the years to his women and to other women he shared; but only two of them, two boys, were considered to be his sons. They believed that babies were given to them by the spirits and had no connection with copulation. Tiny stars were faraway twinkles of babies waiting to be born and the big stars and constellations, which they all knew well, were majestic figures of the Dreamtime.

For many years Jack lived at peace with his chosen people and they covered such a vastness of land at such a leisurely pace that he had almost forgotten the country around the Namoi when they finally returned. Visitors to their camps told them that black people could still go on from the Namoi across the plains and the mountains and down into the sweet valley; it was true, there was nothing to stop them, but the white men were everywhere, and they could be very cruel.

'This can not be so,' Moorego said. 'Why have you let this happen? This is Kamilaroi territory. If the white men take it all where can we go?'

'They come forward like a flood,' one man said sorrowfully. 'How can we stop them?'

Jack now understood the territorial rights of the different tribes. Land was a birthright. Even if the white men took all of the Kamilaroi territory

277

the people still could not move onto land belonging to another tribe. It would be unthinkable, and besides, their totems and their burial places and all their sacred places were within their own tribal land. If they left these familiar places they feared their spirits would get lost and would not be able to find a home in the Dreaming.

Men from other tribes came into the vast Kamilaroi country only by invitation. They usually came on trading expeditions and when they did the Kamilaroi told them of tragedies that seemed to have no end. The white men had passed the Namoi and gone on to the Gwydir River crossing other big rivers with their thousands of animals as if they were creeks. They now occupied more than half of the land of the Kamilaroi who now feared they would be engulfed like other tribes to the south.

Desperately wanting to help, Jack said to Dimining: 'They're close enough now. Perhaps I can get down and steal a gun and some ammunition.'

'No,' his friend said. 'You must not do that. You are safe with us as long as you do not have a gun. That would only remind the people you are a white man and someone might take fright and kill you.'

Jack sat by his camp fire feeling afraid and isolated, knowing the group was preparing to go east, towards the sea. They were only waiting for stragglers to arrive before leaving. He stood up beside his fire, his hands raised for their attention. 'Don't go that way,' he begged them. 'Let us go out instead to the Warrego, on to the big river, far from the white men.'

But they told him they must go. It was time to go that way and there were families to see again, friends who would know they were coming, and it would be an exciting journey. He knew they were all looking forward to visiting the valley they called the sweet valley, which he knew to be the Hunter, and he also detected a curiosity among them to see the white men and the wonders they surrounded themselves with. Only Dimining understood his pleas and supported him.

Ngalla could not understand why he made such a fuss. 'We just go to sit down for a while with the Warrain people in the sweet valley. The white men give them good food,' she added archly.

'They'll give you a kick in the backside too, or worse!' Jack said.

The men argued for days and Dimining was losing ground. 'The white men are dangerous. They will shoot a black man for less reason that they will kill a barndoo [black duck].' But he was not able to call up their anger against a foe which to them seemed non-existent. With their own eyes they could see blackfellows who had walked among the white men and returned unharmed; look at Dimining himself! With their own ears they had heard stories of tucker, white man's tucker, to make the mouth water. They were impatient to be on their way, to see all these wondrous things for themselves.

The impetuous ones clapped Jung Jung when he spoke. 'There is no argument. That is our path. We must stay on the old paths so as not to confuse the spirits. From here we go through the long grasses and over the mountains to the valley where the Warrain people will be waiting for us at the grove of the yellow blossom trees. We never go any other way,' he admonished Dimining, 'not my father nor his father. How can you be so cruel as to tell our people that they must no longer travel towards the morning sun from this place. Who dares to say that Kamilaroi people may not cross their own land?'

Ngalla cried for days when Jack announced his decision. He would not go with them. He tried to explain to her that the white people would lock him up if they caught him, but she did not understand the idea of being locked up. It was outside her experience. So he talked of the shooting stick, the gun that would kill him and her eyes grew round with interest at this weapon. Then the loving Kana came to him on Ngalla's behalf bringing special delicacies she had cooked for Jackadoo, and lying with him she whispered to him how sad it would be for Ngalla to go without her husband.

'Then she stays here with me,' he said and that caused so many more tears he relented, but he knew he would worry all the time they were away.

Travelling by night he had examined the station homesteads and the rough cottages that were growing up in the area and some of them he saw had augur holes cut though the planks, places for guns. He wondered why white men would want to build houses in black man's country, surrounded by thousands of hostiles, and the elders asked Jack the same question, but knowing nothing of the fever for land he did not have an answer.

Some of the blacks who visited the camp claimed they had worked for the white men who had paid them in delicious food and Dimining strode away, too angry to listen to them any more. Moorego was shocked. 'We are hunters and warriors! What is this you do, to have food handed to you like crippled toothless crones?' The argument dissolved into laughter when it was explained what the work meant and in the dance that night they mimicked the workmen straining and toiling and looking up at the sun all day and in return being handed a lump of meat.

The leader of the dance, the spokesman, called. 'What is this toil when the spirits give us all the food we need? This can not be right. If the white man has food to share he is simply sharing it with you. Do not read too much into their ceremonies. I beseech you my people to walk alone, stay apart from them and return to us at the third moon.'

Jack questioned newcomers about redcoats and they seemed to abound, also mounted troopers, and that settled the matter for him, he would wait in the hills. He knew now that his spirit was free, like theirs, that chains would destroy him, so he had to be very cautious and stay well out of reach. One day maybe he would cross over to that other world again and he accepted that the day would be shown to him by the spirits. His life was becoming bound up with the mysticism of the Aborigines. Sometimes they astonished him with what they did know and he had a grudging respect for the Dreamtime fables.

There was plenty of time to think about things. Take for instance, his stories. He spoke of the white man's world, of houses so high and of ships that carried many people and animals as well, and of all those things they called it his magic, part of his Dreaming.

Many a night he had lain awake watching clouds move away to reveal the stars. What if their Dreaming is as real as mine? Their mysteries and their magic awed him and he began to take steps not to upset the powerful spirits on his own behalf without waiting for instructions.

Kamarra came back with a hunting party one night and brought with him a good supply of kidney fat taken from speared cattle, just the fat. It had become the greatest delicacy of all. He told Jackadoo the story of an archway with white man's drawings on it that had been built across a trail and Jack was intrigued. He instructed the next hunting party to bring it back for him.

'Why?' Moorego asked him.

'A joke that's all. To read their drawings.'

'Ah plurryell!' Moorego laughed.

So the prize came back. It was a large polished board, hardly windworn yet, with the name of the station burned into it in large letters 'CARLTON PARK'.

The night before the friends left they sat around their fires singing, clicking sticks to the drone of a didgeridoo, while the children, who were never chided, ran madly about and Ngalla sat across from Jack looking at him with her big mournful eyes. Suddenly there was silence as if the sound had been stopped in mid-air. Not one voice trailed.

Jack saw a huge fearsome-looking blackfellow standing on a boulder above them, his face and body covered with ash and slashed with white paint. There was a bone through his nose and his hair was piled into a clay cone; dingo fangs hung around his neck and strips of fur hung from his hips and ankles. Jack could see him as could any others who were facing towards the boulder but no-one else turned to look. They sat waiting.

'Who is that?' Jack whispered to Ngalla but she sat cross-legged, taut with fright at his question. No woman could say his name.

'Ilkepala,' Dimining whispered. 'Warrigal magic man.'

If he hadn't seen it for himself, Jack would not have believed it. One minute Ilkepala was standing on the boulder and the next he was in the centre between the fires. It was not possible to jump that far. At first Jack thought there must be two of them but often over the years he heard of the very special magic men who could be in two places at once.

The figure in the centre began to chant and they all listened and echoed him with subdued sounds coming from the backs of their throats.

'He is giving us the moon blessing, a great honour,' Dimining said and tears of emotion ran from faces all around them, and black eyes glistened with awed joy. Jack wondered if he were included in it and decided to accept all the good luck that was going – that was how he interpreted the ceremony.

He jumped in fright when he looked again. Ilkepala was replaced at centre stage by a big dingo, fangs bared, eyes red and glaring, reflecting the fires, and the chants began again, swelling, too many voices he knew, for the number in the camp; it seemed to him that thousands of voices were singing the full-throated songs but no-one else seemed to notice. And then the wind blew up and smoke swirled around them and normal conversation resumed and Jack wondered if he had imagined the whole thing. No-one wanted to talk about it. Too sacred.

Neither Ngalla nor Kana came to him that night and he went looking for them and found them curled up with the children. 'Warra warra,' they said. 'Go away. Sacred tonight.' The camp was silent. Even the yapping dogs were quiet.

In the morning Jung Jung was waiting for him. 'Ilkepala says you must go to find the Tingum people.'

Jack laughed. 'What? And get my bloody head cut off? No fear!'

Jung Jung picked up a handful of earth and let it trickle through his fingers; he suddenly looked very old. 'Ilkepala says you *will* leave the Warrigal people.'

'Not much chance of that,' Jack said. 'You look tired. Don't go today, stay here with me.'

'I must go, my spirit is waiting.'

Irritated by the conversation, he watched them all leave and offered no farewells. They would have a good time and he would have to wait up here for months. Soldiers and the squatters were to blame for depriving him of his friends, there were only a few visitors left in the camp now. Moodily he held his spear like a gun and pointed it at trees, pretending they were troopers. 'Bang, bang, bang!'

# CHAPTER FOUR

Jasin Heselwood boarded a coastal ship for Brisbane with Arthur Appleby and two other young men in tow, all very impressed to be travelling with a Lord and, Jasin thought, being ill bred about it, but then of course, they were. To be free of them, he walked off to the stern of the ship where he stood watching the wake churn the blue waters.

Bourke had sailed for England but the new Governor, George Gipps, had kept Bourke's promise of assistance and the expedition so far had been a simple affair. The Governor had sent a message ahead that Lord Heselwood and his three companions should be provided with horses and equipment by the Moreton Bay military establishment and a black guide assigned to them.

He thought of the Forrests back there, and Milly's anger. Dermott would do well to keep that tongue of hers in place. 'They are fortunate I did not serve them with an eviction notice when I returned to Newcastle,' he muttered. In fact he had done nothing at all about them. His visit had shown him what he wanted to know – that Dermott was keeping the station in good order and the stock healthy. It didn't concern him that they had discovered their names were not on the title to Carlton Park, they could shout for all they were worth. The courts were full of boundary disputes and land-ownership claims and legislation tried to keep up with squatters, claim jumpers and 'cockatoos'. He understood that the system in theory was workable but no-one kept to the rules and one man's description of his boundaries was never the same as his neighbour's. When it came to the crux only God would know who got there first and who owned what. He grinned, oh yes, the Forrests were welcome to the courts.

He would also make certain that the title deeds were re-written giving his full title. He had, in his own mind, divided the colony into two classes. Those who enjoyed to associate with titled people and those who were immediately antagonistic, but of the latter most harboured a secret envy.

The court benches were full of gentlemen of the first issue, who would think twice about ruling against the Earl of Montone.

The Forrests had established a good life for themselves at Carlton Park and he was at a loss to know why they complained. He had made this possible for them. They could retaliate by withholding his share of the profits this year, in which case an eviction notice would be dispatched and they could fight him from their bootmaker's shop. But if he could just get

Dermott on his own and show him that they had the life they wanted, he would succumb. Of that Jasin was certain.

The only disappointment he felt at leaving Carlton Park so soon was that he had missed the opportunity to see Dolour. He smiled. He had a vague recollection of a couple of drunken days spent with some derelicts outside Singleton when he had growled about disposing of MacNamara and some old sod had volunteered. He had gathered from stockmen they had met on the road that MacNamara was still hale and hearty. Not that he had expected much else, the old soak would have been hardly capable of shooting his own foot . . . but it would have been convenient.

The London ladies, he had found, were bolder these days, quite wanton and up to all sorts of intrigue but he still thought of Dolour from time to time. None of them was a match for her. He sighed. Perhaps his imagination was overdoing it. Maybe she had simply awakened the real vitality in him. Hard to say. But he would still like to see her again.

Their passage through Brisbane was uneventful. Troopers escorted them up-river from the penal settlement and took them by boat to the other bank while convicts swam their horses across.

Jasin was glad to get away from Brisbane. Two days there had been long enough; he considered the place to be repulsive. The state of the hundreds of prisoners clanking around was disgusting and the visitors were consumed by fleas and mosquitoes. How these officers could even consider bringing their ladies to such a place was beyond him. He declined the Commandant's offer to dine with the company and refused an invitation to be shown over the prison. 'I think I have seen enough, Captain.'

Their Aborigine guide, an old fellow called Zed, was waiting for them, dressed in ragged trousers with a necklace of sharks' teeth.

'It's only about sixty miles from here to Limestone,' Arthur said, 'and we've plenty of company on the river, so I can't see us getting into much trouble.'

Jasin agreed, but they found the track more difficult to navigate than the river. The green undergrowth was as thick as thatch and thorny in patches. Zed hacked at the scrub ahead of them with a machete but often he made only enough room for himself and disappeared from their sight, forgetting they needed more space for the horses. They forded creeks and detoured away from the river through timbered hills, and then came back to the river and waded through paper bark swamps, slashing at thick creepers and clinging green tendrils.

'Is this the right track?' Jasin cried.

'Right track boss. Everything go fast-growing in the wet.'

'We should have gone by boat to Limestone,' Len Almond complained, and his friend Robert agreed. 'This is a bugger of a track.'

'There are no horses to be had at Limestone,' Jasin said angrily. His companions were getting on his nerves.

283

When they finally arrived at the little outpost, Arthur joined Jasin to enquire as to the route ahead and purchase more supplies but the other two repaired to the inn where they got drunk.

'Don't worry about them,' Arthur apologised. 'They'll be all right in the morning.'

'They had better be,' Jasin snapped.

From Limestone they descended to easier terrain but the thorns on the acacia scrubs tore their clothes and their skin and the horses were irritable. Running ahead of them Zed pointed to the high range in the distance. 'Him Downs country boss. Up there!' and Jasin was amazed it was so close. He was delighted, congratulating himself, and that put him in a much better humour. Wentworth may have done him a great favour after all. They had not seen any blacks except for a group of about twenty filing away in another direction, taking no notice of his small party. Jasin felt he could almost reach out and touch the famed Darling Downs.

They cheered and rode towards the looming plateau with more enthusiasm, and the closer they got, the higher it seemed. But it did not matter to Jasin, he knew that up there was this kingdom to be won. They passed some isolated farm huts where settlers were clearing small blocks for crops and although their presence made him feel safer it disturbed him that farmers too were aware of these new territories. He had learned from the Macarthurs that these little family groups were likened to flocks of cockatoos that sat on their fences because they encroached on station properties and the authorities were inclined to leave them there.

When they began the climb into the foothills Jasin thought the heights seemed very close but tall trees obliterated their view until they came to a sheer cliff face.

Zed pointed to the skies. 'Up there boss.'

Jasin stared. 'Very good. Now how do we get up there?'

Zed skipped to a ledge. 'Easy boss. Climb up.'

'That won't do. The horses can't get up there you fool.'

Like his compatriots Zed had no use for horses. 'No boss. Leave horses here.'

Jasin sighed, trying to be patient. 'We must take the horses. Now there is a path up there, show us where it is.'

Their guide was bewildered. 'This man go up many times, many places. No horses.'

'I don't think he knows where the gap is,' Arthur said, and Jasin shook his head angrily. 'Oh never mind. We'll find it ourselves. It's marked on the map. We'll make camp here and search it out.'

Arthur took the map and studied it 'The trouble is Mr Heselwood, this map shows how to find Cunningham's Gap from the direction of the Downs. It doesn't say how to find it from this direction.'

Len and the third rider, Robert, were already starting a fire. 'We'll find it,' Len said. 'It must be around here somewhere. I'm starving, we'll eat.'

Jasin glared at him, he was always starving and it was only mid-morning.

He decided to follow the face of the plateau and sent the other two to the east while he and Arthur rode westwards. But both parties were confronted by blind gorges and impenetrable scrub. The massive cliffs rising high above them seemed determined to stay aloof. Several times they thought they had found the gap in the range but after leading their horses through the forests and across the steep ridges they always came to another dead end. Jasin studied his map until it was ragged, but the scale was small and it was no help in this difficult terrain.

Zed hung around the camp ashamed that he had failed them and sat well away from their tent at night, ignored by the white men.

'We ought to give it away,' Len said, but Jasin would not hear of it. 'There is a way up there, we'll find it.'

Robert laughed. 'We've been riding up and down this country for days. We've found everything but the Gap. I don't reckon we're much good as explorers.'

Suddenly Zed came running into the clearing and hurled himself at Jasin. The two men crashed backwards into the bush rolling down the slope.

'What the hell?' Arthur cried and ran to help Jasin. Len and Robert were too shocked to move until the crack of tree trunks gave warning of the boulders that were thundering down on them. Len managed to get away but Robert was struck by a huge jagged rock and pinned against a tree.

When only a few dislodged stones remained to rattle down from the cliffs Jasin looked around him, stunned. 'What happened? Was it an avalanche?'

'No boss,' Zed said. 'Blackfellers up top. More better we go from this place.'

Robert's leg was broken and Arthur bound it as best he could and made a stretcher from saplings which he and Len took turns in carrying with Zed while Jasin rode ahead with the spare horses. It was a long slow trek back to Limestone where a doctor was found to re-set the leg and Robert was sent by boat to Brisbane.

Jasin was depressed. Wentworth had made a fool of him. He could find another guide, he supposed, to take him directly to Cunningham's Gap but he knew now that the Darling Downs would be settled from the south, not from Brisbane.

Having seen the port for himself he still wanted land within range. Why travel hundreds and hundreds of miles from Sydney and Newcastle when there had to be equally good land within a reasonable ride of Brisbane? It was rumoured that the port of Brisbane would be opened soon and that would create a land rush. The facilities were already there, good wharves and stores and the township well established. It was wasted on convicts, who of course would provide a ready source of free labour. The Governor

285

had said there were a thousand or so prisoners in Moreton Bay. Wentworth had been right, the best use of convicts was to put them to work. The incorrigibles who would not work should be packed off to Norfolk Island. It was something Jasin planned to discuss with the Governor on his return to Sydney.

The three men rode into a rough timber-getters' camp on the journey from Limestone to Brisbane, with Arthur and Len anxious to get back to Brisbane but Jasin was not prepared to give up so easily. He sought out the camp boss. 'What's up river from here?'

'No use looking at that country mate,' the timber man replied. 'A lot of our blokes have marked off land for themselves all along the Brisbane Valley and they're already fighting over it. To the west of the river some blokes have claimed a big spread and built a bloody fort on it. They won't let anyone near the place. But why don't you go straight up north?'

'I keep hearing this but what about the blacks?'

'Jesus, if you're scared of the blacks up this way you might as well go home now. They're a fact of life like floods and fire only they won't be around forever.'

'Where would you go up north?'

'Just follow the coast.'

'Only about eighty miles and no walls of China to bar your way,' he laughed. 'Nothing wrong with that country at all. If you make it worth my while, I'll take you up there myself.'

Jasin hesitated for only a second. 'When can we go?'

Within four days, an easy ride to the north, they were in the green and fertile country that bordered another fine river and although it was winter the days were warm and the skies blue. Jasin marvelled at the balmy climate realising that Newcastle and Sydney would now be suffering from cold wet weather.

The timber-getter returned to his own camp and Jasin, with the help of Arthur and Len, began the job of marking boundaries while Zed kept watch at the base camp.

'It's bloody good country here,' Arthur said for the hundredth time, but Jasin would only nod, keeping them working. Len was already tiring of the job, finding surveying work much harder then he had imagined and Arthur was very slow on the uptake. Jasin missed Clarrie and Snow, nothing had impeded the two old bushmen but this pair complained about everything, the scrub, snakes, broken axe-handles, the time it was taking, and he knew they were not making much of a job of it but it would have to suffice for the time being.

'The only thing that worries me,' Arthur told him, 'this country might get a bit damp underfoot for cattle.'

'That doesn't matter,' Jasin said. 'This will only be the head station. From here we look inland for drier runs.'

'Oh no!' Len cried.

'Not this time, later on,' Jasin said. 'This station will feed us and out there to the west in the drier country I'll get bigger runs. This one will be the saver if there's a drought.'

Zed was able to tell them the Aborigine name for the district, they called it Gimpi Gimpi but he could not translate it. They occasionally saw wild blacks but there were no signs of hostility, nor did they come near the camp. Jasin was always curious about what lay beyond the ever-present horizon of hills. 'Next time you see them, ask them what's out there,' he told Zed but the Aborigine shook his head. 'No fear boss. Them Tingum men.'

'Do they speak another language?' Arthur asked, but Zed shrugged, having nothing more to say on the subject. When they had done all they could to mark the boundaries, Jasin announced, to their relief, it was time to go. 'I shall call this Montone Station,' he said and they carved the name into a tree.

He was satisfied. What more could one ask? Free land, free labour and a ready-made port to hand. Georgina would appreciate travelling most of the way by ship and river boat, and she would enjoy this temperate climate. By the time he had the station fully stocked the homestead would be completed and neighbours would be settling in. Land like this was too valuable to remain hidden for long.

While they waited for a ship to take the three young men back to Newcastle and carry Jasin on to Sydney, he wandered around the penal settlement looking for anyone or anything that might assist him to establish the station. He recruited a Sergeant Krill who was due to sign off from the army and wanted to stay on in the colony. 'I can't say I know all that much about cattle sir, but I can learn, and I can take orders so I'll keep your station in good marching order. I'd fair love a job as a foreman.'

'Then the job's yours Sergeant,' Jasin said. Krill would be ideal, he was a strong fellow and with his military background would not put up with any nonsense from the men – the sort of man who became a loyal family retainer. And besides, he had years of experience in Moreton Bay.

'Captain Barry tells me,' he continued to Krill, 'that an acreage the size of Montone Station would entitle me to twenty convicts. I'd like you to keep an eye out for some reliable men, if you can find any.'

'There are plenty of good lads'd be willing to work to get out of here sir.'

'Excellent. I'll send tools and equipment up to you by ship and you can store them here until I arrive. The cattle will be coming overland. But find me some carpenters. I want my house built properly. Are there any in the convict ranks?'

'We've got every type of tradesman you'd ever need sir. Leave it to me.'

Jasin was pleased to do just that. At last he had found a right-hand man he could trust. An Englishman and respectful. Montone Station would be a going concern within a year.

# CHAPTER FIVE

At the same time as Jasin was returning from the north Pace MacNamara was making the long overland journey to meet up with O'Meara. He joined bullockys, settlers and timber-getters on the trail, helping them where he could and appreciating their company. Being a station-owner himself, he was welcome at homesteads along the route, and given assistance with directions. He crossed through New England and went up to the Darling Downs to a huge newly established station on the Condamine River known as Canning Downs, owned by Patrick Leslie.

The Leslies were the sons of a laird from Aberdeen who had followed Cunningham's blazed trail to the land which had been described as 'better than you have ever dreamed'. They had not found it wanting.

Not one to place all his eggs in the one basket, the old Laird, worried by his family's failing fortunes, had sent his eldest son to Hong Kong where he was doing well in the legal opium trade and his three other sons he sent to the colony of New South Wales.

With a retinue of twenty-two men, all ticket-of-leave men, or convicts, these incredible Scots had pushed north with four thousand breeding ewes, a hundred ewe hoggetts, a thousand wether hoggetts, a hundred rams and five hundred wethers. The scope of such a drive astonished Pace, and Patrick Leslie, proud of his men, introduced them to his visitor. 'They're as game a lot of men as ever existed,' Leslie said, 'worth any forty troops.'

They were a cheerful group of men taking the natural hazards of the land in their stride as they recounted their adventures to him and Pace was interested to hear that the blacks in that area were 'tame enough' but there were alarming tales coming from the north.

'It's difficult to know whether the blacks are hostile ahead of you because the local blacks won't talk. Half the time they don't know, because it is a different tribe with different ideas, all you can do is keep alert.' That was Patrick Leslie's comment.

Armed with a new map and fresh supplies Pace set off for the next station about eighty miles on. It was a lonely trail and when he made camp that night he wished he had some company. Besides being nervous of the blacks, being alone again brought thoughts of Dolour to his mind, and of the hopeless situation they were in. He could see no answer to it.

In that high country the nights were freezing so he wrapped himself in his blanket and huddled close to the fire, too miserable to sleep.

The camp fire had attracted attention and in the morning with the frost still white on the ground six troopers woke him demanding to see his papers.

Pace showed the sergeant the letter of introduction from Patrick Leslie to Ephraim Duncan the owner of the next station and their surly attitude changed to politeness. 'I'm sorry sir,' the sergeant said, 'but we've got to be on the lookout for escapees from Moreton Bay.'

'Are you just riding around up here looking for convicts?' Pace asked. 'It'd be worse than the needle in a haystack.'

'No sir. We've been sent up here to see if we can find marauding blacks. A bullocky was killed up here a couple of weeks ago and all his team slaughtered and they speared a shepherd the week before that. You shouldn't be travelling alone, I could give you an escort.'

'I wouldn't like to put you to any trouble,' Pace said, fearing that he might bring troopers down on top of O'Meara.

'It's dangerous country Mr MacNamara,' the sergeant said. 'Two of my lads will ride with you. They know the trail.'

'We don't mind sir,' a young trooper said in an aside to Pace. 'At the station we'll get some good grub, better than we've got at our camp.'

They rode until nightfall. 'We go west here, towards Oakey Creek,' the troopers told him. 'All this is Mr Duncan's land and the homestead is only a few miles away. We'll be able to see it from that hill up there.' The corporal, Jim Cheel, urged his horse on, eager for the journey's end but as they emerged from the scrappy tea-tree for the downhill run there were no lights to be seen.

'Are you sure you fellows know the way?' Pace asked.

'It's down there all right,' Jim said and the trooper agreed. 'He'd be right sir. The corporal's got a natural sense of direction.'

Pace shrugged. It was a dark night and dangerous for the horses to be trying to pick their way over rough ground; if he were not careful, he would end up with a lame horse. He remembered that on their first drive, Heselwood had gone off to visit a station, which had turned out to be Chelmsford, on that superb horse Prince Blue and had come back without him. Heselwood had never said what became of the horse. The lads had figured that he must have been offered a good price and sold him, but his new horse had not been nearly as fine an animal. Pace had always wondered about that, he must ask Rivadavia one day. But there he was thinking of Heselwood again. Lately every thought he had, seemed to trickle from the one source.

A shot rang out and the lead horse reared. 'Jesus!' Pace cried, 'that was meant for us. Pull back and we'll light a flare.' He found some dead brush and lighting it, held it aloft.

'Troopers!' the corporal shouted. 'Don't shoot!' And they waited for the answering call.

289

A stockman was waiting outside for them with a lantern. 'Did you see any blacks out there?'

'Not one,' Pace said.

'Well either they're gone or you're the luckiest blokes alive.'

'Why? What's happened here?'

'Something terrible,' the man said. 'Bring your horses around the back. Stay close to the house. The blacks attacked here today while we were out mustering. Mrs Duncan and her sister were killed and Sandy, their youngest boy, and the Chinese cook. All speared to death. It's bloody terrible. One of the station gins ran for miles to get us but by the time we got back it was all quiet. We've been out after the murdering bastards, we found tracks everywhere but they've disappeared.'

He led them into the house, and through the gloom they could see about ten men standing around the kitchen and in the passageway. Inside, in the dining room they met Ephraim Duncan who was sitting at the table reading a Bible by the faint light of a small child's lamp.

They shook hands with him mutely, feeling as helpless as Duncan's own men in the face of such a tragedy, and backed away.

The next day a funeral was held for the victims and as soon as it was over Duncan despatched his other children to the safety of Canning Downs under the care of the troopers and a guard of four stockmen. Pace offered his condolences to Duncan and went on his way, riding hard this time with his rifle and pistol ready and his stockwhip coiled carefully on his saddle.

O'Meara had told him to find a Scot called Jock McArdle at one of the timber-getters' camps on the Brisbane River. It took him a full day to locate the man but he got the directions he needed and was on his way again relieved that O'Meara had waited. He turned away from the Brisbane River travelling west across the Valley looking for the homestead at every rise and when he saw it he reined in his horse. 'Oh bejesus, did you ever see the likes?' He patted his horse. 'There's a good fellow, only a bit further now and you'll get a good feed and a drink.'

The gate in the timber fence was wide open and Pace rode into a square shaded by an enormous tree, splashed with glorious bright orange blooms. The place looked more like a barracks than a station homestead and there was activity everywhere. A blacksmith pounded his metallic song over to the left, men walked by leading their horses, while Aboriginal women rested under the central tree watching their children play.

Pace had been so open-mouthed at this strange oasis in the isolated valley he hadn't realised the gate was guarded.

'Where do you think you're going?' a voice grated at the back of him and he turned to see a grey-bearded stockman menacing him with a rifle, but O'Meara came striding across the square in a red shirt, battered trousers and Hessian boots. 'Let him be, Alf, he's a friend. And about time you turned up, MacNamara.'

*　　*　　*

290

On the return journey Pace picked up with other men who had been searching for land and had claimed runs far to the north of his station. Many were squatters from New England and exhilarating company. Prosperous but adventurous men, they sang the praises of the near-north country that would turn them into millionaires. Anxious to be home, they travelled fast, preferring to camp on the trail rather then delay by socialising at homesteads and their camp-fire talk gave Pace yet another perspective on this new life he had embarked upon.

One of them was an American, Jonah Willoughby. 'Won't-Work Willoughby' the other men dubbed him because he sat down at each camp and expected to be waited on, claiming his age earned him the right. They let him get away with it because they liked him. Willoughby seemed to know a great deal about this business of expansion besides being a horseman of note. 'Do you notice they're calling it the near-north already?' he said to Pace. 'I'll bet you never rode this far in your life before.'

'I'd have fallen into the North Sea,' Pace laughed.

'See how quick it takes to adjust then. You guys have to think high, wide and handsome before it's too late. You think you're smart grabbing these penny-ante blocks. What's twenty square miles, thirty square miles in this territory? How many head of cattle have you got down there on the plains?'

'I don't know, about a thousand I'd say.'

'Kid stuff,' Willoughby said. 'Have you had a look at a map of this coastline? A good look? And taken a ruler and measured it from the Pacific to the Indian Ocean? You could have ranches here that would take a half a million cattle, and still not run out of room.'

'Is that what you have in mind?' Pace asked him.

'My bloody oath I have and I'll do it too.'

Pace looked at him gloomily. 'It takes money.'

Willoughby glared at him, his white eyebrows and moustache quivering. 'There you go. Beaten before you start. Find the money! If you haven't got any friends who'll stake you, go and see the merchants at Goulburn. They're the boys who're financing enterprising men. If I was this government I wouldn't be paying fares for grubbing little immigrants, I'd be scouring Europe for the money men, men with foresight who'll expect your grandchildren to be in the same league as them. Big money.'

'Where do you live?' Pace asked, intrigued.

'I live on my horse. I can write an IOU on a piece of brown paper and no bank in this colony would knock it back. Back home I've seen what can be done so I've got a new lease of life here, you lot are just new boys.' He looked at Pace and laughed. 'It's not as bad as it sounds. I've got a wife and two daughters, they've got a fine house in Sydney and live well. I always turn up for Christmas. They're glad to see me come and glad to see me go!'

Talking to him Pace felt a roll of excitement, with dreams and ambitions lurking nearby and Willoughby assuring him they were not out of reach. 'If you mean to stay with cattle, boy, you'll have to leave the south and use the

Brisbane Valley only as a staging area. The big ranches will be far to the north. I'd give my eye teeth to know what's up there. For sure it can't be too much different from cattle country in the States or even Argentina.'

'Now that's interesting,' Pace said. 'My partner is Argentinian, Mr Rivadavia.'

'I know him!' Willoughby cried. 'What he doesn't know about cattle you could write on your thumb but he's cautious. Thinks twice or three times before he moves. Sometimes you've got to get up and run or you miss the boat.'

Pace parted from them near Armidale station. Deliberately he headed for the Hunter Valley, telling himself it was important to talk to Rivadavia as soon as possible but he knew he was postponing his return to Kooramin, to Dolour. He ached to see her but the hurt was still with him, hurt that he translated into anger.

Rivadavia rode out to meet him. 'Welcome back! Did you have a successful journey? Did you buy the land?'

Pace leaned over to shake hands with him. 'The answers are yes and yes,' he laughed. 'We won't ever be sorry about that run.'

'That's good news. We'll go back to the homestead, you must stay over. How are things at your station?'

'I haven't been home yet.'

Juan looked at him curiously and let that pass.

'I've got a full description of the land,' Pace continued. 'So I'll take it on to Newcastle and leave it with Batterson to register when the time comes. At least we'll have it on record.'

'What about payment?'

'O'Meara wants the money paid into a bank account in Brisbane, name of McArdle Timbers.'

'Why?'

'Because they're outlaws,' Pace laughed, enjoying the startled look on Juan's face. 'But don't take it too hard. He was a political prisoner, banished from Ireland and he didn't take kindly to being a slave on Mudie's station so he took to the bush.'

Juan smiled, 'What about his cattle? Are they worth buying?'

'They're in good condition, believe me, and that did my heart good but they've got some very strange brands among them.'

'Don't tell me they're rustlers?'

'You call them rustlers, we call them cattle duffers and they call it making a living the best way they can, but I'd just as soon have no part of their cattle.'

'That would seem wise for both of us.' Juan was looking at him again as if wondering whether to speak. 'Have you heard from Kooramin at all? From Mrs MacNamara?'

Pace felt a sense of foreboding. 'I have not.'

'We've had a dry winter, hardly any rain. It's very dry out on the plains, not a lot of feed about.'

'So I've noticed. What else is wrong?'

Juan sighed. 'You've been away all winter Pace and you've ridden across half the country. I'll take it from here. I'll go on into Newcastle and make the arrangements, you can pay me when you're ready. It's the least I can do to let you go on home now.'

'What's wrong out there?'

Juan seemed to study the track which wound around the gums towards the rear of his homestead. 'Your foreman was killed,' he said quietly.

'Who? Jim Connelly?'

'Yes.'

'Dear God. How did that happen?'

'They tell me he was riding along a high bank of the river, it must have been undermined by erosion. It collapsed and the horse fell on top of him. He was badly injured, he died a few days later.'

'When did this happen?'

'Only a few weeks after you left. Fred Forrest came by, he told me about it.'

'Who's running the station?'

Juan looked surprised. 'Of course. You wouldn't even know that. Your wife is, Mrs MacNamara.'

As he rode through the pass from the Hunter Valley, the tall gums hung over him dry-leafed and listless. He should have been able to come home triumphant. The acquisition of the magnificent northern run was like having a lump of gold in the cupboard, but now Connelly was dead. Like Brosnan he'd never had a chance, pushed out of his own country to die in a strange land, without the proper mourning of his family and friends.

And Dolour. At the thought of her his mood darkened, he'd have to face her soon, a crisis point.

Everything worried him, the dry country, even the blacks. The massacre at Duncan's station was still on his mind. It was doubtful if the wild blacks would come this far south but it would be as well to see that the women and children at the station were protected during the day while the men were out on the range. O'Meara had convinced him that he was wrong to refuse shelter to even a couple of convicts, he could have them assigned to him, treat them well and pay them. It was exactly what Connelly had tried to tell him but he'd been in no mood to discuss anything.

O'Meara had been less deferential. 'It's only your own bloody pigheadedness, not saintliness,' he had said. So Pace decided he would get a blacksmith and a maintenance man to work around the homestead, and arm them.

'It's a peculiar world,' one of the outlaws had said to him. 'I got transported for poaching and brought out here where it's legal to poach on blackfellers' land. And if he objects he's the one who gets it in the neck.'

One of the outlaws had known the names of a few tribes of the north. 'Our blacks are Kamilaroi,' Pace had said. 'But they're a peaceful lot, we don't have any trouble with them.'

'Bully for you,' the outlaw had snarled at him, and Pace realised that had sounded patronising.

The bushrangers were a cantankerous lot and not pleased that a squatter had ridden in among them, but it was O'Meara's camp, a man to whom authority had become second nature and he was backed up by his loyal offsider, Scarpy. A friend of O'Meara's (or Minogue as he was known) had to be accepted; grudgingly though, Pace noticed. As the days went on he too began to enjoy the free and easy way of life. He had no responsibilities except to mark out the boundaries and he had help from plenty of volunteers, who had nothing else to do. O'Meara had set up a shooting match backing Pace against the best shots in the camp and, of course, O'Meara had won all the bets, while, at the same time, demonstrating to his companions that his friend should be treated with respect.

'What will these boys say at you selling up here?' Pace asked.

'You don't listen MacNamara,' Dinny said. 'These fellers are not the originals who came here with Scarpy and me. This is just a temporary sanctuary, they stay a while and then they go. They move cattle for me and they move on. I see to it that the really bad lads move on faster than the others, but the world's closing in on them.'

Pace passed the turnoff to Carlton Park. He was curious to know how the Forrests had coped with Heselwood, that name again, and wondered if Dermott had recovered but he was not ready to deal with their problems. He had enough of his own. The one bright spot in his life was his sons, John and Paul, he was looking forward to seeing them.

For months now he had been pondering the confrontation with Dolour. What choice did he have? He would have to forget what she had told him or the marriage was finished.

'Forgive her,' a voice said in his head. 'Forgive those who trespass against us.' He reacted impatiently, jerking the reins and talking to his horse, who had become accustomed to these conversations.

'Forgive?' he asked, wondering where that thought had come from. 'There's nothing to forgive. I'm not God. I'm not the parish priest.' Dolour had led a life of tribulation and he had hoped to make it up to her. Everything that had happened to Dolour was part of the misery of Ireland. She had gone to the priest for her confession the night before they were married and she had taken communion the next morning but she had not questioned him when he had declined to join her.

The old tyrant of an Irish priest at Newcastle had glared at him when he had turned away from communion but he still married them.

'He had breakfast Father!' Dolour had spoken up in his defence, and

Pace laughed now, remembering her quick thinking. He wished they could put things right between them, to turn things back to what they were before. He wished too that he could set things straight with the Church, as it had been when he was a boy, but life was not simple. 'When I was a child, I thought as a child,' he quoted. 'Now that I'm a man – well that's a different story.'

It had not been possible for him to go with her to communion, as a husband should, beginning a good marriage. Pace MacNamara, the marksman, the sniper, had been excommunicated.

Pace had discussed this with O'Meara, the only person he knew who understood the rules and O'Meara had laughed. 'And you still managed to get married in the Church? That old priest you told me about would have had a fit if he'd known. And you'd better be nice to that beauty of yours, Dolour. You wouldn't want her to find out that in the eyes of the Church you're not married.'

'What are you talking about man? Of course I'm married.'

'I wouldn't be too sure about that my lad,' O'Meara roared, laughing at his dismay. 'You can't take the sacraments when you're not in the state of grace you know, and the state you're in you'd need the Pope to open the door again. And marriage is a sacrament don't forget.'

It annoyed Pace still, that O'Meara had seen this as a huge joke. 'Of course I'm married,' he echoed as the horse plodded on; it was tired now and so was he. It would be good to get home.

The homestead was quiet, dozing in the afternoon sun, and he shuddered, remembering the tragedy at Duncan's station on the Darling Downs. He resolved again to see that the household had protection during the day.

A stablehand wandered out of a shed, ignoring the horseman until he realised who it was. 'Ay! Good day Mister MacNamara. I thought you was one of the blokes. You home eh?'

'Yes, I'm home,' Pace said grimly, still worried about the vulnerability of the station.

A young girl popped her head out of the dairy, staring at him. 'Who's that?' he asked.

'That's Sheila, a servant girl the Missus brung in, to help around the house. The black girls try but they're not much good you know.'

Pace nodded. Sensible of Dolour, she always did work too hard. He dismounted and handed over his horse. 'You're Claudie aren't you?' he asked. 'I didn't know you behind the beard.'

Claudie grinned and fingered his curling ginger beard. 'They bet me I couldn't grow one.' Then he stopped. 'Did you hear Jim Connelly was killed, boss?'

'That I did, Claudie, God rest his soul.'

He walked around the deserted outbuildings to the house, where the black girls were sitting, grinning, on the back steps. Behind them the two boys John and Paul were asleep head to toe on a bunk under a thick

295

mosquito net. He peered in at them, smiled at the girls, put his fingers to his lips and went into the house but there was no-one around. Feeling let down he came back to the verandah. 'Where's the missus?'

The two girls giggled. 'Missus out working boss.'

With nothing else to do, he wandered through the house, noticing Dolour had fixed it up comfortably, pleased with the results of his labours. The shingle roof was holding well, no sign of leaks, the floorboards had come up well with waxing and the doors and windows opened easily. It was a big house, by Irish standards, with a wide passageway running through from front to back to catch the breeze, but then there was no shortage of space to put a house.

He heard horsemen coming up from the south paddocks and wandered out to greet them.

Dolour rode in with them, sitting astride her horse, and the men grinned, leaning down to shake hands with the boss on his return, but tactfully kept moving as Pace stared at his wife, dressed in trousers. 'What in God's name are you doing, got up like that?' was the first thing he said to her.

She pushed the stockman's hat back on her head and swung down from her horse, ignoring the question. 'So you do come home, you bastard!'

'You use that language on me woman and I'll ride out again.'

'And what's stopping you?'

He turned on his heel and strode back to the house, seating himself at the white-scrubbed kitchen table to wait for her, but she took her time.

When she did come through the door it was like a whirlwind. She slammed it shut and faced him. 'What have you got to say for yourself MacNamara? Walking in after all this time as if it was only yesterday you left and never a word from you.'

'More like it what have you got to say now?' he growled. Things were not turning out the way he had imagined they would. Even though he disapproved it was hard to keep his eyes from her, the open-necked shirt and the dungarees made her look younger, more active, more desirable.

'About what?' she asked defiantly. 'About how your sons are? About Jim Connelly? About how we've been managing here?'

'You know that's not what I meant.'

'Oh. I see. I'm still doing my penance am I? Well I'll tell you what I have to say about that. I'll be moving the twins into my room and you can sleep in their room. You'll not sleep in my bed. Last time you saw me you looked at me like I was a harlot. Well I'm not. I'm mistress of this house and don't you be bloody forgetting it.'

'Your language has improved since I saw you last,' he said quietly.

'What do you expect? I've had to run this place and keep those men work-ing,' she yelled.

'We've got another station up north now,' he said, hoping to settle her down.

'*You've* got another station up north. I don't want to know about it. I've got enough to do here. Kooramin is my home.'

296

# PART ELEVEN

## THE BLACK WARS II

# CHAPTER ONE

Lord Forster had promised his grand-daughter, the Honourable Delia Francombe, that when she turned eighteen he would take her to visit his friends in Argentina, but they had arrived at an inconvenient time. Jorge Luis Rivadavia was ill, and although his wife, Ester Maria, was gracious and hospitable, she was distracted with concern for her husband and the political unrest on the pampas. Bandits and rustlers harassed their herds and unsettled the villagers.

Forster was warned it was no longer safe for him to ride away from the hacienda, even with an escort, for fear he might be kidnapped. He decided to shorten their visit and take Delia, who was accompanied by her maid, Miss Lee, and return to Buenos Aires. Then he planned to extend their travels to include New South Wales, sailing back to England via Capetown.

The Rivadavias were sorry to see them go, but delighted that Forster and his granddaughter would be visiting Sydney and insisted they call on their son, Juan.

'He has several estates in New South Wales now,' Jorge said.

'I am pleased that he is doing so well,' Forster replied. 'It doesn't seem so long ago we were discussing the plan for him to leave.'

'And the Islas Malvinas,' Jorge added wryly.

Forster smiled, a little embarrassed. The British had annexed the Islas Malvinas and now called them the Falkland Islands.

'But we will look at that another time,' Jorge continued, 'we have enough troubles with Rosas, who is now a dictator and taking Argentina back to the dark ages. Juan got away in time, many of his friends did not. Others have had to flee to Chile.'

'How long do you think this regime will last, Jorge?'

'Years yet. The people will not believe that Rosas had a hand in the political assassinations, they don't understand the corruption and by the time they do, he will be too powerful. We can only stay in the background and wait. But I must not worry Miss Francombe with our problems. Juan has turned his exile into a triumph and that is our joy.'

'You must be very proud of him indeed,' Forster said. 'I believe New South Wales is far more civilised these days. We are looking forward to our visit.'

'What does your son do there Mr Rivadavia?' Delia asked.

'He has varied interests including sheep and cattle ranches.'

'How exciting,' Delia cried. 'He must be a very clever person.'

'Yes. And good looking too,' Forster laughed and winked at Delia.

'Grandfather! Really!' Delia chided, but her eyes sparkled with interest.

Jorge wrote to his son but did not include the letter among the gifts he sent to Juan to be delivered personally by Lord Forster. He arranged to have it carried to New South Wales by the ship's captain.

*My dear son,*

*Your mother and I send our blessings and as always our great love. We are proud that you have a successful and satisfying life in New South Wales and have maintained the high standards of your beloved family and we are overjoyed that your letters arrive so frequently, allowing for the vagaries of shipping. I cannot tell you what a comfort this is to your mother. But I do not know how much longer we shall be able to correspond. Rosas is turning the country inwards, under the guise of encouraging a national spirit. He has become excessively antagonistic towards outsiders and contact with foreigners. We no longer hear from our friends in Chile, the post is not censored but burned, we are told.*

*We send our deep love to our grand-daughter Rosa and are pleased that you take your responsibility seriously and with the obvious love you have for her, but we feel it is time you were married. No doubt you have considered this and your mother feels that no suitable lady could have been presented to you. We have met a young lady, the Honourable Delia Francombe who is the grand-daughter of Lord Forster. They are en route to Sydney and will be visiting you. Your mother says to inform you that the young lady is very beautiful and would make an ideal match. As for myself my fatherly advice is to commend a betrothal and if you consider the young lady suitable then tread carefully as there is no family spokesman to ascertain feelings in advance for you and to protect your good name against rejection. You must keep in mind that in some cases union with an Argentinian might not be seen as acceptable to the British however that statement might hurt. But then we have similar prejudices.*

*We hope you will give thought to our choice of a wife for you and you will pray to God for guidance. I shall be interested to see if my son can arrange this marriage, which we believe will enhance his life and reputation.*

*To send with this, your mother is writing the news of your brothers and the family. We pray to Mary for you and our love transcends the great distance of the oceans. God go with you.*

*Jorge Luis Rivadavia*

On their arrival in Sydney, Forster and the Honourable Delia stayed for some weeks at Government House. Sydney was a welcome surprise. Forster found the town charming and the spectacular harbour idyllic. The climate suited him well and there was no end to the hospitality. Delia was captivated by the social whirl, with the young blades of the town standing in line to escort her to soirées and balls in her honour.

When he tired of the parties, Forster left them to Delia, preferring to sit quietly in the evenings with Governor Gipps, discussing with him difficult matters of state. Forster found him to be a just and honest man, who kept a firm hand on the finances of the colony which was, after all, the mainstay of the community. In London they were very pleased with Gipps's handling of New South Wales affairs and the letters of complaints about his rule, which were the lot of all Governors, the colonists being prolific letter writers, gathered dust at the Colonial office in Westminster.

'I'm working on new legislation,' Gipps told him one night, 'and they'll be after my neck on this so I have to get it right. I know you are well respected at Westminster and I could do with your advice, if you could spare me the time.'

'My dear Gipps, I am at your disposal.'

'My problem is this, we need legislation to protect the Aborigines.'

'Why is that?'

'Because they are being over run, killed by the white man.'

'I rather thought it was tit-for-tat out here.'

Gipps sat down at his desk. 'That was the opinion I held until I came here. It is not correct. Though it might appear in Sydney that we have no trouble with the blacks we do in fact. Not a great deal, not battles like in India but we still have to face the fact that we have colonised their land and a great number of them have been killed needlessly.'

'In fights?'

'Not on a large scale, nor organised; but random shootings, yes, and disease. I really have no idea of the extent of it but they are disappearing from the civilised sector at an alarming rate. I know of an element here that shoot the blacks for the sheer sport of it. And they do it because they are confident they are above the law.'

'I think it goes deeper than that. These fellows are ignorant, they don't even see it as a crime. It's a problem the world over.'

'Then I shan't permit this ignorance to be used as a defence. I want to make it quite clear that any man who kills a black person must face the full consequences under the law.'

'Why then should you need more legislation? You already have laws covering murder. They do not specify colour or creed.'

'Because a white jury will not convict. I need to strengthen my powers to force a jury into behaving with integrity.'

'I should be very cautious there. You can't direct a jury.'

'There must be something I can do.'

*Kana was always timid. She'd jump at her shadow. When the white man came riding down to the waterhole at the place of the big wattles she ran and hid but the others laughed at her. White men often came there for water, to let the big beasts of* horses cool off, to sit at their fires and to have loving with women and it was an event, exciting, something different. The Warrigal people from the mountains were fascinated, some of their friends could even talk to the white men although they kept away from the huge animals they sat upon.

Moorego sighed and walked with the elders to welcome these white men, astonished at the way they galloped in, not waiting to be invited. It would not do among the mountain people, a few spears would have taught them manners in no time. But down here the blackfellow mobs said things were different. They said only bad blackfellows got into trouble with the whites.

Moorego had been wanting to leave, and Dimining too because there was little hunting here any more. They were told that if they went out with the spears, the white men saw that as war-like and became frightened and they would try to shoot them. It was better to stay here and eat the white man's food which was good, and it worried Moorego that some of his people might not want to come back home.

The old men were smiling at the white men who were riding towards them and Moorego, with no smile, was standing, stiff and polite, but then out of the blue heavens about them, silver flashed like lightning thrusts, and the horses rode right over them and guns banged.

Kana saw the blood gush from Moorego's neck and her husband came running but his chest gaped blood as his body flew backwards like on a great wind and Kamarra came to help him, shrieking, and everyone was running and a sword slashed Kamarra to the ground. She sprang out of the bushes running now to grab the children but the men were down from their horses, booting, clubbing, stabbing the old men, children, anyone in their way, in a frenzy of blood. A huge man grabbed her arm and pulled her along, calling out something about the 'gins' and he handed her on to a grinning bearded face and all around her Warrigal people were being slain, even the little children, and tossed onto the fire and white men were beating the bush for the people who had fled. She twisted loose and ran the other way down towards the river, flying through the trees which in their magic gave way for her, not one stood in her path as the ugly white voices roared and stumbled behind her and at the high bank she dived into the mercifully deep river.

Away in the hills Dimining still hunted. It was his life. This was still Kamilaroi land no matter what the white bosses said. When he began his walk back to the sit-down place he was uneasy and closer in he smelled fear in the wind.

There was no sound in the camp so he crept nearer in the darkness calling his presence but he met silence and the smell was now of blood. Fires were still smouldering when he came upon the carnage, the bodies of his friends piled up to burn, dirt shovelled on them, his wife and child dead, and Moorego. It was too horrible to search any further.

He wailed the high dingo howls and the animals themselves echoed his anguish and he moved away from the terrible place and washed himself in the river and sat down to cover himself with white mourning paint. He slashed his arms and chest, mixing the blood with the paint and smearing it across his face and then he stood with his spear and his boomerang and faced the mountains. Fully prepared and armed he strode across the land with the morning sun at his back.

He saw his first target rounding up sheep in the distance and kept straight ahead and when he judged the distance to be right, the Kamilaroi warrior took his boomerang and hurled it with all his might. The weapon hissed through the air and the hard blackwood broke the stockman's neck. The horse screamed, reared and bolted, dragging the body behind it, making for the homestead, and the sheep scattered.

When the horse arrived at Chelmsford station with its bloody cargo Juan Rivadavia ordered all his stockmen to take cover and the homestead was shuttered like a fort. They had heard whispers of killing from the station blacks who had mysteriously disappeared and Juan expected a native uprising, believing the blacks were entitled to fight back, an eye for an eye, but coming across the paddock was a lone black in what looked like full war paint. Juan wondered if he were a fore-runner of that attack and decided it would be best if he talked to this black man, to find out what had happened.

'Mind the child,' he said to Dora. 'I'll go out and talk to him. We don't want any more killing.'

'Don't do it boss,' Andy warned. 'That bloke doesn't look as if he is in any mood for talking.'

'I'll go out unarmed. He will see that, he will see your guns trained on him so it is possible to talk. I must, or God knows what will happen around here.'

Dimining was still marching straight towards the homestead. He saw the white boss come out and recognised him as a peaceful man. He had been to this station many times but things had changed. He was a true black man again now and he would live by the black man's law. He saw the boss come out, his arms stretched wide, no weapons, as it should be, in the correct manner, inviting payback. In a lightning move Dimining's spear shot forward embedding itself in Rivadavia's thigh but even as it hit, Dimining was dead in a hail of rifle fire.

'Killed twelve of them,' Governor Gipps said. 'An awful business. The mongrels must have gone berserk by the sound of things. Your friend, that fellow Rivadavia, reported the massacre but nothing was done about it. I have ordered an enquiry but the trail's cold. No-one will talk. The first thing I will have to do is sack the police magistrate, I'll begin there so that if this sort of thing happens again the troopers will know they have a job to do.'

Forster nodded. 'It's a disgraceful situation but right is with you. There must be decent people in the colony who will support you. I'll see what else I can find out from Rivadavia himself while I'm there.'

'Thank you, that's what I had in mind. I would appreciate it. When are you leaving for the Hunter Valley?'

'As soon as I can prise Delia loose from Sydney society. She is having the time of her young life.'

# CHAPTER TWO

Kana travelled upstream and left the river on the other side under cover of tall reeds and ran across country to the next camp around the bend of the river but that camp was deserted, the fires out. She ran on and on again, hysterical, alone in the world of terror until she saw a gunyah in the bush and friends sitting smoking and humming small songs. Even while the men were talking to her trying to make sense of this shocking story, the women were packing up, stamping out the fires and soon they all disappeared into the high country and across the wide plains to find safety in the big mountains to the west.

Runners raced ahead of them and the news spread through the Kamilaroi nation. Jack Drew had been on a walkabout with some friends, relations of Jung Jung, they said, but he had long ago given up trying to work out their complicated families and whether they were related by blood or by totem. This mob were Goanna people but they didn't expect him to camp alone, only men in disgrace camped alone.

They were all crying when they brought Kana to Jackadoo so that she could tell him what had happened, her eyes still deep in shock, her body trembling and her wide mouth twisting at the agony of having to recall the horror.

He couldn't believe it! 'Why?' he cried as grief-stricken and bewildered as they were. 'Why?'

They named to him the ones who had escaped.

'Where's Ngalla?' he screamed, 'and Moorego and . . .' But they shushed him, the names of the dead must not be mentioned. He broke away from them calling, 'Dimining? Where's Dimining?' but they turned their backs.

'The children?' he asked, describing with his hands the two little brown-skinned boys, his sons, the ones he had taken for granted, there were always so many children around, and they turned back to him shaking their heads. He looked at the tears in their eyes and the beaten slump of their shoulders as they crept away mourning. And he was filled with hatred. If he could only find the men who did this, he would kill them himself.

The Aborigines had converted Jack Drew to the ideas of family support and group endeavour and he had embraced their way of life willingly, not only because among them he felt needed and was looked up to, but because they cared about him. Even loved him. It was an awkward word for Jack Drew to contemplate. What was there for him in the white world but jail? And even if he eluded that, he would have to scratch out a living without money. He had thought about these things many times until the subject bored him and faded, overtaken by the freedom of the life he now embraced.

To have his family torn from him in such a cruel and senseless manner was a bitter blow and he wandered now with Kana on the fringe of other mobs, feeling at a loose end. Even Jung Jung was dead. Jack seemed to have lost that precious sense of belonging but he could not go back east, there was no place for him in the white man's world and he hated them for it. He would make them pay one day.

They were travelling now towards the place for a big sit-down, Kana told him, a great corroboree, and they journeyed north, high into the mountain ranges where the trees streamed green, past the borders of Kamilaroi territory. He had never been so far north before and he remembered the warnings of his friends. 'We had better turn back,' he said to Kana. 'We're going into Tingum land.' But Kana was unconcerned. She pointed to converging tracks tramped flat by bare feet. 'This time big meeting. All people go.' She was looking forward to the corroboree where there would be singing and dancing and stories told, but Jack was still nervous. They joined with other bands and there were hundreds of strange blacks on the trails and the hills puffed smoke from their camp fires and he wondered how safe he really was, but the strangers seemed to know him and no comment was made about his presence.

When, finally, they emerged from the bush to a high plain bordering a lake, Jack was amazed, there seemed to be thousands of blacks camped along the shores reaching right to the dense forest at the far end. 'Bloody hell,' he said in English and then continuing in Kamilaroi, 'We'd better stay up here.'

Kana pouted. 'Bloody hell' were the only two English words Jack ever used any more and she still had not worked out what they meant. Sometimes he used them in anger and sometimes in laughter. 'No. We must go down. I told you this time a big sit-down.'

'There are too many strangers here, they might kill a white man.'

She laughed. 'You're a funny-looking white man!'

They fell in with their mob ambling to a camp site and Jack sat down quickly, praying he was invisible, his spear handy, and the sharp knife he had fashioned for himself sitting firmly in his belt.

There was much activity in the camp with preparations for a feast and the decorating of dancers for the evening's entertainment, and traders came by with their wares. One man sat down with the women to display his basket of necklaces, beads, coloured stones, shells, combs and other adornments. The women laughed and shouted and argued, trading baskets and fishnets and dilly bags and plaited waistbands. Jack turned over the stones, idly at first, just pretty pebbles and milky stones with fiery colour in them, and blue glassy lumps that looked like dark sapphires but never having seen them in their natural state his opinion wavered, and shifting them, he came across a pitted untidy lump of metal that felt heavy in his hand. 'What is this?' he asked the trader, but the word 'gold' was not in their vocabulary, all stones were called by their colours.

He became as excited as the women, scrabbling in the basket to see if he could find more but there was just this one lump. He rubbed and rubbed at the stone fearful that the colour might come off or that, it being as heavy as lead, he had in his hands something as worthless as lead, but the yellow glinted even more on its sharp little points. It was not at all what he had imagined gold should look like but in his heart he knew, he laughed so much he rolled in the grass, and, delighted, the others laughed with him, but when he traded his knife for the yellow misshapen thing that wouldn't make much of an adornment they thought he was mad.

Kana reached out for the little ornament thinking it was for her but he refused to hand it over. Making a game of it she tried to grab it from him and she would not stop until he slapped her hard. While she sulked he made a little skin bag to keep the stone in, and this he placed on a strong string around his neck. Then he went to see the trader again. 'Where did you find the yellow stone?'

The question achieved nothing. The trader's descriptions were lost on Jack who knew nothing of the territory to the north but he was determined to find out. He was not so disenchanted with the white world that he would not re-enter it a rich man. 'What man are you?' he asked the trader.

'Tingum,' came the reply and Jack jumped. The name terrified him but the trader didn't look fearsome, more like the genial meat seller from the market at home. While they talked Jack looked around at the trader's companions and realised he had come galloping into this circle like a clown, without taking proper cognisance of their mood, which was bad manners, and dangerous. The other men were carefully applying red ochre and white paint and white feather-down to a two-foot-high headdress, built on a bamboo frame in the shape of a cone. As he watched, they added gaudy feathers and bright shell pieces from oyster casings. Beside them, only a few feet away from Jack, a large man sat cross-legged allowing the artists to paint his body for the celebrations. They spoke a different language but the sound was still strong and guttural like the Kamilaroi language as if words of great strength needed the barrier of their strong white teeth to make them resound. Jack had often practised with words like Warrego, the name of the great river, and it seemed to need every muscle in his mouth to puff his cheeks and bring the sound from his chest to roll into the word, and he was never able to get it right. His voice sounded feeble compared to theirs.

The fellow who was being decorated turned and spoke to Jack who stared at the large white teeth. They could bite a man's arm off, he thought.

'What did he say?' Jack asked the trader.

'He said what people are you?'

'Tell him Kamilaroi.'

When the trader gave the answer the big man looked at Jack and laughed but there was no humour in the laugh. Jack decided it was time to leave.

'We'll talk another time,' he told the trader.

'You stay!' the stranger ordered and the circle was quiet.

'You speak the same tongue as the Warrigal people?' Jack was surprised.

'Better than you,' the man commented impatiently.

The trader leaned forward. 'He speaks many languages. Like me,' he told Jack. 'The chattering birds who fly from one homeland to another teach us.'

The stranger interrupted, addressing the trader in his own language. Jack could see they were discussing him; the trader making a saga of their conversation, with sweeping actions. Jack guessed he must also be a storyteller of some note. He hoped he was telling a true story, these fellows were apt to exaggerate and embellish the most minor events. At any rate, he thought, whatever he's telling them, he's got them interested. Others gathered as the tale went on and he saw the listeners smile occasionally and then a great groan went up and the stranger near him pummelled the ground in a rage. Jack wished the trader would quit, he could see himself being used for target practice.

The stranger asked a question and the trader pointed to Jack. 'His name is Jackadoo.'

But the other black shook his head, 'He is not Kamilaroi. Never Kamilaroi.' He poked Jack in the chest. 'You prison man? You run away?'

'Yes.' Jack threw up his hands to make his reply interesting. He hoped the interrogation was over, these men made him feel insignificant, their eyes were hard and uncompromising and he had already noticed their spears were barbed and their tomahawks reflected the sun; few of his friends carried tomahawks.

Suddenly the atmosphere changed. The stranger clicked his tongue and white flowers were handed to him. He chose one with care and reaching over, placed it gently in Jack's hair. 'For your crying,' he said, his eyes brimming with tears, and his companions bowed their heads.

Jack nodded his thanks. It still hurt him to think of what had happened back there. 'What is your name?' Jack asked and the men around him sucked in their breaths in surprise at the question.

'I am Bussamarai,' the man said. 'Of the Tingum people.'

The white man was impressed. Here was the very man he needed to get permission to go north with the trader and search for that gold but he judged it was not the right time to be asking favours. 'I am pleased to meet you, your honour,' he said, mixing in a couple of English words in an effort to impress.

That night the big corroboree was a spectacular affair. As usual Jack took his place just behind the great circle of men, close to the women, trying to work out what the dances were all about. Often these dances bored him, men leaping around pretending to be kangaroos or snakes or borobis, the bears that never drank water, and less obvious spirit characters, but this night there was a new quality about them, more fire in the movements, more determination and he felt a tension building up.

'What is happening?' he asked Kana.

'There have been more killings,' she said. 'In Kamilaroi country. Families again.'

Jack was shocked; he had thought that first assault on their tribe had been an isolated event, some drunken pigs gone mad. 'Who was killed?'

'We do not know yet. Message sticks bring the crying news. All the people here are very sorry for Kamilaroi.' But as Jack watched he saw it was more than sorrow.

The main feature of the evening began with a great silence. The didgeridoos stopped, the clacking sticks and muttering voices were stilled and figures drifted about dressed in long thin sheets of bark, white-painted, all wearing masks. He knew those masks depicted dead people. Men lay still depicting water and others stood by, their heads and shoulders covered in small branches and Jack, understanding now, waited breathless, like the rest, knowing what was to come.

The play went on. Attackers flew into the stillness shouting horrible cries and the music began again and all the tribes were shown what had happened to Kamilaroi people and then they were all on their feet stamping and droning sorrow. When it ended Bussamarai entered the circle now in his full regalia, the head-dress making him tower over the others. He spoke to the people in Tingum, his voice roaring across the lake and echoing in the hills and his message was plain. Jack shivered.

One of the Kamilaroi mob stood up before them and cried: 'Bussamarai says why have we let this happen? He says too long we have stood aside and let the white man take our land and kill our people.'

The man listened again as Bussamarai continued and there was a shout from the gathering. 'He says the men of the northern tribes are warriors, who will fight. They will not creep under bushes to hide and wait there for the white men's swords.'

From the circle other men addressed them in their own languages and Jack could see that whoever they were and wherever they came from in this northern land they agreed with Bussamarai. This time the white men were in for a war. He found himself standing and stamping his defiance with the blacks, caught up in their excitement. He too would fight the invaders.

In the cold light of morning he was not so enthusiastic. If they were to have a war he would prefer to be as far away as possible. He could see himself with a bullet in his chest or a spear in his back. It would be better to backtrack and then go further west, far inland. It would take the whites years to get out that far, if ever. But then there was the gold. He touched the little bag at his neck. It would be a sin not to try to find it.

The days went by in socialising and feasting and in the background the elders and the tribal leaders held meetings, but Jack stayed close to the trader. Years back he had dreamed of becoming a leader himself but that dream had faded. It was hard to match them at anything in this environment and leadership here depended on strength, family relationship and the ever-present magic.

He mentioned to the trader that he would like to go walkabout with him into the grand Tingum country, but the trader was non-committal. Then he tried another approach. 'It is too dangerous for me back in Kamilaroi country now. The white men are looking for me. They will lock me up.'

He knew that in their eyes that punishment was worse than death and the trader looked at him with troubled eyes. 'I will speak to Bussamarai for you.'

The tribes were beginning to vacate the meeting place. Kana told him their mob would be leaving soon and they would have to go with them so Jack hurried back to the trader who took him to Bussamarai. The leader did not waste words. 'You, white man, Jackadoo. You will come with this man. We will chase the enemy out of our land.'

When they said goodbye to their friends Kana boasted that her Jackadoo had become very important, a friend of the great Tingum chief who was even now summoning up the fiercest warriors of the land of the hot sun to smite their enemies.

# CHAPTER THREE

Juan Rivadavia's leg had healed but the muscles still cramped and he now walked with a slight limp. He inspected every corner of Chelmsford station before the arrival of Lord Forster and his grand-daughter, and Dora was so nervous she was all of a dither.

'They're still only people,' Andy told her.

'Not the way the boss is fussing around. You'd think angels were coming to visit. And Rosa with all those new dresses, what's the use? I can't get her to stay in them, she'd rather wear britches. Her father has given strict instructions that she must wear dresses every day while the visitors are here and she's already digging her heels in.'

'Come inside Rosa!' she called as the child tramped up the back steps dragging a basket. 'And leave those fleabag kittens outside!'

'It's too cold for them out here,' Rosa cried and Dora went out to take them from her.

'You're mean Dora,' Rosa said, 'the poor little things.'

Rivadavia was at the kitchen door. 'Dress the child now please,' he said. 'I am informed our guests are on their way.'

Rosa pulled a face and he bent down to pick her up. 'Don't you want to look pretty?'

Dora smiled. Whenever the father spoke there was no further argument from Rosa, he was the only one who had any control over her.

Juan and his daughter stood before the house to await the company, flanked by Andy and Dora and the excited black house girls in new dresses, and stockmen and field workers stopped to watch the arrival of people so important that they rated an escort of troopers.

Juan stepped forward to help down Lord Forster and then the grand-daughter the Honourable Delia Francombe, and smiled. His father's choice met with his approval. This lady would be his wife. Her first glance at him had been one of surprised appraisal, so he took her gloved hand with cool politeness, giving no indication that he too was impressed. She was very beautiful and, he was sure, accustomed to admiration, and as he escorted them into his home, he knew how he would court her. He would be the good host, the essence of politeness, entertain them as best he could and, in the evenings, the dinners would be romantic, with fine food, wine and music, and he would keep her at a distance.

Rosa was charmed to meet this lovely lady and she immediately attached herself to Delia whom, Juan noticed, was young enough not to mind. She went with Dora to show the lady her room.

'I didn't know you had a child,' Lord Forster said.

'Oh yes. Her mother died only a few days after she was born.'

'My dear fellow, I am so sorry. And what a shame, such a pretty little girl.'

Their days were well spent looking over the station and testing the wines Juan had produced from grapes grown and pressed on the station.

'I had hoped to see Cormack's station while I was out this way,' Forster said.

'They are away,' Juan said shortly.

'But I believe the foreman is in residence, James Mackie . . .'

'I do not have any dealings with him.'

'Oh. And why is that?'

'He is a renegade that fellow. He was mixed up in the murder of the blacks on my property, everyone knows it, but we were never able to prove anything. I have made it plain he is not welcome at Chelmsford.'

'I quite understand, we'll give him a miss then. The Governor was very concerned about that incident.'

Juan looked at him thoughtfully. 'I would have thought that "incident" was too mild a word.'

Forster nodded. 'You are quite right to correct me, my boy, I remember you correcting your father's English when I first met you. I am afraid I was just repeating the word parrot-like.'

'If the blacks had killed white people, we would have called it a massacre, so that's what it was.'

'Very true. But tell me, has anyone been charged?'

'There's no hope of that. But there has been a shake-up at the watch-house in Newcastle.'

'I'm pleased to hear that. Governor Bourke read the police magistrate the riot act so it looks as though his warnings have worked. Let's hope the new fellows have more control.'

On an evening when Lord Forster was laid low with a cold, Delia and Juan dined together. He had been treating her with great consideration but had maintained a formal distance, pretending not to notice Delia's lowered lashes and the occasional flirtatious glances she gave when Forster's back was turned. He had also been circumspect in seeing to it that, until now, they were never on their own, seeming to prefer the company of her grandfather. Nevertheless, when he could not be observed, he had studied every inch of her, his favourite spot being his own room where he could watch her on the lawn under the trees with Rosa. Delia was indeed a beauty. He longed to reach out and touch the flawless skin and her fine blonde hair that she tied in a soft loop at the nape of her neck, and looking back at his large four-poster bed he could see her with him there. He daydreamed of how he would go about loving this delicate creature, this pale English rose, with her long legs and willowy body. It would be done, gently and discreetly, the loving to awaken a virgin, because he did love her, passionately.

He was finding it difficult to keep his eyes from her but he had to attune himself to English ways or his cause would be lost. Delia was a spoiled young lady, accustomed to getting her own way. Juan had no quarrel with that. Her rank required it. When she was his wife he would spoil her too. He realised that if Delia herself chose a husband, then she would allow nothing to stand in her way.

'One hardly got any sleep at all in Sydney Town with so many balls and parties,' she told him, 'I had so many beaux too.'

'I am sure you had and in London too I presume?'

'Of course, simply dozens.'

Dora brought in the dessert and disappeared into the kitchen. 'I suppose you have quite a few lady friends here?' Delia asked.

'Yes. They come quite often, with their husbands to look over the horses and choose a mount for themselves. They like to help me choose names for the foals.'

'I should adore to do that.'

'Then you must come back in the spring.'

'We shall have returned to England by then.'

Juan made no comment on that. 'Would you care for another glass of wine? It is very light.'

'Thank you, I would.'

He watched as she twirled that fine hair around her fingers, lifting it to brush close to her lips. 'Do you not find me pretty?' she asked.

'I would not presume to remark on your beauty,' he said in a voice that sounded sombre but Delia heard that one word and her eyes shone.

'Why not?' her voice and eyes were arch, teasing, playing the flirting game but he answered seriously. 'If I were to speak to you in such terms it would not be the voice of a teasing dandy from Sydney or from London. I only speak of such things from the heart. If I were to tell a lady that she is the most beautiful of all I would mean it.' He looked at her, watching her eyes widen with delight. 'To be able to say such things to you I would have to have the permission of Lord Forster.'

Delia rose from the table and Juan stood to take her chair. He followed her into the parlour and she stood in front of the fire looking lovely, he thought, in that blue silk dress, and she knows it. She picked up a small ivory elephant with jewels set in the red saddle-cloth. 'This is beautiful.'

'It is yours,' he said.

'But it must be worth a fortune.'

'If you like it, you have it.' He had thought about purchasing jewellery for her but that would have been too forward. However it was not unseemly to give the lady something she admired. He had hoped it would take her eye.

311

'You are very generous.'

'Only with people I like.'

'Then you like me Juan?'

He decided the game was over for that evening and excused himself. 'I am so sorry to leave you but I must talk to my foreman.'

Lord Forster rose late the next day and seemed preoccupied at lunch. 'I believe you know the Heselwoods?'

'Yes. Quite well.'

'They say Heselwood now has solid backing from London what with his title and the estates he has out here. Is his station in the north as big as Chelmsford?'

'Much bigger. He has Montone Station operating now. I have a property up that way too, in the Brisbane Valley. I share it with a partner but when we get it working we'll split into two stations, there's almost limitless land. This station is considered small, but I like it because it is neat and manageable, the ideal place for a home. I have cattle runs on the Peel and Gwydir Rivers also, but strictly for pasture as yet.'

'No wonder your father is pleased with you,' Forster said.

Juan had to wait several days before Forster brought up the subject of Delia. 'I have a delicate matter to discuss with you Juan, so I might as well get it out, awkward you know. Delia seems to be very taken with you and she seems to think you might reciprocate. Now I know you have been the soul of decorum with her, she has told me that herself, but young girls, you know how they are, she insists I speak to you . . . dear me . . .' he wiped his brow with his handkerchief, 'she is threatening to speak to you herself.' He looked at Juan, who gave him no assistance.

Embarrassed, Forster continued. 'Well sir, what do you say to this now?'

'It places me in a difficult position. We are not accustomed to making any declarations until such time as we are sure a courtship would be approved.'

Forster tapped the table, his eyes fastened on his own gold and ruby ring, aware now, that this was no surprise to Rivadavia. 'I can't speak for her parents,' he said, 'but I can't go home and say she's run off on me. She's very strong willed this young lady.'

Once again Juan made no comment and Forster had to take the lead. 'To put the cards on the table, it appears that Delia wants to marry you, and for my part, I can see no objections. You're a Catholic too, good family, you can afford to support her, and you're a gentleman. That is what I shall be telling her parents. If you care for Delia, you are within your rights to speak up. If you do not, then we shan't discuss the matter further. I say, could I have a glass of that good port of yours? This has been one of most difficult pieces of diplomacy I have ever been engaged in. It was hard to decide how even to broach the subject.' Red blood vessels stood out on his cheeks and he loosened his collar, looking flustered.

Juan handed him a port and poured one for himself. 'In that case sir, I have the honour to request the hand of your grand-daughter in marriage. And I can assure you that I shall maintain the dignity of her station and she will want for nothing.'

'Capital!' Forster said, relieved. 'Congratulations dear boy! I had better write a letter to her father and if I were you, I'd speak to her before she changes her mind.' He winked at Juan and went off to his room but Juan found that remark unsettling. A sudden gust of wind blew smoke into the room from the fireplace, irritating him while he brooded over the remark, worrying it until it became abrasive. 'If she is inclined to change her mind, then I shall give her more time,' he said to himself. 'She can wait, strain a little, find out what it is to really want something not quite within reach. But if she wishes to change her mind now that her grandfather has approved, so be it.'

Lord Forster was at a loss to explain to Delia why it took Rivadavia days to speak to her of a betrothal, and during those days she was nervous, fidgety, even tearful.

# CHAPTER FOUR

A willy-willy was building up on the horizon and the black girls were already hurrying around shutting down the house. To them a willy-willy was fun, to Dolour it was dust, debris and damage. They pulled chairs inside and closed all the shutters and doors, putting blankets and sheets and rugs, anything they could find, against the doors to prevent the dust from seeping in. Dolour had learned this from the big red-dust storms that came howling out of the west, dumping tons of dust on them. She looked out of the back window to see that Claudie was putting the shutters up on the henhouse, and Tom Gates, the new blacksmith, had locked up the stables.

These days there were more men around the homestead during the day. Pace had a large vegetable garden under irrigation and employed two convicts, full time, to look after it and that made a big difference with all the mouths to feed. Tom's wife had charge of the cookhouse, which left Dolour free to look after her own family but there was still plenty to do. The dairy herd was bigger now and Dolour made butter and cheese which she sold to travellers and to other stations. On the whole the station hands, one and all, were an easy-going lot, they worked well with Pace and since Mrs Gates was a good cook there were few complaints.

The new baby, their third son, was a month old. The black girls seemed to think that each child was entitled to his own nursemaid so they had brought a new girl to the house. 'This nursie, Maia, missus. She mindem new baby good,' they told Dolour. It was no use arguing with them, the girl, having been allotted her place on the station, was not likely to let anyone else have the job. It would cause fights.

Maia was interesting. She was taller than any of the local women, and more serious. She listened to everything that was said and picked up English quickly. 'Where does Maia come from?' Dolour asked Lena.

'Owl people missus. That girl owl people.'

Dolour already knew that most of the blacks on the station were dingo totem and all their magic talk fascinated her, reminded her of her grandmother's legends of the Druids, that were not all so different. 'Yes, but what tribe?'

'Tingum, missus.'

'Tingum,' Dolour repeated. 'And you are Kamilaroi?'

'Yes missus.'

'Now Maia is married to old Bulpoora?'

314

'Yes missus.' All three of the nursemaids were married and their husbands did not seem to care that they spent most of their time at the house.

'Where do the Tingum people come from?'

Lena turned about her and pointed north. 'That way. Long ways.'

'Then where did Bulpoora find her if she comes from so far away?'

Lena went to speak but suddenly Minnie was standing in the doorway and Lena turned her head away quickly without answering. Minnie was standing very still, unusual for her. It seemed to Dolour a silly thing to get upset about so she answered the question herself.

'Did he meet her on a walkabout?'

Lena rolled her eyes in fear, cringing away, not wanting to reply.

'Yes,' Minnie snapped and Dolour knew that for some unaccountable reason that was a lie. But it didn't matter. She sent them about their business. She didn't like Maia's husband. He was an ugly old man with a cold baleful stare who never spoke to any of the white people, but the black stockmen told Pace he was respected in the mob and it would cause trouble if he were sent away. Not that Dolour really wanted him to go, he would take Maia with him and she was a good nursemaid.

The willy-willy rattled and banged at the house and she saw the dogs racing for cover but she had seen worse, and in a few minutes it went zigzagging on its silly way. They began to open up again and she went into the bedroom to let some air in there.

Over the double bed was a picture of the Sacred Heart and whenever she was alone like this, with a little time to spare, she sat on the hard wooden chair and prayed. She prayed that her husband's heart would be softened. Gradually he had come to her for a night here and there and she had allowed him and then he moved back into the bed; what else could she do? Keep her husband at arm's length forever?

But it was never the same any more, their love-making had lost its charm. Should not even be called love-making, she reflected sadly. It's his conjugal rights, no more, he does not care, we're not even real friends. We talk now like business partners or parents, but not lovers and it's easy for a row to start. Sometimes he talks to me as if I'm the housemaid. I try to ignore him, but my temper will not allow it and I tell him what I think, letting him know he is not so high and mighty. I wish I could stop doing that.

She had had a fright when the invitation came to attend the wedding of Juan Rivadavia and the English girl. Dolour had even considered burning it before Pace saw it. She was afraid Heselwood might be there. But a blessing came in the form of Milly Forrest who was all talk about the wedding, and what she would wear.

'What if Jasin Heselwood is there?' Dolour had whispered.

'He's not coming. I found that out first. He's up north on that station of his.'

Dolour was so relieved she only half-heard Milly's woes about the legal argument they were having with Jasin and the time it was taking to get the case to court, but the thought of the trick he had pulled on the Forrests sickened her and made her feel even more guilty. As if she had wished him on them. And she knew that every time Milly came over with her brother-in-law complaining about Jasin, Pace remembered. Afterwards, he would not look at his wife.

She wished there was something she could do to ease things for him. The men were worried about the cattle, it had been a dry winter last year and this one was just as bad. The creeks were drying up and feed was getting low. Pace was talking about moving the herds to the north, leaving Kooramin empty.

She loved working out there on the range with them, in all the noise and excitement of the big stockyards, and she was determined that as soon as she stopped feeding the baby she was going out again. Since she had been forced to ride with the men when Jim Connelly died, Pace could not very well stop her now.

They had waited until Father Caimen Court could get out to the station for the christening, it being important to them to have a priest they both knew perform the service and when Caimen arrived, riders were sent out with invitations to all for the following Sunday.

The Rivadavias were away, but friends from the stations on the plains came riding in all that Sunday; owners, workmen and mobs of blacks who had been invited by the Kooramin blacks. It was more like a bush carnival than a christening with the young men challenging one another to horse races and wood-chopping competitions and the women out in their best bonnets and shawls weighing down the trestle tables with their contributions to the 'breakfast'. The Forrests brought Dermott over in their buggy and transferred him to a wheelchair and everyone rejoiced with the MacNamaras when their third son was baptised 'Pierce.'

A keg of beer supplemented the other drinks and it turned into a great party with fiddles and flutes and a squeeze box setting feet tapping and couples dancing. Pace was in good form, the genial host who sang for the company and, Dolour noticed, even put an arm around his wife. For her it was a grand day, to think she had come this far up the road from the miserable little cottage back home to a great station with more cattle, she was sure, than they had in the whole of Ireland. But the happiness was flawed by the rift between husband and wife, the proud parents. To make it worse Milly started on her troubles with Heselwood again, telling everyone at the table what he had done to them, as if they hadn't all heard it many times before, and what she had written to the lawyers and what they had written back to her. Dolour stole a quick glance at Pace relieved to see he was still smiling, usually the mention of Jasin would throw him into one of his dark moods.

'And him a Lord!' Milly cried, exasperated. 'and that son of his, Edward, will be a Lord too!'

316

Everyone laughed, including Pace, who stood up glass in hand. 'Is that so? Well if Heselwood's son can be a lord, my son can be a duke.' The company cheered and Pace picked up the baby . . . 'Meet Duke MacNamara!' They all enjoyed the joke and Dolour, her nerves tingling, smiled too, hoping Pace would leave it at that. He did. There was no more mention of Heselwood that day, but the name stuck. Her Pierce became known as Duke to everyone.

Before Father Court left, he sought Dolour out. 'Is everything all right with you girl?'

'Everything is fine Caimen. Look at us, we're lucky people.'

'Are you now?' he said. 'It's not the impression I get of the pair of you, for all the good front you are putting up.'

Dolour shrugged. 'It's nothing.'

He rolled his soutane into an unclerical swag and smiled at her. 'I'll pray for you and your family.'

Two days later bushfires broke out in the dry scrub and raced across the plains burning out hundreds of acres of the best remaining pastures and tore on towards Batterson's Run, as the station was known. Batterson had died a year back and left his station to the Craddocks.

With the smoke still hanging in the air, days after they had put out the fire, Pace came home exhausted. 'That does it,' he said. 'I'll see Rivadavia as soon as he gets back from the north. I've got to push the cattle off here while there's still feed on the trail.'

317

# CHAPTER FIVE

Georgina surprised Jasin. She took over the management of the isolated household at Montone Station with enthusiasm and immediately began planning a garden and an orchard, inspired by the magnificent tropical flowers that grew in abundance on their land. Jasin himself was wary of eating the strange tropical fruits in the beginning, but Sergeant Krill had assured them that the mangoes and papayas had been tried out on convicts who had suffered no ill effects and by this, the second mango season at Montone, they had become his favourite fruit, displacing even the delicious bananas.

He loved Montone. It was like owning your own village, as his forebears had done before the rot set in. He owned this green land as far as the eye could see, and thriving herds of shorthorns, and near a hundred horses. Krill was performing well in his role of foreman and had more than fifty acres under the plough for crops, corn, pumpkins and potatoes, worked by convicts, while the better types had been elevated to stockmen.

As Jasin had predicted, immigrants poured into Brisbane and the first rush had settled close to the port. The market for Montone cattle was consolidated. Other pastoralists had taken up runs in the Brisbane Valley and further north, and all of them were from the south, some even from the other side of Sydney. There was a hostelry called the Planters Arms out on the trail, where Jasin occasionally met up with his fellow graziers. They were already the elite of the district and the hotelier had wisely set aside a saloon for them, and, rough and ready though it was, it separated them from the hoots of stockmen and bullockys who were the main trade.

He enjoyed the early morning rides with Krill, on inspections, and the evenings when he could sit down to his desk after dinner and attend to his books. He kept a detailed account of his stock losses and gains and sales and it made him feel like a banker, counting out his money. He kept records of everything: the dates of the clearing of more tracts of land and his own small maps of their precise location, of how his crops were progressing, of his staff, convicts and free men, and of the number of blacks who had been 'let-in' on a bond of good behaviour, and until recently, he had controlled the provisioning of the station but Georgina had taken that over.

'Those men have to be fed well or you'll have trouble. I've heard them grumbling Jasin. They complain about the cook and he says it's not his fault. You don't give him enough supplies.'

Georgina had sorted that out very quickly. She had brought in extra supplies and then sacked the cook. Now they had two, a fellow to cook for the men, and his wife for the household and it was a common sight to see Georgina marching down to the cookhouse to taste the fare that was to be served to the men. It pained Jasin to hear them call her 'Missus', his wife should be addressed as Lady Heselwood, but she found it amusing.

'I learned years ago here, my dear,' she had told him, 'that they don't care who we are.'

Jasin was surprised. 'What an odd thing to say. The reverse is more appropriate. What *they* think is immaterial. Just don't take any nonsense from anyone on the station.'

And indeed she did not. Tiring of her skirts forever trailing in the dust, she had taken them all up to ankle length and now strode about in her polished boots, carrying a shooting stick which she used to point imperiously at neglected chores, and no-one seemed to mind. The homestead station hands worked feverishly to accomplish all the things she set them to do, vying with each other to please her.

Jasin had been surprised to find there was no twilight in this land. The sun went down behind the inland ranges in a rush leaving a wash of pinks and reds and yellows to sort themselves out. As he sat at his desk he watched the moon come up through the open doors of his office casting a vivid night-light over the countryside.

'It's beautiful isn't it?' Georgina said coming quietly in, having sent the kitchen staff off. 'I had no idea this country would be so beautiful. I haven't seen Carlton Park, is it as scenic as Montone?'

'Oh, my dear, no. Compared to this it's rather stark. Which reminds me I must get after those wretches, the Forrests, they still haven't sent me my share of the cattle sales. I hear there's a drought down that way. We'll see how the Forrests handle that, the fools. Had they been more co-operative they could have driven a herd up here for agistment.'

'But won't it cost us money too, I mean if they have a drought?'

'Can't see there's much difference if I can't get my money out of them. They're still responsible for my cattle, though, and it will put them deeper in debt to me and lessen my repayments on their loan.'

She looked over his shoulder. 'You still at those books? You'd putter around with them all night if I let you.'

'Oh well, I remember what Macarthur told me, this is where you make sense of the station.'

'Then tell me, bookkeeper, how is the station going?'

'Wonderfully well. A few years here and we'll be independent of the banks. And some of the fellows tell me there's even better country north of here. Thousands of miles of territory!'

'Well let's leave it there for the time being. Do you think you could get the men moving on those stables, that roof is useless, make them thatch it over. The way it is, the next bit of rain and the horses will be soaked. It's a disgrace.'

319

'I'll get them onto it first thing,' he said, impressed by her observations. He had a feeling that her new energy had to do with their parting from Edward who was now at school in England.

The carpenters had built the Montone homestead almost to Georgina's design, with large rooms and high ceilings for coolness, but they had disobeyed her instructions and placed the kitchen away from the house, which had caused an eruption when she found out. The interior kitchen had only recently been completed but in the meantime Georgina had put the rest of the house in order.

'Is there anything else you need before the visitors arrive?' he asked her.

'I'll always need something here. I don't think I'll ever have the house the way I want it, but it will suffice. We can make them comfortable enough. After all it's not supposed to be Mayfair. I just hope they remember to bring some books. It would be nice to start a library.'

Jasin sighed. 'Where?'

'Why, straight out there, with a garden in front, fenced down as far as those palms. It would be very appealing.'

'I suppose it could be done,' he allowed. It was a relief that Georgina enjoyed this country life, he had feared that if she objected to living out here, he would have to provide her with a household back in Sydney, since Brisbane was still a rough village and out of the question.

He was grateful to her; it was a lot to ask of a woman of her standing to have to set up house in the wilds, in the middle of nowhere, with no females of her own class within calling distance. They had both been delighted to hear from Lord Forster and the invitation to visit Montone had been issued immediately.

'Have you thought where to put Delia's maid?' he asked.

'In the fourth bedroom.'

'In the house?'

'Where else can I put her? She can't stay in Cook's quarters and I can't bunk her on the verandah, the woman would probably die of fright.'

'What bathroom will she use then? She can't use ours. I mean, we can't share a bathroom with a maid.'

Georgina began taking some flowers out of a vase. 'She will have to stay in the house and if that bothers you, then you'll understand why I wanted to build maids' quarters in the first place. The black girls are willing enough, but I should have brought in a couple of properly trained maids before this. Cook will have to help me with our guests. Now look at these flowers! I told those girls not to bring these big tropical blooms inside, they close up! They're not house blooms.'

She threw the shrivelled flowers into a bin. 'They will be here tomorrow won't they? There's been no word.'

'Yes, as far as I know.' He turned around in his chair. 'I still can't get over Forster allowing his grand-daughter to marry the Spaniard.' He laughed. 'It's peculiar. I mean to say, it looks as if Forster were touting the

320

girl around the world to collar a husband, she must be as plain as a jam tin.'

'I doubt if Juan would settle for an ugly wife, not him.'

'Why not? He took on Adelaide didn't he? She was years older than him.'

Georgina glanced at him, annoyed, feeling a personal hurt at that remark, but he kept on. 'Besides, your friend Mr Rivadavia would marry his horse if she had a title, I'd bet on that.'

'You might also wager that Lord Forster is not unaware that Juan is a very wealthy young man, that could tip the scales.' She had meant that remark to sound scathing but Jasin agreed. 'Ah yes, the Forsters backed the wrong church long ago and came off second best. Never recovered. They're well down Short Street.'

'Like another titled family I know,' she commented.

'Now now, don't get tetchy. You must have noticed I didn't resort to marrying money, and as for the Heselwoods being broke, I am remedying that as you can see. My son will never be poor.'

Georgina shrugged. It was difficult to get the better of an argument with Jasin. But he had reminded her that the Forsters were Roman Catholics. That could have been the deciding factor. She decided not to mention it to Jasin, and give him grounds for another chip at Juan. Since Jasin inherited the title, credit was easier. The bank, she surreptitiously discovered, had lifted Juan's guarantee, and she had written a note of thanks to him, but she had never mentioned the subject to Jasin. It would only create hostility. He had believed her original story, so it had not seemed necessary.

And now, after all this time, Georgina was looking forward to seeing Juan again, being able to welcome him to her own home at last, and on top of that, even though she had given no sign to Jasin, she was bursting with curiosity to meet his bride. She wondered if young Delia really were a plain girl. And realised she rather hoped she was.

The next morning dragged while they waited, with everything in readiness for the arrival of the visitors. It was rare for Jasin to be in for lunch. Although he never admitted it, Georgina knew he enjoyed the camp-fire meals out on the range with Krill and the stockmen and he had become addicted to billy tea.

Georgina's letters home these days were full of joy at their new life in the country, tempered by her sadness at the enforced absence of Edward, who had only spent a year at Montone in its early stages, but she wrote to him about the animals, the livestock, the milkers and the big herds and the native bears and kangaroos and the big emu they called Clarence, who hung around the house like a giant hen and who had become a pet, and the dogs, the clever cattle dogs, but fierce, and the snakes . . . there was no end to what she could write about.

Her mother had remained sceptical about Jasin. She had never liked him. In London, Jasin had slipped easily back in to his old way of life, disappearing to the clubs with his cronies and dashing off to the turf club meetings in stylish clothes. His mother-in-law could never believe that this same Jasin was truly in control of his life as a pastoralist. Georgina was hard put to find the words. 'He's as game as any bushman,' she had said, but even the word 'bush' needed translating. It was as impossible to describe the extent of New South Wales to her mother, who never listened anyway, as it was to describe her husband's activities. All her parent would admit was that Jasin looked healthy, not seedy, as she had previously described him.

Apart from Krill, who idolised Jasin, Georgina knew from expressions and overheard remarks, that the men on the station didn't really like Jasin, but they respected him, because, astonishingly, as she had tried to explain to her mother, he knew what he was doing. He watched over his cattle like a broody hen, counting, checking, worrying about them and keeping the men out on the range when the cows were calving.

He had found a convict, one Victor Passey, who had a way with sick or suffering animals and had promoted him to veterinarian and Passey now had his own role to play in the life of the station, joining Krill as a trusted employee.

Georgina worried about all these men, even though they were convicts, with no women to bring some gentleness into their lives, to soften the harshness of their exile; it horrified her that quite a few of them found consolation with the poor black gins, information that had come to her in giggling delight from her house girls, and which she chose to ignore, not even mentioning it to Jasin, because she could see no answer to the problem. She had heard that a shipload of spinsters was being brought from Britain and was due to arrive in Brisbane shortly and had mentioned to Jasin that some of the better types should be permitted to go down to see if they could find wives, but he would not hear of it. 'We'd have to build married quarters and then, with only a few women among all these men, we'd be asking for trouble. There'd be chaos in no time.' And she supposed he was right.

All through lunch, Jasin was restless. 'We should have heard something by this. I was sure they'd send riders on ahead to announce them.'

'They might have had trouble with the carriage. It would be a slow journey on these trails. I still think they should have come on horseback, it would have been so much simpler.'

'Perhaps Mrs Rivadavia is not the horsewoman you are my dear. And I suppose Forster is a bit old for long rides. In his letter Forster said Rivadavia had located a comfortable coach in Brisbane, they have with them some men from Chelmsford as well as the trooper escort provided by the Governor. Between them they could practically haul it themselves.'

But later in the afternoon his patience had run out. He took Krill and Passey and went out to meet his guests.

Georgina found herself wandering restlessly around the quiet homestead, listening to the wind rattle bamboo canes which she had retained

322

near the house. She lit the lamps and sat down at her piano to practise her pieces, filling in time.

Before long she heard whispers on the verandah and knowing that the blacks liked to sneak up and listen to the music, she felt less anxious, playing Chopin études for her audience and smiling at their sighs of pleasure. If she acknowledged their presence they would scatter because Jasin didn't like them hanging around the house, so they kept very quiet until one man, ignoring the logic of his situation, commented quietly . . . 'Boss coming missus,' in a conversational tone.

Georgina closed the piano and went outside. There was no sign of her audience nor of any horsemen, but she waited, confident that the anonymous black man would be correct and after a while, she heard the horses in the distance and voices on the light breeze. As the riders approached Krill whistled and shouted to the station hands, who came running, and the station seemed to come alive.

'Where's the coach?' she called to Jasin.

'Bogged down the road,' he replied dismounting to offer his hand to Mrs Rivadavia. 'You take care of Delia.'

They were all with him, Juan, Lord Forster, Delia and her maid.

Forster was grey and tired, looking ready to drop, so Jasin took him straight to the parlour for a drink and a rest in a comfortable chair, and Georgina turned her attention to Delia, taken aback by the stunning blondeness and fragile features of Rivadavia's wife, who was not at all as she had expected.

The girl was flushed and nervous, but her maid seemed quite excited at their adventures. She was a stout, red-faced English woman, in a tweedy outfit and felt hat, looking conspicuously dowdy against Delia's pearl-grey riding habit with black velvet lapels and cuffs.

Delia wished to retire immediately and the maid swept her charge away with an air of determined cheerfulness, following Jessie, Georgina's cook, who was acting as housekeeper, since Georgina could not trust the first introduction to the homestead to her black maids.

After all her preparations, she was disappointed at this unseemly start to their visit. To have them all stumbling into the house exhausted and dishevelled, was a pity.

Juan touched her on the arm. 'I'm sorry to be bursting in on you like this at such a late hour, but it is good to see you again. I was very much looking forward to visiting Montone.'

'Juan, no . . . don't apologise. I'm worried about Mrs Rivadavia. Is there anything I can do for her?'

'Miss Lee will look after Delia. She is quite well, just tired.'

'Do come inside then,' she said and he followed her into the parlour. 'Now, what happened?' she asked. 'You all look exhausted.'

'What didn't happen to them!' Jasin said. 'They were attacked by bush-rangers and had it not been for Juan's foresight in having a group of his

323

own men trailing them, they should all have been robbed and murdered.'

'I don't think the bushrangers were in a killing mood.' Juan smiled. 'Don't disturb yourself on that account Lady Heselwood. They just wanted our horses.'

'And how long would you have survived out there without horses?' Jasin cried.

'Until my men came along,' Juan replied simply.

Jasin was preparing the drinks. 'One's pouring hand is still shaking at what might have happened.'

'What did happen? With the bushrangers I mean,' Georgina asked.

'They were chased off, so there is nothing to worry about,' Juan said. 'This is a very pleasant house.'

'My word it is,' Forster agreed. 'It's good to get the feet up. And the countryside up here is very different from down your way, isn't it Juan? Far more tropical than I imagined with all those waving palms, reminds me of Colombo.'

'Yes. Very rich vegetation,' Juan replied, 'and it is so much warmer.'

Georgina watched him as he spoke with Jasin about the station, noticing that his new wife had not altered his very individual style of dress, he still wore his classic black, well-cut clothes, and his hair was still kept well in place with the help, she guessed, of oil. Forster's white hair was fluffed out from his exertions and Jasin had given up trying to keep that one lock of fair hair from his face. Georgina rather liked that, it gave him a boyish look, although he now wore a thick moustache. Most men in these parts wore beards and she was pleased to see that Juan too, had resisted the fashion, his swarthy skin was as smooth and attractive as ever. He was shorter than Jasin, but more robust, stronger, more interesting, and, finding she was dwelling too much on this man, she checked herself and came back to the conversation, realising there was more to their journey from Brisbane than they had told her.

'What else happened to them Jasin? It is obvious Juan and Lord Forster will not elaborate so you must tell me.'

'There are blacks out there,' Jasin said. 'Hundreds of them!'

She saw a flicker of anger on Rivadavia's face, obviously he did not want to discuss this in front of her, but she had to get it out of Jasin, now. Later he would have time to fabricate.

'Wild blacks you mean? But we hardly ever see any on this station. And even if they are out there, no-one seems to have come to any harm.'

'They would not let Lord Forster's party pass. They were forced to travel more than ten miles out of their way. That's how they ended up getting bogged. Krill will take some men and bring the coach in tomorrow.'

'Were they aggressive?' she asked Juan.

He shook his head. 'Not really, more stubborn. They looked fiercer than they were, I think. But it was plain they had decided not to allow us to ford the river at that point.'

'Where Jasin? At Massey's Crossing?'

'Yes,' he said indignantly. 'Right there, where we always cross. They'd better not stand in my way next time I go through there.'

Forster wheezed and took another brandy. 'It was a matter of numbers dear fellow. There were a good thirty blackfellows standing in our way and quite a few on the rocks above. We were not able to establish exactly how many.'

Juan intervened. 'We did not wish to cause any trouble. Lord Forster was very good with them.' He smiled at Forster. 'Our diplomat. He rode down to them and was extremely polite, and bowed to them, requested their advice on an alternative route.'

'Could they speak English?' Georgina was astonished.

'No,' Forster laughed. 'We talked in charades, sign language and they became quite affable. You know, I had the impression those fellows were under orders, but not sure what they were supposed to do. And they knew what guns were, they watched our troopers carefully. Anyway, we gave them some gifts, a couple of saddlebags and fish hooks and bits and pieces . . .'

'Gifts!' Jasin snorted. 'I'd have ridden right over them.'

Rivadavia studied him. 'Maybe so. But they didn't have any women with them, which is a dangerous sign and I had my wife with me, and her maid.' He turned to Georgina. 'Lord Forster made a very correct remark, which now I can't recall. Something was the better part of valour . . .'

Georgina saw that brilliant smile of his again and reflected that Delia was a very lucky girl.

'Discretion, my boy,' Forster called, laughing, but Jasin was still angry. 'Tomorrow we shall ride out and if they are still there we shall disperse them.'

Forster was troubled. 'Please forget it Jasin, it's not as if they committed any crime. Don't stir up any trouble on our account. Governor Gipps is trying to find ways to keep the peace with the natives, based on goodwill, so I don't want to be involved in any fuss.'

'Gipps is a fool!' Jasin said. 'We're not going to put up with their posturing. Armed blacks! Threatening my guests! Poor Delia must have been frightened out of her wits.'

'Jasin's right there,' Georgina said. 'What an experience for her. She might prefer to have supper in her room this evening would you think Juan?'

'I'll find out,' he said.

As he left, Georgina noticed he was limping. 'Have you told me everything?' she accused Jasin.

'Well we haven't heard about the boat trip from Newcastle to Brisbane or the less exciting section of the journey my dear, but we have to give Lord Forster time to catch his breath.'

'Why is Juan limping?'

'Is he limping? I hadn't noticed,' Jasin said.

325

Forster explained. 'He had a bad experience with a native. Got a spear in his leg. Severed part of a muscle, something like that I believe, but it was fortunate the fellow wasn't much of a shot.'

Jasin was stunned. 'Good grief! What is happening? Don't tell me this happened down in the Hunter? They don't have trouble with the blacks down there surely?'

'Not really. They had trouble with the whites; killed a family of blacks. Seems they killed some innocent blacks in retaliation for losing sheep and caused one poor blackfellow to seek revenge. He broke a stockman's neck and then went for Juan before they shot him. A sad affair, but he's quite a fellow, Delia's husband. He bears them no grudge, he says the native was within his rights. There's your goodwill, Jasin, Rivadavia refused to retaliate. Oh quite a fellow! I'm very fond of him. Of course, his father's a great friend of mine, you know.'

'Yes, I did hear that,' Georgina said, interested. 'How did that come about?'

As Forster was explaining, Juan returned. 'Delia would be very grateful for a light meal in the room this evening, Lady Heselwood. Now that she's safe and warm here, she's had time to think about the journey and is a bit shaken.'

'So am I,' Georgina said. 'We'll have to make it up to her. I feel responsible. But we've been here two years now and this is the first sign of trouble.'

'Except for when they spear our cattle!' Jasin growled.

'Oh for goodness sake! We have so many cattle, what difference does it make if they kill a few here and there for food?'

Jasin turned to Juan, exasperated. 'I keep trying to explain to Georgina they don't kill for food, just to be bloody-minded but, of course, we never see the culprits. What am I supposed to do? Let it go on?'

'I'd give your station blacks more presents, more food, let the wild ones see what a good chap you are,' Juan suggested.

'It didn't seem to help you,' Jasin said, making reference to Juan's leg, but the Argentinian shrugged.

'I don't believe that native meant to kill me,' he said quietly.

'What rot!' Jasin retorted and Georgina was nervous. When Jasin was angry he said the first thing that came into his head and she worried that his underlying resentment of Juan would upset everyone.

Forster tried to come to her rescue. 'I say Juan. Now that we are up in the sub-tropics, where is your northern station from here?'

'South-west of here, I think. Maybe not more than a hundred miles.'

'*You've* got a place up here?' Jasin sounded as if the Argentinian had stood on the Union Jack.

'Yes. On the Brisbane River, in the valley.'

'How many acres?'

'I'm not too sure, about fifty square miles. Not a lot.'

326

Georgina felt herself sinking into the chair. That was all Jasin needed, Juan's property was bigger than Montone. But, once again, thinking he was being helpful, Lord Forster joined in, chortling. 'Not a lot for an Argentinian with their great ranches, but vast for an Englishman, what?'

Georgina warmed to Forster. She hadn't seen him for many years but he was such a sweet man, and obviously proud of his grandson-in-law. Jasin, on the other hand, she could see, was furious. She felt she should go out to the kitchen and tell the cook to hurry with supper, but decided it might be a better idea to stay where she was and try to keep some control over the situation.

'You got in early,' Jasin said, his voice silky, not quite complimentary. 'How did you come by a run up here if you've never set foot in this country before?'

'I have a partner,' Rivadavia said, 'he located it for me.'

That pleased Jasin. 'Oh I see. It is not all yours.'

'No. I am sorry, my English sometimes lets me down.' Juan explained, but Georgina saw a hard glint in his dark eyes and she wished Jasin would leave it at that. For all Juan's polite replies to Jasin's questions, she knew that he was irritated.

But Jasin persisted. 'And who is your partner, for God's sake? Don't tell me you're in one of those syndicates picking up impossible tracts of land just for speculation?'

'Certainly not Lord Heselwood. I never speculate. The run will make a good head station for cattle when we have time to move some herds up.' From the downward inflection of the last few words, Juan had indicated that the subject was closed, it was not interesting enough to pursue. He had just turned to speak to Lord Forster, when Jasin, swallowing his brandy, insisted on another question.

'Since you and this partner of yours will be in this region, you could tell us who he might be? Another of your compatriots perhaps?'

'No,' Juan said quietly, his eyes wide, deceptively child-like, as if wondering why anyone would be interested. 'He's an Irishman. I believe you know him. Pace MacNamara.'

Jasin's glass fell from his hand and smashed on the floor.

That night in bed, with Jasin fast asleep, Georgina mulled over the conversation again and laughed. Jasin had asked for that. But it was still very strange. There had been an antagonism between Pace and Jasin since the first time they had met on the ship. To be honest, she recalled, initially she had disliked MacNamara too, feeling he had no place in their company, but after a while she had relented a little. The Irishman had a deceptively sharp wit and when she came to think of it, he had always been pleasant, far more manly and helpful than Dr Brooks or that pathetic Dermott Forrest. Perhaps she had misjudged him. Life in the colonies did give one a different outlook. But here was this strange business with Jasin, who had employed the man, even though he had been a thorn in his side.

The odd thing was that Jasin's cranky regard for MacNamara had turned into hatred. Of that she was certain. The reason could only be put down to the fact that his employee had taken up a station near Carlton Park, by all accounts a much poorer effort, but surely that was not enough for Jasin to go off like a box of firecrackers every time the man's name was mentioned. She really felt Jasin was over-reacting. It made no sense, any of it.

Two doors away down the passage, with his arm around his bride, Juan Rivadavia wondered about that too. And he knew a little more. He knew that the hatred was mutual.

Juan Rivadavia had his own plans for this visit or he should not have accepted the invitation. He found Georgina charming but did not enjoy Heselwood's company, nor would he have volunteered to remain idle on Montone station when he had so much to do at home. When courtesy permitted, he planned to take his men and ride down to inspect the Brisbane River runs. He wanted his stockmen to be familiar with the country there too, because they would be bringing the first herds north and, if Pace agreed, would begin to work the station.

The first few days at Montone were uneventful. Delia recovered her spirits and was very much at home in the company of English friends. They all found they had a great deal to talk about, and Juan was pleased, he would have no qualms at leaving his wife with them for a few days. There weren't too many people even in the Hunter Valley district to whom Delia could relate and he wanted to do all he could to make her happy, understanding from his own experience what a sacrifice she was making by agreeing to live in New South Wales. On the whole he found the colonials rather crude, even the people with money. They had little idea of genteel living. He missed the music and gaiety of Argentina. For himself, he did not expect too much, however from now on he would have to make a greater effort to find and entertain people whose company Delia might enjoy, women especially. She would be able to take up residence in the seaside house at Newcastle in the summer, and she needed friends of similar interests to invite to join her since he could not be there all the time.

On the third day of their visit, two hardy Scots arrived in from their station out on Burnett Waters and Juan was introduced to them. They claimed that at least forty of their cattle had been killed by blacks in one night and that had brought in large numbers of dingoes. The five men, including Juan and Lord Forster, sat around the dining room table to discuss the matter.

Davey Morrison was very certain what they should do. 'The squatters in this district should unite and take action against the blacks, give them a good lesson.'

Lord Forster cautioned against it. 'You would be wiser to call in the military rather than take matters into your own hands.'

'We have already appealed to the Governor for support but we haven't even had the courtesy of a reply. They don't care what happens up here,' Davey said.

'But your problem is in finding the real culprits. If you retaliate against innocent blacks and some of them are killed, you could be arrested for murder.'

Laddie Morrison, Davey's red-bearded brother, roared his anger, 'You can't be serious man! No-one would want to try arresting me for shooting a black on my land.'

'We're peaceful men,' Davey Morrison said, 'but we can't afford to let this go on. Lord Heselwood agrees with us.'

'Of course I do. The runs are too big to patrol, we can't chase them off and we don't want to. The day might come, when they get some civilisation, that they'll work for us.'

'Don't hang by your thumbs waiting for them to work,' Davey snorted. 'We didn't come here to talk airy-fairy nonsense, we have to retaliate.'

Lord Forster was worried, remembering his talks with Governor Gipps. 'What exactly do you mean by retaliate Mr Morrison?'

'The only way we can. If we catch any of them at it, which is more than unlikely, we'll grab them and give them a hiding but if not . . .' He looked to his brother who replied. 'Then we have no alternative but to shoot a couple of them as a warning.'

'Human lives for cattle?' Lord Forster said.

'Human lives!' Davey Morrison muttered derisively stuffing tobacco furiously into his pipe, but he did not look at Lord Forster.

'What is your solution then Forster? That we sit back and let them decimate our herds?' Jasin was in no mood for compromise.

'We lost two of our best bulls,' Laddie Morrison said. 'Don't you understand, sir, that those animals are invaluable to us. We can't replace them up here. We have to go back down to Newcastle or even to Bathurst to get good stud bulls.'

'That's right,' Davey said and he laughed. 'We'll have a hard time replacing the bulls but we wouldn't have any trouble replacing a few blackfellows.'

Forster turned to Juan. 'What do you think?'

Juan searched for a solution. 'I understand your position, but remember this, retaliation breeds retaliation. You kill some of their men it stands to reason they'll kill your men next, not just cattle.'

That weakened Jasin's resolve. He had only lost a few cattle and the Morrison brothers were further west than Montone, perhaps the blacks out there were fiercer. 'Maybe we should just let it ride for a while. That was a good idea of yours, Davey. Give the guilty ones a flogging.'

Davey Morrison turned on him angrily. 'That's easy for you to say because you're getting off bloody light so far, but don't bank on it staying that way, something's up I tell you. Our station blacks have gone bloody quiet, no talk at all, and whole camps have disappeared.'

'They could have been frightened off though, thinking we'd pull the same trick they served on the blacks at Kilcoy,' Laddie said.

'Oh forget about that!' Davey scowled at his brother but Lord Forster intervened. 'Just a minute, what trick did they pull on the blacks?'

Laddie grinned. 'They fed 'em poisoned pudding, Kilkoy pudden they call it, laced with arsenic.'

'My God!' Forster was shocked. 'I can't believe anyone would do such a thing!'

'We had no part in it,' Davey Morrison was quick to say, 'but you have to realise that all this unrest among the blacks happened before that episode, they were having trouble with the blacks too.'

'It is still an absolutely bloody foul thing to do. I want no part of it,' Jasin said. 'I suggest we look after our own stations. I'm not lining up with fellows who resort to that sort of behaviour, vile bloody creatures, certainly not gentlemen. And that,' he suddenly remembered, 'was probably the cause of the problems your party experienced on the way up here, Forster. You passed through that country.'

'My God! Had I known this I doubt we should have left Brisbane!' Forster replied. 'Those murderers have placed all white people at risk here. I shall report this to the Governor and there will have to be an enquiry.'

'Then I'll ask you not to mention where you heard the story,' Davey Morrison growled. 'We've got enough trouble without falling out with other squatters.'

'Despicable behaviour,' Forster said, still worrying about the poisoning. He shook his head as if trying to make himself believe that it was not true.

Juan got up and walked to the door, looking out over the peaceful countryside. Georgina had placed ferns and gum tips all along the wide verandah and it seemed so quiet and restful, a country retreat one might imagine. 'The retaliation you spoke of has already begun then,' he said, 'so if I were you I would prepare to defend yourselves.' He remembered the Indian wars in Argentina had begun in much the same way.

'Against what?' Davey Morrison said. 'They wouldn't dare attack the stations. You're getting off the track. It is our stock we have to defend.'

'I wouldn't be so sure of that,' Juan warned. 'The Aborigines are no less men than any of us. If their people have been murdered in this district you're in for trouble.'

'If they wake up to what killed them,' Laddie said hopefully and Juan turned to glance at him with such contempt that Jasin moved to adjourn the discussion. 'Let's get a bite to eat. Georgina has set up tables in the breezeway. It is very enjoyable there in the warm winter sun. And I should appreciate it if this subject is not mentioned in front of the ladies.'

He presided over the luncheon, doing his best to entertain. Georgina had gone to a great deal of trouble, handicapped by a cook who belonged, Jasin felt, in a soup kitchen, but she had managed to set out delicious cold meats and vegetable aspics, with hot bread, cheeses and good wine. The usually urbane and talkative Forster was quiet and Rivadavia brooded in his irritating Latin way, while the Morrison brothers talked only of cattle. He was pleased when they left to get back to their station.

'Well what do you think?' he asked Forster, in the quiet of the afternoon.

'I don't know. You would be better to talk to Rivadavia, he's more experienced in this sort of thing than I am.'

'Not much point in that. You can't compare Aborigines to Indians, these fellows don't even have horses. We could run them down if we wanted to. No, if they leave my stock alone, I've got no quarrel with the blacks.'

They walked down the track that led to the house and stopped at some towering red gums, with their smooth trunks mottled grey and white, and Forster gave an involuntary shudder. 'They must be very old, these trees,' he commented. He looked back to the timber house which seemed vulnerable with all the French windows opening out on each side to the verandahs and he remembered Juan's sandstone house, that was built inwards around a courtyard. Juan had rebuilt the original homestead along the lines of the haciendas, aesthetically more attractive and easier to defend. He had disposed of the side verandahs, choosing the design more from nostalgia than for protection but Forster now thought that this might have been a better design for Montone. Then again, he appreciated that an enclosed homestead would block out these lovely mountain views. He sighed. His thoughts were only an old man's rambling and really not worth mentioning.

In the early morning the three men went on a turkey shoot and returning with the bags full of plump birds, they were looking forward to a sumptuous meal when Krill came galloping down to meet them. 'Something's up sir,' he called to Jasin. 'Everyone's in, all the boundary riders too. They reckon the station is crawling with wild blacks.'

They stared across the cleared land to the line of pale green bush silhouetted against the cloudless blue sky and then back at the darker green of the hills. 'Are you sure?' Jasin asked. 'Everything looks normal to me.' Two lorikeets screeched overhead in swift food-spotting flight. 'Morrison's men could have spooked our fellows with their talk.'

'No sir. My lads tell me it's no ordinary mob. They're all painted up to glory and silent as shadows. I don't like it. The station blacks have disappeared, every last one of them and some of our boys are all for bolting right now. What do you reckon we should do?'

'Arm everyone. Put men on to guard the stables, we can't afford to lose the horses, and get the rest of the men in around the homestead. We'd better be prepared, just in case.'

He turned calmly back to Juan and Lord Forster. 'I'm sorry, there seems to be a bit of a fuss going on. We'd better get back, it's a nuisance but I think it would be best to be cautious.'

Back at the house they closed the shutters and barred the doors and Jasin insisted that Georgina, Delia and the other two women, Miss Lee and the cook, be seated in the master bedroom while the men gathered in the kitchen and parlour.

Delia was pale with fright but Georgina calmed her. 'I think that would be a good idea. We'll have breakfast in there, just the ladies.'

'Why on earth should we?' Delia asked. 'I would far rather stay with Juan.'

'Oh dear no, leave the men to their fun. I'm sure they're thoroughly enjoying themselves, there's nothing to be worried about.' She hurried Delia into the bedroom and closed the doors as the men began handing out firearms.

By midday there was still no sign of the blacks and the women began moving about again serving sandwiches and tea. The house had become a fug of tobacco smoke so Jasin allowed some doors to be opened.

'Do you think we should send someone out to see what is going on?' Jasin asked Krill.

'Very well sir,' Krill replied and turned to give an order in true military fashion but Juan intervened. 'Not just yet,' he said. 'If they've gone, there's nothing to worry about, if they are still there it could be dangerous for scouts.'

'It's damn silly to be sitting here locked up like jailbirds if there is no cause for concern,' Jasin argued.

'But it doesn't hurt to be patient,' Juan replied. 'We don't know these people or their habits. They might be peaceful for all we know, then again if they are thinking about attacking they might wait until dark. The blacks we met on the way up here spoke a different language from the ones I've heard at home, which surprised me. I thought they all spoke the same language. I wonder who they are, the blackfellows up here?'

'I know that sir,' Krill said. 'The blacks down your way are Kamilaroi . . .'

'Yes, that's right,' Juan said.

Krill nodded. 'Yes, well these boys are a different lot, they call themselves Tingum.'

Bussamarai and his warriors appeared like a white wash along the long line of trees and stood waiting in the moonlight, their white-painted shields held firm and their spears aloft.

Jack Drew had been forbidden to join them because he was not initiated, for which he thanked his lucky stars, because he had begged Bussamarai not to do this. 'They will kill you all. Let me show you a better way.'

'There is no better way,' Bussamarai had said, standing tall in the small circle that composed the council of war.

'It is madness,' Jack had shouted at them and the Tingum men had growled their disapproval. It was impertinent of this stranger to question their ways even if he were a friend to the great Bussamarai.

All Jack could do was to stand at the edge of the forest, well back, and watch as Bussamarai's four hundred warriors took their places, wanting to run across the paddocks to that house and call out to the white men not to shoot, but that presented the old nightmare, the one he had feared for years. It could not be done, he would not get very far, a spear or a bullet.

When the four long rows of magnificent warriors were in position the chanting began and behind them sticks began clicking and from far off in the forest Jack heard a didgeridoo droning. Bullroarers took up the score bringing thunder down with deep-sounding shattering ferocity, and he shuddered wondering what effect this racket would be having on the whites sheltering in the house. And then there was an abrupt silence. The black regiments took four strides forward and eight hundred bare feet began stamping in unison and the rhythmical thumping echoed through the earth and rolled out into the hills.

'God Almighty!' Forster said, peering through the slats. 'They look like bloody Zulus. Did no-one warn you that there were such tribes in this country?'

'No-one,' Jasin said stiffly.

'I was under the impression that these natives only went in for a bit of a skirmish here and there,' Forster continued, fascinated. 'But look at those shields. They're six foot if they're an inch. I've seen shields like that in Africa. Helluva weight to carry, they must be strong fellers. What I'm saying is, it would have taken time to make them, and those blacks, all painted up like birthday cakes, they've been preparing this for a while.'

Juan listened to the Englishmen. Here they were facing a serious attack and Lord Forster was carrying on a running commentary as if he were a tourist and not, himself, in danger. 'Have you sent for help?' he asked Jasin.

'Yes, six riders have gone in three different directions. But it will take time. Pray those black devils keep up their prancing.'

As Juan watched, the warriors moved forward another twenty paces and continued their stamping, their guttural voices resuming the monotonous threatening chant.

Heselwood's foreman came into the front parlour where all the furniture had been pushed aside to allow the defenders room to move. He placed spare guns and boxes of ammunition against the wall. 'Some of the men have bolted,' he said.

'Who? Those damn convicts I suppose?' Jasin said angrily.

'No, stockmen, the convicts are still at their posts.'

Lord Forster turned to him, aghast. 'Not Englishmen I hope?' and Juan stifled a laugh. There was something unreal about all this. The cook went past the door carrying another tray of tea for the ladies. He looked again at the advancing warriors and wondered why he felt they didn't seem to be real either.

Hiding in the forest, Jack waited for the next move. He heard

Bussamarai throw out the challenge and the warriors take up the call, shouting at the white men to come out and fight like men so that this war could be settled right now. Keeping under cover he ran forward and up the trunk of a fallen tree to pull himself across to a higher vantage point, and he cringed as he heard his friend Bussamarai shouting to the white men to come and fight, spear for spear in the correct manner. 'Oh Jesus,' he moaned. 'You bloody fools. They'll never understand.' He prayed that there were some station blacks in the house who could interpret the challenge and he cursed the stupidity of these white men who had just marched into Tingum country without any parley with the blacks. 'All they want is the challenge,' he cried as the chanting resumed. 'When a man is killed on one side the battle is over. The losers have to back off.'

'They're getting closer,' Forster said to Jasin. 'They might be trying an old native trick, to mesmerise us into letting them get close enough to charge.'

'Fire over their heads,' Juan said. 'A warning volley.' But Jasin ignored him. 'If they advance again they'll be within range. We won't let them get any closer.'

The homestead was in darkness as Bussamarai's warriors advanced that one last time, once again shouting their challenge and hurling insults at the cowardly white men quaking inside their walls.

'Fire!' Jasin cried and the guns cracked in short sharp bursts and the warriors fell where they stood, toppling in their lines, bowled over like toys and the guns kept on firing, on and on.

And in the forest Jack screamed at them to take cover. He jumped down to the ground away from the terrible sight, hating the smugness of the white men who were still firing although not a spear had been thrown, and after an age, survivors ran past him, grey ghostly figures, disappearing into the night.

The homesteaders kept up their vigil until dawn. The blacks had taken the bodies of the casualties under cover of darkness but the scores of shields and spears left lying around told the story.

'That will teach them a lesson,' Jasin said. 'They won't come near Montone again in a hurry.'

The staff and the 'bosses' at Montone celebrated their victory that morning with a generous issue of rum and milk but Delia was still so terrified Juan took her to the quiet of their room to comfort her.

When the cook went on a tour of the house to open up all the windows again she barged in there and quickly retreated. Red-faced, she tore out to the kitchen. 'I can't do anything about their room, they're in bed, and not just sleeping either! In broad daylight!'

Georgina flushed. 'Get on with the rest of the house then,' she snapped, and as she passed a mirror, seeing her own stern face she laughed suddenly. 'Why madam,' she said to her reflection, 'I do believe you're jealous.' And why not? she thought. In the last few days she had become very bored with Delia's company, the silly slip of a girl. She was beautiful, there was no arguing with that, but she was also wilful, self-centred and extremely arrogant. Georgina wondered if she had been as bad as that when she was young and found that line of thought a little too close for comfort.

Delia had treated Georgina to endless lists of what Juan was yet to buy for her, and then of course there was her opinion of the beach house at Newcastle where she and Juan had stayed on their honeymoon. 'The decor,' she had told Georgina, 'is appalling. All white and bare like a snow storm, looking as if one couldn't afford to furnish it decently. I'm going to do the whole place over myself. Juan doesn't care how much I spend to make it look pretty.'

Georgina had told Jasin about that and he had almost choked laughing. 'There you are my dear. You completely wasted your time on the house. If Rivadavia had really liked your decor, he would forbid her to touch it.'

And that had made Georgina cross with all of them, although she hoped it was simply that Juan wished to please his wife. He had liked the style she had put into it, surely. Now she was uncertain. It was disquieting. Delia was irritating as well as clinging. Georgina decided she would have a good rest and then wash her hair and take extra trouble in dressing for dinner; everything Delia did made her feel old and unattractive. This evening, after all that excitement, she would give the young madam a run for her money.

'I hate this place,' Delia said to her husband. 'I want to go home. Those terrible blackfellows might come back. You will take me home.'

'Very well. We will leave as soon as possible,' he said, and Delia curled into him, delighted. It was wonderful to be married and to have a husband so eager to please her. It was far better than being single where one's parents argued the point at every turn.

Juan's announcement was not unexpected. 'I am sorry to miss the opportunity to inspect my land but I really feel we should go.'

Forster agreed. 'You should come with us Georgina. This is dangerous country. Why don't you retreat for a while, you too Jasin, until we can get some troopers up here.'

'Definitely not,' Jasin said. 'I can't leave Montone. Not at this stage. But if you wish to take a break, Georgina, by all means.'

'You can come down and stay with us at Chelmsford,' Delia said to her. 'Little Rosa will be thrilled to have us back so soon. She dearly wanted to come with us but Juan said the journey would be too hard for her, and, of course, he was right. I had no idea what we'd be getting into.'

Georgina heard a patronising note in her voice; the last thing she wanted to do was to go anywhere with Delia. 'I'll be staying here. No-one on the station was hurt. But thank you for your concern.'

'Good show,' Jasin said. 'There really is no need for Georgina to uproot

335

herself. I am quite capable of taking care of things here.'

'Please be careful then,' Juan said. 'I think you could have more trouble here. I am wondering if that demonstration last night was just that, a show of strength.'

Jasin laughed. 'You could say that indeed. It was a show of strength, on our part. We've sent them packing and we're well protected.'

When they were leaving, Juan kissed Georgina on both cheeks and she felt the sincerity of their friendship. 'I'm sorry to see you go so soon,' she said. 'Now don't forget us.' She watched them leave in their coach with their own escort and an extra guard of stockmen from Montone who would return to report their safe arrival in Brisbane from where they would return by ship to Newcastle.

Two weeks later Laddie Morrison was speared to death within a hundred yards of his homestead . . .

# PART TWELVE

## THE BLACK WARS III

# CHAPTER ONE

After the mourning, Bussamarai sought out Jack Drew to ask his forgiveness and then his advice, promising, this time, to take heed.

'They've got too many guns,' the white man told him. 'You would be better off to leave this district. Let them have it.'

'Never. This is our land.'

'Well then hit them when they're not looking. None of this walking out in front of them any more. You swoop now, like the eagle.'

Kana was standing shyly nearby, waiting politely to be acknowledged by the great man and Jack called her over.

She ran off and came back with a boy, copper-coloured with lank brown hair, and Jack picked him up. 'This is my son.'

Bussamarai tickled the child. 'He is a fine boy. What is his name?'

'Wodrow,' Jack said and Bussamarai tried the word. 'Wodoro.'

'Yes. That's it.'

'What does it mean?'

Jack was startled. 'I don't know. It is a name of mine. I don't know what it means.' Bussamarai laughed and looked at Kana. 'You like that name?'

'Yes. Wodoro is a good name. It means black rock.'

'Black rock?' Jack cried. It was the first he'd heard of it. 'The name means bugger-all,' he muttered lapsing into English. But he was pleased to present the boy, it gave him a better standing in the community.

For months after that, Bussamarai's men attacked and killed lone stockmen and scattered their stock. The white men retaliated by shooting any blacks they saw, so all the people pulled back, far into the west out of reach and there they stayed. Only the warriors ran down in war parties to attack the stations right across the panorama of the Burnett and Mary Rivers and the Brisbane Valley, and tribes from the high country bore down on the Darling Downs stations. But every time, the white men fought them off.

The black squads could cover up to fifty miles in a day so no-one knew who would be next. This kept the stations on constant alert and demoralised the workforce. The attacks were called mosquito raids because none of them caused too much damage. The squatters called meetings and arranged to have fast horses kept ready for any sign of hostiles so that a messenger could race to the nearest station for help. Even if they were not in time to stop the raid then riders would go after the retreating blacks and run them down.

Montone station was attacked again by a band of about twenty blacks just on dusk one night, but Jasin was ready for them and they were quickly driven off after six of them were killed by gunfire before they reached the outbuildings. The quick despatch of the attackers was thanks to Krill who had drilled the men to take their posts immediately the alarm bell was sounded.

Bussamarai was suffering heavy losses and the Tingum men were unhappy with him. Jack explained that he had too few men spread over a large area and once again suggested that the Tingum should stay out west, away from the whites. The warrior chief still refused to admit defeat but he realised he did not have enough men.

'We will travel into the hot sun and speak to the Mandanggia and the Kungai and the other tribes and I will tell them that if they do not help us they will be next. Is this not so?'

'It is certain to happen,' Jack said.

'Good. You will come with me and help me to explain this to them. I have given this matter great thought. Since the white men are not frightened by our raids then I will ask the tribes to rise up in one fierce attack and we will sweep all the white men before us like dead leaves. We will come down like a flood from the hills. When I return I will call all the Tingum men together, but in the meantime let them go on swooping and snatching if they wish. It will have the white men thinking that they are winning, but gradually they must stop altogether. This will be the eye of the storm.'

Jack understood. He had seen the ferocious rain storms that swept over Bussamarai's country, torrential rains and great winds that smashed and uprooted trees. When it seemed to be over the blacks waited. They drew pictures of this ring of wind explaining to him to stay in the shelter of the high caves because there was always more to come, and they were right. He was fascinated at how much they knew about their land.

This plan of Bussamarai's sounded fine in theory. But then again what else could they do? Lie down and die? No fear, they might as well take some of the white bosses with them. He remembered Ngalla and his sons and Dimining and the others, they still hadn't been properly revenged.

'Tell them, the men of those other tribes, that it isn't just the white men, but the sheep and cattle they bring with them that despoil the land and destroy the waterholes. Once they understand this, you should get them on your side,' he said. 'And if they won't believe us, we'll bring them down here to see for themselves. But I'll have to get some guns, to show them what guns can do. A lot of your warriors died because they still didn't understand what guns can do, running out into the open with their spears. You have to stop them doing that.'

'You are very wise Jackadoo,' Bussamarai said. 'Sometimes I think I am not very wise and I ask the spirits to show me the way, but what do they know of white men? Nothing at all, so that is why they sent you.'

This was news to Jack but it could be right for all he knew.

He took a band of warriors and travelled fast, heading for the coast until they came across a well-used trail. Then they settled down to wait.

The first travellers that came by were in a heavy German wagon, a family of settlers, and his black men were eager for the ambush but Jack couldn't bring himself to let them kill women and children. If they killed the two men with them, what chance would the women have to get the children to safety? There were others beside blacks roaming these wild lands.

'But they've got guns, we came for guns,' his warriors argued.

'They're not the right sort of guns,' Jack said quickly. 'No good. I know what I'm doing.'

He allowed the settlers to pass, watching them curiously and listening to them talk, they seemed to be unsure of their route. He thought of telling them that the best way would be to turn around and go back but that would give him away as a white man and bring the soldiers.

The blacks were patient. They waited with him for another two days, and he marvelled at their quiet acceptance of duty. At last their real quarry came along and Jack could not believe his luck. He had been waiting for a couple of men, stockmen or squatters, he did not care, but here were a pair of troopers, and one was a sergeant. These were the ones who deserved to get it in the neck. He nodded his approval and watched as the blacks took up their positions.

The troopers never knew what hit them. The great spears thudded into their backs and they fell like sacks of potatoes, the horses galloping away in fright, to stop, hesitant, further up the track. The Tingum men pulled the bodies into the scrub and hid them, while Jack collected the guns and walked down the road to take ammunition and rations from the saddlepacks.

Just in time, Jack stopped his men from spearing the horses.

'Don't do that. They are good animals.' He took the saddles and bridles from the horses and hurled them into the bush, slapping the horses to send them away and stood back, grinning, as they sped away, free.

Bussamarai and Jack went among the Tingum people showing them the guns and how they worked. Then they sat down with the elders of the tribe to discuss Bussamarai's proposal to invite the northern tribes down to fight with them. That caused a great deal of discussion, a lot of it Jack gathered, was to do with taboos and totems. The idea wasn't as simple as he had thought it would be. And all the time the whites in the district were becoming more numerous.

Pacifists argued that perhaps they should negotiate with the northern tribes to be allowed to take refuge in their lands and that angered Bussamarai. 'What is the use of that? The white fellers will keep on coming and in the end we will have to cross the water and hide in the gunyahs of the Kebishu men? Do you want that?'

They all shook their heads in fear. The tribes across the straits at the far north were notorious headhunters. Their cruel and bloodthirsty rites were well known.

'Then you must let me go for help,' Bussamarai cried. 'I will take my friend and counsellor with me into the hot lands and seek out more warriors, then I will come back and this time the white men will know about us. And if I fail I will never return.'

Jack wondered how far they would be going. He was in his forties now, and he wondered how much longer he could keep up with Bussamarai who never seemed to tire although his hair was showing grey. After all this, he decided, he would pick up with a mob and go well away into the west and find a safe and settled camp. Not all of them wandered around like gypsies he had discovered. It would be better to take Kana and Wodrow out of reach of the whites. He fingered his little gold trophy. Although he was always searching and his friends helped him search he had never seen any more gold and had long since lost touch with the trader.

Message sticks were handed to heralds who fanned out over the land to advise that Bussamarai was coming, that he wished to sit down in a big corroboree far to the north of his own territory and that he wished to be told of a suitable meeting place.

Weeks passed before Bussamarai informed him they were ready to go and a party of six Tingum men were chosen to accompany their leader. No preparations were needed. They simply began the trek by following the river until it reached the sea and then went north along the coast. The journey was a delight to Jack. The travellers swam and fished in the warm clear waters and ran for miles along white beaches until they came to headlands or mangroves that forced them inland temporarily. They went so far that Jack was certain any day they would come to where the land ended and face the dreaded Kebishus. The others laughed, it would take moons to get there, they told him, not days. Sometimes, when he thought of England, he wondered if he had stumbled off the earth into another place. How could it be, he asked himself, that the towns back there were crowded with poor starving people when this land was so huge and empty and so full of good food? Meat, fish and fruit, and such fruit, all for the taking. It surely must be another earth.

His companions were excited, they told him that the Wanamara men were coming and the Kokokulunggur and the Barbarum and the Merkin warriors.

'And many who heard me speak the first time too,' Bussamarai added 'who went away and forgot. Now they will see how wrong they were.'

This time the meetings were held in a flat bay like an amphitheatre and there were few women present. Bussamarai slapped his thighs with joy. It was obvious they were taking him seriously now. Jack was not permitted to attend the crucial talks, his role was simply to demonstrate the guns.

At the appointed time he strode out in front of them, making them all stand well back, pointing to some wallabies that were grazing on the hillside. Creeping closer to the animals, he fired and missed. He felt a fool. But the tribesmen got such a shock at the loud report that they yelled in fright, then finding everything seemed to be normal again they clapped

341

him. Rather than waste any more ammunition Jack sent his friends off to catch a wallaby and bring it back alive and with the animal tied to a tree, he shot it. That did the trick. After that he brought down a possum and a bear and Bussamarai explained to them what had happened.

While Bussamarai and the other men went on with their talks Jack had a lazy time of it, there was always plenty of food around and their hosts, while speaking another language, were anxious to please, they brought him all manner of tasty food including his favourite, oysters. He asked them to show him where to find them. In the afternoon he sat on a beach prising open the marvellous oysters, gloating over them; until his companions pointed excitedly seawards. A sailing ship was coming into the bay.

Jack spat. 'There they are!' he shouted. 'The white men who are in Bussamarai's land, now they are coming into yours!'

He ordered them to light fires everywhere in the bush and to send up as much smoke as possible to make certain the white men saw their camp fires and think twice about landing. This they did and when the ship retreated Jackadoo was the hero of the day.

That night he talked to Bussamarai again. 'It's no use bringing all these blackfellers down and setting them against one station at a time. Sure you'll win the first round but they'll be waiting for you next time. You tell them you need as many warriors as you can find. And you attack the stations in one district all at the same time so they can't send for help. And you don't attack at night when they're wary and on guard. You attack in the afternoons when the men are scattered working and the rest are hot and sleepy, when the flies are buzzing. But you have to strike all on the same day and at the same time. I've been thinking about this for a while . . . something like that . . .' His voice trailed off.

He rarely made long speeches, it was still hard and he never knew how Bussamarai would react, but he was getting tired of their endless discussions. He did not see what they had to talk about all this time. And the presence of that ship had unnerved him. It reminded him that although living by the seaside was a great pleasure, it was not the safest place to be and his original plan of making for the inland was far more sensible.

The new war plans were at last settled and timed for three moons away to give the tribes time to rally their men.

The Tingum group took their leave. They sped down the coast again, this time cutting through the forests and over the hills, swimming the rivers with ease until they came to the mouth of their own river where by another of their mysterious arrangements Tingum men were waiting for them with canoes, to take them swiftly and silently up river.

They camped overnight in the bush and in the early dawn they ran along the sandy banks to drag the canoes from the hiding places.

One of the Tingum men caught up with Jack. 'I found them,' he said proudly, grinning broadly through matted whiskers.

'Found what?' Jack asked.

'The yellow stones. I found your yellow stones.'

Jack stopped and stared. The guide, a man in his fifties, was pleased that he could do better than the young ones. He opened his hands and on each lay a gold nugget. One was a jagged piece about six inches long and the other a lump as big as the man's palm.

Jack cried, 'Where did you get them?'

'Back here,' the man said and took Jack to the bend of the river and there in the crumbling bank Jack saw the gold. He had always known he would find it sooner or later but now that it was right in front of him, the dull yellow just sitting there laid bare by the river, it seemed too easy just to reach for it. A blasphemy, like stealing a jewelled chalice from an unguarded and open church. He looked around him furtively as he dug nuggets from the bank and stuffed them into his dilly bag but no voice of authority shouted at him, no hand of the law clamped on his bare shoulder, only a quiet voice whispered to him. 'Bussamarai say you come.'

He wanted to throw himself into this golden river, to revel in it but there wasn't time. With his knife he gouged out another nugget from the lower bank and looked despairingly around, knowing there had to be more but he was being urged to hurry. He took stock of the land marks, especially the booka booka tree. He would remember that, booka booka trees were precious, they supplied the bark for canoes and shields. He twisted the string tightly around his dilly bag and ran down to a canoe. 'Has this place got a name?' he asked.

'Gimpi Gimpi,' Bussamarai said. 'Now get in, we have to go.'

Bussamarai was not interested in Jackadoo's find, he was intent on his own plans. The nearest stations would be attacked at the same time by large forces of men so that the white men on their fast horses couldn't ride for help, they would be too busy protecting their own hides. Then the warriors would all be pulled back out of harm's way to regroup and a second strike would be made. But the first attack was all important. If it failed, he would have trouble keeping the other tribesmen active in his district. For that matter he would have trouble keeping his own men fighting. He could not afford any more mistakes. He sighed looking down at the waters rushing by like his life, there was little time left. He was getting old and could not afford to be wrong. The young are never wrong. They do not believe in being wrong. Their hearts beat so fast they do not have time to be suspicious of their own judgement. 'My heart beats slower now,' he said to Jack.

'Mine doesn't,' Jack laughed joyfully, clutching his dilly bag, 'it has wings today.' And Bussamarai smiled, pleased with his enthusiasm.

Back at their own camp he explained the plan in more detail to Jack who had difficulty concentrating. Jack Wodrow alias Drew, highwayman and tribesman, was rich. How rich he had no way of knowing. This heavy gold must be worth thousands of pounds.

Bussamarai drew a map on the dusty ground explaining which stations were to be attacked by mobs of one to two hundred warriors, depending on the number that answered his call, and each mob would have Tingum guides so there would be no mistake. Jack whistled! He had no sympathy for his own kind. When the word got out among the blacks about the Kilkoy pudding they had gone into a frenzy of grief. Corroborees were held demonstrating the agonising deaths of the victims. Hatred for white men had reached such a level that Jack's own life was in danger. Had it not been for the protection of Bussamarai they'd have shoved some of that dirty poisoned flour down Jack's neck. Oh no lads, he thought, you white fellers have done nothing for me but put me in chains like a slave and nearly sent me to the devil with a belly full of arsenic or strychnine or whatever it was you used on the poor buggers. You fight your own battles.

He had been carrying the nuggets in a possum skin pouch but they were too heavy and ungainly hanging from his rope belt so now he began making a wide money belt from layered strips of hide and stitching each piece into the belt so that they would sit snugly into the contours of his body.

He'd had a good time wandering with the blacks but once these battles were over he would have to work out a way to get back into the towns – now that he was a rich man. Kana and the boy would not want to go, life in a town would be no good to them. He would take them to an inland mob and settle them down first and then leave. They would be well looked after, the blacks shared everything. Dozing by the campfire, he remembered his first and best friends in the Kamilaroi, all dead now, and he began to think about the war plan. If everything worked out the way it should, the squatters in the Burnett River and Mary River districts are in real trouble, he mused. And if Bussamarai has enough men, he'll strike into the Brisbane River valley too, the fate of the settlers was in the lap of the gods. He recalled that the blacks had mentioned a strange station in the Brisbane valley but he'd been too busy day-dreaming about the gold to take much notice. Now he shivered. The way they described this place it could be a barracks, it could be filled with troopers. Bloody hell!

He ran down to Bussamarai. 'I need some guides to show me the strange station in the big river valley, quickly. If it turns out to be full of troopers, you'll get your heads blown off!'

'Go then,' Bussamarai said. 'There is still time.'

'One more thing,' Jack paused. 'What about the Kamilaroi people?'

'What about them?'

'We have to avenge them. You promised.'

'This will be their revenge.'

'No. It must take place in Kamilaroi country or no-one will know.'

'I am sorry,' Bussamarai told him. 'We do not have enough men to go that far. You know that, you told me yourself small parties mean big risks. But we can send messengers to them to tell them of the beginnings of our war.'

'That's it then,' Jack cried. 'Tell them to stir up as much trouble as they can down there too, kill the cattle, burn the crops. It will further confuse the white men. They won't know what is going on.'

'Ah to have the wings of an eagle to see this great sight,' Bussamarai's eyes shone. Jack suddenly felt depressed, particularly now that he had made up his mind to leave these people. 'You understand this war is only payback,' he said nervously. 'The white fellers will never leave your country, there are too many of them.'

'I know that now,' Bussamarai said. 'But I also know that the things you told me about long ago, the towns full of people and the big ships that can carry so many for months on end, all these things are real. They are not magic. Here, where I can see what I am doing, I know I am fighting ordinary mortal men. The fear that kept me stupid has gone. I will explain this to everyone. The guns are not magic either, they can miss like you did. That was a good lesson. But hear what I say now. As long as the spirits allow me to live here I have a duty and my duty is to stop the white men from roosting in our trees. As long as I live no white man will be safe in these valleys, along this river, or in any part of Tingum country. A man can only do so much. And this I can do, you will see.' He chuckled. 'It is not magic either, my war will be won by the swiftness of the spear and the fleetness of foot.'

In the morning Jack went with two young blacks down to the Brisbane River valley travelling through the scrub quickly and efficiently, their bodies dusted grey, and streaked with silvery white paint that camouflaged them into invisibility.

When he first saw the place from a distance, Jack was worried. It looked like a barracks with a high sapling fence surrounding the buildings. He moved forward into the long grass to watch for uniforms. Bushmen came and went though the wide gateway, black gins ambled outside with their children but there were no troopers. Cattle grazed in mottled groups in open country or rested, nosing in under tall trees for shade, huddled together, their backs to the world. He could not understand what this place was. It was nothing like a station homestead, he had seen plenty of them. To make certain he waited for hours. Perhaps the troopers were out on patrol. But then it was strange they had no guards or lookouts on duty. No-one was even keeping watch at the gate as far as he could see.

He was almost ready to turn away convinced that this was just another cattle station, when a rider came out on a fine chestnut horse and headed across the saddle-high grass towards the river.

Jack kept very still so as not to disturb the horse but as they approached he saw something familiar about the rider. He almost moved to scratch his head but years of hunting had taught him not to move a muscle. He peered through the tips of the grass to get a better look at the rider's face, and then he squinted again to make sure, trying not to laugh because there was no doubt about it. This man was Scarpy the sailor, his mate from the ship; last seen at Mudie's slave farm.

He moved down to the river bank where Scarpy was watering the horse and prepared to speak but found himself searching for the English words. He wanted to say something appropriate to this great joke of meeting Scarpy out here in the never-never but he had been using the blacks' language for so long it was hard to remember any English and harder still to form the words.

'You'd be deaded by now,' he said and Scarpy leapt out of the water staring around him in fright. Spear in hand Jack slid down the bank to the sand, to confront his old mate.

'Don't kill me,' Scarpy cried. 'I ain't done nothing to you.'

The ferocious-looking black man doubled up laughing, and Scarpy made a feeble attempt to join in while trying to lead the unwilling horse out of the water.

From habit, Jack barred his way with the spear. 'You Scarpy?'

Scarpy's eyes widened like a great owl. 'What did you say?'

'I say you Scarpy, my mate,' Jack said carefully, his tongue tripping.

'Oh yeah. That's right, mate. Good on you, mate. I'll see you later,' he tried to move away but Jack stopped him. His English was beginning to flow back.

'Think again,' he said. 'The ship, the *Emma Jane*, from London. Don't you know me Scarpy?'

His words only shot more fear into Scarpy's face as he backed away into the water. It was bad enough being faced with a cannibal but one who talked magic as well was too much. He went down on his knees in the shallows. 'Let me go. Look, I'll give you my neckerchief.' He pulled off the dirty red cloth but Jack brushed it aside.

'Shut up Scarpy. I'm Drew. Jack Drew. Remember?'

Scarpy stared at Jack. He shook his head. 'You can't be. He got lost in the bush. Died. Years ago.'

'The hell I did,' Drew said, remembering his status in that world. 'I got away. I always said I would.'

Scarpy struggled to his feet. 'You don't look like Jack Drew. You're a bloody blackfeller.'

Jack shrugged and walked over to stroke the horse. 'Is this your horse?' he asked Scarpy, still needing to know if there were any troopers around.

'Yes. I learned how to ride and I'm bloody good now. I've got two horses of my own.'

'That your camp over there?' Jack pointed towards the stockade.

'Yeah. Me and O'Meara and a lot of blokes live there. You remember O'Meara?'

Jack nodded. 'The Irishman.'

'By Jesus you are Drew or I'm going mad!'

'It's me all right.'

Scarpy laughed, tears coming into his eyes. 'Well whadya know? Wait till I tell O'Meara. Listen, why don't you come back with me? We'll give the bugger the shock of his life. I'm bloody pleased to see you Jack.'

He reached out to shake Jack's hand, waiting a little gingerly while Jack transferred his spear to the other hand. 'Can you use that thing?'

'Too bloody right I can,' his friend said and Scarpy was dizzy with delight. 'Oh Jesus Jack, you always was a smart one.'

'Any troopers in your camp?' Jack asked, remembering his mission.

'You'd be joking. We built that stockade in case they came after us. Hey come on Jack, we'll go up and see O'Meara.' He led up the bank, and Jack followed, but he had made up his mind, he would not go near Scarpy's camp, it was too dangerous with a money belt full of gold.

'I'll tell you something Scarpy. For you and O'Meara. Get the hell out of that camp. Run for your life.'

'Why?' Scarpy asked, startled, staring at the painted body.

Jack stood straight now, took his spear and hurled it at a tree. It thudded into the trunk and stayed there with hardly a quiver. Scarpy flinched. Jack retrieved the spear and turned back to him. 'That's your warning. Take your horses and go. Today. Now!'

When Scarpy looked again he had disappeared, there was no sign of him anywhere.

At first O'Meara laughed at him. 'You're drunk Scarpy.'

'I'm not, I swear.'

'Then you're seeing things, going bush-mad.'

'No, listen to me O'Meara. He said we have to get out of here and fast. Run for your lives, he said. I swear he did. And I reckon he knows what he's bloody talking about too. You should have seen him, looked more like a blackfellow than a white man and a wild black at that.'

O'Meara walked to the gate of the stockade and looked out. All seemed quiet. 'What if we just batten down for a while?'

'Jack Drew's no fool. If that's all we needed to do, he would have said so. You can stay if you like, O'Meara. I'm off. I'm not hanging around.'

'What about our cattle?'

'Bugger the cattle. You've got your money for this place. MacNamara won't care if we leave now. Let's pack up and go.'

'We could go down and mix in with the cedar cutters and drift into Brisbane with them, but I wasn't quite ready to go yet. Look at the prime animals we got out there. It's walking money.'

'Right, you stay. I'm going and I reckon the rest of the blokes here are entitled to know something's up.'

Scarpy was so sure of imminent danger that O'Meara gave in. 'Right then. Tell them the party's over. Start packing!'

Within an hour the stockade was deserted and crows came down to pick over the discarded gear thrown around the compound and to peer in the open doorways in search of food.

# CHAPTER TWO

When the attack came it was not precisely as Bussamarai and his council had instructed but it was just as devastating. Large parties of warriors filtered through the scrub by night. There were so many people moving about that Jack was amazed that the whites were not alerted, but native scouts reported everything was normal on the stations.

Bussamarai himself led the attack on Montone Station as a matter of honour. There was a debt to be settled. This was where he had challenged the white men in the first place and sustained terrible losses.

It was made clear to Jack that he was expected to take an active part in the battle; 'permitted' was the expression they used but he knew it would not be worth his life to refuse. This was to be a united fight, no man could be neutral, even those who claimed the white men had been good to them.

Keeping to the original plan, Bussamarai's men began their attack in mid-afternoon, bursting with pride that they were part of this great flood of warriors. Jack shared their excitement but was relieved to see that they had taken his advice. There were to be no more lines of warriors exposed to fire. They moved quietly on the station from the rear, flicking swiftly from tree to tree, edging closer to the outbuildings in the quiet of the bush which was lulled by the heat of the day.

Two stockmen were ambushed at the river bank before they had time to get to their horses and the main mob moved on. A woman came out of the henhouse with a basket of eggs and a Tingum man silently felled her with a massive blow from his waddy, but the fowls made such a racket that the blacksmith stepped out of his shed to see what was happening and a spear threw him to the ground. By that time someone was ringing an alarm bell and the warriors broke from cover and hurled themselves at the station. Jack ran with them hoping to find protection from the bullets that were already beginning to fly, by staying within the mob.

Inside the homestead Jasin was shouting instructions and barricading the house, as men close enough to make it dashed for the back door. Passey was in, but there was no sign of Krill. He could see some of the men, remembering Krill's instructions, had battened down the stables and were firing from there.

While Passey handed out more guns and ammunition, Jasin pushed Georgina into the main bedroom dropping the heavy bolts against the already shuttered French windows. 'Stay here,' he shouted, 'so that I know where you are.'

At first it was difficult to get a line on the attackers because they kept to the cover of the rocks, trees and outbuildings. Spears rained on the house but it seemed to Jasin that little real damage was being inflicted by either side. But the blacks soon became more reckless, running along the verandahs smashing at the walls with their axes and dropping burning branches on the timber decks. He remembered the auger holes in the first bunkhouse Clarrie and Snow had built at Carlton Park and wished to God he had kept that in mind when building this house.

Passey had already thrown open the shutters in one room and put his men behind the upturned dining-room table where they were now beginning to account for careless natives judging by the shrieks, but the men in the kitchen were taking the brunt, firing through the smashed windows. All around him Jasin could smell burning but was unable to see where it was coming from. He joined the men in the kitchen, firing from one of the two windows, frantic now that he could see this was no small attack. There seemed to be hundreds of blacks surrounding them. He prayed that the men who had been assigned by Krill to ride for help at the first sign of trouble, had remembered their duty and gone, and he prayed too that they would bring help in time. Beside him a station hand screamed and fell back, hit by something that had caved the top of his head in, blood pouring from the frightful wound. Jasin turned back to the window as Passey dragged the body away.

Outside he could see all the outbuildings had been overrun except the stables. He heard the screams of men captured by the blacks.

'How many men have we got in the house?' he shouted.

'Only eight now,' Passey cried, but then they heard the unmistakeable sound of splitting timbers. 'They're at the front door,' Jasin shouted and went racing through the house firing into the smashed panels.

Jack Drew was in the second onslaught on the house and he was with a mob at the back while the main group forced their way through the front door. Pushed along by his comrades, he stumbled into the homestead which had become chaotic with gunfire and hand-to-hand fighting and ran around a passage. He threw open a bedroom door and a white lady was standing there by the shutters frantically trying to reload her pistol. He had a sudden, strange feeling that he knew this woman and without a word, he grabbed her and threw her onto the floor and pushed her under the bed. No time to think why.

He ran out the door slamming it behind him to turn back to the fray in the house. As he did so Jasin Heselwood shot him point blank in the chest and he crashed to the floor.

Jasin leapt over the body and wrenched open the bedroom door terrified of what he might find in the room but saw that Georgina was safe. From the doorway he fired into the passage, killing a painted black who had just come storming around the corner from the back. He went down on his knee, blood dripping from his shoulder where a tomahawk had glanced against him in the first fight at the front door, preparing to defend his wife.

The dying Jack Drew beside him, looked into his face. 'Wodrow,' he whispered. 'Wodrow.'

But Jasin didn't hear him over the noise and shouts and curses as his men battled with rifle butts and chair legs to force the blacks out of the house.

Suddenly as if an invisible bugle called, the blacks pulled back and ran from the house.

Passey ran in to Jasin. 'We have to get out. The house is burning and they've fired the stables.'

'Get all hands working to put the fires out then,' Jasin yelled.

'No. It's too late,' Passey cried. 'That's what they want us to do. Then we'll have no cover and they can bring up more men.'

'No,' Jasin screamed, 'I won't leave this house. I order you to get them working. Now!'

'It's no use boss,' Passey said. 'Come on Mrs Heselwood!' he called past Jasin to Georgina. 'We've got to get the hell out of here.'

As he spoke, flames crackled from the roof and a cloud of smoke sent them running outside for air. Passey rushed them to the side of the house where the men, already mounted, were waiting with three spare horses.

'We'll have to make a dash for it,' Passey said. He nodded, approving, as Georgina swung into the saddle, astride, her skirts pulled up over her knees. Jasin reluctantly mounted his horse. 'Now we're all going out together,' Passey shouted. 'We stick together and stop for nothing. If they're in our way we ride right over them, you got it?'

Jasin edged his horse over to his wife. 'Are you all right old girl?'

'Yes, Jasin, I'm quite ready.'

'Well hang on, we'll get out of this. I always said you could ride better than most men.'

He looked around him as the horses pranced impatiently while Passey handed out ammunition. There were only ten men in the group out of a company of almost fifty but there was no time to search for stragglers, a good few would have been out on the range. He hoped they got away. 'Has anyone seen Krill?' he asked but they shook their heads. 'Right then, everyone ready?'

'Yes boss,' the men called grimly.

'Then we ride hard and head for Jackson's station.'

The riders galloped away just as the combustion in the house sent a blaze of flame through the roof. They tore across the home paddock leaping over a small stone fence to head for open country, the terrified horses as eager to get away as they were. They kept up the pace until they turned onto a trail miles from the homestead.

Some horsemen came galloping towards them. 'The Jackson station's been sacked,' they shouted. 'Burned to the ground and old man Jackson's been killed. We were coming to warn you.'

'Too late,' Jasin said. 'You might as well turn back. We'll head south instead.'

They stopped at a waterhole at dusk but the horses were fidgety. 'They're here boss,' Passey muttered. 'We have to keep moving.'

'Fire a few volleys into the bush to scare them off,' Jasin said, but Passey was worried. 'They could have hit us if they wanted to. If we just keep going they might be satisfied.'

Wearily Jasin climbed back on his horse as Passey helped Georgina to remount and they set off down the road again in the darkness.

They rested at a shallow river crossing until morning, and then were joined on the road by other retreating settlers with horrific tales to tell, but Georgina rode in silence.

'What say we make for Brisbane?' Jasin asked her. 'At this rate all the stations will be bedlam. Do you feel up to it?'

'We might as well. We have to get there sooner or later.'

Jasin pulled away to talk to the men and Georgina thanked God that Edward was safe in England. Her thoughts turned now to the house. She had looked back once to see everything they owned going up in a huge bonfire. The women on the wagons stared at her, ladies did not ride astride even in these circumstances, but Georgina didn't care. What was left for them now? More weary years of living in other people's homes?

Krill had been working cattle out of a dry gully with two convict stockmen, when a rider appeared high on the ridge and gunned his horse down the dangerous steep slope at a headlong pace.

'What are you doing!' Krill shouted, spurring on his own horse. 'You'll kill that horse you bloody fool.' He was so angry he was ready to pull the madman out of the saddle.

But the cowboy was screaming. 'They're attacking the station! Hundreds of blacks!'

'Let's go!' Krill called to his other men, as he loaded his rifle.

'Not me,' the rider said, 'you'll never get near the place. I ain't even got a gun.'

Frustrated, Krill looked to the others. 'What about you blokes?' Neither of them were armed.

'We're game if you are,' the first man said, lifting a small axe from his saddle. The second one, a cockney by the name of Barrett, held up his stockwhip with a grin, and the three men set off as one, galloping for the station.

Within a mile of the homestead, with the horses galloping fast towards the billowing smoke, they were caught between the retreating blacks and another mob racing to join them. The first stockman was brought down by a spear, while Krill fired into the advancing mob, but his horse, swerving to get away from them, put his foot in a hole and went down, throwing Krill heavily to the ground.

Coming up on a wider course, cracking his stockwhip into the faces of blacks who got close enough to him, and riding low on the neck of his horse, Barrett broke free, looking back, terrified, to see a mob of blacks attacking Krill with clubs.

He saw the house explode into flames and pulled the horse away heading for the cover of the bush, riding wildly, losing all sense of direction. Dismounting and too afraid to lead the horse through the shadowy bush, he held the reins and clutched a stirrup as he walked, taking some comfort in the presence of the horse, hoping it knew where it was going.

Barrett had only been on the station a few months, after years at the Moreton Bay penal settlement, and Krill had discovered he had a talent. Krill had put him to counting cattle in a big muster. Where other blokes lost count or went wrong as the herds, adding up to thousands, were brought in, Barrett was never wrong and kept it all in his head. Krill had made Barrett his assistant for the muster and given him a horse. Barrett was proud of his achievement and proud of his horse – only the gentry rode at home. Now with Montone burnt down, what would happen? If he could keep clear of the blacks and get to a station, he'd be safe. Then he'd have to make sure he got assigned again. No more prisons for me, he thought. No way. I'd bolt first.

He felt sick thinking of Krill and the other bloke back there, killed by the savages, and drank his waterbag dry to wash the taste of bile from his mouth.

As they rode down into the hot and steaming Brisbane Valley, it teemed with rain and the hills surrounding them were blotted out by a wall of hissing grey rain. The horses slipped and skidded in the mud and wagons became bogged, while men, drenched and sweating, struggled to haul them out. Soaked to the skin, Georgina found herself in a long line of bewildered refugees heading for the township. Jasin had no jacket to give her but a stockman had ripped a hole in a saddle blanket and slipped it over her head. She was grateful for the spontaneous gesture.

Troopers in oilcloth coats rode alongside them shouting over the rain, asking questions, trying to discover what had happened. It seemed to Georgina that the officers with their swords clanking uselessly by their sides were more agitated than the survivors.

Jasin was riding beside her, past caring about the rain. It's warm rain at least, she thought and looked down at her muddy clothes. She didn't have a shred to change into when they arrived at their destination, whatever that would be, and it didn't seem to matter any more.

The men from Montone flanked them as they rode, their own loyal and gallant band now, it seemed. She wanted to cry for the people who had died at Montone, even the cook, the poor convict woman Jessie, who had done her best, and the men, mostly convicts too.

An officer reined in beside the men but they deferred his questions to Jasin. 'Where are you from?' he asked.

'Montone Station,' Jasin replied, looking grimly ahead.

'Your name?'

'Lord Heselwood,' Jasin announced angrily and his men grinned at the discomfiture of the officer.

Georgina wondered again at the peculiarities of the station hands, who set such store in being 'their own men', wary of bosses and yet she was sure that if Jasin turned about and said he was returning to Montone they would go with him. It was all to do with a point of view, she supposed as her horse plodded on. They had been riding for days, one had to think of something to stay awake and stop panicking about the future. The Heselwoods were homeless again and on their way to a strange town where they did not know a soul.

'What tribe attacked your station sir?' the officer asked.

'How the bloody hell do I know?' Jasin said. 'I didn't ask for their credentials.'

'I'm sorry sir. What we're trying to find out . . . I mean, it appears that this attack was part of a well-organised series of simultaneous attacks on stations across the frontier. It is quite out of context you understand. Unheard of for blacks to attack in this manner.'

'It's heard of now,' Jasin snapped and Georgina thought this young officer might be wiser to move off before Jasin's temper got any worse. The rain had sunk to a thick drizzle and clouds hung low over the miserable township ahead of them, beside the churned and muddy river.

But the officer pressed on. 'They must have had a leader, someone in charge, but we can't even pick up a name. If we could just find out who is running the show we'd have something to go on. You had no warning sir? Not even from your own blacks?'

'The only name I need,' Jasin said, 'is the name of your commanding officer,' and the soldier wiped water from his face. 'I'm sorry sir. I beg your pardon.' He backed his horse away from the angry squatter.

Nevertheless he must have passed the word along because when they finally entered the waterlogged streets of Brisbane the commanding officer, Lieutenant Gravatt, sought out Jasin. 'If you and Lady Heselwood would accompany me sir, I have accommodation for you in my quarters.'

'I should prefer you found accommodation for my men!' Jasin said.

'Of course sir. The barracks can put them up.'

'Good. I hear you have a new hotel in the town. My wife and I would rather go there. Could you arrange that?'

'Certainly Lord Heselwood.'

The last half mile is always the hardest. Georgina remembered someone had told her that once and they were right. She would have settled for the barracks if they were closer but she followed Jasin to the hotel, ready to fall from the saddle by the time they arrived.

Thanks to the lieutenant, who had dashed on ahead, they were taken to the best room in the house where maids were frantically cleaning up and clearing out the belongings of some unfortunate who had just been deposed. Georgina sat listlessly on a hard sofa while sheets billowed and fresh pillowcases were swept under chins to encase plump pillows, and windows were thrown open in the false hope of acquiring a breeze.

The monotonous rain hammering on the iron roof in the early morning was comforting. It gave Georgina an excuse not to get up and face the day. A grey day she thought, and fitting, probably the greyest day of our lives. Her wet clothes were still hanging limply over the chair where she had thrown them and she remembered that Jasin had collapsed on the bed in his wet breeches. He was still asleep, dead to the world, and she felt his breeches, surprised to find they were only slightly damp, steamed by the heat of the room in this monsoonal weather. She wondered if she should wake him, afraid that he might catch a chill, but left him be. If either of them were to be afflicted by colds it was too late now to do anything about it. He would be better to rest. She remembered anxiously Jasin's break-down at their last setback. This time things were a great deal worse. It was essential that he get all the rest he could.

Eventually she slipped from the bed and went to the window, clutching her bedcover around her, thankful now for the hot weather. She had decided it was time to do something constructive, so she went to the door and hissed to a maid. 'Would you ask the publican's wife if I could see her for a minute.'

The maid stared at the white-draped guest and scurried away. Within minutes a large bony woman in a black dress, with keys jingling from her belt, was at the door.

The woman took no notice of her strange garb. 'Ah, Mrs Heselwood, you're awake. Are you feeling all right?'

'Quite well Mrs . . .?'

'Pratt madam. Mrs Pratt. You're in a bit of a fix aren't you?'

'We are indeed,' Georgina said, closing the door behind her, not caring that she was standing in a public passageway looking like someone in a play. 'I don't want to wake my husband,' she explained, 'but could you get someone to dry our clothes? We only have what we stand up in.'

'Of course I can. I'll arrange for that immediately.'

Georgina went back inside and collected their clothes and boots which were handed to the maid.

'The hotel is full,' Mrs Pratt said. 'But come down to my room and you can have a dressing gown and we'll get you some breakfast.'

Mrs Pratt's room was no different from their room, so neat it looked as if no-one lived in it, but Georgina sat at the small table in the corner wearing

354

Mrs Pratt's large rough dressing gown and trying to stomach the breakfast that had been set in front of her. Hot cocoa, fresh bread and butter and chops and eggs were the usual breakfast, in the country areas she had already found, so this one didn't surprise her. With nothing else to do, she worked her way through the chops and finished off the eggs.

They had no money, but they would have to buy clothes, that would be the first thing, on account at that. She shuddered, remembering the attitudes of Sydney tradespeople and merchants to that sort of transaction. She would have to find a lawyer and have him get in touch with their Newcastle lawyers. He could arrange with the banks to transfer some funds up here, then they could take a ship from Brisbane to . . . where? Sydney? Government House? Bourke had gone and there was a new fellow in residence, Gipps. They didn't know him. Newcastle? Land on the Burnetts again? Or Juan Rivadavia? She wondered if his beach house were occupied. That could be the answer. She fought back tears at the thought of being beholden to people all over again.

Mrs Pratt came in without knocking. 'Ah! That's good.' She swept the tray away. 'I hate flibberty-gibbet eaters. The girls have washed your clothes and are drying them by the fire. Is there anything else I can do for you? They say downstairs that you're a Lady. Is that right?'

'Yes.'

'And your husband is a Lord?'

'Yes.'

'Well I never! What should I be calling you then?'

'Mrs Heselwood will do,' Georgina said. She needed this woman.

'You lost your station and everything?'

'We were fortunate. A lot of people lost their lives, including my cook.'

'A woman?'

'Yes.'

'Oh God help us. What you must have been through.'

'Mrs Pratt. We will have money sent up from Newcastle but do you think a shopkeeper could bring us some clothes? We shall have to buy some clothes. On credit,' she added nervously.

When Jasin awoke, new clothes, not too fashionable, were ready for him and a hot breakfast followed. Georgina, wearing a black dress, her hair plaited around her head and pinned with a tortoise-shell comb, was trying on shoes that had been delivered to them. Jasin was quiet over breakfast and ate only one egg, pushing the plate away. 'I should prefer tea,' he said. 'I'm not fond of chocolate,' and Georgina hurried out to find some for him. When she returned he had drunk the cocoa anyway.

'We have a lot to do today Jasin, one hardly knows where to start.'

He nodded, sitting uncomfortably on the light bedroom chair that was far too small for his frame. He was very tense.

'After we sort out everything here we will take a break. Go south and stay with someone for a while, have a holiday,' she said lightly.

'This is no time for holidays. What are those rags over there? Are they meant for me?'

'It was all I could find, I was thinking we might visit the Burnetts in Newcastle,' she tried again.

'You were thinking,' he said, 'that the Heselwoods are homeless, you mean.'

Georgina was flustered, not wanting to upset him.

Jasin stood up. 'Have a look at this scratch on my shoulder, I'd better get it washed and put some ointment on it.' She undid the bandage Passey had wrapped around it. The cut was wide but not deep, more of an angry graze.

'It looks very sore,' she said, 'but not infected.'

'It itches more than anything else,' he said. 'And my arm aches. As for the other matter, we are not homeless. You forget we have another station. Carlton Park. Since Montone will be unsafe for a while we shall take up residence at Carlton Park.'

'But what about the Forrests?'

'What about them?' he picked up the new clothes impatiently. 'Carlton Park is ours and we now need and require it; any magistrate will lean our way on hearing of this tragedy if it comes to that. I shall instruct the lawyers to send them an eviction notice, reluctantly forced on me by these events. The Forrests and their relations will be out by the time we are ready to leave here, and we shall go directly to our own station on the Liverpool Plains.'

Georgina sighed. Heselwood was his old self. For better or worse.

The weather did not improve, nor did Jasin's temper. They found themselves still in Brisbane at Christmas, because Jasin steadfastly refused to leave until they had completed all their business. There were endless enquiries and interrogations, hampered and delayed by a lack of staff and interference from army officers who had instigated their own investigations. No-one was able to give the names of the Aborigine leaders and the possibility that the raids were part of an invasion of the area by other tribes was considered.

Troopers were sent out to 'bring order' to the Mary River district. This meant getting rid of the blacks by whatever means they chose but they ran into fierce attacks before they neared the valley, suffering four dead and three men wounded, and they were forced to turn back to headquarters. The squatters on the Darling Downs had survived less organised raids, and things were quiet enough there but no guarantee of safety could be given to any white men travelling north. Jasin engaged a lawyer to communicate with the Newcastle firm and spent hours writing letters in their hotel room, in between frequent visits to the police magistrate, but Georgina had nothing to do.

Sometimes she walked with him and sat outside in anterooms just to get away from the four walls of their temporary home, but it bothered him to have her waiting, he felt it was undignified.

There was still no money forthcoming, Jasin had taken out a temporary loan with the local lawyer but they had not been able to pay the publican a penny and Mrs Pratt was showing signs of impatience. Although she had not as yet mentioned their account, Georgina felt that a request for payment was imminent. For some reason Jasin kept delaying their departure, and it irritated his wife that they were running up bills at the hotel for no apparent reason.

As Georgina was walking to the post office, the long way round to fill in time, she saw a ship preparing to leave, with passengers making their farewells on the wharf, so she crossed the road and walked down to the gangway.

Two men, dressed in new clothes with the packing creases still evident, came towards her.

'Excuse me,' she said, 'are you travelling in this ship?'

'That we are madam,' the taller of the bearded pair replied, in a broad Irish voice, and she marvelled at the daring she had acquired these days, talking to anyone she felt like addressing. 'I wonder if you could take these letters for me?' she asked. 'I will have missed the mailbag in the town.'

'No trouble at all,' the smaller fellow said, but his companion held up his hand. 'Are you sending your letters home to England?'

'Yes, they're just family letters.'

'Then you'd best wait on another ship. We're bound for the Far East, going in the wrong direction.'

'Oh! I am sorry. I beg your pardon.' Georgina went to turn away feeling very foolish.

'Just a minute,' the Irishman said. 'I never forget a face. You were one of the ladies that came out on the *Emma Jane* were you not?'

'Why yes. That was a long time ago, you have a good memory.'

'We didn't have much else to brighten the day,' he said boldly and Georgina felt a redness rising in her cheeks. Convicts! They must have been convicts!

'It's all right,' O'Meara lied, grinning. 'We've been given the royal pardon long ago.'

'That's nice. I am pleased,' she said politely, wanting to run, but having caught herself in this conversation, she could hardly turn her back on them now.

'Would you know Pace MacNamara then?' O'Meara asked.

'Yes, or rather, I know where he is,' Georgina said.

'That'll do. Would you tell him that Minogue and his mate have gone to China. He'll be sorry to hear we've gone, he was a great friend to us. We've had a fine time in New South Wales.'

357

'Come on Dinny,' the other man said. 'You don't have to make a speech.'

Georgina saw the twinkle in the Irishman's eyes as he spoke. She didn't believe a word of it and she wasn't meant to. She returned the Irishman's bow with a small smile, trying to look serious. 'I shall give him your message sir,' she said.

As the ship swung out into the river the Irishman looked down at her and winked. He gave an extravagant mock salute, not to her she understood, but to the prison colony he was leaving and she put her gloved hand over her mouth to suppress a laugh.

In a better mood now she went on to the post office where she met Jasin. 'How much longer are we staying here Heselwood? I'm sick and tired of this place.'

He took her letters, disposed of them and came back. 'We'll be here a while yet,' he said, lowering his voice.

'For heaven's sake why? Tell me why?'

'Because I'm going back after the cattle,' he whispered.

'What? You are not sir! It is far too dangerous.'

'Passey and the other men have agreed to come with me. They're broke, they've got no work now. I'll pay them well and a bonus.'

'Have you gone mad? What is the use of money if you all get killed? I distinctly heard the police saying all that area and Wide Bay is out of bounds.'

'They only mean they can't offer protection. They can't stop us. But I don't want anyone to know about it.'

Georgina felt faint. Perhaps this was another manner of nervous breakdown on his part. A wild excursion into danger for a few cattle. 'I won't have it!' she said.

'Listen to me Georgina. The pickings are too good to miss. We'll go armed and we'll be careful, not blazing up there like those mad troopers with colours flying. The blacks wouldn't have destroyed all the cattle, not a chance. All the other squatters in our area have run off, if they're still alive, so any cattle we find will be ours. The blacks hate cattle; once they see what we are doing, removing them, I think they'll let us go. Every beast I find will belong to me. There must be thousands running loose, abandoned. I'll bring them down past Brisbane and sell them to the cattlemen from the south coast. They'll pay in cash and don't tell me that we don't need that.'

'I hope you know what you are doing.'

'My dear. I always know what I am doing.'

Georgina looked at him as he strode down the street, expecting her to keep up. Jasin always sounded so convincing. She wondered, if he were always right, why they got into so many difficulties.

# CHAPTER THREE

Dolour handed Pace the letter when he came in for supper and he read it and shoved it in his pocket. She put the soup in front of him and stood, waiting, but he made no comment.

'Who was the letter from?'

He took it out of his pocket and dropped it on the table. At first glance the name Heselwood sprang out at her and her heart lurched and then she saw it was from Georgina Heselwood, the wife.

'Dear Pace,' she began, reading aloud, and stared at him. 'I didn't know she was a friend of yours.'

He brushed that remark aside with a wave of his spoon, and went back to his soup, ignoring her.

Dolour was too afraid of the contents of the letter to read any more of it aloud, and walked behind Pace to examine it, her hands shaking. The very mention of the name Heselwood still caused thunder in the house.

*Dear Pace,* she read again. *By the time you get this letter it will be well into the New Year so I send my best wishes to you and to your wife and family for the coming year.* [She doesn't know, Dolour breathed. She can't know. Oh God. Why did she have to write to him and start this all up again.] *I heard it is very dry down there but I can't say the same for Brisbane, it has been raining ever since we came here. No doubt you heard we lost our homestead at Montone.* [Dolour raised her eyebrows in surprise, they hadn't heard.] *It was burned to the ground. We were attacked by blacks and quite a few of our people were killed but thank God our lives were spared.*

'That must be a disappointment to you,' she said to Pace.

'What must be?' He was pretending to be uninterested.

'That Heselwood survived the attack.'

'It is as a matter of fact. If the blacks had shoved a spear in the bastard it would save me the trouble.'

'I knew you'd say that. You never give over do you?'

'Not on that boyfriend of yours who tried to have me killed.'

'I never believed that story,' she cried. 'God knows it never made a speck of sense you believing an old drunk fool.'

'So next time I see Heselwood he'll have a chance to deny it after I knock him down. What's for dinner?'

'Steak and kidney pie. I ate with the boys.' She reached into the stove with a flour cloth and brought out his meal.

359

'Why is it I'm never permitted to eat with my family any more?' he asked. 'No matter what time I get in I'm always too late. What sort of an upbringing are you giving my sons? I'm treated like a pariah in my own home. I'd be better off and have a better time eating with the men.'

'That can be arranged,' she said and went back to the letter.

*Of course we were not the only ones, everyone in the district is in the same boat. We all had to pull back to Brisbane and very sadly, quite a few families did not escape. I recall Mr Rivadavia telling us you took up a run in the Brisbane Valley. This area was also attacked. I hope you did not have any people there.*

'Oh no!' Dolour cried. 'Dinny O'Meara's in the Brisbane Valley!'

'Dinny O'Meara's got nine lives,' Pace said drily. 'Read on.'

*But what I am writing about (and no doubt you are surprised to hear from me): I met some friends of yours here in Brisbane, two very cheerful fellows, one an Irishman who said his name was Minogue, but in such a way as to lead me to believe that it was not. However, he requested I inform you that he and his Mate were off to China and they had a great time in New South Wales. I am certain the conversation was all tongue-in-cheek, but they were men from the* Emma Jane *who amazingly recognised me.*

'They got away!' Dolour, completely engrossed with the letter now, threw up her hands in delight. 'Oh glory be, they made it! Oh I am so pleased.' Forgetting their own troubles in the excitement of rare good news, she ran to Pace. 'How could you read that with a face like a turkey tail? He's free! Can you see that Dinny O'Meara now, turning up in America and rallying all the lads? He'll give them buggers back home a run for their money.' She heard Pace suck in his breath. He still hated her to swear. 'But how will he get from China to America? Is it very far?'

Pace was forced to smile. 'Not the way we think these days. It's just one ocean away. To get out here, we sailed three oceans.'

'Did we now? I wish't I'd have known that.'

Embarrassed by these rare pleasantries she went back to the letter but that was all save for the formalities and the signature 'Georgina Heselwood'. She wanted to remark to her husband that she had always thought titled people had a grander way of signing letters but the barriers were settling into place again.

'How long are we going to keep this up?' Pace asked her, his voice softer now.

'Keep what up?'

'Oh Jesus, Dolour! We can't go on living as if we're in two different worlds. I've got enough to worry about.'

'For good, if you like,' she said. 'Until you apologise to me.'

'Christ almighty. You were the one in the wrong and you want me to apologise to you. I never heard such front!'

'All right then. Tell me this. If I'd told you about Heselwood back there in Newcastle, would you have married me?'

360

Pace looked squarely at her. 'You want the honest answer?'

'I do that.'

'Then the answer is no. I would not have. Not for anything.'

She flinched as if she had been struck. 'Well then. I have my answer haven't I? There's no love lost in this house. Best you get on up to your northern station as soon as you can.'

'Dolour, you asked me how it would have been then and I told you the truth. You wanted the truth.'

'Sure I did, and I got it. I'm not complaining.' The bravado was obvious but she had to keep on talking or run from the room, defeated again. 'This place is as dry as a chip. I thought you were going to take the cattle to better pastures up north. So go. Take them!'

He finished his meal. 'We can't take them. Rivadavia warned against it and from this letter it is clear he was right. There's too much trouble with the blacks up there now.'

'So you bought a pig in a poke?' she taunted. 'Trying to be the big man when it's all we can do to keep going here.'

Pace shouted back at her. 'I did not. Land is land. When will you ever learn that? Our sons will benefit.'

'While we starve. This station is going backwards and you know it. There's no feed for the cattle. The blacks are getting worse lately, killing beasts and setting fire to crops. You should have bought land down south, you could have bought us a small farm in proper settled country but no, you have to own a county!'

'Will you shut up, woman! You're always nagging.'

She slammed away outside and sat on the verandah steps. So I am always nagging, she thought, but what else can I do? The only time we get to talk is when there's an argument, except for a few soft moments like just now, but I can't let him ride roughshod over me. If I can't make him back down, there's no chance for me. I'll always be the sinner and him the sinned against, and I won't have it. He'll leave me one day, sure as God, if I keep this up, but a woman has to keep a price on her head and it is up to her to name that price. My price is the apology for I did him no wrong. I might have sinned against God, but I never shot a living person dead.

Before the marriage he had told her why he'd had to quit Ireland, but she had already known he was one of the men resisting the English. And he had been a dab hand at it too by the sound of things and to Dolour he had been one of the heroes of Erin. But now that she had time to think about it, she wondered why the worst sins of all had to do with women in bed. Only women. And all the time it was the men who lusted and the women who searched for love.

And there inside he sat, the bastard, and her heart and soul ached for him and her arms wanted to reach out to him and draw him to her and she wanted to tell him how much she loved him, but what would that achieve? Hadn't he just said he'd never have married her? That was plain enough.

361

She felt the hot tears in her eyes. Will the crying ever stop? she wondered.

The boys were playing bat and ball with Henry, an Aborigine about their own age, and some of his friends from the camp, while the nursemaids cheered and dashed around, exasperating the children. Those black girls will be still working as nursemaids when they're ninety, Dolour was sure. And there will be some howling when John and Paul go away to school. The baby, Pierce, she still refused to call him Duke, was being washed in the tin tub by Maia, who was now the self-appointed boss of the house girls, and watching them all, Dolour felt extraneous. A spare toe, she thought.

'Missus!' Maia was whispering to her, but not looking at her. 'Missus, you lockemup them horses this night. Blackfellers come chasemup.'

'What was that?' Dolour asked but the girl had closed her bottom lip over the top one and Dolour knew there would be no getting any more out of her. She ran inside to Pace. 'I think the blacks might come down to try to get at the horses tonight,' she cried. 'One of the girls told me.'

'Oh Christ. Get her in here.'

'No don't do that, she's frightened. She's said enough already.'

'It might not be just the horses they're after. Get everyone in and we'll lock up. I'll put men on patrol all night with lanterns so they know we're onto them.'

'You don't sound too worried?'

'If the station blacks aren't spooked we've got time. I'm going down to their camp to see that old Bulpoora. I'm bloody certain he is at the bottom of all the trouble around here. It's just the sort of thing he and his mates would do, let out all the horses just to annoy us.'

He rode down to the blacks' camp about a mile from the homestead, relieved to see they were all going about their business as usual.

'Where's Bulpoora?' he shouted, remaining on his horse to look down at them.

A large fat woman with a baby on her hip grinned at him. 'Bulpoora gone.'

'Gone where? Has he gone walkabout?'

She laughed. 'No. Bulpoora gone hunting.'

'Bulpoora hasn't been hunting since he was a pup, the lazy old coot.' Pace was deliberately keeping the conversation light, he didn't want to stampede them.

The woman agreed. 'Bulpoora lazy coot too right,' she said and turned back to the others to enjoy the joke. They all grinned at him.

'Good tucker you got there?' he asked, pointing at the fish the women were placing in the coals.

'Good tucker boss,' she echoed. 'You want some good fish?'

He beckoned her to come closer: 'Hold up your hand.'

She did so curiously and he said pointing to her fingers, 'That's five.

Five days. In five days we have a big feast. Plenty meat, plenty pudden, and the missus make you toffee. You know toffee?'

She rolled her eyes and rubbed her hands together. 'Toffee good stuff boss.'

'Will you tell them all about the big feast in five days?' and the woman nodded, her face shining with excitement. 'You tell Bulpoora if he brings bad blackfellers onto Kooramin, no feast, no more tucker, all finish.'

Her expression changed to disappointment, and she looked around her, worried now.

She straightened her shoulders and flexed her muscles. 'Bulpoora!' she said and spat and, without bothering to finish talking to Pace, she bounced down to the women, her arms flying to tell them what was happening, setting off shouts of dismay. Pace laughed. Women were the same the world over. Old Bulpoora was in for trouble when he got in, these gins would not be above belting him.

Nevertheless all the horses were brought in, guards placed and the cattle dogs released. He put chains on the gates in the home paddocks and had the men bring down mobs of cattle to roam the perimeter. For some reason the cattle were far more sensitive to danger than horses, and they would react quickly. He had sent riders out to warn the other stations that there could be trouble and that was about the best he could do, but he was still very nervous.

Georgina's letter had shocked him. He had almost forgotten the scene he had witnessed on the Darling Downs after the squatter's wife and son were murdered, but now it came back to him.

But from what Georgina had written it looked like there was a full-scale war going on up north, and there was no reason why the wild blacks down this way would not hear of it. Probably they already had, they knew everything that went on, but you could never get much out of them. When they wanted to you'd think they'd all been infected with lockjaw. If the wild ones of the Kamilaroi tribe, and there were plenty out there yet who hadn't come in, got wind of the triumphs up north then it could put some spirit in them to try something down here.

He was watching the stockmen drive the irritable cattle closer to the homestead, where the animals knew there was no feed. The men were shouting angrily and cracking their whips, whistling and cursing, their own nervousness showing in the urgency of their movements. It was getting dark.

Pace reflected on their isolation: newspapers were months old, turning up haphazardly with wagons or bullockies or brought out by anyone from Kooramin who happened to have been in town. There was even some mail inside for the Forrests at Carlton Park which he had forgotten to give to the riders to pass on, but they could wait.

All he had done so far was based on bluff. An organised attack could be disastrous. Fire could wipe them out. He went inside and picked up his rifle.

'Where are you going with that?' Dolour asked.

'I'll get up on the roof and have a look around.'

From that vantage point the station seemed to bristle with activity. His thoughts went back to the Curragh and his disrupted life. 'You're fighting on the other side now MacNamara,' he told himself. 'Here, the dispossessed want *you* out of their country. This time, you're the landowner, the squire, ready to kill them for fighting back just like you did, but with nothing but their bare hands and poor spears. Is it a miserable world or are you a miserable person MacNamara? It's easily seen you do not know what you want.'

He sat on the roof for a while in the clear crisp night and he could hear Dolour talking to the children, taking them inside with the women. When he had a chance he would apologise to her, he was only making both of their lives miserable, carrying on with this vendetta, and it was awkward for his friends, none of whom had any idea what it was all about. He scanned the dark fields, trying not to feel too sanctimonious, after all it had taken this fear of attack to make him realise he did love her, and was prepared to tell her.

As he slid down from the roof a rider came hurtling into the yard. 'You're right boss, they're out there. The cattle are ready to stampede, pushing and shoving in all directions.'

'Don't worry about them,' Pace yelled. 'Pass the word to everyone to start firing.'

'There's no point, they're still out of range.'

'That is the point, we don't want to kill any of them.'

'Since when?' the stockman laughed.

'Since I say so,' Pace barked. 'There's no need for killing. Make as much noise as possible. Let them know we're ready and waiting.'

'You're the boss.' There was a sneer in his voice, and Pace reacted angrily.

He pulled the stockman from his horse. 'And don't you bloody forget it,' he said. 'You get inside and stay with the women. I'll see to it myself.'

The firing commenced even though it was impossible to pick out any of the blacks from that distance. Pace ran along the fence telling his men to keep it up, hoping the intruders would stay back, but then the blacks emerged from the dark bush carrying flaming torches. 'Oh you fools,' he groaned. 'Go back. You're making it hard on yourselves.'

As he watched, the torchlight procession faltered, some moving ahead, some falling back, wavering. 'Keep firing,' he shouted. 'They're having second thoughts.' Then over the intermittent firing he could hear shouts and yells echoing across the paddocks. It confused him.

'What are they screaming about?' one of his men said. 'We haven't hit any of them yet. We couldn't have.

Clutching his rifle Pace moved cautiously around the sheds peering at every tree and bush that might hide attackers and went across to the last fence. 'What's going on out there?' he asked of the men.

'We don't know, boss,' a voice answered in the darkness. 'It ain't no war dance. It sounds more like they're having a fight of their own.'

Gradually the torches went out and the firing stopped and they waited, everyone on edge, listening to the racket from the bush.

Pace kept up his patrol, talking to the men on guard, but they saw no more sign of the blacks. The noise had stopped and the bush seemed as quiet as the grave.

'Five days boss,' a voice said to him and he turned so quickly he whacked his elbow on a fence post sending a current of pain into his arm. The fat black woman, Narana, was standing beside him.

'Holy Mother of God!' he yelped. 'Where did you come from?'

She looked mystified and pointed across the paddocks to the bush. 'Five days, big feast boss,' she reminded him.

'Yes, all right. But what's going on out there?'

'Bloody mad blackfellers. Old Bulpoora. We kickem out. Kick Bulpoora in bum.' She put her hands on her hips and laughed. 'Bloody good fight.' She had an ugly gash across her chest, and blood was seeping over her full breasts. 'You're hurt?' he said.

'Yeah. Crackem heads out there.' She was carrying a waddy as thick as her own solid thighs.

'Have they all gone?'

'Yeah. Kooramin mob pissem all off.'

Pace started to laugh and she joined in with a rumbling chortle, proud of the night's excitement.

'Come on then,' he said. 'I'll get the missus to fix you up.'

She trotted after him, still carrying the waddy. 'Did you really come across that paddock?' he asked again.

She had walked right under their guns. He wondered what hope they would have if enough blacks chose to attack by stealth.

The station was on alert all night, in case the blacks returned, and morning broke bleakly. Pace thanked his men for their vigilance. They now had six convicts working on the station and he thanked them especially for their co-operation, announcing that he would be applying for tickets-of-leave for all of them.

They cheered this news and Pace felt a spasm of sorrow. He had another reason for the move. If the drought continued he might not be able to support them too much longer, so the least he could do was try to steer them towards their freedom.

By mid-morning Dolour still had not slept, and was looking very tired. 'Why don't you go and have a sleep?' he said.

'I will, but I've got a few jobs to do yet.'

'Can't they wait?'

'They won't take long.'

Lena poked her head in the window. 'Miz Forrest come missus, along a jinker.'

Dolour laughed. Milly's sulky, painted red with black upholstery, was well known in the district. It was more of a nuisance than it was worth in this country but she insisted on driving it everywhere, with two outriders as escorts, who spent their time pulling it out of bogs in the winter and repairing broken wheels in the summer. Milly did not always have an eye for the track.

'Fred's riding with her,' Pace said, as Milly drove quickly up the drive. 'It's rare for him to come visiting.'

'Ho!' he called. 'What brings you to Kooramin?'

'Everything Pace, everything! They raided us last night!' Milly sounded hysterical as Pace helped her down, disentangling her cloak from the whip rack.

'Didn't you get my message?'

'Yes,' Fred said dismally. 'We did what we could. But they burned down the outbuildings, the stables, the hayshed, the dairy's gone too . . .'

Dolour ran forward to help Milly inside. 'Was anyone hurt?'

Milly began to cry. 'Some of the men were burned trying to get the horses out, although not too badly, but Dolour, those black devils burned down Dermott's workshop. He could have been killed.'

It was Fred's turn to speak. 'It's a shame,' he said. 'I'm really upset about all this. What are we going to tell Heselwood?'

'Damn Heselwood!' Pace growled. 'How many blacks were there?'

'It's hard to tell. The lads say about fifteen, they shot four of them, the rest got away. Riders are out looking for them now. But that's another thing. The boys reckon that one of the blacks they shot was from here, one of your station blacks.'

'An old bloke?'

'Yeah that's right.'

'Bulpoora,' Pace nodded. 'He was the troublemaker, the rest were blacks from another mob he must have joined up with. What time did they hit your place?'

'About one o'clock this morning.'

'That'd be right. They must have gone straight from here.'

'What? They were here?'

'Indeed they were. It's a long story but they ended up in a fight with the Kooramin blacks so they retreated in your direction. I'm sorry.'

Fred looked wearily around him. 'You suffer any damage?'

Pace shook his head. 'Come in and I'll get you a drink. I think you could do with one.'

'I could do with a few hands to help us out. The house is the only building left standing on Carlton Park.'

'My lads'll be over and I'll come back with you myself. What about your horses?'

'Scattered to the bloody winds. We caught a few and the stockmen are

366

looking for the rest of them. But the blacks speared a lot of cattle too just for the hell of it.'

'Is Dermott all right?' Dolour asked.

'Oh yes, but it was terrifying,' Milly wailed. 'Absolutely terrifying, all that noise and the fires.'

'Did they try to burn the house?' Dolour asked.

'No, Dolour,' Fred said, wiping the perspiration from his balding head. 'They burned all the sheds and ran off.'

'How do you know, Fred Forrest?' Milly cried. 'The men ran them off or we should all have been murdered in our beds. It was frightful!' And Milly charged through the house to the kitchen, with Dolour close behind.

The two older MacNamara boys, seated at the table for their lunch, were fascinated.

'Did you shoot any Mrs Forrest?' John cried eagerly.

'Dad didn't get any of them,' his brother added, disgusted.

'You boys be quiet now,' Dolour told them. 'Why don't you go outside and play?'

'No. We want to hear what happened,' John replied, but Pace appeared in the doorway with Fred. 'Out!' he said, and they departed, reluctantly.

'Would you like a cup of tea?' Dolour asked her.

'No. I'll have a rum with some milk please. I feel quite sick. Oh those villains! You should see the place! The men's quarters and their kitchen were burned down, with all the equipment and the stores.'

'We'll help you rebuild, Milly,' Pace said. 'It's not as bad as it sounds. Worse things have happened elsewhere.'

'That is easy to say, Pace MacNamara. But how would you feel with everything burning around you and your husband in a wheelchair?'

Dolour gave Pace a warning glance and he judged she was right. This was not the time to mention Georgina's experience. 'How is Dermott?' he asked. 'How did he take it?'

'Dermott's fine, he took it all very calmly,' Fred said, 'and my Bess is a treasure. She's already out there seeing what she can salvage.'

Milly's flushed face seemed to grow purple. 'Of course she's a treasure. Why would it worry her? It's not her place. You tell me, Fred Forrest, who's going to pay for the rebuilding? We can't get any money out of Heselwood. Do we have to foot the bill for bunkhouses, stables and store-rooms – the whole damn lot? Have you thought of that?'

'Have another drink Milly, we'll sort it out,' Pace said but he understood what she was saying. And by the sound of things, if Heselwood's own station had been burnt out there'd definitely be no cash coming from that direction.

Dolour prepared a meal for them while they talked. She got out some cold pickled pork and went to the pantry for some potatoes and, as she reached up for some of her home-made pickles, she saw her hands were shaking. It was always the same, at the mention of Jasin she could not help trembling. She loitered in the pantry to regain control of herself but when she came back Milly was still going on about the 'high and mighty' Heselwood, and she felt her husband's eyes upon her.

All through the meal the men tried to work out how they could rebuild at the least cost, with despairing interjections from Milly, until Pace found a reason to change the subject. 'Milly, I nearly forgot. There's a bag of mail here for Carlton Park. One of the stockmen brought it from town. I meant to send it over to you yesterday but I forgot.'

He went inside and returned with a small canvas bag. 'Here you are.'

She grabbed it and unceremoniously tipped the contents on the floor, newspapers and catalogues and letters scattering, and stooped down to sort them, handing the papers to the men. She found three letters addressed to Dermott and herself and salvaged them while Dolour put the remainder, for Carlton Park staff, back into the bag. 'Two from home,' Milly said, pleased at last. 'And what's this one? Nice handwriting and good paper.'

She opened the letter with the aid of a knife, read it and re-read it and started crying hysterically. The boys came rushing into the kitchen to see what the noise was about, and Milly abruptly jumped up knocking her chair over.

'Who is it from?' Fred cried, startled.

'Heselwood!' she screamed. 'Here. You read it!' She thrust it at Dolour, who pulled away as if she had been scorched.

'No!'

Fred took the letter since Pace made no move to look at it either. 'It is from him.' He looked at Pace to explain. 'He never writes direct to us. Always through his lawyers.'

He turned back to the page and began reading aloud. 'Dear Mr and Mrs Forrest. As you are no doubt aware, there has been serious trouble in our district with the blacks, resulting in considerable loss of life and property. Montone station has been destroyed and my wife and I, with our staff, were forced to withdraw to Brisbane.'

'Pity they didn't put a spear in him,' Milly said angrily.

'He says he has consulted with a magistrate,' Fred said, 'but I can't see what that has to do with us.'

'Will you read the damn letter or give it to me,' Milly cried.

'All right Milly, hang on. Now let's see . . . he consulted with a magistrate . . .' He raised his voice. 'And am informed that since our own residence has been destroyed we are now within our rights to occupy our station at Carlton Park. This is an unfortunate setback for all of us, and without malice I therefore instruct you to vacate Carlton Park within one month of this date as my wife and I shall be taking up residence. An eviction notice will be forwarded by my solicitors. I regret the necessity of this action but you must realise we have no choice.'

Fred dropped the letter as if it were on fire. 'Is he forcing us out?'

Pace picked the letter up angrily, and stared at it to make certain that

Fred was not mistaken and in the heat of the moment he caught Dolour's eye. 'You've got some nice friends haven't you?' he snapped. 'We're going to have him for a neighbour after all.'

Milly didn't understand what it was he had said to Dolour but she was pleased to see the black anger on his face. 'I'll burn the whole place down first,' she shouted.

Fred put a hand on her arm. 'Steady on girl. We'll have to talk to Dermott. Work out what we'll do. Maybe Heselwood's only bluffing.'

'He's not bluffing,' Pace said and turned to Dolour. 'Is he? *Is* he, Dolour?'

He glared at her as if it were her fault and for a minute she stood stunned and then went quietly outside. Perhaps we're all getting above ourselves, she thought, with Pace and the Forrests trying to be big squatters and me thinking I could be a squatter's wife. I live with a man who despises me. He lives for his station and his sons, and they'll be going away to school soon and then what? With Heselwood next door there will never be any peace in this house and if Jasin turns up here Pace is likely to put a bullet in him, he always said he would. She felt sorry for the Forrests but it was not the end of the world for them, they were a family, they could go back to Sydney. It'd be better for their little girl living there anyway. Milly's daughter Lucy Mae seemed to cling to Bess more than Milly. As for my own sons, Pace can do no wrong. They hardly listen to me and why should they, given their father's example? And the Heselwoods would be taking over Carlton Park. Maybe the lords and ladies were meant to have it all, and people like us should not be trying to get above ourselves. Right now they could have it all, she thought. The Forrests, the Heselwoods, Pace, the lot of them. She was tired of the heartache and this was not the end of it, this was only the beginning. She yearned to go home to Ireland, to the green country where there was singing and laughter, but she would never see Ireland again and that was certain.

And had not Pace said he would never have married her had he known she'd been with Heselwood? 'Oh dear God,' she wept. 'I am so sorry about that. So terribly sorry. I've asked your forgiveness Lord, but you will not allow it to me, you've just gone on punishing me until I can't bear it any longer.'

Inside, the three sat grimly at the table and continued the discussion. 'We can't start rebuilding until we sort this out,' Fred said.

'What about Dermott?' Milly was even more worried now. 'This will kill him. It will bring on another attack. We mustn't tell him.'

'We have to tell him,' Pace said. 'He'll have to know. It'll be a sad blow to him just the same.'

Milly took her hat off and pulled her hair back from her face. She looked exhausted, defeated.

From the yard they could hear screaming, the girls were running around in a panic and Lena crashed into the kitchen shouting. 'Boss! Come quick! Missus die. Down in the toolshed.'

Pace was out of the seat, running across the yard in a second. He found

Dolour collapsed in the dirt and as he lifted her up, her head fell back. 'She's unconscious,' he cried, still unable to take this in, as Fred Forrest puffed in the door behind him.

'What's the matter with her?' Fred called. 'What's happened Pace?'

'I don't know,' Pace was almost screaming. 'Send someone to get the doctor fast, take two horses.'

He cradled Dolour to him, trying to rouse her, then heard a rasping breath which relieved and terrified him at the same time. Her face had lost all colour save for a blueness around her mouth.

Milly pushed him out of the way. 'Is she still alive?'

'Yes,' he whispered. 'What in God's name has happened to her?'

'Get some milk quick,' Milly cried and grabbed Dolour roughly, turning her over. 'Get the damn milk when I tell you!' she screamed at him. 'She's poisoned herself. She's drunk poison!'

# CHAPTER FOUR

Jasin Heselwood's immediate and desperate plan was to muster as many cattle and horses as he could find, no matter what brands they carried. His stockmen, armed with rifles and pistols, rode out with him, excited by this daring escapade. Even Barrett, who had been brought in by a bush constable, joined the party.

Jasin was disappointed to hear of Krill's death. He had been certain that Krill would have gotten away, somehow. But then, as Barrett insisted, if the horse hadn't fallen, Krill, an experienced soldier, would have fought his way to safety. It seemed so stupid to him that this skinny little convict had bumbled through, even after being lost in the bush for a week, and Krill had been killed. Bad luck that's all it was. He would miss Krill, he had come to rely on him. Thank God Passey had survived.

They left Brisbane before dawn to avoid questions, carrying rations in their saddle packs, and rode hard the first few days but once they were well away from the settled areas they rode quietly and deliberately.

Jasin tried to be cheerful. 'There's a possibility the wild blacks have all bolted by this,' he told Passey.

'Not from what I hear,' Passey said. 'The black trackers reckon they're dug in.'

Every brush of a bush and every mirage-like shift of tree trunks made Jasin more nervous but he was determined to carry on. He had to carry on or face ruin. With ten stockmen in the party there would be no limit to the number of cattle they could drive out of the valley and the surrounding hills. The cattle up this way were fat and thriving, not like the herds he had seen coming up from the south. They'd fetch a good price.

The familiar perfumes of the tropical flowers reminded him of Montone and the garden Georgina had been so proud of. At night the frangipani and jasmine had given their house a pleasant bouquet. The thought of how Montone might look now frightened him, but he steeled himself against any emotion. It was no use grieving over a house; it was only a house. The situation, once again, simply required a change of plans.

Didn't they always? he asked himself.

He had thought that after two years at Montone everything would go smoothly and now he cursed the blacks. After this he'd never allow any of the bastards within miles of his station.

'There are plenty of cattle around, boss,' Passey said, interrupting

Jasin's thoughts 'We were wondering when you want us to start rounding them up.'

'We'll go straight to Montone and work back from there,' he replied. 'It's safer to stay together.'

They passed other homesteads, some burned, some deserted and Jasin decided it would be better to camp in the open than go near them. 'If we keep moving past, they'll think we're travelling through, I hope,' Jasin said. 'And once we start mustering they'll realise what we're doing, given they've got any brains at all.'

Despite his expectations of ruin, Montone was a shock. Out of the charred wreck all that remained standing were the two chimneys. It seemed strange to be able to see right through to the high rails of the bull pens in the distance.

Beside this stark scene, magnificent gold and purple bougainvilleas curled and wove along the trellis that led down to the orchard – reminiscent of a brilliant formal wreath.

Black crows cawed, picking through the debris and flapping angrily into the air as Passey fired shots overhead, and suddenly dingoes swerved out of the ruins running for the bush.

A sickly odour blew down from the house and the men reached for their neckerchiefs, to tie them around their faces. Jasin let the reins drop to follow suit automatically as he identified, with a shock, the source of the putrid smell.

'Would the bodies still be there?' he said to Passey, leaning across to him so as not to have to raise his voice.

'If you want to stay down here, I'll go up and have a look,' Passey offered, but Jasin needed to stay in control. 'No. I'll come with you.'

He turned to the men. 'You fellows start mustering.'

'We can't do that,' one of the stockmen said. 'We have to bury our mates first, what's left of them.'

'Yes, of course,' Jasin said. He looked distastefully at the homestead ruins.

'We might as well get it over with,' Passey said, and the men urged their horses on.

They placed two men on guard, while the others tramped across to the charred remains of the house. Leaving the men to their gruesome work, Jasin stepped into the area where the front entrance had been and followed the line of the hallway to the site of the main bedroom. With a heavy stick, he began examining the wreckage.

Behind him the men went about their tasks using battered shovels retrieved from what was left of the tool shed, and hessian bags. 'Ah gee,' he heard one of them call, 'look at the piano! The Missus'd break her heart if she could see this.'

Jasin shook his head. That damned piano had been tugged and lifted and dragged halfway across the world to suffer this ridiculous fate. He pushed aside some blackened timbers to get to the remains of Georgina's dressing table.

'Hey Passey,' he heard Barrett shout. 'We only bury our own, right?'

'Yes,' Passey called back. 'What we can find of them but I think the blacks have taken theirs.'

Jasin found a brass lock and poked further into the debris. Georgina had kept her jewellery in a lacquered box so he didn't hold out much hope. The dressing table had burned to a heap – but there, covered in ash, he could see the remains of a few pieces. Some had been costly, some worth little, mostly silver, but now they were fused together by the heat. He took a handkerchief and bundled the lot into it with the ash and dirt, to be cleaned and examined when he could get them to a jeweller.

He stood up and looked around him angered by the wanton destruction and tried to re-create the events of that day. This was where he had finally stood, in the doorway, where one of the savages had fallen at Georgina's door. He recalled he had shot the fellow at point blank range. He had seen him lying at this spot. Passey was right, the blacks had recovered the bodies of their own men, there should be one here. He could still see the ferocious white-painted face. God knows how I got through it all, he wondered.

There was a glint of brass in the ash and he poked at it with his stick. A doorknob probably, Georgina had a liking for ornate doorknobs, but the brass seemed to be encased in leather, badly seared but recognisable. He crouched on his haunches and gingerly tipped the leather over with his stick and then brushed the dirt from it. The leather was a good five inches wide and looked more like a belt. His head swam, the smell of death still lingered in this spot, but then it was everywhere in the ruins of his home. He tried to recall what they had owned that was brass encased in leather and idly brushed the ash from it. He did not want to have to join the men at their ghastly labour so it would not do any harm to look busy, engaged in searching through his own property.

He tried to pull the piece of brass out, but it was only partly exposed and was firmly seated in its casing so he scooped underneath, to lift it up, dragging the belt or whatever it was, through the debris, surprised at its weight. It can't be a belt, he thought, it's too damned heavy, need an ox to carry it, and then with a shock that almost amounted to fright he looked again at the brass. It was not brass, it was gold. He was sure of it. Years ago, as a boy, his father had shown him a piece of gold from a mine somewhere and he remembered his disappointment, he had always expected gold to be smooth and shiny like his father's gold watch.

For a minute he did nothing, stunned. Then he looked warily over at the men. They were intent on their own work. He changed position so his back was towards them and felt along the leather band realising it had several thicknesses and it bulged in places. There was something familiar about it.

Yellow glinted from another burned section. At the ends of the band he found frayed and burned strips of hide and he sat back realising what he had, what was so familiar about it: this was a money belt; rough, but strong and constructed with care. He took his knife and prised the first weighty lump free and found he was holding a gold nugget at least a half a pound in weight. At least half a pound, he told himself, excitement rising.

Feeling along the belt, he found some smaller pieces in the hard thickness of the leather. Sweat streamed from his face. He had found a fortune. It must have belonged to the blackfellow whose body had been lying right here. No white man could have worn such a rig without attracting attention, it was wider than a prize-fighter's belt. And what was a blackfellow doing with gold? And more importantly, where had it come from? Was there gold on Montone Station?

Jasin was trembling now as if in a fever. He had been thinking of selling up Montone and returning to Carlton Park, but whatever happened now, Montone was not for sale.

He remembered that black man, seeing only the white-painted face. 'If I'd known you had these,' he murmured. 'I'd have given you the bloody house.'

Lord Heselwood, Earl of Montone, covered the belt with ash and dropped a lump of timber over it and walked casually back to his horse.

'Did you find anything boss?' Passey asked him.

'Nothing much,' he said sadly. 'I found some of my wife's jewellery, a molten mess but we might be able to get a jeweller to save some of it. Sentimental value really, but I promised her I'd pick up what I could. 'He took his saddlebag and went back to his find, making his steps look as despondent as he could. Then at the site he pulled the money belt out again and stuffed it in the saddlebag, covering it with rags and placing on top of it again Georgina's pathetic little swag of pieces.

They seemed to take an interminable time to bury the bodies and hold a short service. 'Do you want us to go through the house now and see what we can collect for you Mr Heselwood?' Passey asked him.

'No,' Jasin said. 'What's the use? We can't carry anything on a cattle drive. We'll make camp and get out of here first thing in the morning.'

By morning they were all eager to leave. They jolted the grazing cattle into life, whips cracking, horses racing into the scrub to cut the cattle out, as birds wheeled and screeched, and kangaroos bounded out of the way, but no blacks were seen. Hundreds of cattle were mustered at the perimeters of the station within a few days and the big drive south began. Jasin and Passey set off along the trail with the herd while the men on the flanks brought in more and more but it was far more difficult than Jasin had imagined. The cattle were rebellious, cranky at being taken so suddenly from their home territory and there were not enough men to cope with the numbers being mustered. Also the party, with no cook wagon to support them, was not equipped for a long slow drive.

Well into the second week Jasin abandoned the idea of pushing on past Brisbane to Ipswich (as Limestone was now called) as a precaution against owners recognising their brands. Jasin and the men were living off the land, eating game and what fruit they could find, and robbing fish-traps set up in the rivers by the Aborigines. There was no time for butchering or the comforts of damper to accompany the charred meat, and rain had forced them to spend wet depressing nights in the open.

Only Passey was worried. 'We might get complaints over some of these brands,' he warned.

'To hell with them!' Jasin said. 'They're abandoned cattle and we found them. The saleyards are on the outskirts of the town. We'll drive them straight in and sell them without further ado. First come, first served, and I don't give a damn if they have to buy back their own cattle.'

From the bathroom in the hotel Georgina saw Jasin ride into the yard and she flew downstairs to throw her arms around him in front of everyone, tears of joy and relief in her welcome.

'Careful,' he grinned. 'I'm absolutely filthy, it was a rough drive.'

'I'm so relieved you're back. You've been away weeks, I was terrified something had happened to you and afraid to go to the police because you'd insisted I should not. Are you sure you're all right, you look very tired.'

'Of course I am,' he said, dragging the saddlebags from the horse and lifting them onto his shoulder. A stablehand came for his horse and they went into the hotel through the back door, passing Mrs Pratt who looked at them coldly and turned away.

'She wants her money,' Georgina whispered.

'My dear, we have her money,' he said. 'In two or three days we'll be out of here.'

After he had paid the men, Jasin realised more than a thousand pounds from the sale of cattle, ignoring the mutterings of the squatters on the last day of the sale, and the hesitant enquiries of the district constable who had been sent to investigate the jumble of brands. The next day, having paid their debts, although still angry that no money had been forthcoming from their bank, he and Georgina boarded a coastal steamer for Sydney.

'That damned bank manager will pay for this,' he said. 'We could have been destitute for all he cared. I'll see to it that he's out on his ear the first chance I get. I will insist upon it.'

But Georgina was confused. 'Wouldn't it be better to take it quietly Jasin? We're not out of the woods yet. And I thought we were going to Newcastle to stay with the Burnetts and then out to Carlton Park.'

'The plans have changed,' he said merrily. She had noticed that he had been very happy on his return from Montone, spending money freely as if the cash he had raised on the cattle would last them forever.

'You're always changing our plans. For once couldn't we just go right

375

ahead as we were going? Really Jasin, you are quite beyond me.'

Their cabin was small and musty. Jasin dropped the saddlebag on the grubby linen-less bunk, and with it the valise carrying their few clothes.

'And how can we go to Sydney in these awful clothes?' Georgina asked. 'Heselwood, I do think you should reconsider.'

He checked the door but there was no lock on it. 'Stand here by the door my dear and don't let anyone in. I have been bursting to tell you about this, but I thought I'd wait until we were well on our way.' He took a canvas pouch from his saddlebag and emptied the contents onto the bunk.

'What's that?' she asked. 'What have you got there?'

He laughed. 'It's gold, pure gold. We're not poor at all.'

Sydney turned on a glorious day for the Heselwoods when they arrived back at the harbourside town for the first time in years. They took a carriage directly to the Australian Hotel.

'It's so wonderful to be back,' Georgina said, 'and what a surprise to find such a comfortable hotel suite. I shall just adore being here. We shall be able to look up our friends and invite people in to dine with us. I feel quite carefree again. How long are we staying?'

'Until we can find a decent ship to take us to London.'

'Are we going home again? I had no idea.'

He lowered his voice. 'I want to take the gold to London and sell it there. We'll get a better price in London I should think. I don't want even a hint of it getting out here or it'll start a rush to Montone, blacks or no blacks. If I produce gold nuggets the news will leak out and it will be taken for granted that it came from Montone. We can't allow that.'

'But what about Carlton Park?'

'We'll still get rid of the Forrests. The loss of Montone is the ideal excuse to shift them. Passey can run it for us; the other lads from Montone are out of work so they can come down with him. I'll get the lawyers to sort out the finances once and for all, I can't be worried about it any more, but I won't lose it. Carlton Park is still an excellent station. And given time, Montone can be resurrected, the troops will chase the blacks out. There's always the possibility too that there's gold on Montone but we can't bank on that. The blackfellow could have brought it from anywhere.' He reached over and pulled the bell cord. 'I think we should have some sherry before dinner. For that matter it might be better to dine up here. We can hardly go to the dining room in these rags.'

'I'd like nothing better. We can sit up here and watch the sun go down. Tomorrow we'll look at the Sydney fashions, which will still be years behind London, of course.'

A waiter came to the door and Jasin asked him to send up the manager. 'I'll explain our predicament to the fellow,' he told Georgina, 'and tell him to send us up his best from the kitchens. You know, we'll find it rather chilly in London after this balmy clime. One tends to forget the cold and

376

fogs. I was wondering if you might prefer to purchase a house in Sydney? You could decorate it to your own tastes.'

'Jasin! You're going too fast for me. I'm now looking forward to seeing Edward and you start talking about staying here.'

'No I'm not. We'll proceed to London but we should get a place here before we go. Prices are going up all the time, and we'll have our own home to come back to. We could rent it to some high-placed civil servant who wouldn't dare but look after it.'

The manager was at the door followed by a waiter who brought in complimentary champagne and hors d'oeuvres for the illustrious guests. There were already gentlemen of the press waiting to interview them, the manager informed Jasin. 'I hear you and your good lady were in the midst of that great northern massacre milord,' he said. 'It must have been a frightful experience.'

'It was,' Jasin told him, seeing an opportunity. 'We had to ride off in what we stand up in. So you understand why we are loath, as yet, to receive anyone. Tomorrow it would be helpful if you could send me a tailor of repute and suggest to Lady Heselwood who might be able to provide her with a reasonable wardrobe.'

'It shall be done, milord. Leave it to me.'

There was another gentleman at the door. 'Who are you?' Jasin enquired.

'Governor Gipps presents his compliments sir and extends the hospitality of Government House to Lord and Lady Heselwood,' the young man recited and the hotel manager looked crestfallen.

'Would you be good enough to thank His Excellency,' Jasin replied, 'and tell him we should be pleased to accept his very gracious invitation at a later date but for the present we are in very good hands.'

The gentleman bowed and left, and the hotel manager was grateful. He wrung his hands and peered around Jasin at her ladyship.

'That will be all for now,' Jasin said, cutting off any further conversation. Their host withdrew.

'I shall dine out on our adventures for years,' he laughed. 'I should have told that fellow no beef for dinner, I am sick of the sight of beef. But we can always send it back.'

Georgina had been thinking about these announcements of Jasin's . . . off to London . . . buy a house in Sydney. When he was in high spirits, Jasin had grand ideas but they were not always successful.

'Jasin. Why don't we sell Montone when we are in London? You can truthfully say you found the gold there and the price would go heavenwards.'

'I thought of that, old dear, but the real gold is land.' He looked at her seriously. 'Once upon a time the Heselwoods were immensely wealthy. What we have now, compared to my ancestors, even with the gold, which will only keep the wolf from the door temporarily, is neglible. I intend to see to it that no Heselwood of our line ever has to suffer the indignities that we have undergone. We shall keep Carlton Park and Montone and expand.'

'How?'

'You know, Georgina, so don't pretend. I intend to acquire more land, and get it cheaply. There are still millions of acres out there waiting to be claimed.'

Georgina stiffened. 'Very well, you can do that to your heart's content but once I have my own home here, never again will I go out into the bush. Sometimes I think I must have been mad.'

'You won't have to my dear! That's exactly what I have in mind. We shall live in Sydney and I shall find the land. There is no need for us to operate them ourselves. I discovered that at Montone. I need to find reliable fellows who can read and write, as old Horton told me, remember? Resourceful men who understand the bush. They can run our stations.' He took a glass of champagne. 'You know I always wondered why Horton wanted me to run his place. And now I know. I thought he'd gone off his head at the time but he had more faith in me than I had in myself. If John Horton arrived on the scene now, fresh from England, I'd give him a job managing a station straight off, without a qualm. Let's drink to dear old Horton!'

Georgina smiled. 'I'd far rather drink to the fact that we didn't have Edward with us at Montone. What a frightful experience that would have been for the boy. I don't want to go on about this Jasin, but I still think that blackfellow who broke in on me was trying to protect me.'

'Stuff and nonsense. He knocked you down. You had the bruises to prove it.'

'Jasin, he threw me under the bed out of sight and then he ran off!'

'You're letting your imagination run away with you Georgina. Feeling sorry for him now. I shot him at your door. God knows what he had in mind. It was all so confused it doesn't bear thinking about. Do think of something pleasant. What say tomorrow we go househunting?'

Lord Heselwood was welcomed at the Sydney office of the Bank of England by Mr Wilfred Luton and taken into the Board Room for a pre-luncheon drink. 'My dear Lord Heselwood, I heard you were back, and I was hoping you would call.'

Jasin smiled at him. I'm sure you were, he thought. The fellow looks decidedly nervous, worrying about my affairs. He placed a small steel deed box on the table with a bump.

Luton fussed. 'I read about the catastrophe in the papers, what an appalling thing to happen.'

'Don't believe half of it.'

'But you were attacked by blacks! And your station was burned down!'

'The house was burned but the station is still there. You can't burn down land. It is still a magnificent property.'

'Oh quite. Yes, of course. But it does make it rather difficult for us. I mean to say the station is not operating, Lord Heselwood. And one is loath to mention this at such a time when you have suffered so much, but the interest has to be paid and you are behind in your payments of the capital. Dear me, I have been racking my brains to think how best I can assist you but I fear the situation is now rather grave.'

Jasin put a hand on his shoulder. 'Not at all dear fellow, not at all.' He would not mention the sale of cattle or the miser would try to snatch the proceeds from his very pocket. 'It was bad luck losing Montone and our personal effects, a great trial for my wife.'

'Is it true that you and your wife, I beg your pardon, Lady Heselwood, had to ride for your lives with the savages at your heels?'

'Yes! It was quite a saga, that's why I am pleased to have Lady Heselwood resting up here in Sydney.'

Luton's face was round and his eyes rounder with interest at this news from the Earl himself. 'You must stay to lunch and tell me all about it!'

'Sorry, that's not possible. We are moving into Government House today, the Governor insists. Perhaps you might come over there and lunch with us one day?'

'I should be delighted. Now, there is this matter of payments. Can you do anything in that direction?'

'In a few days the cash will be flowing again. There's no problem. We still have Carlton Park remember? The tenants there owe me quite a bit and that settling up is under way. I am replacing them with my man Passey from Montone who has proved to be an excellent fellow, reliable and knows what he's doing. He'll improve things at Carlton Park. And as soon as the unrest in the north dies down I shall open Montone up again. But I really must leave now.'

There had been nothing but silence from Carlton Park. The eviction notice had been issued by the lawyers, who had not yet received a reply. Jasin had been assured that this was the best way out of the problem and they had admonished him for being too soft on the Forrests in allowing them to take up residence in the first place.

'One more thing,' he said to Luton, 'before I go. Would you place this box, temporarily, in your safe. I have a key, here on my fob-chain, but I'm a devil with keys, so I'll leave this one in your care. But I must insist that the box be not opened. It contains private papers and jewellery we recovered from Montone, you understand.'

'Of course. I shall see to that. You can rely on me.'

'Very well, once we are settled at Government House I shall return. To tell you the truth that affair at Montone was rather a shock to the system, I'm just beginning to get my bearings again. And I thank you for your patience, it is much appreciated.'

Outside the bank, he laughed. Human nature being what it is, that fellow finding the weight of that box will be sure to secretly open it and see the gold. That will turn the tide and he won't dare mention the contents to anyone. Oh yes, Mr Wilfred Luton, we'll have no more nonsense from you and next time I come in, you'll get an earful about that wretch of a representative in Newcastle who refused to draft some money to us when we were in need. Who would have left us destitute! What was his name? Jackson. Yes that was it, Mr No-Christian-name Jackson. Well Jackson, he thought grimly, you'd better start packing your bags.

He strode off down the street feeling pleased with himself. They had in fact moved into Government House that morning. Gipps planned to return to London as soon as he completed his rounds of farewells because his health was no longer up to the strain of the colony, and he had invited Lord and Lady Heselwood to travel with him on one of Her Majesty's naval ships. Delighted, Jasin had accepted the offer. Not only would they have every comfort and good company, there would, of course, be no charge. He was walking with a spring in his step in the morning sunshine, when suddenly he was confronted by a stranger.

'Heselwood?' the man shouted and Jasin stared down at him, a stocky fellow in bushman's attire, but before he could reply the stranger struck out at him with a horsewhip, lashing at his face and as Jasin, falling back, put up his arms to defend himself, the whip lashed across his neck.

Unable to defend himself from the sudden onslaught Jasin turned to run but the long, vicious whip cracked again and ripped across his back, jerking his body into a spasm that caused him to stumble. He could feel blood streaming down his face and he heard shouts and screams around him as hands dragged him into a barbershop and shoved him into a chair, but the assailant pursued him. 'That's for my brother,' the madman shouted, his bearded face almost on top of Jasin's. 'For Dermott Forrest!' Then he stalked away into the street.

Men were dabbing at him with wet cloths while Jasin was trying to push them away, and the doorway was crowded with onlookers.

'You'd better stay still sir,' a voice cried. 'We've sent for a doctor. That cut across your cheek might need stitching.'

'What about the one on his neck?' someone else said, and a woman cried, 'Ah, what a cryin' shame! Look at that lovely coat ruined!'

No-one thought to call the police. Horse-whipping was an accepted practice to settle differences, and Jasin could think of nothing beyond the pain and humiliation. 'Leave me be!' he thundered. 'And shut that bloody door!'

# CHAPTER FIVE

When Fred Forrest returned to Carlton Park he did not mention his attack on Heselwood, there was no need to, he had achieved what he had set out to do, and he knew Heselwood would not prefer charges and bring all this out into the open, even into the newspapers.

Milly was listless, clinging to Lucy Mae now, and fussing over Dermott. She still couldn't face the fact they were leaving Carlton Park.

'But what if we don't go?' she asked Fred for the umpteenth time.

'I told you Milly. We can be forcibly evicted and you wouldn't want that. Until we can prove Dermott's claim, Heselwood is the owner of this property, cut and dried, that's all the local magistrate needs to know.'

'The magistrate?' she shrieked. 'He couldn't make the magistrate order us to leave?'

'That's what Fred has been trying to tell you Milly,' Dermott said. 'Anyway we'll have the last laugh yet. We're not broke. It hasn't cost us anything to live out here and with this drought going on and on, we couldn't pick a better time to leave. We'll still take him to court and if we don't get satisfaction here, we'll put it to the courts in England. I won't let up on him.'

'Good on you Dermott.' Fred patted him on the shoulder. 'I can't see much point in staying here any longer. The cattle are sold, they'd never have survived anyway, and I told the lawyer why we had to sell. He said we were lucky to be able to offload them to Dangar, so we're covered there and I see no reason why we should rebuild.'

'I should say not,' Milly said angrily. 'But you'd think Heselwood, being the shifty wretch he is, would want us to stay now and rebuild for him.'

Fred looked at her sadly. 'You have to let go, Milly. He's sending his own men to take over. I'd like to get away before they come.'

She looked around her wildly. 'But what about our things? All my furniture? Everything here?'

'I've got a horse-team coming, we'll take what we can,' he said.

'Oh no,' she cried. 'We'll take everything. We'll strip the place of everything that can be moved if it takes three horse-teams. I won't leave them a single thing!'

'Then we're all agreed,' her brother-in-law said, relieved that the decision had finally been made. He would be glad to get back to Sydney and

381

earn some real money again, this time it would be a leathergoods factory.

'But where are we to live in Sydney?' Milly cried. 'You sold your house.'

'I've taken a lease on a place in Clarence Street, for the time being,' Fred told her.

'Oh good,' she said, her spirits bouncing back up again. 'That will do while we look around for another station.'

Juan Rivadavia rode across Kooramin Station feeling the misery of the dry dusty land. The few hungry cattle he could see were nibbling at thistles, which would cut and scour their mouths and their insides. The two-year drought had also hit the Hunter Valley but not as severely. He felt sorry for the graziers on the Liverpool Plains, it was a terrible situation to be in with the long dry summer ahead of them. And he was sorry for Pace in particular, knowing he had other troubles as well. He wondered what could possibly have caused Dolour MacNamara to try to take her own life. She had seemed such a robust person, so self-assured, and a beautiful woman too.

Word had reached Chelmsford that the station-owner's wife from Kooramin had tried to kill herself. Juan had been sure that was a mistake until Andy had met up with some stockmen from Kooramin who confirmed it. They were mystified too. Pace and his wife were well liked. There seemed to be no reason. And with three sons . . . that had shocked Juan. It still did.

He wanted a son so much. Delia had suffered two miscarriages in the early stages of pregnancy and he had been broken-hearted, unable to understand how she could take the losses so lightly. Then Delia took everything lightly. She took no interest in the station and seemed to have a talent for choosing the busiest times to demand they go to Sydney or at least to Newcastle. She was already complaining about the heat and wanting to go to the seashore house in Newcastle but he insisted that they would not be going until Christmas. He was sorry now that he had bought that Newcastle house, Delia preferred it to their home.

In the distance he saw a man in a buggy riding away from the homestead and his heart gave a bump. It was Tom Green, unmistakeable in his white dustcoat. Juan turned the horse and rode after him.

'Good day to you Mr Rivadavia,' Green called, pulling up his buggy. He was always ready for a chat.

'Good afternoon doctor. Have you been to the house?'

'Ah yes. Making my rounds.'

'Is everything all right?'

'Mrs MacNamara you mean? Ah yes. Her lungs have taken a belting. The Irish never have strong lungs at the best of times, it must be the damp over there, we could do with some of it here couldn't we?'

'But is Mrs MacNamara well now?'

'Sure she is. Her husband took it hard though I tell you. It's been a month now and he's still walking around as if it was all his fault. I told him he shouldn't blame himself. It isn't an unusual event in the bush. A lot of women chuck it in. They come from faraway lands and the bush gets too much for them. Some of them walk out into the rivers until their hats float and others stride off into the bush and are never heard of again. Lost in the bush is the verdict, but I have my doubts about that. I don't think they want to be found, some of them, mind you, not all. Are you going to visit them?'

'Yes.'

'That's good, cheer MacNamara up a bit. There's little cheer for the squatters these days. Look at it. Not a cloud in the sky. How's that wife of yours, in the family way again yet?'

'I don't think so.'

The doctor chewed on his pipe. 'Well, next time keep her in bed for the first couple of months. It's not as if she's got a lot of work to do. But it's a funny thing though, I see women out here working like bullocks but they still turn out a child a year. Just the way they're built I suppose. Mrs Rivadavia's a bit skinny though. Feed her up a bit, give her a glass of stout every night, get a bit of condition on her. Well I've got to get going. One of the men at Carlton Park, one of the stockmen, had an accident, broken a leg and a couple of ribs by the sound of it.' He reached over and shook Juan's hand. 'Nice meeting up with you.' He flicked his whip gently at his horse and the sulky bowled and bumped down the track.

Dolour met him at the front door. She seemed to be pleased to see him at first but looked away from him, trying not to catch his eye, as she led him into the parlour offering to get him some coffee and send for Pace all in the one breath.

'No, wait,' he said. 'How are you?'

She gave him a wry smile. 'You heard did you? Everyone seems to have heard about it. I wonder if the King of England knows?'

'It's a queen now,' he corrected.

'Ah well so . . . her too.'

'I thought I was a friend of the family,' he said carefully, 'not just a dull business associate. If it is impolite of me to ask how you are, then I must apologise.'

'Oh!' Dolour clutched her hands together as if she had just been slapped on the wrist. 'Oh I am sorry. I'm well now, thank you. I'll get Pace.'

'Don't go yet. There's no hurry. Stay and talk to me awhile.'

'What I have to say wouldn't be very interesting,' she answered, defiance in her voice.

'I suppose not,' he said and she gave a small gasp. Since it had happened everyone was treating her with kid gloves, and his remark sounded more like an insult than polite agreement. She felt the need to defend herself, but did not know how to respond.

He sat down and Dolour, trapped into remaining in the room, sat uneasily across from him.

383

'Did you know there are a lot of Irish people in Argentina?' he asked.

'I did not,' she answered stiffly.

'Well there are, and they have married harmoniously into our families. It is a good mix because the Irish understand us. They too, like life to be dramatic. Like us, they are either very gay or very sad; very serious or deliberately uninterested. You're in one of those moods now. Is it just me who is not interesting you today or is it everyone?'

'Everyone,' she said with a shrug.

'I thought so. Is that why you tried to kill yourself? Is your life so boring?'

She stared at him, hardly believing that someone would march in on her thoughts like this but afraid to leave because she felt he was getting the better of her. 'Of course not,' she said angrily. 'It was far more complicated than that and I would just as soon not talk about it.'

'As you please. What else shall we talk about? What is happening now that you are better? Has life improved?'

'Yes I am going away. I'm leaving.'

'Going where?'

'Back to Ireland.'

'Oh? Why? You've had your punishment so why are you now punishing your husband?'

'Because he deserves it,' she blurted out without thinking. 'No, I mean, he doesn't want me. I'm just going away. It's too late.'

'It can't be too late. It was too late when you tried to kill yourself, but the moment passed. That game is over. Concluded. This is another game you are playing now. You made a fool of yourself. Your pride is damaged so you run away. I do not blame you. Pride, for people like us, is most important.'

Bewildered, she searched his face. His voice was so soft and thoughtful that the confrontation he was provoking seemed to be within herself, not with him. Was he really telling her she should go?

Pace came rushing in to shake hands with Rivadavia. 'Juan, I'm so pleased to see you, I was coming over as soon as I could.'

'I'll get some coffee,' Dolour said but Pace took her arm. 'Don't you be bothering, Dolour. You stay and talk to Juan. I'll get it.' He looked at her earnestly, wanting to please and she shrugged, averting her eyes from him as she had from Juan, so he retreated to the kitchen.

It was obvious that Pace cared a great deal about her and his display of affection was an embarrassment to her so Juan smiled. 'Your illness doesn't seem to have done you any harm though. You look as beautiful as ever. I don't believe he wants you to go. What can we do to keep you with us?'

'You're teasing me now,' she said. 'You're making me feel foolish.'

He jumped up, 'I wouldn't do that. Never! That's another thing about us, we do not like to be teased. We like to be taken seriously. Isn't that so?'

Dolour laughed. 'Talking to you is like ring-a-rosie! I don't know where I'm going to end up.'

Listening as he walked back into the room Pace was astonished. It was the first time he had heard her laugh in ages and was afraid he might break the spell but Juan was in a mood to entertain. 'I have come from Henry Dangar's place,' he said.

'They say it's a big house he's got,' Pace said. 'The girls are bringing us some coffee, if they don't put tea in it.' Dolour half-rose as if to go and check but Pace stopped her. 'No, let them do it.'

'It's not just a big house,' Juan went on, 'it's a mansion. Huge and horrible. They're calling it Dangar's Dance Hall. And, by the way, he's buying out all the squatters around here. Have you been approached?'

'I told him I won't sell,' Pace said.

Dolour got up to leave, 'Excuse me, I have to see what they're doing.' And she was gone before they could stop her.

Pace looked after her, misery in his face and, with an effort, continued. 'Not that I'm doing any good at the minute, but it has to pass. I won't give up my land.'

'How bad is it?' Rivadavia asked him.

'You've seen the countryside. I never could have believed it could dry up so fast. We're shooting our own cattle to put them out of their misery.'

Juan nodded. 'I'm sorry I can't help, my runs up the other side of Dangar's spreads are too dry to carry cattle. I'm sending sheep up there, Chelmsford's too small to carry them in a drought.'

'What are you doing with your cattle?'

'Dangar's opening up a cannery. I have sold him my herds and it might be a good idea if you did so too. Skinny cattle are only good for boiling down. I'd sell them quickly while they still have beef on them. Keep only enough for breeding stock.'

'A cannery eh? It'd be better than watching them die. I was thinking of slaughtering my own beef and opening a salt works, to sell beef for export, that wouldn't take much capital, but if he's got a cannery . . .? What do you think?'

'I'd sell.'

'Then what? What becomes of the station?'

'You can survive here. Seasons change, the rain will come and with it new life, new herds, give the land a chance. We had a good plan. It is just unfortunate that we can't use the runs in the Brisbane Valley, all that green feed, it drives me mad to think about it. But until the area is safe we have to wait.'

Dinner that night was subdued. Pace had never heard Juan talk about Argentina before and knew he was making an effort to overcome the strained atmosphere. He prayed that Juan would not mention Carlton Park, and fortunately he did not, possibly not wanting to discuss more unhappiness in the district. He wondered how Juan himself was getting

385

along. He'd heard that Dora was unhappy at Chelmsford now, and disliked her mistress intensely. She was only staying because Andy refused to leave. Rivadavia has a good foreman there, he thought, it is a wonder he does not prevail on his wife to be a bit kinder to her staff. But then that was only a minor worry compared to his own problems.

That night he tried again with Dolour. 'You don't have to leave, Dolour. I don't care about Heselwood. Forget about him. That's all over now. I need you, and the boys need you.'

'There are plenty of people to look after the boys here, and then they'll be going away to school. I'll not take them with me, they're better off the sons of a squatter than an Irish pauper.'

'Dolour. I'd never see you a pauper.'

'And that would ease your conscience wouldn't it?'

He walked across the bedroom, away from her. 'Nothing will ever ease my conscience. Have I become such a despicable person that you had to try to kill yourself to get away from me?'

'Yes. You and Heselwood. Between you, you killed Dolour Callinan. I am only Mrs MacNamara now. A thing to be abused and ignored.'

'Don't say that, Dolour. I love you. Everything will be all right here now. Everything will work out fine. I'm selling the cattle so we can all rest up through the summer. Juan has invited us to bring the boys and stay at his house by the seashore for Christmas. Do you realise our sons have never seen the sea?'

'You can take them. All I want from you is my passage home to Queenstown. And I'll find me own way from there.'

Her face was set hard with anger. 'I was stupid to try to kill myself,' she said. 'I should have left then, but I didn't think of it. I'm well enough to go now and I'm leaving this week. There's nothing you can do about it so leave me alone.'

In the morning she thought Juan had gone off early to look around the station with Pace as they usually did, but she found him lounging on the verandah. 'Where's Pace?' she asked him.

'Checking the stock,' he replied. 'Stay and talk to your guest.'

'So you can tease me again?'

'No. So you can tell me why you are so unhappy.'

He stood up, waiting for her to sit, and she gave in again. He was very persuasive and had a good humour about him that she could not resist. Not carrying the face of doom like everyone else on this miserable station.

'Why didn't you ask Pace?' she said.

'I did. I had a talk with him this morning, he is so upset that you are leaving he can't think straight. But he couldn't tell me the reason for all this drama. He said it was too personal.'

'It is.' She was crying now, and embarrassed. 'Oh God, it's all such an unholy mess.'

'I tell you what I'll do,' he said. 'If leaving is what you really want I'll take you into Sydney myself. You can rest up at Chelmsford on the way. But you have to tell me why New South Wales is so bad that you have to go running home to a country where people are dying in the streets of famine.'

She blinked. She hadn't thought of that. Ireland, the green and lovely country, was still, to her, a place of friends and family. She had forgotten the suffering. A hawk soared effortlessly in the distance against a background of unremitting blue. Juan was younger than she was but he seemed so much wiser, and more of a conspirator than an inquisitor, offering to take her to Sydney. She doubted if anything would shock him. 'Oh what does it matter?' she said. 'He wouldn't tell you, it's too shameful for him. But the truth of it is that he said he would never have married me if he'd known about my life beforehand.'

'How very interesting. A woman with a past. That makes you very mysterious.'

She looked up at him from behind her handkerchief. 'It's not that interesting. And don't say "I suppose not". You're getting me all tangled up again.'

He was grinning, leaning back in the chair with his hands behind his head. 'You smiled. I saw you. You don't believe your past is so bad any more than I do.'

'Being told your husband wouldn't have married you is though.'

'I agree,' he said, and appeared to be thinking about it. 'Yes, I'd have to say that's just about unforgiveable. If I said that to Delia, I'd be paying for it for the rest of my life. But then Delia punishes me for my faults by making me buy her presents. There's no chance of Pace buying you off?'

'None at all.'

'So was your life beforehand something to do with Heselwood? Perhaps an affair?'

Dolour shrank into the chair, shocked. It was the first time that anyone had ever guessed at it let alone mentioned the subject. 'How did you know that?'

'It isn't hard to see how much Pace hates Heselwood, out of all proportion, given that Pace only worked for him. And don't forget, I know Heselwood. The hatred is reciprocated.'

She stared at him, surprised that he had divined the truth so well but intrigued that he was taking it so calmly, and then she nodded. 'So now you see how the land lies . . . Pace said he wouldn't have married me if he'd known about Heselwood.'

'And for that remark you can't forgive him? Or did you drag it out of him?'

'I asked him straight out.'

Juan sat forward and looked at her very seriously. 'Sometimes people ask the wrong questions. Let me give you a question. Would Pace have married you if you were not a Catholic?'

'He would not have, no.'

'And would you have gone off and killed yourself?'

'Of course not.'

387

'Then I think you're making too much of this whole thing. The MacNamaras should try talking some more yet. And I'm tiring you, I sound like my father.'

Dolour was still confused and she was sorry he had ended their conversation. 'Would you like to see the horses? Pace said you might take some of them for a while.'

As they entered the wide stable doors she saw a saddle hanging on a peg. 'Whose is that?' she asked. 'Oh it's yours Juan, of course. 'She reached up and touched the handsome black leather saddle with its intricate stitching and flamboyant silver trim. 'Is this real silver?'

'Yes. The saddle belonged to my father. It was his farewell gift.'

She saw Pace riding across the paddock. 'I'd better get up to the house. And thank you Juan, but I don't think talk ever fixes anything.'

'It does if you learn to ask the right questions.'

She looked around her, bewildered. 'I wouldn't know what to ask.'

'Then Pace will have to think of them.'

Dolour smiled. 'You're talking in riddles again.'

'No I'm not. If I were Pace I wouldn't let you go.'

'And what would you do about it?' she asked.

'I'd tie you to the bed,' he laughed and wandered down the centre of the stables peering into the stalls.

'You never even talk to me,' Pace said, 'unless there are persons around.'

'So now you know what it feels like,' she replied. She was seated at the end of the old cane couch at the far corner of the verandah as if to place herself out of reach.

'I don't like it, does that make you feel better?'

The needle flashed as she concentrated on her embroidery.

'Dolour. I'm begging you not to leave. What can I say to make you change your mind?'

'You can save your breath.'

He lit his pipe and leaned against the verandah post. 'Very well then, we'll all go. I'll sell up here and we'll all go back.'

Her hands dropped to her lap in surprise. 'To Ireland?'

'The same.'

'You can't go back, you'd be spotted in no time.'

'I'll take the chance they've forgotten me.'

'Then the others would have you back doing the same work for them in no time. The fight's still going on.'

'We'll forget all that. I'm a family man now. We'll buy a farm in Ireland. Would you like that?'

She looked at him, disbelieving. 'I can just see you with six cows and four pigs.'

'Never mind about that. I can't lose you Dolour, there'd be nothing here for me without you. Can't you see there's nothing I wouldn't do for love of you?'

Her voice was small as if testing the air. 'It'd be a funny sort of running away, everyone running with me.'

'Will you think about it then?'

'Would you do that for me? Sell up your precious land?'

'Haven't I just said I would? And do you mind if I sit down here beside you, I'm a bit weary tonight.'

She shrugged. And she sat for a long time trying to think what to do, feeling tired and washed out herself. Then she realised he had dozed into a quiet sleep. She touched him on the arm and he awoke with a start. 'I was thinking,' she said, 'perhaps we could start again.'

'And where would that be, here or in Ireland?'

She looked out over the quiet of the station. 'Here would be the best, wouldn't you say?'

# PART THIRTEEN

## VALLEY OF LAGOONS

# CHAPTER ONE

A gala dinner was to be held at Chelmsford in honour of Governor Sir Charles Augustus FitzRoy, who was visiting the Hunter Valley with the Colonial Secretary, Edward Deas Thomson, and staying a few days at Cormack's station.

Sir Charles FitzRoy was known to all the right people in the colony as a very accommodating chap who rarely interfered in the day-to-day business of the colony. Shock waves were still lingering over Gipps's conflicts with the squatters over land policy and his desire to expand the education system to embrace all children, rich and poor. Though he had not mentioned black children everyone felt that given time, he would even have gone that far. Especially since he had demanded a second trial of the men arrested for the Myall Creek massacres of some forty or fifty blacks. The second trial had upended the first jury's verdict and they were found guilty and most of them hanged. Even to the last minute, the murderers and most of the colony had expected a reprieve but none came.

Within the first year the squatters were finding FitzRoy amenable to their expansionist plans and the man in the street saw him as no better or worse than the rest. And that was the way FitzRoy wanted it. He and his wife would stay their term in the colony and return to England with honours, not under a cloud as so many others had done before him.

Where Gipps had been quiet and retiring, FitzRoy plunged into the Sydney social scene, meeting as many people as he could and entertaining at Government House on a grand scale. He enjoyed the races, and cut a fine figure driving his own phaeton around Sydney. It was evident to all, that this Governor was enjoying life in New South Wales and they appreciated him.

Although there was still trouble with the blacks in the far north, settlers were moving inland from Brisbane and ports to the near north of Moreton Bay. But every man who sailed down Cook's Whitsunday Passage, inside the great coral reef, told of the magnificent uninhabited country they viewed from their ships.

'A thousand miles of lush and inviting coastline,' the Governor was told, 'land that must be explored.' And FitzRoy agreed to send an expedition, led by Edmund Kennedy, to explore this far region which extended from the Tropic of Capricorn right up to the straits. Explorers captured the public imagination, and FitzRoy was always aware of popular causes.

As his coach spun up the drive to Chelmsford homestead along the tall windbreak of trees, FitzRoy was thinking of the strange German explorer, Ludwig Leichhardt, who had made the fantastic journey inland from the Darling Downs right up to the Gulf of Carpentaria and around the Gulf to the doomed Port Essington, which was slowly being crushed by disease and isolation.

Relaxing after his incredible expedition, Leichhardt was wandering the gentle Hunter Valley collecting botanical specimens, and the Governor had made it known to his host, Mr Rivadavia, that Ludwig Leichhardt would be a welcome addition to the guest list.

The glazed lattice windows bordering the massive doors of Chelmsford homestead glowed a welcome as the Governor's coach pulled in and a liveried footman, Delia's innovation, ran down to assist.

On cue Mr and Mrs Rivadavia stepped forward to welcome their viceregal visitor and inside, guests were lined up waiting to be presented.

The genial Governor marched through, taking note of the bowing and bobbing heads and smiled at a Mr MacNamara who remained erect, and his wife Mrs MacNamara who seemed to be caught between bowing and not bowing. It didn't bother him that MacNamara had refused to bow, rather gave a little zest to the evening.

He strode through to the parlour. 'Very pleasant place you have here sir. Spanish looking, I like that style. But I see you chose an English rose as a wife. A wise choice sir, and the colony's good fortune.'

Delia blushed with pleasure.

FitzRoy looked around the room as he talked to them. There were some squatters he knew, the Dangars, the De Lisles, the Barringtons and Cormacks and some hard-jawed Scots. The men looked as if they had just come in from the frontier while the women were stiff and reserved in black, in contrast to the hostess's gown of pearl-encrusted blue satin. He toured the room, taking his time to talk to the guests, with a genuine interest fuelled by curiosity. 'I have not been in the colony so long,' he announced, 'that I should tire of hearing tales of high adventure and surely to pioneer new lands must be the greatest adventure of all.'

He came to Pace MacNamara and spoke easily with him but found it hard to keep his eyes from Mrs MacNamara and harder still not to compliment her on her beauty. His instincts told him the husband might not appreciate it. 'There's a woman,' he told himself. 'An artist could never do that cream and auburn colouring justice.' He gave her a delicate passing smile and noticed that his host Rivadavia, alone of the men present, seemed also to share his admiration of the Irish woman. He raised an eyebrow at Rivadavia and was pleased to see that he picked up the sentiments. No doubt about these Latins, he mused, they have an eye for women, more so than the cold fish that frequent Government House.

'Do you come to Sydney much?' he asked his host.

'Quite often,' Juan said.

'Then you must call. We shall go to the races, make a day of it. Now where is Mr Leichhardt?'

'He has not yet arrived Your Excellency,' Juan said. 'If you wish we shall start dinner without him.'

'Very well,' FitzRoy said, disappointed. He would have preferred to wait but he loathed cold meals.

They were just commencing the main course of juicy racks of lamb, ovenbaked in white wine and spices, a dish that FitzRoy found delicious, when Leichhardt came striding in, the footman trailing behind. 'Good evening ladies and gentlemen,' his voice boomed in a thick German accent and they all turned to stare. He was dressed in a tall hat, mismatched clothes and Hessian boots.

The Governor had insisted that a place be kept beside him for the explorer since he had not had a chance to meet him prior to this evening, and now he regretted that decision. 'One can not expect perfect table manners of people who are forced to reside in the wilds,' he told his wife later, 'but the man ate like a pig, snuffing and snorting through his moustache, and he stank. But on the other hand utterly fascinating. Once the ladies retired I can't recall when I've had such an entertaining evening.'

Leichhardt was the centre of attention. Juan was appalled at the boorishness of the man and amazed that the Governor did not take offence. The British were a mystery to him. He was more at ease when the ladies left because some of Leichhardt's comments and accounts were rather crude, much too close to the bone for propriety.

With only men in the room and the port flowing freely, Leichhardt talked of his great expedition and then turned to philosophy, of the effects of isolation and loneliness in the vast lands beyond the settlements and his listeners hung on every word.

'You would have to place great reliance on your companions,' FitzRoy commented, 'one for all and all for one so to speak.'

'This is so, one comes to love them dearly, but then the love of man for man is the greatest love of all.'

The Britishers around him nodded wisely.

'And never shown better than on the battlefield where a man will lay down his life for a friend,' De Lisle said, and Juan stared at them. Did they really not know what this German was talking about or were they pretending?

'Yes. This is so, the soul and spirit of man invokes the greatest admiration in those closest to him, not forgetting God's greatest creation, the body of man. A wonder in itself.'

Juan almost laughed aloud as the conversation continued at cross-purposes and the worldly FitzRoy, choking on his cigar, mischievously encouraged Leichhardt to continue. In the end the Governor seemed reluctant to leave but with the ladies waiting, he could hardly turn the evening into a men's club night.

As the Governor was leaving he turned to Juan and laughed heartily. 'What a night! I must compliment you on an excellent dinner and superb wines, quite the best I've come across in the colony and the conversation was far from dull was it not?'

'I am pleased you enjoyed the evening,' Juan said, careful not to make a personal comment on any of his guests. 'I have put a case of our wines aside for you. This is ideal country for wine-growing and you might care to sample more of them.'

'Thank you. They are of such good quality you should think about exporting them. We'll discuss it when you come to Sydney.'

Juan smiled, satisfied. That had been the point of the dinner party.

He had invited the MacNamaras to stay over so that he could talk business with Pace. When at last the drought had broken, Pace had restocked Kooramin and Juan had opened up his runs north of Dangar's holdings, and, using that station as starting point, they had sent more cattle over the Darling Downs to the Brisbane Valley since the area was now considered safe. His own foreman Andy was in residence on the Brisbane River property with his wife Dora. The promotion of Andy from foreman to station manager had pleased everyone and solved the problem of the feud that had developed between Dora and her mistress, Delia. Between them now, Juan and Pace had more than a hundred thousand head of cattle and were preparing to expand north-west. There was still no end to the available land and they were determined to diversify their holdings so that never again would they be brought to a standstill by the ravages of drought.

Juan said his farewells to the other guests and was irritated to discover that Leichhardt had made his way back to the dining room and was now settled in talking to Pace about his explorations.

'What do we do with him?' Delia asked.

Juan clicked his tongue impatiently. 'I can't very well ask him to leave. Perhaps you and Dolour should just quietly retire. I don't think his conversation at this hour is suitable.'

He joined the two men and sat down to wait out the last guest but in no time he was just as impressed as Pace, and was listening intently. The Gulf country Leichhardt had mostly spoken about earlier had seemed nothing more than a traveller's tale of a faraway exotic land but now that he was speaking of the exact route it became more real.

'It is no use talking,' Leichhardt said. 'I have maps in my saddlebag I will show you.' He dashed outside and returned to unroll a folio of maps which he spread out on the table and began explaining his journey in relation to the coastline. 'Now here is the great Burdekin River which I named after a lady in Sydney who gave me financial and moral support and on this you can see how we went on to the Gulf. See, here is where we all nearly expired.'

'I've got to hand it to you,' Pace said. 'It's a marvellous journey you have taken there. But what about the blacks?'

'As I told you, Gilbert, dear chap, was speared to death but he was our only casualty, thank God. If it had not been for the savages in the top end there, we would have died. They led us out of the wilderness to Port Essington. And just in time. You should have seen their faces! We were like phantoms come out of the dark continent.'

Juan shook his head in wonder. 'I too am impressed. Magnificent!'

Leichhardt grinned at him. 'And I was impressed with your meal. Are there any of those chops left?'

'I'll see,' Juan said and went himself to the kitchen and came back with cold chops, cheeses and bread.

The three men talked late into the night, Leichhardt not needing any prompting. 'You must stay over,' Juan said. 'It is too late to go now.'

Leichhardt took that for granted. 'Of course. You see I am preparing myself in spirit for my next journey which will be the greatest feat of all. I will cross the continent from there, on the Mitchell River, right across to the Indian Ocean.'

'It's not possible!' Juan breathed.

'Everything is possible if the mind is in the right state of order. And you sir, I am shocked at you, an Argentinian, clinging to the heels of towns when there is magnificent cattle country in the north.'

'We have a place here,' Juan said, pointing to the Brisbane Valley.

Leichhardt exploded. 'Call yourself a cattleman! There is far better land than that to be had. It's as wide open and fresh as your own pampas and you sit down here wasting your time. Fiddling about with pocket-handkerchief runs. Now see here, from the Burdekin . . .' He swept his hand across the map, inland, as the two men listened carefully. 'You could have a cattle station out there of a hundred square miles and you know what? No-one would notice it. A speck on the map.'

Pace looked again at the well-worn maps, perplexed. 'It is so huge that country, on such a scale I see now, I never realised it before. But where in God's name would you start?'

'I know where I'd start,' the German said. 'I'd begin with the ripest plum of all.' He cut a hunk of cheese and bit into it. 'Good cheese, did you make this yourself?'

'No it is imported,' Juan said absently, waiting for his guest to proceed. Finally Pace asked the question. 'Would it be in order for a man to ask where this land might be?'

'Certainly and I will tell you. I have told a lot of people but no-one listens or cares, it is too far away.'

'Where is it?' Juan was so excited, he was whispering.

'Here!' Leichhardt's bony finger stabbed the map. 'It is the most beautiful pasture land in all the world. Never in my life have I seen such a paradise, sweet green grass, plenty of water and lagoons teeming with birds. When I first looked over this Eden I was so overcome, so surprised, that I called the mountain far in the distance, over the other side, here, Mount Surprise. For that was what it was, the biggest surprise of my life.'

The other two men sat, completely spellbound.

Leichhardt continued. 'An oasis in the wilderness. And I named it myself. I called it Valley of Lagoons.'

Dolour was awake on and off during the night, waiting for Pace to come to bed. As the dawn breezes began to blow through the open window, she wished she were at home so that she could get herself a cup of tea. The morning light filtered into the room giving the walls a pink glow and a richness to the heavy black furniture. The floors were of stone but thick red-black patterned rugs compensated for any lack of warmth. She thought they were very attractive and clean-looking but still preferred her own timber floors. As the seasons improved and the station flourished, she had been able to furnish her own house comfortably but it was always inter-esting to look at other houses and think what else could be done.

The door opened quietly and she called: 'Don't bother to tiptoe, I'm awake.'

'What are you doing awake at this hour?' Pace asked wearily.

'I've been expecting you every half hour. I've got something to tell you.'

'Then tell me tomorrow. I'm too tired now. Just let me get undressed and get to bed.'

'Did you talk to Juan?'

'What about?' he yawned. 'We talked to the German . . .'

'Then he didn't tell you?'

Pace didn't bother to answer. He pulled off his boots, discarded his new suit with the long coat and fancy lapels and took off the waistcoat but that was as far as he could go. He fell on the bed, exhausted.

'Don't go to bed in your good shirt, Pace,' she pleaded but got no response, so she leaned over him and shook him. 'Pace! Listen to me. Delia is leaving. She told me last night. She is going back to England because she hates this country, and nothing will change her mind. What can we do?'

But he was fast asleep.

She waited until she could hear people stirring in the household and then dressed carefully, pinning her hair up with only a few wisps escaping. Then she went out to look for Juan and she spied him talking to some station hands, one foot resting on a tank stand.

'Could I see you a minute?' she called to him, hoping Delia wouldn't come out from the house just yet.

'Of course you can, Dolour. You look splendid this morning. Did you enjoy yourself last night?'

'It was a lovely evening and everything was perfect. I never expected, when they carted me out here, that I'd be sitting down to dinner with the Governor, never in my wildest dreams.'

'His Excellency was very taken with you.'

'Come now, he was not, you shouldn't say such things. But I want to talk to you about Delia. She says she's leaving.'

397

He sighed and lifted his hands in an expression of resignation. 'She wants to leave. I think she is very homesick, she doesn't like it here, she doesn't like anything about New South Wales. I can't even persuade her to stay in Sydney.'

'Then she is just going home for a holiday?'

'No. This is not a sudden decision. I've seen it coming for a long time now. She wants to go home and she will live with her mother. I will support her, I've told her I'll buy her a house in London if she wishes, or wherever she wants to live over there.'

Shocked, Dolour took his arm as if to stop him taking that course. 'You sound as if you want her to go.'

'I don't want her to go,' he said. 'It is not right, but I don't want her to be unhappy all her life. And I can't stop her.'

'But you must!'

'How?'

'I'm surprised at you,' she said. 'It seems not so long ago you stopped me from going. You had all the answers then. What has happened to you?'

'If you think about it, I didn't stop you from leaving. It was Pace who was prepared to make the sacrifice so as not to lose you.'

'Good then. You must do something like that. You'll think of something.' She was more cheerful now, sure that Juan would overcome the problem. It was hard to understand how a woman could want to leave such an attractive man, who was always kind and respectful to her; and she remembered in Delia's rush of complaints about everything – the heat, the insects, the distances she had to travel to get anywhere, the discomforts of travel – she had hardly mentioned Juan. She recalled too, amused at Delia's tactlessness, that the English girl had said she loathed all the people she had been forced to associate with in the colony, even in Sydney. 'There are only a handful of people out here of my social standing, and they're always away when one wishes to call. Sometimes I think that Rivadavia is not as well accepted in the right circles as he likes to believe.'

'That's not true Delia,' Dolour had said. 'Juan is well thought of. Why there has been a lot of talk lately about asking him to become a Member of Parliament.'

'Oh don't worry. He thought about that too, but he would have to become a British subject. However, I can't see that representing the roughnecks around here would alter his status to any great degree.'

Dolour had escaped from her, feeling that Delia had said enough.

'You'll talk her into staying, won't you?' she said to Juan.

He shook his head. 'I can't. And I was just thinking of Pace. I'm not prepared to make those sacrifices, so it appears that I don't love her enough.'

That thought seemed to depress him even more, and Dolour felt guilty, as if by her kindness she had just managed to make matters worse.

# CHAPTER TWO

The two-storied mansion with its sturdy stone verandahs overlooking the harbour was so pleasant and comfortable that Georgina was happy even when Jasin and Edward were away. She had studied the architect's plans herself before giving permission for the renovations to go ahead and remembering Cormack's chilly town residence, insisted that this house be secure and warm in winter, as well as a defence in summer against the unbearable heat. Even now it was necessary to shade the breakfast room from the morning sun, and she was watching as the men put up striped canvas blinds that could be raised or lowered outside the room when required.

Thanks to the Forrests, and Jasin's stubborn refusal to negotiate, they had been forced to stay in England much longer than they originally planned and all the time she had been worried about Jasin's health. He had suffered several bouts of influenza but refused to return to New South Wales until the matter was settled once and for all. He had won the first case but Dermott Forrest had taken the matter on to a higher court which found that the Forrests were partners with Lord Heselwood in Carlton Park. The original contract was clear, though, that the Forrests were silent partners and not entitled to occupy the premises. They were ordered to sell their share of the station to Lord Heselwood at the price per acre on average, at the time they left the property, and Heselwood was ordered to repay the monies borrowed on a rising scale of interest.

Edward had been jubilant that it was over at last. He disliked living in England and yearned to return to New South Wales. Georgina worried that his childhood memories might have become greatly exaggerated over the years. 'It's not as wonderful as you seem to think, Edward.'

'Then why are you going back?'

'Because I like living in Sydney and I have a lot of friends there now. And your father loves the stations and getting out into the country and being terribly clever at finding new land that he doesn't have to pay much for.'

'That's why I want to come back with you. I want to live on a station too. Father says I can live at Carlton Park to learn the ropes and go with him to re-open Montone. It's far more exciting than this boring place. Father says that with my help, we can end up with a string of stations in the north. Really big cattle stations.'

She had hoped he would remain in England and continue his education but on the other hand she would have missed him terribly. And, now that they were back, Edward had become more enthusiastic and more ambitious than his father, if that were possible, and the two of them got along so well. They had got Montone operating again and Edward was back at Carlton Park. Jasin, as healthy as a horse again, was enjoying Sydney.

'What are you doing here?' he came sauntering across the garden.

'You're back?' she said. 'I didn't hear you come in. They're putting up the blinds I ordered. Remember we saw some like this on that charming house in Bath?'

'Oh yes, so we did. I met your friends, the Rivadavias, in town today.'

'Good. Did you invite them over?'

'The Miss invited herself. She's coming to call at five o'clock.' Jasin always referred to Delia as 'the Miss' even though she was a married woman.

'What about Juan? Isn't he coming?'

'I think not and I didn't push it. Could be embarrassing. FitzRoy told me she's leaving him.'

Georgina was amazed. 'But why?'

'I gather she's fed up. I don't know. Ask her yourself. His Excellency will be glad to see the end of her. She is inclined to button-hole him, seems to regard him as an ally in her condemnation of everything colonial. The way he tells it is highly amusing. He spends a lot of time moving from one end of the reception room to the other to get away from Delia and her highly vocal criticisms which give the impression that he agrees with her, and leave a trail of dark looks.'

'And how is Juan taking this?' Georgina was very concerned.

'The Sphinx my dear. No-one knows. She does enough talking for both of them so it would be hard to tell his reaction.'

'I am so sorry. It's a shame. By the way, there's a letter from Edward, I put it in your study.'

'What does he say?'

She smiled. 'What would you think? The weather, and cattle, and the new horned breeds he wants you to import, and a new agricultural publication he needs, and all sorts of things for you to do.'

'Good! My word he's shaping up well. I'll have a look at it. Now if Lachie Cormack comes along send him out to me. He's starting up a Cattleman's Association, a sort of lobby group more than anything else I'd say. I'm not very interested but it would be a good idea to get Edward into it, on the ground floor so to speak, just in case it is successful.'

As he was leaving, Georgina called him back. 'There's one thing in Edward's letter that worries me Jasin. I want you to speak to him about it. He says they put opium ash into the flour and tea they give the station blacks, and he seems to think it is funny. "Keeps them docile," he says. It's an awful thing to do. You tell him it has got to stop.'

400

'They all do it. I couldn't stop them. The blacks only get the leftovers anyway, a lot of those squatters out there smoke themselves into a stupor. Their Saturday night treat.'

'That's disgusting! You never did.'

'I didn't need to, I think it's rather sickening.'

'But what if Edward takes up the habit? He's only eighteen.'

Jasin laughed. 'No he won't. He knows all about it. I took him to an opium shop and showed him some of the customers lying around the back rooms doped to the eyeballs in their so-called euphoria and he found it pathetic.'

'You actually took him to one of those places? Jasin, really! You never told me.'

'So I'm telling you now. There are opium shops everywhere, and supplies go out to the stations with their provisions, it was better that he saw the condition of those smokers so that he won't go trying it.'

'They should be banned, those places. I'll speak to the Governor about it myself.'

'You do that,' he laughed. 'But I don't think you'll get far.'

He wandered out and left Georgina to think about that, but as she turned back to the workmen she saw that they'd hung the blinds back to front.

That afternoon she waited impatiently for Delia, rehearsing the pleas she would make on Juan's behalf, if indeed the gossip were true. It was possible that Delia was only going home for a visit.

But when she arrived she made no apologies for her decision. 'It's no use, Georgina. I find this colony a most tiresome place. If Rivadavia wishes to see me he can come to England. The whole thing was a mistake from the beginning and really I blame my grandfather. I was too young and impressionable to make a commitment to live in a strange country.'

'Others might think you were very lucky to have married a man as charming and well-off as Juan. Surely he has always been good to you?'

'And why should he not be? I'm his wife. But then if I wanted to do something that he didn't want to do, it was like talking to a stone. And he's impossible in the house! Everything has to be just so and if there is a mess anywhere he raises the roof. I told him time and again it's not my fault. The servants are useless. We got rid of that terrible Dora woman and we've had four cooks since then, each one worse than the last. And they give cheek! You've never heard the like! Servants out here don't know their place. And even my own maid, Lee, turned against me. She's staying here in Sydney you know, refusing to come back to England. My mother will have something to say about that.'

'Did you give any thought to taking a house here in Sydney?'

Delia turned on her angrily. 'You've been talking to Juan!'

'I have not even seen Juan since he arrived in Sydney,' Georgina said quietly. 'But listen to me. When I first came out here I have to admit I hated it . . .'

'There! You see,' Delia interrupted. 'I knew you'd see it my way. The whole atmosphere out here is coarse and ugly. We don't belong here.'

'What I was trying to say, is that you should give it more time. I prefer New South Wales to England now. I enjoy living here, I don't find the atmosphere coarse; rather, I find it invigorating. And your husband is a very refined man.'

'My husband would like to see me a brood mare. He'd have ten sons if he could. I've told him we Forsters are not great breeders and I can't see why it is so important. He already has a daughter.'

'Some people like to have quite a few children, it is understandable.'

'You didn't. You've only got one child.'

'I consider that my misfortune,' Georgina said stiffly, becoming increasingly exasperated with her guest, but for Juan's sake she tried again. 'Juan must be upset that you are leaving.'

'Naturally he is upset. But I can't help that. He suggested I should stay awhile in England and then return when I'm feeling better, but he knows now I have no intention of returning. Ever.'

'Delia. Do you realise he could divorce you?'

'Don't be silly. He won't divorce me, we're Catholic. And I don't want to get married again. I've had quite enough of it. I'm lucky to escape without having some squalling baby on my hands.'

And where does that leave Juan? Georgina wondered, finding it difficult to be polite to her guest but Jasin came to the door, looking for Lachie Cormack who still hadn't arrived.

'Come on in Jasin,' she called quickly. 'You have to say goodbye to Delia.'

'Ah yes. Mrs Rivadavia. You're off soon?'

Delia sat up and primped her hair under her bonnet. 'The day after tomorrow. I'm so excited.'

'And how is Mr Rivadavia?' Jasin said, a pointed remark that Georgina knew was designed to irritate but Delia answered it airily. 'He's very well. Busy now with his great new scheme.'

'What scheme would that be?'

'We had that awful fellow Leichhardt to dine, the night we entertained the Governor and he told Juan about some land. Well I tell you Jasin, it was the worst thing he could have done. I've heard nothing but Valley of Lagoons since he left.'

Jasin sat down quietly. 'What's the Valley of Lagoons? A swamp somewhere?' His voice sounded bored but he was not. He was watching Delia intently.

'By no means. Apparently it is some paradise out in the middle of nowhere. You know Juan, land and more land, that's all he thinks about. The German discovered it and now Juan, with that Irish friend of his, Pace MacNamara, is mad to get it.'

Georgina tried to change the subject. 'What ship are you taking Delia?' But Jasin waved her aside. 'Now I come to think of it, I have heard mention of that place,' he lied. 'Up north, up past Montone somewhere.'

'It's a lot further north than that. Into black country. I told Juan he is stupid to even think about it. They'll get killed, but he said Leichhardt went there and lived to tell the tale.'

Jasin left it to Georgina to see 'The Miss' off, pleased that her prattling had been of some use for a change. He had read of Leichhardt's expedition but there had been no mention in any of the accounts of a Valley of Lagoons. If Rivadavia and the Irishman were interested there must be something to it. What a slap in the eye it would be to them if he could get there first.

He went back to his study, a large airy room set apart from the house with its own entrance, rather like the arrangement John Horton had. It was easier, he now knew, to have people come straight to his office rather than disturb the household and out here he kept his guns, his riding boots and all the paraphernalia for his back country journeys as well as his files on the stations and his investments. He often thought of Horton, how he died far too young, and how they both would have enjoyed comparing notes on their progress. He wondered which one of the two of them would be richer by this. 'Me old chap,' he said to the empty room. 'I'll wager I've beaten you to the stakes.'

He sat down and began writing to Edward. He told him about this place, the Valley of Lagoons, a prospect of good land going begging again. And as he wrote he became more and more enthusiastic. 'I shall find out where it is and let you know. If it is country as rich as I am led to believe, then we might consider an expedition.'

It wasn't easy to obtain more information on this valley, no-one seemed to know anything about it, not even the Colonial Secretary, but a chance meeting with Major Mitchell the Surveyor General gave him the opportunity to view copies of Leichhardt's maps which had been placed in the hands of the government surveyors.

'His journey was far more extensive than I had imagined,' he told Mitchell as they pored over the maps. 'I had no idea! What an achievement! The fellow deserves a medal.'

'If we ever find him,' Mitchell observed drily.

'Now look here. What about this country up here?' Jasin was intent on his own enquiries. 'I wouldn't mind establishing a run up on the Burdekin River.' He had spied the Valley of Lagoons, so far to the north he'd almost missed it. 'They say Leichhardt himself claims it is great cattle country.'

'Oh yes, he does. And he waxes lyrical over this place in the upper reaches of the Burdekin, Valley of Lagoons, but it is too soon to be thinking about that country. If you thought you had trouble with the blacks on the Mary River, that country would be a waking nightmare. It's a thousand miles beyond the frontier.'

Jasin nodded. 'I can afford to wait a few years. It will give me the time to make preparations and gather more information. But what a challenge, eh Mitchell?'

That night an excited Jasin wrote to Edward again. 'I have located the valley I spoke of and am enclosing my own rough sketch of the location, well out of reach of anyone just yet but I am quite determined that the Heselwoods will lay claim to it due course. I have been speaking to Mitchell, the Surveyor General, and he will keep us advised of progress in the north, especially as regards ports. By the looks of things we could get close to the Valley of Lagoons by ship, to Halifax Bay. Leichhardt is to be complimented on the name he has chosen, I would not wish to alter it. When you come in at Christmas we shall discuss the matter further, and by that time I shall have copies of official maps to show you.'

The foreman at Carlton Park was not as enthusiastic about the boss's son as his parents believed. Edward, known on the station as Eddie, was tall, like his father, and beginning to fill out to man size, but from Passey's point of view the lad was far too big for his boots. They would have been better off to send him to another station where he would be treated as an ordinary stockman, to learn the ropes, but here, he was only playing at being a station hand, while living it up at the homestead.

What's the use of a stockman who thinks he doesn't have to take orders? Passey worried. As far as he was concerned, Eddie could hang around the station all day and do nothing, have a holiday, please himself, but he insisted on joining in the work, when it suited him. And that was the trouble. He was unreliable. When he was rostered to do a job, chances were it wouldn't get done, or it would be left half-finished. He was muttering when he walked into the kitchen. 'That bloody Eddie,' he said to his wife. 'I told him a week ago to take some men and dig out the waterhole in Blackman's Gully and it hasn't been done. It's almost dried up now and there's a bullock bogged in it.'

'Don't be too hard on him,' she said. 'He's only young.'

'He's old enough. Those MacNamara kids could have done better at half his age.'

'They're different. They've been brought up out here.'

Passey poured some rum into a tin mug and went outside to light his pipe. The men were coming out from supper but Eddie hadn't shown up yet. He spent his time with a couple of stockmen, who heeled like dogs for the boss's son, and were a wild pair of show-off roughnecks. Eddie had no place in their company. Passey knew that the trio went to the blacks' camps every so often, screwing the poor gins. He had spoken to Eddie about it. 'Nothing much I can do about the other blokes Eddie, but you don't want to be hanging around down there.'

'I only go for a lark,' Eddie had said. 'I never touch them.'

Passey knew he was lying. 'I hope you don't son. They're not too clean. You could get sick.' He knew he was wasting his breath so he tried another angle. 'If you feel you're needing a woman,' he counselled, 'maybe it's time you thought about getting married.' He hoped he was saying the right thing.

'It's not my job,' he told his wife as they climbed into bed, 'to be wet-nursing station hands. If they get into strife they have to sort it out themselves, but if Eddie buys trouble I'll have Lord Heselwood blaming me. There were a couple of drovers threatening to give Eddie a hiding, last week, you know.'

'They're only jealous of him.'

'Jealous or not, what's the difference? He rubs the men up the wrong way. And he's got those two young bucks as cheeky as himself.'

'Which two?'

'The brothers. Ben and Max Belcher. They sit on their brains, that pair.'

'But they're good stockmen.'

'They're two-bob bloody lairs! Bill Craddock was complaining about them yahooing over at his place last Sunday. They nearly caused a fight.'

'The Craddocks are always complaining about something. I don't know why you worry so much,' she said. 'I think Eddie's a very nice boy. He's always polite to me. Anyway he's going down to Sydney soon, to spend Christmas with his parents.'

'It can't come soon enough for me. I hope he bloody stays there.'

# CHAPTER THREE

Sir Charles FitzRoy planned to hold a gala ball at Government House on Christmas Eve and make it a grand occasion to round off a successful year. He had managed to keep the squatters quiet and still pick up more revenue on their stock and leases; the first regular steamship run between Sydney and Adelaide had been established, the Turf Club at Five Dock was well established, and another at Parramatta; and he was the patron of all sorts of civilising associations.

All in all, his reign to date had been highly successful. He had presided over the establishment of Victoria as a separate colony and there was now a clamour afoot for the north to become yet another state. While keeping his cards close to his chest, because there was bound to be controversy, he had already recommended separation to the Home Office. It was impossible to administer towns popping up six hundred miles away. He had even suggested that the colony be called Queen's Land.

He still felt great remorse at the loss of his wife, a weight he would carry forever. There was no escaping the blame, he had been driving the phaeton when it overturned, killing dear Lady Mary and his aide-de-camp. The shock had almost overwhelmed him. He sighed. One has to press on. He had continued with the decoration of Government House, as Lady Mary would have wanted, and with his duties as Governor but the grief was still with him, which was why this tragedy and its repercussions were more hurtful to him than he would admit. Edmund Kennedy and ten of his companions had perished on their expedition to the north. Most of them, including Kennedy himself, had been murdered by blacks. It had been awful news, Kennedy was much loved in the colony and his expedition had caused great excitement. Major Mitchell, the Surveyor General, blamed the Governor for having permitted the expedition, and his criticism was merciless.

'It is unfair of Mitchell,' Sir Charles told his aide, 'to claim that I should have sought his advice first. He was out of the country at the time. Most unfair.'

He left his private rooms to find the ladies of the Royal Benevolent Society departing from a meeting in the Green Room, being farewelled by his daughter-in-law, and he spied Lady Heselwood, one of his best friends. 'Ah Georgie my dear. Just the one I wanted to see. I'm arranging a small dinner party this Saturday night, just a few friends, to discuss the Christmas Eve Ball. You and Lord Heselwood must come along.'

'We should be delighted, Sir Charles.'

'Very good. You'll know most of them I think. Our friend Rivadavia will be in town. He'll escort the newest addition to our Sydney circle, Lady Rowan-Smith. Old Sir Percy's widow. Do you know her?'

'Oh yes. Her first husband, John Horton, was a friend of ours.'

'Excellent. She's back from England with her daughter, forget her name, and Rivadavia's daughter, Rosa. Seems the girls went to the same school in Paris. This Christmas we'll have a grand collection of young people to join us. Your son Edward is in town isn't he?'

Georgina nodded.

'He must come and he must bring his friends so that we have plenty of dancing partners for the young ladies.'

The other ladies of the Benevolent Society were waiting nearby to pay their respects and Georgina stood back while he swept forward to make a fuss of them and thank them for their endeavours.

'I will not sit at table with that woman,' Jasin said. 'What is Rivadavia doing squiring her around, anyway?'

'He has to take someone.'

'Why couldn't he take one of the Courtney girls? Poor Mrs Courtney has a house full of them. Now that the old boy has died she's got her hands full trying to launch them.'

'Your solicitude for the Courtneys is touching, my dear,' Georgina murmured. 'I didn't think you'd notice.'

'One does. Courtney was a canny old Scot. It must irk him to be at the pearly gates leaving his fortune to those silly women.'

Georgina laughed outright. 'And you have a solution?'

'It wouldn't do any harm to invite a couple of his daughters to meet Edward.'

Later she broached the subject of the dinner party again but he would not be persuaded, and Georgina was disappointed. FitzRoy's parties were always fun. He loved to surprise his guests with games or entertainment. They sent their apologies to Sir Charles but Georgina felt it was a mistake on Jasin's part. He had allowed Vicky to get the better of him again.

Lady Rowan-Smith's homecoming to Sydney after all those years was far more exciting than she had imagined. It was a joy to bring home her daughter Marietta who had grown up in England and was a beautiful young lady. She had expected her old friends to rally around, and she was not disappointed.

They were staying at the Majestic Hotel while Wilkin House was being remodelled and refurnished. It really was a very happy homecoming and made more interesting for Vicky by the presence of Juan Rivadavia who had been at the wharf to meet them.

While she was living in England, the Rowan-Smiths had insisted that Marietta attend St Cecile's Convent in Paris, an expensive finishing school, and on one of her visits to her daughter, Vicky had noticed the name of Rivadavia on the list of students. It was such an unusual name. She had never forgotten him, the handsome young Argentinian who had bought Chelmsford. She had sought out Rosa Rivadavia, finding that she was indeed Rivadavia's daughter from New South Wales, and invited her to visit them in England. The two girls had become the best of friends. And when they graduated who better to accompany Rosa on the long voyage home but Marietta and her mother? Rivadavia not only approved, Rosa told them, he was delighted.

Of course she heard all about the Rivadavia family; how Rosa's mother had died, that he had married a young English woman but the marriage was not a success, that his wife hated New South Wales and now lived in England; and that Rosa reciprocated with her dislike for her step-mother.

Rivadavia was as handsome as ever, more so perhaps, Vicky thought, more elegant.

He had taken over the burdensome arrangements of landing their belongings and sported them to a celebration dinner at the Majestic Hotel with gifts and flowers for all three ladies.

Vicky had been stunned, on opening a small silver-wrapped package, to find a slim fob watch set with diamonds. 'Mr Rivadavia, this is too much,' she had said.

'My gratitude for delivering my daughter safely home and for your kindness to her,' he had replied.

The girls were still ecstatic at their presents: a pearl necklace with a tiny diamond clasp for Marietta and a magnificent diamond and ruby necklace for Rosa.

Vicky could not get over the change in Sydney, the new buildings, the stylish shops, the gas-lit streets, and then there was always Chelmsford. Rosa had insisted that she and Marietta come out to visit the station and Vicky was looking forward to seeing it again.

To please his daughter Rivadavia had agreed to stay on in Sydney for the festive season and it seemed natural that he should escort Vicky to various functions since they shared the company of their daughters. They were all looking forward to the Christmas Eve Ball at Government House.

Vicky's neighbour, Mary Cormack, was intrigued that the mysterious Rivadavia should be at Vicky's beck and call. 'He's very friendly with the Heselwoods,' she said. 'There's even talk that he seems more friendly with her than him.'

'That wouldn't be difficult,' Vicky scowled. 'She's the better of the pair.'

'Oh now, you must forget all that unpleasantness,' Mary told her. 'We all get along so well. Wait until you meet the Governor. He's charming,

408

and a widower, Vicky. Don't forget your friend Rivadavia is married.'

'Good heavens,' Vicky protested. 'I'm hardly on home shores yet. I'm not thinking of marriage.' Which was almost true. It was too soon to think of marriage, but he was a charming and attractive man.

He took her to the Governor's dinner party and she realised that he and FitzRoy were firm friends, in part due to their mutual interest in racing and cards. She wondered what else they got up to, since it was obvious they both also enjoyed the company of ladies. At one stage she heard them arranging to go to a race meeting at Parramatta and was surprised at the anger she felt. It was the first time she had experienced jealousy for many years and it hurt. By the time Christmas came Vicky was deeply in love with Rivadavia and feeling very insecure. She was afraid of losing him and uncomfortably aware that no further mention had been made of her visit with Marietta to Chelmsford.

The ball was a glittering occasion. All of Sydney society had turned out in their finery; crinolines of silk and satin swirled in the ballroom under the huge crystal chandeliers, and magnificent jewellery glittered in the brilliantly lit room.

Sir Charles, looking dashing in full dress uniform with an array of impressive medals, led Georgina and Jasin over to a large silver punch bowl. 'You must try this, it is a special recipe of champagne and strawberries and curacao and sundries, and is delicious.'

'Thank you, we will,' Georgina said. 'It is a magnificent evening Sir Charles, you've really outdone yourself this time.'

A woman tapped Sir Charles on the arm with her fan and he turned to her without a trace of irritation at her rudeness. 'Why Mrs Paget, I was just coming over to chat with you. You know Lord and Lady Heselwood?'

'Indeed I do Sir Charles. Our station is not far from Carlton Park. We had hoped to see Lady Heselwood out our way sometime.' She looked past him at Georgina. 'Or do you never venture out west milady?'

FitzRoy answered for Georgina. 'My dear! Lady Heselwood has ventured further into the wilds than any of us.'

'Oh quite,' she replied, unimpressed. 'I forgot. But Sir Charles, we are very civilised out our way now. They say our place, Blair Station, is quite outstanding.'

Georgina saw a twinkle in his eye as he spoke. 'So I have heard. I believe Mr Paget has built a castle on the property, absolutely intriguing! And how wonderful for all the Pagets to be living in a castle out there on the plains. Don't tell me you haven't seen it Lady Heselwood?'

'No, Sir Charles,' Georgina said, not daring to utter another word; she had heard of the Paget castle, a monstrosity, a two-storied, twin-towered, turreted castle of blue stone.

'What remarkable ingenuity,' Sir Charles was saying. 'Where did Mr Paget get the idea?'

'He's entitled to a castle, Your Excellency,' Mrs Paget said. 'I have been waiting for an opportunity to tell you all about it. On his last visit to Scotland, Mr Paget discovered that one of his ancestors was a baronet.'

Mrs Paget launched into her tale, a familiar story among the colonists who had acquired wealth and were now anxious to shake off their humble origins. They were paying fortunes to British genealogists to search out, by hook or by crook, some aristocratic bloodline. Georgina found it sad that people could not accept that their own achievements were sufficient. The Pagets had amassed immense fortunes in Australia, and that took brains and energy.

Beside her Jasin was talking to, or rather listening to, a Colonel Norbert and a slight pressure on her arm indicated that he wanted to move on but through the crowds, directly ahead of them, Georgina saw Vicky Rowan-Smith, looking very elegant too; a different person, her face, now free of freckles, a shining ivory, and the unruly curls formally dressed behind a glittering tiara. As a delaying tactic, Georgina turned back to Mrs Paget. 'You must tell me more about the castle.'

FitzRoy used the pause to escape and was soon engulfed in an adjoining group. 'I feel remiss,' Georgina said, 'that I haven't had a chance to visit Carlton Park. It was our first station you know. I thought I might pay a visit sometime next year.'

Mrs Paget was delighted, her fan working overtime. 'You simply must visit us too. We shall arrange some entertainment for you. A race meeting perhaps.'

'That would be most enjoyable.'

'Do you see who we have ahead?' Jasin hissed.

'Mrs Paget was saying we should visit their station my dear,' Georgina said, hoping to distract him.

'A splendid idea,' he said absently. 'Would you excuse us madam.'

He manoeuvred Georgina steadily through the crush, taking his time, chatting to acquaintances on the way. 'Would you look at her,' he whispered to Georgina, 'decked out like a Christmas tree.'

Georgina sighed. Vicky's dress of dark green and silver taffeta was spectacular, the beading alone was superb. They were now moving inexorably towards Vicky who was standing with Rivadavia. She had seen them, Georgina knew, but was making no attempt to avoid their company, so perhaps all was well.

'Lady Rowan-Smith, I do declare,' Jasin said, nodding to Juan.

'Jasin.' Vicky inclined her head, ignoring his title. 'And Georgina. How nice it is to see you again. You know Mr Rivadavia, of course.'

At least Juan was pleased to see them and he called to a waiter to bring them champagne, which gave Jasin a chance to address Vicky. 'Sorry to hear of Sir Percy's death. What a miserable thing to happen to you, poor Vicky, to have a second husband pass away on you.'

'I was brought up not to dwell on unhappiness Jasin,' she said, and as the music commenced Georgina hoped they could move away.

But Jasin persisted. 'And how is Delia, Juan? What is she up to these days?'

'Quite well, as far as I know,' Juan said with unaffected nonchalance.

'Lovely girl,' Jasin said to Vicky. 'You have been in England all this time. Did you meet Mrs Rivadavia?'

'I did not have the honour,' Vicky replied, her eyes cool. She turned, and seeing a woman friend, threw out her arms in what seemed to be a spontaneous gesture, turning her back on the Heselwoods – without apology.

'She hasn't changed,' Jasin snapped as they walked towards the supper room.

'On the contrary,' Georgina replied. 'I think she has changed a great deal.'

Lady Rowan-Smith attended social functions with Juan Rivadavia over the holiday season, mostly at the instigation of their daughters, but their relationship had not developed beyond the use of Christian names. Marietta was still talking about going out to Chelmsford Station and working out what clothes she should take when Vicky drew her attention to the fact that they had yet to be formally invited.

'But I have,' Marietta said. 'Rosa is talking about it all the time.'

'Mr Rivadavia hasn't said a word to me.'

'He will, Mother. You know what men are like. They forget.'

Vicky couldn't imagine Juan Rivadavia forgetting so she waited for a chance to approach the subject, tactfully. He had hired a cutter for a Sunday cruise on the Harbour. About forty people had been invited and they were having a very enjoyable day with plenty of good food and refreshment and a quartet of musicians to entertain. 'This is your last Sunday in town isn't it Juan?'

'Yes. It's time to go home.'

'You will forgive me for asking, but Marietta seems to think she might be going with you. I don't want her to force her company on you.'

'Marietta could never do that, she is always welcome.' He took her down to the bow of the boat where they sat on richly cushioned benches. 'When you have time, I should like to invite you also to Chelmsford, Vicky, but you understand, I am married. It is awkward for me. I must set an example for my daughter, and also people talk.'

'I am not concerned about what people say.'

'You should be. You have a good reputation. I am considering having my marriage annulled. What do you think of that?'

'From what I hear it is about time,' she said directly, pleased at the news.

'I suppose it is,' he laughed. 'I shall miss your company when I leave. But we will be down at Easter for the Agricultural Show so I hope to see you then.'

By chance Vicky met Mrs Forrest, at a charity morning tea. She was the wife of a wealthy merchant, and, Vicky realised, these were the people who had been feuding with the Heselwoods over Carlton Park. Before long Milly was

411

telling her all about it. 'He's an oily customer Lord Heselwood,' Milly said, 'and that son of his is no better. They say he's quite the rake, even in town, and we hear all sorts of stories about him from station people. But I hear you owned Chelmsford before Juan Rivadavia, Lady Rowan-Smith. Isn't that fascinating?' She giggled and almost nudged Vicky in the ribs. 'Of course, Rivadavia himself is fascinating too, wouldn't you say?'

'He's a charming man,' Vicky allowed and Mrs Forrest nodded. 'You'd be ideal for him. He should get out of that other marriage and snap you up while the going's good.'

Although she found Mrs Forrest too brash for her taste, Vicky warmed to her. One could hardly dislike such an obvious ally. And the Forrests were well known to Juan. Old friends, it seemed.

Marietta went out to Chelmsford for a few weeks, stayed longer, and came home bubbling with excitement about her wonderful holiday, the strangeness of the countryside, the kindness of Rivadavia, and the fun they'd had with other station people. She was glowing with news. 'Rosa has a beau now.'

'Who?'

'The Honourable Edward Heselwood, no less,' Marietta crowed. 'And it is serious too, but they're not saying anything for the minute. Edward will be taking over Carlton Park himself, any day. We went out to visit and it's a big station and the house is lovely. It will be Rosa's home when they get married. The manager, Mr Passey, is going north to manage another of the Heselwood stations.'

Vicky retired to her room to think about this. At first she was relieved that young Heselwood had set his cap for Rosa and not her own daughter but then she thought about the connections. Heselwoods again! If she married Juan they'd be members of the same family group. Almost enough to make one think again. And another thing, by all accounts Edward Heselwood, the Honourable or not, was by no means the white knight these young girls saw. That was a worry. Rosa was too young to be involved with him in this silly flirtation. Juan really ought to be told. Vicky thought of writing to him but feared that any intrusion on her part would be resented.

And then she softened, amused at herself. What did it matter? None of them mattered except Juan himself. And there were many problems to overcome before he could think of marriage.

But the next time she met Milly Forrest at St James's Church fete, Vicky couldn't resist mentioning that young Edward Heselwood had his eye on Rosa Rivadavia. In passing of course, just in passing. She seemed to have forgotten Milly's remarks about his reputation.

It didn't take long for that shot to reach its mark.

Marietta received a distraught letter from Rosa, that there had been the most awful row at Chelmsford and her father had got it all out of her. He had accosted Edward at the yearling sales and threatened to horsewhip him for daring to discuss marriage with his daughter. 'It seems,' Rosa wrote, 'that people have been telling lies about Edward. Father even went so far as to say his reputation in the district was unsavoury, but I'm sure he didn't mean that. He was just angry. Nevertheless I have had a note from Edward and he is still quite determined. When I am of age it will be a different matter.'

'Marietta,' the letter went on, 'your mother knows Lord and Lady Heselwood. Do ask her to put in a good word. And with Father too, for that matter.'

'It is such a shame,' Marietta said. 'They make a very handsome couple. Will you speak for them, Mother?'

'I'll see,' Vicky said, using the age-old parental reply. 'I'll see.'

# PART FOURTEEN
## WARUNGA COUNTRY

# CHAPTER ONE

Juan Rivadavia walked into his office and stoked up the fire. It was a cold night, Rosa had gone off to bed early and the station was quiet, which would give him a chance to read the pile of Sydney newspapers awaiting his attention. He placed them on the wide desk and put the lamp alongside, turning up the mantle so that the room was as bright as day, and sat down to read.

He saw that there was great excitement in Sydney, the railway line had been completed between Redfern and Parramatta, and Sir Charles FitzRoy had made a speech about how the railways would open up this country, so lacking in navigable waterways like North America, and he nodded, Sir Charles was right. Once the railways reached inland there would be no stopping the expansion of the colony.

He turned the pages and read on. Gold! That was all people could think about since they found gold at Bathurst. There were success stories and hard luck stories. It seemed that if a writer could get the word 'gold' into his copy then it would be printed.

Irritated, he passed over a few more pages and then he saw it! He grasped the page and read it again. A gentleman by the name of Christopher Allingham had set out from the Liverpool Plains with two Aborigine guides, taking the route mapped out by Ludwig Leichhardt, and had ridden to the far north and back. He had followed the great Burdekin River but had not ventured into the tropical jungles of the Cape York Peninsula where no white men dared roam since Kennedy's death. Instead, he had turned back at a green and fertile valley which he said had already been named by Leichhardt. It was called Valley of Lagoons.

Juan stood up and walked over to a cupboard and from a wide deep drawer he took out the plans that he and Pace MacNamara had been working on. A Sydney chartmaker had transposed Leichhardt's chart onto a linen scroll, which he now unrolled from its varnished wooden pins. That had been his own idea at the time since insects and mould destroyed paper in this climate. What had happened to their dream over the years he wondered? I suppose we all get too busy. Now look at this! Here it is in a newspaper – Valley of Lagoons. For all the world to know about! What fools we have been! We should have gone years ago.

He turned up the other newspapers of around the same date, searching for more details. There it was in the *Gazette*, with their usual inattention to

416

detail. Mr Christopher Allingham had set off northwards, from Canning Downs . . . 'Oh damn!' Juan cried, talking to himself now in his excitement. 'That's the Leslie station!' . . . through the Toowoomba swamps, journeying inland with Brisbane to the east.

'Right past our station!' Juan snorted. 'Wait until Pace hears about this!'

*Mr Allingham,* he read, *traversed the waterholes and channels of the wide Burdekin River and discovered a tributary which he named the Starr River and at the end of the trail he stood looking down at the Valley of Lagoons. Only the second white visitation of the area after the Leichhardt expedition, to gaze on these splendid pastures. Mr Allingham marked out two large runs and calmly turned about for the fifteen hundred mile ride home.*

Juan thumped the table. It was the same place! And Allingham had done it on his own!

He wondered how they had come to let this idea lose priority, and studied the chart again. Valley of Lagoons was still far beyond the frontiers, they'd assumed that there was plenty of time, and now an intrepid young man had ridden out unnoticed, a David taking on Goliath. Juan grinned at the audacity of such a ride. What a feat! While all he and Pace had done was to talk about it.

He pushed the newspapers aside. What was he doing sitting here like an old man with this challenge staring him in the face? Allingham, it had said, had taken up two large runs, so there was more land available. He would ride out to Kooramin Station tomorrow and show Pace the newspaper articles. He wanted to see his face.

Pace MacNamara did not disappoint him. He stared at the paper and then threw it down. 'Well I'll be damned! We've been left at the post! I'd always banked on getting some of that land.'

'We still can,' Juan said. 'Why don't we go anyway? As soon as possible.'

Pace looked doubtful. 'I can't go for a while yet. Not until after mustering anyway. And I've got a big mob to bring down from the Peel.'

'So what? Send your men to do it – wind things up here and then we'll go.'

'Go where?' Dolour came in, untying her apron.

'The Valley of Lagoons,' Pace said, and she laughed. 'Lord help us! You're not on about that again?'

They showed her the cuttings about Allingham and she read them with interest but shook her head. 'Over a thousand miles away. That's ridiculous.'

'It's less from our Brisbane Valley station,' Pace said.

'It might as well be more for all the good it will do you. You're too old for a journey like that MacNamara.'

Juan stood back and listened to them. If he had needed a persuader, Dolour was now filling the role expertly. He tried not to laugh as

MacNamara exploded. 'Too old am I? I tell you woman I'm a better bushman than any man on this property and I can outlast any of them in the saddle. Too bloody old? I haven't had a day's sickness in my life and I've still got my own teeth.'

'All right then, maybe you could do it, but it's dangerous Pace. And you don't need to go. We've got enough land now.'

'Oh I give up.' Dolour sighed. 'What would you do with runs so far away.'

'One day there'll be cattle stations in the North ten times the size of the biggest stations down here,' Juan said. 'It will be the land of the few.'

'Just so's we're among the few,' Pace said. 'I won't be left out of this.'

Within weeks Juan was in Newcastle searching out the latest maps. The next time Pace came to Chelmsford Juan showed him the route he had worked out. 'We'll go over the Darling Downs and on to our station in the Brisbane Valley where we'll pick up supplies and go north from there. Overlanding all the way.'

'Why don't we go by ship?' Pace said. 'We could probably land here at Keppel Bay, there's a village, Rockhampton.'

'I thought of that. But we don't know how far inland we can get from Rockhampton. Leichhardt and Allingham both kept away from the coast. My plan is to change horses at the Brisbane Valley station. And from there we leave the packhorse behind and make a dash for it.'

Pace was still not convinced. 'There's one thing wrong. Andy would only have stock horses on that station, and we won't be able to buy better mounts. Good horses will be essential up there.'

'I thought of that. We will take a pair of thoroughbreds with us. We'll leave the packhorse and our first-stage horses with Andy and that's when the fast horses will be used. They can rest till then. I've got two very special horses I've chosen for the ride.' He put his head out the window and whistled to a station hand. 'Tell Jimmy at the stables to bring up Sonny,' he yelled.

They walked out into the courtyard and the groom came running in leading a chestnut stallion. 'This is Sonny, Pace. What do you think of him?'

Pace smoothed his hand along the horse's gleaming neck. 'He's magnificent. What a beauty!' He stood back to admire the horse again while the groom trotted Sonny proudly around the yard.

'He's yours,' Juan said.

'What do you mean, he's mine, man? He must be worth a fortune!'

'A gift horse MacNamara, you've heard of them. When we leave the station we'll be racing and I don't want to leave you behind. Sonny is the only horse in my stables that is a match for my horse Vencador. He's down in the fields.'

'Vencador! I've seen him. Are you bringing him? Well now I would need Sonny and I thank you. What a ride this will be. And we're not taking guides?'

'No. They'd slow us up. The compass and your bushmanship should get us there.' He laughed. 'And if there are any hostile blacks on the trail, we'll be moving too fast for them to be worrying us. All we have to do is mark out the runs, come back and wait.'

He arranged for Rosa to go down to stay with Vicky Rowan-Smith during his absence. The letter from Milly Forrest had been annoying but a timely warning. Unfortunate that the Heselwood son should have such a reputation (stockmen being notorious gossips, everyone in the district knew he used opium and consorted with blacks) and rather embarrassing now that he'd decided to single out Rosa for his attentions, but he would not be permitted to see Rosa again. Under no circumstances. Even if it meant breaking off the friendship with the Heselwoods, the son was their problem not his.

Jasin, Lord Heselwood read the newspaper account of Allingham's ride too, and decided to charter a boat to take him up there, but it was difficult to locate the type of craft he required. Finally he called on Major Mitchell at his offices where he was presented with a copy of Mitchell's book, *The Australian Geography.*

'Where were you thinking of taking this ship to?' Mitchell enquired.

'To Halifax Bay. I'm determined to get to the Valley of Lagoons. I've always had my eye on it.'

'Yes I remember,' Mitchell said quietly. 'But keep in mind, poor Kennedy's expedition set off from Rockingham Bay just north of Halifax. But we don't go into that now. Suffice it to say, that behind your Halifax Bay is a mountain range and there's no pass. You won't get over those mountains. The eastern side of that Seaview Range is high and sharp, no waters come down, which suggests that the land on the western side is good fertile country.' He shook his head. 'The Valley of Lagoons might seem to be close to the coast but approaching it from there is out of the question.'

'Then how do I get to the Valley?'

'I wouldn't have it on my conscience sending you into that territory. Go and see a fellow called Dalrymple. He has just arrived in Sydney and is keen to get up that way. Better still, I'll introduce you. He's very much aware of the prospects up there but he's cautious. The blacks in the north are dangerous. Leichhardt's east to west expedition has never been found. God knows where they perished.'

'Why Dalrymple?'

'Because he's forming a syndicate. I'm only recommending you because you can afford it. There are vast pasture lands up there but they will need considerable investment to be effectively used. My advice to you is to

419

throw in your lot with Dalrymple. You'll never look back and you'll live to see the dawn of a cattle industry in Australia that will rival the sheep barons.'

Everyone on Kooramin station turned out to witness the departure of the boss and his friend Rivadavia on their expedition into the unknown in spite of winds that heralded a welcome storm. Rain clouds were building up over the hills and the intermittent rolls of thunder added to the excitement. Station blacks roamed the yards while their children thirstily drank the lemonade the missus always put out for them on special days.

Paul MacNamara had been begging Pace for days to let him come with them. 'There's still time Dad. I can ride with you. I won't hold you back.'

'I keep telling you,' Pace said, 'you're to stay here and run the station for your mother. Let up on me, John's not nagging me like this. And you keep your eye on young Duke, your mother can't be everywhere.'

Juan was waiting patiently for him, talking to the men who were admiring Vencador. Pace knew Rivadavia would understand the delay. Dolour had been upset and he'd had to sit and quieten her, not wanting to leave her with the miseries, he'd done that to her once before.

At last she came out looking reasonably calm and they prepared to leave. Juan walked over and kissed her on both cheeks and she took a little cloth shamrock she had made and put it in a buttonhole of his black leather waistcoat. 'That's for good luck Juan. Now don't go taking any chances. If it's hard going you'll turn back won't you? And look after that husband of mine.'

He patted her on the shoulder. 'You take care while we're away. I won't let him get into any trouble.'

Pace laughed. 'I'll come second to that horse of his. If Vencador gets his feet wet Rivadavia'll probably turn around and come home.'

'We'll see about that MacNamara.' Juan slid his rifle into the saddle pouch and swung into the saddle.

Pace kissed Dolour goodbye while the audience cheered, and he looked up, laughing. 'You'd think I was going to England instead of a fine ride into the country.'

# CHAPTER TWO

South from Kooramin, at Carlton Park, the new manager, Edward Heselwood, was having trouble, but it was trouble he blamed on his Maker, an act of God. They'd had a fortnight of heavy rain and the Namoi rolled down from the hills and rushed into dried-up creeks, pouring across caked and cracked mud too swiftly to be absorbed, surging into blind gullies trapping cattle that had wandered into the cool patches of green.

There were men who said Passey would never have allowed this to happen. But it was not said to Edward, who entered a loss of forty head in his journal where it should have been eighty. There was no-one to contradict him.

Nevertheless the accident worried him. He knew his father was concerned, overly concerned he considered, about accounting for each and every one of his livestock. To make up the loss he picked up fifty head from a fast-talking drover, who complained that he was sick of the trail, and who sold them to Edward cheaply, for cash.

With the Belcher brothers, Edward swung the cattle about to take them home to Carlton Park and by the time the trio arrived on their home station, the herd had almost doubled, since they had collected unbranded cattle on the way through the fenceless properties.

'Finders keepers,' Edward had laughed and his friends had agreed. The only rule to respect in cattle duffing was not to get caught.

A week later, Jack Temple, the head stockman, baled Edward up. 'Where'd you get that last herd? Half of them are diseased. We'll have to shoot them before they infect the whole bloody station.'

'Don't shoot any of my cattle,' Edward warned. 'You leave them alone.'

'We have to shoot them, otherwise you'll have none. You've been sold someone else's trouble, a right mess.'

Edward watched as the stockmen cut out the diseased newcomers and shot them, while others toiled in the mud digging a huge pit to burn the carcases, and he turned away in disgust.

A few days later, to stop Temple's grumbling he promoted him to foreman and allowed him to choose his own head stockman which caused Ben Belcher to complain. 'I thought you'd be making me head stockman, us being mates and all.'

But Edward would not interfere. He realised if he were to keep the place in order he would have to rely on men like Temple or he would have his father to answer to. And the Belcher brothers were not his mates, they were simply the only company around. He was looking forward to his next visit to Sydney when he would be a man with his own station. Sydney went mad over squatters and with good reason. He had been astonished to see just how much his father was earning from cattle and he now understood the perpetual urge to acquire more land, more runs, more herds.

Remembering his altercation with Rivadavia, he laughed. He would marry Rosa, it was a fine feeling to have one's future mapped out, it gave him time to plan. Rosa was beautiful with her dark eyes and rosebud mouth and she was no colonial clod, having spent two years in Europe.

His parents, of course, had heard about the row, God knew who had pimped on him, and his mother was worried but his father was amused. 'The damn cheek of the Spaniard eh? You'll probably forget about her when the next beauty comes along but if not, marry her. Your choice of wife must be your own. It is possible though that he'll cut her off without a penny.'

'I don't care if he does,' Edward said stoutly, but sometimes he wondered about that. Everyone knew Rivadavia was immensely wealthy, Rosa would inherit a fortune one day. The combined fortunes of the Heselwoods and the Rivadavias would give the Honourable Edward Heselwood considerable influence in the colony.

It was Sunday again and the weekend was a disappointment. Edward had been invited to revels over at Paton's castle, a hideous place but they entertained in style. At the last minute a rider had come in with a note of apology, the party had been cancelled, several of the family were down with mumps. Now he was stuck with Ben and Max for company.

He never invited them into the house, they understood that, it was enough to sit up on the wide verandah with him. He watched some horsemen ride out. 'Where are they going?' he asked.

'After brumbies,' Max said, 'they reckon now the river's up, a lot of them can't get back to the hills. They're cut off like.'

'What happens when they catch them?' Edward wanted to know.

'Finders keepers, fair game the wild horses,' Max told him.

'Let's go and watch,' Edward said. 'Saddle a horse for me Ben.'

'Righto boss.' Ben lumbered off.

'If those horses are on my land they should be my property,' Edward said but Max shook his head. 'No, they move too fast, you never know whose land they're on after a while.'

They joined up with the others and followed the chase, but just when the men thought they had caught a small herd of ten brumbies, the horses broke loose and were away again. By midday Edward had had enough. 'They'll never catch them.'

'Oh yes, they'll get them,' Ben said. 'It looks like a lot of backing and filling but they're narrowing the circle all the time. In the end the horses'll have nowhere to go but in through the gates down there.'

'Bull!' his brother said. 'Those weak rails won't hold them. The stallion will kick the shit out of them. Or throw his mares at them. He won't care if his women get hurt, plenty more for him to shove it into. Hey Ben,' he started to laugh, 'did you see that big red bull yesterday in the rear paddock?'

'Ah Christ yes,' Ben laughed. He climbed down from his horse and pulled a bottle of rum from his saddlepack. 'You want a drink boss?'

'It's not that overproof stuff again is it?' Edward asked but he kneed his horse into the shade, dismounted and reached for the bottle, pleased at least to get first drink from the top, he really didn't like having to share but was chary about wiping the mouth of the bottle. They had laughed at him about that once before. 'God!' he choked. 'It tastes like kerosene.'

'A few more swigs and you won't notice,' Ben said.

They sat propped on whitened tree trunks and handed around the quart bottle. 'Firewater,' Ben nodded appreciatively.

'What did the bull do anyway?' Edward asked, and the brothers began to laugh again.

'He's a real ripper that one,' Max chortled. 'If he can't get at the heifers he goes up the steers, he's got a donger as big as a leg and he don't care where he puts it as long as he puts it somewhere.'

'We got a couple of blokes in the bunkhouse much the same,' Ben snickered, handing on the bottle.

They were right, Edward noticed, by the fourth swig it wasn't tasting too bad at all.

'What do you mean?' he asked, and the brothers roared, pleased to be one up on the boss.

'What do you think we mean? If it's standing up you got to do something. You can't blame 'em.'

'Passey was heavy on it though, wouldn't have it,' Max said.

'Oh Passey was a bloody old prude. All right for him with his missus waiting.'

Edward listened to them, not wanting to show his disapproval but at the same time feeling a stirring, an excitement, as they talked. Ben struggled to his feet hitching at his bulging crotch. 'Cripes. Look at me! I've got the hots myself.'

For one second Edward thought, feared, Ben might unleash his pants.

'We call him horse,' Max laughed. 'Horse,' he cackled. 'You should see it! Hey, show us, horse!'

But Ben was pointing down the gully, distracted. 'Look down here.' He pointed to a small herd of cattle filing through the scrub into the gully. 'We're way out on the perimeter of Craddock's station. The road's only a half a mile away.' He took off through the scrub.

'Where's he going?' Edward asked, nonplussed at this sudden change.

'To see if they're branded,' Max whispered. 'Hidden away out here they could've been missed.'

423

'And if they're not?' The play dawning on him, Edward asked only as a matter of course.

'We could grab them.'

Edward walked forward to get a better look. Why not? It had been a boring wasted day. He could see Ben walking through the herd looking for brands.

'Craddock'd never know,' Max urged.

Ben was waving to them, his hands clasped above his head in a victory salute. 'Do you want them?' Max asked.

'Yes,' Edward said. 'Bring them out.'

'Right you are,' Max laughed. 'Let's get them.'

'It was a lark,' Ben whined to Jack Temple. 'Just a lark.'

'That's right,' Max said. 'We were only fooling around.'

'Then you tell me again what happened,' Jack Temple snarled, 'and if you tell me any more lies I'll break your bloody jaws.'

So Max began again . . .

'We were bringing these cattle down the road, a joke that's all it was, we'd had a few drinks and it was hot.'

'Bugger the bloody cattle. What happened?' Temple shouted.

'It's got to do with it though . . .'

Temple had brought his head stockman, Taffy, and a drover called McGinty in to witness the statements, and they were tiring of this slow process. Taffy walked to the end of the empty shed and picked up a whip. 'We'll thrash it out of them.'

Ben started screaming. 'You got no right to touch me, you bastards.'

'Take him out of here McGinty,' Temple said. 'We'll get the story again one at a time.'

As McGinty pushed Ben to the door, Taffy suddenly lashed out with the stockwhip giving Ben a neat cut across his backside which sent him yelping forward. Even Max laughed.

'You'll laugh on the other side of your face in a minute,' Temple said. 'This time we'll have the truth or Taffy'll pick every stitch off you with his whip.'

'I'm trying to tell you,' Max complained. 'We were out on the road with the cattle when Mrs MacNamara comes trotting along and she's got a little nigger kid on the horse with her. Well I lifts the lid and say good day to her but she's staring at the cattle. "What are you fellers doing?" she asks.

'Eddie's across the other side of the road and he says, "We're just bringing in some cattle for the Craddocks."

'Well Mrs MacNamara gets down off her horse and starts looking at the cattle and Eddie climbs down too, and they have an argument because it turns out we were on MacNamara's land, still a mile off Craddock's. Now I gave Eddie the wink that we'd better bolt, no-one gets into grips with MacNamara, he'd put a hole in you quick as look at you, but he takes no

424

notice. She's going crook that we're duffing her cattle and that she'll set her husband onto us and that's where Ben joins in. He's laughing. "MacNamara's gone walkabout boss. Her old man's gone up north with Rivadavia from Chelmsford."

'Then Mrs MacNamara wakes up who Eddie is and she's wild, got the real Irish paddy up by this. "You're Edward Heselwood!" she says. "You ought to be ashamed of yourself. I'm going to report you to the police."

'But Eddie's talking as if she's not there. He looks back at me. "Is this Mrs MacNamara?"

' "Yes," I say. "Maybe we made a mistake eh?" I'm giving him the out.

' "You sure have," she shouts. "You leave the cattle here and get going or I'll have you up for stealing them."

'Now we're all a bit boozed remember, only got the rum in our bellies, and I thought Eddie was just wound up with Dutch courage when he refuses to let go the cattle, but he had to go one better. "You won't pimp on me," he says to her. "My father told me all about you, you were his convict whore, weren't you?" '

Temple stiffened and looked at Taffy. 'Jesus!'

Taffy glared at Max. 'He was lying, the little shit.' But Max shook his head. 'I don't reckon he was, Taffy.' He shifted from one foot to another. 'Can't I sit down?'

'Not until you finish,' Temple said.

'All right then. Well, this was news to me and Ben, and it stopped her in her tracks, just for a moment though. She whirled on Eddie and gave him a crack across the face and would have followed through with another only he grabbed her and he was laughing at her. He pulled her off the road into the bush and her kicking like a wild filly. "Get hold of her," Eddie yells, so Ben and me grab hold of her. Now the black kid must have bolted, we didn't even see him go, with all this fuss going on, because now it's got into a real free-for-all, she was struggling so much her shirt was just about ripped off.'

He licked his lips and grinned, remembering. 'She's a real good sort, I tell you.'

Temple punched him in the face and he crashed to the floor. Taffy yanked him to his feet again. 'Let him finish, Jack. The damage is done now.'

Max rubbed his jaw. 'You didn't have to do that, Temple, I only said . . .' He looked at his interrogators and decided to continue. 'Well anyway, we've got her, the three of us and she's calling us for everything. She's no lady I tell you, you should have heard the language. I never even knew she was a convict until then. But anyway the struggling is going on and we're holding her down like for branding, that's what it seemed like' and it musta put the idea in Eddie's head because he says, "Let's see what's inside these britches." She was wearing britches you know, men's pants.

So it was just a lark and Ben's chuckling away while Eddie gets her boots off and then we get the britches off but she's got ladies drawers on underneath, and now we're all getting a bit hot and it's gone quiet, because she's still struggling but tight-mouthed now, not making a sound but she took some holding. We get the drawers half off and Eddie's unbuckling his pants. I swear we wouldn't have touched her, not Ben and me, no fear, but Eddie's the boss and he wanted her and she was there for the taking.'

'He's being real quiet to her. "We're not going to hurt you Dolour," he says. "It is Dolour isn't it?"'

'And I thought it was funny she was so quiet but all of a sudden she shouts, "Get the gun!"'

'We didn't know who she was talking to. I thought the black kid had come back, he wouldn't be much help, and we looked around and there was no-one. But next thing this big black gin looms up, that Tingum woman, Maia, from Kooramin and she's got Mrs MacNamara's rifle.'

'I told her to bugger off and Eddie turns around. "Put that gun down," he says to her but Mrs MacNamara's fighting mad.'

' "Shoot," she yells and the gin didn't need a second telling she just fired the bloody gun. She didn't take aim or anything, just pulled the trigger and bang! Eddie's down on the ground screaming, the bullet went straight into his knee. I mean the stupid bitch could have killed any one of us.'

'Or she could have missed,' Taffy scowled.

'That's right. But Mrs MacNamara cuts loose while we're trying to look after the boss. She stood there pulling the shirt and drawers into place, grabs the gun and sent the gin to get our guns. Then she told us to get going. She wouldn't let us do a thing for Eddie and him crying with the pain, so we had to get him on his horse with him bleeding like a stuck pig.'

'Why didn't you take him to Craddock's place? It was closer,' Temple asked.

'He wouldn't let us. We stopped down the road and bandaged him up and brought him home. And you know the rest.' He looked from one to the other. 'Is his leg gonna be all right?'

'I don't know,' Temple said. 'We have to wait for the doctor to get here. Ah you stupid bastards. What a bloody mess this is.'

'Too right it is,' Max said. 'You want to get that gin. She'll go up for shooting a white man.'

Jack Temple stared at him and then hooked his head at Taffy. 'Get him out of here before I shoot *his* bloody knee off.'

A week later Sergeant Buchanan rode into Kooramin station to have, as he put it, 'a little talk,' with Mrs MacNamara, and Dolour brought her foreman, Joe Donnelly, and his wife, Sheena, in to witness the conversation.

'I hear there has been a bit of an altercation out here,' he said to

426

Donnelly, who nodded. 'Yes, the wife and I know about it, but Mrs MacNamara hasn't mentioned it to anyone else here yet, especially not her sons.'

'That's sensible,' Buchanan said. 'Makes it easier to sort it out. Now I believe one of the Kooramin gins shot Mr Edward Heselwood in the knee. The leg will be stiff for life, the Doc tells me.'

Dolour sat resolutely in her chair and the Donnellys, taking her lead, had nothing to say.

Buchanan took out his notebook. 'The name of the gin is Maia. Is that correct?'

'It is,' Dolour said.

'And I suppose she's gone walkabout?' Buchanan grinned.

'She has not. She is here in the house. Maia has no reason to run.' Dolour's voice was firm.

Buchanan coughed. 'I got the full story from Jack Temple, and in the case of you being worried Mrs MacNamara, I thought I'd do best to call in and tell you that Mr Heselwood will not be preferring charges.'

'That's good news,' Donnelly said. 'Maia was just trying to aid her mistress. She didn't even take aim.'

'So I heard. We'll write it off as an accident.' He closed the book.

'Can I get you a drink and something to eat, Sergeant?' Mrs Donnelly asked him.

'That wouldn't go astray now,' he replied and settled back, the business concluded.

'Would you open your book again,' Dolour said.

Buchanan was surprised. 'What would that be for?'

'Because I want to prefer charges.'

'What charges?'

'I want to lay charges against Edward Heselwood and those two men . . . what were their names again Joe?'

Dully, Joe intoned the names as if he were already in court. 'Max Belcher and Ben Belcher. But Dolour, why?'

'I am charging them with duffing cattle from Kooramin and with assault upon my person with intent to rape.'

Buchanan's complexion took on a ruddy hue. 'Oh now, Mrs MacNamara, you should be a bit careful about these things. Dear me, hang on a minute.'

'Isn't it you I should be telling?'

'It's me all right, but as a friend let me tell you. I can understand your anger, but put it this way, Edward Heselwood came off second best.'

'And the other two got off scot free,' she added.

Buchanan tapped his knee and appealed to Donnelly. 'You better talk this over with Mrs MacNamara.'

'There no need,' Dolour said. 'My mind's made up. It's the legal answer, otherwise there could be more trouble. How do you think John

427

and Paul MacNamara are going to react when they find out what happened to their mother?'

Buchanan was annoyed. 'It's for me to keep the peace around here Mrs MacNamara. I'll talk to your boys myself. Besides, if you prefer charges everyone will be talking and that's not very nice for a woman in your position. It could be downright embarrassing.'

'What happened to me wasn't very nice,' she snapped.

'That's true, it was a shameful thing and I'm very sorry,' he said. 'But you see now I'm only trying to spare you any more upsets.'

Dolour stared at him, waiting.

He sighed. 'Oh well, I'll take your statement. And a statement from Maia.'

'We'll give you that.'

He stared at his small notebook. 'I'll need a bigger sheet of paper. You've had a nasty experience, Mrs MacNamara. Can't you leave it at that?'

Dolour stood up. 'There's paper here on the desk, ready. And pen and ink too.'

When Buchanan departed looking irritated at having to retrace his steps to Carlton Park to do his duty, Joe Donnelly still tried to dissuade her. 'Don't do this Dolour. Wait until Pace gets home and talk it out with him.'

'Pace? Could you imagine me trying to talk over something like this with Pace? He'd be off to Carlton Park with a shotgun!'

'I suppose so. But Dolour, you could tell him . . . God Almighty, this is hard to say to a woman. But they didn't really get to you. You weren't raped. After all you weren't hurt.'

She looked at him, her eyes wet with tears. 'But that's where you're wrong Donnelly. I was hurt, desperately hurt. And I'll thank you to mind your own business. I'll fight my battles my own way. They won't beat me again.'

Dolour's decision caused an argument with her sons. They were all for riding over to Carlton Park immediately. But Dolour forbade them to leave and insisted that they abide by the law.

Another week passed, without incident until Sheena Donnelly came racing out to the storeroom where Dolour was cleaning down shelves to tell her a carriage was coming along the drive.

'Who is it?' Dolour said.

'I'm sure I don't know,' Sheena replied.

'Well you put them in the parlour, whoever they are, while I tidy myself up.'

She washed her face and hands in the laundry and slipped inside to the bedroom to comb her hair, grabbing at a small lace collar to brighten her plain brown working dress, pinning it into place with a cameo brooch.

Sheena put her head in the door. 'It's Lady Heselwood,' she breathed, and Dolour nodded. 'I was thinking it might be.'

She took off her work boots and put on a pair of soft leather pumps and went quietly down to the parlour. 'Lady Heselwood is it?' she asked, and Georgina smiled. 'Yes. And you're Mrs MacNamara? I'm very pleased to meet you after all this time. We've known your husband for many years.'

'So I believe. Won't you sit down?'

Georgina sat. 'And how is Pace?'

'He's very well, as far as I know. He's up north with Juan Rivadavia looking for land.'

'Oh yes, I heard. So is my husband. He's in Brisbane. I think they love the constant search for new land more than the actual acquisition.'

'That's true,' Dolour said, surprised that Heselwood's wife had the same opinion as her. 'They'll never have enough land.'

Dolour surveyed her visitor as she knew she was being surveyed, or assessed. Lady Heselwood looked very smart in a blue-grey silk dress with a soft hoop that allowed the dress to settle gently around her. She wore her years well, the creamy skin unlined and her fair hair swept back in neat rolls at the nape of her neck under a dark hat with a wide brim holding blue-grey plumes. It looked very elegant on her.

'Would you like tea?' she asked.

'Not just now thank you.'

Georgina clasped her gloved hands together and began. 'Mrs MacNamara, I have come to offer you my most abject apologies for the behaviour of my son.' There were tears in her eyes, and unaccountably Dolour felt a lump in her own throat. All she could do was nod as Lady Heselwood struggled on.

'I believe I have a true rendition of events from the foreman at Carlton Park, Mr Temple. I can't tell you how sorry I am that you were subjected to such indignity.'

Dolour was silent and Georgina took a deep breath. 'In all my life I have never felt so ashamed. I hope you will accept I am most sincere in this.'

The apology was unexpected and Dolour felt sorry for her. Temple would have told her what happened, but not all. Not the bit about being her husband's convict whore, surely, not the bit that Dolour would never forget. None of the men would dare mention that.

'Edward will apologise to you of course when he is able,' Georgina continued, 'God knows what his father will say.'

At that, Dolour's nervousness left her, remembering it was Heselwood who had caused the whole thing by boasting to his son, making their affair sound dirty.

'Is there anything I can say or do to make amends?' Georgina asked.

'There is not,' Dolour said. 'But I thank you for asking.'

They sat in awkward silence then Georgina spoke. 'Do you still intend to prefer charges, Mrs MacNamara?'

Dolour looked away. She didn't want to hurt the mother, but her voice was firm. 'I do.'

Georgina gave a heavy sigh as if there had been tears and this was a lingering aftermath. 'Don't you think Edward has been punished enough? His knee can't be restored. He will have a stiff leg for life.'

'That has nothing to do with it.'

'The other two have run off,' Georgina continued, 'leaving Edward to face the music on his own.'

'His choice of friends,' Dolour commented.

Georgina leaned forward. 'Mrs MacNamara. Let me tell you, in all honesty. You can't win cases like this. The cattle were not stolen in actual fact and you have them back. And no matter how appalling their handling of your person, you did not in fact suffer any personal injury.'

Dolour opened her mouth to speak but Georgina put her hand up. 'No, just a minute. I would agree with you that injury was involved, but the courts will not. They will not. And it isn't just the men, if there were women on juries they wouldn't convict either. You must understand you will lose on both counts.'

'I know I will.'

Georgina blinked, and stared in surprise. 'Then why on earth . . .?'

'British justice, Lady Heselwood. Did you know I was a convict?'

'No I did not.'

Dolour smiled, that answered the other question. The men were still all looking after themselves.

'The fact that you were a convict should make no difference Mrs MacNamara. I'm at a loss to know what to say here, except that you are a respected person in the community, don't put yourself through a dreadful court case which you cannot win.'

'I don't need to win,' Dolour said. 'I just want them brought up before the courts, then everyone will know what they are. They'll find the other two louts and bring them in.'

Her words left no doubt that she considered Edward Heselwood was also a lout and Georgina flushed.

'I will bring witnesses who will testify as to the character of the three of them, including Aborigine women,' Dolour said grimly, 'and Lady Heselwood, if I were you I'd stay home.'

'Mrs MacNamara, I beg you not to do this.'

'Now you wait,' Dolour said. 'A while ago you worried about what your husband will say. Can you imagine Pace? I don't want him in trouble over this. He's bound to want to retaliate and he'd be arrested for assault or worse. No, I am attending to this myself legally, it is the best way.'

Georgina shook her head. 'You might have convinced yourself you believe that but not me. I think you are simply being vindictive. You want to keep your revenge in your own hands. You've even produced a valid reason for being vindictive and everyone will believe you, but not me. Never.'

Dolour was not uncomfortable with that assessment. 'What if I am? I'll have them in the courts like any common criminals, that's all that matters.'

'I'm sorry you are taking this attitude,' Georgina said. 'Can't I appeal to you not to do this? Isn't there some other way?'

She looked surprised when Dolour replied, 'There is one other way.'

'What would that be?'

'Your son could go home to England.'

'Mrs MacNamara, this is his home. He was born in Australia, in Sydney.'

Dolour pushed her hair back from her face and her eyes took on a faraway look. 'I was born in Ireland and I was forcibly taken out of my country, and I hurt no-one.'

Shocked, Georgina drew back. 'Oh my God. Is that what this is all about?'

'I suppose we could say we've arrived at the cause and the solution in the one breath Lady Heselwood. You tell that son of yours to get out of the country now because I won't let up on him. If I lose the first time I will appeal and then anyone who missed the case the first time will hear about it the next time around. There'll be no-one left that will spit on him.'

'And you insist on this?'

'You English made the rules, not me.'

'Do you hate us so much?'

'I think I am being very reasonable,' Dolour said. 'He won't suffer like I did. Just tell your son to make himself scarce.'

'And you'll drop the charges?'

'Oh that I couldn't do. They're my insurance that he stays in England. But I'll delay to give him time to get going.'

Georgina stood up to leave. 'I will not retract my apologies to you but I think you are being very hard.'

'Convict ships make you hard.'

'My lawyers will probably offer you an out-of-court settlement.'

'Tell them not to waste their time.'

Georgina nodded as if expecting this reply. 'Then I'll bid you good day Mrs MacNamara.'

431

# CHAPTER THREE

With no packhorses to slow them down after they left the Brisbane Valley station, Pace and Juan travelled swiftly across open country, noting the weird shapes of mountains that jutted up from the horizon.

The next day was harder as they threaded their way through heavily timbered forests and on into endless hills that dropped down to wide gullies and streams, but by the third day they came to the Dawson River, right on schedule.

Leichhardt's route then took them through rich river flats and on to harsh brigalow scrub and then on a rough climb into the Christmas Ranges and down again to follow the Comet River.

Day after day they travelled northwards as fast as the terrain allowed, finding the journey strenuous but not as difficult as they had expected it to be, and on the grassy plains they were able to let the swift horses out to a steady gallop, making up for lost time.

The land seemed to be uninhabited but they knew it was not, and while they were now out of reach of bushrangers they kept watch for blacks.

It was not until they got past the Isaac River, and were searching for a gap in the ranges that they blundered into a blacks' camp.

Women screamed, the horses plunged, and black men grabbed their spears running forward to bar the way.

Pace kept his hand on his pistol while Juan dismounted and walked forward towards the Aborigines who stood tall, their coal-black bodies poised to react. Juan smiled and bowed and tried some Aborigine words to no effect. 'Wrong language,' he said to Pace. 'Pass me down a can of beans.'

Pace did so, all eyes on him, and Juan plunged his knife into the can. He fished out some beans with his fingers and began to eat with a show of relish and handed the can over.

The nearest Aborigine followed the instructions and ate some, passing the can around, but gave no indication of appreciation. It was obvious that they were not in awe of the white men.

'Ask them where the pass is,' Pace called.

'It would be a much better idea to just get out of here,' Juan replied.

'We could waste a day looking for it.'

'I'll try,' Juan said. He began to draw a map in the powdery dust and the blacks watched, understanding the map immediately. One man stepped

432

forward to add the sun, drawing with the point of his spear. The others grinned. Juan drew the river, adding drops from his waterbottle for effect, and scratched up dirt to make the hills. Then he took a great step across the hills and threw up his hands asking 'How?'

To their amazement, the charade worked. Juan pointed in various directions but they shook their heads. Finally a young man was brought forward and he beckoned them to follow him.

Juan led his horse and Pace followed, turning to say farewell to the blacks, who stared at him in astonishment.

The guide ran on ahead, anxious to get this chore over and done with and took them through the gap in the range where they looked out over flat land and a river in the distance. 'That will be the Suttor,' Juan shouted. 'We're half-way. That takes us to the Burdekin and the Burdekin will deliver us to the Valley of Lagoons!' He patted the guide on the shoulder and went back to his saddlebag. 'What can I give him as a reward?'

'You're too late. He's gone. I gather they think we're a couple of ratbags wandering around not knowing where we're going.'

Two days later they found the junction of the Suttor and the Burdekin and began to follow the great river north. They were into the northern dry season and the river flowed effortlessly but the bordering sandbanks were immense and the far banks high, a half a mile across.

'This river makes me nervous,' Pace said. 'Would you look at the great banks? Wherever the hell it comes from, in the wet it would have to be a torrent like I've never seen in my life.'

Juan agreed, but for their present purposes it was easy going through flat country spotted with tall anthills and dusty trees; still, quiet country that erupted suddenly whenever a flock of birds were disturbed or when a mob of kangaroos sped across the land.

They camped overnight within a few miles of their destination and in their enthusiasm were up at the light hour before sun-up to get on their way. By sunrise they were standing on a ridge overlook a misty expanse, which they knew had to be the Valley of Lagoons.

'There it is,' Juan cried.

Pace reined in his horse. 'By God it is. I knew we'd do it.'

'And so we must celebrate,' Juan said. 'I have come prepared.' He took out a silver flask and handed it to Pace. 'The best brandy, to drink to the Valley of Lagoons.

Pace took a drink and held up the flask. 'To us! It's not at all what I expected.' He handed the flask back.

'You're not disappointed MacNamara surely?'

'Indeed I'm not. I'm stunned. I was thinking of a valley you know, a long green valley like we have in Ireland, that you look down like a tunnel. This isn't a valley, it's an expanse.'

'Coming from a place as small as Ireland you'd have to think small wouldn't you?' Juan teased. 'It's a wonder you can find your way around this country at all. Look at those lagoons out there. Leichhardt was right. It's magnificent cattle country.'

'What are those ranges out there to the west?'

'I don't know. How far are we from the coast then?'

'Only about a hundred miles but it might as well be a thousand.'

They stared up at the heavily wooded Seaview Ranges behind them, dazzled, as the sun lifted to full strength.

# CHAPTER FOUR

He was known as Wodoro. He could pronounce his name correctly, Wodrow, because his father had taught him, and even shown him the white man's symbols for it, often carving them into trees for all to see. It amused him that none of the other boys could get their tongues around his name, but he didn't mind because he thought Wodoro sounded much better, more musical.

Wodoro was well connected. His father was the white warrior who had brought the message from the Kamilaroi to the Tingum, and who had fought so valiantly in the great wars. The good spirits had seen to it that his funeral pyre lit up the skies for miles around when he died in battle at the white man's big house. The fires had been lit by the warriors but the magnificent sky-leaping flames had provided a fitting tribute to the great man.

After the mourning Wodoro had been adopted by the great Bussamarai, to demonstrate his loyalty and gratitude to his friend Jackadoo.

Wodoro knew his initiations would be of the highest order because of these connections so he suffered through them with dignity, using humility to cover his fear, but he did not feel humble. The tests and trials had taken him into manhood and now at sixteen he could speak Kamilaroi, Tingum and many words of the white man's language.

The great Bussamarai had kept his word, no white men could camp safely in the Mary River and Wide Bay country while he lived. Any intrusion brought fast and fierce punishment because his scouts were everywhere and his warriors obeyed him without question. But when he died, his authority went with him and his tribesmen knew the end had come, their district was now surrounded by white settlers.

When the invasion did come, some Tingum people stayed, while others sought refuge in the hills, in country too rough for the white men's cattle or for the sowing of crops, and Wodoro's family went with them. He now lived with the tribe, his heart beating fiercely for love of his people, and his soul despairing because he had always dreamed of being a warrior.

Against the wishes of Kana, his mother, who was still terrified of the white men, even though she had married one, Wodoro walked boldly down to the stations and joined his people so he could have a better look at the whites he had heard so much about. Kana had told him the story many times of the murder of her family and friends and how she had escaped the clutches of murderous white men. The anger in him burned fiercely.

The white men ignored him, except when they laughed at his hawk-like nose, so different from the flat noses of his people. He listened to their words, practising them, understanding them, and taking delight in not revealing that he could speak this language. Wandering from station to station, watching and observing, he became known as 'the dummy', the boy who could not speak, but often in the blacks' camps, when there were no whites around, Wodoro would entertain his friends with a speech in English. Not for him the pidgin, his tongue sprang deftly around the English words and he could mimic the bosses better than anyone. The people slapped their sides and rolled around laughing and no-one ever gave away his secret.

'The dummy' hung around the stock yards and stables, never offering to help, never so much as picking up a bucket of water. Some of the blacks who had become stockmen suggested to him he should stay and get a job. 'Why should I work?' he asked. 'I can get fish and game whenever I want it.' Then he turned to them with a broad grin, saying, in English, 'Tingum are gentlemen. We do not work.' That became the big joke of the station blacks, they doubled up laughing whenever they saw him.

He heard the strange word 'opium' at Montone Station and watched the white men laughing as they tipped ash into the mouldy flour and tea set aside for the station blacks and he was afraid. Everyone had heard of poisonings; they would never forget or forgive that.

When no-one was looking he took handsful of the ash and distributed it liberally into the horses' feed, deciding that if the horses dropped dead he would warn the people to run for their lives.

In the morning the horses were half asleep, one old mare was even staggering and it was funny to watch, with the whites muttering and swearing, thinking the drowsy animals were sickening with something. Wodoro now understood what this opium was, remembering the glazed faraway look he had seen in a lot of them, especially the women, who ate more of the white man's food because the men took the first share of the fish and meat. He tried to tell them what was happening but they didn't care; they didn't want to know.

Why the white men were doing this remained a mystery to Wodoro. The blacks knew of many native leaves and bulbs that could produce the same effect, but did not usually choose to use them. The whites were certainly very strange people, not as warlike as he had imagined, but he had seen their guns in action and realised the Tingum could only survive now as guests on their own land.

He made his way back to his own mob, taking note of fields of corn which were easy pickings for fast-moving blacks from the hills on dark nights, but the people had moved on. The trail took him north to the big lake almost at the perimeter of Tingum country and his mother welcomed him home with tears of relief and the news that the elders wished to see him in the secret place.

He dressed himself respectfully. Mud-pasting his hair into a topknot, out-

436

lining his chest and arm scars with yellow ochre and putting on his necklace of the single dingo fang, symbol of the Warrigal people; he put his boondi club into his belt of manhood, which was made of Kurrajong rope with a frontal fringe that came almost to his knees, and took up his spear, one stride taller than himself. He tested his hunting boomerang, the span exactly the distance from his belt to the ground and, satisfied all was correct, he went to the elders.

Moolingi sat a few feet in front of the other two men, being the oldest and therefore the spokesman. He invited Wodoro to sit and took his time getting to the point. The conversation was good natured, with enquiries about his travels. Wodoro sat more easily, answering questions about where he had been and what he had seen, although he knew there was little they did not know of his movements.

'And what do you think of the white men?'

'I cannot see how they can be forgiven,' Wodoro said. 'They are not a moral people. They do not keep their promises. They use abusive languge to our people and they are cruel to our dogs.'

Moolingi looked at him shrewdly. 'And do you seek revenge?'

Wodoro shrugged. 'What's the use? There are too many of them. Killing one is like taking one possum from the forest.'

'And yet you speak of wishing to become a warrior. Do you wish to kill only hostile black men and not hostile white men?'

Wodoro froze. His mother always said he talked too much.

His inquisitor allowed him to think on that, but did not require an answer. 'What do white men talk of?'

'Horses mostly.' Wodoro would not volunteer more information now, unless specifically asked.

Moolingi smiled, approving. 'You are a Warrigal man. You know of Ilkepala?'

'Yes.' He knew of Ilkepala. His father had even seen him, he would have been proud to say, but he held his tongue.

'Ilkepala has been here and consulted with us. You are to be appointed a messenger because of his respect for your father and because you understand several languages which is essential for a messenger. Are you willing to undergo the training?'

'Yes.' Wodoro was excited. A messenger could travel anywhere.

'You understand you may not take up arms except in defence of your person, your family or your honour. Once you have received the official designation of a herald you cannot be a warrior.'

'Yes. I understand that. When do I start?'

'Your training will commence when the first knock-em-down storms begin so that it will not interfere with your hunting.' Moolingi turned to the others who nodded in agreement, and then continued. 'It is a mournful fact that a herald is rarely required to go south into the cold countries any more but you will have much to learn. The hotlands and the wetlands and the stony deserts where the sun sinks are still ours.'

When Wodoro told his mother she was thrilled. Once again she was in the centre of attention. 'This is a great privilege Wodoro. After a few years you will be promoted to special envoy, held in great awe by even the strangest tribes. What wonders you will see and what magnificent gifts you will be able to bring home to your mother.'

It was Kana who kept him at it. The training, which Wodoro had imagined would be as easy as catching fish in a trap, turned out to be physically and mentally arduous. He had to learn to run longer distances at great speed without food or water, because, as he was advised, messages were often crucial and speed vital. He had to study the stars for finding directions in strange lands and learn the laws covering intertribal ceremonies, meetings, punishments and battles because it was the duty of the messenger to arrange the time and the place of such events.

He was shown how to arrange hawk feathers in his hair and to decorate his spear so that he could be recognised as a messenger, and warned to carry a firestick at night to ward off evil spirits.

His mother was assigned to teach him the songs of the Kamilaroi and he was tested in the songs and stories of the Tingum. He would be expected to deliver them at corroborees in other lands. It was always interesting to hear new songs and tales. He had to go over them time and again at the camp fire with everyone listening, and laughing at his mistakes, until he got them right and overcame his shyness.

So many other things they taught him, it seemed a life-time of learning all over again. He realised that this was to be a lonely life and only clever men could survive the pitfalls. He doubted his ability to cope and worried that he would end up getting his head cut off by some far-off ferocious tribe. Or be eaten by them. Everyone knew the plainsmen ate their enemies.

When the training was over Moolingi told Wodoro to say his farewells and Wodoro thanked the God-in-the-sky for that. The lessons had become boring. Moolingi was a nit-picker, afraid that he would offend the powerful Ilkepala if he neglected to educate his student correctly; while it was considered cruel to smack a defenceless child, Moolingi thought nothing of cracking his hulking pupil across the head for not paying attention.

At the end of the wet season when the land was steaming in the heat two strangers came, two Kalkadoons it was said, from the land of the tall gins. It was now revealed to Wodoro that these men were messengers and an exchange was about to take place. The younger Kalkadoon would stay with the Tingum to learn their ways and he would now travel with the senior Kalkadoon, whose name was Gumurra, to their land, to do likewise. He would be expected to learn the Kalkadoon language. With what seemed like a heavy stone sinking in his chest, Wodoro discovered that his apprenticeship was beginning all over again. New people. New ways.

Gumurra hurried him north through other tribal lands explaining who they belonged to, on and on until they saw the sea as richly blue as found only on the feathers of the most brilliant birds. Trees groaned with luscious fruits and the people brought them tasty sea foods. Wodoro thought they were a most fortunate tribe. Gumurra led him over mountains that seemed never to have known a human foot. This was Kalkadoon country and Gumurra ran steadily on, down to drier pastures which he said he preferred because there were not so many mosquitoes and sandflies.

In their turn the Kalkadoons politely handed him on to the Jangga people but not before they were certain he was well taught in their language and customs so that if arrangements needed to be made he would know not to trangress their laws.

Each tribe he met looked more fearsome than the last so he was very careful. The Jangga tribe lived in open country, hard country he thought. The soil was red and hot with trees scattered across it like little knots of green but the Jangga did not seem to mind. They were a cheerful lot and sat in their dusty gunyahs waiting for the big wet that would turn their river into a sea. Then they would go walkabout.

Men from other tribes were brought to him since it was not possible to visit them all and he began to get an overall picture of the black nation. His role was never that of an adjudicator, rather a master of ceremonies but he felt proud when people came to him for advice. One day a Jangga man came to him with his woes. 'I brought home a Mandanggai woman, married her and now my father will not spit on me. He won't have a woman here from that tribe and he says her totem is impure for my family. Because my father disapproves, my friends won't speak to me. Some of them have even shown me their backsides. What can I do?'

'There is nothing you can do to obtain your father's good graces, except to send her back where she belongs,' Wodoro told him wisely.

Several hours later, the savage Mandanggai woman stole up behind him and clubbed him senseless. Wodoro was the laughing stock of the camp. With his head aching he discovered the elusiveness of wisdom.

As the days went on the Jangga men intrigued him. They liked to talk of life and its relationship to death and the world beyond. They understood the Dreamtime better than any other men he had met and they taught him about thought. 'Through thought,' they told him, 'being wide awake with your eyes closed you can travel up the rainbow to the sky world and across man's world and into men's minds.' And when he felt he was just coming to the edge of understanding these things, it was time to leave.

The wise men of the Jangga people invited him to return when his tour was completed and he was awed by the compliment. These men he now knew were mystics, who understood the universe. Such a subject he had never discussed before, his prior experience only took in three dimensions. Who knew what lay beyond?

There were tears in his eyes as he sat with them on this last evening waiting for the women to bring his food while across from him sat two strange men of the Warunga tribe who were to take him on, ever north.

He heard a growl in the camp, and whispering, but no-one approached the official group.

'What's wrong?' he asked.

'You don't know?' one of his teachers asked, interested in his reaction.

'No.'

'You don't feel it?' another asked.

'No. Should I?'

'Probably not. It is too soon. But there are white men in the vicinity.'

A year before he would have shown his anger and surprise, but he had learned that a herald should be calm.

The Warungas were bristling, nursing their weapons, but the Jangga men quietened them. 'They are but passing by. Two men on horses. Do not be alarmed.'

Wodoro smiled. So often he had been forced to explain that there was no such animal as a man with four legs. Somewhere in the past black men had taken their first glimpse of horses, alien to this land until the white men came, and seeing humans atop them, had come to the conclusion that the human and the horse were one animal. A horse with the head and shoulders of a man. But the Jangga men, even though isolated from the whites, were not fooled.

'If they are here it is dangerous,' he warned. 'It makes for a dangerous dawn.'

'There have been others,' the Jangga head man said. 'They always leave. The earth is for men. Do you begrudge men to stand on the earth? Have they not heads and ears and toes?'

'And no manners,' a Warunga growled. 'They should be punished.'

Wodoro was curious. 'Would you not punish a black man who intruded on your land without permission?'

Munjundi of the Jangga people looked at him with his one good eye. 'Evil is intent. They do not know any better. But too long have our people blindly punished, creating and enforcing divisions in myriad laws. Totems are important so that relatives may not marry and bear poor fruit but man-made divisions which grow in profusion like reeds choking rivers must be examined in these times and discarded for the common good. The white man is upon us. You, Wodoro, son of Jackadoo, know this. Your father was a white man.'

There was a shocked silence at the campfire. The black faces, tinged a gleaming red from the reflection of the coals, stared at Wodoro who felt as if he had been clubbed. His pride in his father seemed now a guilty secret. He was amazed that these people up here at the ends of the earth would know. His colour had never been discussed before.

Munjundi placed a hand on his arm. 'All in love,' he said. 'Do not flinch. Tell me this. Had we been one nation of black men under one law with one language, vast in numbers, knowing our earth as we do, would we have failed in such a miserable manner?'

440

Wodoro felt his heart heaving with tears. 'I don't know.'

'Of course not,' Munjundi said. 'See how far you have come. No ready answers any more. The question was just a Dreaming thought. But you as a messenger should contemplate it. Do not search any more for answers but rather questions. The answers were decided back in the Dreamtime. Everything you are being taught is designed to keep things as they were and you know it is not possible. Ask people as you travel to be more willing to be part of our brotherhood, and less caring about trivial things like border transgressions and ceremonial attire. Ask them to unite, all of the tribes. In that way we will never conquer but we will survive.'

As it turned out the Warunga men were only scouts, sent to take him through their land. They were to follow a wide river with huge sandy banks to a camp at the headwaters where, they explained, their tribespeople were waiting. The Warunga travelled great distances and only gathered together every few years and their people were looking forward to his visit.

All three of them had picked up the trail of the white men as soon as they left the Jangga camp and, without meaning to track them, they followed them right into the heart of Warunga country. Wodoro's companions became angrier at each step. 'We'll go faster and catch them,' one of the men said. 'Kill them before they go any further.' But Wodoro cautioned them. 'No, wait. They might just be passing through as Munjundi said.'

'I didn't understand a word Munjundi said,' the older scout told him. 'The Janggas are peculiar people. They live in the dust with their heads in the clouds. Is this not better country?'

'Yes it is,' Wodoro said. He was not sure that he had understood the lectures either, but as Munjundi had said, thinking was necessary.

They climbed into the low hills and looked out over a country of lagoons and watched the white men riding down to the flats, the Warungas stamping with rage. 'It is our job to watch the boundaries. Why are we letting this happen?'

'Where could they be going?' Wodoro asked. 'What is in that direction past the lagoons?'

'Four, five days' march is the big river country and then the sea.'

'But I thought the sea was to the east.'

'Yes, over the big mountains about us also is the sea, only two, three days. But what about those white men?'

'Tomorrow,' Wodoro said. 'If you like we'll stay here and watch.'

They camped in the hills looking down at the smoke from the white men's camp. In the morning, they moved closer.

'Be careful,' Wodoro said. 'Those sticks they carry will kill you dead in a second.'

The intruders made no attempt to pack up their tent in the morning, instead they left their camp intact and went out examining the land, returning to their camp that night.

'See, they are staying!' the Warungas cried, becoming impatient with Wodoro. 'We will kill them while they sleep.'

'There is no hurry,' Wodoro said. 'We must make sure. Where are the juicy fish you told me we could get here?'

He did not understand why he was postponing the inevitable. Perhaps the Janggas had put a spell on him. Or perhaps being forbidden to attack any man had spoiled such adventure for him. Unless the white men attacked him, they were safe from the spear of Wodoro the messenger, but the Warungas were becoming tired of his talk. They were not much for talking.

The next day the intentions of these intruders were clear. They rode through the land blazing trees with axes, and dismounting to carve symbols on other trees.

'Stay here,' Wodoro said. 'I'll go down and listen to them.' He slipped among the trees and into the long grass and listened to the men talk. They were two squatters, marking out Warunga land for stations, going into raptures about this beautiful land that didn't even belong to them.

'Bloody hell,' he whispered to himself, and at one stage he thought of going down to talk to them, that might be amusing, but then the Warungas might take offence. They were easily offended and still suspicious of his copper skin. They had never encountered such a thing before.

The men sounded like bosses, although their voices were not in tune, different tribes, he thought, probably different white men's tribes. And he wondered where they came from. And then for the first time he wondered where his father had come from to this land. A question he might put to the Jangga men one day. Where did the white men come from anyway?

Other Warunga people came down and were shown the intruders, but the white men were left unmolested while a feast was prepared. It took days to gather the emu eggs and fish and fruit and choose a fat kangaroo. As far as Wodoro could make out, since they spoke a tongue very similar to the Janggas, a special day was coming up. They captured huge lizards and brought them into the camp. Wodoro had never in his life seen lizards as long as a man and they were killed and hung in the trees safe from dingos.

The feast was held deep in the hills and Wodoro was expected to entertain. This he did now with great confidence and they were delighted with him, the women praising his talents and fussing around him, and a young woman was brought to him as was the custom. The next morning it was discovered that the white men had shifted camp. This caused a stir but the scouts said they were still in the valley. Perhaps the singing and the music of the didgeridoos had made them nervous.

A council sat down and it was decided that it was time to do something about the white men. There was now no doubt in anyone's mind that the white men were marking out the country in precise directions and this could only be for occupation. It was agreed that they should be killed and their horses too. They would be confronted the first thing in the morning and led away for punishment.

'No!' Wodoro cried. 'You can't do that! They won't come quietly, they will kill the first man who even raises a spear and any who follow.'

'Then we will fall on them when they are asleep.'

'A coward's way. That cannot be done,' another man argued and so it went on, but whatever way it went it was clear to Wodoro that the white men would not get out alive. And he began to think about that.

'Kill one of them,' he said. 'Only one.'

They looked at him in astonishment. 'But they have both transgressed.'

'They don't know any better,' Wodoro said, echoing Munjundi. 'Kill one and let the other go free. Send him back where he came from as a warning. Otherwise more will come thinking this is a safe place. They would not know what happened to these two.'

'Other white men have already come here and we let them pass. This is too much now. They must die.'

But the esteemed messenger won the day, the decision was made to kill just one of the white men as an example. They then began arguing about which one to kill, the one in the black or the one in a shirt the colour of flowers.

Since he could take no part in the action, Wodoro went back to find Djeni the Warunga woman, surely the most beautiful person he had ever encountered, a gentle girl but strong and loving.

The Warunga people had presented her to him with great pride. Even the women had refrained from the usual giggling scenes when she stepped forward, treating her with great respect, and in the placing of the flowered mantle on her shoulders, whispered advice to her.

Thinking of her now, her full firm body, her thick hair tangled like curling vines around her sweet face, he felt a glow like the warmth of the morning sun stealing through him. He had already decided to take Djeni for his wife, Djeni being only one of her string of class and kin names, the one he liked best.

The names indicated that her mother's side of the family was dominant and therefore he would have to obtain permission for the marriage from her mother's brother, and his gifts would have to be acceptable to her brother. Being a skilled negotiator Wodoro knew he would have no trouble arranging the marriage but taking Djeni away from the tribe would be another matter. He could not stay in their land, nor did he wish to. He would have to see to it that he maintained his position of authority so that they would readily volunteer the woman to impress him.

Djeni had promised to show him the great waterfall, the spring of life and strength for her people, and they would go there together to bathe and fish when this vexed problem of the white men was done with: he was impatient to be alone with her.

# CHAPTER FIVE

They had already decided what to call this station before leaving home. The blacks at Kooramin station had told them the word for lagoon was Mungowa, so they worked methodically along their new boundary lines searing or chipping an 'M' and Roman numbers into the exposed trunks of trees, keeping clear of Allingham's markers.

'When I get home I'll tell them all those "M"s stand for MacNamara,' Pace called as he worked.

'Sure you will,' Juan laughed. 'And you'll have me squatting on your land.'

Pace stood back and looked around him. 'I've been thinking. The boys, John and Paul, can run Kooramin. There's little for me to do there now and I want to set this place up myself. It's a few years off yet but I'll bring young Duke with me to get it established. He's keen that lad.' He wiped the sweat from his face with his handkerchief. 'Let's head back to the camp. We've done all we can here, no point in being greedy. We should get going first thing in the morning.'

They caught some fish and cooked them, tired after the long day in the heat. 'Ah it's a great prize we have,' Pace said. 'It would be a fine place for a house through there, right level with this ridge. Over there. They'd get the view we have now with lagoons turning pink in the sunset. What do you say about that?'

'A good choice. I'll put a house about ten miles to the south of here, facing into the morning sun.'

Pace was surprised. 'I didn't know you were thinking of building up here. I thought you just wanted the land, leaving it to your old mate MacNamara to look after your stock.'

Juan looked around him as if evading the answer. 'It's even better country than I had imagined. God knows how far it stretches into the west.'

'Hold on, now, I'll have my wife with me. What would you do up here without your lady friends Rivadavia?'

'I might not be alone,' Juan grinned. 'I've decided to do something about Delia. I might get the marriage annulled.'

Pace approved. 'About bloody time. You need a real wife. But it's not an easy thing to get an annulment is it?'

'Not with your damn pig-headed Irish priests. I wouldn't have a chance with them. I'll organise it through Buenos Aires. The bishops there are not so sour. It's time I went home to see my parents anyway. I have been transferring my father's funds back to Argentina now that the dictator has gone.'

'Would you want to stay there?'

'No. It wouldn't work any more. I am my own man, used to my own estates.'

'That's true. But tell me, this annulment. If and when you get it, have you got a new lady in mind? I heard tell that you and Lady Rowan-Smith, the widow, have been seen about Sydney.'

Juan nodded. 'She used to live at Chelmsford you know. Her father built the original homestead.'

'There's a common interest you have then. And she's native born, no shocks like poor Delia ran into.'

'Delia!' Juan snorted. 'Delia would complain if she lived in her own palace.' And he laughed. 'Marriage cured that love affair, I've never wanted to spoil them since.'

'But you're thinking of Lady Rowan-Smith?'

Juan looked into the camp fire. 'I don't know. I like Vicky but I'm not in love.'

'Ah come now Rivadavia. That's for boys. The love comes later, like it did with Dolour and me. We had our bad times but it is sweet now to be with her. Anyhow we'd better turn in, we'll have a long ride tomorrow. I won't be happy until I see these runs legally notarised ready for registration.'

He wrapped a blanket around his shoulders. 'It's surprising the nights are so cold. I thought up here it would be hot all the time.'

In the morning Pace kicked over the coals from the fire and unhitched Sonny but the horse twitched nervously. 'Steady boy,' he said, 'everything's all right.' He put his foot in the stirrup but Sonny reared in fright and Pace plunged backwards. At the same time a spear whistled past his face. 'Jesus!' he shouted to Juan. 'Where did that come from? Let's get out of here.'

Even as he spoke Juan had his saddle on Vencador and was frantically buckling the girth.

Pace led down the hillside and Sonny didn't need any urging. The horse bolted forward, raced through the scrub, up and over a huge log and out into the open, with Vencador crashing after him. Then Pace heard a shout and looking back saw Juan fall from his horse. He wheeled Sonny around passing Vencador who had kept up his momentum for a few paces and then stopped, confused.

In seconds Pace was off his horse, his rifle in his hand, heart pounding in fear. He turned Juan over, relieved to see that he was still alive. 'What happened to you?' he yelled.

'I don't know,' Juan said, blood seeping through his hair. 'Oh – yes I do, something hit me on the side of the head. A stone. God, another inch and it would have taken my eye.'

Pace helped him to his feet but suddenly the horse, Sonny, screamed and collapsed with a spear in his side, his legs threshing in agony.

'Oh no!' Pace cried, and ran back to the horse. 'Oh Jesus Mary, no!'

He dragged Juan to a crevice of rocks and raced after Vencador to pull him to safety. For the first time he saw the attackers, as a black man ran straight at him, spear raised. Pace shot him. Behind the casualty other blacks came out and, taking careful aim, he shot another one and that sent them all scattering out of sight.

From the clearing Sonny screamed again. 'Poor Sonny,' Juan said. 'Keep me covered and I'll finish him off, we can't leave him there in pain.'

'Take Vencador and keep going,' Pace told him. 'We won't get far on one horse.'

'Don't be stupid.'

'I'm not being stupid. Our most valuable possession is Vencador, and our most vulnerable. Get him out of here. I'll catch up with you downstream in a day or so.

Sonny was still alive, quivering. Broken hearted, Juan saw he was dying, the big eyes bewildered and hurt. He raised his pistol and fired and ran back through the undergrowth.

'A grand horse he was,' Pace said as if in epitaph and Juan edged into their shelter feeling sick, his head aching.

'How many blacks are out there do you think?' he asked.

'Too many,' Pace said. 'And I told you to get going.'

'Why don't you take the horse?'

'Because you're the cavalry, I'm the sniper.'

'Is that what you were in your war?'

'Yes, but I'm not used to people firing at me you see.'

There were often times when Juan was unsure whether MacNamara was joking or not.

They crouched low as a barrage of spears came at them again and retaliated as the blacks fell back.

'If you don't mind me saying,' Pace said. 'It'd be better if you load and I fire, that way we'll make our mark. My ammunition is all down there with Sonny.'

'I got one of them,' Juan argued.

'You didn't you know. He won't be able to sit down for a while that's all. But can't we stop this? I don't want to shoot them. They're to be our neighbours and it's not the best start in the world.'

'You're not suggesting we stand up with a white flag?'

'I think that'd be a bit foolhardy. Have you got any of that brandy left?'

'No, it's finished.'

'And I suppose we haven't got any water?'

'That's right. I was going to fill the waterbags on the way out.'

'Well, we will have to stay here awhile. You guard the horse and I'll watch this way. They may decide to leave. It's been known to happen.'

'When?'

'Ah – I couldn't rightly say just at the moment.'

It was a long day, the blacks attacked every so often, acts of bravado it seemed, and Pace fired steadily. They heard shouts from the bush all around them as the afternoon crept on and still there seemed no way out.

As night closed in the bush was alive with movement and the red eyes of dingoes glared at them. 'They're after the horse,' Juan whispered and fired in the direction of Sonny. A dog yelped and others snarled.

'They'll smell Vencador next,' Pace said. 'Those brutes will cripple him. He's too highly strung to fight them off, he'll panic.'

'He's not the only one,' Juan said. 'We have to go. Question is, night or day?'

'We've got no hope in the dark. We'd never out-steal blacks. Day it is. We can't sit here until we're down to throwing rocks too.' Every so often a spear attack would be interspersed with a shower of rocks that cracked and racketed around them.

'We'll go in the morning then,' Juan said.

They stayed, crouching and uncomfortable in their shelter through the night. 'Look at those stars,' Pace said. 'There seems to be a million more tonight and they hang low in the sky, don't they? Everyone talks about the Southern Cross in this country but I've never been able to find it.'

'Up there,' Juan said. 'See the pan-shaped stars and then a big star?'

'Yes.'

'Now follow your eye. There's the Cross.'

'Will you look at that! So it is, a cross indeed! What a marvellous place the world is.'

Juan scoured the tree trunks that reflected white in the moonlight trying not to listen to the growls and snaps of dingoes feeding. He fired into them again, expecting Pace to remark on wasting ammunition but he made no comment.

When the first light slid into the valley, Juan was worrying about Vencador. 'He must be thirsty.'

'Have you got a plan then?' Pace asked him.

'Yes. We just go,' Juan said.

'We might as well,' Pace replied. 'They'll be getting impatient by this. They could always burn us out. They love fires.'

In the morning Wodoro came down to join the men who were keeping vigil over the whites and listened to their bitter complaints. They bared their teeth and hissed and spat and cast baleful glances at him. They had lost nine warriors. Never in the history of the tribe had such a calamity come upon them and Wodoro trembled. More tribesmen gathered, blaming him in whispers for not allowing them to kill the white men in the first place.

'It is your own fault,' Wodoro announced. 'Did I not tell you about the guns?' He used the white man's word to intimidate them. 'Did I not come from far away to warn you? And who listened to me? But your young men have gone into the Dreamtime with great honour, as warriors, and they are

447

proud. They will live forever in the Dreamtime as strong men, not dried-up old sticks.'

They digested this moodily among themselves until Wodoro held up his hand. 'But I have spoken to the good spirits for you and they say to keep your warriors well back, the solution is simple, we will use fire, surround them with fire.'

Suddenly there was a great commotion and Wodoro forgot his awesome role to run with them down the scrubby hillside. 'They've broken out!' the cries went up. 'The white men are getting away!'

Wodoro raced, fear thudding in his chest. If they got away he would be in disgrace, maybe his own life would be in danger. He cut across the hill to head them off, knowing the horse would plunge down the slope and then turn to speed away on the flat, but he was too late. Some Warunga men had the same idea, running swiftly with him. They hurled their spears as the big black horse with the two white men on his back, galloped across the patchy grassland. Wodoro panicked. He screamed angrily at the Warunga men and grabbed a boomerang, made of blackwood, huge, sharp and strong. As he stepped out into the open he felt the fine balance of it and blessed the maker, then he stood back and hurled it after the fleeing men.

The throw became one of the legends of the Warunga people. They said it was beyond the range of mortal men, that it soared, dipped and attacked like an eagle. The Warunga were of the eagle totem.

The boomerang hit the ground, not quite in front of the racing target as Wodoro had meant it to, but a little to the side where it renewed its force in the ricochet, regaining its momentum as a lethal weapon. It struck and felled the white man at the back, the white man in the flower-coloured shirt, the one they had chosen to kill all along.

Surprisingly the other white man made no attempt to escape, he wheeled the big black horse and came back and leapt to the ground to kneel weeping beside the bloody body of his friend whose head was almost severed.

Wodoro walked calmly to the horse and led it back. He also picked up the guns and gave them to the people. 'Destroy them!'

One of the Warunga elders came forward. 'Now we kill this one.'

'No,' Wodoro said. It was essential to maintain his authority; now it was for the woman. 'You have forced me to break my vows not to take up weapons but I had to do that to save your honour. Have you forgotten already we promised the spirits we would kill only one of the whites and let the other go? We had our reasons. It was decided. This one cannot harm you any more, you must let him go.'

Wodoro didn't much care one way or another, but his own prestige was important. The Warungas looked doubtful so he produced his master stroke. He looked down at the white man, kneeling there in the centre of them, helpless. 'I have told them to let you go.'

Rivadavia stared at him, almost uncomprehending, as amazed as the audience of blackfellows, who nudged each other in surprise.

'You speak English?' he cried.

'My father was a white man,' Wodoro said.

The white man shouted at him, 'Why didn't you speak sooner? You could have stopped all this. We didn't mean them any harm.' He was in such a rage he grabbed Wodoro by the throat and had to be pulled off him and held until he quietened, and Wodoro was taken aback. Everyone seemed to be blaming him. He reasserted himself. 'You are ungrateful. I am trying to help you.'

'Like you helped my friend. Which one of these bastards threw that boomerang?'

Wodoro translated. His version: 'He says he is very sorry and if you let him go he will never intrude on your land again.'

The blacks conferred and Wodoro turned back to Juan. 'They say you can go if you promise never to intrude on their land again.'

Still shocked, Juan nodded vaguely. 'I have to bury my friend.'

'We will help you,' Wodoro said and Juan shook his head as if to shake off the confusion of a nightmare.

Never in his life had Juan been so shocked, so distraught. The horror of Pace's death would not leave him. No matter how hard he tried he could not eradicate the bloody picture from his mind. He prayed, but he didn't know what he was praying for. Pace was dead, it was too late. He shouted and cursed and when night fell he was afraid to close his eyes. He could hear the mournful singing of the blacks and the drone of the didgeridoos and he felt out of place in this macabre setting, but he could not leave, he could not bring himself to desert Pace lying beneath the rough cross.

As the days went on he watched the blacks going about their business, now released from their purposeful invisibility and he suffered the madness of having this English-speaking savage for company and hurled away the food the black woman brought him.

There were times when he thought he was their prisoner, and there was an awful guilt that he should be still alive, wandering unmolested among Pace's murderers. He lay in the gunyah they had constructed for him wrestling with his nightmares and an overwhelming remorse.

'Was your friend not a good man?' Wodoro the blackfellow asked him.

'Of course he was,' Juan muttered, annoyed at the stupidity of the question.

'Then why do you despair so? He has gone to a good and powerful dreaming. All men die.'

'He should not have died,' Juan screamed at him. 'Leave me alone.'

'Drink.' Wodoro gave him a bowl of sweet coconut milk, insisting that he drink it all.

Juan snapped awake in the gunyah. The woman was seated cross-legged, beside him, brushing at flies with a feather seeming not to notice that his eyes were open. Cockatoos screeched from the trees and the sounds ripped through his head. He groaned and shaded his eyes from the light.

The pain was familiar, like the aftermath of too much whisky and he

449

recalled the drink Wodoro had given him. 'That's all I need,' he groaned, 'a grog headache.' It was the worst he'd had since the time years ago, when he and Pace had drunk the night through at Carlton Park, the night Dermott Forrest had suffered the heart attack. In the morning he'd been in a worse state than the older man, and Pace had laughed at him. The Irishman had laughed a lot. Except for the time when he'd been upset about Dolour.

'Oh God,' he whispered. 'Dolour! And the children!' He sat up so suddenly it had the same effect as if his head had collided with the branch of a tree. The shock of Pace's death had been so great he had been transfixed in this valley and had not given a thought to the outside world. Tears ran down his cheeks, desolate tears, and the black woman crept away.

'I'll never tell them,' he said, 'never. They must never know how he died. I will not give them that burden.'

Wodoro was standing in the light. 'Why do you cry now?'

'For them. For his family.'

And Wodoro nodded. 'You are better now. We must go from here. They will put down their crying in time too.'

That night he talked to Wodoro for the first time. 'Who was your father?'

'Jackadoo, a great warrior who fought with Bussamarai in the wars.'

'What wars?'

'Near Gimpi Gimpi, your white man's names are Mary River and Wide Bay. Bussamarai swooped like an eagle. He had a thousand warriors.'

Juan remembered the first failed black assault on Montone and was careful with his questions but the information excited him. 'Tell me about Bussamarai.'

Wodoro was a magnificent story-teller and Juan sat listening far into the night, trying to concentrate to find some relief from his grief. He realised he was probably the first white man to hear the true story of this black leader and to finally discover the name of that elusive man.

When it was time to leave he and Wodoro stood beside the grave of Pace MacNamara.

'Where did your father come from?' Juan asked.

'I do not know where any white men come from,' Wodoro said simply.

'We came on big ships,' Juan said. 'This man who is buried here came on a big ship called the *Emma Jane* from a country far far away called Great Britain. It is likely that your father came from there too.'

Wodoro was enthralled. This was something to think about and to tell the Jangga men.

# CHAPTER SIX

Jasin, Lord Heselwood, was attending to his affairs in Brisbane and enjoying the new mood of the town of which he regarded himself an elder statesman. Queensland would soon be a separate colony and Brisbane its capital city. He was staying at Newstead House which had been built by Patrick Leslie of Canning Downs. Newstead was a languid single-storied house overlooking the river, but extremely comfortable for the climate, catching every breeze, and an ideal place for discussions with Dalrymple and other members of the syndicate.

He was pleased now that he had listened to Mitchell, despite his earlier objections to shared exploration. The experience of Montone had taught him it was wiser to march forward from the rear. Now that Montone was flourishing again and the hostile blacks overrun in that district, his knowledge of the country north of Brisbane carried a great deal of weight in their discussions.

Who would have imagined, he mused as he walked down William Street, that this wretched little port could have improved so rapidly? McConnells, squatters from the Brisbane Valley, had built a fine residence called Bulimba House and the Russells of Cecil Plains had their town residence, Shafton, at Kangaroo Point, so there was no shortage of hospitality. It was even tipped that Newstead House would become the residence for the first Governor until a Government House could be constructed.

Ships of the Hunter River Steamship Company came into Brisbane regularly and paddleboats, sternwheelers and lighters plied back and forth from Ipswich carrying freight and wool, and, of course, passengers. Jasin had taken a private cabin for six shillings to view the countryside along the river again. He was delighted to see the population growth, markets for his cattle.

But it was Edward he was thinking of, he would bring Edward up this way to meet the men who would be the power in this colony. The cattle business could only expand; Edward was now in the right position to begin to look at the seats of power and young enough to take his time about it. He strolled back to his waiting carriage and instructed the driver to take him to the Victoria Hotel, where a special dinner was to be held for the shareholders in the new syndicate.

Most of the gentlemen were assembled in the private lounge when he made his entrance and he was welcomed warmly, as he had expected. He

451

had already invited several of them to visit Montone with him in the succeeding weeks. Albert Reynolds, who hoped to be appointed a director eventually, hurried over to him. 'Lord Heselwood, I believe there is a letter for you at the reception office. Shall I get it for you?'

'Do,' Heselwood said, and turned to a fellow who was claiming he had some interesting news. 'What's the furore about?' he asked.

'Sir, there's a gentleman in town who has just returned from the far north, claims he has staked out runs in the Valley of Lagoons.'

'Not another one?' Jasin replied angrily.

'At the rate we're going there'll be nothing left,' another man complained. 'I said all along there's too much mucking around here. This syndicate had better talk less and act more or I'm pulling out.'

'What has Dalrymple to say about this?' Jasin asked.

'I believe he has been trying to persuade the gentleman to address the meeting but he will not do so,' he was told.

'Damn'd unsporting of him I say,' another voice interjected.

Jasin looked around the crowded room but Dalrymple was not to be seen, so he moved back towards the lobby. Reynolds intercepted him. 'Your message Lord Heselwood.'

Jasin opened it up and read it, irritated. The message letter, marked 'URGENT', had been hand delivered from the ship. It was from Georgina requesting him to return home immediately as they had problems at Carlton Park. He shoved it into his pocket. Where did the woman think he was, Parramatta? He was not about to rush home for some bother on the station. Edward was in charge, he would have to sort it out. There was too much at stake up here, the return on his investment would depend on the people chosen as directors and he would be staying for the vote. Besides he was going on from Brisbane to Montone with his guests. What nonsense wanting him home! By the time he took ship and got back to Sydney the problem, whatever it was, would probably be solved.

He saw Dalrymple with a group of men at the main entrance and made straight for him. He was nearly on top of them when he saw they were talking to Rivadavia.

'What brings you to Brisbane, Rivadavia?' he asked without bothering to address the rest of them.

'Mr Rivadavia has just returned from the Valley of Lagoons, Lord Heselwood,' Dalrymple said in a low voice, sounding quite depressed. And with good reason too, Jasin thought, this will give you all a shakeup. If it were true, of course.

He laughed. 'Don't tell me you've done an Allingham, my friend?' he said to Juan. 'There and back on your own?'

Rivadavia looked at him in that strange intense way of his. 'I did not go alone, I was with Pace MacNamara.'

'And you marked out runs?'

'Yes.'

Jasin looked around at the other men and shrugged. 'And we're expected to believe that?'

Dalrymple intervened. 'Just a minute Lord Heselwood, I have to tell you Mr Rivadavia ran into trouble. His partner was killed by the blacks. We're very, very sorry to hear this.'

Jasin was stunned. He stepped back. 'MacNamara was killed? Good God! Well of course, I'm very sorry too.' He realised now, on closer inspection, that Rivadavia looked grey, as if he'd really been through the mill.

'You're not sorry,' Juan said bitterly. 'You've always hated him.'

'I am not his keeper,' Heselwood retorted,' so don't take it out on me. Did you really mark out runs up there?'

'Yes, we did,' Juan said. He turned to leave, Dalrymple making way for him in respectful silence but Jasin had to have the last word. 'Oh well, you'll own the lot now.'

Juan stopped and looked at him, incredulous, and then slammed his fist into Jasin's face sending him staggering into a table and crashing to the floor with it, smashing and scattering a huge bowl of flowers.

It was weeks before Jasin was well enough to venture out of Newstead House. The attack by Rivadavia had smashed some of his teeth and dislocated his jaw. He had considered charging him with common assault but Rivadavia's story was in all the newspapers and he was the latest hero in the town. Dalrymple had persuaded him to let the matter drop, explaining that the Argentinian, who had left for Newcastle anyway, had been overwrought because of the tragic circumstances.

Nevertheless, when he was next in town Jasin went to the Lands Office to discover just how much land, and where, Rivadavia intended to claim. He was amazed to find there was no claim at all in the name of Rivadavia, he had put all of it, thousands of acres, in the name of Duke MacNamara.

He had called the run Mungowa Station, placing the MacNamara family fair and square in the middle of this much-vaunted cattle country.

Jasin marched out the door and went straight down to the Victoria Hotel, his decision made. He found Dalrymple and wrote him out a cheque for a sum much larger than the one that had already been discussed. 'Count the Heselwoods in,' he said.

'A wise decision,' Dalrymple told him. 'It's an exciting prospect. We'll build one of the biggest cattle stations in the world. Queensland will be a great colony.'

# CHAPTER SEVEN

Few Governors left New South Wales with so much good will and so many farewells as Sir Charles FitzRoy. His term of office had been extended but now it was time for him to return to England, handing over to Sir William Denison who would guide the new colony of Queensland into existence.

He had extended an invitation to Lady Georgina Heselwood to call for morning coffee, knowing that Lord Heselwood was still in Brisbane negotiating with Dalrymple.

'Georgie, my dear, have you written Heselwood of the problem?'

'Sir Charles, this is not the sort of thing one commits to paper. I have requested that Heselwood return immediately on two occasions and he has chosen to ignore me. Nothing, you see, is ever as important as his estates, so he couldn't conceive that anything down this way could really be wrong. But to avoid a scandal, Edward must leave the country.'

The Governor nodded. 'And you are going too?'

'Yes, I shall be returning with Edward.

'But surely you could wait until Heselwood returns.'

'There is not time. It took me a while to convince Edward of the seriousness of this situation and get him back to Sydney from Carlton Park.'

'But he's not a boy any more. He must realise he can't go tramping about rough-shod like this.' He laughed. 'He really trod on Rivadavia's toes you know, proposing to the daughter, Juan was highly indignant!'

Georgina sighed. 'Don't I know it. So foolish.'

'Georgie,' FitzRoy said seriously. 'You know I have tried, don't you? Once these legal charges are set in motion there's nothing I can do. If I interfered there'd be the most frightful hue and cry. Worse here than in England. I had a chat to the police magistrate but even he can't help. At home, they don't mind a bit of tidying up, but out here the papers would pounce if they got wind of it.'

'I know that. You've been most considerate.'

'It's a hellish situation. I'd invite you and Edward to travel back in my party but I am turning a blind eye at his departure, so I must not have him on board. Much as I should have enjoyed your company on the homeward journey.'

Georgina smiled. 'You are the nicest man Charles. I can't thank you enough.'

'Is there no way to persuade Mrs MacNamara to change her mind?'

She shook her head. 'It's probably the last thing on her mind now, since Pace was killed.'

'Yes, I believe she is in a state of utter shock. And for poor Rivadavia to have to come home with that news! Horrible! MacNamara was speared, they say, like young Kennedy. I haven't seen the report on it, that I'll leave to Denison. It's too sad.'

A French window banged shut, picked up by the westerly wind and FitzRoy went over to anchor it. 'Why don't you write a letter to Lord Heselwood and I'll get my people to deliver it personally under my seal, then it will be entirely safe.'

'Thank you, but it wouldn't help. The summons has been issued. Heselwood couldn't do any more than you've done. The *Plymouth* leaves in two days, we're booked on that. We must go.'

'Ah well, it will all blow over. Why don't you stay to lunch with us? Forget your worries, we'll have another farewell party.'

'Charles, I appreciate that, but not today. I have a few calls to make.' She stood up. 'You are right, it will blow over. Compared to Mrs MacNamara's grief my worries are trivial. That's the dreadful part. That we should be involved in adding to her unhappiness.'

'You're a generous soul, Georgie. We'll see you before you leave won't we?'

'Of course.'

As the carriage left Government House the wind brought sweeps of rain and Georgina pulled her woollen cloak around her. Generous? she thought. I don't think so. It's hard to be generous, especially with Heselwood.

She had long remembered the name Dolour, from Jasin's first visit to Camden, and in later years had heard the name of Pace MacNamara's wife, realising that this was the real cause of the animosity between the two men.

But Dolour, angry and hurt though she might have been, was not really calling all the shots.

Of course Georgina had known she was a convict, transported from Ireland, it was difficult to keep these things quiet. It would have been unkind to admit to that knowledge. And pointless. But in the flaming row she'd had with Edward at Carlton Park, lying abed feeling sorry for himself, he had claimed that a convict whore should not be permitted to cause all this trouble.

Georgina had felt like slapping him herself. She had, instead, prised out of him the source of that remark.

Then, Georgina knew, as well as did Dolour, that the real culprit was Jasin. Whatever he had done in his younger days was forgotten, should have been forgotten; it was unforgivable of him to pass on a story to his son that was a humiliation to his wife and a scandal on the reputation of a neighbour's wife. She had considered it best to have Dolour believe that part of the incident had not been repeated.

So Mrs MacNamara was handing out her punishment, mostly aimed at Jasin, and had Georgina been in her position she would have done exactly the same. There would be no letter to Jasin. When he returned he would find his wife and son had left the country. And it would be up to him to explain that away.

They were travelling South Head Road and on impulse Georgina called to the driver to turn into Wilkin House. She decided it was time to call on Lady Rowan-Smith.

She was shown into the sitting room which she remembered so well, it had been redecorated but was still a pleasant room, and Vicky came in. 'This is a surprise, Georgina.' She seemed to have no objection to Georgina's visit but looked tired.

'I hope I am not inconveniencing you,' Georgina said.

'No. Not at all.'

'Vicky, I have come to ask you a favour. Several, in fact.'

'If you want me to appeal to Dolour MacNamara for you, I can't do that.'

'You heard then?'

'Yes. I've just come from Kooramin. It was dreadful. Juan sent a message from Brisbane asking me to bring Rosa home to Chelmsford immediately, so I knew something was wrong. I went with him to Kooramin Station to break the news to Dolour and her family.'

'Poor woman.'

'Yes. While I was there the boys mentioned the trouble with your son. Dolour didn't discuss it at all.'

'I'm not surprised. But I didn't come about that. I wanted to ask you to tell her one day, when things settle down, how dreadfully sorry I was to hear of Pace's death.'

Vicky shrugged. 'When I see her.'

'Oh! Well also, I'm leaving for England in a few days, but before I left I did want to hear how Juan is, he has always been a good friend to us. How is he after that terrible experience?'

Vicky stood up and rang the bell for the maid. 'I don't know about you Georgina, but I need a glass. I've had as much as I can take the last few weeks.'

'I feel much the same way,' Georgina said.

The maid knocked respectfully. A change for this house, Georgina recalled.

'Serve sherry and wafer biscuits would you please Anne,' Vicky asked and turned back to Georgina. 'I am sorry you've been having trouble with Edward.'

'Thank you,' Georgina said. 'It has been rather unpleasant lately. He seems to have me in bother everywhere just like Jasin used to. He even offended Rivadavia and that's quite an achievement. Jasin didn't even manage that.'

Vicky shook her head. 'You haven't heard?'

'Heard what? I am always the last to hear.'

They waited until the drinks were poured and the maid left.

'Juan struck Jasin.'

'Where was this?'

'In Brisbane.'

'What about?'

'I don't know. Juan didn't enlarge on it.'

Georgina drank her sherry in large sips. 'I don't think I want to know. I've got Edward at home now, confined to the couch, still claiming he will marry Rosa one day.'

'Not much chance of that, Juan's taking her to Argentina.'

'Really? With everyone at odds that's probably a good idea. But you didn't tell me how Juan is.'

'He's shattered. The Memorial Service was a terrible ordeal for him. He's taking Pace's death badly, blames himself.'

'Then the voyage to Argentina will be good for him too. I wanted you to give him my regards, once again when things settle down. You seem to be very friendly with him these days. I'm so pleased about that, he's a fine gentleman and I wanted you to know that I think you two would go very well together. We all move in the same circles, so don't take any notice of Jasin and his remarks.'

Vicky was quiet. 'We had a lovely Christmas,' she said. 'We were like a family with the girls. But it's over now.'

'That's understandable, it must be a difficult time for him, but everything will come back to normal soon.'

'No, it's over between us, I've lost him. That's why I left Chelmsford so soon. It was hard because I had become so fond of him. I will miss him terribly.'

Georgina was startled. 'Oh dear, that's a pity. I rather thought he'd divorce Delia and marry you.'

'So did I. I'm not the best company today. It seems to hurt more when you're older. I'm feeling rather miserable.' She looked thoughtfully at Georgina. 'Did you ever know such a man for not realising how attractive he is to women?'

'Oh he knows, I'm sure he does, but he likes women. And we all respond to that.'

She looked over to the French windows but tall bushes and hedges now obstructed the view. 'I remember we used to be able to see right down to the gate from this room,' she remarked.

Vicky walked over to look out. 'Yes. I used to watch for Horton from here, and run all the way down to greet him.'

'In the rain,' Georgina smiled.

'Yes, even in the rain.'

# THE VALLEY
# OF LAGOONS

# CODA, 1958

The Trans-Australia Airlines plane flew low over the incredible blue waters of the Whitsunday Passage that lies between the Great Barrier Reef and the east coast of Australia, and over Magnetic Island to circle the red-brown landscape of Townsville with its stunted trees and dried-up creek beds.

Hank Wedderburn looked down eagerly. Apart from the family connections he was looking forward to returning to this strange country that had resisted change from its ancient ways until less than a century ago.

Elena and Luke MacNamara were waiting for them outside the corrugated iron shed that served as the airfield terminal building and it was an exciting reunion.

When Luke came over to shake hands with him Hank felt an eerie prickly sensation on the back of his neck.

'You didn't tell me you were here in Townsville during the war!' Luke cried. 'I was amazed when Maria wrote and told us. You're no stranger to these parts after all.'

'I didn't want to bore you on your wedding day,' Hank laughed.

'I'm thrilled you've visited so soon,' Elena said. 'Now Daddy can't go on claiming I've moved into outer space.'

Luke explained to Hank that they'd decided to go straight out to the station and to return to Townsville for a few days later on, which would give the visitors a chance to go out to see the Reef.

'Fine with me,' Hank said, feeling better now.

'How do we get to the station from here then?' Maria asked.

'By plane,' Elena told her. 'We've got an airstrip on the station. Luke will fly us home. We have to have a plane out there, the roads over the ranges from here are impossible.'

'Can't you get there by road at all?' Maria was amazed.

'Sure there's an easier route, but it's a roundabout trip, it takes ages.'

'I'll settle for the plane then,' Hank said, looking around at the quiet airfield with its border of low-lying mangrove forests, the echoes of the noise of a full-scale military base ringing in his ears.

As they followed the other passengers into the shed, the voices surprised him, he had forgotten the accent. Luke had a soft slow voice. 'A country voice,' Maria had said, 'with a timbre and timing like Jimmy Stewart's,' but now she was having problems, she couldn't understand a word anyone was saying.

'It takes a while,' Elena said. 'You'll get it, Aunt Maria.'

Hank went through with Luke to collect the luggage that had been dumped onto an old utility truck and left outside. A tall cowboy was leaning against the fence rolling a smoke. He nodded his head at Hank. 'How're you goin' mate?' and Hank grinned, touching his hat in acknowledgement, remembering now that this strange form of address didn't require an answer. He had come across it first on the Kokoda trail, from diggers as they tramped past him, and had finally worked out that it was more a form of encouragement than just a greeting. And he felt encouraged now, cheered.

They climbed into the small plane with Luke at the controls and Hank squatting in a dicky seat behind the pilot while Maria and Elena settled into the two passenger seats.

Luke took the plane down the runway and up over the scattered trees, heading north. 'We'll go along the coast for a bit, for the scenery, Elena likes this view of the sea and the islands.'

Hank pointed down. 'That's where we were based, and by God, look at that, some of the old quonset huts are still there.'

'Yes. They're not taking any chances now, it's going to remain an army base. They're rebuilding it as a permanent base.'

It was a glorious blue day for the flight with not a cloud in the sky and a few fishing boats and yachts dotted the calm sea.

'That's Halifax Bay down there,' Luke said, 'we're going inland now.'

From the coast the mountains had seemed dense and green with a fringe of ragged trees along the skyline but as the plane climbed higher Hank could see uneven crags and ridges and deep gorges. 'What's the name of this range?'

'Seaview,' Luke called back.

As he looked down Hank was glad they were flying, he could do without a ride over those mountains where there was not a road to.be seen.

'There it is. Valley of Lagoons,' Luke announced.

Hank was trying to look every which way at once. The valley was a surprise, more of a great plain between two distinct mountain ranges with clumps of trees posted all over as unreal looking as toys, and with lagoons, milky blue in the distance.

Luke allowed the plane to lose altitude over the foothills and then flew low along the valley. Startled, grazing mobs of cattle with wide ferocious horns cantered a few yards and then stopped, to glare after them for disturbing their tranquillity and a flock of black cockatoos lifted from a bare tree and winged away into the blue.

'This is the Dalrymple Shire,' Luke went on to explain. 'Named after the first of the big-timers to come in here. The MacNamaras were lucky to get a look in. The Heselwoods came with Dalrymple. You may have met a couple from that family at the wedding.'

Maria was leaning over listening to him, just as interested in everything

461

as her husband. She had to report back to her brother Eduardo Rivadavia. 'I wondered what the connection was there,' she said. 'But he was Lord Heselwood wasn't he?'

'Yes. They've got a big station on past Mount Surprise. A colossal spread. One of the biggest cattle stations in the north. Down there now is Allingham's Station, they got in first over at Mount Surprise and that forced the Heselwoods to go further west. But nothing's changed much here over the years, the few that got in stayed, and the families are all still here.' He laughed. 'They call it the land of the few.'

'Is there a town out here?' Maria wanted to know.

'Further south. They started a town called Dalrymple but it lost out to Charters Towers in the gold rush.

'We're over Mungowa station now, we'll soon be home.'

'What does Mungowa mean?' Hank asked.

'It means lagoon but the blacks up here argue about that. They say it is the wrong language. They've got another word for lagoon. It must be a word from some southern tribe.'

'Mungowa is the head station,' Elena informed him. 'Luke's got another ranch further west and we're building our own house out there now. So for the time being we're living with his mother and grandfather. You'll like Mac, Hank. He's a really nice old man.'

'When he wants to be,' Luke laughed. 'There's the homestead over there. We fly over it to the strip. The house used to be closer to the river but it got swamped in a flood so Mac rebuilt the house up here and handed it over to my father and then the silly bugger went off to the war and never came back.'

Luke's voice jarred. He sounded so bitter that Hank was shocked. He glanced at Luke and saw that his jaw was set and his tanned face tense and uncompromising at the mention of his father.

'We all had to do that,' Hank commented.

'He didn't!' Luke snapped. 'Cattlemen were exempt. Primary industry, they needed beef as much as they needed men.'

Elena and Maria were peering down as they swept over the red roof of the large house set among the trees and Hank drew back in silence feeling angry and hurt.

When they landed at Mungowa station Luke's mother, Elizabeth, and his grandfather were waiting for them in the Landrover. 'Mac' climbed down to greet them. He was in his seventies but he still stood tall in his tweed jacket, moleskin trousers and elastic-sided boots. Some black stockmen sat on their horses nearby to get a look at the newcomers but took no notice of the plane, a commonplace sight to them, Hank supposed.

He was quiet as they drove to the house, listening to them talk.

'I don't suppose this is much different from the ranches in Argentina,' Maria was saying.

'I shouldn't imagine they would be,' Elizabeth said. 'They'd have to be practically self-supporting too wouldn't they?'

'Yes indeed. But why is the house built up off the ground?'

'A number of reasons,' she explained. 'It's cooler and keeps out the damp in the wet weather.'

'And don't forget the snakes,' Elena said. 'They keep out the snakes.'

Mac turned to her with a grin. 'A snake'll get in if he wants to young lady. Just you learn to shoot first and ask him his name afterwards.'

They climbed the steps to go into the house, Mac taking a heavy walking stick to help him up the stairs, refusing any other assistance. He lowered himself into a cane chair on the wide verandah. 'You sit down here with me,' he said to Hank, but Elizabeth disagreed. 'It's too hot out here Dad. Come inside.'

'Don't take any notice of them,' Mac grumbled. 'You sit here Hank. Just because they've got electrical fans to re-arrange the hot air they think they're cool.'

The others gave up and went inside. 'We'll have our lunch out here,' Mac called. 'Pull up a chair Hank. Would you like a beer?'

'Sure. A beer'd be great. Will I go and get one?'

'No. I've got young Luke well trained.'

As he spoke, Luke brought out the beer and two glasses. 'Would you rather have a whisky Hank?'

'No. Beer's fine.'

When Luke went back into the house Mac poured the drinks. 'She's a good girl, your Elena,' he commented, 'rides well.'

'She seems to be happy. I'm glad you like her,' Hank said. The old man seemed to be studying him with his calm grey eyes and Hank forced himself to make conversation. 'Were you born up this way Mr MacNamara?'

'Yes. Call me Mac.'

'Your father must have been a pioneer here?'

'Ah no, he was born here too. His father was Duke MacNamara, he opened up these runs, my grandfather that is. Before him though his old man, Pace MacNamara, found this property with a mate, but Pace was speared by the blacks. It starts down there at John's Ridge.' He pointed with his stick to an outcrop in the foothills. 'That's the landmark for the east boundary of this station. Old Duke, he reckoned they spelled it wrong when they drew up the proper maps of the district, used to get bloody cranky about it too, but we could never figure out any other way to spell John.'

He looked out dreamily. 'I was born in the old house that used to be down there before the flood. It was a lovely old place, beautiful timbers, not the rubbish they use now. There used to be an old cemetery down there when I was a boy but that got washed away too. This river's got

463

some force in it when it gets going. You were here during the war?' he asked suddenly.

'Yes.' Hank felt guilty again and looked away. 'Yes. I spent quite a bit of time in Townsville. I even got as far as Charters Towers.'

'You did? My word, good on you. Of course Charters Towers was in full flush in the gold rush days, they used to call it 'The World'. Had its own stock exchange and all.'

'It wasn't so quiet when I was there either,' Hank laughed. 'Did you ever know an old guy called Bony Jack?'

'Bony Jack? Yes. Everyone knew him. An old prospector, only died a few years back. Got thrown from his horse. Those old fellers, you couldn't get them out of the saddle. Old Duke MacNamara went the same way. My father used to say once you find out you don't bounce any more, it's time to hang up the spurs. But you met Bony Jack eh?'

'I sure did.'

Mac's eyes twinkled. 'So tell me son. Were you smart enough to buy any of his gold?'

'You bet! I meant to take it home with me, there were thousands of GI's being flown home from all over the world, no-one had time to look in kitbags, but I didn't get it any further than Townsville. All the guys were after souvenirs and gold was a world-beater! They went crazy! Name your price man! I hitched rides out to Charters Towers on Air Force planes after that and old Bony Jack kept the supply coming. But one thing I never figured. Why he sold to me so cheap.'

'He was set in his ways, that's all,' Mac said. 'He couldn't read or write and he was getting his dough without having to fill in all the Government forms and pay all those wartime taxes. And he was fronting for other prospectors too. Simplifying the system they called it.'

Hank laughed. 'They sure did that! Did you ever find gold on this ranch?'

'Not gold but we got a push along with silver. This old country is bulging with minerals and precious metals. Of course Charters Towers had enormous deposits, they're still going, and they reckon there's gold under the main street waiting to be picked up. And north of here, the Palmer was a river of gold. But like the Californian gold rush, some were lucky, some had to plod on. Now you take the Heselwoods, further out from here. The old Lord, he never missed an opportunity to expand his holdings, he could never get enough land.' He sucked on his pipe and winked. 'They always reckoned he knew about the gold on his Montone Station, north of Brisbane, but he never let on.'

'Why would he do that?'

'I suppose he didn't want diggers swarming all over his property, he'd have wanted it for himself. But anyway, once the gold rush started, prospectors were everywhere and sure enough there was a big strike at Gympie, right in the middle of his territory.'

'Did he live to see it?'

'Oh sure. He did it in style, hired miners by the dozen. He even had his portrait painted standing by a mine with his crew. The family's still got that old picture out at their head station. Still, we can't complain. It was gold that made this country, brought the people see, built the towns, created a market for beef, put our cattle stations on their feet for good and all.'

After lunch Mac insisted on taking Hank on a tour of the station. He walked around, pointing out the various buildings and talking with the station hands, introducing Hank to everyone. 'The stockyards are down there,' he said, indicating a maze of high rails, familiar to Hank. 'I'll take you down later. You're a Texan, you can tell me what you think of our cattle.'

He wandered into a shed and came out with a bottle of rum and two dusty glasses which he rinsed under a tap. 'Come and sit down,' he said, leading Hank to a bench under a wide flowering tree. 'Have a rum. It's good for what ails you.'

Hank sipped on the fiery neat rum.

'We like rum in the north,' Mac said, 'because we reckon it's the only spirit worth drinking without ice.'

Hank nodded, swallowing some more, hoping it would revive his spirits.

'You went off to the war from here?'

Hank nodded again. 'The second time, yes.' His hands were clammy and cold. He wished he had never come to this place. Luke had disappointed him, put him on the defensive.

'My son died in the islands in the war,' Mac said simply.

The American reached for the bottle and poured himself another rum. 'And I suppose you think he shouldn't have gone too?' he asked, his voice harsh, and the old man looked surprised.

He dabbed at his white moustache with his handkerchief and stuffed it back in his pocket. 'No I don't think that at all. Where did you get that from?' Then it dawned on him. 'You've been listening to Luke's talk.'

'What about?' Luke was standing behind them.

His grandfather looked at him steadily. 'I was just going to explain to Hank here that you still fret after your father.'

'I do not,' Luke said angrily. 'I am just of the opinion that he didn't have to go. It was stupid and unnecessary. There were plenty of others.'

'Like Hank. He went,' Mac commented.

'Did you have a family?' Luke asked Hank.

'No I didn't.'

'Then it was different for you.'

'Here, you have this rum,' Mac said, handing his glass to Luke. 'I'm going over to see Billy Flynn over there. He keeps putting his junk in my

465

storeroom. You see if you can talk some sense into this fellow, Hank. I'm sick of arguing with him.'

When Mac left, Luke apologised. 'I'm sorry Hank. It's not worth talking about.'

'I think it is,' Hank said quietly. 'You've got sisters, where are they?'

'One lives in Brisbane and the other one is married, they live on a property down on the Fitzroy River.'

'You all seem to have survived the war quite well.'

'That's not the point.'

'I suppose not. So, do you think that if your father had really loved you, he wouldn't have gone off to the war?'

Luke was embarrassed. 'I don't know about that. It's history now anyway.'

'Gee thanks,' Hank said. 'I was there, don't turn me into history. I'm not that old.'

'I'm sorry, I didn't mean it that way. It's just that I still say he had no right to go.'

'He had every right. But I don't think you're mad at him for going. You're mad at him for getting killed. If he'd come home you'd have thought it was okay. You'd have gone around boasting "my father went to the war" like any other kid.'

Luke stared sullenly into the dust and Hank felt sorry for him but then the anger returned when he thought of the father, Sergeant MacNamara. 'The trouble with you Luke, you can't forgive him for getting killed. Or that's how it seems to me. I think it hurts so much you're finding it easier to blame him, get mad at him instead. He doesn't deserve this bitterness. As you people say down here, give the guy a fair go.'

When Luke had nothing to say, Hank continued. 'He must have felt it was his duty to go. Maybe it was his family he was thinking of all along, his way of looking out for you.'

He offered Luke a cigarette which he took, seeming to dismiss the conversation.

Luke straightened up. 'Here comes Grandpa. I'll see you later Hank.'

Mac watched him leave. 'You smarten up his ideas did you?' he asked, referring to Luke as if he'd been eavesdropping.

Hank shrugged. 'Maybe. Just different ways of looking at things.'

'It's hard to get through to him,' Mac said. 'But never mind. The bullock trains used to come through here in the old days. You ever seen their rigs Hank?'

'No.'

'Come on then and I'll show you.'

He took Hank down to an old shed, leaving the double doors open to let in some light, and propping open the wooden window shutters with poles. 'This is my harness room. Where I keep all my treasures. I'm always going to clean it up but I never get around to it.'

The shed was a museum of rigs that hung around the walls and lay in dusty heaps on the floor, stock whips and strangely shaped iron rods were everywhere. There was even an old jinker in the corner.

'Have a look here,' Mac said. 'See these leather braces. They were used by Cobb and Co coaches instead of steel springs. Made for rough roads.'

Hank walked around with him, examining the pieces, and saw saddles hanging from the rafters. 'What are they doing up there?'

'Keeps the mice away from them. There's another one down here somewhere. I keep meaning to hang it up too.' He dragged some hessian bags from a dark corner, threw aside what looked like the upholstered seat of an ancient buggy and pulled out a saddle wrapped in canvas. 'This one's a beauty!' He dragged it outside into the light and unwrapped it, wiping mould from it with his hands. 'All the stuffing's gone. Hey Billy, bring me a wet rag.'

The station hand gave him a chamois and he wiped it clean standing back to admire it. 'The trim's real silver,' he said. 'It's a beauty isn't it?'

Hank went down on his haunches, intrigued. The saddle was huge, old-fashioned and ornate, the black leather embossed with intricate designs and the silver was a work of art. 'It's magnificent!' He frowned. 'It shouldn't be left in there to rot.'

'I know, I know,' Mac said, circling it. 'I have to send it away to a good craftsman to get it restored. One of these days.'

'Where did it come from?' Hank asked rubbing the silver.

'We're not too sure. You never see saddles like that in this country. We think it might have belonged to a South American feller. He was Pace MacNamara's partner, and after Pace was killed he married the widow. It must have been late in life because she already had grown-up sons. But that was their way then, no widow worth her salt stayed single. That's what I keep telling Elizabeth, Luke's mother. She's a fine-looking woman, she should be looking around now.'

Mac's reference to his son's widow was another jolt for Hank who was trying to accept these constant reminders, part of his penance for coming here in the first place, he told himself. But there was no doubt Mac had loved his son. Maybe as you get older, he mused, you get a better grasp on reality, on what has to be.

'My father was never much interested in family history,' Mac was saying. 'I got this information in bits and pieces from my grandfather old Duke when I was a kid. He said his mother would never come up this way, they lived down in New South Wales in the Hunter Valley somewhere. And there's another branch of the family lives out on the Liverpool Plains.'

'Are they in cattle too?' Hank asked.

'Oh sure. Got big stations out there I'm told. Very swanky, not bushies like us.'

'How did the saddle get up here?'

'It belonged to Duke. He went down south to a funeral at one stage, to his step-father's funeral and his mother gave it to him. That's why I think it must have belonged to the South American husband.'

Hank was intrigued. 'Where did he come from in South America?'

'That I couldn't tell you. In fact it's a bone of contention. One of my sisters, she was named Dolour after Duke's mother, she claims he was a very rich South American, an important fellow. Spaniard. My wife, God rest her soul, was always going to write away for the records but she never even finished sorting out her own family without starting on the MacNamaras.' He laughed. 'She found out her mob were convicts.'

Hank looked up and there was mischief in his voice. 'And your great-grandfather, Pace, was he a convict?'

'I don't know. He could have been. It wouldn't be hard to find out. The English were good at keeping records and they're still intact. He was a mystery man Pace, he must have spent half his life on a horse blazing trees. There's another big property in the Brisbane Valley, prime country too. Duke's sister, Mary, got that and they say she was a real tartar. Ruled her family with an iron hand. But old Pace did good by us, my oath he did.'

'What are you going to do with the saddle now?' Hank asked. 'You're not putting it back in the shed?'

'No, we'll take it up to the house.' He went to pick it up but Hank stopped him. 'I'll carry it. Maria would like to have a look at this.'

And Maria was fascinated. 'It is very valuable. We'll have to get it restored. Let me take it home. The silversmiths might be able to tell us more about it.'

Mac looked doubtful but Hank reassured him. 'Maria loves projects Mac. Let her take it to Argentina and get it fixed up and we'll personally deliver it into your hands again. What do you say?'

'Thank you,' he said. 'I'll never get around to it, but I'll be looking forward to seeing it in trim.'

On their last night at Mungowa station Hank sat outside with Mac in their favourite chairs. It was a hot clear night and fruit bats squabbled in the trees. They had been sitting quietly for a while when Mac made a remark that made Hank stiffen in his seat. 'We never told the kids how John Pace died because of Luke.'

Allowing that to sink in he continued. 'You've softened him up for us Hank, I'm grateful. He took it so hard we never had the heart to tell him what really happened, and as he got older, he seemed worse. And his mother can't bring herself to talk about it. One day when he can handle it he might want to enquire into the exact circumstances and he'll either ask or look it up for himself. But he's coming out of it now, I can feel it. You know that photo of John Pace in uniform in the parlour?'

'Yes?'

'Luke's never acknowledged it and yet I heard him point it out to you. "That's my father," he said.'

'Yes, he did,' Hank mumbled. An effort to speak.

'You acknowledged it too,' Mac said.

'What did I do?' Hank asked, startled.

'You looked at the photo and you said, "Yes, Sergeant MacNamara." No-one else noticed but me.'

'Wasn't he a sergeant?' Hank asked.

'My word he was, but when that photo was taken he was a corporal.'

Hank felt himself drifting. He had done well. He had seen the face in that photo the minute he walked into the house and he was handling it. He had been able to look at the face without terror. It didn't seem so bad any more, as if he had finally laid the past to rest. And he felt that by coming here he had been able to speak to Luke on behalf of Sergeant MacNamara. And he had also experienced an unaccustomed fatherly satisfaction that MacNamara's son was happy with his new wife, in a good sound family environment. And now this? He glanced at Mac without a word, wondering now if he should have stayed away.

The old man smiled and placed a strong hand on Hank's shoulder. 'My son, John Pace, you came across him didn't you?'

Hank hesitated and then admitted, 'Yes'.

'It's all right Hank. Let go. I'm his father remember? I sifted through every report. You have to know these things no matter how bad they hurt. And I always hoped I'd meet the bloke who got away. We MacNamaras are bad losers. When I read that report I thought, "You bloody beauty Yank you got away". That would have pleased John Pace.'

'You knew it was me?' Hank said.

'Not at first. The name rang a bell when you got here, so I called up a friend of mine and had him look it up again for me. I've got a bottle of good brandy stuck away inside, what about a snort?' He stamped off into the house, tramping noisily on the polished timbers and Hank knew it was to give him time to adjust to this new and emotional situation.

When he came back Hank was waiting for him. 'I feel I should have told you but I can't talk about it.'

'There was never any need,' Mac said. 'Your report was clear enough. Don't carry it around with you. You're fretting just as bad as Luke only he won't admit it and you can't stop. Take a look out here at this peaceful valley. It wasn't much different here in the old days from a war. In the struggle a lot of good men on both sides came to grief.

'You know,' he continued, 'the blacks say those little stars up there are

469

babies waiting to be born, and when a good man dies he walks up the rainbow to his Dreaming. I like that. We're too precise. They see more wonder in life and death than we do. Let's drink to John Pace. He did good by us, too. My oath he did.'

# AFTERWORD

The Irish poet Aidghagan O'Rathaille was known as the Dante of Munster. As he moved around Ireland in the early eighteenth century receiving the hospitality traditionally accorded the poet, he expressed for those among whom he lived, the whole spirit of a vanished past and a wounded present, using the rich music of spoken Irish to convey an intensity of pride, of a people's dreaming:

> *I will cease now; death is nigh unto me, without delay*
> *Since the warriors of the Laune and the Lein and the*
> *Lee have been laid low.*
> *I will follow the beloved among the heroes to the grave,*
> *Those princes under whom were my ancestors before the birth of Christ.*

The haunting sadness of O'Rathaille's verse speaks for all the tribes of humanity that have suffered at the hands of their fellow men.

In the case of the Australian Aborigines they outlasted great civilisations over their known existence of 40,000 years, but that is no consolation when your Armageddon happens within living memory.

Most cultures base their pride of race on the heroes of the past. The Aborigines concentrated on the spiritual side of life, seeing nature as heroic, rather than mere man so it has been difficult for them to get through to the invaders that their civilisation is equal in honour and dignity. It is only in recent years that the world has come to appreciate the wonderful legends of their Dreaming.

This book introduces the great Aboriginal leader, Bussamarai, who really did exist.

The Governors of New South Wales whom we meet in this book plot the years for us. William Wentworth, the Macarthurs, Alexander Macleay, and 'Major' Mudie with his prison farm, Castle Forbes, are all well-known figures in Australian history.

Macarthur's home in Parramatta still stands as do the superb residences of William Wentworth, Vaucluse House, and Macleay's Elizabeth Bay House. They are now owned by the Historic Houses Trust of New South Wales.

The fate of Ludwig Leichhardt is not known. The 'Prince of Explorers'

471

disappeared during his attempt to cross the continent from east to west.

Christopher Allingham did make that fantastic 1500 mile ride from Armidale in New South Wales into the dangerous and unknown territory of the tropic north, and returned unharmed. His family was among the first pioneers of the Dalrymple Shire which encompasses the Valley of Lagoons.

J. Elphinstone Dalrymple led the first official expeditions into the far north, later the new State of Queensland. Around that time gold was found at Gimpi Gimpi, now known as Gympie, and the big gold rush began.

Hard on the heels of Dalrymple and his team came more pioneers, among them one James Atkinson who first took up a pastoral settlement at Mount Surprise, and his son opened up other cattle stations. To this day the Atkinson family own and manage a large cattle station in the area. The name of that cattle station?

## VALLEY OF LAGOONS.

The narrated story in the first chapter of this book is based on fact. An Australian Digger did go to his death exactly as described. He gave that warning: 'Lower mate' to an Allied soldier, a stranger to him, who was hiding in the jungle, and strode on to his execution. The soldier took his warning, fell back into the jungle, made it back to his own lines, and survived the war.

Although most of the characters that appear in this book are fictional, where historical figures appear they have been fictionalised in ways that are consistent with what is known of their personalities and experiences.

It only remains now for me to thank Sally Milner for her assistance and advice. And I have to thank Lorraine Poynton and Laurie Paul, and Mary and Geoffrey Neath, my progressive readers, for their encouragement as the manuscript developed.

Patricia Shaw 1988